OFFSIDE

By
Bianca Sommerland

Copyright 2013, Bianca Sommerland

ALL RIGHTS RESERVED
Edited by Lisa A. Hollett
Cover art by Reese Dante

Copyright © 2013 by Bianca Sommerland

Offside (The Dartmouth Cobras #4)
First Edition, Paperback-Published 2013
Edited by Lisa Hollett
Cover art by Reese Dante

License Notes

All rights reserved. No part of this book may be reproduced in any form or by any electronic or mechanical means including information storage and retrieval systems—with the exception of short quotes used for critical articles or reviews—without permission in writing from the author.

This book is a work of fiction and any resemblance to persons, living or dead, or actual events is purely coincidental. The characters are products of the author's imagination and used fictitiously.

Warning

This book contains material not suitable for readers under 18. In also contains scenes that some may find objectionable, including BDSM, ménage sex, bondage, anal sex, sex toys, double penetration, voyeurism, edge play, and deviant use of hockey equipment. Do not try this at home unless you have your very own pro-athlete. Author takes no responsibility for any damages resulting from attempting anything contained in this book.

Also by Bianca Sommerland

The Dartmouth Cobras
Game Misconduct (The Dartmouth Cobras #1)
Defensive Zone (The Dartmouth Cobras #2)
Breakaway (The Dartmouth Cobras #3)

Also
Deadly Captive
Deadly Captive (Collateral Damage)

Rosemary Entwined
Rosemary & Mistletoe

The Trip

Dedication

Le Bleu-Blanc-Rouge. This year we have hope.

Acknowledgements

Rosie, for vanilla and sprinkles! Lol! Our little thing. You know how much you mean to me! To Cherise, so much love and respect. You taught me the meaning of affectionate revenge. ;)

To my betas, Missy, Ebony, and Stacey. You've become such an important part of this series and I'm so happy to have you along for the ride. To the fans of this amazing hockey team, thank you for cheering them on, for giving the team what it need to thrive. Because of you there are many books still to come!

And this last acknowledgement, probably the most important one I will ever make, is to my daughters. It will be a long time before you pick up one of these books, but by the time you do I hope all this hard work has gotten us where we need to be together. Sharing a bright future in which I can help you make all your dreams come true. There's a lesson in this juggling act you see me perform every day. No matter how hard things get, you *can* do so much more than even you believe. Don't doubt that no matter what anyone says. You're *my* girls and that means no one will ever hold you back. I love you so much!

Dartmouth Cobra Roster

Centers

No	Name	Age	Ht	Wt	Shot	Birth Place
27	Scott Demyan	28	6'3"	198	L	Anaheim, California, USA
45	Keaton Manning	30	5'11"	187	R	Ulster, Ireland
18	Ctirad Jelinek	26	6'0"	204	L	Rakovnik, Czech Republic
3	Erik Hjalmar	23	6'3"	219	R	Stockolm, Sweden

Left Wings

No	Name	Age	Ht	Wt	Shot	Birth Place
16	Luke Carter	22	5'11"	190	L	Warroad, Minnesota, USA
53	Shawn Pischlar	29	6'0"	200	L	Villach, Austria
71	Dexter Tousignant	23	6'2"	208	L	Matane, Quebec, Canada
5	Ian White	25	6'1"	212	L	Winnipeg, Manitoba, Canada
42	Braxton Richards	18	5'11	196	L	Edmonton, Alberta, Canada

Right Wings

No	Name	Age	Ht	Wt	Shot	Birth Place
22	Tyler Vanek	21	5'8"	174	R	Greenville, North Carolina, USA
72	Dante Palladino	34	6'2"	215	L	Fassano, Italy
21	Bobby Williams	33	5'10"	190	R	Sheffield, England
46	Vadim Zetsev	26	6'0"	203	R	Yaroslavl, Russia
66	Zachary Pearce	32	6'0"	210	L	Ottawa, Ontario, Canada

Defense

No	Name	Age	Ht	Wt	Shot	Birth Place
6	Dominik Mason	31	6'4"	235	R	Chicago, Illinois, USA
17	Einar Olsson	27	6'0"	200	L	Örnsköldsvik, Sweden
74	Beau Mischlue	25	6'2"	223	L	Gaspe, Quebec, Canada
26	Peter Kral	27	6'1"	200	L	Hannover, Germany
2	Mirek Brends	33	6'1"	214	L	Malmö, Sweden
47	Tony Brookmann	24	6'3"	212	L	Winnipeg, Manitoba, Canada
67	Owen Stills	22	6'0"	217	R	Detroit, Michigan, USA
39	Rylan Cooper	23	5'11"	198	R	Norfolk, Virginia, USA
11	Sebastian Ramos	29	6'5"	227	R	Arlanza, Burgos, Spain

Goalies

No	Name	Age	Ht	Wt	Shot	Birth Place
20	Landon Bowers **	25	6'3"	215		Gaspe, Quebec, Canada
34	Svend Ingerslov	32	6'0"	205		Lillehammer Norway
29	Dave Hunt	20	6'2"	210		Hamilton, Ontario, Canada

Chapter One

Early July

I can't do this. Rebecca Bower hunched down, arms crossed tight over her stomach, keeping her voice low so her five-year-old daughter, who sat in the backseat of the car coloring, wouldn't hear her. Her eyes burned as she glanced up at her mother. "Mom, I can't do this."

Lifting her hand from the steering wheel, her mother, Erin Bower, patted her shoulder. "Yes, you can. I know it will be hard, *ma bichette*, but Patrick is Casey's father. He has some rights."

A length of barbed wire seemed to wind around her stomach, around her heart, digging in and tearing her insides apart. The last time Casey had been with her father, she'd ended up in the emergency room. *I almost lost her because of him.*

"Becky, get out of the car for a minute, please." Her mother opened her door and stepped on to the parking lot. A big straw hat sat on her head, shielding her pale face from the glare of the sun until she tipped her head back to stare up at the planes leaving the airport. The fine lines around her mother's eyes deepened with tension and exhaustion. She lived for her children, had dropped everything in her own life to come to Dartmouth, but as strong as she was, the weight of all she'd pulled on to her slender shoulders was beginning to show.

"I'm sorry, Mom," Becky whispered as she came around the car to stand beside her mother. "You'd be on your way home if I'd kept this to myself."

Her mother pursed her lips. "I would have been very disappointed if you'd kept this to yourself. You're staying with your brother because he needs you, which makes me very happy, but don't be too proud to accept help yourself."

"I'm not, I just—"

"You tried to hide how upset you were about this. You wouldn't have told either me or your father if I hadn't insisted. I understand your not wanting to talk to your brother, he's dealing with enough,

1

but since when can't you talk to me and your father?"

"It's not that I can't talk to you . . . it's just . . ." *Ugh, how the hell am I supposed to make her understand?* "This is my mess. I need to show my daughter I'm strong enough to manage on my own."

"No. Right now, you need to show your daughter she doesn't need to be afraid of her father." Her mom took her hand and squeezed tight. "It's as simple as that. She doesn't remember much—if anything—about what happened last time she saw him. She'll feed off your reactions, so you need to get better at hiding how you really feel from her. I know it's hard. I wish you didn't have to go through this, but you do. His mother will supervise the visits. She might be blind where he's concerned, but she'll keep your daughter safe."

Becky swallowed hard, nodding slowly. She couldn't argue with that. And Patrick *had* gone to a few parenting courses. Enough that her lawyer pointed out he was entitled to visitation, and denying him would put her in contempt of court. *Again.*

The fines, the threats from Patrick's lawyer, she could deal with. But the judge at their last hearing had warned her that she could do jail time if she refused to respect the visitation order. The judge had shown some sympathy when she presented him with reports from the doctor and the social workers who'd been involved when Casey had nearly drowned in the bathtub while in her father's care. Because he'd left her alone. But the fact was that he'd eventually taken steps to become a better parent. The court believed it was in Casey's best interest to get to know her father. The only concession was supervised visits since contact had been limited for so long.

Maybe he's changed. Maybe he can be a good father.

Her instincts all screamed at her, fierce voices like a dozen fists pounding at the inside of her skull, telling her not to believe it.

But she didn't have a choice.

"All right, I got it." Becky leaned into her mother's hug, then planted a broad smile on her face as she caught Casey peering out at them from the back window. She opened the door and unstrapped her daughter from her booster seat. "So, *poupée*, are you excited about going to Marineland with Daddy?"

"I like dolphins." Casey picked up her little purse and her stuffed

Shrek. Her tiny white dress shoes clicked on the pavement as Becky set her down. She tucked the purse and the toy under her arm to straighten the skirts of her pink floral sundress. "But I'd rather stay with Uncle Landon. I want to see the baby. And Silver is fun."

Holding in a sigh, Becky crouched down to her daughter's level. "You'll only be gone for three weeks, Casey. The baby won't be here yet."—*I hope*—"Besides, you promised Silver you'd take lots of pictures for her. Since she's stuck in bed, you'll need to tell her all about your trip when you get back so she won't be bored."

"And I can talk to her, and Uncle Landon, and Uncle Dean every night," Casey said, repeating what Silver had told her before they'd left Dean's house. "But what if Daddy doesn't let me use the phone?"

"He will." *He'd better.* "You'll talk to me too though, right?"

"Well, duh." Her daughter giggled, sounding a bit too much like Silver Delgado for Becky's liking. Then she topped it off with a statement that set Becky's teeth on edge. "Silver said you need a break. Can't you come with me?"

"I just started a new job, baby. I can't take time off now." She continued before her daughter could remind her she worked for Silver—well, more specifically, she worked for the Dartmouth Cobras as the Media Relations Coordinator, but her daughter didn't know the difference. "Besides, this is a special trip for you, Daddy, and Nanny."

Casey wrinkled her tiny nose, winding her pink beaded necklace around her fingers before sticking the end in her mouth and speaking around it. "I guess . . ."

Way too serious for a five-year-old. Becky laughed and took her daughter's toy and purse. "Come on. Daddy's probably waiting."

Her mother held Casey's hand as Becky retrieved her suitcase from the trunk, then chatted excitedly with her as they made their way into the airport. All Casey's reluctance seemed to disappear as she caught sight of her father. Her face lit up. She pulled away from her grandmother and bolted toward him.

"Daddy!"

Becky moved to run after her daughter, but her mother halted her with a hand on her arm, shaking her head. Patrick met Casey halfway, bending down to look her over as she skidded to a stop in front of him. The noise in the crowded airport made it impossible to make out what he said, but Casey ducked her head shyly and moved in for a hug.

As Becky and her mother approached, Patrick straightened, rubbing his thick, brown beard and reaching out for Casey's suitcase. "Anything I need to know?"

Don't let her out of your sight? But no, he knew that. His mother had spent hours on the phone with Becky, assuring her he knew he'd messed up when he'd left Casey alone in the bath so he could make a move on his latest girlfriend. That he wanted to be a good father. That he was ready to try again. Undermining his efforts wouldn't improve the situation.

"She's allergic to strawberries. She has an EpiPen in her suitcase. Check everything she eats." He knew that too. Her brow furrowed as he nodded distractedly. His phone buzzed, and his slid his hand into the pocket of his black slacks. The buzzing stopped.

"Does she still wet the bed?" he asked.

Casey gave him a horrified look. "*Daddy!*"

"No, but no drinks after six." Becky smiled at her daughter. "She's good with that, though. She usually gets herself a glass of milk and some cookies around then."

"Do you have cookies, Daddy?"

"I can pick some up." Patrick ruffled his daughter's hair, then pointed toward the escalator. "Nanny went to get an iced tea and some croissants. You still like croissants, don't you?"

"Yes! Uncle Dean makes them for me almost every morning!"

"'Uncle' Dean?" Patrick arched a brow at Becky. "Exactly how is he her uncle? I didn't know Landon swung that way."

"He doesn't," her mother said tightly, speaking up for the first time. "But Casey has become very close to him lately and decided to call him 'Uncle' out of respect. He's family."

"I'm not sure I like you having all kinds of men around my daughter." Patrick put his hand on Casey's shoulder. "Especially the kind of men Silver Delgado would be involved with. I've heard things about her—"

"She happens to be involved with my brother." Becky did her

best to keep her tone pleasant. "And this is a conversation we can have some other time."

"Whatever. I'm just telling you now, I plan to take a much more active role in my daughter's life. I will have a say in who she spends time with. And I'm not comfortable with her being around *that* woman."

"But Daddy, I love Silver. She's having a baby, and it's going to be my cousin and . . ." Casey pulled away from her father, the soft roundness of her cheeks going red as she inched closer to Becky. "Silver promised I could see the baby after it comes out of her belly. She promised, Mommy!"

"You will, *poupée*," Becky said, wishing she could pick her daughter up and bring her home. Home being Dean's place, even if only temporarily. But she'd set up their new house while Casey was gone. And Casey had to go. So Becky had to find a way to get past this little setback. *Damn Patrick for not dropping it.* "Daddy just doesn't know Silver. He's looking out for you."

"That's right." Patrick made a face and grabbed Casey's hand. "Come on, Nanny's waiting."

"No!" Casey sobbed, pulling away from her father once again, throwing herself against Becky's leg. She clung to Becky with one arm and hugged her Shrek toy with the other. "I don't want to go, Mommy! Daddy and Nanny can visit me here!"

"This is ridiculous. We're going to miss our flight." Patrick checked his watch. "Come on, Casey. You're acting like a baby."

She is a baby. Becky's throat locked as she gently pried her daughter off her leg, then bent down to cup her tear-streaked cheeks in her hands. "Go with Daddy, *poupée*. You'll have so much fun you won't want to leave."

"Please don't make me go." Casey's tear-filled eyes broke her heart. "I won't watch SpongeBob anymore. I know you hate it."

This isn't fair. Becky felt her own eyes moisten and blinked fast to keep the tears at bay. She glanced over at her mom, grateful for her presence as she bent down beside them.

"Casey, your daddy misses you." Erin wiped away her granddaughter's tears. "Be my big girl and go with him now. You can call us as soon as the plane lands. You love plane rides. And I'm sure

Daddy will take you to see the falls. I haven't been to see them in a long time. Will you take pictures of them for me?"

Casey hiccupped, then nodded shakily. "I'll take lots of pictures. For you and Silver and Mommy."

"Good girl." Erin rose and placed Casey's hand in Patrick's. "You know, Daddy needs to learn a lot more about hockey. Maybe you can teach him?"

"You need me to teach you about hockey?" Casey peered up at her father, eyes wide. "I have all the *Rock'em Sock'em* DVDs. We can watch them together if you want?"

"Great." Patrick scowled at Becky. "Thanks for making this easier for me."

Becky ignored his sarcasm as she stood. She hugged and kissed her daughter, determined to make it as easy for *Casey* as possible. "Chin up. No more tears. Show Daddy how tough the Bower women are."

"She's a Dubois," Patrick said through his teeth.

And you're an asshole. But thankfully, Casey managed to go with her father without any more protests, though she sucked her thumb and held Shrek tight as she followed him. Becky watched them step onto the escalator. Her whole body trembled as she retreated. Her back hit something solid.

"Hey, Becky." Firm hands on her shoulders steadied her, and her eyes widened as she glanced up to see Scott Demyan, one of the Dartmouth Cobras. The *last* one she wanted to see right now. Just being around him made her feel like the whole world had tilted beneath her feet. And she didn't have the strength to haul up the walls she needed to put between them. He seemed to notice, because he wasn't stripping her with his dreamy blue eyes like he usually did. Actually, he sounded concerned. "You okay?"

"I'm fine." She managed a shaky smile. "My baby's first trip without me."

"Ah." He glanced up toward Casey and frowned. "He should be holding her hand."

Becky nodded, following his gaze. Her breath caught in her throat as Casey dropped Shrek and bent down to pick him up near the top of the escalator. Patrick was on the phone. He didn't see

Casey's necklace catch on the steps as they reached the top.

"Patrick!" Becky bolted for the stairs, Scott a breath behind her. She heard her mother scream.

"Zach!" Scott launched up the steps, then threw something to a man about to step onto the descending stairs. The man snatched it out of the air.

The escalator stopped. Casey let out a high-pitched cry, struggling against the necklace cinched around her neck. Patrick shouted.

Beads covered the floor as Becky dropped to her knees and pulled her daughter away from the escalator and into her arms. A blade flashed before it was tucked away, and her breath lodged in her throat as she gaped up at the man standing over her. Zach Pearce. Another player. He took a knee beside her.

"Becky, look at me." His bright green eyes were hard. "Calm. Down."

Casey was still crying. People were gathering around them. Panic clawed at Becky's chest, but she knew she couldn't let it take over. The command latched on to her racing pulse, forcing it to slow. Zach was right. She needed to calm down for her daughter.

"Shh. You're okay, *poupée*. Mommy's got you." Becky rocked her daughter in her arms. "You're okay."

"My necklace is broke, mommy." Casey sobbed and picked up a handful of pink beads. "It got stuck."

"I'll get you a new one." *Damn it, why did I let her wear it? She could have—*

"She's too young to be wearing something like that." Patrick snarled as he raked his fingers through his hair. "I don't know why you let her get all dolled up like that. Are you determined to make me look like a bad father? If she hadn't grabbed for that stupid toy—"

"Mister, there's a sign reminding you to hold your kid's hand." An old man who had come off the escalator behind Patrick glared at him. "You weren't. If you ask me—"

Patrick's face went crimson. "Nobody asked you."

"Is the little girl all right?"

"Some people shouldn't have kids."

All around them people were talking, looking at her, at Patrick, condemning them both. Becky rose shakily, cradling Casey in her arms, using one hand to cover her daughter's ear, not wanting her to hear all the things she wished she could say. A solid grip on her shoulder led her away. She found herself sitting in a small room, aware of nothing but her daughter's tiny hand in hers. Then she heard Casey laugh and the world snapped into place.

"Don't let Mommy see. She hates SpongeBob."

"You better eat it quick then," Scott said.

A crunch. Becky frowned and focused on her daughter. She had a huge SpongeBob lollipop in her hand, staining her lips yellow. A few blinks and Becky made out Scott and Zach, standing on either side of them. A woman in a crisp white uniform stood a few feet away, holding a bottle of water. She was staring at the men with pure worship in her eyes.

"May I?" Zach took the bottle and uncapped it. Then he knelt in front of Becky while Scott distracted Casey with a bag of gummy bears. "Take a few sips, then pull yourself together. Your mother looks like she wants to kill your husband."

My husband? Becky glanced over at her mother, who had Patrick backed into the corner. Mrs. Dubois, Patrick's mother, lingered close behind, wringing her hands. Becky took a few gulps of water, then shook her head and laughed. "We're divorced."

"I got the impression you were a smart woman." Zach grinned. "But that's beside the point. He's the little girl's father. She had a bad scare, and she needs to know it was an accident."

It's always "an accident" with him. Becky gritted her teeth, then cleared her throat. "Mom, remember what you said?"

"I was wrong." Her mother huffed and took a step back. "What was so important that you had to take that call not even five minutes after you were with your daughter?"

"That's none of your business." Patrick squared his shoulders. "Not that it matters. She's not going to want to come with me now."

"I'm okay, Daddy." Casey wiggled out of Becky's arms and smiled at her father. "We didn't miss our plane, did we?"

"Not yet." Checking his watch again, Patrick sighed. "If you still want to go, we better make it quick. And for fuck's sake, hold your grandmother's hand. We've had enough drama."

"Patrick—" Mrs. Dubois pressed her hands to her pale cheeks "—please don't be like that."

All the muscles in Becky's body turned to steel as she stood. Casey was staring at her, looking for guidance. And damn it, as much as it killed her to hand her daughter off to a man she hated more than she'd ever thought herself capable of hating anyone, she would be strong for her daughter.

"Patrick, things happen. Casey's been looking forward to spending time with you. Right, *poupée*?"

Casey gave a hesitant nod.

"There you go. Give me a call when you land." Becky stepped past Zach, somehow feeling stronger with him behind her. She hardly knew the man, but he'd saved her daughter. Said exactly what she'd needed to hear to pull herself together. She gave her daughter more hugs and kisses. Managed a big smile for her brave little girl as Casey approached her father. "Do what Daddy said. Hold on to Nanny's hand."

"I will." Casey hiked up her chin, her loose curls slipping over her shoulder as she glanced back at Zach. "Thank you for saving me from the escalator, Mr. Pearce."

He grinned and reached out to tap her nose with his finger. "You don't need to call me 'Mr.', angel-face. And I'm just happy I got there in time. Take care of yourself, okay?"

Patrick made a rough sound in his throat, gesturing impatiently as he headed toward the door. "Come on, Casey."

Mrs. Dubois followed him, holding tight to Casey's hand while awkwardly fumbling in her purse. She pulled out a flattened croissant and passed it to Casey, bending down to whisper something before breaking into a mock run to catch up to Patrick's long strides.

"Fucking douche bag," Scott mumbled under his breath. He stuffed his hands in the pockets of his jeans, then ducked his head at Zach's dirty look. He turned to Becky's mother. "Sorry, Mrs. Bower."

Her mother winked at him. "That's quite all right. He *is* a douche bag." She latched on to his arm. "We haven't been properly introduced—which doesn't surprise me. You're Scott Demyan. My daughter's told me *so* much about you."

Scott arched a brow at Becky. "Really? Anything good?"

"Not if she can help it."

"*Mother!*" Becky dropped her head back, whispering a prayer as her mother cajoled Scott and Zach into walking them out to the car. Erin Bower was loyal to her husband, but she'd always been a bit of a flirt. Becky didn't know how her father put up with it.

I wouldn't.

Past the doors exiting the airport, the summer sun glared down and the morning air became humid and sticky. Zach walked beside her, not saying a word, but somehow seeming completely aware of her. He slipped on a pair of aviator Ray-Bans, hiding eyes that were a startling pale green, the inner iris like leaves in the fall before they faded to yellow, circled by the darker shade of evergreens. She'd seen him in pictures and on TV often enough to avoid staring the first time she'd interviewed him, but the sunglasses were a welcome relief now that she wasn't distracted by her daughter.

Sunglasses! Damn it! Becky stopped and dug into her purse. She pulled out Casey's pink-framed glasses. "I'll be right back."

"Rebecca." Zach caught her wrist before she could rush back inside. His firm tone made her knees quiver, and she had to fight the urge to kneel gracefully before him, to offer surrender in a way she hadn't in far too long. "*Yes, Sir*" was on the tip of her tongue. His grip on her wrist was as secure as a shackle, slightly roughened with callouses which reminded her of supple leather. "You've said your goodbyes. Going back will make it harder."

"I know, but . . ." Becky hauled in a rough breath and took a big step back to get away from the effect he had on her. His grip slipped from her wrist to her hand, giving her the choice to retreat even farther. A choice she didn't want. But she never submitted outside of a club—well, *almost* never. And she certainly didn't blindly obey when it came to her daughter.

Not that he expects me to.

"Casey gets very whiny when the sun hurts her eyes. Patrick can't stand it when she whines and—"

Zach nodded slowly. "Well, you're her mother. You know what's best. But I think it's a bad idea."

It *was* a bad idea. Casey had seemed okay when she left, but would she be if she saw Becky again? "You're right, damn it. Sorry, I'm just not used to this."

"Believe me, I understand. My sister, Tracy, was like that the first few times she had to let my nephew visit his father, and he's a decent guy. Just really young. After he graduated high school, he got a good job—gave her more than he had to because he wanted to prove he could be a good father. But Tracy had a hard time leaving her baby with anyone and it took a court order for her to finally let him see his son."

"I can't blame her. If a full-grown man can't be responsible with a child, how can a teenage boy manage?"

"The same way a teenage girl can, I imagine." The edges of his lips twitched as her face heated. "Kev has two amazing parents. And he's a great kid. My sister is fine leaving him with his dad now. They've learned how to get along, even though they can't be together."

If only it were that simple. "Tracy trusts Kev's father?"

"After ten years? I certainly hope so."

"Then it's not the same." Becky's gaze followed a plane rising into the sky. Not Casey's plane. Not yet. *But soon.* She hugged herself. "I can't trust Patrick."

Zach slid his hand to the nape of her neck, massaging the tense muscles, speaking quietly. "But the courts granted him visitation rights?"

"Only supervised." Becky found herself leaning against Zach's side, his touch alone bringing her to a peaceful place. There was something about him that had her letting down the guards she erected with most men. Probably had something to do with the fact that he was gay. She let out a deep sigh. "His mother has to be with them for the whole visit."

"Do you trust *her*?"

She nodded without hesitation. Mrs. Dubois has always been great with Casey.

"Then try to focus on that. Take some time for yourself while she's away."

For a split second, she considered going to the club Dean

Richter owned. Maybe she could find a Dom who could give her the release she craved, who could give her the illusion of freedom. Freedom from all the pressure closing in on her from all sides every single day. Not from her family; they were wonderful. But quitting her job, moving, starting over . . . the list of things she had to take care of was endless.

Zach could do that. He goes to the club.

Looking for men. But there were other Doms.

"Maybe I will." She took a deep, bracing breath as they met her mom and Scott by the car. Scott was chatting away with her mother, slouched with his back against the driver's side door. In a tight white T-shirt and ripped jeans, he played the part of any woman's perfect wet dream.

My perfect wet dream. Ten years ago, when I was young and stupid.

His lips slanted into a half-smile as she stepped up to her mother's side. "Your mom says you haven't been out in a while, so I was thinking you and me could catch a movie or something." The subtle drop in his tone implied the "or something" was more likely. "What do you say?"

Finally, a chance for my very own notch on your belt! Every time she was around Scott, she found the smartass she'd been as a teen coming out. But he was cutting back on the sleaze. So she'd be polite. "Dean's going to the club tonight, so I need to stay with Silver and my brother. Maybe some other time?"

"Bower's a little too old to have his big sister babysitting him." Scott hooked his thumbs in his pockets. "One night won't hurt."

Becky frowned. "He just had surgery. And Silver's on bed rest."

Her mother nudged her. "I'll be there, *ma bichette*. It will do you some good to get out."

Not with him. Becky chewed at the inside of her cheek. Her mother had her trapped. "I guess—"

"Naw, I get it." Scott shook his head, rolling his shoulders as he backed away. "If you change your mind, I'm sure my cell number's in that big portfolio you've got on me."

"Scott." Zach's eyes narrowed. Caution edged his tone.

Scott rolled his eyes. "I'll wait for you by the car, Zach. Mrs. Bower, it was a pleasure to meet you."

"Likewise." Her mother smiled sweetly at Scott. "You should come by for dinner some time. I'm sure Landon would like to see you."

"Ah... I'm not so sure about that, but I'll keep it in mind."

After Scott walked away, Zach opened his mouth, his eyes widening slightly as her mother threw her arms around him. Becky's cheeks blazed as she struggled to find a way to explain her mother's odd behavior.

"I will never forget what you did for my granddaughter. Whether or not Scott comes, you must promise you will before I head back to Gaspe."

"I would love to, ma'am." He let her mother pull him down to kiss each of his cheeks, then gently hugged her. "Enjoy the rest of your day, ladies."

Once the men were gone, Becky climbed into the car, inhaling deeply before she glanced over at her mother, who looked much too pleased with herself. Becky thought she'd gotten past being embarrassed by her mother's matchmaking hobby, but apparently not.

"Mom, you've got to stop—"

"You know, I really don't understand why you and your brother have a problem with Scott. He's such a nice boy." Mom shook her head and clucked her tongue. "But if you aren't interested in him—which I find hard to believe—you should definitely go out with Zach. You were quite friendly with him."

Becky smirked. "You know what? You're right. I think Zach would be perfect for me."

"I'm glad you agree."

"He's easy to talk to, and I won't ever have to worry about him pushing for more than friendship."

Her mother's brow shot up. "And why is that?"

"He doesn't play for my team."

"He certainly does! And even if he didn't, that's a silly reason not to..." A blush rose high on her mother's cheeks. "Oh."

"You still want him to come over?"

"Why wouldn't I?"

"Because Dad..." She hated to say that her father was a little

13

homophobic, but with the stiff way he'd been acting toward Dean ever since he'd found him in bed with Landon, there was no denying it. Her father was a wonderful man, but some of his beliefs were very old-fashioned. "I don't want things to be uncomfortable."

"They won't be." The determination in her mother's tone convinced her. Becky grinned. Mom knew how to handle Dad. But that being settled left her mother free to latch on to the original topic. "So, about Scott..."

* * * *

Zach stood in the doorway of the bedroom turned gym of his condo, watching Scott on the weight bench, muscles straining as he lowered 120kg worth of weights to his chest. He lifted them slowly, fit enough to handle several reps with good form, but doing it without a spotter was still stupid. Moving quietly across the room, Zach observed the way Scott's jaw tensed with the next rep. His cock stirred as his gaze ran over the man's sweat-slicked chest. They'd only fucked once, but he could still recall exactly how it felt to have Scott's solid body under him, taste the salty, slick moisture of his flesh, smell the musk of sex and the spice of his cologne.

Scott never turned down sex, so Zach could have had him any time before leaving to visit his parents. He could have him now. But joining the long list of Scott's lovers didn't appeal to him. And Scott wasn't ready to offer more. Yet.

Not to me in any case. Zach moved swiftly to straddle Scott's waist, curving his hands under the weight bar for extra support as Scott jerked with surprise.

"What the fuck, man?" Scott gritted his teeth, pushing against the bar as Zach forced it down. His eyes narrowed. "Let me up."

"No." The corner of Zach's lips edged up as Scott panted. He could already feel Scott's dick hardening against his ass. Gaining the upper hand with Scott wasn't easy, the man wasn't submissive—still, he reacted to being overpowered. But it wasn't his physical response that Zach wanted. "We need to talk."

Beads of sweat formed on Scott's temples. "You sure about that? Feels like you want something else. Get off me so I can get you off."

"What did you do while I was gone?"

Scott let out a rough laugh. "You mean *who* did I do. Was I supposed to keep track of names and report back? Guess I forgot. Can't even give you a number. Too many to count."

"Jesus, Scott." Zach's throat tightened. He knew Scott wasn't bluffing. Not that he'd really expected Scott to wait for him to come back; they weren't in any kind of relationship, but it made him feel a little sick to know Scott still let men and women use him as if he was good for nothing but a quick fuck. "You can't keep doing this. One day—"

"What? I'm gonna catch something?" Scott's whole body shook as he tried again to lift the bar. "You know I'm careful."

"It fucks with your head." Zach eased the weight bar onto the stand over Scott's head. "Don't forget, you were in my bed when you woke up screaming."

"Give it a break. I had a fucking nightmare." Scott groaned as he tried to sit up, and Zach shoved him back down. "Look, I appreciate you letting me stay here since my place has been taken over by Vanek's woman, but tone it down, okay? I didn't get away from a Domme just to deal with a Dom. You need to play that way, go to the club. You want uncomplicated sex? I'm all over that."

Clearly. Zach wrapped his hands around Scott's wrists, jerking them over his head to pin him down. "Is that what you want with Becky?"

Baring his teeth, Scott thrust his hips up to grind his dick against Zach's ass. "Yes."

Not fucking happening. The way Becky had reacted when Zach had slipped into command mode had all his protective instincts on overdrive. In her vulnerable state, Scott could do a lot of damage if he wasn't careful. And in his current mind-set, he wouldn't be. "She needs more."

"Then give it to her." Scott rolled his eyes. "You're fucking jealous, aren't you? It's obvious she wants me, but I'm no good for her."

"No, you're not. Not like this." Zach pushed away from Scott, threw his leg over the bench, then straightened. "Why would I be

15

jealous? You've got absolutely nothing to offer."

"Nothing?" Scott sat up, grabbing his erection through his shorts. "I've got plenty to offer, pal."

"You keep telling yourself that."

As Zach reached the doorway, he heard rapid steps behind him and turned just as Scott's body slammed into his. His eyes drifted shut as Scott pressed against him, lips hovering close as he whispered, "You want me."

Curving his hand around the back of Scott's neck, Zach hissed through his teeth. "Yes."

"Then what's the problem?" Scott undid the top button of Zach's jeans, tugged down his zipper, then reached down to grab his dick. His lips were feverishly hot as he kissed Zach. "I'm right here."

"No. You're not." Zach latched on to Scott's wrist, even though his dick was throbbing with need, and roughly jerked his hand away. "We'll talk again when you are."

* * * *

Sitting in the spare room of Zach's condo, Scott stared at his suitcase, all packed up and ready to go. His black T-shirt clung to him, already soaked through with sweat. Every inch of him felt disgusting. Tainted. Somehow, Zach had a way of reminding him of all the things he fought so hard to forget. Ever since that one fucking hot night. Sebastian Ramos, the massive defenseman the Cobras had acquired not long after signing Scott, had thrown a party and let them play with his sub. But Zach's end goal hadn't been the young woman.

It had been Scott.

"I want you." Zach shoved him against the wall in Ramos' basement, tearing at his clothes, the same hot mouth that had been on his dick moments before now on his neck, teeth closing on corded muscle, pain mingling with lust. Scott fisted his hands in Zach's shirt, jerking him closer, groaning as the man kissed him. Zach's lips tasted of the woman they'd pleasured together, of the cigar he'd smoked which had Scott growing harder every time the tip touched his lips.

Zach always seemed so cool. So aloof. But his control seemed to have snapped as he jerked Scott's jeans down to his knees and shoved him over the back of a sofa. There were supplies left for them by Ramos on a small table nearby. Zach found a packet of lube and used it to slick his dick before pressing the head into Scott, filling him with a smooth thrust.

"Fuck." Scott tore himself away from the erotic memory, then stumbled to the bathroom to jerk off. He came hard and fast, but it was shallow compared to the satisfaction he'd felt with Zach. He slumped against the bathroom sink and pressed his eyes shut. The sex had been great, but going home with Zach after had been... different. Scary different. He'd gotten way too comfortable. They'd lazed around in bed for hours, talking about the game, about all kinds of shit Scott didn't usually share with anyone. Somehow his brother, Jimmy, had come up. Scott caught himself right after he admitted he was worried about his brother's gambling addiction. He'd tried to laugh it off, but Zach was fucking perceptive. He hadn't pushed, but he'd made it clear Scott could talk to him if he wanted to.

Fuck that. Bile rose in his throat as he considered other things Zach would probably expect him to share. Like details from the nightmare. The echo of long, manicured nails scratching his flesh made his dick twitch. He shuddered and slammed his fist into the sink.

"People want me. They always have." He lifted his head and sneered at his reflection in the mirror. "I'm a man. I have needs. It's all good."

It hadn't always felt good, no matter how his body reacted. But he'd learned to deal with it in his own way. His life was made up of the game and sex. The sex didn't mean much. The game meant everything.

No one had ever asked more from him. Except Zach. The man saw something in him that wasn't there. Maybe because he'd been there when Scott had woken, gasping for air as he dreamed of hands and breasts all over him, of the scent of a woman's cunt smothering him, dreams that hadn't plagued him in years, but for some reason came as he slept with his head on Zach's chest.

I wish I could give you more, man. Scott drew in a shuddery breath, turning on the faucet to splash cold water on his face. *But I've given you all I've got.*

Chapter Two

"Fuck!" Becky winced as she stepped into the living room, just barely evading the remote which smashed into the wall near her head. Batteries rolled across the floor, coming to a stop by her sensible black kitten-heel pumps. Her brother slumped on the sofa and buried his face in his hands. She crossed the room to shut off the replay of the playoff game where the Dartmouth Cobras had been eliminated. Landon had torn muscles in his thigh, which had kept him out of nets in the second round. His replacement had been good, but not good enough. The team would have gone farther with Landon between the pipes. All the sports analysts said so. And Landon couldn't seem to let that go.

His injury had happened the same night his fiancée, Silver, had gone into early labor. For the longest time, he'd been focused on Silver and his baby, but now that both were doing well, he couldn't seem to get past failing to bring his team to the final stretch. To the Cup.

It wasn't his fault. He'd given everything he had to the team. But everything was never enough. Not for any player who loved the game. And her brother loved it more than anyone she'd ever known.

"Landon . . ." Becky inched into the room, holding her breath as her brother stiffened and stared out the window, past the crutches propped on the couch cushion beside him. "Don't do this to yourself."

"Do what? Face the fact that I failed my team?"

Becky felt a presence behind her and stepped aside as Tim, Dean's brother and the head coach of the Dartmouth Cobras, stepped into the room.

"Get over yourself, Bower. Making it as far as we did was a long shot." Tim braced his hands on the side of the sofa, his gaze fixed on her brother until he finally looked up. "We wouldn't have gotten there without you."

Landon fisted his hand over the brace on his leg. "I'll be useless for months. I can't do anything for the team."

"Bullshit." Tim rested one knee on the sofa and grabbed Landon's shoulder. He spoke through his teeth. "You can work on getting better."

Becky backed out of the room, smiling at Dean as he rubbed her back before joining Landon and Tim on the sofa. He leaned close to Landon, speaking low. She didn't know if the two were lovers. She didn't want to know. All that mattered was Dean was there for her brother. And so was Tim.

There wasn't much more she could add, but there was someone else that might need her now. Someone who would never ask for anyone's help.

Pretty messed up that we've got something in common.

Becky made her way up the stairs, quietly, in case Silver was sleeping. She poked her head into the bedroom, grinning as Silver gasped and hid her laptop under the comforter.

"You're supposed to be relaxing." Becky slipped into the room and perched on the end of the bed. Not many would feel sorry for Silver, not with her opulent surroundings. A 50-inch TV on the wall. Egyptian sheets, and a thick quilt in pastels made by Dean's mother to keep her warm. Magazines and books pre-release for her to read. The whole world at her fingertips.

But she was trapped in that bed. Doing her best to care for a baby who meant more than a brand new life. This baby was everything Landon had lost when his first child had been stillborn. Everything Silver did was monitored. Judged.

Must be exhausting.

"Please don't tell Landon." Silver pulled the quilt up to her chin, eyes already tearing. "I'm trying not to stress, but I'm going insane in here. The doctor said I can keep working, but neither Landon or Dean are willing to take any chances. I feel useless. I never thought being pregnant would be like this."

"It isn't usually." Becky reached out and took Silver's hand. It was hard to put Landon's feelings aside, but Silver was carrying a little niece or nephew Becky would love no matter what. Which made it easier to come to Silver as a mother. "Men can be impossible when you're pregnant. I didn't have to deal with it when I was pregnant with Casey—Patrick was always pretty detached. But I saw how Landon was when *she* was pregnant. With what happened, I'm not surprised that he'd be overprotective now."

"He needs to focus on himself." Silver hugged the comforter to her chest. "I'm okay."

"I know you are, sweetie." Becky smiled and arched a brow at the laptop. "But you're being sneaky."

Silver slumped back onto the pile of pillows behind her. "I know. But my dad keeps calling me. He's cryptic—Dean wouldn't even let me speak to him until he swore not to discuss the team—but I know something's up. Do you know what's going on?"

Aside from the new owner? But if Landon or Dean had wanted Silver to know, they would have told her. The only thing was, keeping her away from her family wouldn't make things easier. Becky couldn't have gone through her own pregnancy without her parents. It wasn't fair that Landon and Dean were restricting Silver's contact with her family.

"My father isn't well. He needs me. And Oriana..." Silver frowned at her white-knuckled fists. "She's all over 'accepting' Ford as our brother. I'm... I'm scared that he's going to use her. And I don't know what I'm supposed to do."

"You're supposed to focus on this baby." Saying so was easy. But Becky knew very well it wasn't that simple.

Silver frowned at her. "You have a kid. Tell me you don't still look out for Landon. Hell, you've made it obvious you don't think I'm good enough for him."

Becky winced. *Have I?* She'd tried really hard to accept her brother's choices, but Silver seemed so self-centered. Becky was accustomed to reading portfolios and making her own judgments, but going by Silver's had proved her wrong again and again. Silver was nothing like how she came off in public. And it was hard to believe Landon would love a woman who was nothing but a Hollywood whore.

Which left her with nothing but what she'd seen of Silver firsthand. Silver was young. She expected more from herself than anyone would ever ask of her. She was desperate to prove she could manage the team, but also desperate to give Landon a healthy baby. The stress of feeling so completely helpless couldn't be good for her.

And if the doctor said she was fit to work, then maybe Landon and Dean should give her something to do.

But until then...

"Would it make you feel better to go see your father?"

A hesitant smile grazed Silver's lips. "Maybe. I mean, he hasn't seen me in months. The baby isn't real to him yet. It might give him something to..."

Something to live for. Becky couldn't argue with that. What parent wouldn't be excited about their first grandchild? And after his family losing controlling interest in the team, Anthony Delgado needed to be reminded that there was more to life than the game.

"Tell Dean and Landon you want to see him. One of them could go with you and—"

"And make things very uncomfortable." Silver rolled her eyes and shook her head. "But you're right. I've just been so worried about upsetting Landon that I... anyway, time to pull on my big girl panties and let them know what's what. Not like they'll spank me if they don't approve."

Becky laughed with Silver, but just the mention of that kind of discipline drew an ache deep within, the kind of ache she had before she ditched the latest fad diet which restricted her to boring food. Even having a Dom give her *that* look before pulling her over his knee would be like that first slice of cheesecake after a calorie-restrictive diet. Damn it, she really wished she could go to the club.

No. Not while her baby was with her father. What if he called? What if something happened? She'd never be able to forgive herself if she was out having fun while Casey...

"Becky?" Silver took her hand, brow furrowed. "You look awful."

Blinking, Becky laughed. "*Thanks.*"

Silver groaned. "I didn't mean it like that. You came in here to check on me, and I didn't even think to ask how you were doing. I know letting Casey go with Patrick was hard. You need a distraction."

So everyone keeps saying. They just didn't get it. She'd had plenty of distractions after leaving Patrick. Being active at the local club kept her busy on the weekends when Patrick had taken Casey before.

Fine, she'd only been on a lunch date with a fellow reporter when Patrick had called from the hospital, but... she shivered. What if she'd been at the club? With her cell phone off. She wouldn't have a leg to stand on in court if she couldn't be reached. Casey needed at least one responsible parent.

There was no way she was getting into that with Silver. So she simply shrugged. "With all you've got planned for the Ice Girls, I have plenty to do. The press is going to be all over the cruise in a few weeks. Keeping the Cobra players involved was brilliant."

"Why, thank you!" Silver beamed and the pink glow of her cheeks made her even more beautiful, despite the fact that she was no longer the perfect Hollywood size 0. "I'm glad I spent so much time setting this up during the season. The mansion thing didn't do all that well—hard to compete with Big Brother—but I have three cable companies airing the cruise. People in Canada are starved for hockey during the summer. Having the guys making appearances will bring up ratings, and you know the male fans will love seeing all those girls in bikinis."

Yeah. Sex on a deck. They'll eat it up. It had been years since Becky had worn a bikini, but she didn't miss it. Much. Fine, sometimes she wished the stretch marks would fade away, and the softness she'd gained with age could be toned down, but she was too busy being a mother and a career woman to obsess.

It would be nice if men looked at me like they'll look at those girls, though.

Patrick had at first. But he'd lost interest. The Doms at the clubs were more attracted to her submissiveness than her body, which had suited her after her divorce, but still...

Being lusted after as a woman would be nice. To have a man want her whether or not she was willing to kneel for him.

What about Scott?

Becky fingered the quilt covering Silver's legs, glancing up once to see Silver distracted by something on her laptop. Scott's teasing smile flickered behind her eyelids every time she blinked. The heat of his lips on hers returned, drifting down her flesh like a featherlight caress. She'd kissed Scott in defiance of Landon's overprotective attitude, but all she'd managed to do was make herself want the man her brother warned her away from even more.

Wanting him wasn't enough. She knew very well she couldn't have sex with a man who wouldn't commit to her unless it was during a scene. Because, during a scene, at least she knew the Dom was focused on her. She'd been with a man for six years who'd never given her that kind of attention. Who hadn't cared about her needs. No. Worse. Had mocked them when she'd finally opened up to him.

Scott wouldn't do that, but she couldn't get past feeling she'd be nothing but an interchangeable body with him. They'd have hot sex, and the next day she'd see him all over another woman. And she knew she couldn't deal with that.

Dean tapped softly on the door and stepped in holding a tray with two bowls. He set the tray on a swiveling, hospital-style table which could be positioned over Silver's lap. The rich scent of stewed beef rose from the bowls, and Becky's mouth watered as she took in the thick, beef bourguignon.

"Eat up." Dean folded his arms over his chest, his black silk shirt clearly outlining his biceps, nicely sized even though they weren't as big as Landon's. Then again, very few men on the team had her brother's build. And as the Cobras General Manager, Dean Richter didn't really need it. But he kept as fit as his men, and between his physical strength, and the sheer power of his presence, he was quite intimidating. Even more so since his command had been directed to Becky. Along with his next words. "We're going out."

Becky stared at him. Her face heated, and she looked over at Silver. "But—"

Silver licked gravy off her spoon, letting out an appreciative moan. "This is delicious, Dean! Oh, and I think that's a great idea. What did Landon say?"

Dean chuckled, bending over to kiss Silver's forehead. "He obviously didn't want details, but he vaguely implied Becky should spend some time at the club."

"*Landon* suggested this?" Hell, if Dean wasn't with Silver and her brother, Becky would be flattered. More than a little tempted. But he was and this could get unbearably awkward. "Sir, I appreciate the offer, but—"

"You won't play with *me*, pet." Smoothing his hand over her hair, Dean gave her a level look. "But I will find someone to take you out of your head for a little bit. All your focus has been on your daughter, on your new position with the team. You need some time to let someone take care of you."

"Dean, I can't—"

"You can and you will." Amusement sparked in his eyes. "I trust you don't need help getting dressed?"

All she could do was shake her head and stop herself from smacking Silver when the younger woman giggled.

* * * *

Not in the mood for leather and props, Zach slid onto a bench at the bar in Blades & Ice, dressed in worn jeans and a faded grey Cobra T-shirt. The BDSM club was ringing with excitement, with life, but none of the energy reached him. A heaviness settled on his chest, as though he'd lifted too much weight and didn't even have the strength left for the roll of shame. All he could do was let it crush him.

You knew Scott wouldn't stay.

Resting a hand on the motorcycle helmet he'd dropped on the seat beside him when he'd come in, Zach waved to the Domme manning the bar. Chicklet came over but paused with the whiskey bottle in her hand.

"You sure?"

Zach arched a brow. "Did I give you the impression I was here to play?"

"With the right sub? I don't see why not." Chicklet propped her elbows on the bar, her black, partially shredded metal studded T-shirt stretching around her broad shoulders. Not big enough to make her butch, but close. Between her beer league and practicing with the whip, the woman was in excellent shape. She intimidated most—even the Doms—but not Zach. He simply respected her as the equal she was. And had come to value her opinion. "I could have told you getting mixed up with Demyan was a bad idea. Find yourself a nice, passive twink that will appreciate you. Wayne's got the flu. His sub would love some attention."

Swiveling on his chair, Zach searched the room for the big bouncer's lithe sub, Mickey. The young man was serving drinks. Keeping him busy was the only way to prevent him from approaching every Dom and Domme in the club with pleading, puppy-dog eyes. Without his Dom around to rein him in, he practically reeked of desperation.

Taking Mickey on would be worse than accepting the little Scott was willing to offer. Easy. Shallow. Zach needed substance when he played, a connection even if it wasn't long-term. Mickey couldn't give him that.

He was a little surprised Chicklet had suggested it. She usually seemed more perceptive. But he'd play along. "Someone should take care of the boy. He looks lost."

Chicklet straightened. "Yep."

"And he'd be easy to deal with."

"Very true."

Zach nodded and pushed his shot glass aside. "All right. This should be interesting. I'll see you—"

"Fuck off!" Chicklet threw her head back, laughing as though he'd said something hysterical. "Nothing fazes you, does it? I was just testing the water, sport. You need to get back in the game, but doing it with him would be stupid. There aren't many male subs available here. You object to a woman?"

His whole body went stiff, but he kept his expression neutral. Ever since he'd confessed to the press that he preferred men, people treated him differently. No one would have questioned him taking on a female sub before—it was considered "natural." Now everyone acted as though doing so would be going against his . . . inclinations.

He gave Chicklet a level look. "Do you prefer men or women, Chicklet?"

"Women." Chicklet frowned. "Why?"

"I guess Tyler's shit out of luck then." Zach lifted his glass, tipping it slightly toward her before taking a blazing sip. "Such a shame. I would consider him if he was available."

"He's not." Chicklet gnashed her teeth, eyes narrowing as she studied him. "And that's not fucking funny."

Leaning back in his chair, Zach regarded her steadily. "It wasn't meant to be. I was making a point."

She folded her arms over her chest. "Which is?"

"My preferences don't restrict me anymore than they do you. I need a sub who needs me. And not just for one night."

Chicklet's lips slanted slightly as she glanced toward the door. "Good. You're in luck." She jerked her chin. "I'm sure you've met Rebecca Bower."

He frowned at her, then followed her gaze to where Becky stood, close behind Richter, wearing a provocative slave dress. The white cotton was threadbare at the hem, so thin it was almost see-through, but unlike many women with the curves Becky had, she didn't seem uncomfortable in her own skin. Not that she should be. Her curves made her luscious and soft. Unlike his teammates, he didn't find himself attracted to the puck bunnies that made themselves available after every game. In his thirty-two years, he'd only had a relationship with one woman. Sue. The woman he'd seen himself spending the rest of his life with, whom he'd given his heart to. But they'd both been young. Ambitious. She'd moved to Washington to pursue a political career, and the long-distance relationship had been hard on her.

Hard on us both.

Their breakup had been amicable, and he still considered her a friend. But he'd never found another woman like her, one he could confide in, one he could share everything with. She'd been the first person he'd experimented with in the lifestyle. The first person he'd come out to. He smiled as he recalled her reaction. Sue had rushed to her bedroom and brought him all the gay romance novels she'd read. Breathlessly admitted she'd love to see him with another man.

But he hadn't wanted anyone but her. To him, it didn't matter if he was with a man or a woman. He was faithful.

Still, he'd been tempted.

After seeing so many on his team find happiness in ménage relationships, he wondered if things would have been different if he'd considered the idea. What if they'd found a man they could both love? A man who could have been with her while he was on the road.

But Sue was happily married, so there was no point in looking back.

Looking forward, all he could think of was Becky. She stirred something inside him that no one had in a long time. He reflected for a moment, realizing it wasn't simply a sexual allure. As she looked to Richter before signing in, as she followed him with her head down and her gaze lowered, Zach felt the pull of her submissive nature. A need that went beyond sex. A need he was desperate to fulfill.

"I have met Becky." He handed his helmet to Chicklet so she could stash it behind the bar. "Please excuse me."

Across the room, Becky trailed Richter as he checked in with each of the DMs, both Dommes. Richter overlooked a piercing scene, then moved to a sitting area, motioning for Becky to kneel as he gestured toward the bar for a drink. He idly stroked Becky's hair, reclining on a leather sofa, speaking softly to her as she relaxed at his feet, resting her head against his thigh. Just being in that position seemed to bring her to a peaceful state.

But Zach knew he could give her more.

"Your pet is lovely, Sir." Zach clasped his hands at the small of his back, resisting the urge to touch the woman he knew was under Richter's protection for the night. "May I speak to her?"

"You may." Richter rubbed his hands on his leather pants, his tone light, but hesitant. "But first, I have to admit I'm a little confused. You've made your preferences clear."

"I'm not sure I have." Zach forced his tone to remain neutral. "I appreciate a precious gift, and it doesn't much matter who gives it."

Lifting her head, soft brown hair drifting over her shoulders, Becky looked up at him, lips parting slightly, blinking as though she couldn't quite believe the word "precious" could possibly be aimed at her. She drew in a soft inhale as he regarded her steadily to make it clear this was exactly how he saw her. Precious and beautiful. He caught uncertainty in her gaze. Something vulnerable.

You didn't come of your own accord, did you, little doe? He tightened his grip on his wrist behind his back. He needed to touch her, more than he'd ever needed to touch anyone. Her eyes were a soft grey, like the fur of the kitten his sister had as a child. But something about her eyes reminded him more of a doe, something he hadn't noticed when they'd first met. Out in the world, she came across bold. Fearless—except when it came to her daughter. Here she was timid, exploring the darkness with wide eyes, ready to dart away at any careless approach. The part of her that would brave out a scene just to satisfy her baser urges would shield the tender side which would run for cover.

But he didn't want her to hide. Not from him.

"There are many Doms here you could play with, Becky. And then there's me. I've thought about you a lot today, hoping you weren't alone, dwelling on things you can't change. Seeing you here . . . I think I can help you." He glanced at Richter, waited for his nod, then held out his hand. "And I promise you won't regret it."

Her throat worked as she swallowed. She lifted her hand, lowered it, nibbling at her bottom lip. "What do you want from me?"

"Only what you're willing to give. We'll start slow."

"This is just for tonight. I'm not sure if I can come back." Her brow furrowed. "I'm not sure I should be here now."

"But you are here. And we'll see if you'll be happy with 'just tonight.' Because I already know I won't be." His breath caught as she laid her wrist in his palm. His skin tingled under the warmth of her smooth, delicate flesh. He pulled her to her feet and brought his other hand up to cup her cheek. Then he smiled. "I haven't scared you away?"

"No. Damn you, you said exactly what I needed to hear." She looked down at her bare feet. "I didn't want to come."

She hadn't seemed all that resistant when she'd arrived. He stroked her cheek with his thumb. "Why not?"

"Because, if I'd wanted something meaningless, I could have made one phone call and had it." She glanced up at him quickly, then away. "But I don't want that."

He knew she was thinking about Scott. Which made it even more important that he keep the man out of his head. So he teased the hair at the nape of her neck with his fingertips and chuckled. "I take it you wouldn't object to talking, before and after? And perhaps a date, even though it could be considered a little backward?"

"I don't mind doing things backward." She grinned. "My mom still wants you to come over."

"And I plan to take her up on the invite."

"Good." She nibbled her bottom lip. "But tonight . . . ?"

"Tonight I'd like to explore your needs." He already had something in mind. Something that would leave her fulfilled, yet wanting more. "Make you happy you came."

She turned her head and pressed a light kiss on his palm. "I already am."

"Good." He leaned close, brushing his lips over hers. "Then I guess it can only get better."

Chapter Three

The music screamed, but Becky hardly heard it. It was nothing but white noise in the distance. And the scenes around her were nothing but echoes of movement in the shadows beyond the sectioned off area Zach led her to. A gasp tore her away from the tranquil state she was in for a beat, but then he picked her up and sat her on the leather, padded table, tapping her cheek lightly so her focus returned to him.

"We should discuss the rules."

Her eyes widened. More rules than the obvious? Unless he didn't know she had experience? *Maybe I should tell him.*

She opened her mouth.

He shook his head and placed a finger over her lips. "Listen first, little doe. It's clear you aren't new to this. But I am new to you. I feel more comfortable going over what I expect from a sub before I play with him or her. I do enjoy certain formalities, but no more than you're comfortable with."

"I'm comfortable with it all. I've been taught well."

"Have you?" He rubbed his chin, nodding slowly. "You seemed surprised when I mentioned discussing rules."

"I apologize. I'm used to Doms knowing how experienced I am."

"So they assume you'll know what they want."

"Exactly."

"I try not to assume anything." He glanced over at a scene where a Dom spoke harshly to a sub who fidgeted as she knelt before him. The girl gave her Dom a blank look, like she really didn't get what she'd done wrong. Zach shook his head. His lips thinned. "I need to know what you expect from me."

"I don't understand." And she really didn't. She was here. He was a Dom. All she expected was for him to take control and let her please him. Not that she was sure anything she could do would.

What if he's settling for me because there's no one else?

"Do you need me to help you forget what happened today, Becky?"

She winced. *Oh, Casey. I hope you're okay, baby.* Her gaze lowered to her bare feet. "I'm not sure that's possible."

"It is. All you have to do it lose yourself to what I do to you."

Do to me? She held her breath, more than a little confused. He'd asked nothing of her yet. Other Doms expected her to kneel gracefully, to dress just right, to anticipate their commands. At the clubs she'd gone to before, she never had a problem finding a Dom because she made them look good. Fine, some Doms wanted a challenge, but dealing with a young, bratty sub could get tiresome. She didn't need to act out to get attention. Actually, she didn't really need attention at all. She just needed to settle into the nice predictable zone where she could turn over control to someone else.

It wouldn't take long to show Zach she could do the same with him.

"Tell me what you need, Sir." She let her hands rest on her knees, utterly passive, ready for him to tell her what to do next. The only thing that made her uncertain was his being gay. Most Doms would tell her to strip right off. He might not need her naked to play.

To him you're a sub. Not a woman.

Her throat tightened slightly. She'd wanted a man to see her as more. To want her as a woman. She'd be missing out on that with Zach.

He did mention a date.

Great. Maybe they could go shopping together. Or see some chick flick. It would be just like hanging out with a woman. He could be her new best friend.

And what's wrong with that? You don't have many friends.

"I will tell you, pet." Zach took hold of the bottom of his T-shirt, then pulled it over his head. "When I'm ready."

Her mouth went dry. He was . . . *damn.* A pure work of art in muscle and ink. She drank him in like gulps of fresh, spring water after a long hike. The tattoo covering most of his right arm caught her attention, and she found herself drawn in to the intricate details. A weeping angel perched on a tombstone, beneath a tree with limbs that seemed barren at first, but looking closer, held tiny pale green buds. The dead grass among the graves gave way to fresh patches. New life amidst death.

She reached out to touch it, then pulled her hand back. One did not simply *touch* a Dom. Not without permission.

"Go ahead, little doe. As long as your hands are free, you may touch me whenever you'd like." The edges of Zach's lips twitched when she hesitated. "Not something you hear often?"

"Not really. Usually a Dom's all about touching me. Getting me naked as soon as I've agreed to scene with them" Her cheeks heated. She lowered her hand to her sides, fiddling with the hem of her dress. "Not that I'm complaining."

I need you to touch me. But only if you want to.

"You make me wonder how many 'real' Doms you've been with, sweetheart." He tossed his shirt aside and placed his hands on the table by her hips. "They sound rather selfish."

She shook her head. "Not at all. They gave me what I needed at the time."

His head tilted to one side. "So you never needed to touch them?"

An ache settled between her eyes. She wasn't sure what to say to that. Yeah, sometimes she wanted to touch them, but once they shackled her wrists, she didn't really think about it. It was all about the scene they orchestrated. And in pleasing them, most of her needs were met.

He took her hand and pressed it to the center of his chest. His skin was smooth, cool, like velvet molded over flowing steel. His pecs tensed slightly as she explored the fine, dark curls covering his chest. He rested his hand on her shoulder as she continued touching him, massaging lightly as she trailed her fingertips over the tattoo on his arm, then grazed them up his neck and along his jaw. Freshly-shaven, nothing hiding the sharp angles of his face. The rich, warm scent of cologne with dark, earthy tones, drifted in the air, so alluring she had to fight not to press her face against his throat to breathe it in. She smiled as she felt the small cleft in his chin.

Sweet mother, he's gorgeous.

"Go ahead. Say it." Zach tugged her hair, light creases forming around his eyes as she looked up, the only evidence she could see to prove he was actually a couple of years older than she was. He was the type of man who only improved with age.

"Say what?" She ran her thumb over his bottom lip, soft and silky and warm in contrast to the rest of him.

He kissed her thumb. "It's a shame."

"Why? Do you hear that a lot?"

"Yes. All the bunnies are in mourning since I 'came out.'"

"I believe it." She laughed. "Actually, I was thinking you're one of the most handsome men I've ever met, but it's probably a bad idea to say so. Your ego doesn't need any more stroking."

He grinned, gathering her hair in one hand, using it as a handle to tip her head back. "I have a feeling that mouth of yours has gotten you into a lot of trouble."

She made a face. "Umm . . . not really. Not at the clubs anyway. I don't usually—I'm sorry."

"For what? If I didn't want you to talk, I'd gag you." He leaned closer. "Or find another way to keep you quiet."

His hand framed her jaw as he slid his lips over hers, brushing back and forth, light as the caress of a feather. Her lips tingled, parted slightly as the tip of his tongue teased them. She closed her eyes as he kissed her, gently at first, then deeper, tasting her, holding her jaw and hair firmly so she couldn't move. Her pulse raced as he pressed his body against hers, stealing her breath. He teased her upper lip with one last flick of his tongue, then eased back.

The room spun like a carousel out of control, with her at the center, Doms in leather with whips and chains taking the place of the pretty ponies, the music a hard-core beat pierced by screams. The atmosphere of a club usually brought her closer to the right headspace than the Dom alone, but with Zach, it wouldn't matter where they were. If he could do this with just a kiss . . .

"I won't restrain you tonight, Becky." He stroked his hand down her spine, watching her face as he laid her down on the padded table. "I'd like to see how well you can follow basic commands. Like, 'don't move.'"

What is this, Submissive for beginners? She knew better than to frown at him, but by the way his brow rose, she'd come close. "I've never had a problem with restraints."

"Good. Then you should do just fine without them."

"But—"

He put a finger over her lips and shook his head. "Come to think of it, I believe we *should* have some speech restrictions. You are permitted to speak to discuss limits. To use the club safeword—though I doubt you'll need it during this scene. If you don't understand a command, you may ask me to clarify, but I think I've been clear so far."

Don't scowl at him, dummy. She inhaled slowly, then nodded. "Yes, Sir."

"Do you have any limits I should know about?"

"Ah . . . no blood, scat and such, no heavy impact or anything that leaves marks that last more than a day or so." Her cheeks heated, but she knew she had to be honest. And her last limit could end things before they'd even started. "No anal."

The edge of his lip twitched. "Was that something you expected me to want?"

"Well, you're . . ." *I really hate this part.* Negotiating with someone new meant talking about embarrassing things. She preferred writing it all down and letting the Dom read the list ahead of time. Discussing only what she'd marked as "uncertain." But Zach hadn't even asked Dean for her limit list. "Do I have to say it?"

"Yes."

"You're gay. I figured the only way you would . . . I mean . . ." Hell, she didn't even know if gay men did that with women. But he wanted to play with her, so he had to be getting something out of it. "I understand if you're no longer interested."

He sighed and bent over, bracing a hand on the table by her head. "There will be no penetration of any sort tonight, little doe, but once we reach that point, I will enjoy your body, however you are willing to give it to me. If that is a limit, I will respect it. However, we will discuss why you're not open to trying it."

"I have tried it."

"I see."

"I didn't like it. It hurt and I'm not into pain." She spoke in a rush, not sure he could possibly understand since that was the only way he could be with most of his lovers. "That's another problem, actually. Some Doms aren't interested in a sub with no tolerance for pain. Not that I mind a light spanking now and then, but—"

"Shh." Zach kissed her, then let out a light laugh against her lips. "It's okay. That's enough for tonight. I know you're not comfortable sharing all this. But I will tell you one thing."

She swallowed, her whole body trembling as she realized he wasn't ending things and sending her off to someone else. He still wanted her. She dented her bottom lip with her teeth, hissing through them. "What?"

His lips grazed her cheek. He spoke quietly in her ear. "It doesn't have to hurt."

She shivered as he straightened, leaving her arms slack as he drew them up to lay on the table above her head, stretched out much like they would be if she *had* been restrained. He did the same at the bottom of the table with her ankles, setting them far apart, making her all too aware of how short the dress she'd borrowed from Silver was. Thankfully, Dean hadn't told her not to wear panties, because the dress was snug enough to bare her to the hip with her thighs spread. Since she hadn't planned to play tonight, she hadn't thought to shave during her shower this morning. Her legs weren't too bad, but she'd have been humiliated to show any Dom that she'd neglected to shave her privates.

If I'd known Zach would be here—that he'd want to—

"You stiffened up. What's wrong?"

I did? She tried to relax. Zach had already decided on no penetration. But as much as she didn't want him to see her unkempt, she couldn't help being a little disappointed. It had been a long time since she'd wanted a man this much. A thought of Scott had her rolling her eyes. Okay, not *that* long, but Zach was the first one she wouldn't feel cheap with in the morning. She had a feeling he—unlike Scott—would still be there when she woke up.

"It's nothing." She forced a smile. "You just have me feeling a little reckless."

"Do I?" He chuckled. "Don't tempt me, Becky. It would be easy to forgo the whole scene and simply make love to you, but that wouldn't satisfy either of us."

She nodded. "Because I'm a woman."

His jaw hardened. "No. Because I'm a Dom, and I need to give you more." He raked his fingers into her hair, tightening his grip to the edge of pain. "As you said, you could have had that with a phone call. I could have had it with less."

Perfectly still, needing to show him, at very least, she could follow instructions, Becky wondered exactly what Zach's relationship with Scott was. There were whispers that Scott would do anyone, anywhere, but was he really bisexual? Zach didn't seem the type of man to take on casual lovers, but Scott wasn't the type of man to take on anything but. Her attraction to Scott was frustrating as hell, because she knew nothing could come of it. How much worse would it be to be used by him when he was also a friend? A teammate?

Scott had been seen with more women over the summer than in his whole career. A different one every night. It had started not long after Zach had come out to the press.

If the two were connected, Scott wasn't just a player. He was a coldhearted son of a bitch. He'd blatantly rejected Zach. And that had to hurt.

"Zach—*Sir*, I didn't mean to . . . I didn't think that you and Scott were—"

"Serious? We're not." Zach sighed. "Please don't apologize. You have the right to know if I'm involved with anyone—I'd expect you to tell me if you were. Can we agree that we're both single, that we both have similar interests, and that neither of us is interested in a one night stand?"

"Yes."

"Good. Then shall we start? Do you understand what I expect from you?"

"Don't move. Don't speak unless for clarity or to safeword."

"Excellent." He gave her a slanted smile, then slowly circled the table, his hand moving in an outline of her body without touching her. "That dress looks lovely on you."

"Thank you." She groaned when he clucked his tongue. "Sorry, Sir."

"Do you often have difficulty submitting?"

She shook her head.

"Hmm. I see." He stopped by her side. Drew his finger up her arm from her inner wrist to her elbow. She twitched. Clenched her fists. "But you are finding it difficult to obey me?"

"No, Sir."

"Neither safeword or clarification." He smoothed his hand over her cheek. "All the Doms you've been with haven't asked for much, have they? No, don't answer." His tone was rough, but not with anger. More . . . carefully restrained. "I'd love to push you. Challenge you. But not yet. First you have to prove you can handle this."

She almost said, "I can," but then remembered she wasn't supposed to say anything. The restrictions suddenly felt more imposing than any gag or restraint. She settled into the sensation, relaxing because giving him what he'd asked for was really very simple. No guesswork involved.

The approval in his eyes was like a bright golden star bursting in the center of her chest. She inhaled deeply and held her breath, waiting to see what he'd do next.

He circled the table again, stopping at her other side. Hooking his fingers into the thick straps of her dress above her shoulders, he pulled it down, moving her as he pleased, taking one arm, then the other, until both were free of the dress. Only the neckline covered her breasts as he placed her arms. Her nipples tightened into sensitive little points as she waited for him to expose them, but instead he walked to the end of the table and traced his fingertips down the soles of her feet.

A giggle escaped her, and she squirmed as he did it again.

"Be still."

And again. It tickled, but she pressed her eyes shut, ground her teeth, and fought not to move. His hands curved around her feet and she bit back a groan as he pressed his thumbs into her soles. He stroked, massaged, then tickled, alternating until the pleasure edged on torture. Yet, somehow, she kept still. Sank into a place where all that mattered was his touch. As it moved up to her calves, she sank even deeper, responding to his slow, even breaths, to his soft praise. She needed to know she had it in her to please him. To be everything he needed and wanted by doing nothing but what came naturally.

"I was right. You are precious." He kissed her bare shoulder, then rolled the material of her dress down over her breasts. "This isn't just sex for you. It's so much more."

"Yes." She absorbed the satisfaction in his tone like earth soaked in rain after a drought. She knew she shouldn't speak, but she had to make sure he wasn't just doing this for her. "Am I . . . do I make you happy?"

"More than I can say." He lowered his head to her breasts, resting his forehead between them. He kissed the side of one breast and she shivered. The sensation was both tender and erotic. Lingering, building as he kissed his way up to her nipple. "Don't forget what I've asked of you."

Don't move.

Pleasure speared her as he sucked her nipple into his mouth. Her eyes teared as she struggled not to arch up. As she pressed her lips together.

"No man or woman has pleased me as much as you have."

He pinched her nipple between his finger and thumb as he sucked the other.

"I won't be easy on you, little doe."

He shifted down her body, drawing the hem of her dress up over her hips, over her belly, kissing the exposed flesh as he worked his way down.

"But if you are mine . . ."

His fingers traced the edge of her panties, along the sides of her pussy lips, close to where the material had grown damp. He bit down just above the slight swell of her stomach, rubbing her panties into her clit.

"I will give you what no one else can."

The muscles in her thighs tensed. Pleasure curled up in her core, sizzling like a live wire in a shallow pool, electricity zipping across the surface.

"Come for me, little doe. Lose yourself. Give up control. It belongs to me."

Becky opened her mouth wide and choked back a scream. She came as though he'd pulled a trigger, set off a spark which ignited everything inside her. A sob tore from her throat as she shook, her hips bucking, her core tightening and releasing sporadically, the sensation fierce even though nothing filled her. Nothing grounded her. And suddenly she needed that. Something to hold her down before she shattered.

"Come here." Zach gathered her in his arms, carrying her to a chair to hold her tight as she came apart. It felt like she'd been torn open, exposed in a way she didn't know how to handle. She shuddered, gasping as she curled into a ball on his lap. His dick pressed into her hip, and she blinked fast.

She'd done nothing for him.

Nothing!

"Don't cry." Zach pressed her head against his shoulder as another sob tore out from her chest. "Rest for a minute, then tell me what's wrong."

A hysterical laugh broke free as she lifted her head. Blinded by tears, she tried to meet his eyes. "Not for me. It's not okay if it's just for me."

"It wasn't, little doe. Believe me." He kissed her forehead. "You have no idea what you've given me. And it's not over. There will be more. So much more."

"It's not enough!" The tears stung her eyes. And she didn't know why. It was so wonderful, but taking more than she gave felt so wrong.

"For tonight it is." Zach kissed her forehead, "Come home with me, Becky. Let me hold you while you sleep. I need to see you when I wake up."

Casey ... Becky's throat locked around a hard lump. Zach *had* managed to make her forget. Her daughter was away. Would be for three weeks. She had nothing to go home to. Except her brother—who had Silver. And her parents—who had each other. Waking up alone in a house that wasn't hers, thinking of the moments she'd spent not thinking about her daughter at all. How could she . . .

"I can't . . . Sir, I screwed up. I shouldn't have done this. What if—"

"What if what, Becky? What could have happened while you were with me?"

"I don't know. Something bad."

"No. Your mother is still at Dean's. He has his phone. Someone would have called him."

"I'm her mother."

"And Casey is with her father. You had no choice."

Helplessness ripped through her, like someone had cracked open her chest. "It's not fair."

"No. It's not. And we can talk about it more in the morning."

Zach dressed her, then held her close to his side as he approached Dean. He spoke low, and she couldn't make out a single word. All she could think of was what a horrible mother she was. She knew Patrick would screw up. Her daughter would need her. And she'd been so incredibly selfish—

"Rebecca, look at me." Dean took hold of her chin, trapping her with his gaze until his words were all that mattered. "You know my number. I will call you if there's anything. Swear to me you'll do the same."

Why would I need to call you? She blinked at him, confused. She was a grown woman, not a little girl who needed protection. But Dean obviously didn't see it that way.

"I will."

"Good." Dean turned to Zach. "Make sure she gets some sleep. She hasn't gotten much at my place since that asshole called her."

"I'm not surprised." Zach pressed her head against his chest. "But she's tough. Don't hesitate to call if—"

"I won't."

"All right." Zach's arm was heavy on her shoulders. Solid and steady. More so than the ground beneath her feet. "Any more objections, Becky? Tell me now."

All that she'd thought was stable within crumbled. She rasped in a breath as she shook her head. It was ridiculous to need aftercare after the little they'd done, but she knew she did. If he'd sent her home without letting her . . .

What can I do for him? He'd mentioned talking in the morning. That could work. She could make him breakfast. Maybe clean for him.

Which was funny, because she'd hated cleaning up after her husband. He'd always been a slob. And doing things for him never meant anything. But doing things for Zach would. She relaxed against his side and let out a sigh.

"No objections. I wouldn't have liked for the night to end like this."

Zach chuckled and kissed her hair. "Sweetie, we're nowhere close to the end."

* * * *

The central air in the condo kept the temperature comfortably cool, but as Zach watched Becky step up to him, shivering, he wondered if he should turn it off. He studied her face as she took hold of the bottom of his T-shirt. She didn't seem cold.

Nervous?

No. Excited. Maybe even impatient. Her cheeks were flushed, eyes wide and bright as she quickly pulled his shirt up over his head. She hadn't hesitated when he'd told her to undress him. He grinned as she dropped the T-shirt and moved closer to him, exploring the muscles of his arms and chest like she couldn't stop touching him. His eyes drifted shut as she pressed a kiss to the center of his chest, and blood pumped steadily into his dick. There was something so close to worship in the way she kissed him. The way her hands caressed him. And the look in her eyes as she lowered to her knees and undid his belt . . . it was as though, in that moment, he was her whole world.

How long had she needed this for the little he'd done to mean so much? He kept his expression neutral as he fought the urge to pull her into his arms and ask her. This wasn't the time to force her to think about what had been lacking in her life. With how she'd reacted to receiving more than she gave, the best thing he could do was let her serve him.

He stepped out of his jeans, then clucked his tongue as she flung them aside. "Is that how you treat your Master's things, pet?"

Becky gaped up at him, blushing even as a shy smile graced her lips. She shook her head. "No, Sir."

After she'd folded his clothes and placed them on his dresser, she returned to him and hooked her fingers into the elastic of his boxers. She bit her lip as she eyed his erection, barely contained by the snug, black cotton.

"Wait."

Blinking at him, she rested her hands on her thighs. He could tell she was trying to hide her disappointment—she might have succeeded if he hadn't been watching her so carefully.

He motioned for her to stand. "I need to see you. All of you." Letting out a sigh of relief, she held still while he eased the slave dress off her shoulders and let it drift to the floor.

Chuckling, he tapped her chin with a finger. "What was that for?"

"It's just..." Her brow furrowed. She stared at her bare feet. "I don't understand why you waited so long to get me naked."

His lips curved slightly as he let his gaze travel slowly over her lush body, from her ample breasts to the swell of her hips. He cupped her cheek. "You were already naked to me, little doe."

Her breath caught as he kissed her, and he smiled against her lips as she moaned softly and leaned into him. She went still as he took a knee, and he heard her swallow hard as he pulled down her skintone, silk panties. A shadow of stubble covered her pussy and he glanced up, taking note of her blush.

"I'm sorry I didn't—"

"Don't be. It pleases me that you didn't go to the club ready to give yourself to just any man. And you haven't tried to cover yourself from me. Very nice." He traced a finger over her stomach, pressing his lips together when she stiffened. "What's wrong?"

"It's just... my stomach is gross."

His brow lifted. "I don't think it's changed since the club."

"No, but it was dark. You couldn't see all the stretch marks and—"

"Stop right there and listen carefully." He straightened, putting a hand on her hip to hold her in place. "You are beautiful. Each and every inch of you. As long as you are with me, this is my body. And I won't accept you saying—or *thinking*—anything negative about what is mine. You bear those marks from carrying a precious child. You should be proud of them."

She inhaled, then nodded. "I never thought of it that way. But I will now, Sir."

"Good girl." The way she glowed at the simple praise quickened his pulse. Suddenly, he had to show her, with more than words, that he meant exactly what he said. Tonight she was his, and he was desperate to claim her. But not with sex. He'd only ever fucked one person in mindless lust and passion, and he still regretted it. He refused to go there with Becky.

But there were other things he could do to her which would satisfy them both.

"I always shower before bed. Would you care to join me?"

The fact that he'd asked seemed to throw her off, but he would only go so far on taking her choices from her on the first night. Eventually, he could see them falling into a peaceful routine. But not yet.

Her fingers curled, then straightened, as though she'd resisted making fists at her sides. She dropped her gaze to the floor. "Yes. I would."

He gave her a level look.

"S-sir." She drew in a sharp inhale. "Sorry."

"Don't be sorry. If you have a problem with my requests, say so."

"I don't. It's just..." Her forehead creased. She clasped her hands in front of her. "There are things I'd do for you if—"

"Like what?"

"I..." She bit her lip hard. Then released it as soon as she caught his frown. "I'd like to wash you."

"I've never had a sub do that for me." He let out a soft laugh at her scowl. He'd openly criticized her former Doms—which was bad form, but he couldn't help it. They'd shamelessly used a sub who desperately wanted to serve. Her actions and words condemned them to his mind. He had a feeling his own words had just condemned every sub that came before her.

She gave him a heavy-lidded smile. "Let me take care of you, Sir. After me, you won't accept any less."

He hooked an arm around her neck and kissed her forehead. "I don't doubt that for a second."

In the shower, beneath the hot spray, he stood, relaxed, letting her soap his body with a facecloth covering her hand. The mist surrounding them picked up the subtle aroma of his orange and ginger body wash, fresh and invigorating. She scrubbed his back, then rubbed the tension from his muscles with slick, surprisingly strong hands. Up on her tiptoes, she washed his hair, using her fingertips to massage his scalp. He let out a soft moan as the soothing sensations slowed his pulse. As she shifted closer, he held on to her waist, partially because he was afraid she'd slip. Partially because he couldn't help himself. Already he was making plans for what he would do with her in the days, the weeks, to come. Having all her focus on him, drawing all his focus to her, created a level of intimacy he'd never felt with anyone.

After rinsing him off with the showerhead, she knelt gracefully, gazing up at him as she wrapped her hand around his dick. He nodded, and she took him in her mouth. Jaw clenched, he held off release as long as he could, then dropped his head back, a rough sound escaping him as he came down her throat. Pleasure rocked his body so hard all his strength went to just staying on his feet. Her hot mouth held him until he went slack. And as she drew away, the selfless contentment in her eyes humbled him. He could bring her to bed and do nothing for her and she'd be happy. Because this wasn't about her at all.

It wasn't enough for him though. A sub like her could give again and again, expecting nothing in return. But he needed to give it.

Not that his needs weren't a little selfish.

Tone rough, he pulled her to her feet and latched on to her thigh. "Put your foot on the ledge of the bath."

She obeyed without question, trembling as he dropped hard to his knees. He molded her ass in his hands and buried his face between her thighs, tasting her with a loud groan he knew she would feel, deep in her core. He flicked his tongue roughly over her clit, then took the nub between his teeth, tugging gently. She whimpered. Her feet slipped.

"Hold on to me." He slipped his tongue between her slick folds as she braced her hands on his shoulders. "For as long as you can."

He dipped his tongue in deep, over and over until she cried out. The muscles of her cunt tightened around his tongue as he thrust in. Her juices covered his face, sweet and hot and so fucking delicious. He drank her in as she trembled, catching her as she fell and lowered her so she could sit on the edge of the bath. With long strokes, he drew out her pleasure, dipping, sucking as she came again. He knew he could force another orgasm, but that would be cruel. She was exhausted. Barely able to stand even as he pulled her to her feet.

And she wouldn't be happy until she knew she'd done more for him than he'd done for her. He caught the subtle stiffening of her shoulders as she stepped onto the bath mat. Part of him wanted to simply carry her to bed and curl up with her in his arms, but he couldn't rest until he knew he'd fulfilled that baser instinct she had to please.

"I can't go to bed like this, pet." He glanced over at the towel hanging by the bath, then let his arms fall to his sides. "If you don't mind?"

"I don't." She grabbed the towel, fumbled with it, bowing her head as she dropped to her knees. "You don't even need to ask."

Fuck. Good job, Pearce. He'd helped her reach the level of submission that satisfied her, but a request, rather than a command, shifted the balance. This was new to him, but he had to adapt quickly or he'd throw her off.

They still had so much to learn about one another. He reached down and tipped her chin up. "I won't ask next time. But you have to promise to tell me when you've had enough."

"I will." Her eyes twinkled even as she rubbed the towel down his thigh. "I'm not interested in a 24/7 arrangement. On our date, I'll be Miss Independent." She laughed, and the carefree sound made his heart skip a beat. He hadn't found himself a slave. He'd found a women with many layers he wanted to explore. Her next words proved it. "That's when my mouth gets me in trouble."

He grinned. "Hmm. Well, I should warn you. I tend to punish mouthy subs."

"You will *not* punish me for speaking my mind."

"Of course not. So long as you do so respectfully." He placed his hands on his hips. "'Yes, Sir' and 'No, Sir' resolve most debates rather quickly."

Her eyes went wide. "You're not serious, are you?"

"No. I already know you're a very intelligent woman, Becky." He took the towel from her as she stood, using it to wipe the beads of moisture from her cheeks. "Challenge me. I look forward to it."

She placed her hand over his, holding the towel against her face, her eyes searching his. "I've never had a real relationship with a Dom. Was never sure I wanted one. Sometimes, the way I get when I'm in a scene . . . I'm afraid to lose myself."

"I won't let that happen." Pulling her into his arms, he rested her head against his shoulder and kissed her damp hair. "I want you, little doe. All of you."

Chapter Four

"Hey, Demyan?" Light sliced through Scott's eyelids and cracked into his skull like a pickax as a familiar voice came from the open door. He groaned, rolling away from the body pressed against his side, practically gagging as he ended up with his face too close to the wide open mouth of the man snoring on his other side. Morning breath with a side of ashtray and vodka. Nasty.

He squinted toward the door. "What is it, Vanek?"

Tyler Vanek, a superstar rookie whose career had likely been ended by a concussion, took a step into Scott's bedroom and gave the men crowding the bed a look of disgust. "Fuck, man. You've sunk to a new low."

Scott snorted and shoved at the man sleepily grinding against his ass. He knew his roommate wasn't homophobic—even in the darkness, it was obvious the guys Scott had picked up were hookers, cokeheads, or both—but the poor kid still thought Scott had standards.

"I'm as low as I can get, sport." Scott sat up and tried to smile, but a throb between his eyes at the movement made it more of a grimace. "What's up?"

"Richter called. Your 'keeper' is on his way."

"My what?" Scott scraped his tongue with his teeth. Damn, how much did he drink last night? His stomach lurched, and he took a deep breath to settle it. "I'm not up to this shit. Call him back and tell him I've got the flu. May be fatal."

"You're shitting me, right?" Vanek inched closer to the bed, glanced back over his shoulder, then leaned over, speaking low. "You're meeting the new owner in two hours. You blow it off, and you might as well pack your stuff."

The meeting. *How the fuck could I forget the goddamn meeting?* His head cleared slightly, despite the sharp, pulsing pain. "Christ. All right, I'm up. Thanks for the warning."

"No problem." Vanek shook his head and tossed Scott a pair of boxers from the pile of clean clothes on his dresser. "You want me to call them a cab?"

"Naw, I'll take care of it. Get back to bed before Chicklet comes looking for you. She already don't like me. She'll be ripping if she finds out I'm exposing you to this shit."

"I'm her boyfriend, not her kid."

"You're her sub."

"And? Seriously, all that time you spend at the club and you still don't get it, do you?" Vanek squared his shoulders, solid, though not broad. He was a good looking kid. But his angel face made him look really young. "Yeah, I'm her sub. But I'm still a man."

I do get it, but . . . Hell, Scott wasn't getting into the fact that *he* wanted to protect the boy from the depraved crap he did. Besides, saying so wouldn't mean much since he'd brought it into the condo they shared.

"Just get out." Scott crawled to the bottom of the bed, pulled on his boxers, then reached into the mini-fridge by his dresser for a bottle of water. He took a few long gulps, then grunted. "I'll get rid of them."

As he fumbled blindly through his mostly empty drawers for a T-shirt, he heard the bedsprings creak. The alcohol in his system had him moving too slow. From the corner of his eye, he saw the bigger guy on the bed grab Vanek's arm.

"You're pretty." The man slurred, roughly pulling Vanek onto the bed. "You suck dick as good as your friend?"

"Let me go, you nasty piece of shit!" Vanek twisted in the man's fumbling embrace, snapping his head to the side to avoid a slobbery kiss. He threw his elbow at the man's face, missed, then did his best to roll off the bed when the man loosened the grip on his arm to grope him. "Scott!"

The door hit the wall just as Scott lurched toward the bed. He slammed into Vanek as Chicklet jerked him away from the man. Blood red nails flashed in the light glaring from the hall. The meaty sound of a fist hitting flesh filled the room.

"You son of a bitch!" Chicklet snarled, punching the man again. His nose caved under her fist. She bared her teeth and wrapped a hand around the man's thick neck. "You've got five seconds to get out before I take a razor to your fucking balls."

"You bitch! You broke my nose!" Eyes wide and wild, the man shoved Chicklet off him and lunged for her.

Scott threw himself into the man and they crashed into the wall. The bedside lamp hit the floor and shattered. The man pushed against him. Scott pushed back. The other man scrambled from the bed beside them, tipping over the night table. The drawer slid out and crashed on to the floor. Scott cursed as the man he held spotted Scott's gun, going for it even as Scott scrambled to snatch it away.

A small, slender hand grabbed the gun before the man closed his hand around it. Laura, Chicklet's other sub, skidded backward, then lifted the gun, holding it steadily.

"Hands up. All three of you." Even in a long, nearly transparent white lace nightgown, Laura didn't look like a chick you wanted to mess with. Despite the chaos, her tone was dead calm. Her cold gaze showed that she saw Scott as no different than the two scumbags he'd fucked earlier. Not as the guy she'd joked with the day before over breakfast. Scott took a step back and put his hands up. The other two men straightened and did the same. "Clasp your hands behind your neck and don't fucking move. Tyler, get my zip ties."

Vanek hesitated by the door, subconsciously rubbing the stark red marks on his arm. "Not Demyan, Laura. He fucked up, but this isn't his fault."

This is all my fault. Scott stared at the marks, already picturing the nasty bruises they'd form. *I did that.*

Laura's jaw tensed. She glanced at Scott, in total cop mode. "This gun registered?"

"Yeah." *I'm not that stupid.* "Do what you've got to do. Getting hauled in will just make my fucking day."

"He didn't *do* anything!" Vanek took a step forward, but Chicklet hauled him back. He groaned. "Nothing happened. I'm not pressing charges. I just want them gone."

"Assault is *not* nothing, Tyler." Chicklet put her hand on Vanek's shoulder. "I'm not letting them get away with this."

"You nailed the guy before I had a chance." Vanek wrenched away from her. "Just leave it alone."

Gun still on the men, Laura glanced over at Chicklet, then jutted her chin toward the door at Chicklet's nod. "Out."

The men grabbed their clothes, slamming into each other as they scrambled for the door, still naked. After they were gone, Laura checked the barrel of the gun, then arched a brow at Scott.

"One bullet?"

Scott shrugged. "Didn't figure I'd need more if someone came after me."

"Why would someone come after you?"

"It doesn't matter," Chicklet said before Scott could come up with an answer. Her brow creased as she looked at Vanek, who folded his arms over his chest and avoided her gaze. "This is your place, Tyler, but I honestly think it's a bad idea for Scott to keep living here. You don't need this. You've been working so hard to get better."

Vanek pressed his eyes shut. Bowed his head. "You're right. I'm sorry, Demyan."

Swallowing hard, Scott nodded. "Don't be. I don't blame you. Just . . . just give me a few days to find a new place?"

"Yeah. Sure." Vanek sighed. "And this stays between us. The team needs you."

Right. Like they need more bullshit. "The owner has no reason to keep me, man."

"Silver put her neck out for you." Vanek ground his teeth. "Give him a fucking reason."

As soon as Vanek walked out, Chicklet strode up to Scott, practically spitting in his face. "I don't know what's wrong with you. And honestly, I don't care. You wanna trash your life? Go for it. But I'll be damned if you bring him down with you."

"Got it." Scott watched the two women leave his room, then sank to his bed and dropped his head into his hands. His throat locked and he swallowed back a sob. Vanek was the only person who gave a fuck about him. He'd started to think about the kid like a brother. He'd gone to physical therapy sessions with him, more invested in the kid's career than he was in his own. He just couldn't accept that Vanek wouldn't recover, even though all his diagnostics seemed hopeless. But like always, Scott didn't fucking think about how his own actions affected anyone else. After leaving Zach's place, he'd hit the closest bar and gotten hammered. He didn't remember anything much after that.

A buzzing from his jacket, hanging on the hook behind his bedroom door, drew his attention. He dragged himself off his bed, fetched his phone, then checked the number.

His brother. He answered. "This is a bad time."

"It always is." Jimmy let out a shaky laugh. "Spot me twenty K and I'll leave you alone."

"Only twenty this time?" Scott's stomach heaved. He dropped the phone and stumbled toward the trashcan under his desk. He puked, then picked up his cell, shaking hard. "I'll put it in your account."

"Thanks, bro."

Jimmy hung up. Scott numbly dialed his bank and transferred the money. Like he always did. Not like the massive paycheck he got from the team went to anything meaningful anyway. And he didn't want to deal with the people his brother borrowed from. Not again.

He managed to make it to the shower before he broke down. Hunched over, muscles trembling, he let the water pound on him. He emptied his stomach over the drain. Bile seared his throat.

When will it end?

Never. Jimmy needed him to be strong. Hell, his brother had lost his daughter. Scott couldn't even begin to grasp how much that must hurt. He'd cradled Ashley in his arms moments after her first breath. Gone to her first dance recital while she was still healthy. Watched the leukemia steal her life away and held his brother as he fell apart the day she died. They had both been through so much, he couldn't expect Jimmy to pull himself together after he'd lost the only person he'd truly loved. They were both fucked up. Not worth much. But Ashley's short life had been worth something. And he'd give his brother whatever he needed to get through the loss. For as long as it took.

Hauling in a lungful of warm mist, Scott forced himself to stand and scrub his body hard enough to get his blood flowing. Being clean made him feel a bit less pathetic. He had to pull himself together and make himself presentable if he wanted to stay on the team. Might not show it much, but he loved the guys. Playing for a rival team wasn't an option.

A soft tap on the bathroom door came just as he was turning off the shower. Someone was in his bedroom. Not Chicklet, she'd had her say. Maybe Laura wanted her turn. He grabbed a towel as he stepped out of the bath and called out, "I'll be with you in a sec."

After wrapping the towel around his waist, he opened the door.

"Well, at least I've got something to work with." The short, skinny man waved Scott into the painfully bright room. He held up his hand when Scott opened his mouth to ask who the hell he was. "My name is Stephan Vaughn, and I'm your new image consultant. Mr. Vanek let me in."

Stephan circled Scott, one long finger thoughtfully tapping his pointy chin. His silky, dirty blond hair fell across his forehead, neatly styled with not a single flyaway. He wore a shiny, midnight blue suit with a pale blue shirt and a creamy yellow tie that stamped him as metrosexual. The suit bag draped across Scott's bed made Scott a little nervous. He could so see this guy having fun dressing him up like some Ken doll.

The man's next words confirmed Scott's fears. "From this point on, you do not go out in public wearing anything aside from what I've picked out for you. We will discuss anything you say to the press to make sure you are giving a good impression. I will be monitoring every aspect of your life."

You've got to be shitting me! He might as well head out to the kitchen, bend over, and let Chicklet peg his ass. Giving himself over to the Domme sounded like more fun. Was this guy fucking high? Scott's lips curled away from his teeth as he folded his arms over his chest. "And I'm going along with this why?"

"Because the team won't keep you otherwise. Silver's lawyer contacted me and explained the situation. Asher and I have worked together with some of his unsavory, yet high profile clients in the past. He managed to talk the new owner into giving me a shot at you. Silver doesn't know how precarious your position on the team is. Or how your reputation reflects on her. In her delicate condition, it's best that she doesn't find out."

"Yeah . . ." Scott ducked his head and water droplets sprinkled from his hair to his cheeks. He swiped them away with the back of his hand. Twice now he'd been reminded that Silver had done a lot for him. She'd taken plenty of slack for signing him. She didn't need more while she was pregnant and not supposed to be stressed. He didn't want to let her down, but still, this seemed like a bit much. Unless... unless it worked. "You think you can keep me from getting traded?"

"So long as you're willing to cooperate?" Stephan's neat brows lifted. He smiled at Scott's nod, flashing toothpaste-ad-white teeth. "Yes. As far as the press, and the new owner, are concerned, you're cleaning up your act. You are a humble man, well aware that he's 'fucked up.' You will listen to whatever the owner has to say and reply politely, always addressing him as 'Sir.'" He sniffed. "And I will do my best to make sure he can't tell you're hungover."

"Some toast and Gatorade and I'll be fine." Mostly. He cursed himself again for drinking so much, but he was feeling a bit better already. Things weren't hopeless, not if Stephan could pull this off. All the attitude he'd wanted to give the stuffy bastard vanished as he considered how fast he'd have been shipped out without his help. "What else do you need me to do?"

"For now, just get dressed." Stephan gestured vaguely toward the suit bag on the bed. He looked around room, nostrils flaring, lips pursed. "We will focus on the meeting, then discuss new accommodations. Is there a reason you share a condo with a teammate and his... girlfriends?"

Scott laughed. "I was renting, but I got kicked out. Vanek gave me a place to stay, but now he wants me gone."

"Ah. Well, I will find you appropriate lodgings. We need you to be completely accessible to the press. I'd like them to see you in a more permanent setting. To make it clear that you've made a home in Dartmouth and you plan to stay."

"I do."

"Good. Perhaps this job won't be as difficult as Asher implied. You have a reputation for being quite... unpleasant to work with." Stephan shook his head. "I've spoken to several of your teammates. None of them had anything good to say about you."

Damn. Not that Scott should be surprised. His teammates on his other teams hadn't liked him either. And he always tried not to care. It was harder with the Cobras though. He liked a few of them—

enough to want to stay even if they'd be happy to see him gone. Zach automatically came to mind, but Scott wasn't sure where he stood anymore either. Did Zach want him gone too? Would he have had anything good to say if Stephan had talked to him?

Probably not.

Scowling, Scott moved to the bed and unzipped the suit bag. Charcoal black. White shirt. The blood red tie was a bit much, but nothing he couldn't deal with. He snorted as he pulled out the small silver bag containing a pair of snug black boxer briefs and socks that matched the suit perfectly. The man had thought of everything. "In other words, they all told you I'm an asshole."

"Flirting with married women is considered bad form."

"The chicks like the attention."

"Let them get it from someone else. I can't force your teammates to like you, but you will do everything in your power to keep them from hating you. Let them see how dedicated you are to being an asset to the team."

Seriously? "I *am* dedicated."

"Are you? Are you on the ice before the rest? In the gym longer? Do you follow the instructions from the dietitian?" Stephan made a sharp motion with his hand before Scott could answer. "Don't bother. I've done my homework. You are the laziest, least disciplined player on the roster—"

"I'm a loser. I got it."

Stephan just kept talking. "—talented, but that hardly matters when you show up drunk. Or call in sick. That. Ends. Now."

Fuck, if you weren't such a fairy, you'd make a good Dom. Scott pulled on the incredibly soft dress shirt, then dropped his towel and stepped into the boxers, grinning when Stephan looked away. "Got it. Anything else?"

"We need to find you a nice girl."

"A what?" Scott stared at the man who'd just officially reached certifiable. "I don't do 'nice girls.'"

"You do now." Stephan propped his hands on his hips, then sighed and brushed Scott's hands aside as he fumbled with the tie. He tied a perfect knot, then smoothed it over Scott's chest. "You've given the media too much raunchy material to work with. They'll get bored of you once you start courting an acceptable young woman seriously, and that's exactly what we want. But don't worry about that now. I'll present you with a list of potentials by the end of the week."

"Okay, this was too much. "You get to choose who I fuck? What if I need a 'nice' stiff cock."

Stephan sputtered. "No! Oh no, that can't happen. I'm sorry, Scott, but if you are homosexual, you'll have to hide it for now. You can't afford to draw that kind of attention. We can work on you 'coming out' once you've become a fan favorite, but at this point—"

"I got it." Scott shoved his hands into the pockets of his slacks. "Wanna fit me for a chastity belt now?"

The bastard's lips quirked. "Don't tempt me."

"So do I get to have a life at all, or is that not on the agenda?" Damn it, Scott would do just about anything to stay on the team, but it grated to have everything he did under a microscope. Being a good boy in public, he could pull off. But Stephan was talking like he couldn't do shit without his stamp of approval. "I appreciate what you're trying to do, but I need *some* privacy. Down time, you know?"

"You've had plenty of 'down time,' Scott. And you've used it to become the most disreputable player in the league." Stephan tugged Scott's hands out of his pockets, straightened his suit, then stepped back to look him over. "Don't waste my time or Silver's money. She may not know it, but she's paying me *very* well to remake you into a man the team and the fans can be proud of. If you're unwilling to do what it takes to become that man, tell me now."

Still slightly dizzy from the vodka still in his system, sore everywhere from fucking and being fucked all night. Scott straightened and considered Stephan's words. How bad did he want this? Bad enough to fit into the mold Stephan wanted to force him into? Could he really pull this off?

Did he have a choice?

"I'm willing to do whatever it takes."

"Good." Stephan followed him out into the hall, frowning when Scott grabbed his dress shoes from the rack by the door. Without a word, he took a knee and opened what looked like a big square brown leather purse. He pulled out a container of clear polish, a cloth, and jerked at Scott's ankle to place his shoe on his other knee. "I have a feeling I'm going to have to inspect you from head to toe every time you go out in public. And a shopping trip is in order. How old are these shoes?"

Scott shrugged. "I've had 'em for a few years. But I don't wear them much." He laughed at Stephan's wide eyed look. "What?"

"The team expects the players to wear suits to all games."

"I know. And I do."

"Please tell me you don't wear running shoes—"

"Fine. I won't tell you." The way the veins at Stephan's temples bulged out couldn't mean anything good. Scott quietly offered up his other scuffed and dirt-streaked shoe. "Look, I'll wear whatever you tell me to, okay?"

"Yes. You will." Once Scott's shoes were as shiny as he could get them, Stephan stood and fussed with his suit a bit more. Then he checked his watch. "Go before you're late. I'll stay here—bring someone in to pack your things and figure out what you need." He pulled a business card out of his breast pocket. "Call me as soon as the meeting is finished."

"Will do." Scott tucked the card in his pocket, eager to get the hell out of there. He spotted Chicklet, in the doorway of Vanek's room, watching him, lips twisted with disdain. He missed the doorknob at his first grab, unable to look away from her. The woman hated him and he couldn't blame her. He lowered his gaze and muttered, "I'm sorry."

She took a step back and closed the bedroom door.

"Prove it, Scott." Stephan patted his shoulder, then squeezed it in a way that was strangely comforting. "I'm not sure what you did wrong, but we'll make it right. I'm here to help."

"I appreciate that." Damn it, he couldn't resent the guy anymore. And worse, he owed Silver, *again*, whether she knew it or not. And the best way to pay her back was by proving to everyone that signing him wasn't the biggest mistake she'd ever made.

He'd always been a mistake. A screw up.

But that was about to change.

* * * *

The forum was dead quiet this early in the morning, no one around besides security. The place would be full in a few hours with the hard rock bands scheduled. The new owner of the forum had plans to use the place for more than games, which was damn *brilliant*. The Delgado family had lost a lot of money using the building for nothing but games and a few local events. If nothing else, the new owner was business-smart.

Scott fiddled with his tie as he crossed the gleaming marble floors with long strides. On the drive over, he'd thought over Stephan's instructions. "Yes, sir." "No, sir." Sounded so simple, but it wouldn't be. The new owner had his shit together, and he'd know Scott was a bad investment. Nothing short of a miracle would save Scott at this point. He'd gotten a fresh start with the Cobras, and he'd wasted it.

Fuck off. You weren't that bad.

Waiting for the elevator, Scott's lips twitched as he considered some of the crap he'd pulled over the last year. If he was lucky, the new owner didn't know the half of it. But his luck hadn't been all that good lately. Too bad he couldn't just deal with Richter. At least Silver could smooth the way with the GM, since she had him wrapped around her little manicured fingers.

She's done enough for you.

His thoughts wondered to Stephan's plans for his future. To the "list" of appropriate chicks he'd be given. Out of all the parts of his life Stephan was taking over, that part rankled the most. Vanek had joked once that Scott was a sex addict. And maybe he was. Having a random body in his bed every night made him feel less . . . alone. Yeah, getting in a serious relationship could do that too, but whenever a man or a woman looked at him like they wanted to go there, it was like they were putting a noose around his neck. He got away from them as fast as he could. And even when he was tempted to make things real, he somehow fucked things up.

Like he had with Zach.

Then again, according to Stephan, Zach wasn't even an option anymore. He needed a "nice girl." Which was funny. A *real* nice girl wouldn't want him. He had nothing to offer. Even Zach, who seemed to want more, had pointed that out. Out of everyone he had to make things right with, Zach would have been first in line. Zach thought he was worth something. The last time they'd talked, he'd given the impression that he'd be there when Scott figured that out.

I should call him.

Scott slid his hand into his pocket, fisting it around his phone. A few words with Zach and he could make it through the meeting, confident that at least someone believed in him.

Not an option.

Until he cleaned up his image, he'd have to be all about "the woman" in his life. He enjoyed sex with women enough to deal, but it would be like being on some weird fad diet, stuck with the same thing night after night, deprived of his favorite food. And after just one night, Zach ranked right up there with steak and pot roast. Being with a "good girl" would be like eating nothing but crackers and chicken broth.

Why do people care who I fuck? Scott jerked his suit jacket straight as he stepped onto the elevator, groaning as a button popped off and hit the floor. Why couldn't he have it easy like Zach? Coming out publicly made the man a goddamn hero to the team, because they all knew he'd done it to take the focus off Luke Carter, a kid who'd just lost his rookie status, who'd gotten in deep with defenseman Sebastian Ramos. He wasn't ready to tell the world he was bi. Whatever. Scott couldn't care less if people knew he was, but *he* had to stick to the status quo. That very night, his agent had called him and told him to make it clear he 'liked pussy'. His exact fucking words. It hadn't been all that hard to find some bunnies to flaunt and fuck.

But he'd hurt Zach. And he kept hurting him every time he went out with a bunny under each arm. Even worse when he snuck out and found some stud to fool around with.

How would Zach feel when he saw Scott with the woman Stephan chose for him? He pictured himself with some pretty little thing by his side, smiling for the cameras. With Zach on the sidelines, watching him, pain in his eyes.

I can't do this. The elevator doors slid open and he forced himself to move forward. He glanced at the doors lining the hall, dragging his feet as he headed toward the new owner's office. If he didn't go through with this, where would that leave him? In some other city, far away from Zach? If he found a way to stay, maybe he could make things right. *I have to try.*

Scott rapped his knuckled on the door to the owner's office. This was it. Time to face the man who would decide where his life went from here.

"Come in."

Stepping into the office, Scott glanced around, taking note of the classy setup. The owner's desk was huge. There were three leather chairs set in front of the large, gleaming mahogany structure. Black and white portraits of hockey greats covered the walls. The man knew the game. Had a passion for it if the pictures with him and Roy, and Lemieux, and Richard were anything to go on. But that wasn't what filled Scott with dread. He looked over the tabloids spread across the man's desk. Pictures of Scott, drunk, half-naked, none of the headlines flattering. Scott stared at them as the man stood and leaned across the desk, offering his hand.

"Lorenzo Piers Keane. It's a pleasure to meet you, Mr. Demyan."

Yeah, Right.

"Scott." With the shit he was about to get into with the man, informal would be good. He swallowed, tearing his gaze away from the papers.

I'm fucked.

He shook the man's hand, then dropped into the chair behind him. "Umm . . ."

"Yes. Umm." Keane sat, then rested his elbows on the desk and steepled his fingers. He wore a simple, black Italian suit, tailored to fit his tall, trim frame. A bit of grey streaked through the brown hair along his temples. His dark brown eyes assessed Scott for several excruciatingly long moments before he let out a heavy sigh. "Scott, your stats make you worth every penny we're paying you, but this . . ." He motioned toward the papers. "The team *cannot* afford your reputation." His lips curled slightly with disgust. "I have to admit, the charges of statutory rape concerned me the most. I considered sending you to the farm team on waivers without—"

"There were no charges!" Scott shoved his chair back, rage

sizzling through his veins as he grabbed the tabloid with a huge picture of him making out with a girl whose face was blurred out. A smaller one of her slipping underneath the table. The last of them heading for the men's room. "She was seventeen. We met at a bar and she had ID. I was set up!"

"Set up?" Keane arched a brow, his expression showing mild interest. "How so?"

"A reporter paid her to come on to me, then made a big deal about it. Believe me, she didn't look like a kid. You know so much?" Scott jerked his thumb at the papers. "You've gotta know Hayley Turner is gunning for the team because she thinks Silver fucked her husband. *Everyone* knows that."

"More than one media outlet covered the incident."

Yeah, Becky had picked it up from some "source" for a behind the scenes sports special. News was slow. He guessed she had to give them *something*. But it pissed him off that she had to make him look like a goddamn cradle robber to get ahead.

"What can I say, I'm fucking fascinating." Scott ran his tongue over his teeth, lowering back into his seat as he caught the way Keane's eyes narrowed. He wasn't making himself look any better to the man. He rolled his shoulders. "Look. Don't think I don't understand where you're coming from. I need to smarten up. But some of this stuff isn't as fucked up as it looks. They—"

"Ah, the infamous 'they.'" Keane let out a tight laugh. "I have teenage daughters, twins—which you seem to enjoy." He picked up another newspaper which showed Scott in a limo with a pair of hot redheads. After crumpling the papers in his hand, he tossed it aside. "But I won't let my personal bias affect my decision. Especially since you feel targeted by the press. Let me see . . ." He tapped a colored photo of Scott and cocked his head slightly. "Please explain to me how the media managed to get you drunk and onstage at a strip club. Did someone forcibly remove your clothing?"

Scott winced. He'd forgotten about that night. He'd been pretty wasted. "No. That was just me being an idiot."

"I see. And the brawl you were involved in at a . . . karaoke bar? Let me guess. You planned to sing professionally once you'd destroyed your career as a professional hockey player, and some asshole told you not to quit your day job."

"No. I just got drunk and—"

"Stupid. Yes, that seems to happen a lot with you. And the street racing—which there *were* charges for." Keane flipped open a folder. "According to your file, you spent several days in jail."

"I was sober." Scott's jaw tensed. "I don't drive drunk."

"Commendable, but that doesn't change the fact that you seem to have an alcohol problem. I trust you weren't sober when you went streaking in downtown Montreal?"

"Actually . . ." Okay, it was really hard not to laugh at that one. Middle of winter, he and a few of the guys had been hanging out with the Habs. The Cobras had a friendly rivalry with the Canadiens. Some French guy had dared Scott to a race down Saint Catherine. Naked.

He never turned down a dare.

Keane shook his head, flattening his hands on the desk. "Scott, I could tolerate these antics from a rookie, do my best to take him in hand. But you've been in the league for ten years. You've proved to be immature and, frankly, unstable. If it was limited to your actions in public, I would consider giving you a chance to improve your image. Unfortunately, your behavior on the ice is no better. You instigate fights with your own teammates. The amount of penalty minutes you racked up last year is unacceptable. And I've never heard of a professional athlete calling in 'sick' as often as you have. The only reason I haven't already traded you is because Silver Delgado made the choice to sign you, and she's done so much for the team, I can't believe she would have done that without a good reason."

The situation looked pretty damn hopeless. There was no point in lying to the guy. Scott slumped in his chair. "She didn't know much about the game when she signed me. She was told I was good on the ice and figured I'd help change the team's image. Bring in the younger crowd."

"You have. But so have other men on the team, and they've done so without it reflecting negatively on the whole organization."

Right. Time to go home and pack. Scott rubbed his hands over his face. "What can I say? I'm willing to change, but the way you're

63

talking, it's too late."

Keane stood, pushed his chair back, and gathered all the newspapers into a neat pile. He reached down, picked up the trash can from under his desk, and set it in front of Scott with a sharp *clink*. Then he stuffed all the papers into the stainless steel bin.

"Give me one good reason to let you stay."

Lips parted, mouth dry, Scott gaped up at the man. Why even give him a shot? Why risk millions on someone who could potentially bring the whole team down?

Why question it, man? Give him a reason!

Scott swallowed and lunged to his feet, speaking in a rush. "I already told my image consultant I'd do anything he asked me to. Change my attitude, my clothes, my whole life if it means I can be a Cobra. I want to be with this team when they make the Cup. I want to retire with this team. I'll take a pay cut if it means I can stay. Just tell me what I have to do and I'll do it!"

"Why? Why does it matter so much? There are other teams that would have you."

"Because . . ." He frowned, searching for the truth. And then he found it. "Silver believed in me. She took a lot of flack for it, but she stood by her decision. I need to prove to her that it wasn't a mistake. That everyone was wrong about me."

Slapping his hands on the desk, Keane smiled. "That is exactly what I needed to hear. I need to know you have solid motivations to make all these changes. Following your IC's advice will go a long way in convincing me to offer you a contract. The season doesn't start for months. I want to see your face in more papers, but I want every article to express what a positive addition you've become to the team. I don't care if you're kissing babies or setting fashion trends. You will be a man young boys can look up to. Let the other teams hate you. I don't give a shit how much you chirp on the ice. But your fans, your teammates . . ." He took a deep breath. "They will love you. I won't accept any less."

That's it? Scott's head reeled at the abrupt shift. It had all seemed utterly hopeless, but in the end, he'd gotten the chance he'd so desperately wanted. His lips moved soundlessly, then he nodded quickly. "I can do that."

"I've faxed your IC a list of appearances I've set up for you and several of the other players. Can I trust you to be at each and every one?"

"Absolutely."

Keane inclined his head. "Very well. You may go."

Just like that, Scott was dismissed. He thanked Keane again and headed out, practically knocking Sloan Callahan, the team's captain, on his ass in the hall.

"Watch where you're fucking going, Demyan." Callahan snarled before striding into the office and slamming the door behind him.

Scott righted himself, glanced over to the other man who stood by the door, Dominik Mason, the team's most vicious defenseman, and muttered a vague greeting. Mason spared him a brief glance before pulling out his phone. He sighed and dialed, then spoke softly.

"I'm here, love. Sloan's with Keane." He pressed his eyes shut and nodded slowly. "I'll do what I can, but I can't promise anything. If he's determined to . . . I know. But he won't listen to me—I love you too."

Leaving Mason, Scott hunched his shoulders and headed to the elevator. The shit going on between Mason and Callahan was pretty serious. Unlike him, they deserved to be here. They'd worked their asses off for this team. Oriana Delgado, Silver's sister, was a sweet chick. And the trouble with her men made Scott's seem even more pathetic. He'd brought this on himself. The captain and Mason's problems stemmed from loving the same woman and barely tolerating one another. Keane was probably trying to convince Callahan to stay.

Scott kinda hoped the owner succeeded. Because the captain was one of the few people Scott respected. One of the people he hoped would be around if he actually managed to pull this off.

* * * *

Dominik rested his head against the pristine white wall of the hall, pressing his eyes shut as Sloan stormed out of the office, slamming the door for a second time. Part of him wanted to go to Sloan, to force him to see they didn't have to come to this. They loved the same woman. The same team. They could make it work.

But Sloan wouldn't listen. Things had become tense in the house they shared. Max Perron's house. Oriana was Max's wife, and that meant more than the fact that Dominik had collared her, or that Sloan had marked her. No matter how much Oriana cared for them both, she would follow her husband. And Max had done the unthinkable by making leaving the team an option.

It's not an option for me.

Dominik hauled in as much air as his lungs would hold and pictured Oriana, kneeling before him, pouring her heart out.

"I *don't* want to go, but Sloan . . ." *Her face crumpled and tears spilled down her cheeks.* "Sloan may never play again. I can't let this be the end for him. He needs me."

"*I need you.*" *Even on her knees, she had all the power. He'd accepted that when he'd let her into his life. His heart. As long as he shared her with two other men, she would never be his alone. Which felt so wrong as he watched her suffering between the three of them, desperate to please them all.* "Tell me what you need me to do."

"Come with us."

He'd looked away from her then. That wasn't what she really wanted. She was telling him what she thought he needed to hear. Nothing would change if he followed her to Calgary with Sloan and Max. He would still be an obstacle. The man who challenged Sloan, who made sure the fucking sadist never pushed too hard, went too far.

But what was too much for Dominik wasn't too much for Oriana. Her husband might cringe at the marks Sloan left on her, but he simply tended to the wounds and accepted that the extremes satisfied Oriana, so there was nothing wrong with them. Dominik had tried, so very hard, to do the same. But there were times when Sloan sank so deep into his needs as a sadist that he couldn't handle the aftermath. Which left Dominik holding Oriana, blinking back tears as he carefully bandaged the marks on her body, trying not to hate Sloan for making her bleed. He'd taught Sloan as much as he could, but the pupil had outgrown the teacher. Become a master in his own right. Begun to question everything he'd learned because Oriana needed more.

"Be honest with me, Oriana. Do you really want me to come with you?"

She refused to look at him as she answered. "They need you here."

"Do you want me to stay behind?"

"Yes."

"Then I will."

Eyes tearing, she blinked, then rested her head against his chest. "This is one of those times where I want you to take control. Where I don't want to have a choice."

"Sweetheart, I wish I could tell you what to do." He kissed her forehead.

"But I can't. Not with this."

"Mr. Mason?" Keane held the door open for him, then quietly followed him into the office. The door clicked shut, and Dominik took a seat, waiting for Keane to take his place behind the desk.

Instead, Keane stepped in front of him, arms crossed over his chest, hip resting on the edge of the desk. Despite the silver streaking the man's dark brown hair, something about his bearing made him look younger than forty. He was tall, fit, but not especially muscular. Clean-cut, always well put together, the man had a presence that made it hard not to sit up and take note when he spoke. He'd only had one meeting with the team so far, but already, he'd made quite the impression. Men who'd whispered about "getting out" before the team folded were singing a different tune now.

Except Sloan. But Dominik knew Sloan wasn't leaving because he'd lost faith in the team. He was leaving because he needed to regain the control he'd lost. Over his career and his personal life. The man wasn't known for his patience, though it had improved over the years. He wouldn't let an injury hold him back.

Or another man.

"Do you know why I worked so hard to acquire this team, Mason?"

Dominik frowned. *What kind of question is that?* "Honestly? You're a rich man. There aren't many other teams for sale. I assumed you wanted to own one badly enough you took what you could get. Even if the team fails here, there are other places you could move it to where it would thrive."

Keane nodded. Chuckled. "Mr. Richter told me you don't pull any punches, so I appreciate your tact. But there are plenty of teams for sale. I wanted the Cobras, and I've been making offers to the Delgado family for years just to get a piece. Ford Delgado—"

67

"Kingsley." Dominik ground his teeth. "The little bastard only took on the name to make his new daddy happy."

"Legally, he *is* a Delgado. Which is beside the point." Keane's tone lightened with amusement. "He's not too crazy about 'you kinky fuckers' either. But he acted in the best interest of the team. Do you know he asked me if I could handle the alternative lifestyle most of the players are involved in? He seemed quite relieved when I told him not only could I handle it, but I could relate to a majority of the players."

Rubbing his jaw, Dominik laughed. "Really? So you and your wife like to play?"

"No. I'm not married." Keane gave Dominik a level look. "But I uncollared my slave of five years months ago. My point is that I understand where you're coming from."

Rising slowly, Dominik faced the man. "No disrespect, sir, but if you brought me here to discuss my relationship with Oriana, I'm not interested. As openly 'kinky' as the team may be, I value my privacy."

Keane held up his hands in a calming gesture. "I don't expect you to. But the team needs stability. I asked Mr. Callahan to come here because he is the team's captain. The uncertainty in his future creates unrest with the men. That is no longer an issue. He is leaving—all that remains are a few contracts to be signed." His eyes darkened. "I need to know if you are staying. If you are, I'd appreciate your help. The team needs a leader."

Fuck! Dominik paced away from Keane, then back, shaking his head. "Why me? Ask Richter, or our coach, Tim. I'm the most volatile player on the team. The men expect me to protect them on the ice, to throw my weight around. Not to lead them." He let out a harsh laugh. "Besides, *you* have no fucking say in who leads the team."

"I've spoken to both the coach and Richter. Granted, they hadn't considered you as a suitable captain, but things have changed. They've both seen how you handle yourself at the club—"

"The club is not the goddamn ice. I'm not the same man out there."

"You can be."

I don't need this shit! With a few strides, Dominik went up to the window and stared out at the streets below, crowded with cars, tourists, all basking in the blazing summer sun. This place had become home. With Oriana, and Max, and . . . even Sloan. Without them, he had no idea where he belonged. Put him on the ice and he could forget everything else. But now, Keane was asking for more. For renewed dedication in the game, in the team.

He wasn't sure he had it in him. For the first time, his summer hadn't been devoted to training, to making himself a better player. He spent every moment he could with Oriana, feeling her slip further and further away from him. His jaw tightened as he blinked against the burning in his eyes. When she'd gone with Sloan and Max to visit Sloan's father, he'd declined the invitation to join them and headed down to Chicago to visit his mother, spend some time with his sister and his brothers. His mother knew something was wrong. She'd asked him why he hadn't brought his "sweet girl" with him.

All his life, he'd confided in his mother. There wasn't much about him she didn't know. But he couldn't bring himself to say it out loud.

He'd lost his sweet girl to another man.

There wasn't much left for him besides the game. Keane was giving him an opportunity to focus entirely on the team. Not the imposition it first seemed. Maybe a blessing in disguise.

"I'll do it." He kept his back to Keane as he spoke, needing a few moments to compose himself. Accepting the position brought him one step closer to saying goodbye to Oriana. But it was a step he had to take. "Tell me what you need from me. I hope you've got a fucking list because I need the distraction."

Keane stepped up beside him. "I need to ask you to do something rather . . . unconventional for me. But I think you're up to it."

"Go on."

"The Ice Girls are a hit. They've kept the spotlight on the team, even after the season ended. But the most talented girl has certain . . . issues. Issues that distract from her abilities."

"Is she a sub?" Dominik pressed his lips together, not sure he could stomach being involved with a woman, even if it was good for the team. But why else would Keane ask?

"She may be. However, that is irrelevant." Keane's lips curved at the edges when Dominik glanced over at him, confused. "I'm no matchmaker. Your skills as a Dom will be useful, but she may be a little young for you. Not that I care if you decide to take her on. All I ask is that you help her get past her fear of men."

Dominik went perfectly still. "Why is she afraid of men?"

"One can only guess. The Ice Girls will be going on a cruise with several of the players. The media will be watching them. I want her on the Ice Girl team, but she won't make it if she's so afraid she won't let cameras catch the beautiful, outgoing woman I know she can be." Keane went back to his desk. "You are already scheduled for the trip, but I'd like you to work with her beforehand. I can give you suggestions if you'd like?"

"I can manage." Dominik tugged his suit sleeves straight. "Let me guess. The girl is Akira Hayashi."

"Yes."

Cute kid. Shy, but a vision on the ice. She couldn't be more than twenty. *Way* too young for Dominik—even though Oriana was only five years older. He recalled the way she'd cringed the last time a male reporter had approached her in a crowded room. Whatever had happened to the girl was serious enough that it affected every aspect of her life. Getting her past that would be a challenge. It would take time. Thankfully, he had plenty of that.

"Leave it to me." Dominik arched a brow at a timid tap at the door. The girl in question peeked in, her olive green eyes wide. Keane didn't look all that surprised to see her. Dominik scowled. "You knew I'd agree."

"I know what kind of man you are," Keane said under his breath, waving Akira in. "And you need this as much—if not more—than she does."

"You wanted to see me, sir?" Akira fidgeted with the buttons of her crisp, beige jacket. The way she lowered her gaze brought to mind every natural submissive Dominik had ever met. Yet nothing about her stirred anything besides his protective instincts. The way she hovered near the door, as though ready to run out to something—or *someone*—who could keep her safe had him crossing the room to stand between her and Keane before his brain could catch up. Being in here alone with Keane, despite the man's good intentions, was the last thing she needed.

Akira trembled as Dominik approached. The door was still open a crack. Dominik pulled it open all the way, biting back a laugh as he caught sight of Jami Richter, the general manager's daughter and Akira's best friend, standing close enough to the door to listen in.

"If you'd like me to deal with the girls, Mr. Keane, then perhaps I should get started." Dominik gave Jami a slow smile as she skidded backward into the hall. "Your instructions are clear. Please excuse us."

Keane nodded and took a seat behind his desk, looking over some folders. "Miss Hayashi, I had planned to introduce you to your new sponsor. I'm sure you are aware that several girls have players in that position for either financial or moral support?"

Did they? This was the first Dominik had heard of it. Ice Girls on other teams weren't so closely involved with the players. Not that the Cobras followed the norm in any way.

"A couple of girls do, sir, but . . ." Akira squared her shoulders. "My parents are quite capable of supporting me. And I just put in an application—"

"I'm sorry, my dear, but you will not have time for a job." Keane folded his hands on the desk, his tone low and full of compassion. "Akira, your father called me to ask if there was any financial aid available. It is becoming difficult for your parents to pay for you to stay here. You have a bright future with the team. I would fund you myself if it wasn't a conflict of interest while you are still competing, but since that is not an option, I strongly suggest you accept Mr. Mason's generous offer."

"But . . ." Akira blushed and ducked her head. "The other girls got their sponsors because . . . I mean—"

"I expect nothing from you, Akira," Dominik said, his tone much sharper than intended. Keane obviously planned to fund Akira in his name, but he didn't need it. And he refused to allow the girl to believe she had to compensate him in any way. The way she paled had him continuing quickly, his voice as calm and gentle as he could manage. "The Ice Girls are important to the team. *You* are important to the team. That's the only reason I'm doing this."

"Thank you, Mr. Mason." Akira nodded quickly, then moved as though to dash out.

"Not so fast." Dominik joined her at the door, speaking softly. "We need to talk."

"About what?" Jami put her hand on Akira's arm and narrowed her eyes at Dominik. "She said thank you. She appreciates your help, but she's got training and stuff. As far as I'm concerned, there's nothing more to talk about."

Lifting his hand, Dominik brushed Akira's fine, black hair off her cheek. He took a step back when she winced and let his hand fall to his side. "I disagree."

"She'll be fine! Just leave her alone!" Jami placed her hand on his chest and shoved, so much like an angry, spitting kitten he had to fight not to laugh. It was sweet that she wanted to protect her friend.

But not very helpful.

Dominik latched on to Jami's wrist and leaned down to whisper in her ear, the short strands of her spiky blue hair soft against the side of his face. "Sebastian asked me to watch over you while he stayed in Spain with Luke. I'll be careful with her. I won't push her too far. But you . . ." He pressed a light kiss on her pale cheek. "Do. Not. Test. Me."

She gulped audibly, fisting her hands by her sides. "Sebastian wouldn't—"

Dominik kept an eye on Akira, who looked torn between making a run for it and staying to protect her friend. "He wouldn't what, Jami?"

Jami glanced over at Akira, then sighed. "Never mind."

So Sebastian *had* spoken to her. Had likely told her to stay away from the club. To behave herself. Dominik knew Sebastian had asked Jami to remain in Spain with him and Carter and had only given in when she insisted Akira needed her. But he'd made sure Jami would feel his presence through Dominik. He trusted Dominik to respect his limits. Not that he would sleep with Jami even if it had been permitted. He'd known the girl since she was little more than a child. But discipline didn't have to be sexual, and he had no problem taking her over his knee if she needed it.

Between Sebastian and Keane, Dominik had been given plenty

to distract him. Which was good. Maybe it would be easier to say goodbye to Oriana when the time came. When he held her at the airport and did his best to let her go with no regrets.

"Sir?" Akira skirted up to his side as he made his way to the elevator, surprising him by touching his forearm, her tiny hand looking even smaller with the contrast of her light olive skin against his dark flesh. He turned and nodded. She drew in a sharp breath. "I'm still not sure why you're doing this. And . . . I'm not sure I'm comfortable taking your money or anything else while giving nothing in return. It's not much, but . . . I can tell something's bothering you. You can talk to me if . . . if you want."

She was adorable. Scared to death of him, but braving her fears to reach out. He put his hand over hers, smiling when she made an obvious effort not to pull away.

"That means a lot to me, Akira. And I may take you up on your offer." He squared his shoulders. "But for now, this is all about you."

Chapter Five

Cinnamon rolls, croissants drizzled with chocolate, fruit tarts, and rum balls. Everyone else in the café was buying iced coffees and smoothies to cool off, but the long line waited behind Zach and Becky as they picked two of each delicious treat on display.

Every time Becky tried to protest that it was too much, that it was all so fattening, Zach just gave her a level look and added even more to the pastry boxes the cashier had out for them. She could already feel the sugar rushing to her brain. Or maybe it was the two cups of coffee Zach had served her in bed that morning.

Or maybe it's just him.

Being around Zach made her feel young. Alive and carefree. His hand on her shoulder warmed flesh full of goose bumps from an AC turned too high. She laughed as he told the cashier to add four more rum balls to their order. She'd mentioned they were her favorites, but he was spoiling her.

"Zach—"

"Becky, if you complain about your weight again, I'm putting you on a strict exercise regimen." His tone was firm, but something in his eyes told her he was at least half teasing. "I think you're perfect just the way you are, but if it's an issue—"

"It's not." Becky smiled and hugged his arm. "It's sweet of you to say I'm perfect though. It took a long time for me to get comfortable with my body after I divorced Patrick. I'm mostly okay with myself now though."

"Mostly?"

"It's nice to hear I look good from a man—and not just during a scene."

Zach hugged her tight and kissed the top of her head. "I'll make a point of reminding you how beautiful you are. But I must say, you look cuter in normal clothes."

"Normal clothes?" She let out an affronted sniff. "What's wrong with my suits?"

"Nothing. They are perfectly appropriate for work, but I like

75

seeing you in something casual."

She blushed, bringing her hand to the V-neck of the white T-shirt he'd brought for her that morning. With a pair of jeans that fit perfectly. And running shoes. Doms had dressed her before, but never like this. Most of her wardrobe consisted of business outfits, with a few jogging suits thrown in for comfort. She wasn't sure she owned any T-shirts, and her jeans had been given to Goodwill after she'd finally accepted that she'd never be a size six again.

"I hope you don't have a problem with my picking out your clothes?" He pulled her hand away from her chest, twining their fingers. "I haven't had the opportunity with many subs, but I do enjoy it."

"I don't mind at all." Damn, the man made her feel all soft and melty inside. Wearing what he'd laid out for her added an edge of his control to every moment they spent together. And that control would linger, even when he wasn't around. A sweet, subtle reminder, like a solid backdrop, while she was still free to be herself. She liked it, but there had to be limits. "I can't have you doing this when I'm working, but I'm fine with it any other time."

"So noted." Zach picked up the three white boxes the cashier handed him, then moved toward the door. "You mentioned getting the keys to your new house sometimes this week—wanting to fix it up? If you'd like, I can help you paint before Casey gets home."

"That would be awesome! I—" Her phone vibrated in her pocket, making her jump. She pulled it out, her breath bursting out of her chest when she saw Patrick's number. *Something's wrong.* "Sorry, one minute." She answered in a whisper, "Hello?"

"Mommy! A dolphin kissed me!"

Becky laughed, her eyes tearing as Zach took her elbow and led her to a chair on the terrace outside the café. "Wow! What else have you seen?"

"Bears and beluga whales. I fed one a fish!" Casey giggled. "He wasn't slimy, but Daddy wouldn't touch him. And he made sure I washed my hands twice after I petted him. Nanny bought me a stuffed bear that looks just like the ones that waved at us! I mean it, Mommy! They actually waved!"

"Did you take pictures?"

"Tons! And Nanny took some with me and the big fish!" Casey paused. "I wish you were here. I miss you."

"I miss you too, *poupée*." Becky turned her head slightly so her daughter wouldn't hear her trying to breathe around the lump in her throat. Zach squeezed her hand and his firm grip anchored her. She gave him a grateful smile, speaking again when she could do so without her voice catching. "How did you sleep last night?"

They'd spoken before Patrick had put Casey to bed. Casey had cried, wanting her own bed. Her stuffies. Her mommy. Becky had heard Patrick in the background, losing patience, but his mother had taken the phone, promising to stay with Casey all night if that's what it took. She'd called back to assure Becky that her daughter was fast asleep.

"Good. Nanny stayed with me all night," Casey said distractedly. "We're going to see a show with the dolphins now. Nanny told me I should call you to tell you how much fun I'm having."

I love that woman. Becky pressed her eyes shut and nodded. "I'm so happy to hear that. Call me tonight?"

"I will! Love you! Bye!"

Becky hung up, put her phone in her pocket, then lowered her head to her hands. She had a hard time believing everything was okay. She'd prepared for the worst and the relief lifted her up, making her dizzy. Maybe she didn't have to feel guilty about enjoying herself while her daughter was gone. She smiled at Zach.

"That's what I like to see." He brought her hand up to his lips and kissed her knuckles. "Ready to go to the park?"

"Yes." She glanced over to Zach's bike, parked in front of the café. A man sitting at the table at the edge of the terrace, hands clasped around a large iced coffee, caught her eye. It was Scott. Dressed in a crisp new suit, looking like death warmed over. She hesitated, glancing back at Zach, who'd followed her gaze and gone perfectly still. "Are you thinking what I'm thinking?"

Zach groaned and tipped his head back, whispering a prayer to the frothy white cotton-clouded sky. "Probably. But you do know we'll both regret this."

"Maybe not." Becky stood, easing her hand slowly from Zach's. "I know we'll both regret it more if we leave him here like this."

77

"Would we? I was perfectly happy knowing I would spend the rest of the day with you."

"You're mad at him."

"No. He's made his choices. I've made mine." Zach arched a brow at her doubtful look. "Becky, I try to keep my life as uncomplicated as possible. There's nothing uncomplicated about Scott."

"There's nothing uncomplicated about a woman with a child."

"It's not the same. I don't have to worry about finding you in the arms of another man. Of you telling me you want me one day, then leaving me the next." Zach raked his nails over the stubble of hair on his scalp. Creases lined his forehead. "You know exactly what he'll want from you. What he'll want from us both."

"Who says we have to give it to him? Who says that's what he really needs?" Becky leaned over the table, close to Zach, and kissed his cheek. "I'll pretend I didn't see him if you ask me to, Sir. I'm happy spending the day with you, too."

"But you'll feel guilty." Zach groaned. "And so will I. I suppose it won't hurt to make sure he's okay."

Straightening, Becky nodded, then moved toward Scott's table, feeling stronger with Zach behind her. There was nothing Scott could offer that she didn't already have. But there was a lot that she could offer him. Someone to talk to. Someone who cared.

Why do you, though? The man's selfish. Shallow. You don't need someone like him in your life.

For some reason, none of that mattered. Overnight, Zach had given her a sense of stability that made her less afraid of the chaos that was Scott. Nothing he could say or do could shake her. She approached his table, then took the seat across from him.

"Hey, you." She folded her hands on the table. "Having a rough morning?"

Scott snorted before sucking at his straw. He licked his lips, then shrugged. "No comment."

Ugh. So much for being pleasant. "I'm not a reporter anymore, Scott. This isn't an interview—I just wanted to see how you're doing. I'll leave you alone if you don't want to—"

"Wait." He put his hand over hers, glanced at Zach, then drew it away. "Sorry, I'm in a mood. You don't have to go."

"Bad news?" Zach asked, dragging a chair up to the table to straddle backward. Becky couldn't help but notice he'd set his chair close to hers, but not cutting into the small space between her and Scott. He rested his hands on his thighs. "You had that meeting with Keane today, right?"

"Yeah." Scott put down his cup. The edges of his lips curled slightly. "Was all right. I'm not off the team."

Zach grinned. "That's awe—"

"Yet."

"What do you mean 'yet'? Don't tell me the bastard's trying to fuck around with your contract. Silver got you for a bargain." Zach lowered his voice as a few of the other patrons glanced over. He hadn't shouted, but the sharpness of his tone carried. "Your agent is an idiot if he's letting this slide. Let me talk to mine. She's a—"

Scott barked out a laugh. "She's a vicious little thing. She's also not taking on any new clients—Carter tried to hire her last year. I'm fine with my agent—he's done everything he can for me."

Becky nodded slowly. She'd heard some rumors her first day at the office about Silver's lawyer, Asher, acquiring an image consultant. No one could deny Scott's value as a player, but he was also a liability. "What does Mr. Keane want you to do?"

"Short version?" Scott sucked his teeth. "Behave. I have to make the team and the fans love me."

"Jesus," Zach said under his breath. Becky smacked his thigh and he blinked at her. "What?"

"That's not helpful."

"Sweetheart, I'll do whatever I can to keep Scott on the team, but there's no use pretending it will be easy." Zach turned to Scott, then reached out to clasp a hand around the other man's wrist. "Tell me what you need. I'll talk to the guys. Some of them are cool with you. We can work on the others."

"Why?" Scott swallowed hard, his gaze locked on Zach's hand. "You don't owe me nothin'."

"You're my teammate. And more importantly . . ." Zach waited until Scott met his eyes, then continued. "My friend."

This man is incredible. Becky squeezed the thigh she'd smacked, smiling at Zach.

"Thanks, man." Scott slid his wrist from Zach's grip, then took hold of his hand in a way that was little more than a friendly handshake. He gave a wry grin, before pulling away and shook his head. "There's not much to do besides listen to each and every thing my IC tells me to do. Like the suit?"

Zach arched a brow. "I noticed your shoes."

"You would."

"Fuck off."

Becky rolled her eyes. "You clean up very nicely, Scott. The tie brings out your tan. But . . ." She glanced over at Zach, not sure if she was doing the right thing. Hopefully, he'd understand. "It's too nice out for such a stuffy outfit. Maybe what you need is some time to relax. Hang out for a bit."

"*I* noticed you're not all primped and pressed." Scott gave her an appreciative once-over, cheeks reddening slightly as he looked over at Zach yet again. He dropped his gaze to his drink. "I mean, you look nice. Hope you two have a nice day. I should—"

"Did you miss the invite, pal?" Zach laughed and punched Scott in the shoulder. "Becky wants you to come with us."

"I didn't miss it." Scott returned the punch. "I was trying to discreetly excuse myself. You two don't need me hanging around."

"We wouldn't have asked if we didn't want your company." Becky pointed out.

"He didn't ask. *You* did."

Zach stood slowly, leaning one hand on the table in front of Scott. "I'm asking now."

Picking up the pastry boxes, Becky eased out of her chair, hugging the boxes as Scott pressed his eyes shut and rubbed his brow with his thumb and forefinger. He mumbled to himself, something like, "This is a bad idea."

He was probably right. The invitation could mean a lot more to him than it did to either her or Zach. But, at the same time, she couldn't stand seeing him like this. For some crazy reason, she wanted the aggravating, outrageously flirty Scott back.

Do you? Really?

Yes and no. She knew how to deal with that man. How to turn

her back on him. But she couldn't do the same when he looked so broken. So lost.

And he couldn't seem to believe anyone would want him around.

But she did. She had a feeling Zach did too.

So she met Scott's eyes and whispered, "Please?"

"Hell." Scott rose and took the boxes from her. "Like I could say no to you."

* * * *

The scream of little kids in the park across from the picnic area rose above the laughter of teens lounging around, smoking near the trees, and the light conversation from the adults seated at the table around them. Several young women had stretched out on blankets on the grass to tan, but Scott hardly noticed them. Damn it, it was almost impossible to look away from Becky, giggling as Zach fed her bits of pastry, making her close her eyes as he picked a new one each time. In the suits she always wore she'd been hot, but there was something sweeter, more approachable, about her in jeans and a T-shirt.

She was still sexy as hell. The way the white shirt molded to her breasts made his mouth water. Her jeans were nice and snug. She had an ass he just wanted to sink his teeth into.

But for the first time, he found himself drawn to her soft grey eyes, to her smile. She practically glowed every time Zach spoke to her, touched her. The two looked good together.

"Want some?" Becky giggled, rising up on the bench across from him, holding half a rum ball between her fingers. His brain didn't kick in until he'd latched on to her wrist and drew her hand closer. The rich chocolate filled his mouth. He groaned as he sucked some from her fingers. Her eyes widened.

"Fuck." He pulled away, chewing and swallowing, hardly tasting the treat anymore. Tension gathered between his eyes as he glanced over at Zach, whose expression was carefully neutral. After the way he'd treated the man, the last thing he should be doing now was hitting on his woman. Even unintentionally. Not if he valued their friendship. Which he did. "Sorry."

Zach shrugged, picked up a croissant drizzled in chocolate, and eyed Scott, as though considering something very serious. He tore a big chunk of the croissant, leaned over the table, feeding it to Scott when his lips automatically parted. "Not sure I've ever heard you say that before. It's all innocent fun. I don't think I have anything to worry about."

Innocent? Scott gulped down the croissant without chewing. "You've gotta test me?"

"You're supposed to behave. Consider this me helping you out."

Thanks, buddy. Scott shifted, trying to adjust his rock-hard dick without making it obvious. Becky and Zach were like a bundle of temptation, wrapped up in a great big hellish bow. He wasn't used to teasing and flirting directed at him when he couldn't do fuck all about it. So much for being a third wheel. The two of them seemed to have made an afternoon sport of driving him completely insane.

He took off his suit jacket, laid it neatly over the bench, then stood. Zach had brought a football from his car, so he picked it up and slapped it between his hands. "We didn't come here just to stuff each other's faces, did we?"

"Nope." Zach stepped over the bench, wiping his hands on his jeans. He rolled his shoulders, and all the tight swell of muscle under his black tank top strained against the material. Scott lowered his gaze so he wouldn't be distracted by the sight, but seeing Zach just as hard as he was beneath his jeans didn't help much. He was on a strict no-man diet—being close to Zach made him want to fucking binge. He bit the tip of his tongue to stop himself from making a million promises, saying anything the man needed to hear to take him back, even though he knew he couldn't keep a single one.

Zach deserved better. Had better. All those sappy songs talked about . . . about loving someone enough to want the best for them. Or some shit like that.

Scott couldn't say he loved Zach, but he cared about him enough not to push. Not to lie. Zach was being a good friend, and Scott would take what he could get. Show the self-control everyone was demanding from him.

"So how we playing this?" Zach moved closer to Becky, running his fingers through her hair and kissing her forehead before holding his hand up for the ball. After Scott tossed it to him, he handed it to Becky. "Every man—and woman—for themselves? Make it to the tree line for a touchdown?"

"That means no passing. Which sucks." Becky wrinkled her nose. "How about we pass back and forth. Start close, then move farther apart after each round. We switch spots every second round, and only the person the farthest from the goal can go for it. Two points each touchdown. The first to ten wins."

Zach gave her a crooked smile. "You've done this before."

"Of course. Landon and I used to play with our cousins all the time, but there were rarely enough of us for a real game. So we made one up."

"Touch or tackle?" Scott asked, then inwardly cursed himself. Neither would do much for his restraint right now. If he got his hands on either of them . . .

Not that there were any other options. At least with touch he might be able to contain himself. A little. Maybe.

"Tackle of course." Becky sniffed. "Just don't crush me. You two are huge, and I didn't have to worry about my brother hurting me when we played. He was a scrawny kid."

"Really?" Scott laughed, trying to picture the hulking goaltender as a boy, playing a rough game of football with his older sister. "I'd love to see pics."

"I'll show you after I unpack." Becky rolled her shoulders. "So are we clear? I don't want to be sore tonight."

Christ. Please stop talking. Scott thought of all the ways he wanted to make her sore, none of which she'd regret the next morning.

"Neither of us would ever hurt you, Becky," Zach said softly. "Thank you for not trying to be all tough. We won't forget we're playing with a woman."

Becky backed up about ten paces, letting out a light laugh as she threw the ball to Zach. It spiraled perfectly, and Zach grunted as it hit him hard in the gut, barely moving in time to catch the hard pass.

"Don't take it *too* easy on me." Becky cracked her knuckles over her head. "I won't be taking it easy on you."

Scott rolled his shirt sleeves up, preparing for a pass from Zach. His palms burned as the pigskin connected with them. He tossed the ball to Becky, careful to hold back, which had the pass falling short.

She groaned, snapping it out of the grass and tossing it to Zach without even looking. "That was pathetic! I didn't know hockey players slacked off so much during the summer. Come on, Scott!"

Looking over at Zach, Scott received the next pass, retreated five paces, then shot the ball toward Becky with a bit more force. But keeping it a bit short so she could avoid it if it was too hard for her.

Swiftly catching the ball and cradling it under her arm, Becky darted forward, heading for the trees. It took seconds for him to realize what was going on. To notice that she was the farthest from the trees. To remember the rules.

Zach took just as long, and they both reached the trees steps behind Becky. Just in time to watch her slam the ball into the dirt and do a little dance. Her cheeks were flushed from the run. Her eyes sparkled. He really hadn't pictured her as the competitive, sporty type, but there was so much he didn't know about her.

So much he *wanted* to know.

"Nicely done, little doe." Zach laughed as Becky gave him a high five. "You've put us 'pros' to shame. I think we both underestimated you."

"Damn right, you did!" Becky laughed, twirling away from him to pick up the ball. "From what I just saw, my five-year-old daughter would put you both to shame. That kid has a wicked arm on her, and she didn't get it from her father."

Scott usually stayed away from kids. It was hard to see them, so full of life, after he'd gone to his niece's funeral and watched that tiny coffin lowered into the cold earth. But for some reason, he wanted to know Becky's kid. Wanted to see her running around in the park, playing football, laughing, looking so like Becky his heart had stuttered when he first saw her. She was part of the woman he didn't really know. The woman who didn't hold a recorder in his face and ask questions he didn't want to answer. The woman who smiled so brightly at him now.

He'd never really been interested in chicks with kids. Something about it just seemed wrong. They were looking for daddies for their babies, and he couldn't see himself taking on that role. He recalled a scene from the movie *Jerry Maguire*. Something about not "shoplifting the pootie from a single mother." He had the urge to take a full five-fingered discount, but *hell no*. Not from Becky. His teammate's sister. And a woman another teammate was obviously serious about. It didn't matter how *he* felt about her. All he could give her was a good time.

A *really* good time.

No.

Becky moved a few yards away from the trees. Zach jogged to the far point. Scott hauled in a deep breath and held it in. All right. He could do this. Maybe Zach was right. Maybe it was a good test. If he could be *just* friends with Zach and Becky, he could do anything. The ball was tossed back and forth a few times. He focused on the game. Found himself farthest from the goal and decided to make a run for it. Dodged Zach, then Becky. Arms wrapped around his legs, and he pitched face-first into the grass. Rolled with the ball and a curvy body in his arms.

He roared out a laugh as Becky straddled him and tried to wrench the ball out of his grip. "You don't expect me to just give it to you, do you?"

Sitting up, Becky batted her eyelashes sweetly. "What if I ask really nicely?"

He grinned. "I might consider."

"Pretty please, Scott?" She leaned down and whispered in his ear. "I'm a very sore loser."

With her lips so close to his cheek, her breath warming his flesh, he forgot his newfound morals. His dedication to the team or anything else. Her name crossed his lips in a breathless gasp. He stared into her eyes, one hand on her arm, holding her in place. "Kiss me and I'll do anything you ask."

She bent down. Her lips brushed his. "Kiss you? Why? It wouldn't mean anything."

He held his breath. Flicked his tongue over her bottom lip. "We both know that's not true."

Setting her teeth into his bottom lip, she tugged lightly, then jerked the ball away from him. He felt her trembling, even as she pushed to her feet. "You're right. It does mean something." She tossed her hair over one shoulder, squaring her shoulders as she looked down at him. "It means I have the upper hand."

From the ground, he watched her skirt away from Zach to make another touchdown. As the game continued, the sky darkened, but they continued even as the park emptied. Becky led the game with eight points. Zach had four. Scott was getting creamed with his pitiful two points. He hunched over, ignoring the raindrops hitting his cheeks, and grinned as both Becky and Zach prepared to chase him.

Long strides brought him to the tress. He whooped as the clouds burst, soaking him in an abrupt downpour. Laughing, he turned to do a little showboating.

Becky and Zach were running for the parking lot.

"Aww, come on!" Scott shook his head and sprinted after them. His shirt clung to him, the thin material completely soaked. He swiped water from his face as he met the pair by Zach's bike. Becky had her arms crossed over her breasts and blushed as Scott grinned at her. Women in white when it rained. Sexiest thing on earth. "I take it we're calling a draw?"

With one arm still covering her breasts—barely—Becky combed tendrils of wet hair away from her face. Stepping up to him, she snorted. "Yeah, right! I win, and that's all there is to it!"

"I was about to make a wicked comeback!"

"Sure you were." Becky spun around and put her hand on Zach's shoulder, ready to mount the big motorcycle behind him. "We'll have a rematch sometime. I suggest you practice if you ever hope to beat me."

"Sounds good." Scott forced a smile. Hanging out with them had been fun. Gave him something to do besides mope over how messed up his life was. He should head back to Vanek's place. Pack up the last of his shit and see if Stephan had found him a place to live. Becky and Zach probably had plans. "Guess I'll see you around—"

Zach used the back of his hand to swipe water from his brow. "You sure you don't want to swing by my place for a bit? I PVRed a few episodes of *The Walking Dead*. Thought we could all watch it."

Scott's smile faltered. Another pity invite. "Becky's not into that. And I'm sure you two—"

"I *love The Walking Dead*." She pulled her T-shirt discreetly away from her chest. "Silver and I just got caught up on season three."

"That's cool, but—"

"Can we please discuss this somewhere dry?" Becky wrapped her arms around Zach's waist. "I need to get out of these wet jeans."

Zach chuckled as Scott groaned. "Speaking of which, you might be better off getting a lift from Scott." He arched a brow at Scott. "You don't mind, do you?"

"No." *Asshole.* What was the man playing at? Sending his girlfriend with Scott, all soaking wet and sexy, was just plain stupid. Scott hadn't done anything to earn that much trust. He held out his hand to help Becky off the bike. "You sure about this?"

"Yes." Zach wrapped an arm around Becky's waist, pulling her in for a kiss before letting her go. "I trust her."

Ouch. Scott nodded, shoulders hunched as he led Becky to his car. Not only had Zach made it clear he didn't really trust Scott, he'd added the extra uppercut that no matter what Scott did, Becky would turn him down. Arrogant fucker. *Care to test that theory, pal?*

Scott opened the door for Becky, then went around to the driver's side, slouching into the seat and draping his arm over her shoulders as she shivered. "Cold?"

"Don't." She frowned at him and pulled his arm off her. "I shouldn't have teased you. Things went a bit too far, and I'm sorry if I gave you the wrong impression."

"You didn't. It was all part of the game." He smirked as he pulled out of the parking lot behind Zach. "Like you said, you've got the upper hand."

"Scott, I—"

"For now."

The windshield wipers moved fast, but the road was hardly visible, forcing traffic to a crawl. Scott lost sight of Zach, but it didn't matter. He knew where he was going. He turned on the radio to fill the silence.

Becky hugged herself, staring out the window, as far away from him as her seatbelt would allow. "You resent me, don't you? You want him."

"I want you both." He ground his teeth, back stiff. "Be honest.

You already knew that. And you both have me a little fucking confused. One minute you're all flirty, the next you're holding me at arm's length. Just be clear with me, Becky. I'm open to a little kinky fun if you're interested. Not so sure the 'just friends' thing will work, but I'll try if that's all you want from me."

"That *is* all I want from you, Scott."

"You sure about that?"

She didn't say a word. Which was all the answer he needed.

* * * *

"You were right. This was a bad idea."

Standing in front of his dresser with a T-shirt and boxers for Becky to change into, Zach nodded slowly, disappointed, but not really surprised. "He came on to you."

"Not really . . . he just offered . . ."

"Arms up." Zach did his best not to grin at the way Becky's nose wrinkled. Her hackles rose whenever he gave what could be perceived as an order outside a scene. But she never offered even a token protest. He had a feeling she secretly enjoyed it. "You may continue speaking, little doe. I just want you out of those wet clothes."

She rolled her eyes. "Yes, *Sir*."

Another reason he enjoyed blurring the lines a little between scenes and daily life. She was so well behaved as a sub he couldn't see himself having many opportunities to discipline her, but besides that, at any given moment she could be cheeky, even a little bratty, and earn some funishment.

Which he enjoyed handing out very much.

"I don't like your tone. Strip off those jeans and bend over the bed." He bit back a smile as she put her hands on her hips and glared at him. "Now, pet."

"No way! Not with Scott here!" She glanced over her shoulder, closing the door almost all the way, lowering her voice so Scott—who was hanging out in the living room—wouldn't hear her. "I can use whatever tone I want outside the scene."

"Absolutely." Zach moved toward her slowly, backing her into the door until it clicked shut. He framed her jaw in his hand and brushed his lips over hers, whispering, "And I can choose to handle that however I please."

"But Scott—"

"Would you like him here as a witness?"

Her cheeks went red. She shook her head and worried her bottom lip with her teeth.

"Five little smacks on the bottom. I'm willing to bet you'll enjoy it." He swept her hair over one shoulder as she bent down to peel off her wet jeans. Her panties went down with them, and his cock, which had been hard most of the day, jerked in his own damp jeans, causing a painful ache to spread into his balls. She bent over the bed, hands flat on the perfectly smooth comforter, feet shoulder-width apart. Her pussy glistened with her arousal. He stroked a finger through the moisture, humming with pleasure as she shuddered.

"It's you that's got me like this." She lowered her head between her hands, drawing in a sharp breath as he stroked her soft, round bottom with one hand. "Not the idea of . . ."

He bent down to press a kiss on the soft flesh at the small of her back. "It's both, little doe. You know I can make this good for you."

"I don't like pain."

"So you've told me." He ran his hands down her back, cupped her butt in his hands, then squeezed. "I think you're afraid that, if a little arouses you, you'll be expected to take more. True?"

"I've tried, Sir. There isn't much I haven't tried, at least once." Regret filled her tone, as though her only fear now was disappointing him. "Floggers, canes, whips. Once it started, I just closed my eyes and waited for it to end. The cane . . . I threw up after the Dom released me. It was humiliating."

Zach forced himself to keep stroking her the same way he had before her confession. Clenched his jaw to hold in a curse. She was so determined to please she wouldn't safeword if she thought she was giving a Dom what he wanted. Pride probably played into it as well. And she obviously hadn't been with a Dom observant enough to catch the subtle hints that she'd had enough.

She had no scars, didn't seem overly traumatized. It could have been so much worse.

Still, the "Doms" she'd been with didn't deserve the title.

He pressed his lips together, not speaking until he could erase any trace of how pissed he was at what had been done to her. Wrapping his arms around her waist, he rested his forehead lightly on her back. "This is for fun, Becky. But for future notice, you *will* use your safeword with me when you need to. I won't play with a sub I can't trust."

Turning her head, she gave him a sideways look. "Will you punish me if I don't?"

"No."

"Then what—?"

"Relationships need trust. We don't have one without it." He watched her face, the transition from hurt to understanding. He smiled when she nodded. "Good girl. We'll work on it. I need to earn your trust, and I'll do that by not pushing your limits any more than you can handle. By paying attention to you so it ends before you need to safeword out. But I can't read your mind. Your comfort is more important than my pleasure. Got it?"

"Yes, Sir." Her lips twisted. "I'm not sure I'm comfortable being spanked with Scott in the house."

He threw his head back and laughed. "Really? How not sure are you?"

"Umm." She groaned, burying her face into the comforter.

Slipping one finger into her slick pussy, he felt her clench around him. Her body told him what she couldn't say out loud. He withdrew his finger. "You need to be as honest about your needs as you will be about your limits. You want me to spank you."

She mumbled something into the mattress.

"I'm sorry?"

Arching her neck, she lifted her head. "Yes, Sir. I need your hands on me. I-I think it will be different with you."

"You're right." He straightened, then gave one ass cheek a smart slap. "It will be."

Her hips thrust back to meet the next smack. She gasped as he rubbed over the light red handprint, then moaned as he dipped two fingers into her.

Another slap. Her cunt spilled with sweet juices, and he let out a rough sound as he brought his fingers to his mouth. She quivered as he bent down to lick her pale pink folds. Spacing the smacks would make her feel them more, but adding pleasure would change the experience into something she would crave again and again. It gave him a deep sense of satisfaction to know all those negative memories would fade with each new one he gave her.

I'll make you forget them all.

Using his fingers to stimulate her clit, he rose, hauled back, and slapped her outer thigh twice. She made a low, keening sound.

"Tell me, pet." He pushed his fingers into her, thrusting hard, drawing her closer and closer to climax. Blood surged into the head of his cock, which swelled and heated, the bead of precum at the tip cooling in contrast. "Do you care that Scott's in the other room?"

"Who?" She whimpered, then collapsed onto the bed as she came. She tightened around his fingers, all her muscles within undulating with the violent climax. He kept his fingers inside her as he slid her completely onto the bed, easing down beside her as he let her come down in her own sweet time.

From beyond the door, he could hear Scott going through the fridge—probably helping himself to a beer. He would be fine on his own for a little longer. Zach gently slid his fingers free, rolling on to his back as Becky turned to her side, facing him. She blushed as he sucked his fingers clean.

"I almost . . . almost feel bad for not doing anything for you. *Again.*" She propped her head up on her hand, giving him a curious look. "But that gets you off, doesn't it? Tasting me. Toying with me."

"It does." His cock didn't agree, but he rarely let it rule him. Having a bit of fun with company around was one thing. But when he made love to her, it would be just the two of them. "Is that enough for you?"

"Yes." She leaned down and kissed his shoulder, her lids lowering as he cupped her cheek and drew her to him for a lazy kiss. "But sometimes I need to do more. It doesn't have to be much."

He smiled. "Believe me, that's not a problem. I have a cute little maid's uniform in mind. I'm not sure how much cleaning you'll get done before I take you on the kitchen counter, and table, and floor, but you'll have plenty of time to finish when I'm done with you."

"Will you ever be?" She traced her fingers up and down the center of his chest, the edges of her lips curving just a little. "Done with me, I mean?"

From her smile, he suspected she already knew the answer. But he gave it anyway. "No."

"Good." She ran her finger over his bottom lip, then let out as husky laugh as he closed his lips around it. "We're being very rude."

Sighing, he nodded. "We are. I suppose we should see to our guest."

"Oh, don't be like that. You want him here as much as I do."

"True." His brow furrowed as he sat up, rolling his shoulders to rid himself of the tension that abruptly gathered between them. "But why? You already said this was a bad idea."

"A moment of weakness. He does need us." Becky quickly changed into the clothes he'd taken out for her. "That's all there is to it."

A lie, but not a conscious one. Zach had seen how things were between Scott and Becky for months, always push and pull, mostly on Scott's end, but part of her was drawn to him. The part she shut off because she was a mature, responsible woman with a child, one who couldn't involve herself in Scott's reckless life. But there was enough between them for Becky to care about what happened to Scott.

As much as I do. No more, no less. But what if Scott changed—became the man they both knew he could be? Would the token attraction turn into something worthwhile? As a Dom, he was compelled to explore every one of his sub's needs. But what if those needs involved another man?

Don't worry about it now. It's not an issue.

But it would be. And he wouldn't make the same mistake he had in the past. Life was never cut-and-dry. Relationships didn't have to be limited to a man and a woman. The fact that a good portion of the team proved it had been a big part of the attraction. His agent, Danielle Trey, knew his past. She'd suggested he use caution with how open he was about it but had taken it in stride when he'd come out.

"I love your non-answers." She'd told him, snickering as she read over his latest interview. "Gets the press frothing at the mouth. That guy, Keane, already asked about extending your contract. Sweet four-year-deal. Not sure your announcement had anything to do with it, but it certainly didn't hurt."

"I didn't think it would." Zach slid on his sunglasses, sure their impromptu meeting was over. They'd meet again once she'd hashed out the details of the contract. "Give me a call when—"

"Sit down, Pearce, we're not done. I'm happy things worked out." Her sharkskin colored eyes narrowed. "But don't ever do that to me again. I had to trash several endorsements I'd been working on for months because of this. Bunch of narrow-minded assholes, but that's not the point. I don't like surprises."

"I understand."

"You get involved with anyone, you better give me a call." She waited for his nod, then continued, her tone suddenly relaxed, her way of telling him all was forgiven. "I've got a few things lined up. Tim Horton's! I think you'll like this one."

Such an offhand way to inform him he'd given up the remnants of his private life. Zach dumped his damp clothes into the hamper, then pulled on a pair of fresh jogging pants. He lifted his gaze to Becky, who stood in front of his dresser, using his comb to smooth out her hair. She smiled at him as he grabbed a few things for Scott to change into. He planned to spend a lot of time with her over the summer, and every spare moment after. Which meant the press would be all over them. He should probably give Danielle a call.

Later.

"Ready?" He put his hand on the doorknob, then waited for Becky's nod before opening it.

Scott eyed them as they came into the living room, his beer tipped against his lips, his throat working in long, slow swallows. Shirtless, slouched on the sofa, he was a great big bundle of sin with a lazy smile. Tiny goose bumps covered his flesh, but Zach knew the man wouldn't cover up even if he was cold. Oozing sex was more important than comfort.

"Sorry we kept you waiting so long." Becky moved closer to Scott, a shadow of guilt darkening her eyes as she ran a finger though his hair. "It's still damp. Let me get you a towel."

"I'm fine." Scott gave Zach a crooked smile when Becky ignored him and went to fetch a towel from the bathroom. "She can't shake that momma instinct, can she?"

"Why should she?" Zach shoved Scott's leg off the sofa cushion and dropped down beside him, tossing the spare clothes on to his lap. "You need someone that gives a shit about you. You're lucky she does."

"You implying you don't?"

"Not at all. But don't push me where she's concerned."

"Whoa, buddy! I got that you've made a claim. I'll ask for permission or whatever first, I promise. I've seen how it works at the club." Scott's lips curled slightly. "But if you think I'll get on my knees first and bow to your überness like Carter does for Ramos, you're gonna be disappointed."

"Did I give you the impression that I was willing to share?" Zach took Becky's hand when she returned, keeping her by his side, pleased that she didn't resist. He could tell she wanted to tend to Scott, but he needed to be her Dom right now. In this mood, Scott might say—or do—something to hurt her. And it was Zach's responsibility to keep that from happening. "More importantly, why would I even consider sharing with you?"

Scott snorted. "Do I need to spell it out?"

"Yes."

"Fuck, man! What's up with the games? This whole day has been leading up to a fucking wild *ménage à trois*. I'm just waiting for the invite."

Becky clung to Zach's hand, her voice strained with remorse as she faced Scott. "I don't know how you came to that conclusion— actually, maybe I do. And if it's my fault, I'm sorry. You two are talking like Zach has the final say in what happens, but he doesn't. I'm not having sex with you, Scott. If that's all you want from me, you can leave now."

"You can't kick me out of Zach's—"

"Actually, she can." Fuck, he was proud of her. Becky was no one's doormat. Zach stroked her palm with his thumb, hoping to convey his approval. Scott was difficult to deal with on his best days. And this wasn't one of them. But she was handling him just fine. "If she doesn't want you here, I'll show you the door. You know I like keeping things simple."

Tonguing his bottom lip, Scott nodded slowly. Stood holding the clothes Zach had given him to his chest. He glanced toward the door, then toward the bathroom. "Got it. Can I get changed first?"

"Go ahead," Zach said, torn between relief and regret. Scott could have stayed with them. Had a pleasant night with two people who'd ask nothing of him but his company. But that didn't seem to be enough.

"Just one thing before you go." Becky pulled her hand free, then hugged herself. "We don't want you to leave. But if friendship isn't what you're after, I don't think we have anything to offer you. I just have to ask . . ." Her eyes were sad, as though she knew there was more behind Scott's crass behavior than his whole playboy front. "Do you really have enough friends to reject what we are offering?"

Damn him if Scott's eyes didn't glisten just a bit before he blinked and turned his head. Scott fisted his hands by his sides. "You two are fucking with my head. You want to be *friends*? Seriously? That's it?"

"That's it," Becky said softly.

"What if I want more? You telling me it's off the table?"

"At the moment? Yes. I can't tell you what will happen a week, or a month from now. I *can* tell you that you scare me, Scott." Becky took a deep breath and inched closer to Zach, threading her fingers through his as though she needed his strength to continue. "I won't lie. I have feelings for you. But I'm not stupid enough to give you the power to hurt me. And looking at you right now, I can tell you will."

Scott's lips parted. He stepped forward. "I won't. This is different from before, Becky. You're not a reporter looking for a story. You're a woman I can't get out of my head. And Zach . . ." The look Scott gave him stilled his heart. Raw and open and honest. For the first time since they'd met. "I need him to be part of my life."

"Then you'll give us the time we need. That might be how you feel today, but what about tomorrow? If you mean it, prove it." Becky put her hand on Scott's cheek. "Don't ask for more than we're ready to give."

"Okay." Scott ducked his head, tightening his grip on the clothes in his hands. "I think I can do that. Blue balls aren't my thing, but I guess I can deal with them if it'll show you I mean what I say."

Fucking incredible. Zach did his best not to laugh, but Becky still gave him a dirty look at the gruff sound that escaped. He cleared his throat. At least Scott was trying. "We'll turn the TV up loud if you need a few minutes."

"Naw, I'll manage." Scott gave Becky a heavy-lidded look. "Do the zombies scare you? You gonna want to snuggle under the blankets?"

Becky smiled and patted Scott's cheek. "Yes. Actually, I'm looking forward to watching the show between two big strong men, rather than hiding behind pillows with another woman. Maybe I'll be able to watch what's happening without freaking myself out at every creak in the house. Or worrying that my brother might pop in, groaning loud enough to give me a heart attack!"

"I always knew Bower was a jerk." Scott chuckled and kissed Becky's forehead. "I'll make sure you feel safe. Wait for me?"

If Zach ever considered adding another man to his relationship with Becky, it would be Scott, as he was right now. The man was better than he knew. Than anyone knew. If he could accept the limits, who knew what would happen? Maybe the three of them could be happy together.

Don't jump the gun, Pearce. You've never seen this side of Scott. It might not even be real.

Time would tell. But for the moment, Becky seemed happy. And Scott had accepted the little she was willing to give. Which seemed to be more than enough as they cuddled on the couch, Scott so well in tune with Becky that he covered her eyes whenever the music changed. That he spoke softly to her before moving his hands. That he laughed with her to ease the tension when she got choked up about a favorite character meeting their bloody end. At one point, Scott looked over Becky's head and met Zach's eyes. And told him, without words, that this woman meant something to him. That he really was willing to do whatever it took to prove it.

This man, the one who wasn't trying to live down to the image he portrayed to the world, was the man Zach had tossed everything aside to be with that night. Was the man who fought for teammates on the ice, who was fighting to keep the Cobra black and gold.

Who just might succeed if his goals were more important to him than falling into old, self-destructive habits.

As Scott fell asleep with his head on Becky's shoulder, she tipped her head back and whispered in Zach's ear.

"I think we're good for him."

Zach nodded and reached over to touch Scott's mussed up hair.

"Yeah, we are."

Quietly rising from the sofa, Zach helped Becky ease Scott's head on to a cushion, then covered him with a light grey throw. Part of him wanted to shake the man, wake him up so he could join them in bed. But a bigger part, the part that was cautious, maybe even a little selfish, forced him to leave Scott there.

Just one more night with Becky in his arms, one more night to show her she didn't have to be afraid to wake up in the morning to a cold, empty space on the other side of the bed.

The clock read 5:03 a.m. when Zach heard the floorboards creak. He stared up at the ceiling, listening to the soft sound of the front door opening, then clicking shut. Sleep weighed on him, dragging him down for a few more hours' rest.

With no regrets.

Chapter Six

Sweat soaked the sheets and cold beads clung to Dominik's skin as he rolled over, opening his eyes wide, welcoming the sun that sliced across his bed through the part in his bedroom curtains. Daylight was a goddamn blessing. He couldn't stand the dream anymore, the same one that came every night, where Oriana passed him in the halls of the forum without any recognition in her eyes, the back of the white practice jersey she wore shredded and soaked with blood.

Sloan would never hurt her that badly. Dominik knew that. As much as he hated the whip drawing even a trickle of blood, Sloan did know what he was doing. He was also *much* better at first aid than he was at aftercare.

The other part of the dream disturbed him almost as much as the blood. Oriana hurt and not coming to him. Not *seeing* that he was still there for her. How long would it take before they became virtual strangers? Weeks? Months? At what point would they look at each other and realize they had nothing but memories?

Groaning, Dominik shoved off the bed, then went to take a quick shower. Oriana and Max were both in Oriana's room, where they typically spent the night. Where Dominik would have spent the night if things were different.

They aren't. You know exactly how this will end.

There was no point in dragging this out. Every single day, he felt things changing. Sloan was already gone, but that wasn't really new. As he'd gained confidence as a Dom, he'd asked for Dominik's advice less and less. Then not at all. He shut down when Dominik ... fuck, there was no other word to use besides lectured. About aftercare. About not distancing himself when his own urges scared him. The more Dominik talked, the less Sloan wanted to listen. They didn't gel at home like they did on the ice.

And now that Sloan might never play again, they didn't even have that. All they had was Oriana. And Max. But Max was an honest, loyal man. He loved Sloan like a brother. Maybe more. If it came to a choice between Sloan and Dominik ...

Dominik wouldn't force him to make that choice. Wouldn't force Oriana. If she'd given any impression that she still needed him, he would have fought harder, but . . . it was clear her future was with Max and Sloan. She still wore his collar, yet, for some reason, when she fingered the leather resting against her throat, he had a feeling it was more for sentiment than security. The meaning behind it was gone.

Maybe it had never been there. He now saw the collar like a child's training wheels, something that had eased Oriana into the lifestyle, given her the strength to find her own balance. It hadn't been that way when they'd gone through the ceremony, but no one could have predicted how much things would change.

He grabbed a protein bar from the kitchen cupboard and headed for the door. He should have known. Sloan was one of his students. How could a lover they shared be anything other than temporary? How could he have looked at Oriana as a woman who belonged to him, even a little?

But she does! She always will!

No. Maybe he still had a small part of her heart. But not enough.

"Want me to make you something?"

Her voice . . . his throat locked, and it took all his strength to turn and face her without tears in his eyes. She stood there in one of Max's T-shirts, all lovely curves, bare feet, and rumpled hair. He laughed as he tossed the wrapper of the protein bar in the trash. "I hope I didn't wake you up? I'm going to meet my brother at the gym."

"You have to eat more than that."

"You don't have to take care of me anymore, Oriana." He moved away from the kitchen counter and cupped her cheek so she wouldn't be hurt by his words. Still, they had to deal with this. "You know that."

"But . . ." Her hand went to her bare throat out of habit and her eyes widened, as though she'd expected his collar to be there, as it had been for so long. As it had been the night before. With a lock only he had the key for. Max must have cut it off for her. But why? "Dominik, I still love you. This is . . . hard. I'm still looking for a way to make this work for all of us. But it can't, can it?"

He tore his gaze away from where her hand rested against her neck. "I would have given you the key, sweetheart. All you had to do was ask."

"I couldn't."

Max might has well have taken those metal cutters to Dominik's chest. Because he wouldn't have used them unless Oriana asked him to. He could feel them snapping their razor-edge deep even now. Making raw meat of all the fragile bits within. Like his heart.

"You'll come tonight, won't you? I need . . ." Oriana blinked fast as she backed into the counter. "I need you there. Because I still don't know if I'm doing the right thing."

"What do you have for you when you go, Oriana? Besides Sloan and Max?"

"The team doctor in Calgary offered me an internship. And if not him, there are sports therapists that talked to me about working with them. Someone must really want Sloan, because I've been offered scholarships—"

"You'll have everything you need."

"Except the team, and . . ."

And me? He automatically added the words, but he really wasn't sure she would have said them. Nothing but wishful thinking. Which he should be past at this point. Her little gestures showed him she was still hanging on, but not in a way that would do either of them any good.

"Not 'buts,' pet. Put how big this will be for Sloan aside. You won't have to deal with your father anymore. You'll be free to live your own life. Don't let anyone hold you back."

"You never held me back, Dominik."

"Yes, I did. Sweetheart, you have something special with Sloan—something I haven't accepted as well as I should have. I've been trying to protect you from him. Negotiating limits that you need to set." He shook his head. "Sloan resents me, and I can't really blame him. You've been using me as a crutch, and that's not a relationship."

"I didn't mean to—"

"I know you didn't." He shoved his hands in his pockets. Fuck, he just wanted to hold her. Tell her he'd fix everything. Except . . .

doing that was what had brought them to this. "Oriana, I want you to be happy. You're not happy here."

She inhaled roughly, then exhaled, nodding slowly. "You're right. But it's not because of you. It's . . . everything. I need to figure things out. And anyway, nothing's set in stone yet. We're just going to explore our options."

"I know." *I also know you're not coming back. Not to me.* He eased his hands from his pockets, then went to the fridge to grab a bottle of water, doing his best to sound casual when he spoke again. "Give me a call when you're leaving, okay?"

"But . . ." She came up behind him and put her hand on his forearm. "You're coming to see us off, right?"

He bent over to kiss her forehead, his tone only a little gruff. He took a big gulp of water. Cleared his throat. "I'll be there."

On the porch, the door closed tight behind him, Dominik stood and looked out at the clear blue sky, letting his eyes drift shut as the sun's rays tipped over the low roofs of the bungalows across the street. The summer warmth caressed him but didn't touch the cold numbness that made him feel dead inside. He drew in a shaky breath and forced himself to walk down the steps. To unlock his car and get in. His brother, Cameron, was waiting for him. Had come all the way down to Dartmouth because he needed a fresh start.

His timing was perfect.

As he started the engine, a soft rap on the window brought his head up. He opened the door and leaned back. "What is it, Max?"

Max looked toward the house, raking his fingers through his overgrown, beach-boy-blond hair. His bright blue eyes had taken on a shadowy cast. His throat worked as he swallowed. "I just wanted to tell you . . . fuck, man, don't come tonight. Oriana will understand. This is hard enough for the both of you, and we still don't know if—"

"I'm coming to say goodbye. Because it will be goodbye, Max. We both know that."

"It don't have to be. We could try—" Max cut himself off and shook his head, holding up one hand. "Naw, don't bother. We've tried it all, haven't we?"

"Yes."

"Then there's really nothin' else to say." Max's jaw clenched. His hand shook as he reached out to grip Dominik's over the steering wheel. "Shit, I didn't realize it would be this hard. I'm gonna miss you. We had it good for a while."

"We did." Dominik turned his hand, fisting it around Max's. His throat tightened. Nothing would be as hard as saying goodbye to Oriana, but saying goodbye to Max came close. He'd never known a man like him. He grinned as he pictured Max, flopping onto the bed over him before an early morning practice, pulling him into a choke hold, laughing as Dominik snarled and did his best to toss the insanely chipper man over the side of the bed. They'd wrestle until Oriana came in with coffee and pronounced a winner. One morning, when Max had come in, Dominik was already up. On the phone with his sister who was panicking because their older brother, Joshua, was MIA. He was in the Air Force, and his plane had to make an emergency landing in hostile territory.

Oriana's father wasn't doing well, so it was Max who had taken the trip home with Dominik, who had sat with him and his mother and sister while they waited for news. He'd been Dominik's fucking rock, helping him stay strong for the women. And damn it if he had cheered the loudest when the call came to tell them Josh had been found. Alive and well.

Dominik laughed and pulled Max down for a rough, back-slapping hug. "I'm going to miss you, you crazy redneck."

"Hey, it's not like we'll never see each other again!" Max grinned as he straightened. "Just keep the hatin' on the ice when my new team kicks Cobra ass."

Dominik chuckled. "Will do. *If* that happens. But you have to promise me something."

Max expression changed. Utterly serious, he said, "anything."

"Take care of her. Make sure she speaks up for herself. She needs more than Sloan is giving her."

"I will."

"And take care of you."

"Right back atcha, man." Max pressed a sloppy kiss on his cheek, then ducked away from a halfhearted punch. "You hear me though, right? I'm not really gone. Just a call away."

"I hear you." But Dominik would never make that call. Because Max needed to speak up for himself, too. He'd stood back too often, letting Dominik say what he couldn't. He'd matured as a Top, could give Oriana most of what she needed in a scene, but still let Sloan take over far too easily.

They'll work it out. Let it go.

"Tell Cam I said hi." Max slapped the side of the car, then took a step back as Dominik pulled out. Through the rearview mirror, Dominik saw Max bow his head, nod once, then head inside. He was a good man. The kind of man Oriana deserved. And knowing Oriana had him made it a little easier for Dominik to buck up and keep going. Because she would be fine as long as she had Max.

We'll all be fine. The steering wheel creaked as every muscle in Dominik's body tensed.

Just fine.

* * * *

Muscles pumping, Akira lengthened her strides, a sheen of sweat cooling her flesh as she gasped in the moist salty air that carried the tropical scent of her suntan lotion. Her lungs burned as she pushed herself to the limit, her only concern making sure Jami could keep up. A light touch on her arm surprised her, because Jami had been doing well up until now. But her cast had only recently come off.

She must be hurting. I should have—Akira dug in her heels, laughing as Jami tried to pull her into the large gym they'd just passed. "It's just another mile to the forum, Jami. Don't be lazy!"

Jami rolled her eyes and jutted her thumb toward the big window. "Dominik's here. And there's a few of the other guys too."

"So?" Akira jabbed her teeth into her bottom lip at Jami's level look. Akira preferred to use the equipment in the gym at the forum rather than go to a public gym. It didn't cost anything. And if they were lucky, they'd be the only ones there besides a couple of Ice Girl hopefuls.

"This is the perfect opportunity to get you around people. Of the masculine persuasion."

No. She could already see all the men inside the gym. Big men, most of them shirtless. A sight that would make most women drool, but all Akira could see was how easily any one of them could overpower her. Her blood turned to liquid ice as she imagined those big hands wrapped around her arms and legs. *I can't—*

"There's only a couple weeks left until the cruise, hon. You need to get used to being around the guys." Jami dropped her arm over Akira's shoulders, giving her a little squeeze. "I won't be with you then. I'm here now. We'll just pop in for a few and leave the second it gets to be too much."

It's already too much! Akira looked down at herself, her tiny, baby blue shorts and white tank top. Showing this much skin was just asking for trouble. Then again, her Ice Girl uniform showed just as much. And she'd be wearing a flimsy little bikini on the boat.

If you're going to be a chickenshit about this, maybe you should get an office job.

A shudder ran through her. She'd been working part-time in her father's office when his partners had . . . She cut off the thought, reminding herself that all the prim and proper clothes in the world wouldn't stop a man from doing whatever he wanted to her. More importantly, she wouldn't let *those* men destroy her dreams. If she made the team, she'd win enough money to put toward starting her own figure skating school. If she was chosen as captain of the team, she'd be set. The position came with a $100,000 prize.

No one would vote for a coward.

"All right, since Dominik's here . . ." Akira hooked her pinky to Jami's, giving her best friend a wry grin. "You knew he'd be here, didn't you?"

"I didn't; I swear." Jami's eyes twinkled as she tugged Akira past the automatic doors. "But I *did* know most of the team comes here to work out off-season."

"You're such a pain in the butt."

Jami smirked. "But you love me anyway, right?"

"Right." Taking a deep breath, Akira followed Jami to the front desk, shook her head before Jami could pay for them both, and took the money out of the zipper pouch cuff around her wrist. She'd gotten a check from Dominik in her mailbox that morning. Enough to cover food and her share of the rent for the next month. *More* than enough.

Least I can do is thank him. Akira squared her shoulders, moving away from Jami, clenching her hands by her sides as she made her way across the gym toward where Dominik stood, spotting a man lifting weights. The man's skin was a few shades darker than Dominik's, but their features held some kinship. She slowed her pace, her gaze travelling slowly over the man's ripped abs and thick chest.

Dominik looked up when the stranger muttered something and caught Akira's eyes. His lips curved into a welcoming smile, which almost got her moving again. She trusted him. She was okay around him, even though they weren't anywhere close to the friendly hug, two-cheek-kiss stage. Not yet anyway.

But a glance at the stranger had her backtracking. There was something hard in his eyes, and the black cross and chain tattoo just added to his gruff appearance. Then again, tattoos had scared her ever since the men who'd attack her had shed the suits that made them look so tame.

Jami stepped up to her side. Took her hand. "You okay?"

Akira nodded. "Yeah. But maybe we should let them finish—"

"Hey, Jami. Finally got out of that cast, eh?"

Spine stiffening, Akira turned, fear drowned in anger. She pursed her lips as she glanced over at Ford, Jami's ex-boyfriend. He had some nerve coming to talk to Jami after what he'd done. As far as Akira was concerned, it was his fault Jami had gotten in the accident that had broken her arm. If he'd told her about the man his father had sent after Jami, she wouldn't have gotten hurt. Wouldn't have almost been . . .

Raped. Akira's eyes burned as the word slammed into her skull. She couldn't say why, but even thinking the word made what had happened to her, and what could have happened to Jami, seem so much worse. The word made her feel powerless. Like there was nothing she could have done to stop it. Her therapist had told her again and again that it wasn't her fault. That there was nothing she *could* have done. But Akira refused to believe that, because if she couldn't have done anything differently, there was nothing she could do to keep it from happening again.

Ford could have—*should* have—done something. Said something. He hadn't, and Akira wasn't sure she'd ever forgive him for that.

Jami, however, had forgiven him the moment he'd brought her baby lovebird, Peanut, back to her. She loved the little bird and had fallen apart when her stalker had taken him. Ford had made himself her hero that day.

While Akira considered all the ways Ford was anything *but* a hero, Jami hugged the man and let him draw her into a conversation about Peanut. And her arm. And her new job at the forum.

The second Akira felt Ford's eyes on her, she hugged herself and headed aimlessly toward the back of the gym, desperately needing to be away from him. Before she'd found out how stupid he really was, she'd . . . she'd been interested. The way he talked to her, the way it felt when he'd touched her hand that one time, stirred things inside her she'd thought were dead.

What had happened to Jami killed those feelings. Which was good. She didn't need a man like Ford in her life.

Not that she'd ever *seriously* considered letting him in.

Her foot thumped into something heavy and she yelped, hopping as she glared at the stack of weights on the floor. Her eyes teared and she cursed under her breath, dropping hard on the mat to rub her abused toes through her thin running shoe.

A man crouched in front of her. "Akira? You okay? Sorry about that. I tried to warn you, but you didn't hear me."

Glancing up, Akira grinned as she recognized Scott Demyan, the Cobra's notorious bad boy. Strangely enough, he didn't scare her. He could have any woman he wanted, and he was so out there with his flirting that he didn't come across as a threat. It was the men who pretended to be all polite in public that had to be watched. Their true form came out when they had you alone. Scott was Scott, and it was refreshing to be around a man who didn't try to hide who he was.

"I'm okay." She pushed to her feet, pretending not to notice the hand he held out as she furtively glanced over her shoulder to make sure Jami hadn't gone too far. Scott might not scare her, but she still didn't like men touching her. Letting them come too close was an invitation to do more. "A little surprised to see you here though.

Everyone talks about how lazy you are."

Scott snorted. "Well, aren't you blunt."

"I'm honest."

"Honest or not, do you really think I'd look like this if I sat on my ass all day?" He flexed his biceps, then wiggled his eyebrows. "Go ahead and touch. You know you want to."

Without thinking, Akira giggled and poked Scott's bicep. It felt good not being scared. And this was why she'd come in here, right? To get comfortable with the players. To convince herself they wouldn't grab her and hurt her.

Big hands settled on her hips, the hands of a stranger, holding her still. Her lips parted, but she couldn't scream. The gym disappeared and she saw them again, dragging her into an empty office, tearing at her clothes. Laughing.

"Damn she's hot, Demyan." The voice behind her was cold. Bitter. Icy fingertips slid over her stomach. He laughed when she shivered. "Think I might have to steal this bunny away. Fair play and all, right?"

Scott reached for Akira, his tone sharp. "You stupid asshole, let her—"

"Son of a bitch!" Ford yanked the man behind her away before she could get a good look at him. Akira winced as the big black man who'd been with Dominik blocked Ford and caught a fist in the gut. Ford shoved at him, his expression wild. "Get out of my way, Cam."

"No can do, boss." Cam's face split into a satisfied grin as Scott nailed a younger man with a swift fist to the jaw, knocking him on his ass. "I'll take him out back if you want me to, but I think Demyan's got this."

Dominik stepped up behind Akira, putting a hand on her shoulder, his brow creasing as she cringed away. She tried to stay still as her mind caught up with her body. Dominik. This was Dominik and he wouldn't hurt her. He was speaking, but she couldn't hear his words. All she could see was the man—little more than a boy actually, on the ground, black curls flattened with sweat, head bowed, spitting out a mouthful of blood. He was big though. Big enough to do damage. And he was getting up . . .

"Akira." Jami elbowed her way through the crowd, then rushed to Akira, smoothing away the hair clinging to the tears on Akira's cheeks. Jami's hands were nice and warm. Her voice reached Akira unlike any other sound around them. "Look at me, sweetie. Are you okay?"

"Fine. I'm fine." Akira's teeth chattered and a cold chill spread across her flesh, making her shake so hard that she was sure her bones were frozen inside. They wouldn't work if she needed to run. And she needed to run. The man was standing. "Let's go. I want to go, Jami."

Dominik cut off her view of the scene with his wide chest and pulled a set of keys from his pocket. "Get her to my car, Jami. I'm gonna get this settled."

"Thank you, Sir." Jami hugged Akira to her side, speaking low as she led her outside. "Damn it, I should have stayed with you. I didn't think . . ."

Akira stumbled along the sidewalk, heaving as much air into her lungs as she could manage. She almost walked right by Dominik's SUV, but Jami gently took her hand, guiding her back. The hot metal was wonderfully solid behind her. The gym was almost a block away. And no one was coming out.

But if he did—Jami was here. Jami would stay with her and Dominik would come. They'd protect her. Only . . . her pulse slowed, and she dropped her head back against the window. No one should have to protect her. Fight for her. Any other woman would have turned around and slapped the guy. *But not me. I just stood there and let him . . .*

"Akira?" Jami unlocked the backseat of Dominik's SUV, concern shadowing her eyes. "Talk to me, girl. Are you okay?"

"No!" Akira pressed her hand over her mouth. She couldn't yell at Jami. It wasn't her fault. "I-I h-hate that I r-reacted like that. I s-should have—"

Jami shook her head as Akira climbed into the backseat, then leaned over to hug her. "Don't do that to yourself. He caught you off-guard."

"I shouldn't have *been* off-guard! I know what men are like!"

"Not all men. Look how pissed Scott was. And Ford—"

"*Ford?* Why should he care? He knows I don't want anything to do with him." Akira gnashed her teeth. "It's his fault you got hurt."

"That's not true." Jami bit her bottom lip and crossed her arms over her ribs. "He didn't know . . . anyway, this isn't about him. You were doing so good until—"

"Yes, you were." Dominik came up behind Jami, resting his forearm above the open door. His muscles tensed and relaxed, and his soft lips turned down at the edges, tight with regret. "I'm sorry that happened, Akira, but you need to focus on how far you've come. I've never seen you so comfortable around a man. What is it about Demyan that had you so relaxed?"

Dominik's calm steadied her, helped clear her mind. She fiddled with the hem of her shorts, blocking out everything but his question. The way Dominik held her gaze, his eyes warm with approval, made her feel like maybe she'd done something right.

"He's . . . I don't know—straightforward?" She wrinkled her nose, not sure that made any sense. Why would a man so overtly flirty be easier to deal with than the men who tried to be nice? "It's clear what he wants from a woman. And that saying 'No' would be okay. He'd just move on."

The skin around Dominik's eyes crinkled slightly. "I can see that." He cocked his head. "But what about the other men? I thought you were coming to see me at first, but then you stopped. Why?"

"The man you were with . . . he made me nervous." The tattoos. Akira shook her head. What a stupid thing to go on. There were evil men without a mark on their bodies.

"That man was my brother, Cameron. He's a good guy."

"He's working for Ford?" *Ugh, why are you bringing him up again?*

Brows furrowed, Dominik nodded slowly. "Apparently. My brother wanted to enlist like our eldest brother, Josh, but he was turned down because of bad blood pressure. He came here to stay with me, get in better shape, and then try again."

Jami laughed. "He looks like he's in pretty good shape to me."

"He is. But he failed the medical and thought I could help him work on his endurance. I'm not sure that will help much, but . . ." Dominik shrugged. "Let's not change the subject. Are you comfortable with me, Akira?"

"Yes." Akira blinked, surprised that she didn't even have to think about it. Dominik was safe. His only interest seemed to be making her stronger. Helping her reach her goals. The only woman he wanted was Oriana. And . . . she frowned. "I wanted to ask you how thing were going with you. Is Oriana still—?"

"She's leaving tonight." Dominik's jaw ticked. His smile was forced. "As much as I appreciate your concern, this is still about you. Who else are you comfortable with?"

Akira considered carefully. Something about Dominik had her wanting to be completely honest. "Luke and Sebastian. I can tell they love Jami, and they don't look at me like . . ."

"Like?" Dominik prompted.

"Like they want me."

"So the only men who scare you are the ones who show interest?" Dominik stroked his chin, his expression thoughtful. "I could be wrong, but Ford has shown interest. And he doesn't seem to frighten you."

He doesn't scare me. I want to slap him. And . . . And nothing. Whatever she'd felt for Ford had evaporated when he'd kept things from Jami that could have prevented the hell her best friend had gone through. "You're right. But I don't want to talk about him."

"Fair enough." Dominik slowly lowered his hand to her knee, watching her face as she inhaled sharply. When she didn't shift away, he brushed his fingers gently over her bare skin. "What happened when that man touched you? Did you freeze up? Panic? Did that happen because it was unexpected, or because you were being touched?"

The answer came automatically, the skin on her belly crawling with the echo of the man's fingers on her. "A little of both. When I went into the gym, I was thinking that the way I was dressed was asking for trouble. But . . ."

"Yes?"

She blinked fast. No way was she going to cry about this. *Nothing* had happened. This time. "I wasn't dressed slutty when I was attacked. I know my clothes don't matter."

"Ah. I see." Rage flashed through Dominik's eyes. "You do know it wasn't your fault? Not what happened before, or what happened today?"

"I guess. But . . . maybe if I hadn't been playing around with Scott, that other man would have left me alone."

"That other man was Dave Hunt. And he lost a woman he was interested in to Scott." Dominik held her gaze, his own hard. "But you are not responsible for how anyone else behaves. I don't believe Hunt would force himself on you, but he still had no right to put his hands on you. Understand?"

No. Akira turned her head and stared at the back of the seat in front of her. In joking around with Scott, she'd given Dave the impression that she was open to more. She hadn't meant to, but that didn't matter. A normal woman would have handled it better. But she wasn't normal.

"Akira, look at me." Dominik patted her knee, then lifted his hand to cup her cheek. "We still have time to work on this. And you've made a lot of progress. Next time, we'll plan this a little better. Start from where you feel safe and go from there. It's very encouraging that you're comfortable with me, because I'll be with you on the cruise. Scott will be there too. If you don't mind, I'll have a chat with him. Which means we'll both be looking out for you. But . . . I'd like to find a way for you to be able to face men on your own. Maybe a self-defense course? Knowing you can bring a man to his knees with a well-placed kick can be empowering."

Damn, that would be awesome. A smile crept across her lips. If only she could have done that when Hunt had touched her, she wouldn't have had to run out like a coward. Wouldn't have felt like a victim. "I'd like that."

"Good girl. I think Scott is volunteering at a women's shelter as part of his new 'image.' Letting chicks beat on him. I'll see if I can get you in." Dominik brushed her hair away from her face. "Listen to me, little one. You should be proud of yourself. Months ago, just me touching you, or coming too close, would send you into a panic. But you're okay with it, aren't you?"

"I am." Somehow, the warmth of Dominik's hands on her flesh made her feel bigger. Stronger. She put her hand over his on her cheek. "Thank you. This . . . I needed this."

"And I needed to give it to you. You said you wanted to help me, and this has. I like being able to focus on things I can change." Dominik moved closer, smiling as he pressed a light kiss on her forehead. "I don't know the details, and I don't need to unless that's something you want to share with me. What's important is you reclaiming what was taken from you. You are a strong, talented young women. You have so much to offer, and I'm more than happy to help you see that."

After feeling so low, so pathetic, just a few words from Dominik gave her a new perspective. Hunt was just a stupid guy who hadn't even known the impact his actions would have. The whole ordeal was over, and Dominik had helped her move beyond the little setback.

But there was pain in his eyes, hidden behind his determination to help her. A pain she couldn't ignore. She slid her hand down over his. "I think I can talk to you, Dominik. Tell you everything. So long as you promise to do the same."

He smiled, a sad, lonely smile. "I will. I promise. But not today."

He'd said Oriana was leaving. And he loved the woman so much, it must be impossible to process right now. Tomorrow he would still be here. And so would she. With all he was doing for her, it felt really good to know he'd accept her giving something back.

"You know my number, Sir." She blushed, not sure if that sounded bad. How socially inept could she be? "I mean—"

"I know what you mean, pet." Dominik chuckled, then gave her a little hug before stepping back. "And I think I'll take you up on that offer."

Good. Akira sat back in her seat as Jami and Dominik climbed into the front seats and they headed out. She still felt the echo of a strange man's hands on her body, but flashes of Scott hitting the man, of Jami and Dominik at her side, of . . . of Ford enraged because he cared about what happened to her . . .

Altogether, it gave her something she'd never had before. She wasn't dealing with this alone. And she had something to offer.

Dominik had turned out to be exactly what she needed. Maybe she could do the same for him.

Chapter Seven

"I left you alone for not even an hour! You were supposed to show the guys how dedicated you are!"

Laying his swollen hand in his lap, Scott tightened his grip on the steering wheel with the other and bowed his head, trying to look appropriately contrite as Stephan continued his lecture about what had happened at the gym.

The man had called him early that morning, again and again, leaving messages every time, reminding him how precarious his position with the team was. 5:00 a.m. had seemed insane, so Scott had tried to ignore him. But by 5:30 he couldn't sleep anymore. Couldn't set aside how badly he'd fucked things up for himself. He'd gotten dressed and snuck out of Zach's house, leaving a note so the man wouldn't think he was running out on him and Becky for something better. Because he wouldn't get better. Didn't want it if it was out there.

Stephan made sure all his shit was out of Vanek's place, then dragged him to a bunch of stores the second they were open. Forced him to donate half his clothes to Goodwill, then spent most of the morning lecturing him on how he'd present himself from this point on. Sounded good, but when Stephan had left him at the gym, he'd kinda forgotten everything. Just gone with the flow. The guys had been cool, and Akira was a sweet little thing. Flirting with her had been a nice break, even though he knew nothing would come of it. Becky and Zach were still on his mind, and even as he played loose and relaxed, he couldn't stop wondering how they'd take the note. Had he said too much? Not enough?

"You're determined to make this difficult."

Of-fucking-course.

Scott made a face as he drove himself and Stephan to the new condo the man wanted him to look at. If he wasn't fucking someone, he was nothing but a goddamn problem. He hated summer. It wasn't like he had anyone to visit besides his brother. And he'd never see his brother unless he had to. Because their relationship was one-sided. Something he'd accepted a long time ago. Jimmy never called unless he needed something. Which was fine, because Scott hadn't been able to be there for Jimmy as a kid, no matter how hard he'd tried. They'd been in foster care together, but what good had that done? Scott had gotten all the attention from their foster mother, because he was "prettier" and "eager to please." And Jimmy had hated him for it.

"I'd have a better life if someone had done for me what she did for you."

Maybe Jimmy would. Or maybe he'd be even more of a wreck. Scott obviously wasn't doing all that well, despite his advantages.

"Are you even listening to me?"

"Yeah. I'm an idiot. Something, something, something. I need to do better. Yadda, yadda, yadda." Scott parked and slouched in his seat. "Oh, yeah. And I shouldn't be fighting."

Stephan groaned. "I'm not being paid enough for this. You do realize you're not a fifteen-year-old boy, do you not? Fighting on the ice is one thing, but it's ridiculous for you to be brawling with other players in a public gym."

No shit? "Got it."

Lips pursed, Stephan regarded him steadily for a few moments. "You never told me why you were fighting with Mr. Hunt."

Scott snorted. Talking to Stephan reminded him of talking to his principal in high school. *"Why can't you get along with the other children, Mr. Demyan?"*

"Because Hunt's an asshole."

As Scott got out of the car and headed toward the large, red wood and gold trim double doors of the condominium, Stephan clipped alongside him at a half run, barely able to keep up to his long strides.

"There has to be a reason, Scott."

"Does there?"

"Yes. And if you tell me, perhaps I can work with it. Put a positive spin on the situation." Stephan made a sharp, irritated sound. "Was Mr. Hunt doing or saying anything that would justify you attacking him?"

"Yep."

"Would you care to elaborate?"

I am going to strangle this man. Why the hell couldn't he let it go?

Jaw clenched, Scott stopped short and glared down at his nosy fucking team-appointed babysitter. "Does it sound like I want to elaborate? Can't you take a fucking hint? I get that I shouldn't be fighting, and I promise I won't do it again. Drop it."

"I'm not here to make this pleasant for you, Scott. Please step aside." Stephan's eyes narrowed, and he stared at Scott until Scott let him pass. "I'm here to make sure you don't lose your job. Which I can't do if you won't speak to me when things like this happen. Reporters will hear about this, and without some kind of statement from you, they will assume the worst. And so will Mr. Keane."

"Let them. I'm not making a statement about this. That poor kid—" Scott scowled and snapped his mouth shut. He avoided Stephan's expectant look as he stepped into the elevator. "I'll talk to Keane if you want, but that's it."

"And what exactly will you say to him?"

"I'll tell him why I gave Hunt a black eye." The satisfying throb in his fist brought a smile to his lips. He clenched and unclenched it, snorting at Stephan's disapproving frown. "And volunteer to give him another."

* * * *

"Oh. My. God. That was . . ." Becky stretched, her head heavy as she shielded her eyes and found the clock by the bed. Almost noon. Sleeping in this late felt so deliciously naughty, right up there with sex and Belgian chocolates. She smiled as she leaned up on her elbow to look down at Zach. He slid his hand into her hair and pulled her down for a kiss. She moaned against his lips as her blood caught fire. "You're corrupting me."

"Not yet." He tugged at her bottom lip with his teeth. "But very soon."

Letting out a low purr, she smoothed her hand over his chest. "Why not now?"

He nodded toward his night table. "Because your phone's been buzzing for a while—and before you panic, it wasn't Casey or Patrick. I would have woken you up."

"Okay . . ." The bed was so comfortable, and she loved being here with him, but she wasn't sure she liked him choosing not to let her know someone had called. Even though he'd checked to make sure it wasn't her daughter, it could still be important. She sat up, holding the blanket to her chest, turning her head so he wouldn't see her frown. Maybe getting involved with a hockey player wasn't such a good idea after all. Maybe he didn't understand that she, unlike him, still had responsibilities year-round.

As she picked up her phone, he rose behind her and caught her wrist. "What's wrong?"

"Nothing. I need to—"

"A little honesty, pet." He caught her chin and studied her face. "You're angry."

Her lips thinned as she pushed off the bed. "Actually, yes, I am. I enjoyed spending the night, but I have a job. Family. I don't appreciate you deciding whether or not I need to take a call!"

The room was too dark and cozy. She strode up to the curtains, throwing them open to flood the room with blazing light even as she checked her phone. The number was unfamiliar, but there were several messages.

Listening to them had her even more aggravated. Scott's image consultant wanted to meet with her to discuss a statement to downplay his "latest public stupidity." Snapping her fist against her thigh, she spun around to glare at Zach. "Scott's not here?"

"No. He left early this morning." Zach stood and pulled on his jeans. While she dressed, he propped his shoulder against the bedroom doorframe, watching her. He didn't speak again until she moved to walk by him. He stopped her with a hand on her arm. "Becky—"

"What is it, Zach? I'm in a bit of a hurry. I can't very well go represent the team like this." She gestured to the rumpled jeans and T-shirt, utterly disgusted with herself now. This wasn't like her. Running late, dressed all wrong, completely frazzled. *I'm too old for this!*

But then Zach looked at her, with his pale green eyes telling her before he said the words, how sorry he was. "You're right. I screwed up, and I had no right to make that decision for you. This isn't how I want things to be between us. I want us to fit into one another's lives, not complicate them. I'm sorry."

Damn it. If he'd done the typical man thing, apologizing just to shut her up, she could have walked out that door without looking back. But he meant every single word. She shook her head, fighting to hold back a smile. How could she stay mad at him?

"I forgive you." She patted his scruffy cheek, then rose up on her tiptoes for a quick kiss. "Just don't do it again."

He chuckled, hooking his finger to the back of her jeans before she could skirt away. "One thing first."

"Yes?"

His breath on the back of her neck stirred all the tiny hairs. His low voice in her ear made her breath catch. "You're fucking sexy when you're all worked up."

She swallowed, suddenly not sure she really wanted to rush out. "I really shouldn't be shouting at my Dom."

"Ah, but it's allowed when your Dom's being an idiot." His lips brushed the length of her throat. "You have a busy day ahead of you, but I'd like you to call when you have some free time. Let me know when you want me to help you paint."

"It won't be today." She bit her bottom lip. Unless she skipped dinner and . . . she glanced up at him over her shoulder. "Actually, I don't have to—"

"No. Keep whatever plans you have, and I'll do the same." He lowered his hand to the base of her spine, nudging her forward. "I have a meeting with my agent tomorrow and my physical therapist. Does Wednesday work for you?"

Two days? Why did it seem so long? She wasn't a teenage girl who absolutely had to see her boyfriend every single day. Spending all this time with him had spoiled her.

Letting out a long sigh, she nodded. "Wednesday would be perfect. My stuff is being delivered to the house, so you can help me bring it in. I'll ask Scott if he wants to help too."

"Or we can ask one of the other guys."

Becky pressed her lips together. Scott taking off obviously bothered Zach. She glanced over at the sofa, grinning as she spotted a folded paper on top of the rumpled blanket. Flipping it open, she laughed and read it out loud. "'Sorry I had to take off, my IC was on my ass. Call you later? Thanks for letting me hang out. Looking forward to doing it again.' Wasn't that considerate of him?"

"Yeah. Not like him at all." Zach folded his arms over his chest, one brow arched. "I won't tell you not to see him, if that's what you choose to do, but please be careful. Once he has you—"

"He can't have me." Her phone buzzed again. She hurriedly pulled on her running shoes, blowing Zach a kiss as she checked the number. Scott's image consultant. Again. She really had to stop stalling. *Responsible adult, Becky. Pull yourself together.* "Until further notice, I'm yours."

"Until further notice?" Zach gave her a hooded look. "I like knowing that you're mine. I take it that means there are limits to Scott showing how sorry he really is?"

"Absolutely." She answered her phone and quickly asked the IC to hold for a moment. Then she winked at Zach. "And when you two make amends, I get to watch."

* * * *

The reporters hovered outside the conference room, reminding Scott of rats waiting for the cat to leave so they could pick up scraps of trash. Stephan was on his phone again, keeping a respectful distance so Scott and Keane could talk. Not being a fucking nuisance for once. Nice change.

"Stephan said that you refused to tell him why you fought with Hunt." Keane's lips curled with disgust as he glanced toward the open door. Another reporter had tried to slip in, only to be stopped by security. He waved for one of the security guards to close the door, then leaned forward, his voice low. "He said you were fine telling me. I suggest you do."

Scott didn't want to tell anyone. Some things should be private, but it didn't work that way in their business. And unless Keane was a complete asshole, it didn't need to go any further. Rolling his shoulders, he hooked a finger to his cardboard-stiff collar and stared at his shiny new shoes. "There's this girl—one of the Ice Girls. She's not comfortable with men, but me and her were chatting and she seemed okay. Until Hunt grabbed her and—"

"Akira?" Keane thrust his chair back, standing even as Scott nodded. "Good enough. I can't say I approve of your actions, but—" A small smile crept across Keane's lips. "You put him in his place?"

Well, fuck! Scott laughed, holding up his damaged hand. "Clocked him a good one."

"Excellent." Keane stroked his smooth chin, eyeing the door once again. "The only problem now is giving the press a story that won't expose Akira or make you look bad. Is there a reason for the bad blood between you two? I assume Hunt didn't make a move on Akira on impulse? He's a hotheaded young man—immature, but not someone I could have pictured doing something like this."

"Ah . . ." Scott ran his fingers through his hair, not sure he wanted to make Hunt look better and himself look worse. But shit happened, right? "This chick Hunt had his eye on kinda ditched him for me."

"Through no fault of your own, of course."

Scott shrugged. "He was doing the whole roses and sweet talk thing. I just asked her if she wanted to fuck."

"And naturally, she did." Lips twisted with mirth, Keane came around the table, hands clasped at the base of his spine. "Stephan has been going on and on about finding you a woman, but I was reluctant to force you into a relationship just to make you appear stable. I'm starting to think it would be a very good idea."

"Yeah, well, I said I'd take a look at his 'list.'"

"A list? Are you telling me you can't find a woman on your own to commit to?"

Becky. Scott shoved his hands in his pockets, thinking about the night before, watching a movie, not trying anything after his first blunt advances. He could picture himself with her, proudly telling the press and anyone who'd listen that she was his woman.

If only she wasn't with Zach.

He refused to hurt Zach again, which meant he'd leave Becky alone unless the three of them . . . only, even if the three of them found something, it wasn't like he could be public about it. Hell, he wasn't even sure Becky and Zach would be public about their relationship. People would assume Zach was using Becky as a cover.

Which would be weird since he'd already come out.

Not an option. So what you gonna do now, Demyan?

"I don't fuck girlfriend-types." Scott winced, all too aware how shallow that sounded. "I just . . . damn, I was all about having fun. I'm cool with choosing someone to go to events with or whatever. Professional arm candy works for me."

"I have someone in mind. If she's open to the idea." Keane crossed the room at a soft rap on the door. He held it open to let a young woman in, frowning as she darted past security, tears glistening on her cheeks. "Sahara, are you all right?"

"I'm fine." The tiny blond sniffled, then buried her face in her hands. "And I'll take the job!"

Scott stared at her, then glanced over at Keane, his lips soundlessly forming the words "What the fuck?"

Keane held up his hand and shook his head. He pulled Sahara aside, his eyes narrowing as he spoke softly to her, too low for Scott to hear. At one point Keane's gaze went to the long sleeves of the cream colored blouse Sahara was wearing. Then he pressed his eyes shut.

"Fine. But we *will* be speaking about this again, Sahara." Keane handed her the black kerchief from his suit pocket, then turned to Scott, his eyes hard. "Sahara has agreed to join the Cobra Ice Girls. I've been looking for someone with experience to lead them, and she finally accepted my offer. I think she would be the perfect woman for you."

A sweet, pink blush spread across Sahara's cheeks as she dabbed away her tears. Eyes wide, she looked at Scott, then back to Keane, keeping a white-knuckled grip on the man's hand. "I . . . *what?*"

"Scott needs a young lady to accompany him to several events. And it will look good if he's with the same woman on the cruise. It's just for the press, and you've always been a media sweetheart." Keane gently pried his hand free. "You have the job whether or not you agree, but I would consider it a personal favor if you could help our top sniper ditch his reckless, womanizing status."

"You would?" Sahara nibbled her bottom lip, then approached Scott, studying him with her big blue eyes, long lashes clinging together with unshed tears. "You're okay with this? I mean . . . I just broke up with my boyfriend. I'm not ready for anything serious and—"

"Babe, if I was ready for something serious, I wouldn't need Keane to set me up." As a tear broke free, Scott lifted his hand to brush it away, then jerked it back at Sahara's flinch. *Fuck.* Her ex had done a number on her. She was so tiny, and he'd always thought she was kinda cute when he saw her around the forum. He moved closer, slowly, taking in her perfectly applied makeup. Must be waterproof of something—her tears hadn't even smudged it. But the skin tone around one eye was applied a little thicker. He could tell she'd covered a fading bruise. His jaw ticked. "Who was he?"

"You don't know?" She let out a nervous laugh as her hand hovered over her throat. "No offense, but I don't want to talk about it right now. The press is waiting for you, right?"

"Yeah." *I want a goddamn name.* A tremor ran through him as he thought back on his time in foster care. One of his foster sisters had gotten just as good at covering up bruises when her boyfriend had decided it was fun to smack her around when he was pissed. Scott had been about thirteen when he'd gone after the eighteen-year-old with a baseball bat. His foster sister had shielded the bastard. *At least Sahara was smart enough to get away from the asshole.*

"Scott, you're not listening to me." She shook her head and snapped her fingers in front of his face. "Just follow my lead, okay?"

Before he could protest, Sahara gestured to Stephan, who opened the door. Letting out a bubbly laugh, she wrapped her arms around Scott's waist. He blinked as cameras flashed, blinding him. Questions were shouted his way. A few of the male reporters shoved to the front of the crowd, and Scott's protective instincts took over. He drew Sahara around the long table at the end of the room, pulling out a chair so she could sit between him and Keane. As he took the chair beside her, she offered her hand, right on the table for all to see.

He laced their fingers together, chuckling as he finally caught one of the questions being shot at them.

"Was I defending someone special?" He brought Sahara's hand, clasped with his, to his lips. "Absolutely."

"You can't approve of your players fighting amongst themselves,

Mr. Keane?" A mousy young man in an ugly brown suit shouted. "Will you be taking disciplinary action?"

"I will. Both men will be fined." Keane smiled. "But I must be frank. I believe Mr. Demyan considers this lovely young woman worth whatever price he has to pay."

More questions. Some of the reporters were eyeing Scott and Sahara suspiciously. One finally said what all seemed to be thinking. A woman with a pinched face and thin, blood red lips. She glared at Sahara with bare hatred. "You're not a man known for long-lasting relationships, Mr. Demyan. Is this a publicity stunt? There've been rumors of you trying to improve your image."

A dramatic gasp escaped Sahara. She blinked fast, putting on the performance of a lifetime as she withdrew her hand. "Is that true, Scott? Are you with me just so you can look good to *them*." Her bottom lip trembled. "Is that all I am to you?"

Scott gave the reporter a cold look, then slid his hand around the nape of Sahara's neck. They went quiet as he rested his forehead against Sahara's. This was his last chance, and even after everything Sahara had gone through, she was willing to help him paint himself as a good guy. It *was* all for show, but damn it, the team, his life here, was worth putting on a good one.

What they needed to see between him and Sahara was something he didn't really feel. He recalled high school drama class, his enthusiastic teacher explaining how to laugh, to cry, on cue.

"All you have to do is think on a time where you truly felt whatever emotion you want to portray. Bring it back. Relive it."

He saw Becky, eyes flashing with defiance as she shoved him against a wall in front of her brother, her lips so hot and sweet as she kissed him.

In that moment, Scott had no other woman, or man, on his mind. All he could think of was how he didn't want to let her go. He lowered his lips to Sahara's, picturing Becky, putting everything he wanted to show her in the kiss. He gently eased away before she did, needing to see the dazed look in her beautiful grey eyes.

But the eyes that gazed up at him were blue.

"That . . ." Sahara touched her lips, then ducked her head.

Not Becky. His lips twitched, but he remembered the act before he could ruin it and brushed a strand of corn silk blond hair behind

Sahara's ear. "Answers your question?"

"Oh, yes." Sahara rested her head on his shoulder. "Can we go home now?"

"Home? Are you living with Miss Larose, Mr. Demyan?"

Scott opened his mouth, but Keane cut him off. "Thank you all for coming, but that's all for now. Another press conference will be scheduled before the Ice Girls' cruise and as you all know, both Miss Larose and Mr. Demyan will be attending. I believe we've answered all your questions."

"If not, please feel free to call me for the official statement." Standing in the doorway, Becky gave the reporters a broad smile, as though they were all great friends. But the smile didn't reach her eyes. "The team will provide several opportunities for you to interview both the players and the Ice Girl contenders."

Dismissed, the reporters filed out. Scott tripped over his chair and slammed his elbow into the table, cursing as he tried to catch up with Becky. She was already out of sight. He had to get to her. Make her understand.

He bared his teeth as Stephan cut in front of him right outside the conference room. "Move it!"

"Can I speak to you for a moment?" Stephan nodded to Keane, who left them without another word, then drew Scott aside. "That was perfect. Don't screw it up by chasing after another woman."

"Are you fucking kidding me? She's going to think—"

"Ms. Bower is a professional. And a mother." Stephan's fingers dug into Scott's forearm. "I'm sure she understands getting involved with you in any way would be a bad idea."

Scott threw his head back, bitter laughter ripping out of his chest. "So I'm allowed to have a fake girlfriend, but not a real one?"

"If you had a girlfriend, why didn't you say something?" Stephan groaned as Scott jerked away from him, holding out his hands in a calming gesture that didn't help Scott at all. Stephan lowered his voice as several reporters lingered in the hall, probably hoping to get a good scoop. "Please, I'm begging you. Avoid getting involved in drama until the ink dries on your contract. Assuming you get one."

After Stephan left, Scott returned to the conference room, closing the door so he and Sahara could have a moment alone.

Sahara stepped up to Scott's side and hugged his arm. "I'm sorry things are so messed up, but they'll work out. You'll prove you're not the asshole everyone thinks you are. I'll help you, and once you get your contract . . ." She smiled up at him. "Becky's a lucky girl."

"Yeah." Scott rubbed his hand over his face, Stephan's words resounding in his skull like a hammer striking a gong. Getting involved with him would be a bad idea for any woman. Right now anyway. But what was the point of doing all this shit if it wasn't to be better? To be the type of man Becky deserved. He ran his tongue over his teeth, then snorted. She already had that man. "You're right. She *is* lucky. Zach's an amazing man."

Chapter Eight

A pile of folders tucked under her arm, Becky checked her watch, then fumbled in her pocket for her key. She threw the door open. Slipped inside. Pictured Scott kissing Sahara with so much passion watching from across the room had made her feel like a voyeur. Half the folders fell from her grasp as she kicked her office door shut. Her throat locked, and she laughed as tears of frustration stung her eyes.

You're being ridiculous. Get a grip!

On one knee, she gathered her papers, putting them in order as she forced herself to take several slow, deep, even breaths. She wasn't *this* upset about seeing Scott with Sahara. Really. Today had just been long. Exhausting because of . . . everything. The days with Zach had just made it so easy to forget losing the job she'd loved because she wasn't cutthroat enough. Moving away from her parents and her friends to get a job that would pay well enough to support her daughter and let her be close enough to help her brother.

The thing with Scott was . . . the last straw. He'd been the first man to make her feel like a woman again after her divorce. He'd teased her, challenged her, and even though she'd turned down all his advances, she'd looked forward to them. She had to admit, part of her had hoped that his changes meant they could have something. Crazy, but being with him and Zach had felt right. She knew Zach was wary of Scott—she couldn't blame him—but she could have bridged the gap between them.

Because the man would change for you, right?

Wrong. And she knew that! Hadn't she learned from her failed marriage? Patrick had always been a little selfish and lazy, but he was so charming, could be so sweet, she'd convinced herself once they started a life together he would step up. After all, he'd been eager to have a child, always talked about their future together as if it was all he'd ever wanted.

He'd talked a lot. But that's all it was. A lot of talk. Their vows hadn't been worth the air it took to voice them.

Scott isn't Patrick.

They had a lot in common though. Like jumping on the first perky young thing that caught their eye. She straightened, moving quickly around her office to put away the folders she didn't need, getting her work for the night, and her thoughts, in order. Zach had warned her, but she'd needed to believe Scott had meant everything he said. She'd been desperate to hang on to how young and alive Scott made her feel.

And what about how Zach makes you feel?

Not until she reached the parking garage moments later did Becky let herself pause, hip rested against the door of her car, clearing all else from her mind until all she could see was Zach. Her cheeks heated as she recalled the press of his lips on hers, the way he claimed her body, the way she slipped into that peaceful place where his pleasure was all that mattered. She smiled, tucking a loose strand of hair behind her ear, picturing his eyes, bright with laughter, then practically glowing with heat. She would say that he was the better choice because he was safe.

Only he wasn't safe at all.

Losing herself to him would be so easy. The tightening of her chest, the way her pulse sped up just thinking of him, told her she was in serious danger of falling fast and hard. And before becoming a mother, she might have let herself do just that.

He wanted to take things slow. Which was . . . perfect. Because she was in no position to dive into anything. Even though she knew her bed would feel big and empty without him in it. Even though just hearing his voice right now would make everything okay again. She could tell him all about her silly little emotional trip, and he'd understand.

Then call him.

She shook her head as she climbed into her car, tossing her files on to the passenger seat. No more talking—or thinking—about Scott. Zach seemed perfectly happy moving forward with her. Just her. And being with him alone fulfilled her. Yes, sometimes a relationship worked with more than two people involved, but sometimes two was more than enough.

Zach was more than enough for her.

Twenty minutes later, sitting at Dean's dining room table for an early dinner, Becky watched Silver speaking quietly to Oriana, who'd been invited over with her husband, Max Perron. The young woman looked so lost. In a few short hours, she'd be getting on a plane to Calgary to begin a new life. Without her family. The team that had once meant everything to her.

And leaving one of the men she loved behind.

However well things worked between Dean and Landon, not every relationship with extra partners worked so well. There were times like this when things got too complicated. Becky glanced over at Dean as he stepped up behind Oriana to rub her shoulders. She was pale, had hardly touched her food, and it was clear she'd been holding back tears all night.

"I'm glad you could come tonight, Oriana." Dean bent down and pressed a kiss to Oriana's forehead. "We're going to miss you, but I've heard about the amazing opportunities you'll have out there. Let's focus on that, yes?"

Oriana gave him a shaky smile. "You're right. I mean, I was taking a night course, but not doing much else with my life. It will be nice to finally use all that schooling for something."

"And you'll visit, right?" Silver stabbed a piece of steak with her fork, brought it to her mouth, then lowered it as her bottom lip trembled. "I need you with me when I have the baby."

"Oh, sweetie." Oriana reached over and took her sister's hand. Her eyes were bright, but some of the sadness faded away as she laid her hand over Silver's on her swollen belly. "Of course I'll be there."

Max exchanged a look with Landon across the table, smiling grimly as Landon took Silver's other hand. Becky couldn't help but catch the uncertainty in the man's eyes. They all knew Oriana would want to be there when Silver gave birth. Unfortunately, there was no guarantee. Oriana would be clear across the country.

Silver needed that promise though. And, more importantly, she needed to avoid stress.

The men clearly couldn't help with that. Becky folded her hands on the table, thankful for the distraction. "Landon mentioned that you haven't gone to Lamaze classes yet."

Pursing her lips, Silver frowned at Landon. "I can't very well go alone. Dean is working crazy hours, and Landon just had surgery."

"I told you I'd go with you," Landon said, staring at the mushroom on his fork. "You and Dean decided it was a bad idea. I'm overruled, as usual."

"Stop being a grouch." Silver wrinkled her nose, turning back to Becky. "I don't get the point of Lamaze, but I was willing to go because my doctor thinks it would be good for me . . ."

Becky inclined her head. "Well, my best friend came with me when I was pregnant with Casey, and I was much more comfortable with her than I would have been with Patrick. I'll go with you if you want."

"Really?" Silver bit her bottom lip, her eyes lighting up. "You'd do that? I mean, I thought of asking, but you seem so busy."

Becky grinned. "My boss might be willing to give me some time off to go with you."

"You're damn right, I will!" Silver laughed. Then she looked up at Dean. "Well, I mean, it's not entirely up to me. I have to clear your schedule with Dean."

And Keane. But Silver didn't know about him, and now wasn't the time to bring him up. Besides, he didn't seem like the type of man that would use his controlling interest to make things difficult for Silver.

Dean simply smiled at Becky, mouthing "Thank you."

A few seats over, Max checked his watch. Took a deep breath. "I hate to cut this short, but we've really got to get going. Thanks for having us over, Richter."

"It was our pleasure," Dean said, standing. "Do you have a few minutes? If everyone's finished, I made a New York-style cheesecake. Silver and Oriana's favorite, if I'm not mistaken?"

Oriana let out an appreciative sigh. "We'll make time."

Dessert was served, but as forks scraped the small china plates, it became obvious that Oriana was stalling. She asked for seconds, then poked the slice of cake with her fork as she drew Silver into a chat about the Ice Girls. "I'm still trying to figure out this whole cruise thing. What's the point?"

Silver rolled her eyes. "Photo ops!"

"What does that have to do with hockey?" Oriana took a bite of cheesecake, groaned as though full, then handed her plate over to

Max. "I swear, you'd have the men playing in nothing but jockstraps if you had your way."

"You're damn right, I would!" Silver giggled. "Picture it. All the female fans swooning in the stands. It would be epic!"

"I have to admit, Silver has increased the female fan base more than I ever thought possible." Dean moved around the table, clearing the empty plates. "But players skating half naked is where I draw the line."

"Even if it's for charity?" The impish grin Silver gave Dean implied that they'd already discussed just that.

Dean tipped his head back to stare at the ceiling, his lips moving silently. "Yes. Even then."

Things had lightened up, but as chairs were pushed back, the whole purpose of the dinner seemed to settle heavily on everyone present. Silver moved close to Landon as he propped a crutch under his arm. Oriana clung to Max's hand. They all moved toward the door.

Suddenly, Becky felt very alone. She had to be strong for Silver. For her brother. But did they really need her right now? Her parents had gone out to dinner, preferring to give the two couples some time alone to say goodbye. Maybe she should have done the same, but she didn't really have anywhere else to go.

You should have called Zach.

Her phone became a heavy lump in her pocket as she followed her brother's slow pace to the door. Calling Zach now seemed too needy. What impact did Oriana leaving really have on her life, besides making things more difficult for Silver? Which in turn, made things harder for Landon. Her brother had been very quiet over dinner, all his attention on Silver, as though he was afraid this would be too much for her. The doctor had put her on bed rest. Had insisted on no stress because of her alarmingly high blood pressure. That she'd been doing well since didn't seem to matter, and Becky completely understood his brother's fear.

She wasn't sure he could take losing another child. She knew he couldn't handle losing Silver. And until he held that sweet little baby in his arms, and saw Silver strong and healthy after the whole ordeal, he would be a complete wreck. That their mother had put off going home yet again proved it.

By the door, Silver wrapped her arms around Oriana's waist, choking back a sob. "I can't—can't say goodbye now. I want to come with you to the airport." She looked over at Dean, her eyes brimmed with tears. "Please!"

"The doctor took you off bed rest. But . . . ." His brow furrowed as Landon and Becky stepped up to his side. He put his arm over Landon's shoulders. "It's not up to me, dragonfly."

Landon shook his head, his throat working as he swallowed hard. "Hell, just say it. I'm being paranoid." He took Silver's hand and kissed her knuckles. "*Mon amour*, you've put up with me long enough. If you think you can handle it, I trust you."

Silver blinked fast, then nodded. "You know I wouldn't do anything to hurt our baby. I'll be okay."

"Let's go then," Landon said.

Dean opened the door. He barked out a laugh. "You're lucky Mrs. Bower isn't here. She wouldn't be happy about you showing up so late."

Becky's heart stuttered as Dean stepped aside to let Zach pass. It took every ounce of strength she had not to throw herself in his arms. Her lips parted as he came to her, holding out his hand, his eyes telling her he already knew she needed him, but couldn't say it out loud.

Lacing his fingers with hers, pulling her to his side, he shrugged as though his presence wasn't all that important. "Your mother called while I was in an impromptu meeting with my agent. I came as soon as I could." He slapped Max's shoulder. "Wanted to see this man one last time before I cream him on the ice."

Silver gaped at Zach, her gaze snapping from his hand latched to Becky's to his face. "Are you two—oh my God, but I thought you were gay!"

Landon glared at Zach. "So did I."

"Enough. This isn't the time for—" Dean started.

Becky couldn't let him finish. Pregnant or not, Silver had some nerve. "Of all people, you're the last to judge my relationship with Zach. If you can accept Dean and my brother—"

"What?" Landon stared at her. "Me and Dean? We're not . . .

fuck, Becky! *Really?*"

Silver smothered a giggle with her hand. "Wow. You thought . . . ?"

Cheeks hot, Becky inched closer to Zach. "Believe me; I try my best not to think about it at all."

Dean let out a rough sound, like a choked back laugh. "All right. I don't think we need to discuss what your brother and I do in bed. Shall we go before Max and Oriana miss their flight?"

"You're an asshole, you know that?" Landon muttered, using a crutch to push Dean out of his way. "Not bad enough you've got my dad thinking there's something after he saw you fucking spooning—"

"Don't want to hear it!" Becky covered her ears with Zach's hands, smiling as she felt him shaking with barely contained laughter. "Let's just go!"

Zach had brought his bike, so he ended up with Becky in the backseat of Dean's SUV, sitting beside her while her brother sat brooding on her other side. Which would have been an issue if it wasn't such a perfect way to distract Landon from worrying about Silver.

"Becky, we need to talk about this," Landon said quietly as they pulled up in front of the airport. "When this is all done, we need to—"

"No. We really don't." Becky sighed, leaning close to her brother as Zach stepped out, following Silver and Dean into the airport, leaving them alone for a moment. "I wasn't sure about Silver at first, but she makes you happy. I really believe Zach can make me happy. Isn't that enough?"

"Damn it, Becky. You lost your job because you wouldn't get the 'inside scoop' about him and whatever man he's with. I respect the guy a lot, but most of the team knows the other guy is Scott." Landon raked his fingers through his hair. "You don't need to be caught up in the drama between them two."

"There is no drama, Landon. Zach could have had Scott." She inhaled sharply, well aware that Zach could still have Scott, if he showed the least bit of interest. But he'd given up on Scott even before she had. "If you really need to know, I was the one who made

Scott an issue. But he's not anymore. He's with someone else."

"And Zach's okay with that?"

"I don't think he'll care. He knows who Scott is. But he doesn't want him." *And neither do I.* "He wants me."

"I hope you're right." Landon threw the passenger side door open, wincing as he stepped out. "Because I'm in no shape to kick his ass if he's using you. But I will be soon."

Becky shook her head and hurried around the car to help Landon with his crutches. Her little brother had always been insanely protective of her. He'd always hated Patrick, and Patrick had given him every reason to. But she didn't want to see the same thing happen with Landon and Zach. They were teammates. "You respect him. Can you trust me?"

"I do, Becky. But—"

"No buts. You either trust my choices, or you don't."

"He's gay, Becky. He came out publicly."

"That's not what he said. And even so, you know why he did that." Becky stopped him outside the automatic doors, her hand on his arm just above the padding of his crutch. "Luke and Sebastian are together. Is Dean worried about Jami?"

"No. He's accepted that they both love her. And he had to accept that she's an adult, and—" Landon groaned. "I get it. I have to do the same."

"Yes. You do." She folded her arms over her chest as they came into sight of Silver and the others. The time for distractions was over. "How about we deal with the real issue here? You're not sure how Silver will take losing her sister."

"She seems okay, but . . . I don't know." Landon squared his shoulders. "We've all got to deal with it. The whole team. And I'm not sure if that makes it worse. Silver managed without her sister for a long time, but now it's losing her, and two of our strongest players. Silver has so much invested in the team, and all together, it's just too much. I'm just glad she doesn't know—"

"You're lucky Keane isn't a media whore like Anthony Delgado. The right Google search and you'd have a crisis on your hands."

"Please don't mention her father in front of her. She wants to see him, but he'll only make things more difficult."

Right. Becky held on to her brother's arm, taking a deep breath as Zach slowed to keep pace with them. Zach's hand in hers made everything so much easier. The muscle in Landon's arm hardened. Becky glanced at him, then followed his gaze and winced as Oriana dropped her bags at Max's feet, rushing forward, all else forgotten.

"Dominik!"

"Fuck." Landon hissed under his breath as Silver stopped short, her hand on her throat as Oriana sobbed and threw herself into Dominik's arms. For a moment, it looked like the man's solid embrace was the only thing that kept Oriana from falling to her knees.

"I can't do this, Dominik." Oriana buried her face into Dominik's chest, her fingers bunched in his T-shirt. "Tell me to stay."

Becky bit her bottom lip hard as cold crept up her side where Landon had moved away to be closer to Silver. Without a word, Zach slid behind her, rubbing warmth into her bare arms as she settled back against his hard chest.

"I can't." Dominik kissed Oriana's hair. "But I promised I'd come. And I brought someone else to see you off."

Oriana lifted her head, letting out a watery laugh as she slipped away from Dominik to hug her brother, Ford. "I called, sent you texts, but you never got back to me."

"My phone got busted." Ford patted her back, shifting away awkwardly, staring down at his boots. The young man made Becky nervous—she'd heard some really nasty things about him—but right now, there was something sad and lonely about him. There were shadows under his eyes, as though he hadn't been sleeping, and his voice was rough, as though he was fighting to keep it level. "My car too. It's been a weird few weeks, but when Dominik told me you were leaving tonight, I dropped everything."

Silver made a sharp, irate sound. "Puh-lease. I don't know why you listen to a word this asshole says, Oriana. He's a liar. And a user."

Ford sucked his teeth. "Yeah, well, it runs in the family. Who called Dad all sweetly after not talking to him for months? How much did you sucker him out of this time, Silver?"

"Don't call him 'Dad,' you fucking mold-infested douche bag." Silver put her hands on her hips. "And I didn't ask him for a cent. I told him how thing were going with the new screens I had put up outside the forum. He *offered* to contribute money we both know he doesn't have."

"He still wrote you a check."

"Which I ripped up! And how do you know that anyway? Can Dad shit without you sticking your nose up there to see how bad it stinks?"

"Silver!" Oriana smothered a laugh with her hand, holding up the other toward Ford before he could voice a comeback. "Will you two stop it? Please? I need you to promise you'll look out for each other while I'm gone."

Ford arched a brow. Silver snorted.

Oriana sighed, then took Dominik's hand, tugging him down the hall with her. "I need to talk to you."

Dominik nodded, but glanced over at Max as though needing to clear it with him before going any further. Max shoved his hands in his pockets, inclining his head.

Silver rested her head on Landon's shoulder, a sad smile touching her lips. "That went better than I thought it would. She's going to be okay, right?"

"Of course she will, *mignonne*." Landon's brow furrowed as he met Dean's eyes over Silver's head. He gave Zach the same look, and it took a moment for Becky to figure out what it meant.

No one doubted that Oriana would get through this. She had Max and Sloan to help her. But Dominik . . . Dominik had no one. Besides his teammates, whose help he'd never ask for. There was no way any of them could tell Silver this. Not for another month anyway.

"She loves him so much." Silver turned to Becky, speaking only to her, as though the men couldn't possibly understand. "I wish I knew why she's leaving him. Why he's letting her."

"It's simple, sweetie." Becky took a deep breath, swallowing against the lump in her throat as she stared out the window into the dark, starless sky. "He loves her too."

* * * *

"I have to go, don't I?"

No. No, you can stay. Dominik pressed his lips together, staring out the huge, fingerprint-smeared window at the planes lining the runway. One of which would be taking Oriana away from him all too soon. His whole chest caved in a little more with each breath he took, closing down on his heart which beat so hard against his ribs he was sure Oriana could hear it. His jaw ached from clenching his teeth to keep his smile in place. He loosened it as he glanced over at Oriana, taking in her wide eyes, glistening with tears.

This wasn't easy for her, which made what he had to do, to say, even harder. A few words and he could play her uncertainty in his favor. Have her go back to Max and force him to leave without her. But then what? Being without him might hurt, but losing Max would tear her apart.

Max would stay. Max would do anything for her. You don't have to let either of them go.

Could he do that to them? Or himself? It would be so simple. All he had to do was pretend the relationship hadn't truly ended months ago. Lie to himself every night as he held Oriana. Make believe she'd chosen him.

"Sloan is waiting for you." He touched her cheek, hanging on to his smile so she would know he wasn't trying to be cruel. All he'd ever asked from her was the truth. And he couldn't hold it against her just because the truth wasn't what he wanted to hear. It was time for him to make her face it. "If you're not getting on that plane, you should call him and let him know."

"Dominik, you know I can't do that." She tucked her hair behind her ears, the faint color in her cheeks vanishing completely. "I-I love him. I can't picture my life without him."

But you can picture it without me. Not a question. It was all too clear. "Then you have your answer."

She caught his hand, shaking her head. "But I still love you. You can come with us and—"

"No, Oriana. I can't. The team needs me." He held his breath, hating what he had to say next. But there was no other way to end this. If all they'd ever had was honesty and trust, they would have that still, even though it was over. "You don't need me. Not anymore."

"That's not true—"

"Look. At. Me." Dominik's voice broke as tears spilled down her cheeks. His own eyes burned as he gave her the last command he would ever give her. "Go. Go build something strong between yourself, Max, and Sloan. Find the life you've always wanted and . . ." He swallowed hard. "Don't look back. There's nothing left for you here."

"There's my family." She swiped her tears away and bit her bottom lip. "There's y—"

"Just your family. And you'll visit. But you know what you have to do now, Oriana." He was shocked that he still managed to smile as he dried her last tears. "Go."

"All right." She inhaled roughly, stepping away from him. She sniffed, then squared her shoulders. "I'm sorry I made this more difficult for you. All I want—all I've ever wanted—was for you to be happy. But none of us have been for a while, have we?"

"No." His smile faltered. He wanted to take all his words back as he saw her physically, and emotionally, pulling away from him. And he would have, if it would change anything. Only, there was no point in dragging this out any further. It shouldn't have been dragged on this long. "We will be though. Door closes, window opens, and all that."

She blinked back fresh tears and nodded. "For you too. You're the captain of the team. And you'll find someone—"

Spine stiffening, Dominik backed away from her. "Don't. Please don't. We've said all we have to say. I'm trying to make this easier, but I can't hear that from you. Not that."

Covering her mouth with her hand, Oriana's face crumpled. "I'm sorry! Dominik, I didn't mean to—"

Brisk footsteps came toward them. Without looking, Dominik knew it was Max. He gave a jerky nod as Max squeezed his shoulder, facing the window as the man drew Oriana away.

"If we're going, we have to leave now," Max said softly, speaking to her. "You know I'll accept whatever choice you make."

"We're going." Oriana never came any closer. Simply whispered, "Goodbye, Dominik."

Dominik's lips formed the word, but the sound couldn't pass the locked down part of his throat. Max's heavy footsteps, followed by the slow scrape of Oriana's heels, faded away. And his whole body shook as he leaned his forehead against the cool glass before him. A broken sound escaped as his heart shattered into a million jagged pieces. He choked on a sob, pressing his fist against his lips.

She's gone. A blazing hot tear trailed down his cheek. *She's really gone.*

Chapter Nine

Mason hadn't come back. Oriana and Perron had said their last goodbyes at security. Their plane had disappeared over the horizon. But Mason was nowhere to be seen.

Zach knew the man wouldn't do anything stupid, no matter how upset he was, but he shouldn't be alone right now. Looking over at Becky, he could tell, by the way her lips parted and her hand tightened on his while she stared down the hall where Mason had disappeared, that she'd been about to say just that.

"I'll check on him, then give you a call later." He leaned over to brush a kiss on her cheek, then nodded to Richter and Bower, who barely acknowledged him. Silver stood between them, staring out at nothing, her face utterly still. Tears would have been reassuring, but this . . . this was a little frightening. Thankfully, her men were capable of taking good care of her. And Becky had been pregnant, so she'd know if there was anything to worry about.

Ford blocked him before he could go any farther. He rolled his eyes when Zach frowned at him. "Cam came with us. His probably with Dominik."

"What if Dominik doesn't want to talk to him?" Silver curved her hand around the base of her throat, lips pressed together so hard they faded into the rest of her pale skin. "What if he just needs time to . . . to deal. I think I need that. Just a short walk by myself so I can wrap my head around this."

"Silver—" Bower reached for her, but Richter drew him back. Bower hunched his shoulders, then nodded. "Go ahead, *ma cherie*. We'll wait for you at the car."

Becky stepped up to Zach's side as Silver made her way out the closest door, her throat working hard as she looked helplessly at her brother. She looked worn out. Zach had been keeping her up too late, and with the emotional rollercoaster of the last few days, she was probably completely drained.

"You should get back to Richter's place and get some sleep." Zach stroked her back gently, warmth filling him as she leaned against his chest, not trying to hide her exhaustion. He didn't mind a clashing of wills once in a while, but with this, he'd have pushed the issue if she'd argued with him. "I know you're going to spend the night worrying about Silver and your brother."

"Come with me?" Becky tipped her head up to look at him, holding back a wince. "Ugh, that sounded pathetic, didn't it? You have a lot to do tomorrow."

"My bike's still back there. I can stay for a little." He kissed the tip of her nose, grinning at the way she wrinkled it. She was adorable when she was all sleepy. "Tuck you in and sing you a lullaby?"

"Mmm. I bet you have a really nice voice." Straightening, Becky rubbed her eyes, letting out a light laugh. "I don't have the energy to say no to you."

Tempting, but no. He wouldn't even tease her about her words. This painfully long day needed to end.

But as he passed the automatic doors, familiar screams told him it wasn't over yet.

"You fucking bitch! Oriana just left!" Silver stood in the middle of the parking lot, facing a woman Zach was sure he'd seen around the forum. "My father sent you for me and Ford? *Tonight?* Why don't you tell him—"

"You've always been so dramatic, my dear." The woman—Anne, Mr. Delgado's secretary or assistant or something—clasped her hands in front of her lime green pencil skirt, her thin lips twisted in a smirk. Her tone was maddeningly calm in the face of Silver's rage. "Please get ahold of yourself. This excitement isn't good for the baby."

"Why didn't he come? She's his daughter and all she ever wanted was for him to say he loved her!" Silver's voice cracked. "It would have meant so much to her if he'd come."

Richter strode ahead, with Bower following as fast as he could, but Silver waved them both back, then completely ignored Ford as he moved up to her side. Zach took Becky's lead, sticking close to Bower in case his leg gave him trouble.

"Why would your father make that kind of effort for a child he doesn't believe is his? And besides, her behavior reflects badly on the family. It humiliated your father that she carried his name while strutting around with all those men." Anne sniffed, eyeing Silver's stomach. "Though I can't say you're much better."

"Listen, lady—" Ford took a step forward, grunting when Silver slapped her hand into his chest. "Fuck, Silver. She can't talk to you like that."

"I don't need you defending me. I—" Silver cringed and hugged herself. She let out a pain-filled gasp as the color left her face. "No. Not again."

"As I said. Too much excitement," Anne said, glancing over at Ford as he wrapped his arm around Silver's back to support her. "Your father would still like to see you at your convenience."

"Tell my father he can go to hell." Ford snarled, nodding when Richter came to lift Silver into his arms. Ford looked shocked when Silver latched on to his hand, towing him along with them. "I got you, sis."

Anne seemed about to follow, but Becky smoothly cut her off, hissing something under her breath that had the woman skittering away as fast as her stick legs would carry her. Bower limped fast toward the car, cursing as his crutch snagged in a wide crack in the pavement. He gave Zach a grateful smile when Zach took one of the crutches and flung Bower's arm over his shoulders, bearing most of his weight.

"Fuck, I'm glad you came, Pearce." Bower let out a strained laugh as he watched Richter ease Silver into the backseat of his SUV. His whole body shook with nervous energy. "You just might be good enough for my sister. Stand by her tonight, let her know she doesn't have to worry about me, and I'll give you my blessing."

"I'll stand by her either way." Zach opened the front passenger side door for Bower, then helped him up. "But it's good to know you approve."

"Shit. This is it." Bower took a few deep breaths, sounding a bit like he was doing Lamaze in preparation to push out the baby himself. "You're okay, Silver. The doctor said you passed the dangerous time."

"Don't tell me I'm okay! Damn it, that woman ruined everything!" Silver panted, then thunked her head against the headrest. "It wasn't supposed to happen yet!"

"Shh. You're ready, dragonfly." Richter smoothed hair sticky with sweat away from Silver's face. "You're going to be just fine."

"No, I won't!" Silver pressed her eyes shut, sobbing breathlessly. "Oriana said she would be here. She's not here."

Zach winced as he took the keys from Richter, who'd taken the seat at Silver's other side. *Poor, kid.*

Ford patted the back of Silver's hand, his voice calm even though he was shaking just as hard as Bower. "I'm here, sis."

Silver cried harder, but laughter broke through her sobs. "But I hate you!"

"Hate me later. Right now, just hold my hand and tell me you're going to be okay, because you're fucking scaring me."

"Don't fucking swear around my baby! What kind of uncle are you?"

A glimmer of hope stole some of the shadows from Ford's eyes, but he simply chuckled. "Shut up and breathe, or push, or whatever you need to—"

"Don't push!" Becky gave Zach a shove toward the driver's side, suddenly all business. "Just breathe, Silver. Kinda like Landon's doing, only slower so you don't hyperventilate." She climbed into the farthest seats in the back, then snapped on her seat belt, glaring at Zach through the rearview mirror. "Go, Zach! She's not having my niece or nephew in this car!"

He grinned at her as he started the car, loving the way she inhaled sharply, her cheeks glowing red with excitement. His beautiful sub was fierce, and he had a feeling even the baby would wait until she gave it permission to come out before moving another inch. The best subs always seemed like Dommes out in the world, but with Becky, he couldn't help but wonder what it would be like to let her take charge in the bedroom.

"I'll have her there in five minutes, Ma'am." He winked at Becky when she gaped at him. That look was priceless. Even the title coming from him seemed to disturb her. She wouldn't be playing his Mistress any time soon.

"Shit." Silver went still, blushing as she buried her face under Richter's arm, while still clinging to Ford's hand.

Richter stroked her hair, murmuring. "What is it, dragonfly?"

"I think my water broke."

Zach's pulse raced. He didn't know much about babies, but the water breaking was universal for "Hospital. Now." "I can cut that time in half if I—"

"Five is fine, Zach." Becky looked like she wanted to laugh. "Don't worry, the baby is not just going to slide out. Drive safe."

"Safe. Got it." Zach felt his cheeks heat as he caught himself breathing along with Bower in short puffs, then long exhales. He supposed it was better than Ford, who seemed to have stopped breathing altogether. Only Richter and Becky still had some semblance of control.

"All right boys, with me. In." Becky inhaled a long, slow, steady breath. "And out."

"Becky." Bower growled. "Focus on Silver."

"Silver is fine. Let's try that again."

"Shut up."

"Watch it, little brother. You're not too old to spank."

Richter snorted. Bower clamped his lips together. Silver stopped panting long enough to giggle.

Zach just did his best to focus on the road as the tension eased out of the car. He'd never met a woman like Becky. Her strength, the way she put others before herself, no matter how she was feeling, her dedication to her family . . . if he looked at her again before he got ahold of himself, she would see something in his eyes that it was too soon to share.

She would see that he was falling in love.

* * * *

Hours passed, time measured by the short spans between contractions, then suffering that seemed endless. Suffering Landon wished he could take away. He limped across the delivery room as Silver bent forward, her face red and beaded with sweat. She bit back a scream as he took her hand, fighting so hard to be brave for him.

He braced his free hand on the bed by her side, leaning over to kiss her forehead. "Let it out, *mon amour*."

"I can't." Silver hissed in a breath through her teeth. "Are you all right? You shouldn't be standing so much. Where's Dean?"

Landon did his best not to react to her asking for the other man. Dean was just as involved in this as he was. The only problem was, Silver didn't seem to think Landon was strong enough to stand by her. His behavior over the past few months probably hadn't helped.

"I'm here, dragonfly." Dean spoke up from where he sat across the room, reading the sports section from that morning's newspaper, tipping down his new reading glasses to smile at her. His calm was driving Landon a little insane, but his level tone had Silver relaxing back on to the pillows and smiling back. "Becky's gone to get some more ice. Did you need something else?"

"Yes. I need you to..." She gave Landon an apologetic look before meeting Dean's eyes. "Make sure he doesn't make his leg worse. I know how bad he wants to get back between the pipes and—"

"The pipes? *Mon dieu*, Silver, do you think I care about the damn game right now?" Landon raked his fingers through his close-shaved hair. "All I can think about is you and our baby."

"Right." Silver panted. "But you were in the hospital not that long ago. You need to take care of yourself. The team's got a lot of money invested in you, and you'll be a free agent in—"

"*You're* in the hospital *now*." He shook his head, eyes narrowing as Dean chuckled. "You seriously want to talk about my contract?"

"Absolutely. I want to extend it—ah!" Silver's grip on his hand tightened. She rasped out the words even as she bent over in pain. "Twenty years. Dean can... work out the details. I don't... don't want any other team stealing you from us."

"No one's taking me away from you." Landon winced as Silver tossed her head from side to side, gasping, then finally letting out a sharp scream. There was an IV taped to the back of her hand, but the damn thing was useless. *Where's the fucking doctor?* "Let me see if Dr. Singh can come and give you something else—"

"Don't want anything else." Silver huffed out a breath, whispering thanks as Becky returned with a pitcher full of ice and a plastic cup. Her eyes fluttered shut as Becky gently stroked her wet fingers across her cheeks and down over her throat. She let Becky feed her a sliver of ice, then relaxed as she crunched on it, looking close to sleep for the first time in over an hour. With her face nuzzled against Landon's forearm, she mumbled. "Talk to him, Becky. Has to be careful."

"*Tabernac.*" Landon gave Dean a grim smile as the man pulled a chair up for him. His leg hurt like a motherfucker, but it was nothing compared to what Silver was going through. "I really messed up. She shouldn't be worrying about me."

"Why not?" Dean laid a hand on Landon's shoulder, his thumb moving soothingly up and down the back of Landon's neck. "There's nothing wrong with her focusing on you rather than her pain. And you're doing very well. I thought you'd be panicking by this point."

Becky laughed as she fussed with the thin blue sheet covering Silver. "The doctor threatened to kick him out if he didn't calm down. Don't give him too much credit."

Landon scowled. "Thanks a lot, sis."

Eyes wide, Becky covered her mouth, then shook her head. "Damn it, I'm sorry, Landon. That wasn't fair, it's just... Patrick made it all about him when I had Casey. I know you're not like that. I know why this is so hard for you."

Sighing, Landon straightened and held out his arms as his sister moved in for a hug. That fucktard had put her through a lot. "It's okay. Actually, I'm glad you're here to make sure the focus is on Silver. Where it *belongs*."

"Yes, but Dean's right. Any distraction is good for her." Becky smoothed her hand over Silver's hair, the fondness in her eyes making him smile. After the rough start between the two, he'd wondered if his sister would ever accept the woman he loved. But they'd bonded during the pregnancy, and Becky obviously considered Silver part of the family. "Poor thing must be exhausted. It's been a long night."

"But it will be over soon, right?" Landon groaned as Becky exchanged a *look* with Dean that couldn't mean anything good. "The doctor said it shouldn't be more than twenty-four hours since her water already broke. It's been—" He glanced at the clock on the wall and groaned again. "Only six? Fuck!"

The door swung open and the short, bald doctor strode in, a broad smile on his face. The nurse behind him fiddled with Silver's chart, her cheeks red as her eyes darted from Dean to Landon.

"Ah good, she's resting. I was a little worried that having so many people around would wear her out." Dr. Singh ambled around the bed, checking the heart monitor and the IV. Silver's original doctor had been a woman, but Silver refused to see her after the woman had made a snide remark about the baby's paternity. Dr. Singh was easygoing and took the relationship in stride. He'd extended Silver's bed rest after both Landon and Dean expressed their concern. Silver had been comfortable enough with him to confess to her past drug use. Luckily, it hadn't affected the baby, but the doctor had warned Silver that the damage to her heart could be an issue. Which was probably the only reason Silver hadn't argued *too* much about being stuck in bed.

"The stress didn't create any problems?" Landon let Becky help him stand, his breath catching as Silver's eyes shot open and her lips parted in a silent scream. He automatically gave her his hand, which had gone numb at some point from being squeezed so often. "Hey, *mignonne*. Look who's here."

"Dr. Singh!" Silver whimpered, pressing her other hand to her stomach. "I need—I need to push. I know you said I shouldn't—"

"Let's see how far along you are, honey." Dr. Singh quickly positioned Silver for the examination. After a few moments, he moved away from her, glancing over at the machine monitoring the contractions. "Very good. You're fully dilated. I'll give you something for the pain and we can get started. Remember what I told you about your breathing?"

Silver nodded, audibly grinding her teeth as the bed was repositioned behind her by the nurse. "I'm ready." Her eyes widened as she looked around her. "Landon? Dean?"

Landon kissed her hand. His eyes teared as he grinned at Dean who'd moved to Silver's other side. "We're both here, *ma cherie*."

Nodding again, Silver pushed her head back into the pillow. "He's coming!"

"Or she." Dr. Singh stepped between Silver's parted thighs. "All right, sweetheart. Push!"

The piercing screams tore right through Landon, and he was grateful for his sister, standing by his side, whispering encouragement to Silver as his voice left him. The crimson towels the nurse held made his pulse stutter. He glanced over, spotting a tiny head, and his vision flashed white. His blood turned to ice as, with one last push, Silver's head dropped back and her whole body went still. The heart monitor showed an erratic pulse.

Then steadied. He let out a rough sound of relief as Silver stirred.

She blinked at him. "The baby?"

He sobbed as he watched Dr. Singh lift the tiny, red-slicked baby up above Silver's thighs. The nurse quickly put a clamp on the umbilical cord, then cut it. Something he'd wanted to do—it was okay though, let them handle it if that's what was best. But as he caught the tight expression on Dean's face, and felt Becky's grip on his arm tighten, he knew something was wrong. He choked in air, blocking out everything else so he could hear his baby cry.

Silence wrenched all the strength from his body. He shook his head. "Dr. Singh?"

The doctor turned away from them. The nurse stood beside him, speaking low. Landon's legs almost gave out, but he forced himself away from the calling darkness. Silver needed him to hold it together if the baby—

"There's we go!" Dr. Singh turned as the baby let out raspy cry. "That was a lot of work, wasn't it, little one?" He grinned at Landon, seeming to move toward him in slow motion. "Silver, gentlemen, you have a beautiful baby girl."

"A girl." Landon's bottom lip quivered as Dr. Singh lowered his daughter into Silver's arms. Tears were flowing freely now, but he didn't bother wiping them away. He sobbed again as Silver stared up at him, her own eyes brimming with tears. "Silver . . ." Dean was right behind him, his grip on Landon's arm helping to take some weight of his leg. He leaned back, glancing over his shoulder to make sure Dean had heard. "Dean, we have a little girl!"

"She's beautiful," Dean whispered, smiling at him. "Strong."

"I know!" Silver kissed their daughter's head, laughing and sobbing at the same time. "She scared me, but . . . oh God, she'd perfect, isn't she?"

"She is." Landon's whole body shook as he stared at them both.

Both breathing. Both so alive. He was afraid to blink. Afraid this couldn't possibly be real. "She's so little."

"Her color is good even though her score is a little low." Dr. Singh slapped Landon's shoulder. "We'll check her again in a few minutes. She may need some help breathing, but I'm not overly concerned. She's small, but Dean is right. She's strong. Her heart rate is excellent."

With every word, Landon felt the ground become a little more solid beneath his feet. He kissed Silver, laid a solid, smacking kiss on Dean's cheek, then gazed down at his daughter, who'd stopped crying, but squirmed and made small, fussy noises in Silver's arms.

"Are you ready to hold her?" Silver whispered.

Landon took a deep breath, then nodded. More tears spilled as the nurse helped Silver place the baby in his arms. She weighed almost nothing, but holding her was a heavy feeling, the sensation of all his love for Silver, of everything they shared, contained in this tiny being. Her head fit in his hand, her unfocused eyes somehow finding his face. Nothing he'd ever experienced compared to this moment. Dean put an arm over his shoulder, lightly tracing his finger down the baby's cheek, speaking soft words that Landon couldn't quite make out.

Then Becky was there, nudging him. "Landon, the doctor needs to check her again. You have to let her go."

Never. But he clamped down on the possessiveness, grinning ruefully as the doctor laughed.

"Not for long, Landon." Dr. Singh winked. "After that, she's all yours. Silver will need a lot of rest." He eyed the heart monitor even as he handed the baby off to the nurse. His brow creased slightly. "Silver, how are you feeling, sweetie?"

"A little dizzy. And tired." Silver licked her bottom lip. "Why?"

"Does anything hurt?"

Silver let out a strained laugh. "She might be tiny, but she didn't feel like it coming out. I'm sore."

Dr. Singh frowned. "You know that's not what I mean."

What's going on? Landon forced himself to look away from where the nurse was examining his daughter and speaking quietly to Becky. Dean still hadn't left Silver's side. And the lines around his eyes had deepened, adding years to his features.

"My chest hurts a little." Silver pressed her eyes shut. Moisture gathered on her lashes. "It's my heart, isn't it?"

Her heart? But, hadn't the problem been just because from the strain of carrying the baby?

"I believe so. I would recommend you staying for a few days, at least until you see the specialist." Dr. Singh's lips thinned as the lines on the heart monitor spiked. "For now, I'm going to give you something to regulate your pulse. It might be nothing, but I'd rather not take any chances."

"What about our baby? Can she go home?" Silver held up her hand before Landon could protest. "I don't want her here longer than necessary. My screwups aren't changing anything for her."

The nurse carried the baby back to them, nodding to the doctor. "She went up two points. Well within the normal range."

"I can make an appointment with the specialist. Come back and be really careful until then," Silver spoke in a rush, as though letting anyone interrupt would trap her here. "Like you said, it might be nothing."

"All right, I'll leave the three of you—" he inclined his head in Dean's direction to include him "—to discuss this. The baby can go home with you tomorrow if that's what you decide. I recommend putting her in the nursery overnight. Silver, you need to take it easy. I don't want to see any more of those spikes. The cardiologist can tell us more. I'll send him in as soon as he's available."

The doctor walked out, the nurse following as soon as she gave the baby to Dean. He cradled the baby, standing close to Landon as he sat on the edge of the bed. Landon studied Silver's face as she slipped her finger into their daughter's tiny hand. He'd expected her to look a little scared, but her eyes were hard with determination.

"There's nothing to discuss. Becky, can you stay at Dean's place a little longer? Help Landon and Dean with the baby in case . . . ?" Silver laughed even as Becky nodded. "Okay, we have to stop calling her 'the baby.' I've been thinking about names." Her eyes filled with mischief as she peered up at Landon. "How about something vintage and hip, like Rainbow?"

Landon stared at her, his own fear momentarily forgotten, not sure why Dean was chuckling. *Rainbow?* "Please tell me you're joking?"

"You have to ask?" Silver giggled as Landon continued to stare. "We all agreed on Lucie—after my grandmother—as a middle name if it was a girl, but I was so sure she was a boy, all I've got as a first name is Adam, after your dad. You were right, so you get to pick."

His ex hadn't considered letting him have anything to do with naming their baby until they'd lost him. He took a deep breath, feeling ridiculous as tears stung his eyes yet again. Silver had already given him so much. He hadn't thought he could love her more, but at that moment, his heart was bursting with all she was to him. More precious than his own life.

"Silver, I love you. I love you so much." He kissed her, then smiled against her lips. "I've been thinking about this for a while and ran it by Dean not long ago . . . what do you think of Amia?"

"Amia Lucie Bower." Silver cocked her head, then struggled to sit up, pressing her lips to the baby's forehead. "I love it. And I love you. Love you both . . . my baby's daddies." She blinked fast, her voice breaking. "If I have to come back, promise me you'll keep her away from here? Keep her home, sing her lullabies, rock her to sleep. You and Dean spoil her rotten. And have Jami spend time with her. Jami's like her sister now." Her eyes drifted shut, but she seemed to struggle to keep them open. The lines on the heart monitor rose and fell slower, but the rhythm seemed off. "I want her to be close to her family."

The door cracked open. Ford cleared his throat. "I . . . ah—"

"Hey, you," Silver said, without opening her eyes. "I thought you took off when Zach left."

"Naw, I stuck around." Ford took a deep breath, swallowing hard. "I'll leave if you—"

"Don't," Silver mumbled, close to drifting off again. "Say hello to your niece. And . . . call Oriana? Amia needs to know our side of the family too." She let out a soft sigh. "I'm glad you stayed."

Ford inched closer to Dean. "Amia. Cute. She's really pretty, Silver."

Landon had never liked Ford, but after how he'd been with Silver the night before, he couldn't deny that the man cared about his sister. That he'd earned the right to be involved in Amia's life. But he wasn't ready to let Ford hold her just yet. Apparently, neither was Dean. He looked at Landon, his eyes reflecting Landon's thoughts as he let Ford give Amia a little pink stuffed kitten he'd probably picked up in the gift shop. Thankfully, things didn't get awkward, because Ford didn't look too keen on getting any closer to his niece. He looked a little afraid of her.

Knowing his daughter was being cared for gave him the time he needed to absorb the situation. He wouldn't disturb her much-needed sleep, but as he lowered into the chair by her bed, he considered what she had asked of him.

"I can promise to do everything you asked, and more, *mon amour*," he whispered, brushing his fingers over the soft, light golden stands of Silver's hair, spilling over the pillow. "But I can't keep her away. She needs you."

Becky came up behind him, wrapping her arms around his chest. "She'll be okay. Take this one step at a time. The three of you will take Amia home tomorrow. Once we know how Silver's doing, we'll talk to her about this. Make sure she knows it's okay for Amia to come visit if she is admitted again."

He nodded, but he wasn't convinced. During the pregnancy, he'd seen how guilty Silver felt about the possible risks her past addiction could have on the baby. Amia being in the hospital when she didn't have to be would just bring that all back.

His sister was right. One step at a time.

First step was bringing his family home.

Chapter Ten

God, I love this house! Becky laughed just to hear the sound echo around her, off the walls of her *huge* living room, through the wide-open space of the dining room, and straight up to the second floor which held the bedroom of her dreams. The bungalow wasn't all that big by most people's standards, but with two and a half bathrooms, two bedrooms, a finished basement, and a roomy, fully-equipped modern kitchen, it couldn't be more perfect. She tromped up the steps, so excited the two cans of pink paint and bag of supplies hardly weighed a thing. Plastic had already been laid out on the floor of the room that would be Casey's. All she had to do now was tape along the ceiling and window frames to keep the crisp white paint clean.

The ladder was a bit of an issue though. The ceiling was much higher than she'd realized. She had no problem with heights, but for some reason, standing at the top of the ladder to apply the tape made the room twirl-a-whirl around her. Her legs seemed lopsided. She took a deep breath and slapped her hand on the wall to steady herself. Something solid latched on to her waist.

She screamed as she was swooped up into the air.

"I don't ever want to see you doing something that dangerous again." Zach's voice in her ear made her shiver. She'd never heard that tone from him before—not anger, exactly, but edging on the brink. He latched on to her wrists, holding them at the small of her back, not letting her turn. "If you insist on doing things like this on your own, you'd better be careful."

The submissive inside her wanted to do some kneeling and foot-kissing, but they were *not* in a scene. And she didn't bend over for macho bullshit. "I *was* being careful!"

"Were you?" Zach released her, leaning an elbow on a ladder rung just a few steps down from where she'd been standing. His expression was controlled, but his tanned skin had taken on a grey cast. "So as soon as you felt dizzy, you were going to come down."

"Not exactly—"

"That ladder is too short for you to reach the ceiling safely, but you planned to keep going. You're here alone." Zach's jaw ticked. "If you'd fallen—if you'd *hurt* yourself—no one would have been here to help you."

So that's what this was all about. She bit the inside of her cheek to keep from letting out a very inappropriate giggle and clasped her hands behind her back to keep from throwing her arms around his neck. "Were you worried about me, Sir?"

His eyes narrowed. "I don't think you want to call me 'Sir' right now, little doe. How I'd handle this as your Dom is very different from how I'd—"

The giggle escaped this time. "That's a yes! You were worried when you saw me up there! So worried you didn't make a sound, just swept me off my feet like some... some damsel in distress..." Which suddenly didn't seem funny anymore. "Zachary Pearce, I'll have you know that I've painted, and climbed ladders, and even used a hammer, all without hurting myself! I enjoy your company, but I don't want you getting the idea that I *need* you!"

"You've made that quite obvious, considering you didn't call when you said you would."

"I figured I'd kept you out long enough the other night at the hospital and you might be busy."

Zach pressed his lips together in a tight smile, shaking his head slowly. Something about the intensity in his eyes flowed through her veins like accelerant, waiting for a match to be struck. He moved forward, invading her personal space, his lips grazing her cheek as he whispered. "Don't make assumptions about me, Rebecca."

It was very, very hard to breathe around the heat building between them. Damn it, she wanted to be mad, to draw a clear line between when she submitted to him, and life in general, but for some reason, she didn't think the line was necessary.

But some clarification was. "What's that supposed to mean? What assumptions have I made? That you were busy?"

"I told you I would come help you. I know very well that you don't need me. The point is, I wanted to be here for you."

She gritted her teeth, annoyed that he still hadn't answered her question. "What. Assumptions?"

"I'm not Patrick." He used the tip of his finger to tuck a loose strand of hair under the bandana on her head. "You don't have to bank favors from me. And you didn't 'keep me at the hospital.' I stayed because I wanted to stay, to be with you *in case* you needed me. Because sometimes, you will. And sometimes, I'll need you. Isn't that how a relationship works?"

That's not how her relationship with Patrick had worked, but Zach was right. He wasn't Patrick. Not even close. Patrick had never talked to her after she got pissed off. He'd either walked away or yelled back. They'd never had heated discussions or tried to work things out. She'd usually just given up because she knew he didn't care.

It's a little soon for Zach to care, don't you think?

She studied his face, nibbling thoughtfully at her bottom lip. "Did I scare you?"

"More than I care to admit." He grinned, latching one arm around the back of her neck and pulling her against his chest. "Don't do it again."

Sinking into his arms, she let herself forget how independent she was supposed to be. Having him to lean on, especially since she didn't really need it, felt nice. And best of all, he'd come here in a faded grey T-shirt, and ripped up jeans, *ready* to work. Even though she hadn't asked.

Hadn't even given him the address, actually.

"How did you find me?" She considered moving away from him to look into his eyes for a split second, then stayed put. She really, really liked him holding her. Much better than yelling at him.

"I gave your brother a call." Zach kissed her forehead, his hand sliding down her back as he shifted over a bit to take in the small room. "He gave me directions while thanking me a dozen times. Then had me speak to your mother. She told me Patrick used to make you do things like this on your own. That having him take out the garbage was a big deal. According to her, being with him was like having another child."

Very true. An ungrateful, miserable child who's sweet only when they want something. She shrugged. "Most men are like that."

"None of the men I've been with."

Strange that he could say that so matter-of-factly. Then again, some said all the good ones were gay. But she didn't believe that. Being bisexual did give Zach a unique perspective though. "I guess you've got better taste in men than I do." She gave him a sly smile. "Maybe you could hook me up with one?"

"Perhaps." The edges of his lips quirked and his eyes filled with humor. "What exactly are you looking for?"

She tapped her chin with a finger, considering. "It may seem a little mid-life crisis, but I'd like a bad boy. Not a *real* bad boy, of course."

He smirked. "Of course."

"I'm thinking a sexy, motorcycle driving, smooth-talking man who plays hard and fast, comes off as rough and dangerous, but is a big, snuggly teddy bear inside." She snickered as his brow rose a little with each word. They both knew she was talking about him, right? "Know of anyone?"

He shook his head with mock sadness. "Afraid not. I know someone with a motorcycle—pretty sexy, but as for the rest . . ."

"You don't consider yourself a smooth-talker?"

"Hmm." He hooked his finger to the front of her T-shirt, lust blazing in his eyes as he drew her toward him. "No. Talking isn't what I want to do with my mouth when I'm around you."

"Oh, nice line."

"I've never been one for lines, Becky." He moved forward, forcing her back, past the ladder, until the wall stopped her from going any further. Her pulse pounded in her ears as he framed her jaw with his hand, fingertips digging in just enough to hold her in place when she gasped and tried to claim his lips. His teeth grazed her bottom lip. "I'm straightforward. I don't play games when I want someone. And I want you."

"Yes," she whispered, letting her eyes drift shut. They'd taken things slow enough. She needed to feel his body, hard, heavy, and so goddamn hot, over hers as he slid into her. She needed to feel him lose control. "The answer is yes."

He chuckled, then gave her a chaste kiss before stepping away. "It wasn't a question. I will have you, but not yet."

"What?" She stared at him, her palm itching to slap him for teasing her. Her voice rose, but she didn't give a damn that she was yelling at him again. He was too fucking much! "You get me all hot and bothered, then say 'not yet'?"

"Put some music on." He went to the ladder, grabbing the tape off a rung on his way up. "We should get started."

"Just . . . wow. You're incredible." She huffed as she stormed out of the room to grab the stereo she'd left on the landing earlier. The heated pulsing between her thighs, the moisture, had her mad enough to scream. She stomped back into the room, muttering under her breath. "I could murder you right now."

"Temper, temper." Zach taped a length of the ceiling, not looking at her as he spoke. "You might be pissed at me now, but you'd be pissed at yourself if we didn't get this done before the furniture is delivered." He was quiet for a while as he finished taping the ceiling. Then he came down the ladder to watch her attack the paint cans with the back end of a hammer. He stood with his hands on his hips until she glared at him. "Damn it, Becky, don't you understand what I'm trying to do? I want us to last."

She dropped the hammer, barely missing her foot. "You think we won't last if you fuck me?"

He hissed in a sharp breath. "You tell me. I could take you on the floor. Against the wall. I could fuck you until neither of us could stand. We could both ignore our phones and our lives and just get lost in one another."

That sounds good to me.

"And then something would happen to bring us back to reality. You'll go back to work, spend time with your daughter, and realize the wild fun you have with me doesn't fit with your life." His brow furrowed. "If that's what you want, let me know. Because I'm invested in this. Probably more invested than I should be."

Her lips parted. Sex sounded good, but what he offered sounded perfect. She hadn't had a real relationship since Patrick and had no idea how to go about it. Her biggest concern had always been keeping things as stable as possible for Casey. Which meant going to the club—maybe every other weekend. Preferably with the same man, but still keeping it all separate. She didn't want a one-night stand, but was she ready for more? She'd let Zach in without even considering how it would work out between them. Her feelings for him had grown so fast, she'd been afraid of losing herself with him.

But he'd told her he would let her. And he'd meant it.

So what now? He'd laid it all out there. The ball was in her court—or, a little more accurately, the puck was in her zone. Zach wasn't the opposition; he was on her team in every way. She only had to trust him enough to reach a common goal.

Which was a future together. She looked around the empty room, biting at her bottom lip as she pictured it, all set up, with Casey in her princess bed, drifting off to sleep as Zach read her a bedtime story. That couldn't happen for a while. No matter how she felt about him, she wouldn't let him until her daughter's life until she was absolutely certain he'd stick around.

Everything else, though . . . She smiled as she thought of all the things they could do together. Before Casey came home. Before he left for the week-long cruise with the Ice Girls. It would be wonderful to have him here, helping her fix up the house. Maybe kidnap him for a few nights, wake up with him in her bed. Knowing he wanted this to last made everything just that much easier. He didn't expect her to put her life on hold for him. He wanted to find a way to be part of it.

"This is . . . this seems . . ." She laughed as she placed her hands on his chest, shaking her head when the words wouldn't come out. "It seems too good to be true. I need time to absorb it, but . . . I want to see if we can have it all."

"We can." He tipped her chin up with the back of his fist and kissed her. "There's no rush."

"I disagree." She ducked her head, squeezing her thighs together, wishing she could show half her restraint. "You're giving me everything I could have ever asked for. But I still want to jump you."

He barked out a laugh, pressing her head against his chest. "This isn't easy for me either, Becky. Since you'd fully intended to do it all on your own, how far had you planned to get before you'd let yourself take a break?"

His hard length pressed against her belly made it almost impossible to think straight, but she forced herself to recall her plans for the day. She had to get Casey's room finished before work started eating into her free time. The paint would need time to dry, and by then, the truck would be here. She'd bought good paint, but wasn't sure if one coat would be good enough, despite the product's claims.

"This room has to be done," she said, finally.

He nodded. "Okay. So is it safe to say I can have my way with you once it is?"

Her pulse raced. He could have his way with her this very moment, but she finally understood why he was holding back. Once the task was done, there would be no regrets to taint whatever they shared. And that would be important to them both in the long run. Eventually, their time would be limited. He was right. She'd have her job and her daughter. He'd be on the road. Every moment they had would be precious.

She exhaled, skirting away from him to grab a roller. "Sir, once this is done . . . I'm all yours."

He came up behind her as she straightened, curving his hands around her waist. His lips slid up her throat, and he nibbled lightly, making her shiver with anticipation. "You're already mine, little doe. And I will prove it soon enough."

Hours went by, but none of it in silence. Zach let her talk about her brother, about Silver, never interrupting, but showing so much interest in everything she said, she didn't feel like she was using him as a sounding board. His brow creased when she let him know that the doctor had wanted Silver to stay at the hospital, and he set down his roller as he asked how Silver was doing since Silver had returned home. Becky gave him the same, scripted answer she'd given her brother when he'd asked the same thing—certain Silver would open up to her. Unlike her brother, who was desperate to believe Silver would be fine, Zach saw right through her.

"The medication won't be enough, will it?" He climbed off the ladder after covering the last bit of white on the walls. "How is she with the baby?"

"Better than I thought she'd be. Amia cries and she's there, but . . ." Becky clenched her fists around the rag she was using to clean her hands. "Not really. Please don't repeat this, but it feels like she's holding back. The way Landon, and even Dean, has connected with the baby is tangible. Silver seems to be going through the motions. It's like she's afraid to let Amia get attached. Like she's expecting the worst."

"I appreciate you being open with me about this, Becky..." Zach frowned. "But why haven't you told your brother? Or at least your mother? They can help her through this."

He was right, but still, she shook her head. "She's only been home a day. I don't want to make an issue where there is none. Everyone's already nervous about what the cardiologist will say when she sees him at the end of the week. Once things aren't so up in the air—I mean, the doctor might tell Silver she'll be fine, at which point, she'll be able to relax and enjoy being a mother. If not... I'll talk to my brother. He's worried about Silver, but he's doing a lot better. You should see him with his daughter." A smile tugged at her lips as she recalled Landon, sitting with Amia in his arms in the middle of the night, singing "Au Clair de la Lune." As their mother had done when they were little. As she still did for Casey almost every night.

Or had until she'd gone away with her father.

"You're missing Casey right now, aren't you?" Zach came over, pulled the rag from her hands, then laced their fingers together. "Just one more week, sweetie, and she'll be home."

Not soon enough. But she didn't want to think about that—didn't want to be sad. She had her house, had a great job, had so much to be happy about. She lifted her gaze, meeting Zach's eyes.

I have you.

All the heat that had dwindled while they worked flared up like a torch at the lips of a fire-breather. She latched on to Zach's shirt, rising up on her tiptoes to press her lips to his. He groaned into her mouth, raking his hands into her hair as his tongue thrust deep, tangling with her own. He sucked on her bottom lip as he tugged her T-shirt up, breaking their kiss just long enough to pull the shirt up over her head. His lips found hers as he unlatched her bra, the bruising pressure driving her wild. She whimpered as he lowered his lips to her throat. Her back hit the ladder, and he gave her a lazy grin as he unzipped her jeans.

"I believe we have some time to play, little doe." He rolled her jeans down her thighs with her panties, a low growl rumbling from his chest as he grazed his teeth up her inner thigh. He picked her up as he rose, sitting her on a ladder rung. "Hands up."

The metal of the ladder warmed under her bare bottom, and she licked her lips as he retrieved the tape from the floor, lifting her hands without question. Her whole body shook as he wrapped the tape around her wrists, and she watched him wrap the long length at the end around the ladder. The tape was thin enough to break if she tugged hard enough, but she wouldn't. She would stay where he put her because there was nothing she wanted more than to let him have his way with her. He tapped her ankles, parted her thighs, then restrained them to either side of the ladder rungs a few steps down from where she sat.

A rung dug into her back, and she shifted to ease the pressure. He observed her for a few seconds, slid a hand between her back and the rung, helping her arch away from it. Then he took a knee, sliding his scruffy cheek along her inner thigh, eyes on her face as he turned slightly to kiss her feverish flesh.

"I couldn't go another day without tasting you, little doe. Every time you clenched your thighs, I knew your pussy was hot and wet and throbbing. It made my mouth water." He let out a low, humming sound as he moved closer to her, inhaling deeply. "You smell so fucking sweet." He used his fingers to part her pussy lips. His tongue slid from just below her slit, straight up to her clit. "Fuck, you're delicious."

She knocked her head against a rung, gasping as he licked along either side of her folds, trembling as he gently closed his teeth around her swollen nub. His tongue flicked over it once, then circled around it before sliding back down. As his tongue plunged into her, she cried out, fisting her hands above her head to keep from tugging at the restraints. Liquid fire spilled from her core, slicking his face as he thrust deeper. He used his fingers to stimulate her clit as he eased his tongue in and out. Her lips parted as the sensations coiled up within. Release was a breath away. All she had to do was let herself go.

"Not yet, pet," Zach whispered, straightening just before she could surrender to the blinding rush of pleasure. He covered her lips with his, swallowing her cries of protest as he jerked his jeans down over his hips. The head of his bare cock pushed against her, and her brain snapped back into place. As much as she wanted him, she wouldn't take any risks. He hushed her as she opened her mouth to tell him. "I have protection. I just wanted you to feel me, flesh on flesh, before something came between us."

Groaning, she nodded, closing her eyes to absorb the incredible feeling of his dick sliding in her juices. She held her breath, slitting her eyes open as he stepped back and pulled out his wallet. He tossed it aside once he'd retrieved the condom. The sound of his tearing it open with his teeth had her quivering with anticipation. When he was covered, he positioned one hand behind her again. She hadn't even noticed the ladder rung digging into her back until his hand cushioned her, his fingers smoothing away the slight dent the metal had made in her skin. All her focus was on his dick, slowing pressing into her.

"Becky." Zach rested his forehead between her breasts, his breath coming out in a hot rush against her flesh. "You're so fucking hot. So tight."

She felt tight. Her hips shifted, the sweat dripping down her back mixing with the spill of her arousal, making the ladder rung under her ass wet. She hadn't been with a man in so long. And the last time she'd been with one, she hadn't had time to wonder how it would feel to be penetrated. Lost in a submissive haze, she'd relaxed into her restraints and just let it happen. Reveled in the pleasure she was giving. But Zach wouldn't be satisfied with taking the pleasure she could give him. As he worked the head of his cock into her with slow, shallow thrusts, she knew it wouldn't be enough for him unless she experienced the same level of pleasure as he did. Everything with him was give and take. And he would accept no less.

"I need you, Zach . . . I mean. I mean, Sir." She rasped in air as he filled her, stretching her around him as he settled his hips between her thighs. "Oh, God! Don't stop!"

He smiled against her lips as he kissed her. "I couldn't if I wanted to. Brace yourself, pet."

His free hand lifted her ass off the rung as he drove into her. The ladder creaked as he slammed in, shifting as he slid almost all the way out. Her lips trembled against his open mouth as she felt every inch of him stroking her deep with every hard thrust. Usually, she needed her clit stimulated to come, but she was already so close, all it took was the unrestrained plunge of his dick against her core to set her off. She threw her head back, her eyes tearing as she cried out, the sound scoring her throat, her whole body shuddering with the intensity of her release. It was like frozen glass dropped in boiling water and shattering within, splinters of pleasure exploding as Zach tightened his grip on her back and thrust in one last time, coming apart with her. He let out a feral sound, cursing as he tore at her restraints, then dragged her to the floor to lay over him.

For what seemed like forever, she couldn't move. All she could do was cling to him, gasping as her core convulsed around him. She never lasted long after she came, which made Doms trying to force her to orgasm again and again almost painful, but Zach holding her, simply letting her come down, was pure bliss. And the way he ground against her, dragging out her pleasure, brought her over the edge again so slowly and unexpectedly she slid into another climax with nothing more than a shudder. The undulating sensation came on so subtly it was like letting the last bite of a chocolate cake that had burst in her mouth with the first bite, melt on her tongue. She sighed as she rested on him, smiling sleepily as he kissed her forehead.

"No regrets?" he whispered as he rolled her on to her side.

"None." Her brow furrowed as something nagged at the back of her mind. For some reason, Silver's words came back to her as she lay in Zach's arms. *"I thought you were gay!"* Her deep need to please him was mostly satisfied, but she couldn't help but wonder if she could be enough considering what she knew. "I just... you enjoy women. And men. Have you ever just been with one or the other?"

"Yes." He pushed up to brace his elbow on the wood floor, his head on his hand. "Why?"

"One is enough?"

"It is. But..." He avoided her gaze as she sat up. "It hasn't always been enough for the ones I'm with. They always wondered if I needed more. But I didn't. When I'm with someone, they are all I need. Can you accept that? Do you trust that I don't need more?"

"I do." She spoke without thinking twice, because she knew Zach wasn't the type of man to stray. If he was with someone, he wouldn't be looking for anything else. But still, she wondered if he wasn't cutting off part of himself because of how he believed a relationship should be. She still had so much to learn about him, but from what she knew, he had two parents who were very supportive. Who had shown him what a normal, stable relationship was. She'd seen men who couldn't admit to being gay, and Zach didn't come off as one of those. She could easily picture him telling his parents that he was attracted to men, could see them telling him they would love him, no matter what. But could he accept needing more? With being with someone who could accept *his* needs?

He smoothed her hair away from her sweat slicked cheeks. "What is it?"

"We've agreed to be honest with each other, right?"

His brow creased. He nodded.

"If ever . . ." She held her breath, hoping he wouldn't take what she was about to say the wrong way. "If you needed something I couldn't give you, you'd tell me?"

"I'd never cheat on you, Becky." His tone went hard, as though he was insulted by whatever he assumed she thought. "I'll never need more than you."

"I know that, but . . . if I told you I never want to try certain things, will you be upset if I change my mind after? If I suddenly decide there's nothing wrong with trying?"

"It's not the same at all. An experience isn't another person."

"But it could be."

He shook his head, then sat up, rubbing his hand over his mouth. "If you want a threesome, I will find someone I trust not to come between us. But it will be something you want to try, not something I need. All I need is to make you happy."

She ground her teeth, not sure what to do with his "point finale" attitude. What if she was making an issue where there was none? All *she* needed was to make him happy. And she was open to whatever it took. But as long as he wasn't, they were at an impasse. "You're telling me you could go the rest of your life without touching another man?"

"That's exactly what I'm telling you." He stood and pulled on his jeans with quick, jerky motions, his tone clipped. "As for honesty?

I'm not sure how to deal with everyone assuming I need a man in my life. I've had several, but they never meant as much to me as you do."

"Don't think I don't love hearing that, Zach." She rose, naked, from the floor, then slipped her hands around the back of his neck. "I couldn't deal with you being with another woman. Which will sound odd considering what I'm about to say. I'll admit, I have my own possessive streak. I can be jealous, and it's going to be hard to let you go on that cruise, knowing all those Ice Girls will be all over you for photo ops. But if there was a man . . . a man I felt could give you even half of what I can—who wouldn't ruin what we have—"

"Please, please don't say that." His kiss was almost desperate as he held her against him. "Don't say it's okay just to have yourself wondering if I'm with someone else when I'm not with you."

"But it is okay." She closed her eyes, thinking it over carefully. It really was. So long as he was honest with her. And himself. "The man better be something special though. Otherwise—"

"Stop." Zach groaned as the doorbell sounded. "Shit. I forgot to tell you . . ."

She checked her watch, frowning. The truck was early? "Forgot to tell me what?"

"You said you wanted Scott to help move everything." Zach rolled his shoulders, as though to shrug off all the tension of everything they'd said. As though just saying Scott's name meant nothing to him. His detached body language was all lies. She knew better. But he gave her a disarming smile, staring at the wall behind her. "I would have called someone else, but you asked for him."

Because I'm an idiot. She swore under her breath as she quickly pulled on her clothes, trying to put her matted hair into some semblance of order even as she skirted away from Zach and hurried downstairs. She hadn't gotten a chance to tell Zach that Scott was with someone else. To tell him if he was interested in any man, she prayed it wasn't Scott. Because Scott couldn't stand by one person long enough to care about them. And she refused to let anyone else close to Zach unless they were worthy. Not a stance that a sub should take, but she was more than a sub with Zach. The first whispers of the words she wished she could say came to her as she twisted the doorknob. *I think I love him. And if you don't . . . you need to stay away.*

Scott stepped over the threshold, sighing as he caught the cold look on her face. "We should talk."

"No. We shouldn't." She glanced toward the stairs as she heard Zach coming down, then spoke in a rush. "You need to understand something. Zach and I are serious about one another. And I know you can't be serious about anything. So let's make something clear."

"Sure."

"Be his friend. His teammate." She met Scott's eyes, holding his gaze to make sure he understood. "But that's it. You had a chance with him and you blew it."

"Crystal clear, babe." Scott let out a self-deprecating laugh. "Just like I blew it with you. That it?"

She shook her head. This wasn't about her. She wouldn't let it be. "You never had anything with me."

"Right. Well, I'm not here to piss you off." Scott stared at his worn sneakers, then glanced over his shoulder as the truck pulled up. "I'm just here to move your stuff."

His failure to flirt and tease made her feel like she was kicking a wounded puppy. He hadn't done anything to make her so defensive. It was what he *could* do that worried her.

"I'm sorry. I didn't mean to be so bitchy . . ." She bit her bottom lip as he shrugged. *Fuck, who is this guy?* Scott always had a comeback. She gave him a hesitant smile and nudged his shoulder with her fist. "Hey, you all right? Not having trouble with your girlfriend already, are you? To be honest, I was a little surprised to see you with Sahara, but she seems like a nice girl. It would be good to see you settle down."

"Sahara?" Zach repeated as he made his way down the stairs. He shoved his hands in his pockets, regarding Scott like he would any other teammate. "She's from New York, isn't she? You haven't been—?"

One side of Scott's lips quirked up as he shook his head. "Naw, I haven't been traded. *Yet.* Keane got Sahara to sign with our Ice Girls."

"And Scott gave her a place to stay." Becky shot her brightest smile up at Zach, ignoring his frown. "Isn't he a sweetheart?"

Scott snorted. "You know me better than that, Becky. I don't do sweet. I wouldn't have a chick staying with me without perks."

Becky swallowed, forcing her smile to stay in place, even though she was sure it must look like it had been welded on to her face. "I'm sure Sahara knows all about your reputation."

"I'm sure she does."

"Whatever makes you happy."

"Being a fucking male whore. That's what makes me happy." Scott's smile looked just as fake as hers was. His gaze snapped to Zach. "Can we get this over with?"

Zach put his hand on Becky's shoulder, his brow creasing as he studied her face. He didn't look too happy with whatever he saw. "Yes. Let's."

Honesty. That's all Zach wanted from her. But how could she be honest with him about her feelings for Scott when she couldn't figure them out for herself.

There's nothing to figure out. You feel nothing.

But she couldn't say that. Because she *did* know how she felt about Zach. And she cared too much about him to lie.

Chapter Eleven

A sharp floral aroma hit Scott as the heavy blanket of sleep dissolved. He groaned, turning his head to the side avoid the scent. If he opened his eyes, he would see *her* in a transparent nightgown, her lashes still caked with mascara, rum on her breath. Her heavy breasts would crush his chest as she climbed over him. Her claw-like nails would rake his stomach as she sought what she'd come for. Maybe she'd leave him alone if he pretended he was still sleeping.

There's my good boy. Did you miss me?

Bile rose in his throat. He shook his head, eyes pressed shut. "No."

"Scott?"

Soft. Her hand felt so soft, touching his cheek. She would be good to him if he gave her what she wanted. But it felt like she was smothering him. Everywhere at once, her hands, her body, until he couldn't wash away the stink of her. He wanted her to stop, but she wouldn't. She wouldn't stop unless he made her, and he never could.

He bared his teeth, eyes snapping open as he shoved her away. "I said no!"

Big blue eyes stared down at him. A small woman, smaller than him, not bigger. Cringing, Sahara shuffled back, holding her hands up as she whispered, "I'm sorry. I didn't mean to—"

Fuck. It was Sahara, not—He moved slowly, making a soft, hushing sound. "Damn, I'm sorry, hun. I didn't hurt you, did I?"

"No, I'm fine." Sahara approached the bed, her smile a little too bright as she perched on the edge of the bed, looking ready to make a run for it if he moved. "I . . . uh, just wanted to know if you wanted to come out with me. You looked really bummed out when you came in."

"Yeah, it's been a shitty day." Scott threw his legs over the other side of the bed. He was just wearing boxers, but if Sahara was gonna stay here, she'd have to get used to it. He stood and stretched, glancing over his shoulder at her. "What time is it?"

"Almost midnight."

"Midnight?" He blinked at her. "And you want to go out?"

"Why not?" She shrugged, flushing as he stared at her. "I figured you were just taking a nap." She fidgeted with the hem of her pleated black miniskirt. "Sorry. I shouldn't have bothered you."

Poor kid's lonely. Must be bad if she wants to hang out with me. He gave her a crooked grin and shook his head. "Naw, it's all right. Just shout next time. Slam some doors or something. Not used to people creeping into my bed."—*Anymore*—"People that *sleep* with me are usually passed out drunk."

Her cheeks reddened. She chewed at her thumbnail. "I'll keep that in mind, but . . . were you having a nightmare?"

"Actually, I was. Kinda. Sexy woman fucked me to death. Seems like a way to go, huh?"

"Yeah. No." She snorted. "You're such a guy." She hopped off the bed. "You coming or what?"

"Can I get dressed?"

She looked him over, tapping her bottom lip with a finger. "Why bother? You'll be naked by the end of the night anyway."

He arched a brow as he pulled some black jeans and a white T-shirt from his dresser, glancing at her over his shoulder. "You hitting on me, roomie?"

"*Hell* no. If we fuck, I'll have nowhere to stay!" She winked at him, smoothing out her tiny skirt as she stood. "I was hoping to take over the bed tonight."

He rolled his eyes. He hadn't been sure about letting her crash at his place until she found a place of her own, but she was fun to have around. And not as annoying as he'd thought she'd be. Except for the fact that she'd hauled blankets and a pillow to the sofa the night before, ignoring his efforts to be a gentleman and let her take the bed. "I said you could have it."

"I know. And I will when you're sleeping elsewhere." She sighed when he rolled his eyes again. "It would feel weird to have you sleeping on the sofa in your own house. I appreciate you giving me a place to stay without expecting anything in return."

Yeah, that was weird. Sahara was a hot little piece, completely available, and yet he hadn't even tried to get in her pants. Something was seriously wrong with him. If he kept this up, people were gonna start thinking he was *decent.*

There're only two people I want thinking that. And they couldn't care less.

He rubbed his hand over his face, a smile forming as though molded in clay. Sahara waking him up was a good thing. He needed a fucking drink. A nice, numbing buzz to get Becky and Zach out of his head.

"We taking my car or you planning on drinking tonight?" he asked after slipping into his well-worn sneakers.

Sahara laughed. "Let's take a cab. I'm getting plastered."

He nodded and took his phone out to call a cab, eyeing Sahara as she frowned at him all the way to the elevator. What had he done now? "Something wrong?"

She shrugged, hooking one finger to the thin strap of her little black purse. "Guess not. It's just weird that you didn't even comment. I'm not sure whether or not to be insulted that you're not hitting on me."

"You want me to?"

"I'm not sure. If you did, at least I'd know you're okay."

The edge of his lip quirked and he threw his arm over her shoulder, kissing her forehead as they went out to the street to meet the cab. "You're a sweet little thing. Don't you worry, by the time you move out, I'll have had you in my bed, with your ankles behind your ears, at least once."

"Ugh." She shoved him away, laughing. "I should have kept my mouth shut. You haven't changed at all!"

He winced as she ducked into the backseat of the cab.

Maybe not. But I'm trying.

* * * *

The bar was bigger than the one Ford Kingsley—or Delgado, whatever—had owned before, but the name and the style was pretty much the same. Lots of gleaming metal and leather. A shiny, dark wood bar that took up most of one wall. The biggest difference was the huge dance floor and the DJ booth. The crowd. And the music. Scott made a face as he trailed Sahara to the bar, the techno slash pop mix enough to make him want to turn around and find his drunken stupor from a bottle of hard liquor in a brown paper bag on a street corner.

Would suit his mood better anyway.

"What are you doing with this loser, Sahara?" Ford asked as he came to take their order. He dropped the rag he'd been drying glasses with and rested his forearms on the bar. "Slumming?"

Sahara hooked her arm to Scott's. "I'm here, aren't I?"

Not really a compliment, but Scott didn't care enough to comment. He put in an order for a scotch on the rocks, then leaned his back against the bar, looking over the bar's patrons with detached interest. An older woman did her best to catch his eye. Something about the predatory curve of her blood red lips made him feel like long, icy worms were crawling under his flesh. He rolled his shoulders and swallowed hard as the images from his nightmare flashed through his skull. He'd done nice, curvy older women before, but after the warped dreams, he tended to stick to men for a while.

Taking a deep breath, he narrowed his search for some hot young stud who might provide some much needed distraction. So long as Stephan never found out. But none of these men were Zach and—*fuck*—that was some high standard to set. Why hadn't he set that standard before? When it would have actually mattered?

While Sahara danced and he finished his first two drinks, three women hit on him, and one guy covertly tested the waters. He shot them all down, only tempted once. A woman with auburn hair and blue eyes that looked almost grey under the black lights drew him into a conversation, and he found himself laughing for real for the first time in days as she teased him. It reminded him of how things had been with Becky before he'd fucked that up. He bought her a drink, ready to seal the deal, ignoring the irritating voice in his head that said she was nothing but a shallow replacement for Becky.

"This will be my last one," The woman, whose name he'd already forgotten, said with a coy smile. "Got to get up with my brats in the morning."

Scott went still. He didn't care that the woman had kids—all he could think of was how Becky was with Casey. The way she'd talked about her baby while they were setting up the little girl's room.

"I really need to do something about all these toys. I'd get rid of some, but

she loves them so much. You should see her tea parties." Her eyes had teared up. Zach had hugged her. *"God, I miss her."*

The love Becky showed for her daughter was all Scott had ever wanted as a kid. He had no idea what it was like to be a parent—hell, maybe it was normal to get sick of your kids—but the little interest he'd had in the woman at his side had died.

"It's been nice talking to you." Scott inclined his head at the woman, then walked away without a backward glance, not even sure where he was going. Sahara shouted for him to join her on the dance floor, giggling as a lanky, fairly handsome man pulled her into his arms. He shook his head, then caught sight of someone familiar, sitting alone at a table by the windows with a bottle of jack and a shot glass. He grinned as he headed over, pulling out a chair and making himself comfortable. The big black man didn't look all that happy to see him.

"What's the occasion, Mason?" Scott helped himself to a shot. Smacking his lips, he smiled at the huge defenseman, pretending not to notice the way his big fists clenched on the table. "You've got a rep for self-control. And ain't you the new captain? Bad example you're giving, don't you think?"

"Fuck off, Demyan." Mason snatched the shot glass out of Scott's hand. "I'm not in the mood."

"In the mood for what? We're just talking." Scott smirked, suddenly feeling reckless. "You want to get in my pants, you better be a bit more generous with the liquor. I'm not a cheap date."

"Leave." Mason snapped, his eyes dangerously narrowed. "Now."

"Mmm." Scott let out an exaggerated moan. "I think I get what Oriana saw in you. That commanding tone is fucking sexy."

"Are you fucking stoned?" Mason pushed his chair away from the table and stood. "Get out of my face before I rearrange yours for you."

"Foreplay. Hell, I don't know why Max and Sloan left you. Or maybe I do." Scott cocked his head, knowing he was asking for trouble. "You were too much for them. They knew they couldn't compete. That's why they—"

"Outside." Mason jerked Scott out of his chair by the back of his shirt and shoved him toward the door. "Fuck, I need this."

So do I. Scott's pulse went into overdrive as he weaved around the crowd and hit the street. He knew Mason could kick his ass, but he didn't give a shit. The whiskey wasn't working. Maybe a good beating would.

As he faced off against Mason on the sidewalk in front of the bar, he couldn't help but laugh. Damn, he wished they were doing this on the ice. He missed the game, missed knowing he could drop his gloves make an impact. Because nothing else he did seemed to matter. He didn't matter unless he was bringing something to the game.

To the team.

He stared at Mason as the man pulled a gold ring off his left hand and tucked it into the front pocket of his blue jeans. Not a wedding ring, but something that had meant just as much. What the fuck was he doing? Getting into a fight with a teammate just because he was messed up?

He closed his eyes as Mason lunged at him. He'd fucking asked for this. Maybe waking up bruised and broken would smarten him the fuck up. He wasn't proving anything to Zach or Becky by being a fucking idiot. All he was doing was showing them that he wasn't worth their time. And maybe he wasn't. But damn it, part of him wanted them to believe he could be. Maybe not now, but some day . . .

Until then, he'd take what he'd earned. If that was a beating, so be it.

He choked on a breath as Mason burst out laughing and slapped his shoulder.

"Damn it, you almost had me." Mason tipped his head back, staring up at the black sky. "We can beat the shit out of each other, but it won't change anything, will it?" He gave Scott a shrewd look. "I'd take you for a masochist, but you're not into pain, are you?" He didn't wait for Scott to answer. "I'd meant to talk to you, but I got too wrapped up in my own thing to call. And I think knowing someone needs you will mean more than getting your ass kicked. You in?"

Someone needed him? Now, *that* was something new. He let out a rough laugh, then nodded. "I'm *so* in."

* * * *

"I'm tired of being afraid."
"Then don't be."

Akira wished she'd kept her mouth shut. As Dominik opened the door to the club, the click of the lock sounded with frightening finality, as though warning her that once she went in, there was no turning back. She glanced over at Jami and took a deep breath as her best friend took her hand. They walked in together.

The club, Blades & Ice, wasn't at all what she'd imagined. From the descriptions of BDSM clubs in all the books she read, she'd painted out elaborate scenes on huge devices meant for torture, but used for pleasure. Cages, racks, iron maidens . . . she couldn't have come if the club was open like it usually was on Friday. Nightmares of violent beatings kept her awake at night, and she'd convinced herself if she came here all kinds of horrible things would happen to her. But all Jami told her threaded erotic dreams through the horror.

They'd agreed the only way to clear things up was for her to see it for herself. Some day. Akira had marked that day on her mental calendar of the very far away future. Before swimming with sharks and right after bungee jumping.

Apparently, Jami had decided to mark the date with a big red X right on Akira's 20th birthday. As she'd pointed out, they needed somewhere to celebrate.

Moving past Jami and Dominik, Akira took in the brightly lit main floor, with a hollow, oval shaped, thick-glass-topped bar taking up most of one section, tables and stools set around it in a semi-circle. There was a large stage, a dance floor, and roped-off areas on the other side with padded tables, spanking benches, and crosses. Leather and some kind of lemony cleaner scented the air. It all looked so harmless. The big wood throne in the center of the room seemed like nothing more than a sturdy piece of furniture.

"It's nothing." Akira exhaled and turned to smile at Jami. "I was expecting . . . I don't know, something bad. I mean, it's cool and all, but I figured there would be more."

Jami cocked her head. "More what?"

"It's hard to say." Akira nibbled on her bottom lip. She wanted to laugh at herself. They'd all come here in jeans and T-shirts—not fetish wear. Had she really expected anything to happen? "The atmosphere in the books seems like it would linger, you know? I thought I'd feel . . . something."

Dominik chuckled as he strolled around the bar. He took out three glasses and poured them each a mixed drink that smelled sweet and peachy. Suddenly, his black jeans and snug, dark blue T-shirt seemed as fitting here as any amount of leather. His tone was deep when he spoke, reverberating right through her. "It's only a room without intent, little one. More comes when you are with someone who knows what you need. You don't need more. *Yet*."

"Yet?" Akira's hand shook as she picked up her glass and slipped onto a stool. There it was. That feeling she got when she read those books. Just a few words from this man, this *Dom*, tapped into the small part of her that wished she was brave enough to experience submission for real. But that would involve . . . *No no no!* "No. I can't. I just wanted to see—"

"All you will do tonight is *see*, Akira." Dominik reached across the bar. His hand hovered near hers, close enough that she could feel the warmth radiating off his skin. He placed his hand over hers when she didn't pull away. His palm was rough on the back of her hand, and she sensed his strength, but wasn't afraid of it. Somehow, she knew he wouldn't hurt her. He smiled, approval glowing in his gold-flecked brown eyes. "I'm here to keep you safe. To make sure you enjoy your party."

"I don't understand." Akira looked over her shoulder at the room. "Why here? Sure, I was curious, but what's the point, really, since I can't . . ." *Don't tell him! He doesn't need to know!* She drew her hand out from under his, then hugged herself. "I mean, I won't do anything."

"You don't have to. This isn't all about sex. There's so much more involved, and I believe you need a taste of that. To see that some of your desires can be satisfied without a single touch." The lights went out. Dominik's hand was there when she grabbed for it, and his voice took on a soothing quality. "You've come a long way."

His thumb stroked her knuckles, making her shiver. "Consider this another step. A tiny one."

I have come a long way. As her eyes adjusted to the dark, she stared at his hand, amazed at how comfortable she felt touching him. It was no more sexual than a tiny boat being tied to a mooring, secured so it wouldn't float away. Still, for the longest time, a man standing too close was enough to bring on a panic attack. *Not anymore, though.*

Not with Dominik anyway. And there were others she'd let close. Very few, but it was a start.

Music filled the room, getting louder, something familiar. She grinned at Jami as her eyes adjusted to the darkness and she recognized the song.

"Candy Shop."

Four men strolled down from the stairs that split the bar area from the sceneing area. All wore matching shiny grey suits with white shirts and grey vests and ties. She knew three of the men fairly well. Scott, who made her smile with the wink he shot her way. Luke, whose appearance made Jami's breathe catch beside her. Jami let out a soft, happy sound, and Akira tore her gaze away from the men to take in the glowing look of love in her friend's eyes. Jami had missed Luke and Sebastian so much—she rarely talked about anything else. Akira hoped Sebastian was here too.

The blush spreading across Jami's face drew Akira's attention back to the men, their smooth, sensual movements timed to the music. She bit her lip as she watched Tyler, a player who'd been injured on the ice a couple of years ago and hadn't returned since, rolling his body down low. Slowly. Provocatively. He'd always seemed so shy and quiet. The last man she knew only by name. Shawn Pischlar, the team's only Austrian player. There was nothing remarkable about him—he was tall, nicely built, yet his looks were almost downplayed by the handsome men beside him.

But *damn* could he move.

As the men came to the center of the bar area, dancing with smooth body rolls even as they undid their suit jackets, Akira hardly noticed the other people filling the room. She caught a few Cobra jerseys from the corner of her eye, but all she could do was enjoy the show. Her blood pulsed hot in her veins as the men tossed their jackets aside, then went to work removing their vests, then their shirts. Sweat glistened on their chests, running in rivulets down their tan flesh, making her mouth water. For the first time in what seemed like forever, she wanted to touch a man. Worse—or maybe better—she had the strangest urge to go straight up to Scott and lick the sweat off his skin. Smooth her hand down Shawn's chest to feel the way his muscles undulated under her palm.

She was actually aroused. And even though she knew she wouldn't act on it, it was awesome knowing she could feel this way again. Hadn't that part of her died, four years ago on that office floor?

Apparently not. Her face heated, and she giggled with Jami as the men peeled down their pants, revealing tight black shorts.

"You get to be with these guys on that boat for a week!" Jami nudged Akira's side as she took a big sip of her drink. "Lucky bitch!"

Akira stuck out her tongue, then swallowed as the men hooked their thumbs to the waistband of their shorts. A laugh escaped her as the song ended and all four men dropped to their knees. Both she and Jami clapped. Akira drained the rest of her own drink, thanking Dominik breathlessly as he gave her a refill. She had to bite her tongue to keep from shouting, "Take it off!" The whole thing was so naughty, so unexpected. Her own reactions even more so.

Maybe I'm better. She smiled as the other players, some with girlfriends or wives, came forward to wish her happy birthday. "Wild Out" by Dijon Talton came on, and the younger players and couples filled the dance floor. The atmosphere still wasn't what she'd expected from this kind of club, but something about it was liberating. She watched Jami as she left her stool to join Luke, still on his knees, and Sebastian, who drew her into his arms for a long, passionate kiss. Chicklet and her female sub, Laura, went to Tyler, Laura kissing him sweetly before snapping a pair of cuffs on his wrists. The trio headed off to the sceneing area, energy and love radiating from them in a way that made Akira feel like she was standing in the shadows on a bright summer day and would only feel the warmth if she stepped out and joined them.

Not just them either. Not all the people here were kinky, but they all accepted the lifestyle. The lifestyle Akira wished she could find a way to be part of. There was nothing scary about any of it. The way Chicklet touched Tyler as she bound him to a large frame was tender. Off to the other side, Luke had a length of rope he was using to bind Jami, laughing as she teased him and wiggled out of the loose loops around her wrists. Others made their way to stations, while the rest of the crowd danced or came to the bar for a drink.

It all seemed so . . . normal. Like something she could have.

Dominik was right. It wasn't all about sex. There was something deeper going on between the couples playing—and most of them *were* playing. Having fun.

I can do this. Any of it. But for some reason, she needed to hear it was okay from the one person whose opinion mattered now. She took a deep breath and turned to Dominik. "I want to try . . . something."

Arching one brow, Dominik nodded slowly, taking a sip of his drink before replying. "Such as?"

Her gaze drifted toward where Chicklet attached clamps to Tyler's nipples while Laura rubbed her cheek against his thigh, moving closer and closer to the erection that seemed almost painfully contained by his tight shorts.

Ah, okay. Not that.

But the scene between Jami, Luke, and Sebastian. Akira's teeth scraped her bottom lip as Luke continued his intricate knot work. Kneeling, her arms bound behind her, Jami's shorts were completely covered by what looked like a skirt made of black and red ropes. The way Luke continued up her body made it seem like he was constructing a dress for her. A *very* restrictive dress. Akira's pulse quickened until she saw the expression on her friend's face. Jami peered up at Sebastian as he spoke to her, responding with a slight smile on her lips.

Akira's favorite books had scenes like this. Bondage that was erotic all on its own, the firm grip of the rope, the texture, the surrender of control, and . . . and so much more she'd never thought she could experience.

Dominik followed her gaze when she didn't answer, then shook his head. "Not yet, Akira. Baby steps, remember? I'm impressed that you're doing so well with all these people—these men around in such a closed space." As some players crowded around the bar, Akira ground her teeth, hating the cold rush of panic that raced through her veins. She tried to keep her expression neutral, but Dominik's shrewd look told her he'd noticed. "This is your party. Mingle. See if you're okay with being close enough to a man to have a conversation with all the music and noise around you."

"Dance." She blurted out, then ducked her head as his brow furrowed. Random much? "I mean, I want to dance. I feel the most confident when I'm dancing, but usually I block out everyone around me."

He nodded slowly. "Jami mentioned that. Try it if you want, but it will help you more if you don't block everyone out. Stay close to someone you feel comfortable with. Who here makes you feel safe?"

"Besides you?" She grinned at his broad smile, reaching out to cover his hand with hers as she stood. She hadn't noticed before, but he looked tired. This was the first time his smile seemed genuine. She wanted to keep it that way. "Thank you so much for—"

"I know that look. Don't worry about me, sweetie. I'm fine." He straightened, jutting his chin toward the dance floor. "I'm responsible for the club since Richter isn't here. I can't dance with you, so I need to know there will be someone close you can turn to if you're uncomfortable."

"Okay." She pressed her lips together as she looked over the throng dancing under flashing strobe lights. So many that she knew as a hockey fan, as an Ice Girl contestant, but few well enough to say she could turn to if she panicked. There was Scott and ... she scowled as she realized she was seeking out someone who wasn't there. Who she didn't *want* to be here. A man she couldn't stand had no place at her birthday party.

Not like he would even know today is my birthday.

He had to know enough players for someone to have told him. Practically the whole team was here.

Maybe he was smart enough to know he wasn't welcome.

Doubtful. Akira glanced toward Jami, a tiny stab of envy hitting her as she watched Luke play with her hair and kiss her throat while Sebastian cupped her cheeks in his big hands and claimed her lips. She seemed so relaxed between them, and they gave her so much.

The envy faded until all she felt was relief. Jami was so much better off with these men. She'd made some bad choices before, and Akira wasn't sure she could have handled the grateful way Jami looked at *him* whenever he was around. Like he was her hero or something.

Even though it was his fault she'd been in danger in the first place.

If Jami can forgive him, why can't you?

Because... because there'd been a moment where she'd forgotten herself with him. She hadn't seen him as he really was. He was a liar. Someone who acted without thinking about the consequences.

Someone she thought about *way* too often.

"What's on your mind, pet?" Dominik put his hand over her wrist, encircling it slowly, giving her the slightest taste of restraint which helped ease her away from her thoughts. But then the sensation distracted her from his question. She ended up staring at his hand, imagining how it would feel to be in Jami's place, to be brave enough to immerse herself in everything without being so damn afraid.

Dominik didn't scare her at all. And after he repeated the question, she forced herself to think of who else she'd be okay with. The answer made her laugh. "Scott."

"I thought so." Dominik cocked his head. "Do you know why?"

That was easy. "He's honest. He might be a total dog, but he's still a sweetheart. He doesn't try to pretend to be what he's not."

"I'm sure he'd be flattered by that assessment." Dominik chuckled. "All right, go ahead. I'll be making rounds, but I will never be too far. Give me a shout if there's anything." He stood, pulling her to her feet. "And have fun."

She nodded, then sprinted away from him, laughing as Scott met her at the edge of the dance floor, twirling her around and kissing her cheek as he said, "Happy birthday." Dancing with him was so easy. And then she was dancing with Shawn. Then Luke and Jami, who'd finished their little scene. Jami, wrists freed, was still wearing her rope dress, but it didn't seem to stop her from moving in a sultry sway to the music. She hugged Akira, shooing Luke away for some girl talk.

"Is this okay? I wanted to do something special for your birthday, something that would make you feel stronger before the cruise." Her noise wrinkled. "I was gonna stay with you, but Dominik said it wouldn't do you much good to have me glued to your side the entire time. And when I saw Luke and Sebastian—"

"This is perfect!" Akira hissed in a breath as Shawn danced close behind her. Not *too* close though. It was like all the men had been given very specific instructions. None would touch her. She'd actually had to grab Scott's hands to put them on her waist during "Bump N' Grind.*"* He'd laughed and smacked her butt, making her jump and giggle. And gave her a sense of freedom she hadn't felt for so long. She could be like any other girl, flirting and having fun.

"You good?" Jami gave Shawn a hard look, and he backed off enough that she couldn't feel him behind her anymore. Almost immediately, Scott was there, dancing like everything was cool, but watching her like a guard dog.

"I'm fine!" Akira rolled her eyes. "You missed your man, Jami! Dance with him! Don't worry about me!"

Sebastian joined them, and Akira could feel his eyes on her as she tugged Scott close and grinded back against Shawn. Everyone was so worried. But she was perfect. She felt powerful, as if everything that had been holding her back had finally let her go.

Still, part of her stayed trapped, looking for the man who wasn't here. Who shouldn't be.

And a quiet, secret part of her wished he was.

* * * *

Leaving Ramos and Carter to keep an eye on Akira, Scott headed out to the parking lot for some fresh air. A few too many drinks, a bit too much exposed male flesh, was making him feel reckless. Seeing the warning in Ramos' eyes when he'd caught Scott checking out Carter's ass had helped sober him enough to take a break. He had a feeling Ramos wouldn't be sharing the boy anytime soon. If ever. And the naughty fun he'd had with Jami before the summer had likely been a onetime thing. There was something tangible between the three, stronger than before—a connection that left no room for outside play.

He took a deep inhale and pressed his eyes shut, laughing at himself for getting all worked up just watching a guy dance that he'd seen naked in the showers a hundred times.

Desperate much?

Hell, he couldn't help but look, even though he knew very well he wouldn't find what he needed from just anyone. Which left him a little antsy, like he had an itch somewhere he couldn't reach and no one would scratch for him. Things had been so much simpler when he could fuck whoever, whenever, get his rocks off, and move on with his life. Sex had never meant anything. It was just something he did.

Not anymore.

Why though? Why did proving himself feel like more of a commitment than being in an actual relationship? Maybe he should just do what everyone expected of him. Fuck Sahara or some random bunny of either sex. Get it over with.

You've got no one to impress.

No one at all.

Steady footsteps came from behind and he caught a whiff of cigarette smoke. He bit into his tongue, the cravings he hadn't had since he'd quite at nineteen adding to the irritation of everything else he'd denied himself. He glanced over his shoulder and spotted Ford, in a thin leather jacket despite the heat, a few days' worth of stubble darkening his sharp features.

Ford arched a brow, then gestured with the pack he'd been stuffing into the pocket of his black jeans. He pulled one out when Scott nodded.

"Everything okay in there?" Ford asked as he lit Scott's cigarette.

Scott shrugged and took a long drag. Letting the smoke out slowly, he angled toward the door, clearing his throat as the urge to cough tickled his throat. "Akira seems happy."

"Good." Ford puffed on his cigarette, his expression thoughtful. "She deserves to be happy."

"You going in to see her?"

"I was thinking about it." Ford flicked his cigarette, his features tense as he brought it to his lips again. "Not sure if I should though."

"Why the fuck not? I thought you, Jami, and her were all friends." Scott rolled his tongue around his mouth, wondering what the appeal of smoking had been. His mouth tasted like he'd taken a big bite of charred toast. "Go on in. I'm sure she'll be glad to see you."

Letting out a sharp laugh with a cloud of smoke, Ford shook his head. "Guess you didn't hear how it was my fault Jami got grabbed. Akira can't stand me."

Interesting. Scott had heard some stuff about what had happened to Jami but nothing about Ford. He could see Akira holding a grudge if Ford had somehow been involved—she was damn loyal, but that didn't explain why Ford had come to see her on her birthday. "I'm missing something."

"Yeah, well . . ." Ford dropped his cigarette and crushed it under his heel, which made Scott feel better about doing the same. "We almost had something. Figure she's got to forgive me someday." He gave the clear sky above a grim look. "Maybe."

"She's in a pretty good mood now. Might as well give it a shot." Scott couldn't help but hope Ford had some success. From what he knew about the guy, he was a fucking thug. But still decent. Hell, he'd saved the team by bringing in Keane. He was trying to go legit.

And if he could pull it off, maybe Scott had a chance.

There was doubt in Ford's eyes, but he inclined his head and followed Scott into the club. Someone had brought out a smoke machine, and a thin cloud covered the dance floor as couples swayed to "Collide" by Howie Day. He saw Jami and Luke in the center of the dance floor, gazing into each other's eyes in a way that made him feel like an asshole for even considering . . .

Ford's hand on his shoulder kept him from going any farther. As he glanced back, Ford gestured to something in the room, beyond the dance floor. Akira, with Pischlar, her cheeks flushed as she held out her hands to let him do some fancy knot work under Ramos' supervision. He was only lacing the slender rope through her fingers, loosely tying her hands together with her sitting across the small table from him, but the taste of restraint seemed to be a little too much for her. The color left her face as he finished the last knot.

Scott felt Ford move behind him but blocked him before he

could pass. Dominik was already there, cutting the ropes, then pulling Akira into his arms. Ford stiffened, but it wasn't until Akira laughed and wiggled away from Dominik to pull Pischlar toward the dance floor that he took a step back. Scott winced as he watched Akira clasp Pischlar's face in her hands, saying something with a big smile on her face—probably assuring him she was all right. He could just imagine what was going through Ford's head. She'd decided on a good, safe man.

The better man.

"Ford . . ." Scott followed the other man back out to the parking lot, snatching the lighter Ford flicked several times without a spark, lighting the cigarette for him. He shook his head as Ford offered him the pack. "You gotta know that meant nothin'. She's not ready for—"

"Fuck!" Ford sucked at the cigarette, then hissed smoke out through his teeth. "I want this for her. I want to know she's okay. I just thought . . ." He sighed. "Doesn't matter. Have yourself a good night, Scott."

"Hey, you're not seriously giving up, are you?"

"No." Ford stared at his cigarette, then snapped it and tossed it aside. "I don't think I can."

Scott nodded slowly. He knew exactly where the other man was coming from. "So what now?"

"Now? Nothing." Ford hung his head, shoulders bowed as though something heavy had just settled on them. "She's too good for me. She might be happy with him, but if not, I ain't going anywhere."

Maybe their situations weren't as similar as he'd thought. Scott wasn't looking for Becky to give up on Zach. He wanted them both.

Still, it came down to the same thing. He was willing to wait until he fit into her life. Into *their* lives.

For as long as it took.

Chapter Twelve

On hands and knees, Becky polished the living room floor, a sweet contentment flowing through her as she glanced up at Zach, who sat on the sofa half watching a baseball game. His hooded gaze kept slipping to her, sliding over her as though she interested him much more than the ninth inning. A blush heated her cheeks and she ducked her head, scrubbing a little harder.

This was the last day they'd be spending together for a while. Casey would come home tomorrow, and Zach would head out on the cruise in a week. He'd asked her to spend the night at his place and surprised her with a cute little maid uniform.

"My place is a mess," he'd said with a smile.

It really wasn't. For a man, Zach was quite tidy. But that wasn't the point. Doing this for him wasn't a chore. As she'd dusted and polished, all she could think of was how nice everything would look for him. There was something deeply satisfying about it, which most would probably find odd, but Zach took her actions in stride, so she didn't feel weird indulging in her need to serve him. She loved that he didn't constantly thank her, or really even acknowledge that she was doing anything extraordinary. She didn't want him to think she was doing this for attention. For gratitude.

The translucent white lace covering her breasts teased her nipples into hard little points as she rubbed wax into the hard wood floors until they shone. The ruffled trim of the skirt tickled the skin at the top of her thighs, and a light draft cooled the dampness between them. Okay, so maybe she was getting something out of this after all. Playing the maid, on her knees so close to Zach, dressed up for him, exposed for his pleasure, was erotic and a little naughty. He hadn't given her panties with the outfit. He could see how wet she was.

Their game would probably end soon. He'd want to take care of her. Which would ruin everything.

She held back a sigh as he picked up the remote and paused the game. Not that she'd mind him making love to her—at all—but she'd sunk into a comfortable zone where what she could give was all that mattered. She needed to stay here, just a little longer. If he focused on *her* pleasure—

"Look at me, pet." His tone was firm, and once she met his eyes, she found herself trapped in them, waiting for his command, all else forgotten. His lips curved as he unzipped his jeans. His dick was long and thick, the head slightly darker than the shaft. She licked her lips and sat back on her heels. He reached out to touch her cheek. "I want those beautiful lips around my cock. My house looks better than it ever has, but it's a waste to have you here, looking so sexy, doing nothing besides cleaning."

All her doubts evaporated. A throbbing ache settled low in her core as she nodded and positioned herself between his parted thighs. He caressed her hair as she took him in her mouth and she shivered, the tenderness in the gesture shifting everything inside her. She flicked her tongue over the tip of his cock, already slick and salty, and let out a soft sound as his hand moved down to the nape of her neck. He guided her motions, urging her to take him deeper, creating a steady rhythm where it wasn't so much giving him pleasure that fulfilled her, but giving up control. She stopped thinking about how much better it would be to do things for him. The tension went out of her shoulders as she let go of all her resistance, simply letting him handle her, enjoying the smooth texture of his hot flesh in her mouth, his pulse beating hard against her tongue through the thick veins around his dick.

"Good girl." His tone turned rough. His grip tightened on the back of her neck, the press of his fingers just short of bruising. He thrust in one last time, holding her still as he came on the back of her tongue, the muscles in his thighs tight against her shoulder. "Ah! Fuck!"

Becky swallowed, smiling a little as Zach rested his head back against the sofa, breathing hard. He looked like he'd come completely undone. His mouth was open, his skin was flushed, and all his muscles had gone slack. *I did that to him.*

She hummed under her breath, rubbing her cheek against the inside of his thigh.

He let out a soft laugh, toying with her hair without sitting up. "I could die a happy man right now."

"Could you?" She peered up at him, loving the way he looked down at her. Like she was someone special, someone who he considered his own. Belonging to a man had always been a scary thought, but not now. Not with him. His sports bag sat by the sofa, the one thing he'd asked her not to put away. She shouldn't let herself forget what he was. And for once, it wasn't the "gay" part that concerned her. "You've got a few years left in you, don't you?"

His brow lifted. "More than a few, I hope. I'm only a few years older than you, pet."

"I know, but that's not what I mean. Would you seriously be happy if you died without a Cup ring on your finger?"

"If I'm dead, I don't think I'll care too much." He winked, then pulled her to her feet as he stood. Doing up his jeans, he watched her curiously. "You have a very busy head, little doe. I have a feeling you're not worried about me dying anytime soon."

"I'm not worried about anything, Sir," she said brightly, heading toward the kitchen. She'd made shaved pork in his Crock-Pot for supper. Should be ready by—

He caught her wrist, stalling her. His tone was level, but the depth to it made her tremble. "Becky."

Just her name, but something about the way he said it told her he knew she wasn't being completely honest. She wished she hadn't said anything. If evading his question would just get her punished, she might try a little harder, but Zach had already warned her that he wouldn't punish her for not being truthful. Trust or nothing.

Fair enough. She expected the same from him.

"You're a hockey player. I mean, it's all romantic for you to say things like that, but we both know I won't be on your mind when you're out on the ice." She shrugged. "I'm just being realistic."

He took a long, long inhale. Wet his bottom lip with the tip of his tongue. Then let the breath out slowly. "You're being very cynical. Yes, the game is a big part of my life. I'm not giving it up. But that doesn't make you any less important to me."

"I know."

"Do you?"

Ugh, so much for his *ruining everything.* He'd given her exactly what she needed, but instead of letting herself enjoy the moment, she'd analyzed it, picking apart his words until she'd found exactly what she couldn't help looking for. Something that could go wrong.

"I do, it's only . . . I don't know." She pressed her lips together, then shook her head and started gathering the cleaning supplies she'd left on the floor. She felt ridiculous, and for some reason, the sexy little maid uniform made it even worse. Here she was, right in the middle of a scene with the Dom of her dreams, and all she could do was question everything he said and did. She hunched her shoulders. "I'm sorry."

"Don't be sorry." Zach took the supplies and set them on the coffee table. Then he straightened and placed his hands on her shoulders, searching her eyes, his brow creased. "Help me understand."

How? I'm not sure I understand. She bowed her head. "Really, it just came out. I guess sometimes it just seems too good to be true."

The edges of his lips quirked. "Imagine how I feel. I have a woman who enjoys cleaning for me and pleasing me in any way I can dream of. My mother would have lost it if she came in here to see me lounging around while you were scrubbing my floors."

Becky's cheeks heated. She peeked up at him. "I think she'd have been a little too shocked to get pissed about that."

He snorted. "You don't know my mother. I think you'll like her though."

Even though she'd gone off the handle a bit, her blood hadn't cooled at all, and the moisture between her thighs reminded her the night wasn't over. She ducked her head, sure her cheeks must be beet red. "I don't really want to talk about your mom right now."

His knuckles brushed her cheek before he used them to nudge her chin up. "What do you want to do?"

You! She looked him over, taking note of the slight bulge in his jeans. She slid closer to him, sliding her hand down over his groin, smirking as he groaned. "You recover pretty fast."

"Sometimes. Mostly with you."

"Hmm." She went up on tiptoes to kiss along his jaw, then whispered in his ear. "I want to feed you."

His laughter followed her as she skipped out of reach and into his kitchen. She grinned as she set out the plates. Her doubt had been nothing but a hiccup. Talking things over with him had helped; he listened, he explained, and he understood.

Her heart was full to bursting, and it didn't scare her quite so much anymore. She'd have her issues, but he was man enough to handle that.

Maybe they'd make it after all.

Chapter Thirteen

Steps away from the Joan Harriss Cruise Pavilion, Zach stood by Becky's side and grinned at the way Casey gaped up at the Big Ceilidh Fiddle, the world's largest fiddle. The little girl had been connected at the hip to her mother all week, even refusing to stay with her Uncle Landon and her new baby cousin while Becky saw him off. When he'd gone to pick Becky up, he'd thought at first that he'd have to say goodbye right there and then, but Casey took charge and insisted her mommy *had* to go to the big boat with him. And she *had* to come along.

He didn't mind at all, but he had a feeling Becky wasn't all that comfortable with it. The few times the three had gone out together over the past week, he was referred to as "Uncle Landon's friend" or "one of the Cobras." Casey saw other players at Bower's place, so she didn't make much of her mother hanging out with yet another one. Every time they went to the park, they saw a few other guys with their wives and kids. Palladino's and Williams' boys had regular playdates, and Zach had been enlisted by Casey as her swing buddy when she saw the boys being pushed high by their daddies. The first time, Becky had told Casey "Mommy will push you, *poupée*," but Casey was a stubborn little thing.

"Mommy, I want to tell all the kids at school I spent all summer with the team! Zach has nothing else to do anyway!"

Ready to leave if that would make things easier on Becky, Zach was a little surprised when Becky simply nodded and went to join the other mothers at the picnic tables. He'd caught up with the guys while the kids played, then found himself drawn into conversation with the precocious five-year-old girl when someone brought up bad calls by refs that past season. Casey had been raised on the game and knew more than most die-hard fans. As they were leaving the park, Casey had held his and her mother's hands, excitedly chatting up a storm about the coming season, and the draft picks the team had picked up, and her birthday.

"You're coming, right, Zach?" Casey gave him a wide-eyed look, so adorable with that pleading puppy dog expression that he was ready to promise

he'd be there even though he wasn't sure what she was talking about, she'd changed the subject so often. She cleared that up quickly. "Uncle Dean said he might be able to have the team there on my birthday, but *you* have to be there!"

"Poupée, your birthday's during training camp." Becky sounded flustered, as though she was torn between giving her daughter what she wanted for her birthday and trying hard to make sure the little girl didn't end up disappointed if she couldn't. "You know the men will be very busy."

"But you and Zach talk all the time! Please make him come!"

Becky couldn't seem to find the right words, so Zach did his best. He squeezed Casey's hand gently and winked at her. "I'll do my best. The whole team will."

The grateful look Becky gave him was bittersweet. There was no mistaking what it meant. She was happy that he'd made himself no different from the other players.

Bringing his thoughts back to the present, he forced himself to acknowledge that, as far as Casey was concerned, he *was* no different. Which he fully understood. It would take months before Becky would be okay with letting Casey know about their relationship. Part of him wished they didn't have to wait, but he wasn't in a rush. He would be there for mother and daughter when they needed him. No more, no less.

"All right, guys. About ready?" Tim called out, looking over the group of players standing by the water. Most of the Ice Girl contenders were already onboard, but the players hung out until the last minute, saying goodbye to friends and family who'd come to see them off. The only Ice Girl he could still see mingling was Akira. She stood with Jami, Ramos, and Carter, cheeks flushed as she made a valiant effort not to laugh at the way Jami let the boy have it. Hand on her hips, Jami faced Carter, bringing up one hand once in a while to poke him in the chest before scowling at the boat.

She obviously thought he was going to get in some kind of trouble.

Zach's lip twitched as Jami cut her lecture short, kissed Carter, then stepped aside so Ramos could move in. Ramos curved his hand around the back of the boy's neck. Their foreheads touched for a moment, and Ramos said something that had a blush staining Carter's cheeks. Carter hooked his arm around Sebastian's shoulders, feigning a hug while pressing a hard kiss to Ramos' throat. Then he laughed, saluted, and headed up the ramp.

Akira hugged Jami tight, then followed, shouting back, "I'll keep an eye on him for you!"

A little hand tugged at Zach's sleeve. He crouched down as Casey gave him that wide-eyed look that made it almost impossible to tell her no. Gusts of warm, ocean air ruffled the child's golden brown curls. "What is it, angel face?"

"You don't really have to go, do you? Grandma wanted you to come over for supper!"

"And I will come over. But right now, your mommy missed you so much she wants you all to herself."

Becky gave him a grateful smile and bent down beside him. "That's right, *poupée*. And you remember Auntie Silver said this cruise was very important. Mr. Pearce has to do this for the team."

"All right." Casey let out a heavy sigh. "But you *have* to come over as soon as you get back. Hockey players are hungry all the time. You're my hero, and we *have* to feed you."

Biting back a laugh, Zach nodded solemnly. The Bower women certainly wanted to make sure he didn't starve. "I'm looking forward to it."

He straightened as the last of the men filed up the ramp, holding out his arm to pull Becky in for a hug. Her breath caught as his lips hovered over hers. Heat filled her eyes. He'd spent as much time as possible loving her body and satisfying her in every way possible, but they were still so new to one another, it never seemed to be enough. After only one day apart he longed to take her somewhere where they could be alone. To explore all the parts of her he still hadn't touched or tasted.

How bad would it be after a week?

Before he could kiss her, she turned her head, biting her lip when he drew back and stared at her. She hugged him tight and whispered in his ear. "I'm sorry, it's just . . . I don't want her to see us being too friendly. It might confuse her."

Nodding, he let her pull away from him. He knew that, but he hadn't even considered what the little girl might think of a man kissing her mother in front of her. And he should have. If he was going to fit into Becky's life, he had to be prepared to let her set the pace.

"Oh good, I didn't miss the boat!" Scott jogged up to them, dropping his suitcase at his feet and bracing his hands on his knees, rasping in air as though he'd run all the way here from his new condo. "Fucking Stephan decided, last minute, that I needed more new clothes."

Becky laughed. "You're going on a cruise! What do you need besides swim trunks?"

"Or a Speedo." Scott winked at her.

Jesus. Zach's gaze skimmed over Scott's tall, lean body. One he knew very well. The man looked pretty respectable—maybe a little *too* respectable—in crisp blue jeans and a white, V-neck T-shirt. But the thought of him in a Speedo was unsettling.

"Umm, eww." Becky wrinkled her nose. "Even you won't look good in a Speedo."

Scott smirked. "Tell me that after you see the pics. I've got the ass for it."

Cheeks a nice hot pink, Becky glanced over at Casey, who'd gone back to the big fiddle and had struck up a conversation with Tim's wife, Madeline. Even though her daughter was out of hearing, Becky kept her voice low. "I believe it. And I like the fact that you'll be taking pictures with at least *something* covering you."

"Hey, you've got to admit, the nude shots were *very* artistic," Scott said.

"You're talented, Scott. You don't need to whore yourself for the cameras."

"Does it bother you?"

"Why would it?" Becky's eyes narrowed as Sahara called out to Scott from the bow of the ship. She didn't seem to care that he purposefully ignored the other woman. Interesting. "You better go." She sniffed. "And have fun."

Cocking his head, glancing over at Zach, Scott moved closer to her. He whispered something in her ear and kissed her cheek. "Don't miss me too much."

She scoffed, backing away. "I won't miss you at all. At least you won't be making my job harder while you're out there. Not with Tim keeping an eye on you."

Scott inclined his head. "There's that. And my lotion—got another bottle. Reminds me of you."

Lotion? Zach eyed Becky as she covered her bright red cheeks with her hands. Lips parted, she shook her head and spun on her heels, not even looking at him before scooping Casey up and heading to the parking lot.

He gave Scott a dark look as he strode past him on the way to the ramp. The man had no fucking respect. And he'd obviously shared something with Becky that Zach knew nothing about. Hell, they'd be apart for a week, and Scott's last words had pretty much guaranteed that she'd be thinking about him.

Get over it. You knew there was something between them. She's earned your trust.

And she'd made it clear she wasn't interested in Scott. Not in any way that counted.

He'd never considered himself a jealous man, but part of him wondered if he wasn't missing something. Becky was so determined to go about their relationship the *right* way. She'd questioned his feelings for Scott several times. He couldn't help but wonder if she was denying her own.

Not that it mattered. Scott had to back off. Zach refused to let her feel pressured by the other man.

With all the camera crews on the boat, Zach knew better than to confront Scott out in the open, but as soon as the cameras were locked on the bikini-clad Ice Girls, he followed Scott to his room, waving Tim away when the man tried to approach him.

The door clicked shut behind him. Scott looked up from where he'd been unpacking his overstuffed suitcase. His brow furrowed as though he'd tried to read Zach's expression, but couldn't. "You're not gonna punch me, are you?"

Zach shook his head, tucking his thumbs into the pockets of his jeans. "No. Most other men probably would, but I don't feel threatened by you."

Scott snorted as he straightened, cramming the last of his T-shirts into the dresser drawers. "You're so full of shit. The only thing I don't know is if you're more scared of how much she wants me, or how much you do."

"We've had this conversation."

"Have we?"

"Yes." Zach wasn't sure what he wanted to do more. Shake some sense into Scott or slam their lips together and kiss him until that cocky smile disappeared. Not that it would do him much good. Scott had a one-track mind, and Zach wasn't in the mood to try to get through to him. *If that's even possible.* Best to keep things very simple. "You know Becky and I are involved."

Scott laced his fingers behind his neck, brow raised. "Yeah, I do. Just making it clear I'm available."

Zach let out a rough laugh. Nothing with Scott was "clear." Becky didn't need this kind of shit messing with her head. "Leave her alone, Scott. She's trying to settle into her life here, and you're doing nothing but complicating things."

"Well, she's not *here,* is she?" Scott inched his body against Zach's, challenge in his steady gaze. "But you are. Did Tim get a chance to tell you?" A small dimple showed in Scott's cheek as he grinned. "We're sharing a room."

Zach's jaw ticked as he did his best not to react to that little piece of info. He waited until Scott ducked out of the room, then walked up to the large window to stare out at the ocean. Scott wasn't going to let this go, and Zach wasn't quite sure why. Did he consider getting under Zach's skin a challenge? Did he want Becky because she wouldn't throw herself at him?

Whatever the reason, Zach had to make sure Scott understood that this had to stop. If he could go through the next week without touching the man, ignoring every advance . . . he grunted, gritting his teeth against the steady throb of his balls. *Yeah, you'll show him, Pearce.*

Okay, so the man turned him on. Him and almost any other man or woman with a pulse. No big deal. He didn't have to act on it.

"*—if there was a man . . . a man I felt could give you even half of what I can—who wouldn't ruin what we have . . .*"

Zach cursed as he recalled Becky's words, right after they'd made love for the first time. She'd been so certain he'd need more. So determined to accept it if he did.

But I don't.

Becky needed stability. Needed a man who would stand by her no matter what. He knew he could be that man. Scott couldn't. Yeah, he was tempting. He was the fucking apple in Eden to them both, and if Zach let it happen, both he and Becky could enjoy what little Scott had to offer. But then what? Becky was already unsure about how her relationship with Zach would work. She'd take his lead if he trusted Scott enough to bring him into what they were building, but what kind of Dom would he be to take that kind of risk?

This wasn't about him being Becky's Dom, though. Her reactions toward Scott weren't something he could control. And negating his own feelings wasn't making the situation any better.

Sitting on the bed, he pulled out his phone, flipping it in his hand several times before dialing. Hearing Becky's laughter before she said "Hello?" brought a smile to his lips. Whatever happened, he knew they had each other. There was no reason for all this uncertainty. All they had to do was talk it over.

"Hello, little doe." He scooted backward to rest against the headboard. "Does Casey still like her room or will we need to paint it a different color?"

"Don't be silly! She loves it—I'm glad we finished in time." She paused and he could hear her shifting about, then the light pad of her footsteps as she went into another room. "Listen, I'm sorry I left like that. I hope you weren't upset?"

"Not at all. I did wonder—"

"About the lotion, right?" She spoke quickly, her tone laced with guilt. "It was nothing, really. Scott was hitting on me once, telling me he had 'needs' so he could perform on the ice. I gave him a small bottom of lotion and told him to take care of it. Then I . . . I guess I sort of gave him mixed signals. My brother ordered me to stay away from him."

Zach bit the inside of his cheek to keep from laughing. That couldn't have gone over well. "What did you do?"

"I kissed Scott. It was more to make a point than anything, but . . ."

"I understand. There's something about him that's hard to resist." Zach sighed. "We should be having this conversation in person, but since that's not possible—"

"Are you finally going to admit you want him?"

"I don't think I ever said I didn't 'want' him. I don't need him when I have you. But I want to be completely honest. I have wondered what the three of us could have if he's serious about all the changes he's making. I've seen the way you look at him."

"He's with Sahara."

"I'm pretty sure he's with her just to improve his image."

"You didn't see the way he kissed her." She cleared her throat. "But . . . if you think you could have something with him, I won't stand in the way. If we're being honest, I have to admit, before I saw him with Sahara, I was wondering what it could be like too. You guys would be hot together."

"We were. But that's not the point." Zach rubbed his hand over his face, not sure she really understood what he was trying to say. "You aren't in the way, love. I need a real relationship, and that's what *we* have. I don't ever want you to feel the way I did when I saw Scott with other men. And women."

"I don't ever want you to feel that way again. That's why I asked Scott to back off." She drew in a sharp inhale. "But it all comes back to him changing. If he has, go for it."

"Not this week. Not until we both have a chance to see if it will last."

"I trust you. I know you wouldn't do anything if I wasn't okay with it. I repeat—" she let out a light laugh, but it sounded strained "—I am."

This wasn't going at all like he'd intended. He shook his head. "That isn't why I called. Nothing will happen. I wanted to clarify things between us. When I found out I was sharing a room with Scott, I—"

"You're sharing a room?" She let out another tight laugh. "And you want me to believe nothing will happen?"

He went still. "I thought you trusted me?"

"I do. But it kinda pisses me off to know you'll be holding him at arm's length when I've told you again and again that I don't mind."

So she said. But her tone told him otherwise. She thought she was giving him what he wanted. He sat up, speaking slowly so he wouldn't be misunderstood again. "I am not a man who enjoys a cheap fuck. That's all Scott can give me right now. I will tell you the same thing you've told me. When—if—you decide to explore things with Scott, I will accept it. But be careful. I won't be happy if he hurts you."

"He's not with me, Zach. He's with you. I won't be happy if he hurts you either, but I think you need to give him a chance."

They spoke for a bit longer, the subject shifting away from Scott, becoming more relaxed as she brought up Silver and how excited Casey had been to see the baby. She mentioned the calendar the team would sell for charity with pictures from the cruise and made him promise to pose for one with Scott.

"Since you're not here, I need some kind of mental image to help me take care of myself at night."

He knocked his head back against the headboard, the image of her pleasuring herself while thinking of him with Scott making his balls tight and his dick hard. "The two of you are going to drive me insane!"

"Easy solution. Stop fighting us." Her voice was deep and husky, resonating down his spine in a way that made him shudder. "Just promise you'll call me and give me all the dirty details."

"If anything happens, Becky, you'll be there to see it."

"If that's true, I'll be a little disappointed. With all the changes Scott's making, I don't want to see him losing his touch. He'll find a way to break through that rigid control you're so proud of."

"Considering my control is one of the things you like most about me, I sincerely doubt that will happen."

"We'll see," she said brightly. Then her tone changed, rough with longing. "I'll miss you."

"Already?" His lips turned up in a sheepish grin. "I thought I was the only one."

"You do know we're becoming one of those sappy couples no one can stand to be around? I don't think anyone expected that from you."

"I don't care what anyone thinks." He took a deep breath. "I'm falling in love with you, Becky. You're everything a man could ever want in a woman. I need you to know I'll never do anything to ruin this."

"That . . . wow. I'm glad you said that. Because it scares me how fast I'm falling for you. This was the only thing holding me back—knowing there was part of yourself you were keeping from me." She paused again. "He won't come between us unless we pretend he's not there. We fit in each other's lives. And maybe he can too."

"Maybe." Zach still wasn't sure. But it was good that they'd discussed the possibilities. "There's only one way to find out. I'll give him the opportunity to prove himself."

"Do. I can't wait to hear how it goes." Her laughter this time was genuine. "Only one downside to all this."

He frowned. A downside she found funny? "And what's that?"

"All the flirting and teasing. All the offers. It worked. Scott's going to think he won."

Grinning, Zach shook his head. The way Scott and Becky pushed and pulled, the way they tested one another . . . he could practically see the sparks fly already when they finally came together. But when that happened, none of them would be playing around. "He hasn't won because this isn't a game. And this goes no further until I'm sure he understands."

* * * *

Scott stepped to the edge of the diving board, inhaling deep as he prepared to take the plunge. After hours under the blazing spotlights in the ballroom, posing with several different Ice Girls, dressed in a suit, then full hockey gear, while they got to wear their cute little uniforms—he'd been more than happy to slip into his swim trunks. Cobra swim trunks, black with gold trim and the logo embroidered on one thigh. Little cheesy, but they'd work for the group photos. And they worked now that he needed to cool off.

The water was a good temperature, waking him without shocking him when he broke through the surface with a splash. He stayed under, crossing the pool with long strokes, coming up for a breath before racing to the other end. A few times he had to stop short when the Ice Girls playing in the water blocked his path, but he got in a few good laps, got his heart pumping, before he stopped. Chlorine stung his eyes and his nose, but the burn in his lungs and muscles was invigorating. He shook water from his hair, then groaned as cameras flashed, slashing white light straight into his skull.

"You haven't gotten enough for today?" he shouted, not all that surprised when the cameramen ignored him and went to blind someone else. "And I volunteered for a fucking week of this?"

"Pretty sure Keane didn't give you a choice, hot stuff." Sahara grinned at him as she perched on the edge of the pool to dip her feet into the water. The sequins on her midriff Ice Girl jersey glinted in the sun. "I know you rich dudes can afford cruises like this whenever you want, but me, I'm happy to suffer the cameras all week long for all this." She tipped her head back, bracing her hands behind her, soaking in the heat with her eyes closed. "Don't mind me if I don't feel sorry for you."

That so? His lip twitched. "Hey, I'm feeling sorry for *you*."

She didn't bother opening her eyes. "Oh? And why's that?"

"They're gonna be so pissed." He scooped his hands under the water. "I'm pretty sure those uniforms aren't supposed to get wet."

The water splashed into her face and soaked her little jersey. Her shrieks rang over the laughter of the other girls. Screaming like an angry cat, she stood, pulling off her jersey and skirt to reveal a golden string bikini. She tossed her clothes onto a pile of towels near the lounge chairs and bared her teeth.

"Scott Demyan, you are a dead man!"

She launched herself into the water, and he back-paddled out of reach before she came up. They splashed and played for a while, attracting the camera crew as the other girls, and a few of the guys, joined in. Pischlar and Akira were in the water now, which tore his attention away from the fun. Akira was flirting, laughing, which was good. She was showing everyone a side of her that wasn't afraid, and he liked that a lot. But her smiles seemed a little too bright, and she seemed to be letting Pischlar get a little too close. Scott eased away from the group to watch her as Pischlar picked her up by the hips and tossed her into the water. There, right before she floated back and slid her body up against the man. A tightness around her eyes.

The determined set to her lips. She'd gone from a nice steady pace into being comfortable with men to a full-out sprint. Being here would give her and Pischlar plenty of opportunities to be alone. She might take a leap just to prove to herself she could.

And he couldn't help but feel that would be a really bad idea. She wasn't ready, and all it would take was one wrong move from Pischlar to trash all the progress she'd made.

But before he could intervene, a heavy hand settled on his shoulder. He glanced back to see Mason shaking his head.

"Leave them for now. I'll talk to her later. She needs you as a friend—let me be the overprotective one." Mason gave him a grim smile. "If she decides to go through with this, she'll need someone to talk to. Since Jami isn't here, I think that should be you."

"Got it." Scott looked back toward Sahara, who had climbed out of the pool and was posing on a lounge chair for the cameras. Behind the man crouching near her feet stood Zach.

Scott's pulse sped up a notch. Zach must have just finished a photo shoot of his own, because he was wearing the bottom half of his hockey gear, his chest bare and glistening with oil that brought out the shadows and ridges of his bulging muscles. Just the sight of him made Scott's dick harden and throb. Leaving the pool would give the cameras more of a show than he wanted to. But he couldn't let Zach just walk away. He had to make every moment they had together count.

"You coming in?" he shouted as he reached the end of the pool closest to where Zach stood. His breath caught as Zach approached him, something in his eyes making Scott feel like he'd just stepped into a lion's den with raw steak strapped around his waist. He hadn't seen that look in Zach's eyes for a very long time. His tone was rough when he spoke again. "I swear, I'll behave."

Little creases formed around Zach's lips as he gave Scott a broad smile. "Really? I'd like to see that."

"Is that a yes?" Scott rested his forearms on the edge of the pool, caught off-guard by Zach's smooth reply. So far the man had shut him down at every turn. Maybe Scott was finally getting to him. "It would be cool to just hang out. If . . ." Hell, one of their issues was probably that Zach wouldn't betray Becky. Scott needed to make sure that Zach knew he that he didn't expect . . . he sucked in a deep breath and lowered his voice. "Look. What I said before was bullshit. I'm cool with nothing happening while we're here. I'm not expecting you to do anything without Becky being okay with it. Same in reverse. I'm not trying to come between you."

"I appreciate that. But Becky's fine with it." Zach chuckled as Scott stared at him. The hard glint in Zach's eyes made him wonder what he was in for. Zach's next words made it clear it wouldn't be easy. "I don't expect you to become a saint, Scott. Doing that would disappoint all your fans anyway. I want to see you having fun here. But not *too* much fun."

Scott scowled. *Cryptic much?* "I didn't have any orgies planned, if that's what you're getting at. I want you and Becky. No one else interests me in the least."

"I'm happy to hear that. Because this is going to be a very long week for you."

"Umm . . . what?"

Taking a knee, Zach glanced over at the girls. At the camera crews. Likely making sure no one was within hearing. "You've talked a lot about proving yourself, but I'm not convinced. You indulge too often for me to believe you're waiting on me and Becky."

"Fuck, I've had nothing besides my own hand since . . ." Yeah, probably better not to bring up the guys that had gotten him kicked out of Vanek's place. "It's been a while."

"Yes. I know what the lotion reference means now." Zach cocked his head, resting his hands on his thighs. "Hand over the lotion tonight. You won't need it."

Holy shit! If Zach meant what Scott thought he did—Scott gulped and nodded. "Not a problem. I brought lube too."

Zach snorted. "How nice for you. But you won't need that either."

"Huh?"

"You'll take what I give you and nothing more." Zach pushed up to his feet. "Have your fun, but know that if you're not getting off by my hands, or mouth, or body—you're not getting off at all."

Okay, that was just funny. Not a night went by that he didn't jerk off to release some pressure. It wasn't the same as enjoying mindless sex, but it fit nicely into his bedtime routine. He laughed. "Listen, buddy. I told you already—you ain't turning me into your sub. I'm not all that into that shit."

"I don't want you to be my sub, Scott. Give me more than words to go on." Zach glanced at the others again, even though the girls were screaming loud enough to cover anything he said. His jaw hardened. "If you can't wait for me, you're not worth my time. Or Becky's."

"I have needs, man." The water around Scott seemed to cool. He wasn't sure he could pass this little test. Sex was his release. Had been for as long as he could remember. "Isn't me saying I want no one else enough?"

"No."

"Then tonight..." He could do that. He could hang on a night—maybe two—if Zach wanted him all revved up just for him. The thought alone had him chewing on the inside of his cheek, struggling for control. "Tonight I'll—"

"Not tonight." Zach patted his cheek. "I never said this would be easy."

Try nearly impossible. But Scott simply nodded, shuddering as Zach slid a hand around the back of his neck and tugged his hair, his eyes dark and full of promise. If Scott could do this, he'd be rewarded. And it made him want to try.

Because the reward wasn't just emptying his sac. Wasn't just cheap, quick pleasure.

It was something that would last. Something he'd never had.

* * * *

Akira wrapped the big, fluffy white towel around her body, shaking so hard her teeth chattered. Shawn had invited her back to his room for "a nightcap after dinner." It didn't really surprise her; she'd practically shoved her willingness down his throat, but she wasn't feeling it. The only reason she was doing this was because she felt like she had to. Hell, she was practically a born-again virgin. The only time she'd... she'd had *sex* was when those men had ripped into her body on that office floor. She needed to do it again just to prove she could. It shouldn't be such a big deal. Maybe, once she got it over with, it wouldn't be.

But she couldn't be near him now. She needed to get her head on straight first. Remind herself that this was something normal people did.

And she wanted to be normal. She wanted to be like all the other girls hooking up with players tonight. Just having fun—not worrying about the consequences. She was too young to take . . . fucking someone this seriously. Yes, someone touching her body was scary as hell, but Shawn was sweet. Made her feel sexy. She kinda wished she felt more for him, but that didn't really matter.

Sex on the 'to do' list. Sounded about right.

Someone cleared their throat and her blood ran cold, like she'd been caught snatching a chocolate bar at the drugstore. She lifted her head, gaping up at Dominik, sure all her thoughts were printed out in black ink on her face. She couldn't hide from him. And didn't really want to.

"What are you doing, little one?"

She shrugged. "Right now? Nothing."

"You know very well what I mean."

She did. But going into it felt like talking to her dad—before what happened with his coworkers. At fifteen, she'd missed curfew. Tried smoking. Had a few drinks. She'd been a normal teen, getting in trouble and driving her parents insane. Working for her dad had been a way to make up for all the trouble she'd caused.

And then . . . then she'd been ruined, and she was sure it was her fault. Yeah, she'd had therapy and everything, had been told she wasn't to blame. But karma came at people in different ways. Her parents were respectable. Responsible. And she hadn't been.

And you paid for it. No matter what you looked like, those men knew who you really were.

Her mind was a great big jumbled mess. Therapy had worked well enough that she could spot the thoughts that didn't fit. It *wasn't* her fault. She hadn't asked to be . . . raped. She had a right to keep living. Within reason. Sending out "fuck me" signals wouldn't help. She really wanted to believe just *doing it* would get her past that last hurdle, but what if it didn't? What if it just made the next hurdle bigger? Harder to pass?

Maybe Dominik would understand. That's why he was here, right? She faced him, her hands fisted around the towel covering her practically naked body. "I have to do this. I have to know I can. Shawn's been so patient, so understanding. I know you've talked to him. He was a good choice."

"I didn't choose him for you, pet. I wouldn't have. Your first time needs to mean something. It won't with him." Dominik traced his cold fingers down her cheek, shadows stealing the reflection of the fading sun from his eyes. "I know you want to move on. But take it slow. You've been through enough."

"I brought that on myse—"

"Don't. You know that's not true. Maybe blaming yourself will make doing whatever you plan easier, but it's not helping you." He moved closer, and she swallowed, overwhelmed by the way her body reacted to him. Heating all over, craving... something. "Baby, you've finally accepted that you can be aroused by a man. And that it's not wrong. Don't cheapen it by taking the first man who comes along into your bed. Sex isn't something that just happens. It should be special."

"It isn't always though. A girl my age should have experiences. Even if she regrets them after." She turned her head, staring out at the waves slapping the side of the ship, already hating her own words even though she couldn't keep them from coming out. "If I can just do it... if I can have sex and act like it was no big deal—"

"Why would anyone want that? Don't do this just to prove there's nothing wrong with you." Dominik's tone changed. Became rough as his gaze followed hers to the dark blue depths. "Even if it doesn't last, there should be no regrets."

Without thinking, she moved up to him, taking his hands in hers. "I heard that Oriana's visiting Silver. Have you talked to her?"

He shook his head. A small smile crept over his lips. "Changing the subject again?" He looked past her, stepped away just as a camera flashed, then groaned. "If you want to talk, maybe we can hang out later. I need a break from the vultures."

She grabbed his arm before he could slip away, something occurring to her that she was surprised she hadn't thought of earlier.

Yeah, talking to Dominik was a bit like talking to a father figure . . . or maybe not. Maybe it was more like talking to a Master. A Master who knew what she needed. She bit her lip, hoping she wasn't making a mistake.

"Dinner with the group is optional tonight. Maybe we can . . . I mean, I won't go to Shawn's room." She took a deep breath. "I'll come to yours."

"You're welcome to, if you want. Being the captain, I was given my own suite. I can . . ." His words slowed and his eyes narrowed. He'd caught on to what she was implying. "Akira—"

"Just hear me out." She dug her nails into her palms, squaring her shoulders and jutting her chin up. "You're my sponsor, right? And you don't expect anything from me in return. That's clear. But you've also become my mentor, teaching me about the lifestyle, showing me I don't have to be afraid of who I am."

"Yes, but there are limits to what I can teach you." His lips thinned as his gaze passed over her, his eyes hooded, but not enough to hide the hint of interest. "I'm not ready for a relationship, Akira. And neither are you."

"Exactly. But that's not what we'll have." She wanted to touch him again. If only the camera crews weren't hovering. Not close enough to hear anything they said, but close enough to snap a shot and make a lot out of nothing. Well, nothing *yet*. "There are other men I feel safe with, but none of them can do for me what you can. I'd never regret anything with you, because you understand me. You'll help me get past all the triggers—you'll catch them before I do. Like you did at the club."

"You have no idea what you're asking from me, pet." Dominik blinked, then shook his head, lips twitching with amusement. "Damn it, I'm already treating you like you're my sub. This wasn't my intention, but I shouldn't be surprised that you'd consider me as someone safe to take the next step with."

"You came to me. You knew I was about to make a big mistake." Her cheeks heated as she considered what he'd stopped her from doing. "I-I would have been too embarrassed to come to you after. I wish I'd thought of this sooner."

"I haven't said yes, little one."

"You didn't say no either." She wrinkled her nose when he barked out a laugh. "What? It's true!"

"It is. But I just realized you're a pushy little brat." He tapped her chin with a finger. "I'm eager to see how the Dom that claims you after I set you loose handles that."

She grinned. "*That's* a yes."

He caught her chin in his hand, rolling his eyes at the sporadic flashes. He bent down so she could feel his hot breath on her lips. "That's a yes. Come to my room in two hours. And you will tell me how your apology to Pischlar went. I won't have my 'pupil' teasing men with what belongs to me."

Her heart skipped a few beats. She panted. Swallowed hard. "I belong to you?"

"Until I find someone who can appreciate you and care for you . . ." He kissed her cheek, then whispered in her ear. "Yes."

* * * *

"I don't see a problem."

Dominik paced around the small table set up with a fondue pot and a tray with tenderized beef and an assortment of vegetables. Having Akira come to his room for dinner wasn't an issue. But what she expected from him was.

So he'd called the one woman he'd hoped would understand his misgivings. His only concern was that her long-standing friendship with Sloan might be a conflict of interest. So far, it didn't seem to be a problem.

But Chicklet was a Domme, first and foremost. She'd approved of his plans for Akira's birthday.

Since when do you doubt yourself so much that you need another Master's approval?

It didn't matter. He did, and she was happy to give it.

"Fuck, Mason. I know it hurts, but what you had with Oriana was exactly this. You prepared her to be with Sloan and Max. The only thing I'm worried about at this point is whether or not you'll be prepared to let her go when the time comes."

He winced. That wasn't how he'd seen his relationship with

Oriana. He'd seen a future between the four of them. He hadn't expected it to be easy, but he'd been prepared to see it through. He'd never loved another woman as much as he loved her.

"I don't want to talk about Oriana. How would you handle this? I can let her go; that's not the problem." He strode up to his bed, sitting heavily and rubbing his temples with the phone propped up to his ear with his shoulder. "What do I do if she gets attached? She's trusting me to help her through this. I won't be helping her if she settles on me."

"She won't. From what you've told me, she knows what she's getting into. Be her mentor. Use this as a way to get past what you're going through. Keep an eye out for the man she needs and be happy for her once she finds him."

"I will be, but I'm still not sure how far I should take this. She's so fragile . . . I know what she wants. I'm just not sure she's ready."

"Bullshit. You know what she's ready for. What you went through with Oriana is just so fresh, you're worried that doing anything will be a betrayal. It's not. I can tell you for a fact that both Max and Sloan are doing everything they can to help her get over you." She paused. "And I told them both that's exactly what they have to do. You've made a clean break. All that's left is to let it heal."

His throat locked. He shouldn't be all that surprised that Sloan and Max had spoken to her. The way she managed her two subs was something to be emulated. "How is she?"

"She'll be fine. It's you I'm worried about." Chicklet made a sharp sound, hissing through her teeth. "Fuck, this whole situation with Oriana sucks. I wish I'd seen it coming so I could have warned you. But I'm happy you're talking to me. Because I'm going to do everything I can to get you through this. And finding a new project is a good start."

"A new project." He snorted. "That's one way to put it."

"You need someone to need you, Mason. Even when you were with Oriana, you still did training scenes at the club. Consider this more of the same." Her tone took on a playful lilt. "Only more 'hands on.'"

He laughed, but he liked the idea. Subs came to the club all the time, single women who wanted a taste of submission, but couldn't find anyone they trusted enough to give it to them. Ramos had handled them before taking on Jami and Carter, but now he had his hands full. Richter was training a few of the younger players who showed an interest in the lifestyle, but none of the rookies had the experience to take charge of vulnerable subs. He did.

Akira would need more attention than most. It would be a challenge to get her past the damage done to her, physically and emotionally. He wasn't sure he could trust anyone else to do it properly.

"You good?" Chicklet asked, his silence obviously concerning her.

He nodded slowly. "I am. And thank you. I thought coming on this cruise would be a good distraction, but it wasn't enough. Maybe doing this for her will be."

After he hung up, he looked around the room, much more comfortable with the setup than he'd been before. One of the most important things he needed to teach Akira was how a Dom should treat her. Granted, scenes at the club wouldn't always be preceded by romantic diners, but they should always be planned with her needs in mind.

Taking a deep breath, he dragged a charcoal grey armchair across the room, pausing when the scent of heated spices rose from the fondue pot and sent a sharp pang straight into his gut. He'd had a fondue night with Oriana once. She'd stripped the second she'd crossed the threshold, fingering her collar with a small smile on lips glossed with his favorite peach-flavored balm. She'd whispered "Master" before lowering to her knees. She'd stayed in that position while he'd fed her every bite, licking the juices from his fingers and staring up at him with pure worship in her eyes.

But she hadn't looked at him that way for a very long time.

A soft tap at the door had him setting the memories aside. He focused on what Chicklet had said.

"She needs you."

Oriana didn't. Not anymore. But Chicklet was right. He needed someone who did.

Lowering into the armchair, he rested his ankle on his knee, smoothing down the lapels of the black suit he'd kept on after the last photo shoot. He'd never scened with Oriana wearing anything but jeans or leather, and every detail that made what he was doing now different gave him strength. Put him in the mind-set required to train a new sub. He became hyperaware of his surroundings. He'd be just as aware of the slightest cue from her.

"Come in, Akira." A half-smile crossed his lips as he spoke, his tone level, giving her no way to anticipate what she was getting into. A little uncertainty would be good for her. He kept the smile in place as she stepped into the room, but his tone hardened slightly as he checked his watch. "You're late."

Chapter Fourteen

Akira's mouth went dry as she stared at Dominik, sitting in the large chair like it was a throne for a king, not quite relaxed, but at ease in a way that made her a little nervous. She wasn't so much afraid of him as she was wondering how she could please him. How she could make up for losing track of the time while chatting with Jami on the phone, all gushy about the opportunity to *be* with one of the Cobras. One that she'd admired for years, who she loved watching on the ice. She'd never been all fangirly about him—actually, the man she'd crushed on had been Max—but she had idolized him. And seeing him as a Dom was more than a little intimidating.

Seeing him as *her* Dom stole her ability to speak.

"Relax, pet. I'm not angry." He pushed off the chair and came toward her, shaking his head when she opened her mouth. "Don't talk. Just let me look at you for a moment."

Pressing her lips together, she shivered under his slow scrutiny as he circled her, resisting the urge to fidget with the pale blue silk scarf Jami had given her to go with her simple, cap-sleeved white dress. She doubted Dominik would mistake the reason for the scarf.

He smiled, fingering the scarf as he stopped by her side. "Very pretty. Jami's?"

She swallowed, nodding quickly.

"Presumptuous brat." He didn't clarify, so she wasn't sure if he meant her or Jami. Instead, he removed the scarf and stepped back to let it flutter to the armchair he'd been sitting in. "I suppose you've been discussing what you're ready for with her?" His brow rose when she nodded again. "I expect you to vocalize answers, pet. Do you really consider yourself ready for bondage after your reaction to it at the club?"

Her cheeks heated, and she stared at his shiny black shoes as she spoke. "I wasn't ready for it with Shawn. Not even that little taste. But with you . . ." She took a deep breath as he tipped her chin up to look into her eyes. "I think it would be okay with you."

"Good girl." His eyes warmed, and she felt that warmth straight down to her core. But she wasn't sure what she'd done right until he spoke again. "I'm glad you said 'you think' it would be okay. I don't want you putting too much pressure on yourself. Neither of us knows for sure how you will react to restraints—or anything else, for that matter. A bad reaction isn't a reason to give up. It simply means we'll need to try a different approach." He held out his arm toward the table set up with fondue that already smelled mouthwatering. "We'll discuss it while we eat."

She hadn't been sure how much submission he'd expect for their first time—would she been kneeling at his feet to eat? He didn't leave her wondering long. Drawing her close to the table with a loose grip on her wrist, he pulled out a chair, waited until she sat, then settled into the chair across the table. He motioned for her to get started, putting a few pieces of meat and vegetables in to cook without another word. She did the same, then occupied herself by unwrapping her cutlery from the crisp white napkin, setting the napkin on her lap, straightening her fork, knife, and spoon, smoothing the wrinkles from her napkin—

"Don't fidget, Akira." His lips twitched when she froze. "You're worrying about what I expect from you, aren't you? I haven't given you any instructions, haven't done any of the things Masters do in the books you read, and you're not sure what to make of it. Tell me if I'm wrong."

"You're not." She blinked at his expectant look, then ducked her head. Too obvious. "I'm sorry, Sir. You're not wrong, Sir. I'm not sure if there's something I should be doing."

"Don't worry, I'll let you know." He winked at her, folding his forearms on the table. "All I want from you now is complete honesty. We'll have a little chat while we eat, okay?"

A chat? She inhaled, holding it in as she prepared for what would no doubt be some hard questions. He'd probably need to know all about what had happened to her. And verbally ripping open all those old scars wouldn't leave her much in the mood for any kind of scene. But maybe he didn't intend to have a scene with her tonight. *Which would really suck.* Maybe she'd gotten all worked up for nothing. She bit back a sigh. "I'm ready."

"I can see that." He chuckled. "When did you have your last

orgasm, pet?"

Her eyes widened. "My last—but I haven't . . ." She wet her lips, sure her cheeks must be glowing neon red. She dropped her gaze to the table, then snapped it back up when he cleared his throat.

"Eyes on me when you answer my questions. You were saying?"

"Never." She had to fight the temptation to look away as she considered how close she'd come while reading. Having an orgasm seemed so easy in all those books, and she'd been aroused, but for some reason she could only reach the brink before her blood ran cold and imagining one of those fantasy Doms touching her brought back horrible flashes of her rape. Her jaw hardened. She wouldn't let that happen with Dominik. "I've never had an orgasm."

"Your mind was going a mile a minute while you thought about your answer, wasn't it?" He reached across the table and took her hand, turning it to stroke over the pulse on her wrist with his thumb. "Do you know what stopped you?"

"Yes." Her eyes teared, and she pushed her chair away from the table. *Fuck, this isn't going to work.* But she needed to tell him—even if he'd be disgusted with her after. "I almost . . . when those men . . . there was a moment when it stopped hurting. I think the man knew I was going to—he pulled out and slapped me. Called me a whore." She choked back a sob. "I believed him and it didn't happen again when the other man got on top of me. He tried though. He touched me and went slow, laughing at me, telling me he knew how much I wanted it." Wrapping her arms around her ribs, she tipped her head back, blinking fast. "I believed him. I must have done something to make them think—"

"Oh, baby." Dominik came to her, kneeling in front of her and pulling her into his arms. "You know that's not true. How your body reacted had nothing to do with you wanting what they did to you. I would cut those guys' balls off if I ever met them."

She let out a watery giggle as her tears soaked the shoulder of his suit jacket. "I can so see you doing that."

He held her a bit longer, then eased her back and kissed her cheek, close to the edges of her lips. "I didn't want to bring out bad memories tonight, but it was inevitable. This is something that we can deal with together. You've had therapy, yes?"

She sniffled, whispering "thank you" when he passed her a napkin to wipe her nose. "I did, but sometimes I wonder if it really helped. There were some things I couldn't tell the therapist about."

"Like?"

"Like the books I read." She rubbed her eyes with her fists. "It helps talking to Jami though. And you."

"Good. That's a very good start." He helped her move her chair back to the table. "But there are things I can help you with that Jami can't. Starting with all that guilt." He went to his chair and pulled his meat and veggies out of the fondue pot—probably overdone by now. He watched her as she placed her cooked food on her plate. "Tell me one thing now, Akira. Do you want to do a scene with me tonight, or would you rather spend some time getting to know one another better?"

A grin stole to her lips before she could stop it. If he was giving her a choice, the answer was obvious. "I'm not sure, Sir. I'd be okay being your shoulder if you want to talk about Oriana, but otherwise—"

"None of that." His eyes took on a far-off look for a split second, his smile fading. But it returned before she had a chance to be concerned. "I've been looking forward to tonight mostly because there are things I can do to you that won't leave much room to dwell on the past. For either of us."

"I like that idea."

"All right then." He put a few more fondue forks in the pot, a wicked gleam in his eyes. "Eat up. You'll need your energy."

* * * *

A soft, warm breeze rose up from the ocean as Zach strolled across the deck. Fairy lights hung from the riggings, lighting up the night for the small crowd. His lips curved slightly as he watched Scott and Carter playing a shuffleboard-inspired drinking game, both laughing in a way that made it obvious they'd been going at it for a while. Across the wide open space at the front of the ship, loud music boomed and the Ice Girls danced provocatively for the cameras. Several players watched them from lounge chairs, chatting over beers and shaking their heads when the girls called for them to join the fun. Most of his teammates had been in the gym with him on and off throughout the day, doing what they could to keep in shape, knowing there wasn't much time left before training camp. None of them wanted to go home and be accused of slacking off by the men who hadn't come on the cruise. Zach had stayed a little longer than the others, because keeping in shape wasn't his only reason for pushing his body to the limit.

He needed the burn of his muscles, the focus of doing each circuit perfectly, to distract him from how badly he wanted to drag Scott back to their room. His control had to be as finely tuned as his form to handle the other man. He hadn't lied when he'd told Scott he didn't want him as a sub, but he had to test Scott's restraint before he let him anywhere near Becky.

Folding his arms over his chest, he leaned against the wall, pleased to see Scott wasn't eyeing the Ice Girls, or Carter, in his usual assessing way. So far, it seemed like he was following Zach's instructions. Having fun. Within reason.

"One sec, man. Gotta take this!" Carter shouted, pulling his phone from the pocket of his cargo shorts. He moved over to the railing, speaking loud to be heard over the music. "Hey, Seb! Fuck, I wish you were here. I swear I've gone blind from the cameras flashing. What? Yes, Sir! Being a goddamn saint!" Carter's laughter cut short. He worried his bottom lip with his teeth. "Sorry, Sir. Not being sarcastic. I'm chilling with Demyan—we're playing shuffleboard. He fucking sucks!" A blotchy red blush spread across his cheeks. "No way! Don't care how drunk I am, I wouldn't... umm, maybe a little tipsy? But still." He nodded and spoke quietly. His features softened and his voice rose again. "Hey, boo! You taking care of my dog? He did what? Aww!" He grinned. "That's my boy. Give Bear a cookie for me and tell him Daddy misses him. 'Course I miss you too." He cocked his head, looked around, then frowned. "I don't see her. Yeah, I'll have her call you."

After Carter hung up, Scott went to him and handed him a beer. He nodded, sympathy in his eyes as Carter rested his arms on the railing, probably telling Scott how much he missed Jami and Ramos. For some reason, seeing Scott with Carter, being a good friend, made

Zach smile. Scott was a decent person when he wasn't cheapening everything he did with sex.

But it seemed like a bad habit. Something Scott went back to when he wasn't sure how to deal with a situation. Almost like it took an effort to avoid turning every relationship into a pure, carnal release.

Why though? The Dom in Zach couldn't help but feel this was something he could fix. Even if he and Scott never went past friendship, he wanted to know what had happened to Scott to make him consider sex an answer to everything. Zach knew Carter had once had issues with relationships. As a young player, he'd been with too many women who wanted him for either money or just to put a notch on their lipstick case. To say they'd "done" a pro athlete. The scars on his face made him even more insecure about why anyone would want him. But Ramos had gotten him past that—so had Jami.

Scott had no scars. No obvious ones anyway. And yet . . . the ones beneath the skin could be the most damaging.

The DJ playing music for the dancing Ice Girls lowered the volume as Sahara called out for their attention. Smiling, she wiped sweat from her brow and drained her beer. "All right, ladies! We've got an early start tomorrow going through our routines. Time to turn in!"

A redhead stepped forward, making a sharp motion with her arm before any of the girls could move. "Who put you in charge? Akira and I are the team leaders. Everyone knows you're just here because your team didn't want you anymore."

"Amy, if you have a problem with me, we'll discuss it privately." Sahara's chin jutted up. "Akira isn't here. I'm telling you, from experience, that you don't want your girls showing up tired and hungover to perform in the morning."

"Screw your 'experience.'" Amy stepped up to her, sneering. "You didn't cover up those bruises very well. You want people to feel sorry for you, don't you?" A cruel smile made her freckled face ugly. "They wouldn't if they knew the truth."

Sahara went still. The color left her cheeks. "The truth? What are you talking about?"

"Your boyfriend found out you were fucking Keane. That's why he hit you. And as far as I'm concerned, you deserved it."

A gasp came from all the girls. Most skirted away from Amy—as though they were afraid to be tainted by her harsh words. Amy seemed to realize, too late, that she'd gone too far. The cameras were rolling, and she'd exposed herself as the bitch she was. Zach straightened as Sahara's shaky hand rose to her throat. She shook her head. Her eyes hardened.

Her fist caught Amy in the chin, knocking her right off her feet. Amy screeched and bounced back up, going for Sahara's face with her nails. Scott and Carter lunged forward to separate the girls. Zach found himself holding Amy after Carter bodily handed her over. The woman was squirming and hissing, and her claw-like nails raked down Zach's cheek. He gritted his teeth against the sting as Pischlar stepped up to help him hold her. Coach's wife, Madeline—who'd come to supervise the Ice Girls—came over and took a firm hold on Amy's shoulder.

"That's enough." She snapped, nodding to Scott as he led Sahara away. She gave Amy a hard look. "The team won't tolerate this kind of behavior. Go to your room. I'm going to suggest you be left off at the next port and sent home."

"Are you fucking kidding me? She hit me first!" Amy shoved away from Zach and Pischlar. "If she's getting away with this—"

"She won't be." Madeline snapped. "I won't say it again. Go. To. Your. Room!"

After the redheaded bitch stormed off, Zach faced Madeline, careful to keep his tone level. "You heard what she said. Sahara shouldn't be punished for—"

"The rules for the cruise are clear, Mr. Pearce. The same goes for the men." Madeline sighed. "But, like with the men, getting kicked off the cruise doesn't change your contracts. Amy will still have a chance to compete for a spot with the Ice Girls. Fortunately, this also means Sahara will still be with the team. And her place is guaranteed. I believe Amy has just lost whatever support she had."

"Well, that's something I guess." Zach inclined his head as Madeline excused herself and went to deal with the other girls. He went inside, finding the hall where all the Ice Girls roomed. He wasn't sure how Scott would handle Sahara—or if he'd really blame him if the girl needed comforting that would last the night. For some reason, he was more concerned with what it would do to Scott to offer that kind of comfort. There were times when it seemed like Scott felt he could give nothing else.

Moments later, Scott came out, looking tired, black mascara streaks on his bare chest. He rubbed his face, stopping short when he spotted Zach.

"I didn't—"

"I know." Zach put his arm over Scott's shoulders, giving him a firm hug. He eased back, studying Scott's face, the taut lines around his white lips. The shadows in his eyes. It was almost as though the verbal attack on Sahara had triggered something for him, something more than him just being angry on behalf of a friend. But a direct approach wouldn't work with Scott. So Zach focused on the young woman. "How is she?"

"As good as can be expected, I guess. She's tougher than she looks, but what happened is still so fresh . . . I think part of her believes that skank is right."

"Sahara cheated on her boyfriend with Keane?" Not that it mattered. There was no excuse for hitting a woman. Not even infidelity. Then again, he really couldn't see Keane fooling around with the girl. Especially while offering her a position with the team. The man was too professional to blur those particular lines.

"No way. I think Keane suspected her boyfriend was roughing her up—it might have prompted him to make her a better offer . . . she really doesn't seem like his type." Scott shrugged. "Either way, just wait until I catch Higgins on the ice. He's gonna need fucking dentures."

Zach smiled and shook his head. This bloodthirsty side of Scott was damn sexy. His pulse quickened as he pictured Scott, dropping his gloves, fire in his eyes as he spotted Higgins, all that energy going to making the loser pay for raising his hand to a woman Scott cared about.

He sucked in air through his teeth, moving forward and fisting his hand in Scott's hair as he slammed their lips together. He held Scott against the wall, gentling the kiss as he explored Scott's hot mouth with his tongue, groaning as Scott pulled him closer.

"Get a room, boys." The sharp sting of Tim's slap on Zach's back cleared his brain of the lust-filled haze. He reluctantly released Scott, knowing Tim was just looking out for him. Tim glanced up and down the hall, tone low. "I hate doing this, but people think Scott's with Sahara. His rep can't take the controversy right now."

No, it can't. And I know better. Zach let his hands fall to his sides, wondering where his brain had gone. Pretty damn far for him to risk Scott's career for a kiss.

Scott eased away from Zach, rolling his shoulders, and nodding slowly. "My own fault. Sorry, Coach."

"Nothing to be sorry about, kid," Tim said, smiling. "Just use some discretion. What you do in your room is no one's business." He winked. "It's not an accident that you two are sharing a room. I know my players."

Well, fuck.

"Really?" A blush spread across Scott's cheeks. "Hell, I thought I *had* been discreet!"

"You?" Tim's brow rose. "Not sure you're capable." He turned to Zach. "But you are. I know why you 'came out,' and I think it was pretty damn decent." His hand curved around Scott's shoulder in a supportive gesture. "Keep this one in line. I don't want to lose him."

Coach might know his players, but he was mistaken if he thought Zach could set Scott straight unless it was something he really wanted. And that remained to be seen. Tim probably thought Zach could take on the same role with Scott as Ramos had with Carter. Their coach was an experienced switch, yet, maybe his time in the lifestyle with his wife had him seeing Doms and subs everywhere. Scott might enjoy a bit of kink, but the firm hand of a Dom would make him balk.

Zach had other ways to handle him though, if it came to that.

More like when *it comes to that.*

Tim didn't need details though, so Zach simply inclined his head. "I'll do my best, Coach."

They left the coach in the hall and went to their room in silence. Scott closed and locked the door. His face was flushed, his half-smile provocative. He obviously expected them to continue where they'd left off.

Kneeling by his suitcase, Zach pulled out his pack of cigars, then went to the bar for a bottle of Crown Royal. He poured some into a tumbler, bringing the drink and his cigar out to the balcony. He settled in a chair, putting his whiskey on the small glass table. Resting his ankle on his knee, he eyed Scott, who had followed him, as he flicked his lighter.

"Something on your mind?"

Scott's brow furrowed. He shoved his hands into the pockets of his shorts. "You're playing, right?"

Taking a long drag of his cigar, he let the sweet smoke out languorously. "What makes you think that?"

A flare of temper flashed in Scott's eyes. "You know why. The way you kissed me—"

"It's something lovers do, Scott."

"Are we lovers or not?" Scott raked his fingers through his hair, then sat hard in the chair across the table. "I'm fucking confused."

"There's nothing to be confused about." Zach took another drag, resisting the urge to smirk at Scott's frustration. Scott might not be a sub, but keeping him guessing, anticipating the next move, satisfied Zach's needs as a Dom. "Consider this foreplay."

* * * *

Akira giggled as Dominik held the chocolate-covered strawberry to her lips, then pulled it away before she could take a bite. Dinner had been nice and relaxed after their first "chat," conversation revolving around the Ice Girl competition and the game. She enjoyed spending time with him, just like this, both of them knowing what they had wasn't serious. She wasn't afraid or overwhelmed with him. All she had to do was trust him to give her what she needed.

Which was a lot easier than she'd thought it would be.

"Stand up, pet." Dominik grinned as he teased her lips with the white chocolate-dipped tip of the strawberry, bringing it out of reach as she snapped at it with her teeth. "I'd like to try something."

As she rose from the chair, he rewarded her with a mouthful of the decadently rich chocolate, his lips twitching at her little moan. The fresh sweetness of the fruit burst in her mouth. She let her eyes drift shut to turn all her senses to the flavor and texture. He glazed her lips with the slick juices, curving his hand along her jaw to tip her head up. Tasting her lips with the tip of his tongue, he moved closer, holding her still as he kissed her.

She whimpered as sensations assaulted her. The heat of his mouth, the tingling of her nerves awaking under her skin as she pressed against him. So very nice. Such a surprisingly normal reaction.

"More." She latched on to his shirt before he could shift away, her lips parted. "Please . . ."

"Soon, little one." He fed her the last bite of the strawberry, then brought his hands to her shoulders, slipping one down her back to the zipper of her dress. "You will tell me if I do anything you're not comfortable with. Use 'red' if you'd like, but any protest will do."

The searing liquid pooling in her core had her squirming as he unzipped her dress and peeled it down her body. She bit her lip as she opened her eyes and caught him watching her. Her cheeks heated and she brought her hands up to cover her breasts, feeling more exposed in her bikini with just him than she had on deck in front of half of the team.

"Don't hide from me, Akira. This beautiful body is mine for the time being." He moved around her, sweeping her hair over one shoulder. He kissed the nape of her neck and she shivered. His lips slid up her throat. His hot breath caressed her ear as he spoke. "I'd like to see what I have to play with."

All of me. Whatever you want. Her lips moved, but he came in front of her and pressed a finger to her lips.

"Not a word unless you need me to slow down." His other hand framed her jaw. "Do you?"

She shook her head.

"That's my girl." His smile broadened and she found herself staring into his eyes, entranced by the gold flecks in the dark brown depths. "Such a sweet little sub." He gave her a light kiss, then caught her bottom lip between his teeth. The slight pressure made her knees shake, and when he deepened the kiss she wasn't sure her legs would hold her anymore. He brought one hand to the small of her back, then pressed something into her palm. "Roll the dice, pet.

Let's see how much you'll owe me tonight."

Owe him? She blinked as she lifted her hand. What would the numbers mean? Should she ask?

But no. He would explain when the time came. Besides, following his instructions kept things so simple. There was no need to worry, to think. All she had to do was let him lead the way.

She rolled the dice onto a bare spot on the table.

"Three. I like that." He chuckled when she stared at him. "With a bigger number, I may have taken pity and saved a few for another time."

"Saved what?" The words escaped before she could stop them. She couldn't help it. The curiosity was killing her!

"You'll see." He smiled in a way that let her know he'd forgive her little slip. He took hold of her wrist and drew her toward the armchair. Sat with his thighs spread. "Lace your fingers behind your neck and sit on my lap."

Swallowing, she laced her fingers behind her neck. But she couldn't go any farther. Not because she was scared, it was just . . .

"What was that thought, pet?"

More than a little embarrassed, she couldn't stop the automatic answer that spilled out. "You told me not to talk."

His lips thinned slightly, and for a split second she wondered if he'd pull her over his lap and spank her. Actually, she kinda hoped he would.

Instead, he shook his head. "Cheeky. I'm happy you're feeling comfortable enough to show a bit of spunk, but now's not the time for that."

"Are you going to punish me?"

Brow arched, he studied her face. "We haven't discussed using punishment in your training yet, but if we do, I promise you, you won't enjoy it as much as you probably think you will. But that's a discussion for later. Tell me why you hesitated."

Wrinkling her nose, she jutted her chin toward his thighs. "I've never sat in a man's lap before. It seems like something—I don't know . . . like something a little girl does with her daddy or Santa Claus."

She really, really appreciated the obvious effort he made not to laugh. "Will it make you feel like a naughty little girl to sit in my lap and let me touch you?"

Well, if he put it that way . . . she clenched her thighs, wondering if her arousal would soak right through his pants. It wouldn't take long for him to find out exactly what he was doing to her. "Isn't that a little dirty? Being turned on while being treated like a child?"

He shook his head. "You're not a child, Akira. And there's nothing wrong with anything you feel. Does my touching you make me a dirty old man?"

"No! You're not that old!"

"I'm in my thirties, pet."

That gave her a little thrill. She knew how old he was, but somehow, the way he said it made her feel young and vulnerable. And yes, a little naughty. She tongued her bottom lip as she perched on the edge of his knee, fluttering her lashes with exaggerated innocence. "I'm okay with you taking advantage of me, Sir."

He threw his head back and let out a deep, rumbling laugh that echoed provocatively deep inside her. Even better, any trace of sadness that remained in his eyes was gone. He gave her a one-armed hug as he caught his breath. "You are too precious."

"Why, thank you, Sir." She wiggled closer to him, resting her head on his chest. "You're happy."

"I am. You have no idea how heady it is that you trust me enough to let me see this side of you."

"There's no one else I'd rather let see it. Being with you . . ." She smiled as he stroked her hair. "I'm safe. I feel like I'm going to be okay."

"Good. Because you will be." He leaned her back against his arm, kissing her in a way that left her so wound up she forgot where her hands were supposed to be. Her nails dug into his shoulders as he claimed her mouth, and the muscles in her stomach jumped as he splayed his fingers over her bare belly. "Damn, you're soft."

A throaty gasp escaped her as his hand skimmed lower and his fingers traced the edge of her bikini bottoms. She shifted her hips, trying to show him she was ready for him to touch her anywhere. Everywhere.

Instead, he pulled one of her hands down from behind him,

whispering. "Since you didn't keep your hands where I told you to, you can help me."

He brought her hand to her bikini top, curling her fingers around the edge to expose one breast. Then he lowered his mouth, flicking her nipple with his tongue. An electric jolt zipped straight down to her clit, sizzling along a taut line of current as he sucked and teased the sensitive flesh with his teeth. He guided her other hand down her belly, slipping it under the golden material so the tips of her fingers touched her moist folds.

"So fucking wet. Can you feel it?" His tone was gruff, his lips sliding over her breast as he spoke. "You smell delicious. I'll need to taste you soon."

"Ah!" She dropped her head back on his arm as he made her fingers press against her clit, then down to her slit. Her own finger pushed against her entrance and his dipped in past it, filling her. "Sir, that feels . . ."

"Feels like what, Akira? Say it." He sucked her nipple into his mouth, thrusting his finger in deep. Something inside her shattered. Her core undulated, so close to the brink . . . but that pressure inside her—

"You fucking whore. I knew it. This was so easy because you wanted it all along."

"No!" She clamped her thighs together, struggling against the hands that held her down, shoving at a hard chest. She didn't want this! She'd fought them so hard, but they wouldn't stop. And her body had betrayed her.

"Look. At. Me." Dominik moved the arm holding her up, curving his hand around the back of her neck, his other hand still holding hers against her pussy, his finger still inside her, though it had gone still. His tone was gentle, but his eyes hard as he trapped her gaze with his. "Who is touching you? Who are you responding to?"

"You!" she sobbed, wishing the other voices would go away. "You, Sir! But they—"

"They can't have you, pet. You belong to me." His palm against the back of her hand put more pressure on her clit. The tip of a second finger, *his* finger, joined the first, stretching her. "Tell me how it feels. How *you* feel."

"Slippery. Full." She shifted restlessly, needing to find that place again, that place where the sensations overruled everything. But to answer him? "Afraid that I can't . . ."

"Do you know why you're so slippery, little one?" His cheek pressed to hers, his hot breath caressed her throat, her ear. The steady glide of his fingers slowed. He curved them slightly, finding a sweet spot within that made her eyes wide and her hips rise in jerky little motions. He smiled. "Because it's my fingers inside you. It will be my mouth on you. My dick inside you. And you want it all."

Her screams scored her throat as she thrashed under the fierce onslaught of pleasure. The fiery ripples within went on and on as he dragged his fingers in and out of her. Her mind went blank, and the faces of those men were like chalk on a sidewalk under a downpour, blurring, washing away until the water cleaned away the last traces. Not for good, but they couldn't hurt her anymore.

Dominik wouldn't let them.

She shuddered as the aftershock vibrated through her muscles, causing her to clench down sporadically on Dominik's fingers. She sobbed again with relief, burying her face under his arm. She wasn't broken or ruined. This wasn't wrong.

It was . . . perfect.

"One more," Dominik whispered against her cheek before bringing his teeth to her throat. "One more and I'll let you rest before you give me the last."

The slow, even thrusts of his fingers made her twitch as all the hypersensitive nerves sparked, but his soft, erotic whispers drew her up again. A hard, deep thrust and she came apart, shaking as he stroked the spot inside her that set her off like a stick of dynamite. This orgasm was merciless, tearing through her with crashing waves of pleasure, draining every last bit of strength from her body until she could do nothing but curl up in his arms, quivering and crying, her tears feeling like a balm over everything that had been ripped open within. She clung to Dominik as he withdrew his fingers and gathered her in his arms to carry her to his bed.

Her voice sounded funny when she finally managed to speak again, small, raspy, but clear enough. She hoped he could hear her.

"Thank you, Sir. What you did . . ."

"I know, baby." He pressed her head against his chest, holding her close as he pulled the blankets over them both. "You did it for me too."

Chapter Fifteen

The weather was absolutely perfect on the third day of the cruise—even better than the first with the sun blazing down from a cloud-free sky. But it might as well have been pissing rain. Scott frowned as he hauled Sahara's suitcases up to the deck, squinting against the glaring sun. And the flashing lights from the cameras. He'd slept well, despite the continuing uncertainty of what was gonna happen with him and Zach, yet, waking and knowing today was the day that Sahara was going to be unloaded in Manhattan—at least she had family in New York—made him feel like a failure. He was supposed to be her friend. He should have been able to do *something* to prevent her being kicked off the boat. This whole thing felt like being hauled to the sin bin after some asshole put on a medal-worthy diving performance.

"Demyan, does it bother you that your girlfriend is leaving? Or does this give you the opportunity to sample the rest of the girls?"

Scott scowled at the reporter. Not one of those invited on the cruise. Scum seeping up from New York, looking for a story. He ground his teeth, dropping Sahara's luggage at his feet. "No comment."

"Higgins has made public statements about how Sahara procured a contract with the Dartmouth Cobra Ice Girls. Would you care to comment about that?"

The next reporter was a woman. The sharp edge to her tone grated at him. As a woman, shouldn't she be at least a little sympathetic? Pictures of Sahara without makeup concealing her fading bruises had gone viral the night before. Rumors about the kinky tendencies of the Cobras had a lot of people speculating that Sahara just liked it rough. A photo of Higgins dragging her out of a club had surfaced as well, but no one seemed to care how obvious it was that she'd been trying to get away from him. Everyone figured it was "a scene." And *everyone* had read all those mainstream erotic books and considered themselves experts. As far as they were concerned, Sahara was a sub, acting out. One couldn't show interest in BDSM, then claim abuse.

Worst thing was, Sahara hadn't said anything about wanting to be in the lifestyle. But if she was involved with the Cobras, she must want it. And she'd get no pity from the outside world.

Scott knew better than to air any of his personal feelings. Nothing he could say would help her anyway. So he stood up straight and glared at the cameras. "No comment."

When Sahara came to his side, his stiff countenance faltered. She looked so broken he didn't hesitate to take her into his arms and kiss her cheeks, whispering things he hoped would make her feel a little better. Starting with "I'm going to bust that asshole's sac."

She giggled and patted his cheek. "Stay out of trouble. I'm heading home tomorrow. I'll water the plants."

We have plants? He grinned at her and cuffed her chin lightly with his fist. Swallowing was a bit hard. This wasn't fair. "Don't leave your panties all over my floor. And do some laundry. Only fair that you clean up since you've been borrowing my shirts to sleep in."

"I can't help it! I love smelling your cologne as I drift off."

"Aww." All the uninvited leeches had taken off. They had to put on a show for the ones here to make them look good. He could do that. "Leave me something of yours that smells like that spicy perfume you wore that time . . ."

Sahara opened her suitcase and fetched a tiny T-shirt and squirted some perfume on it before handing it over. The feigned moment they had was spoiled by the way her face crumpled when she saw Akira. "Oh, sweetie. I'm so sorry! I didn't mean to leave you like this."

Akira braved a smile, glancing back at Dominik, who stood close enough to offer support, but not close enough for the reporters to make anything of it. "I'll be okay. Take care of you, got it?"

"I will." Sahara squared her shoulders, then moved into Scott, hugging him tight. She spoke low, her lips close to his ear. "You're doing good. People are impressed. Don't screw it up."

"I won't." He let her go, happy to see that Zach was lingering at the edges of the crowd, watching him in that way he did, like he knew Scott would trip up and needed his presence to resist the urge to let it all out.

"Are you upset that she's leaving?" One of *their* reporters asked quietly. One that couldn't be ignored.

"I am. But we both understand the rules," Scott said, hoping they'd leave it at that.

Of course, they didn't. "Do you agree that Sahara asked for the treatment she had from Grant Higgins, as was implied?"

"Are you fucking kidding me? What kind of idiot would ask a question like that?" He bared his teeth as he felt a tug from behind.

Carter, shaking his head and saying something like "Don't." Don't what? Make these assholes see that they were making it okay for a woman to be abused because she might be into something different? When was it ever okay? Why shouldn't he make that fucking clear?

"I'd like for that comment to be erased from record and for Mr. Demyan to be given a chance to rephrase his answer." Another suit stepped forward, his voice familiar—Scott was too irritated to do more than give him a scathing look.

Like hell I'll "rephrase." Fuck them all.

But . . . when had Ford gotten there? He acknowledged the man with a nod, wincing as he registered the shock on Akira's face. Mason lunged forward, catching Akira before she could spit whatever harsh words came to her at the sight of Ford in front of the cameras.

"I'm afraid we can't do that." The reporter turned away from Ford, stiffening as Ford stepped up to his side, speaking low. He paled, then nodded, returning to shove his microphone in Scott's face. "You were saying?"

The sound of his breath hissing through his teeth was enhanced by the mike. He met Zach's eyes, caught his short nod of encouragement. And knew what he had to do. Licking his lips, he let his hands fall to his sides, doing his best to take the aggression out of his stance. "When I was a kid, one of my foster sisters was abused by her boyfriend. No matter how bad he hurt her, she always went back to him. Defended him." He held his breath until the sharp stab of regret in his chest dwindled to a dull ache. Shook his head. "She thought she asked for it, but she was wrong. I guess I learned at a young age how wrong it was—and I also learned how easy it could be to think you deserved whatever you got. The way I see it, Sahara found the strength to get out. She realized she deserved to be treated with respect, and she's a good example for all the women out there who still don't believe they deserve the same."

"Are you saying Sahara isn't into 'kink'?"

Scott snorted, cocking his head slightly as he looked the rat-faced little man over. "I think you need to educate yourself about what 'kink' consists of. And I'm not about to discuss Sahara's sex life. Past or present. It's not relevant."

"But—"

"That's enough for now," Ford said, drawing the attention away from Scott. His dark blue suit gave him a professional air, and even though he didn't have any real power, the media hounds hadn't forgotten how well-connected he was as a member of the Delgado family. "My sister's vision for this show didn't include a lecture on BDSM—but I doubt she'd have a problem with some provocative interviews with the girls." He pulled a folded piece of paper from his inner suit pocket, one dark brow lifting as he flicked it open. "Actually, I have a question for the lot of you. Did you plagiarize these questions from *Penthouse* magazine? They look familiar."

The reporters laughed and trailed after Ford to where the Ice Girls were playing in the pool again. Footage for the stupid show was gonna be repetitive. Did they really need to be stuck on the ship for a week for a four-hour special? The fans were gonna be bored out of their minds.

"You did good, Scott." Coach Tim came up from behind Scott, squeezing his shoulder and grinning as Zach joined them. "Might want to take some tips from this man, though. I think the press has given up on him with his short, emotionless replies to every single question."

"I hear you. The guys are starting to call him 'The Droid.'" Scott smirked at Zach's surprised look. "Sorry, pal—hard to tell if you're human sometimes."

"Really?" Zach rested his shoulder against the wall, his gaze going over Scott slowly. "Did you come up with that?"

It was hard to tell if Zach was insulted or just . . . looking to prove otherwise. Scott cleared his throat as the crotch to his jeans tightened around his swelling dick. He was more than willing to let

Zach show him how hot-blooded he really was. "Carter came up with it—before you helped him out though." He scratched his jaw as Carter stopped short right behind Tim. "It was a joke."

"Don't take it wrong, man." Carter combed his messy blond hair away from his brow with his fingers, talking fast. "It's like . . . like a compliment, you know? When the cameras are on you, when you're on the ice—nothing shakes you. I wish I could be like that."

"I'm not taking it personally, Carter. Don't worry." Zach held up a finger as his phone buzzed and pulled it out. His tone gentled as he answered, and Scott heard him say "Becky" before he moved out of hearing.

Carter hooked his thumbs to the belt loops of his shorts, rocking his bare feet on the gleaming wood deck. "He serious? He ain't mad?"

"He ain't mad." Scott laughed and ruffled Carter's hair. "Kid, that man is as straightforward as they come. He's cold and hard when he needs to be, but then . . ." The edges of his lips tipped upward. Zach had mellowed out a lot since he'd gotten with Becky. She brought out the best in the man. And he had a feeling Zach did the same for her. Her sharp little barbs didn't come quite as fast when she talked to Scott, and, unless he was wrong, she was kinda warming to him. The only problem was they never really hung out or talked without Zach around. He was getting plenty of opportunities to get closer to Zach, but none with her.

Maybe it was about time he changed that.

****

"What are you wearing?"

Zach laughed, finding his way to his room for some privacy since Becky seemed to be in a teasing mood. "Swim trunks. You'll be going through a lot of poolside footage from the cruise."

"Mmm, I know. Some of the photos have made it to the fan site." She purred provocatively into the phone. "You look good, Sir."

"Have you been enjoying yourself at night, thinking about me?"

She paused, and he could hear the composure fade from her tone as she replied. "Yes . . . I swear, I bit through my pillow last night to keep from screaming. I'm not sure how thick these walls are."

"What were you doing to yourself, pet?"

A little moan escaped her. "I guess you want details?"

"Naturally." He let out a throaty chuckle, recalling the way she shivered in response to it the last time they were together, hoping it would give her the same reaction now. "Your body, your pleasure, belongs to me. I must know how you're handling it when I'm not around."

"Oh, must you?" Her tone turned cheeky. He could almost see the mischievous glint in her eyes as she tested the limits he couldn't enforce over the phone. "What if I don't feel like sharing?"

This playful, naughty side of her did something to him, something he couldn't quite describe. As much as he loved the purity of her submission during a scene, he enjoyed a little push and pull. He didn't need her trying to be the perfect sub all the time. He needed all of her, before, during, and after, shining through her surrender.

"I believe you need a firm hand to remind you how to behave," he said, voice stern, but not to the point that she'd think he was angry. "Since I can't do much from here, how about we agree that you save your orgasms for when I get back."

"*What?*" She let out an aggravated sound. "That's not fair. Why can you—"

"I won't be, Becky."

"You're going to tell me Scott can't get you off?"

"When I'll allow nothing more than a kiss?" He smirked. "I haven't been that easy since I was a teenager, love."

"Ugh, but I told you to fuck him and—" She stopped herself before he had to, likely knowing she'd gone too far. "I mean—"

He let out a heavy sigh. "Enough. I think I've made it clear that I don't want that kind of relationship. With you or with him. It'll be hard for him to see sex as anything but a release—I'm not sure why, but—"

"Maybe that's because, sometimes, that's all it is." All the fun, all the playfulness, had gone out of her voice. She'd become all business, become a woman he couldn't deal with as a sub, erecting cement walls between them. "You fucked him once, no strings attached. Why can't you just do that again?"

"Because he needs more."

"I think you're wrong." She hesitated, then barreled on as though to make sure she had a chance to get it all out. "I hope you're not, but I can't help feeling it will be so much worse if you're looking for something serious from him. Can't we all just enjoy each other? Let the cards fall where they will?"

"Do you mean Scott, or do you mean you and I?" He could be wrong, but it seemed like she was pulling away from him. Which was why he hadn't wanted to touch this thing with Scott in the first place.

But she was as insistent as ever. "No! I love you. I'm not afraid to lose you to him anymore."

"Good. Because you won't."

"I know that." She made an unhappy sound. "I'm sorry I ruined things, Sir. It would have been more pleasant to talk about how I used my rabbit, pretending it was your nice big cock as I came again and again and—"

He barked out a laugh. "You are a cruel, cruel woman, Becky." He lowered his voice, adjusting his shorts, taking a few deep breaths to regain control. "The restrictions stand. You will wait for me."

"I'm not sure I'm comfortable with that, Sir," she said sweetly, continuing before he could speak. "Unless I know you're getting what you need."

"A disobedient sub is not on the list of what I need." In only two days, he would be with her again. His lips twitched as he came up with a way to make the restrictions just a bit harder. His mouthy sub would benefit from the challenge. "Do you have Ben Wa balls?"

"No . . ." Becky sounded embarrassed. She obviously knew what they were. "Why would I?"

"Their handy for strengthening the muscles you use to pleasure me," he said smoothly. "Go buy some. I want them inside you for a few hours every day. When I come back, the first time I fuck you, they will be inside you."

"While you—"

"Yes." His tone deepened as he imagined pushing into her, feeling the balls shift, stimulating them both. "Can you have someone watch Casey? I want a few hours where I have complete access to your body. So I can take you wherever—and however—I please."

"Oh God." Becky groaned. "And I'm not allowed to—"

"Nope."

"You, Sir, are a fucking sadist."

He laughed. Pouty subs not getting their own way loved to throw that label around, but most wouldn't know what to do with a real sadist if they had the misfortune to piss one off. "It's a shame Callahan left. Seeing a few scenes between him and Oriana would show you what a kind, gentle Master I really am."

"No, thank you. I've heard about their scenes." He could hear the shudder in her tone. "Blood makes me sick."

"I'll never make you bleed, pet." He made his voice calm and soothing. He wanted her worked up. Not afraid. "But I will enjoy making you squirm."

"Mission accomplished."

She asked a few more questions about the Ben Wa balls before they hung up, sounding a bit more eager to go shopping for them, joking about getting a few different sizes. She *had* to test them out to find the ones that "fit just right." She gave him details about how she wouldn't even need lube to slip them into her body.

Vengeful, pet. Well played.

He was satisfied with how their conversation had gone. He truly believed she understood how he would handle Scott. And how he would handle his relationship with her. For the first time, he could see how it would all balance out. It would take some work, but in the end they would all have what they needed.

They were finally on the same page.

* * * *

Insistent buzzing came from Scott's gym bag, laying on the floor next to the weight bench. He could only think of two people who'd be calling him now. Stephan, to bitch about the interview, or Becky, whom he'd texted to get back to him when she wasn't busy. He didn't want to take her away from her daughter.

"Grab that for me, will you?" He grunted, heaving the bar up to the stand, glancing back at Carter who was spotting him.

Carter nodded and bent to fetch Scott's phone. He answered, wandering off with a smirk as Scott dried his hands on his shorts. "Hey, Becky! How you doing, sexy lady?"

"Give me the fucking phone, asshole." Scott lunged at Carter, cursing again as the punk evaded him. "Come on! I'm not playing!"

"He's in a mood. You sure you don't want to talk to me instead?" Carter went still, licking his bottom lip and smiling softly. "She did? Damn, I would have loved to see that. Jami would make a great mother—I mean, not for a long time, but I know my mom would love it!" He laughed. "Yeah, don't tell Dean I said that. I'll end up playing for the Jets if he even thinks I'm gonna knock up his baby girl. Have to put a ring on her finger first . . . yeah, me and Seb have talked about it. Since my mom's doing better, we'll probably wait at least another year, but we both want it. Seb? Oh, he's fine owning us both. The papers won't change that." He blushed. "As long as we're both wearing his collar, he's happy."

Scott stopped reaching for his phone, a smile tugging at his lips as he listened to Carter spilling to Becky. The kid probably needed to talk to someone. Scott should have let him know he'd listen. Good to see the boy was happy, though.

"Fuck no. Once he puts his collar on me, it ain't comin' off for nothing. What happened with Mason and Oriana was fucking sad, but they ain't us. I'd rather be destroyed in the seventh game of the Cup finals than lose either of them. Yes, it's that serious." He cleared his throat. "Damn, Becky. Now I need to talk to Seb. Fuck, I can't wait to go home. I wish I'd stayed there." He grinned. "Sure, here you go. Give my goddaughter a kiss for me."

Taking the phone, Scott slapped Carter's shoulder, then moved over to the stationary bikes. "Hey, babe."

"Hey. I got your text—is everything all right?"

Her voice, something about her concern being aimed at him, had the ground dropping about a foot under his feet. She was probably just being nice, but maybe . . . maybe it was finally happening. Maybe she really cared.

"Everything's fine. Kinda wanted to talk to you."

"Kinda?" She let out a sweet, warm laugh that set fire to his blood. Fuck, he wanted to hold her, to tell her—but she continued. "More like testing the waters. I saw your interview and you're not in trouble. Keane and I spoke about it earlier and agreed to air it. We'd wanted to keep the whole fight between Sahara and Amy off the show, but we might be able to cut out the ugly stuff and keep the drama."

"That's good, I guess..." Scott frowned. "So this means Amy won't be exposed as the heartless cunt she is?"

"Jesus, Scott. Please don't use that word. You're better than that." She lowered her voice. "And I mean that. When I heard what you said about your foster sister... poor girl. Did she get help?"

"Yes. Eventually." Sort of. She'd gotten out of the relationship anyway. Last he'd heard, she'd been working in a strip club. That was years ago. Who knew what she was doing now? He'd lost touch with her in his early teens. His brother had given him updates until she disappeared off the grid. She was just one of the many he'd failed in his pathetic life. But Becky didn't need to hear all that. "Sahara's not in trouble though, right? You guys get why—"

"We do. Don't worry about her. As soon as she gets back, I'll be working with her on the rest of the program for the Ice Girls' final competition. She'll be taken care of." She paused. "What about you?"

His brow furrowed. "What about me?"

"Are you being 'taken care of'?" Her tone took on a slight edge. Almost like she was nervous bringing it up. "I'm sure you know Zach and I talked?"

"Yeah. Doesn't change much. I still need to show how much I've—"

"He doesn't need another sub, Scott."

"I know that."

"Do you? Because you're certainly acting like one. I saw a picture of you with him by the pool—thankfully it didn't go farther than my desk. The way you were looking at him..." She went quiet, and he heard her inhaling slowly. Then let the air out in a laugh. "With how strong you came on before, your being timid surprised me. You have the opportunity to..."

Fuck. She sounded like he'd let her down. Which was freakin' weird. Was she really that anxious for him to fuck her boyfriend? "Zach ain't into flings, Becky. You should know that better than anyone. I thought that's why you chose him over me."

"That's true. But I'll tell you the same thing I told him. It doesn't always have to be serious. I've been thinking about it a lot and . . . and not everything has to be a full-course meal. I think Zach needs a bit of a snack."

Scott pressed his lips together, inhaling slowly. Right. Well, that made sense. Zach liked dick and pussy. Why wouldn't his sub want him to have access to both while ensuring that she was the one he woke up with in the morning?

Better than nothing, I guess.

But . . . "What about you? You want a snack too?"

"This is about Zach." Her voice sounded small, and her next words made it clear why. "I shouldn't have said anything. Whatever happens while you're on the cruise is between the two of you. I guess part of me thought you were calling for more than an update on Sahara. That maybe you needed to hear from me that it's really okay."

"Yeah, that's clear. But you didn't answer my question."

"What question?"

"Not everything's got to be a full-course meal. That goes for you too, doesn't it?" Hell, if she wanted to play this way, he wasn't about to let her back off now. "Enough about him. You're talking to me. You want a snack, babe? I'll be fucking cookie dough ice cream, chips, pretzels—all your favorite junk food. I'll be your naughty indulgence. I'll be anything you want me to be."

"Damn it, Scott. Yes, it's tempting. And I might eventually . . ." She groaned. "It doesn't matter. Be that for him. He needs to stop trying to make this into something it will never be."

"You let me worry about him. All I want you thinking about is what I'm gonna do to you." His smile was feral, and he turned his back on Carter when he caught the boy watching him. "I'm gonna rock you're fucking world, beautiful. Every woman needs that at least one in their lifetime, right?"

For a really long time, she didn't answer. He wondered if he'd gone too far. He'd never really classed Becky as one of those women who just wanted a wild ride from him. His own goddamn stupidity. That's all they ever wanted. No matter how good or sweet they were, they saw right through him, saw all the things they shouldn't want, but did. And they knew he could give it to them.

He'd wanted more with Becky, but at least this was something. Something he could hold on to long after she'd forgotten all about him.

"At least once," she said quietly. She exhaled. "You're doing well, with your image, the interviews, everything. Really well. I need you to know that I'm impressed."

"I try." He made small talk, letting her go with a curt promise not let the cameras catch any more pathetic, submissive looks from him. He remembered that moment, how he'd felt looking up at Zach. Maybe a bit like surrendering, like getting on his knees, swearing to do anything, to be anything Zach wanted him to be. Which was nothing more than a good man when it came down to it.

What a fucking joke. It's all an act. He dropped his phone in his bag, shaking his head when Carter asked him if he wanted to grab a bite to eat. His stomach was in knots. But that didn't change a thing. *I've eventually got to stop pretending to be something I'm not.*

Chapter Sixteen

Being on deck first thing in the morning to watch the sun rise over the ocean, was one of the best perks of being here. Coffee and fresh ocean spray from the wild waves rising up from the restless sea made Akira feel so awake and alive she tipped her head back, soaking it all in.

I'm fixed. She laughed out loud, setting her coffee mug down on a nearby table because she needed to move and didn't want to spill the hot liquid on her white, pleated skirt. Soft music was playing from the speakers above, and she could see the sleepy cameramen creeping out from behind the cabins on the other side of the pool behind her. As the leader of one of the two teams, they probably hoped she'd give them some good footage.

For the first time, she didn't resent them for watching her so closely. Her long, slick hair rose up with the wind as she spun around, singing when she recognized the song that had just started up. "If I Die Young" by The Band Perry. Such a sad song, but she wasn't feeling sad at all. What would be sad would be continuing with the life she'd had before. Short or long, it hadn't really been living. Part of her had already felt dead, but not anymore. She'd been only sixteen when her life had been . . . not severed, but spoiled in a way she'd never hoped to recover from.

But she had recovered. She was living—really living—*finally!*

The three roses on the table where she'd left her coffee caught her eye. She took one, still singing and dancing, pulling off the petals to let them fall into the ocean. Not in a "he loves me, he loves me not" kinda way. More as a way to symbolize the freedom she'd experienced. Four years was long enough to be a prisoner to the experience. It was finally over.

"Akira?"

And yet, it wasn't over at all. Her breath caught and she spun around, tripping back against the railing, holding her hands out, panic clawing at her chest. Dave Hunt, the man who'd seen her flirting with Scott as an invitation to one and all, stood just a few feet away. The cameras were still rolling, but the men behind them didn't seem real. They were like props. There was nothing but her and this man and he saw *her*. Who she really was.

Not who she wanted to be.

"Relax. I'm not going to . . . fuck. I didn't know." Dave fisted his hands by his sides. He didn't look like he wanted to hit her, but she couldn't know for sure. Her instincts couldn't be trusted. Even after he held up his hands and stepped back, she was all too aware that she couldn't run fast enough to get away.

"Please just leave me alone." She flattened her hands over the V of her shirt, wishing she'd covered up more. Or better yet, stayed in Dominik's room. Where she could have kept pretending everything was good. "I'll scream. I won't stop screaming! I won't let this happen again!"

"Shh . . . sweetie, I won't touch you."

"Hunt." A hard voice came from her other side. She was surrounded. She whimpered as a shadow fell over her, but the man didn't touch her. She blinked as Tim stepped between her and Dave. "Get away from her—no, I don't care that you were trying to make things right. It's not happening. Not like this. I see you near her again, I'll throw you over the side of this fucking boat myself."

"Coach, I—" Dave hunched his shoulders and nodded. "I'm sorry. That's all I wanted to say."

It was over. Then it wasn't. Dave turned and a sound, a wild, vicious sound, came from the man who blocked him.

Ford.

"You stupid little shit." Ford grabbed Dave by the back of the neck, jabbing his fist into the other man's gut. Ford wasn't quite as tall, or wide, as Dave, but the younger man wasn't fighting back. An evil smile sliced across Ford's lips. "I've been looking forward to this."

He managed to hit Dave in the face, then again in the stomach, before several players poured on to the deck and pulled him away. Dave was on his knees, spitting blood, not even trying to shield himself from the final kick Ford got into his ribs.

Akira's stomach heaved as she watched Dave crawl over to the wall and slump against it. The cameras kept rolling. Scott got right up in Ford's face, snarling at him to "calm down."

She'd had enough.

"You fucking thug!" She shrugged Tim off when he tried to stop her, shoving past the men until she stood in front of Ford. Who did he think he was? He was as bad—if not worse—than Hunt. Jami could be going through all Akira was because of Ford. Because he'd exposed her to men who hurt women and kept quiet because of his "family business." He might pretend to care about Jami, but he hadn't protected her. She felt a sting in her palm as she slapped Ford, but it wasn't enough. She hit him again. And again. "Do you think I'm impressed? You deserve everything you just gave him. Worse! Why are you here?"

"My sister asked me to come." Ford's gaze shifted away from her. There was a lie in there. Or at least an omission. "She still thinks she controls all this. She needed me to make sure everything was going okay after hearing about two girls getting kicked off."

"She could have sent someone else. Dean—"

"She needs him!"

"She doesn't need you! No one does! Go back to your father and keep doing his dirty work for him! That's all you're good for!"

Ford winced. Blood dripped down his to his chin from a slit in his lip. "Tell me you don't really believe that, Akira."

"I really do. How could you let that happen to her? You could have stopped it!"

"I know." Ford's jaw hardened. His dropped his gaze to her feet. "Believe me, I'll never forget it. I don't deserve her forgiveness. Or yours."

Too many people were watching them, but most of the Cobras knew what had happened to Jami. They must—or should—hate Ford as much as Akira did. So she glared at him, speaking nice and clear so he wouldn't miss a single word. "She still has nightmares." She swallowed as she caught sight of Luke, standing at the edge of the crowd. He pressed his eyes shut, taking a step back as though she'd slapped him too. She knew he'd been there when Jami woke screaming, still seeing the man who'd been murdered in front of her. "But I bet you sleep fine at night, don't you, Ford?"

"I don't. And I know I can't make this right."

"No. You can't. And don't you dare ever forget that either." She felt like she was ripping new wounds into her own heart. She sobbed as she spotted Dominik, coming toward her, the look in his eyes making every man in his path step aside quickly. "Sir, please. I need to get away from here. I . . . I ruined everything."

"No. You haven't." Dominik pulled her into his arms. The cotton of his snug, black T-shirt was soft against her cheek, but beneath it was pure steel-corded muscle. God, he was so strong. And she needed his strength. Because hers was gone. "Ford, I don't give a fuck why you're here. Stay away from her. We clear?"

"We're clear." She heard Ford say before Dominik led her inside. The world was a blur until she was in his room again, the door cutting her off from everything that she was too weak to deal with. Had always been too weak to deal with. All the hope she'd had was like a blown glass vase smashed on jagged rocks, all the pretty pieces scattered in the dirt.

"I need a drink." She took a deep breath and headed toward the minibar. "Five o'clock somewhere, right?"

"Coffee, Akira." Dominik went to the table, which held two covered silver trays and another tray with a coffee carafe and cream and sugar. He poured her a cup, arching a brow as he picked up the creamer. He handed her the coffee black when she shook her head. "Talk to me. What happened up there?"

She took a sip of her coffee, almost spilling it when it burnt her tongue. She scowled into the cup. "I hate him."

"I could see that. And I can understand you being angry with him over what happened to Jami, but it's more than that, isn't it?" Dominik slid his hand down to her waist as he turned her to face him. "Did he do something to you? Hurt you or—"

"No! Ford wouldn't—" *Ugh, really?* With what he'd done to Jami, how could she be so sure he wouldn't hurt her? Not that it mattered. He hadn't.

Not intentionally.

"He's not who I though he was when I first met him." She shrugged. "I guess I'm more pissed that I misjudged him than anything."

Dominik studied her face, nodding slowly. "You have feelings for him."

"*Had.* Past tense." She hugged herself and leaned against his solid chest. "I'd rather not talk about him. I just wish . . ."

"Go on," Dominik whispered, smoothing his hand over her hair.

"I wish I could feel like I did last night. Or even this morning before—" She rolled her eyes at how naïve she'd been. "I thought I was better. Then Dave came to talk to me, and I had a meltdown. It's all gone. Everything I thought I'd accomplished—"

"Is it?" Slight creases formed around Dominik's eyes as he tilted her chin up with a finger. He brought his lips to hers for a soft kiss. "I couldn't have done this a week ago."

"Mmm." *He's right.* And she loved that he could because his lips, tasting of sweetened coffee and cream, so nice and warm, felt wonderful on hers. She smiled as she rose up on her tiptoes to steal another kiss. "That's true."

He grinned, winding her hair around his fist, holding her still with one arm barred across her back. She let out a surprised yelp as he lifted her up with one hand firmly gripping her ass. "Or this."

She swallowed, wrapping her legs around his waist to steady herself. His erection fitting snug between her thighs, with nothing but her panties and his jeans between them, stirred things inside her. Some good. Some more than a little scary. Last night he'd touched her intimately, but it had been all about her pleasure. Her last orgasm had brought things to her lips that she'd never thought she'd say to anyone. She'd practically *begged* him to take her.

He'd decided she wasn't ready. Had he changed his mind?

"Sir, I want to . . ." She shivered as he brought his lips to her throat, kissing and sucking and grazing his teeth down the length even as he carried her to the grey armchair where he'd made her come over and over the night before. Settling down with her straddling him, he picked up the scarf he'd taken from her.

"Give me your hands." His eyes were on her face even as he tied her wrists together in front of her. "How does that feel?"

She tested the restraints, biting back a smile while she shifted her hips so she could feel more of him against her. "Very, very good, Sir."

"Brat." He gave her thigh a light slap. "Are you afraid now?"

"No. I could never be afraid of you."

He combed his fingers into her hair, bringing her flush with his body. His lips brushed her ear as he spoke. "Do you know what I can do to you? What I *want* to do to you?"

Her pulse quickened. She licked her lips. "Yes."

"Nothing's ruined, sweetheart." His free hand curved under her ass. His fingers dipped into her panties, sliding through her wetness, the slight pressure of his fingertips against her entrance almost enough to set her off. "You're so wet for me. You don't panic when I touch you." He filled her with one finger, easing it in and out, bringing his lips back to hers to drink in her little gasps. "It's natural for a woman to resent unwelcome advances. There's nothing wrong with your reactions."

"But . . ." She moaned as his fingers slipped over her clit, not sure her brain was functioning enough for a conversation. She tipped her head back, grinding down on his hand, so close to the edge she couldn't take much more. "I need to know I can . . . handle . . . how I react."

"You do need to learn a little more control." He withdrew his fingers, chuckling when she cursed under her breath. "I don't like those nasty words coming out of that pretty mouth. Stand up."

"I'm sorry! Please, just let me . . ." She put her hands on his stomach, shifting her hips back so she could reach the zipper of his jeans. Her brow furrowed when he put his hand over her bound wrists and shook his head. "I want to give you what you gave me. I'll be good, I promise."

"Don't make me repeat myself, pet. Up."

Nibbling at her bottom lip, she hid her frown behind her hair as she stood. She didn't even consider arguing with him, but she couldn't ignore her disappointment. She'd been hoping—

The sound of his zipper coming down made her jump. She stared at him as he pulled out his hard cock. Long and thick, the same rich, dark shade as the rest of his body, with springy, trimmed black hair around the base. Her fingers twitched as she resisted the urge to close the distance between them to touch him.

"Go ahead, pet." He put his hands on the armrests, utterly relaxed. "I won't be pleased if you push yourself too far though. Do whatever you're comfortable with."

She knelt between his thighs, peeking at him again before she stroked her hands up his leg. This was very different from anything she'd ever done. She'd never had a chance to explore a man before and... fuck, even this part of him was beautiful. Using her fingertips, she traced the veins running down the length of his cock, circled the rim of the large head. The slit of the tip held a shiny bead of precum and she bent forward to taste it, flicking her tongue over the salty slickness, scooting back when he made a rough sound in his throat.

"Don't stop," he murmured, cupping his hand around the back of her head as she lowered her lips once again, kissing the feverishly hot skin at the arrow-shaped indent below the head. He hissed when she touched the same spot with the tip of her tongue. "Fuck. I'm going to hell. Anything that feels this good..."

Her cheeks heated, but she loved how he vocalized his pleasure. Loved knowing that she was giving him even half of what he'd given her. "I think I'm going with you, Sir."

She took him into her mouth, as deep as she could, gasping in air and swallowing when her gag reflex kicked up. Lifting her head, she frowned, wondering how all the heroines in her books managed to "swallow the man's dick whole."

Laughter rumbled through Dominik's chest. "I can only guess that thought. So serious, little one. I enjoy the feel of your lips around me." His knuckles stroked her cheek. "Use your hands and your mouth. With time, you may be able to go deeper, but there's no rush."

Nodding quickly, she wrapped her hands around him, dipping down and swirling her tongue around the heated flesh that filled her mouth. The slight pressure on the back of her head had her clenching her thighs as heat spilled, soaking her panties. Just a little taste of his control made what she was doing just as pleasurable for her as she hoped it was for him. She moved faster, whimpering at the throb in her core.

He tugged lightly on her hair. "I won't last much longer, pet."

If he came, she couldn't take that last step. And she needed to so very badly. But part of her wanted to finish this for him. Take him over the edge. She rose up on her knees, gazing up at him. "I don't know what to do. I want to give you everything."

"You will." He framed her jaw with his hand. "Are you ready?"

More than ready. Restlessness had her shaking. Everything they'd done so far had been to prepare her for this. "Yes."

Nodding, he drew her up to her feet by her restraints. He undid the knots, shaking his head when she protested. "Shh. I need to see you before I take you."

With trembling fingers, she undid the buttons of her sleeveless white blouse. Her skirt joined it on the floor by her feet. By the time she reached the clasp of her bra, her fumbling fingers were useless.

"Akira—"

"Sir, I'm okay." She turned, sliding her bra straps off her shoulders to show him she meant it. "Please help me?"

He undid her bra strap. His fingers hooked the elastic at the waist of her panties, peeling them down. Then his hands slid over her stomach as he pulled her back against him. He kissed the base of her spine, his lips gliding down slowly until she whimpered and squirmed. The feel of his mouth on her skin set her on fire. His teeth sank into her ass cheek and she moaned.

"You're such a tiny little thing." He bit her again, cupping her pussy with his hand and massaging her clit until her knees almost gave out. "There are condoms in my suitcase. Get one."

She tripped across the room, dropping hard to her knees in front of his suitcase. She found the box and took out a condom, fisting her hand around it when she noticed how badly she was shaking. If he saw, he might think she was scared again. But she wasn't. She just couldn't control herself any longer.

"Come to me, pet. No. Don't stand." His tone was rough, and she melted a little more under the heat of his gaze. "You told me the scene in that movie aroused you—when the sub crawled to her Master. Crawl to me. Let me see all that grace and beauty, every movement for my pleasure."

Uncertainty vanished and she held the edge of the condom wrapper between her teeth, focused on making her body move in a slow, sensual way. She crawled to his feet, the whirlwind of thoughts from before becoming a tranquil pool, his calm flowing through her veins, steadying her pulse, her breath.

"Perfect." His eyes glowed with approval. "It became easier when you surrendered, didn't it? In that moment, when you let everything else go, when you simply obeyed, all the voices in your head went silent."

She sat back on her heels and took the condom from between her teeth. "How did you know?"

"I have some experience, pet." He smiled at her. "Cover me, then stand. I'll bind your wrists again—behind your back this time. Giving up a little more control will make this easier for you."

She wanted to give up all of her control, but this would be enough. She tore the condom wrapper, rolled the condom over his dick, then stood, putting her back to him and giving him her wrists. He restrained her with the scarf, more securely this time, tight, but not too tight. His hands on her hips, he turned her to face him.

"Come here," he whispered, helping her straddle him as she had before. He kissed her, his tongue thrusting deep into her mouth, his fingers gliding into her, stretching her as he eased one, then two past the rippling muscles within. His thumb pressed down on her clit, lightly at first, using her own juices to moisten the tiny nub. She cried out as he added more pressure, moving his mouth from hers to pull at an erect nipple with a hard suck of his lips.

"Sir!" Her hips jerked as a jolt of electric sensations sizzled from her nipple to her clit. She was so close, but she held back, needing him inside her before she gave in completely. "Please, please, please!"

He lifted her up, nuzzling his face between her breasts as he positioned himself between her thighs. The tip of his dick spread her pussy lips, but he went no farther. His hands curved under her thighs as he held her in place. "As slow, or as fast, as you need to take me, Akira."

She let her weight down slowly, but the stretching—he filled her so much she wasn't sure she could take more. She rested her head on his shoulder, panting. He kissed her shoulder, using one hand to stroke her back, to lift her sweat-dampened hair over one shoulder.

"I'm too small. You would figure after . . ." Her stomach turned. It had been years, and all her body remembered was how much it had hurt. Dominik wasn't hurting her, but maybe her body didn't understand. Maybe it would never understand the pleasure that could come from having a man inside her. What if they'd spoiled this for her? Forever?

They didn't! I won't let them!

"You're tense and your mind is somewhere else." Dominik pressed his hand against her cheek, drying the tears she hadn't felt spill with his thumb. "Be with me. Feel me. Because all I'm feeling right now is you. You're all I see."

Her lashes clung together as she tipped her head toward him, all that had happened to her so long ago locked away where it belonged, what had happened to him all too recently stealing the tension from her body. "All I see, all I feel, is you."

He let out a sound between a laugh and a sob, his arms around his waist, his lips on hers. They moved together until his thick length fit snugly inside her. She buried her face in his neck, trying so hard not to cry. He'd opened her up and freed a spot in her heart for him to slip inside. It wasn't love, but it was something special.

Something she'd never regret.

* * * *

This was all about Akira. *Should* be all about her. But Dominik hadn't expected his own emotions to get involved. The last woman he'd made love to had been Oriana. She'd climbed into his bed naked, tears in her eyes, though she wouldn't say why.

"I need you, Dominik. Just hold me and tell me how much you love me."

He'd felt the welts on her ass and thighs, but touching them only made her moan and press harder against him. Sometimes she scened with Sloan without sex. It satisfied something deep inside her, but not everything. Even in the darkness, from the moisture slicking some of the welts, he could tell she was bleeding. But she wasn't hurt. And by the way she pressed against his body, he wasn't even sure she needed the emotional connection she was asking for.

Just a different kind of release.

What was happening between him and Akira was more than a release. It was moving on. It was two people drowning, catching the same piece of driftwood that would bring them to solid ground. Finding the shore might be a struggle, but getting there would come that much sooner with them fighting the current together.

Akira's thighs clenched as she lifted up. She held her breath as she took him inside her yet again, and he groaned at how tight she was around him. His whole length was gripped by her snug pussy. His shirt was soaked with his sweat as he carefully guided her up, then down, controlling the pace, reining in the urge to thrust into her hard and fast. She needed him to be oh so gentle. For this experience to be very different from what had happened to her before.

He wished he could say this would be the end for her. That getting here would erase the hell she'd gone through. But it wouldn't. She'd let him in, but they both knew there was only so much he could give her. A safe place to heal, to find herself. Eventually, he'd need to help her find someone who would could help her learn to love. For the first time.

Because she wouldn't get that from him. He wasn't sure he could ever love again. Not the way she deserved to be loved.

She nipped his chin, letting him know he'd done what he'd asked her not to. He'd gone somewhere else when he should be with her. He gritted his teeth as he let the pleasure take over, all too aware that his body couldn't care less where his mind had gone. This beautiful, sweet woman needed to feel his control. And he needed to find it.

He bent her back over his arm, kissing between her breasts, holding her down on him as he ground deep into her body. Then he drew her up, shifting his angle a little, lifting up and holding her there, pleasuring himself with a few shallow upward thrusts as her eyes glazed. Her little whimpers were the sweetest thing he'd ever heard. "Come for me, Akira. We haven't rolled the dice again, so we'll use the number you rolled yesterday."

"Th-three?" She stared at him, then pressed her eyes shut as he brought her down hard. "Ah!"

Her juices spilled over his dick, over his balls, as she clenched and screamed. Pressure built up in the base of his spine, but he forced his own release back with a few deep breaths, holding Akira still so she wouldn't move and set him off. Once she settled down, he pulled her up, gritting his teeth as his dick slid from her body. He stood her up, made sure she was steady, then pulled off his shirt and kicked off his jeans.

Her little scream as he swept her up into his arms made him chuckle. He brought her to the bed, quickly untying her. After he had her on her back, he bound her wrists to the headboard.

"Dominik?" Her back bowed as he kissed down her body, between her small breasts, over the shallow dip of her stomach.

He moved even lower, bringing her knees up over his shoulders. "Shall we work on number two?"

Chapter Seventeen

Scott licked the salt off the wrist of the girl with the chestnut hair before taking his shot of tequila and snatching the slice of lemon from her lips with his teeth. He grinned at Ford, then unbuttoned his blue silk shirt as the four Ice Girls hollered. They were playing cutthroat cricket and Chestnut—Scott was pretty sure her name was April—had closed the seventeen with three darts in one round. Which meant Scott owed her a piece of clothing and had to take a shot. Oh, and a kiss. Things wouldn't get dirty until someone was naked.

Thankfully, the cameras weren't allowed in here. So none of them had to behave all respectable. *A goddamn relief.*

Besides Ford, there were two other guys in the game room. Pischlar and Carter. Scott was fucking shocked that the kid had come along. Even more so to learn that Ramos had told him it was okay. Of course, there was a catch. Carter could play. He could drink and strip. But no touching.

Some kind of fucked-up test? Scott doubted it. More likely, Ramos wanted the boy all worked up for when he got home. Didn't matter either way. Just left more for Scott, Ford, and Pischlar.

Chestnut smoothed her hands over Scott's chest, tipping her head back, her glossy red lips parted. He dipped her over his arm, kissing her hard and fast, laughing into her mouth as the men cheered behind him. She gave him a dreamy-eyed look as he straightened her.

"You. Are. *Amazing!*" She let out a drunken giggle, stumbling back to her friends.

Ford picked up a dart.

"I'm surprised Akira isn't here!" One of the girls—Rachel?—shouted. The music wasn't loud, but the girls had stopped using their "inside voices" after the first few shots. "She's missing all the fun!"

A girl with curly black hair snorted. "Oh, I doubt that. Our potential captain went straight back to *their* captain's room after the rehearsal. And with Mason . . ." She sighed. "You just *know* she's not missing out on anything."

The dart Ford threw hit the center of the chalkboard and stuck in the black slate. None of the girls noticed.

"That lucky little bitch!"

"I know! I would *so* let Mason spank me!"

"Would you?" April cocked her head, sliding over to draw her fingers up and down Pischlar's arm. "I don't know if I could get into the kinky stuff."

Pischlar let out a sharp laugh. "You might want to go snuggle up to Demyan and the Delgado prince then, honey."

April stared at Pischlar like horns had just ripped through the skin on his forehead. She inched away from him, grabbing the bottle of tequila from her friend.

"Don't you know anything, April?" Rachel tossed her head, giving April a superior look. "You want to get with a Cobra, you better like kink. The things that happen at that club—"

"Don't remind me." April shuddered, then turned to Ford. "You gonna play?"

"Yeah." Ford threw the next two darts perfectly, closing the next inning. "I think I will."

Running his tongue over his teeth, Scott studied Ford as the game continued. He was focused, which was good for their team, but something in his eyes had gone hard and cold.

Could mean trouble.

By the time the game was finished, one girl was naked and the other two topless. Carter had fallen asleep on the sofa, and Pischlar had Rachel up against the wall, holding her wrists behind her back and speaking softly in her ear. One of the girls had rushed off to the bathroom, looking a little green.

Ford lit a cigarette, standing by the small bar, and crooked his finger at April. "You owe me."

Cheeks a nice, dark pink, April slinked across the room, dropping to her knees when she reached Ford. She undid the button of his black jeans, then pulled the zipper down with her teeth. Scott noticed that Ford's expression hadn't changed much. Like any man, he liked getting his dick sucked, but it didn't seem to matter much whose mouth was around his cock. Must be nice to be that indifferent. Scott couldn't work up any interest in any of the girls. Or the men. Ford was a good-looking guy, but they had an easygoing friendship that Scott didn't want to mess with.

The last girl—whose name was somewhere in Scott's fuzzy brain—went behind the bar to toss the empty bottle of tequila. She brought out a bottle of rum, gesturing to Scott with it before pouring herself a good helping.

"No thanks." Scott bit the inside of his cheek as something tightened low in his gut. He never drank rum. Just the smell of it made him sick. "You okay getting back to your room . . . ?"

"Shanelle." She gave him a provocative smile, eyelashes fluttering. "You sure you don't want to stay?"

"I'm sure." He smiled stiffly back at her, ignoring her little pout. Over by the sofa, he shook Carter awake. "Come on, kid. Let's get you to bed."

"Ain't going to bed wit' you, Dem—Demmy." Carter slurred, using Scott's rarely-heard nickname since he couldn't seem to say his full last name. "You ain't Seb." He sat up unsteadily and frowned. "Miss Seb. Tell him to come get me."

Fuck, this kid can't hold his liquor. Rolling his eyes, Scott dragged Carter up to his feet. "No can do, sport. But you'll see him tomorrow."

"Good." Carter nodded, slumping against Scott's side. "And Jami. But don't you touch Jami."

"I won't."

"You're a slut, you know that?" Carter laughed as though he'd just told a great joke. "I heard that Vanek kicked you out. You've got to stop fucking whores."

Scott gritted his teeth, reminding himself that he'd seen Carter drunk before. The kid probably wouldn't remember any of this tomorrow. Tequila had just loosened his tongue. He kicked the swinging doors open, pressing his eyes shut as Carter's stumbling almost brought them both to the floor.

"I've cleaned up. Gotta if I want to stay with the team," Scott said.

"All right." Carter took a few wide steps away from him, spinning around suddenly, his brow furrowed. "I still see it, you know. You and Pearce, kissing Jami, touching her, fucking her with your tongues." He braced himself on the wall. "Was fucking hot."

"It was." Scott frowned. What was the boy getting at? "You making a point?"

"Yeah. Was jealous. Seb won't share me," Carter said, confirming Scott's suspicions. "I don't 'need' it. But Jami . . . Jami might. She gets off on her men watching her get used by other men. Freaky shit. Sometimes I wonder . . ."

I so don't wanna hear this. Scott draped Carter's arm over his shoulder, forcing the boy—and himself—to keep moving. He might not be as far gone as Carter, but his inhibitions were all but shot. "Shut up, Carter."

"Fuck you." Carter wrenched away from him, baring his teeth. "I see how you look at me. You never looked at me like that before you found out about me and Seb."

"I don't do straight guys. And you seemed like a fag stag. Cool with it all, but not interested."

"Proved you wrong. But you didn't do anything about it."

"Shit. You don't stop talking." Scott reached for the door handle to the room Carter shared with the Cobra's gritty left-winger, Ian White. "I'm gonna gag you."

"You are one kinky fucker, Demmy." Carter laughed. "I knew it."

"Need help?" Shanelle came up behind him, her lips twisted with amusement as Carter slid across the wall away from her. "Don't worry, cutie. I know you're into dick. Everyone knows Jami's your beard."

The color left Carter's face. His eyes narrowed. "Is not. I love her."

"*Suuure.*" Shanelle winked at Scott, as though they were sharing a secret. "Stay in the closet if you want. Either way, Demyan and I are going to get you in bed before you get yourself in trouble." She lowered her voice. "I swear, guys like *him* think they can turn anyone. Come with me once we get rid of him. I'm sure your skin's crawling by now."

A whiff of rum had Scott's blood running cold. His skin *was* crawling. But not because of Carter.

"Sorry I wasn't clear before, Shanelle." He steadied Carter with a hand on his shoulder when it looked like the boy would fall over. "You have nothing I want."

"Fuck. I was so wrong about you." Her lips curled with disgust. "Fucking fudge packer."

Scott stared after her as she stormed down the hall, not sure he could recall the last time he'd come across someone so ignorant. And . . . shit, what if she told someone?

"Wow." Carter's body stiffened against his side. "Just . . . wow."

"Don't worry. You get used to it." Scott squeezed Carter. "Just get some sleep, okay?"

"But . . ." Carter shrugged Scott's arm off his shoulder, staring up at him, lips thin. "If Seb was okay with it—"

Something inside Scott snapped. He wasn't sure if it was that woman, the stink of rum, or the flashes of heavy breasts in his face every time he blinked, but something had pushed him too far. He shoved Carter into the wall, trapping him with his hands on the boy's shoulders.

He spoke with his lips over Carter's. "Why wait? You need something, kid? Just ask."

"Scott."

The voice came from behind him, low and calming. A voice that got him thinking about how good he was supposed to be. And how messed up he really was.

Zach gently pulled Scott's hands off Carter's shoulders. "Go to our room. I'll take care of him."

Scott got to the room. Somehow. But he was mostly numb, and for some reason the furniture kept getting in his way. Damn, he should have just done it. Taken Carter to an empty hall, or to a bathroom stall, and fucked the shit out of him. Who cared that Seb would kill him after? Or that it would destroy Carter's relationship with the man? And Jami . . .

He was bitter. And more than a little jealous. Carter would go home and probably tell Ramos about everything. Make excuses about how drunk he was—if the tequila didn't create a great big blank in his head. If the kid was just talking like that because Scott had tasted his muffin, he wouldn't be asking Ramos permission for anything. If it was more . . . hell, Scott didn't know what to do with that. Part of the whole complicating his life by behaving deal.

The point was, Carter had it good. And he wouldn't have chanced fucking that up if he hadn't gotten so wasted. A real friend would have just gotten him to bed, like Zach was doing.

But Scott couldn't be anyone's friend. Or lover. Or *anything*.

He could still smell the rum. It was like someone had poured a bottle over his body to lick it off. He could almost feel her tongue, thick and wet, gliding over his concave chest. He'd gotten sick a lot as a kid—hadn't beefed up until he was about fourteen. He leaned against the wall by the bathroom, fists pressed hard to his forehead. The scent got heavier, choking him. A cold sweat cooled his flesh and that reeked of rum too.

He had to get rid of the smell.

In the shower, under the icy spray, he cracked his elbow into the tiles, cursing as the pain reverberated through his bones. He rubbed the soap between his hands, scrubbing his body with the foam. He heard the door open and close as he rinsed. The curtain was shoved aside. The water turned off.

"Scott." Zach held out a towel, latching on to Scott's arm to help him out of the shower. "I need to ask you something. And don't fucking lie to me."

"I wouldn't." Scott fumbled for the towel, a rough sound leaving his throat as Zach pulled him into his arms. He was gonna get wet!

"Did you do time as a kid?"

Time? It took a bit to figure out what Zach meant. Scott laughed and shook his head. "Naw. I wasn't that bad."

"Then what makes you act like that, Scott?" Zach latched on to the back of his neck, forcing Scott to look at him. "Let me help you."

"I don't need no help." Scott jerked away from Zach, skinning his knees on the floor by his bed as he fell. Hands flat on the floor, he hunched his shoulders. "You wanna do something for me? Stop trying to make me into someone I'm not. I'm a quick, easy fuck. I'm a body."

"Jesus, Scott. You're more than that." Zach hefted him up, then sat him on the edge of the bed. He used the towel to dry Scott's face and his hair, his eyes hard. "You're going to tell me. Not now though. Right now, you're going to sleep this off."

Scott tipped his head back and laughed again. "Sleep? Yeah, right. I haven't given you your snack yet. And you're not letting me get what I need."

"Snack?" Zach shook his head, shoving Scott onto his back. "You're not making any sense. What do you need?"

"Things are good after I get off." Still didn't make any sense. Why couldn't he get his brain to work right? "It's over after that. But not until then. You get it?"

"No. But I don't see you making things any more clear tonight." Zach climbed into the bed next to him, his fingers digging into Scott's jaw as he kissed him. He pushed Scott down when he tried to sit up. "My hands, Scott. Are you sober enough to know who's touching you?"

"Like I can think of anyone else while you're here." His throat tightened. *Yeah, I haven't shown that much, have I?* "I'm sorry, Zach. Those other guys were just . . . I don't know. I can't stop."

"Other men. Other women. You just hand yourself out." Zach bit his throat. Hard. Then he kissed away the pain. "That's what got to me. What you do to yourself. It's not right."

"What's right?" Scott held his breath as Zach's hand wrapped around his dick. There was no right or wrong anymore. Just Zach. "Oh, fuck. Please . . ."

"*My* hand, Scott. You fucking look at me while I do this." Zach pushed up on his elbow, stroking Scott in his firm grip. "You look at me and you say my fucking name."

"Zach!" Scott stared at Zach until pleasure blinded him. He pressed his face against Zach's throat, breathing hard as he came. Hot spurts covered his stomach, but all his attention was on that firm grip, not letting go until he went slack. It went away for a few minutes, and then Zach was cleaning him with a facecloth. Covering him with the blanket. Wrapping him up in his strong arms.

"No good. You didn't—" Scott's head throbbed. No pain, just his heart pounding inside his skull. But something was missing. "You have to . . . you can use me."

"Hell, you and Becky have a lot in common." Zach pressed Scott's head down on his shoulder. "Anyone can 'use' you. I plan to keep you."

"Stupid." Scott drifted off, chuckling under his breath. "You're a stupid fucker to think that."

"Yeah," Zach whispered. "Don't I know it."

Chapter Eighteen

The living room lights were turned down low, the small crowd in Dean's kitchen speaking softly so as not to wake the baby. Becky sat on the sofa, her legs tucked under her, a smile on her lips as she watched Landon rocking his daughter and singing "*La Luciole*." She wasn't sure she'd ever seen a father this devoted to his child. Her eyes teared as Casey slipped by her, tiptoeing across the room to sit by Landon's feet. Her own daughter seemed fascinated by her baby cousin and amazed every time she saw her uncle holding Amia, feeding her, or tucking her into her crib.

Casey didn't understand these were things a daddy was supposed to do. Hers never had.

On a shopping trip with her and Silver, Casey had pulled her aside and looked up at her seriously. "Why doesn't Auntie Silver like her baby?"

Becky had made sure Silver wasn't close enough to overhear, then crouched down to speak to Casey quietly. "She loves Amia, Casey. Why would you say that?"

"Because Uncle Landon is always taking care of Amia. That's a mommy's job."

Landon and Casey turned their heads toward the door at the soft click of heels on the carpet. Becky glanced back to see Silver, whose attention was locked on Landon and the baby. She never went closer than this to the baby unless Landon and Dean weren't around. The sadness in her eyes was painful to see.

"Good morning, love." Landon smiled at Silver, cradling Amia's tiny body carefully against his chest with one big, muscular arm, holding out his hand. "She was up a lot last night. She's exhausted. Can you take her up to her crib?"

Silver bit her lip, her whole body stiffening as though she was fighting not to step back. "You need to get some rest."

"I'm fine. Dean got up with her a few times—so did my mom. I slept all right."

"I wish you'd let me take a turn." Silver hugged herself. "It's not fair that I'm the only one getting to sleep through the night."

"Doctor's orders, *ma chérie*," Landon said quietly. "You're seeing him again in a few days. If he says you're doing well enough, I'll let you take over night feedings for a bit."

"Okay." Silver took a deep breath, looking like she was trying to force herself to move forward. "You sure she won't wake up if I move her? I don't want to bother her or something."

"She'll be fine, Silver." Landon's brow creased. "You're her mother. You won't be bothering her."

"I just—"

"Let me take her, Landon." Dean came up to Silver's side, touching her cheek before crossing the room to take Amia. Amia's eyes shot open. She cooed as Dean lifted her up. "Why am I not surprised?" He chuckled and kissed the top of Amia's head. "I knew she wouldn't sleep for long. Did you miss me, baby girl? Your sister's here to see you. So is your other grandmother." He met Landon's eyes over the baby's head. "I think you and Silver need to talk about what we discussed last night."

"What you discussed . . . ?" Silver's eyes narrowed. "Not that again! I don't need a fucking shrink! There's nothing wrong with me!"

So they *had* noticed. Becky held out her hand to Casey, pleased that her daughter came to her without a whisper of protest. She'd been afraid she'd need to get involved, but thankfully, it wasn't necessary. As for Casey, she'd dealt with enough shouting between her own parents when she was little to last her a lifetime.

Becky glanced over at Dean's mother, Verity Richter, as she passed them in the kitchen. Seconds later the woman returned with Amia, gently patting the baby's back as she started crying, then called out, "I'm taking the children for a walk. This conversation will be over by the time we get back."

Jami joined them in the kitchen, "I'm coming with you, Grandma!"

"You certainly are." Verity huffed. "I still consider you one of the children. We'll see if you can convince me otherwise. I've seen the lip you give your man."

"Oh please, Grandma! He loves it when I'm naughty!"

"Damn it, I don't need to hear that," Dean grumbled from the doorway, frowning at his daughter. "Is Ramos coming here with

Carter?"

"Nope. I'm going to his place to see them. Luke might swing by after . . ." Jami ducked her head at the hard look her grandmother gave her. "Just after. That's all I was going to say. Me and Akira will probably do something. Apparently Ford showed up yesterday and . . . ugh, I don't know. She sounded pretty pissed. We need some girl time."

"What happened with Ford?" Silver asked, slipping into the kitchen before Jami could follow Verity out. "He didn't start anything, did he?"

Jami sighed. "I thought you'd heard. He and Hunt got into it."

"Hunt?" Dean scowled. "Damn it, we need the boy. How bad is it?"

"I'm not sure. Uncle Tim didn't call you?"

"No. He didn't."

Silver scowled, heading for her purse on the kitchen table. "Get ahold of Tim. I'll call Ford. That idiot is going to—"

"Silver." Verity returned to the room with Amia in her stroller. She held out her hand for the phone as though Silver was one of her children. None of whom ever questioned her when she gave them that look. "Call your brother later. You're busy now."

"But—"

"Silver, please." Dean slid his hand around Silver's waist, drawing her back to the living room. "We need to talk."

As Jami headed out with Casey, Becky bent to slip on her shoes, jumping a little when Verity touched her shoulder. She straightened, holding her breath as Verity spoke quietly. "Why don't you stay? Tidy up a bit?"

"Ah . . . okay." Becky looked around at the mess of the kitchen, almost feeling guilty for how ready she'd been to walk out. Normally, she would help clean after one of Dean's amazing meals, but she'd thought the whole point of Verity bringing the children out was to give Silver, Dean, and Landon some privacy. Was she missing something? "I wasn't planning to leave it like this, I just figured they—"

"Yes, they need some privacy. But Dean is struggling to be there for them both, and it might help for him to know you're nearby if

Landon needs you." Verity took one hand off the handle of the stroller and rubbed Becky's arm. "Put some music on. Dean will bring Silver up to their room when this is all over. Then you can sit with Landon. Listen if he needs to talk to someone who isn't so close to the situation."

That sounded reasonable. Becky nodded and followed the older woman's advice, turning on the small stereo attached to a base of one of the kitchen cabinets. Then the dishwasher. With that and the water running as she washed the pots and pans, the three adults in the other room would have to scream for her to hear a thing.

Neither Dean or Landon were prone to screaming, but Silver . . . well, she wasn't here for Silver. Not this time. Verity was right, Silver had Dean. Landon was going to need his big sister.

* * * *

Landon cracked his neck, watching as Dean led Silver to the sofa. She seemed calmer. Maybe they'd finally get somewhere with her. *We have to. We can't continue this way.*

Settled on the sofa with Silver beside him, Dean took Silver's hand, speaking in a low, soothing tone. "You're going through postpartum depression, my love. If you won't listen to your doctor when he tells you so, you will listen to me. Don't think Landon and I haven't noticed you locking yourself in the bathroom to cry. This happens every time you spend more than a few minutes with your daughter."

The calm in Silver's features vanished, giving way to a flash of rage. "Of course you'd bring this up with Super Mom here. God! It must be hard for you to see how perfect she is compared to me!"

"No one's comparing you to Becky, Silver," Landon said, trying to keep his voice level, praying Becky hadn't heard any of that. Becky had tried so hard to be there for Silver, and it seemed like all Silver saw was her trying to be superior. "My sister is a single mother. She's been doing this alone for years and—"

"Go ahead! Tell me I'm being a bitch! I suck as a mother, as a sub, and as a fiancée!" Silver sobbed, sounding like she was coming apart at the seams. "I'm glad we haven't gotten married yet, Landon.

It will make things so much easier when I—"

"When you what, Silver?" Landon swallowed when Silver shook her head and turned away from him. His ex, the mother of his first child, had given up too. And she'd done it in a way that would haunt him for the rest of his life. "You don't believe the doctor, do you? You're sure you're going to die."

"If the medication doesn't work—" Silver cut herself off, her tone hardening. "You need to be prepared. Amia needs you."

"Amia needs *you*! You won't let her get close to you, *mon amour*!"

"I can't! I know how much it will hurt her when I'm gone if I do!"

Dean made a rough sound, speaking over them both. "Silver, you listen to me right now. You are going to get through this. If—and that's a *big* if—the medication doesn't work, you have one of the best doctors in the country to perform the surgery. Doctor Singh made it very clear that most patients live perfectly normal lives after the procedure."

"Most of those patients weren't fucking cokeheads! The damage I did to my body..." Silver's cries were muffled against Dean's chest as he pulled her close. "I didn't know. I wasn't thinking of the future when I did it. I'm so sorry. I know Amia needs a mother, but she has both of you. And maybe after, you can find a good woman—"

"Stop it! Fuck, are you listening to yourself?" Landon's voice broke. He shoved out of the rocking chair so quickly it slammed into the wall. "Are you ready to leave us? Ready to fucking give up?"

"I'm not giving up. I'm being realistic." Silver's tone became distant. She drew away from Dean. Rose without looking at either of them. "And I'm tired. The doctor said I should rest when I get tired. I'm going to bed."

"I'll come with you," Dean said.

"No. Stay with Landon. I need to be alone."

Landon slumped against the wall as Silver's footsteps sounded on the stairs. He sensed Dean moving close to him. His whole body started shaking as Dean's arms came around him, one hand on the back of Landon's head, one arm around his back.

"I'll make her see someone, Landon," Dean said, his tone rough.

"This won't be easy, but we'll pull through it together."

"You can't make her fight to live, Dean." Landon's fists bunched in the back of Dean's shirt. "And if she doesn't fight, that seventy percent chance she has of pulling through this doesn't mean anything."

"You watch me." Dean curved his hand around the back of Landon's neck and pressed their foreheads together. "I'll make her fight. And damn it, I'll make you fight too. The only time you're happy is when you're holding Amia. Which is good, but you need to keep living. You skipped your last PT."

"My leg doesn't hurt as much anymore."

"Which is exactly why you need to work on strengthening it. The doctor said you could get back to the game mid-season if you—"

"Fuck the game."

"Landon—"

"No. Dean, I'm serious. Right now, Amia has me and you. But when the season starts, all she'll have is me. If Silver gets better, things might change. But she's right about one thing. There's a big chance she won't." Landon pressed his eyes shut. "And if she doesn't, I'm not leaving my daughter alone."

"Amia has your parents. Mine." Dean shook Landon. "She'll never be alone; I promise you that."

"You're right." Landon pulled away from Dean, his eyes hard and cold. "Because she'll have me. You and the team better get used to that."

* * * *

Becky swallowed and backed into the kitchen, not even sure what she would have said if her brother *had* noticed her standing there. Everything he'd said—he was right. A child needed to know there was one person in their life who put them before all else. As much as Dean loved Amia, he also had his own daughter and the team to look out for. Silver's fear had swallowed her whole. Extended family was great, but it couldn't replace the absolute love and devotion a child needed from at least one parent.

Just seeing the longing in Casey's eyes when she watched

Landon with Amia made it all too clear that Casey knew she was missing out on something. Her father would never be what she really needed. Maybe Becky could find another man—a man like... like Zach—who could fill that place in her life. Zach would make an amazing father. But could he do what Landon was doing? More importantly, could he decide that nothing mattered more than a child who wasn't even his?

It was too soon, much too soon, to know for sure. But they'd already exchanged those loaded three words that meant they had some kind of future together. Or hoped to have it anyway. Becky hadn't planned to go there, but now that she had, she needed to know she was right. That Zach could be that man.

But if he wasn't... she wasn't sure she could shift things between them into something casual. If he wasn't, maybe she'd do what she had before. Go to clubs to take the edge off. Not let anyone get too close. Not let them into her life.

Because her daughter was her life. And either she meant just as much to whomever she let in, or she wouldn't let them in at all.

There was no middle ground. She heard her phone buzz and went to fetch it from her purse.

Zach. He was waiting for her. Wondering if she'd followed his instructions.

She had—for the most part. She'd used the Ben Wa balls, hadn't gotten herself off once. But she hadn't put them in today. This morning her daughter had been all about coming to Dean's house to see the baby. She soaked in the attention from Dean and Landon like a desert plant soaks in the rain. Ever since she'd come back from visiting her father, she couldn't seem to get enough of being the main focus. Becky would have thought she was jealous of the baby, but her eyes lit up every time Amia was around.

Casey didn't want to take anything away from Amia. She wanted to be part of Amia's whole world. A world that was full of love, of devotion.

Becky would do everything in her power to make Casey feel like she could have that, all on her own. Landon and Dean were Amia's sun and stars and entire universe. If all Casey had to herself was Becky, then Becky would shine just as brightly as both combined.

Having another star would be wonderful for her daughter, but Becky wouldn't put too much into hoping for it.

Because the man who should be that star for her daughter wasn't. And asking any man to take that place might be too much.

Damn it, I hope I'm wrong. She didn't pray often, but she did now. *God, prove me wrong.*

She heard Casey's laughter outside as she finished with the kitchen and tipped her head back to repeat her prayer with an added, "Please."

****

There was nothing more beautiful in the world than the sight of Becky coming toward him at that very moment. Her simple pale blue summer dress clung to her thighs as a light breeze moved over her with each step she took. The midday sun brought out the red highlights in her hair which flowed over her shoulders like liquid mahogany with a glorious polished sheen. And her bright eyes, her smile, told him everything he needed to know.

She'd missed him very, very much. Maybe even as much as he'd missed her.

Zach left the luggage with Scott, laughing at Becky's little smirk as she met him halfway across the pier. She'd obviously taken one look at Scott—with his Lacoste aviator sunglasses and bedraggled hair—and figured out that he was hungover.

"Be nice." Zach trapped her chin in his hand, bringing his lips close to hers. "He had a rough night."

"I can see that." But at that moment, she seemed to have eyes for only him. "Casey's spending the night at Dean's place. She loves his mother."

"So I have you all to myself?" He kissed her gently, enjoying the soft press of her lips, the way her breath caught as he slipped his tongue into her mouth. Her cheeks were flushed and she seemed to be having trouble holding still. He drew her tight against his body, whispering in her ear. "You did as I said."

She glanced around as though she was sure all the men disembarking the ship could hear him. And know exactly what he was talking about. She inhaled deeply. Let the air out slowly. "I did. It was hard to . . . to keep them inside."

"That's because you're so fucking wet." He kissed her throat, grinning at her little shudder. "Would you be more comfortable at your place or mine?"

"You're worried about my comfort now?" She groaned as he kissed down to her collarbone. "Zach, everyone's watching!"

"Is that a problem for you, pet?" He lifted his head to kiss her lips again, then tucked her against his side. "You haven't answered my question. We can go somewhere for lunch first if you—"

"Oh, hell no!" Becky poked him in the side. "You've tortured me for days. Take me home. Your place. Before I decide I have plenty of space in my backyard to bury your body."

Zach clucked his tongue. "Poking and threatening your Dom is considered rather unwise."

"Ha! Keep it up, and I'll show you how unwise teasing me is!" She yelped when he pinched her butt. "Zach!"

"Yes, my dear?" God, he loved seeing her all fired up. The "my dear" had her grey eyes flashing like lightning zipping through thick rainclouds. He kissed her before she could say anything else and get herself in trouble. "I'm in a forgiving mood because I'm very happy to see you." He brought his lips to her ear, lowering his tone to let her know he would only let her go so far. "Be my good girl and don't make me punish you."

The lightning faded, leaving her eyes sparkling with mischief. "What if I want you to punish me?"

His lips curved into a slow smile. "Then continue."

Uncertainty crossed her face like a passing shadow. Then she rose up on her tiptoes to whisper in his ear. "I'll take a punishment if it means we'll get out of here faster. My panties are soaked. You've been on my mind every second of every day since you left. No matter how much I wanted to come, I don't think I could have after what you said you'd do to me. My own touch wouldn't have been enough. I need you."

No sweeter words had ever been spoken. He ran his hands through her hair, tugging lightly until her gaze met his, pressing his hard length against her soft belly so she could feel the effect she was having on him. "We'll get going since you asked so nicely."

Her throat worked as she swallowed. She bit her bottom lip, and the shift in her gaze from challenge to surrender squeezed his heart and his hardened cock. They'd come to a good place together, a place where they could have a bit of fun, not take the lifestyle so seriously all the time. But could delve in deep when they needed to.

"Go wait at the car while I grab my bags and let the boys know they won't see me again until training camp," he said, more than a little relieved to see she didn't take his command the wrong way, simply nodded quickly and hurried off to the car. He'd be fine keeping her with him from this point on—though that would be rather unpractical—but she wasn't an exhibitionist. And even though no one knew about the Ben Wa balls held tight inside her dripping wet pussy, she would still feel like she was on display. Which would shift her arousal to discomfort rather quickly if he wasn't careful.

Scott was still with the bags—actually, he'd spread them out to make a bed right on the pier. The media was gone, which was good since Scott seemed to have given up on appearances. The remaining players and the Ice Girls walked around him without so much as a second glance. Most had seen Scott being drunk and stupid.

None of them knew why he was like this. Zach didn't either, but after last night he knew there was a very serious reason. He'd made some strides in finding out though, and he wasn't willing to give that up.

Zach shook his head and nudged Scott with his foot.

Scott squinted over the top of his sunglasses. "Hey. You leaving?"

"Yes." Zach held out his hand and helped Scott to his feet. "How you getting home?"

Twisting his lips, Scott looked over to where the crowd was converging around the parking lot. "Not driving. I'll catch a ride with Ramos and Carter."

Bad idea. With both Scott and Carter hungover, one of them was bound to say the wrong thing. Zach waited for Scott to grab his bags, then nodded in the direction Becky had gone, toward the far end of the lot. "Come on. I'll give you a lift."

Once they got to the car, Zach handed his bags to Scott to put in the trunk and went to speak to Becky. He didn't think she'd mind a short detour, but he'd show her the respect of giving her a heads up. "Scott's in no condition to drive. I'm going to drop him off before we go to my place, okay?"

"You don't have to." Becky relaxed back into the front passenger seat, squeezing her eyes shut and her thighs together. "I won't object if you decide to bring him along. Right now, I don't think I can object to anything."

He caught Scott stumble at her words from the corner of his eye. Scott wouldn't object either. But damn it, he didn't want to share. Not tonight. "Maybe some other time."

Becky opened her eyes. Gave him a curious look. Then shrugged. "It's up to you, Sir."

His brow rose at her blasé tone. "You're right. Perhaps I should take some time to consider . . ."

"No! Please, Sir. I can't . . ." Becky squirmed in her seat, her eyes pleading as he slid in behind the wheel. "Let's drop him off. Or leave him here. Whatever you think is best."

Zach put his hand on her knee, grinning when she moaned. "Much better, pet."

Scott dropped hard into the backseat, shaking his head. "Lucky bastard."

The man had no clue. Someday, he might get one, but not tonight. Every inch of Zach's flesh craved the woman at his side. And every thought in his mind was focused on a single word.

Mine.

****

The engine of the muscle car roared, sending vibrations right through Becky and bringing her close to the edge every time Zach pressed on the gas pedal. His entire focus was on the road, but she spotted Scott watching her through rearview mirror. The heat in his eyes was almost her undoing. She wasn't sure whether or not she liked that Zach wasn't letting Scott come along to play with her. Fighting her own pleasure for so long had finally put her mind in a hazy place where everything that happened around her was arousing.

Not just the vibrations of the car but Zach's laugh at a comment Scott made about a driver that cut them off. The brush of wind coming from her open window which made her nipples grow tight and hard. Even the material of the seat, the texture so rough under her bare thighs, seemed determined to torture her.

She shifted in her seat, whimpering as the engine got louder, the sound reverberating right into the small, sleek glass balls in her core. The bigger, weighted plastic balls she'd tried at first had filled her up more, but didn't engage her inner muscles as much as the glass ones. And they wouldn't have left much room for what Zach had planned.

Her cheeks heated at the thought. She clasped her hands in her lap, trying very, very hard to stop wiggling as moisture pooled down low. Then tensed as a bump whipped pleasure deep inside her.

Scott hissed in a breath, dropping his head back on to the back of his seat as Zach pulled over. He made a not-so-subtle effort to adjust himself in his shorts. "Jesus, Zach. I should have walked."

"I disagree." Zach parked the car, then got out. He helped Scott bring his bags to the sidewalk. "I was generous last night, but that changes nothing."

Generous? Becky bit the inside of her cheek. She wouldn't assume anything. Not yet.

"I didn't expect it to." Scott latched on to the handle of his bag. Becky turned in her seat to watch him glare at Zach. Something passed between the men that she couldn't quite get a read on. "A little leniency for good behavior."

"First of all, getting fucking drunk and hitting on one of your best friends isn't good behavior." Zach grabbed Scott's shoulder, stopping him before he could storm off. "Second, you know there was more to it. I meant what I said."

Their exchange cooled Becky's blood and cleared her mind. She finally had her answer.

She'd needed to know if Zach could put her and Casey first. She knew he would try, but whatever was between him and Scott couldn't be dismissed. It wasn't a passing thing, an itch he needed to scratch once in a while. She truly believed she could have handled them together if that's all it was.

But it was so much more. Too much.

She knew what she should do, but when Zach came back to the car, she couldn't make herself say the words. One look from him and all that mattered was the passion in his eyes and the way he made her feel. She'd pretended Scott didn't matter for this long.

One more night. One more night and she'd do what she knew was right for both of them.

"Are you okay?" Zach asked, taking her hand in his and kissing her knuckles. "Maybe we should talk about the cruise before—"

"No. What happened on the cruise isn't important." She brought his hand to her cheek and smiled at him. Lying to him hurt, but the truth would ruin the last bit of time they had together. And anyway, what he'd done *wasn't* important. She didn't want to hear about it. She wanted the last bit of time they had together to be about the two of them. "To be honest, I'm not sure I'd remember anything you tell me by tomorrow. You've had me waiting so long that . . ."

He didn't make her finish the sentence. "I understand. Tomorrow there are things I need to tell you. But you're right. I've kept you waiting long enough. And there's nothing I want more than to have you all to myself."

"You have me, Sir," Becky said softly.

For one more night.

Chapter Nineteen

The humidity in the condo after a week without the air conditioning and the sun glaring through the huge windows was almost unbearable. Dust sparkled in the still air, and the faint scent of lemon lingered from the floor polish. Zach threw a few windows open while Becky waited for him in the gym. In his bedroom, he went to his closet for his toy bag and some supplies, pausing to admire the chrome-like gleam of the chains he'd added to his collection just last week. Something about the weight of them, the noise they made when a sub struggled against their cold, impersonal grip on leather restraints, appealed to him more that the pliant caress of ropes. Not to mention how quickly they could be adjusted to manipulate a body into the perfect position.

He'd learned the ropes—literally—with Sue while the two of them had first started exploring the lifestyle, but hadn't tried chains until he'd played with his first "boy" years later. But he couldn't even recall how the wiry man had looked all bound up and exposed to him. All he could see was the erotic image of Becky's body spread out. He could almost hear her sweet cries accentuated by the sharp music of the steel links as he took her...

Rein it in, Pearce. He was already hard, with precum a cool smear at the tip of his dick. His jaw tensed as he forced his mind back to the task at hand.

He removed his shirt, tossing it in his hamper before joining Becky in the gym. Naked, on her knees in the center of the room, back straight with her hands palms up on her thighs, she was the vision of a sub patiently waiting for her Master's pleasure. Which brought him into the headspace where he could be the Master she needed. From the color of her skin to the ebb and flow of her breath, nothing about her would escape his notice. If she hadn't been in the right place to begin, he knew many little ways to help her reach it, but she'd put herself there with the same absolute trust a tiny kitten would give before curling up in his big hand to sleep.

He ran his hand over the velvety smooth strands of hair resting on her shoulder, smiling at the way she moved into his touch without shifting position. Her neck curved slightly when he caressed her cheek with his knuckles, but she kept her eyes forward, simply letting him do as he pleased.

Absolutely perfect. "You would make any Master very proud, little doe. Lovely poise. Nice and calm. If I asked you to, you would stay here, like this, all day without a word of complaint."

A tiny twitch at the corner of her lips was the only hint that she wasn't crazy about the idea. Her tone was soft and composed when she replied, "Yes, Sir."

"As always, you will tell me if you're uncomfortable. If anything becomes too much for you to handle." He circled her, drawing out the anticipation while he took his time drinking in how beautiful she was, with her heavy breasts thrust out, her wide hips and the generous swell of her ass a luscious temptation—he could push her forward on to her hands and knees and just worship her body for hours. But he wanted more than her body. This scene would expose all the parts of her she kept hidden. All her desires, all her fears, would be laid out to him. Bringing her to that level would take more than sex. It would require all his experience, would force him to expose own fears.

Which meant he had to trust her as much as she was trusting him. "We've discussed your limits, but I would like to clarify a few things. Anal sex is a limit, but I may choose to touch your ass, use my hands, or toys, to stimulate you. You will use yellow if anything I do comes too close to that limit. Pain is also an issue for you, but I will use a certain amount to increase your pleasure. Yellow if I reach the edge of what you can take. Red at any point when you cannot take any more. Do you understand?"

She nodded. He stopped by her side, not speaking again until she looked up at him.

"You will always vocalize your answers, pet. We've discussed this."

"I'm sorry, Sir." A light shade of pink spread over her cheeks. "I understand, Sir."

"Very good. Is there anything I should know about? Joint issues? Any discomfort in your muscles that would make certain positions uncomfortable?"

"No, Sir. I think I'll be fine in any position." Her tongue flicked over her bottom lip. "But . . . the balls I put in are small. I'm not sure how much longer I can hold them in."

His lips quirked. "I believe I can help you with that. Stand up."

She rose gracefully, the small lines in her forehead and tension in her jaw the only evidence of her struggle to keep the balls inside her. When he patted her thighs for her to spread her legs, she let out a whisper of protest.

"Open." He nodded as she parted her thighs, then he cupped her pussy and covered her mouth with his to swallow her gasp. "Give them to me."

Blushing, she held her breath and went perfectly still. He could sense her trying to relax, but she couldn't seem to bring herself to push the balls out of her body. He kissed her cheek as he pushed two fingers into her, pulling out one ball, then the other. His fingers and the balls were slick with her juices. Erotic to him, enough to make his dick throb and his balls tighten.

But Becky evaded his gaze as though she was embarrassed.

"Everything about you is so fucking sexy," he whispered, his lips close to her ear. "You have no idea how much it turns me on to have you this wet for me."

She gave him a hesitant smile. "Thank you, Sir."

"You're very welcome, pet. I don't ever want you to feel ashamed or embarrassed when you're with me." He left her standing there and went to his toy bag to pull out some cleaning wipes. Leaving the balls wrapped up in one, he took out four leather cuffs and a plain leather collar, then returned to her. "The collar is new, but we'll only use it this one time. From this point on, whenever we play, you will wear my collar. We'll find one together that's a little more personal, but what it means won't change. Once it's on your throat, you are completely under my control. Every worry, everything beyond the scene, is gone."

"But what if—"

"No what ifs. Your phone is in the other room. I'll hear it if anyone calls, and I will tell you if there's an emergency." When she nodded, he continued. "Let it all go. Let me take care of you."

"But only while the collar is on, right, Sir?"

"Right. I think the distinction will make things easier for you. You can say or do whatever you want after I take it off."

Her lips curved into a wry smile. "Within reason."

He chuckled. The collar wasn't on yet, so he was fine with her playfully throwing his words back at him. "Exactly."

As he wrapped the supple black leather around her neck, she held her breath. But then let it out with what he could only describe as relief when he locked it in place. The faraway look in her eyes told him she'd sunk even deeper into her submission.

That she'd let herself go.

This was what he'd wanted from her. And yet, it meant that he had to be even more aware of her body language, of her reactions, her pulse, even the way she blinked. Before long, she'd be too immersed in the sensations to really care about her limits. Or much else besides what she was feeling. Which meant he had to do it for her.

Small beads of sweat covered his chest, which didn't bother him, but the way Becky's hair clung to her temples and her throat made the temperature a problem. He returned to his bag to fetch the Ben Wa balls, then went to adjust the AC. He grabbed a bottle of water from the small fridge at the back of the gym while putting the glass Ben Wa balls, still wrapped up in the cleansing tissue, on a shelf inside. He brought the bottle of water to Becky, let her have a few sips, then set the bottle aside. After putting the wrist and ankle cuffs on her, he brought her over to the steel framed multi-station. Weights filled two sides of the huge cubical structure, and there was a padded bench stretching out from one side, but this area was cleared for chin-ups. And ideal for bondage. The chains wrapped around the top and bottom corners looked a little out of place, but he could tell by the way Becky's eyes widened that she knew exactly what they were for.

He clipped the steel fasteners at the end of the chains to the D-rings on her wrist cuffs, then knelt to do the same to her ankle cuffs. A few adjustments and her entire body was spread open, the chains clinking softly as she covertly tested her restraints. He fit his body against hers, pressing his lips to her throat, smiling against the rapid pulse beating under her soft flesh. The subtle aroma of her sweet, floral perfume, mixed with the heady musk of her arousal, made his nostrils flare.

"Close your eyes." He backed away enough to make sure she obeyed, then brought his hands up to hers, lacing their fingers together. He kissed her closed lids, her cheeks, her lips, drawing his fingers down over her palms, along her inner arms. He traced the pulse of her throat with his fingertips, so very slowly, absorbing her heartbeat through his touch. The texture of her smooth, damp skin. He let her feel the scuff on his cheek against hers as he caught her ear between his teeth with just enough pressure to make her breath catch. Then he tasted her skin, salty and sweet all at once, like some kind of decadent candy he could suck on for hours.

His chest swelled with pride as she shivered and dropped her head, her features softening as she relaxed. He could sense her letting the restraints hold her, feel her sinking deeper into that special zone where there was no resistance, nothing left to hold her back. He knew it wasn't easy for a sub to go there with a Dom, and it would be even harder for Becky because she'd been hurt so badly in the past. That she would do it for him was precious.

There were no words to tell her what it meant to him. But he did his best, wrapping her hair around his fist and letting his tone convey all that what he said would lack. "You're safe with me. I can see you know that, and it means more than I can say. What you're giving me is a wonderful gift. One more valuable than anything I've ever been given. I accept it. And I will keep it. Always."

A single tear spilled down her cheek. "I love you so much, Sir."

He dried the tear with his thumb and kissed her. "I love you too. Now be still. I'll be right back."

She hissed in a breath through her teeth as he moved away from her. He listened to her letting it out slowly as he went to his toy bag. He hadn't taken out everything he would need because, while anticipation was good, the element of surprise added an edge to pleasure. An edge the fear a sub felt when they set eyes on certain toys wouldn't always serve. He brought the toys over to lay them at Becky's feet. Curved his hand around her hip to let her feel his presence. Then brought her heavy breast up to his mouth to suck a hard, thick nipple between his lips.

"Deep breath, baby." He dried her nipple while rolling it between his finger and thumb. Opened the small, metal tweezer clamps and closed the rubber padded tips on the rosy nipple. Becky's whole body jerked, and she shuddered as the clamps pinched her flesh. "Give me a color, little doe."

"Yellow, Sir. I hate these things." Her bottom lips trembled. "They hurt so bad!"

He frowned. He hadn't even tightened it yet. "Is it really that bad, Becky? I haven't added any pressure. Have you used these before?"

"I have, but the teeth dig in and . . ." She swallowed, her brow furrowing. "There's no teeth. No cutting."

Fucking Christ. If he ever found the Dom who'd abused her trust and forced her to experience . . . but no. There was no point in dwelling on that now. He gave her a moment to absorb what she was experiencing with him. Mild pain, if that.

"There's a bit of pressure, but . . ." She exhaled roughly. "Not yellow. I'm sorry, Sir."

"Don't be sorry." He moved the tiny circle to add a bit more pressure. "Tell me when it reaches the point of actual pain."

She bit her bottom lip. Then gasped. "Oh! Enough! No more, please!"

"Good girl." He put the other clamp on, circling both nipples with his thumbs as she adjusted to the sensations. "So pretty. Your breasts are nice and heavy. You should feel them more with the clamps on."

"I do, Sir." Her hair was clinging to her temples again, but this time, it wasn't because of the heat. She gave him a grateful look when he smoothed it back. "I've never been the type of woman to get much out of a man playing with my breasts, but . . ."

"This is different." He smiled when she nodded. Good. Very good. He wanted everything about their scene to be different from the half-assed scenes in her past. "You do know they hurt more coming off?"

"I know." She giggled, a light, happy sound that made his cock strain against the zipper of his jeans. "But I think I can take it."

"Good. Eyes closed." He reminded her. She shut her eyes

obediently, and he picked up the flogger at his feet. From this point on, he would do everything in his power to make every memory she had of all the toys a Dom could use pleasant. "Don't forget it is me touching you. Toying with you."

"I won't forget, Sir. I'm here for you. I just hope all the talking isn't ruining things."

"It isn't, but I think you need to be silent for a while. Find the place where you were before. Stay there. Let me do the thinking for you."

"Is it enough for you, Sir?" She tensed as he ran the strands of the flogger up her inner thigh. "I need to know that I'm giving you something too. I can't . . . I don't feel right just taking."

The way she held on to that tender, generous nature, through it all, was precious. But he wouldn't be satisfied until he helped her let it all go. He flicked the flogger lightly against her flesh. Not hard enough to sting. Just enough to get her ready for what would come. "You're giving me—" He took a step back, flicking the flogger again. Harder this time. "—everything I need."

The tension in her body kept his strikes light at first, just hard enough for a slight sting. But as the tension eased away, he let her feel the leather strands wrap around her inner thighs, over her belly, her breasts. The chains clinked noisily as she arched toward him, silently begging for more. Stark red welts marked her flesh as he let the flogger strike her with a bit more force. Enough that she'd feel it for days. He hit the rosy flesh around her nipples, slowing his pace as the muscles in her thighs tightened. She wasn't a masochist, but her arousal, mixed with the endorphins each bite of the flogger sent pulsing through her veins, brought her closer and closer to her release.

And it was time to give it to her.

"Now, little doe." He stood close to her, flattening her breasts with his chest, filling her with two fingers, slapping her outer thigh with the flogger. Again. And again. "Let me hear you scream!"

Her pussy gripped his fingers convulsively. She threw her head back and let out a scream that sliced straight down the length of his rock-hard cock and speared his balls. He dropped the flogger and withdrew his fingers. She was still clenching, still shuddering from her climax.

The next one would be even harder.

He went to the fridge and took out the Ben Wa balls. While they were still nice and cold, he pushed them inside her, savoring the lovely contrast of the cold glass entering her blazing hot body. Tiny goose bumps covered her flesh as he dropped to his knees, rubbing his cheek along her inner thigh before bringing his tongue up to her slick pussy. He held on to her thighs as he licked her, groaning as he pushed his tongue into her snug cunt, pushing it past the muscles fighting to keep those little balls inside.

"Don't let them go." Breathing hard, he pressed his forehead to her stomach, feeling his grip on control falter. She was so far gone she didn't answer him. Simply dropped her head back and thrust her pussy closer to his face. "Stay with me, Becky. I'm going to take you now."

"Ah!" She trembled as he pressed one last kiss on the plump flesh of her pussy lips. "Zach!"

He stood and undid his belt. Folded it and slapped the length along one if her quivering thighs. Then the other. After unclipping her wrist and ankle cuffs from the chains, he steadied her with an arm around her waist, then turned her to face away from him. He clipped her wrist cuffs above her once again, then drew her thighs together and cinched them with his belt. It would be a tight fit, but it would also make it easier for her to hold the glass balls inside. There was a condom on the floor with his toys. He unzipped his jeans, then tore the wrapped of the condom, peeling it over his feverishly hot dick.

Fisting his dick in his hand, one arm around her waist, he pushed between her thighs, into her wet slit, shoving hard until he was in as far as he could go. He pulled her flush against him. The little balls shifted around the head of his cock and the sensation made him shudder. He drew out, then slammed in hard. The chains sang along with her rough cries.

* * * *

Becky's gasps had hurt her raw throat as the cold glass balls had filled her. She'd been so sure they would slip out, but then Zach had used his tongue on her, bound her thighs together, and filled her up with his dick. For some reason, those tiny balls made her even more moist than usual. And the way they massaged her inner walls, gliding around, stimulating new places within, kept her balancing endlessly on the verge of yet another orgasm.

Everything had passed in quick, erotic flashes, numbing her brain. Her skin sizzled everywhere that the flogger had hit her. Zach's broad chest pressed against her back. He moved around her, and she let out a scream as the tight pinch on her nipples from the clamps disappeared and blood rushed back into the puckered flesh. Pain swelled out through her breasts, making them sore and sensitive as they swayed. She felt his dick between her clenched thighs, driving into her cunt hard, making those little balls move faster, slipping and sliding until the noises coming from her kept time with their every shift.

Control was lost. Belonged to him. All of her belonged to him. Everything except for her mind and her heart. But even the wall protecting them crumbled as she screamed, coming again and again. The tight confines of her pussy were breached mercilessly, and she couldn't stop it. Didn't want to stop it. She dropped her head, shaking as his dick dragged in and out, so slowly that she could feel the silken flesh moving over his steel length. Feel the throbbing of his pulse as he swelled, as he slammed into her and let out a growl of release.

He didn't pull out right away, and she wasn't sure whether it was more for his benefit or hers, but when he finally eased out she realized all her bones had disintegrated. Her body wouldn't do anything she wanted it to. She couldn't stand up straight, couldn't move her arms—her arms, still up over her head with her wrist cuffs attached to chains. Zach unclipped the cuffs one-handed, holding her against him with one arm bracing her back. He carefully placed her arms around his neck. She tried to straighten her legs, but they were stuck together.

"Easy, little doe." Zach smiled, a hint of amusement in his eyes as he picked her up. "Let's get you settled so I can take that off."

She thought he'd put her on the floor or on one of the benches.

Instead, he carried her to his room, laying her down on the bed, grinning as she let her arms flop down at her sides. She groaned. "You broke me."

He unstrapped her legs, then rubbed his hands over the indents left by the belt. Glancing up at her words, he chuckled. "You're still in one piece. You might be a little sore by the time I'm done with you, but—"

Her eyes widened. *Is he joking?* "You're not done with me?"

"I told you, Becky." He shifted, gently massaging her arms and her shoulders. "I'll never be done with you."

His hands on her, soothing, comforting, made her feel heavy. He made her kneel up on the bed and release the Ben Wa balls, then eased her down, tucking her in as her eyes drifted shut. She struggled to open them again.

"Don't fight it. Sleep for a little while." He stretched out beside her, petting her hair, his voice deep and soothing, almost hypnotic in the way it helped her sink deeper into that peaceful place in her head.

"Can't. You need—"

"I need to hold you." He kissed her cheek. "That's all."

* * * *

Soft kisses, a hand massaging her breast. *So very nice.*

Becky turned her head sleepily, smiling against Zach's lips as he climbed over her. She was already wet and ready for him, more than happy to feel his weight settle on her, his fingers gliding into her pussy at a lazy pace. She was still wearing his collar, so he could do whatever he wanted to her. And there was something fulfilling about him taking her in the dead of the night, using her for his pleasure before she was even fully awake.

He rose up on his knees between her thighs. She kept her eyes shut, her body soft and open to him.

Something cool spilled over the moisture slicking her folds. His fingers spread it further, down to her back hole. She whimpered as the tip of his finger dipped into her *there*.

He'd warned her, but she hadn't expected him to toy with her there now. His touch had been so sweet, so loving . . . there was nothing loving about a man fucking her ass.

He said he wouldn't.

"Do you trust me, Becky?" Zach kissed her stomach, his gaze steady on her face as she opened her eyes to look at him. "I know your limits, and you know I won't go past them."

"I know, but—"

"Trust is more than a word. Let me prove that I deserve yours." He brought his mouth down, sliding his tongue along one side of her clit, waking it with the lightest touch. His finger moved in and out of her tight, puckered hole—such a strange contrast to the tender attention he was giving her pussy.

And yet . . . not really. The lube, the slow glide of his finger, wasn't rough or unpleasant. She rested her head on the pillow, gasping in air as pleasure built up inside, more like the flames of a hundred candles than a bonfire, a steady, controlled flame with just as much heat.

His finger slipped out and something hard pushed against her. Stretched slightly, then settled inside. She heard a wrapper as he moved away. Peeked at him to see him cleaning his hands. Another rip as he tore a condom wrapper. He pulled her arms up over her head as he lay over her, holding them with one hand as he filled her.

"Oh!" She pressed her face against his shoulder, absorbing the strange sensation of her body stretching around him with that thing inside her. No pain at all. Just the feeling of every part of her being taken by him in some way.

"Not bad?" His breath stirred her hair as he drew out, then slowly glided back in.

"Mmm, not bad at all."

Their lovemaking was unhurried, but didn't last long. With all those new nerves brought into play, she ended up coming hard twice, her legs wrapped around his waist to bring him in closer. Harder. They lay tangled together for a long time, and she could have stayed that way longer, but he gently eased out, then left the room. He returned with a facecloth to clean her. She was half gone when he pulled the thing out of her—a very small butt plug. He disinfected it with a cleansing cloth, then dropped it in the drawer of the night table by his bed.

"Zach, why didn't you . . ." She sighed as he stretched out beside her, sleepily rolling over to use his shoulder as a pillow. "Did you . . . ?"

"I did, little doe." He kissed her forehead. "But I'm happy that you didn't worry about that until now."

"Too tired to worry." She snuggled close to him. He seemed satisfied, so there wasn't really anything to worry about anyway.

Until she woke up the next morning. She slipped out of bed, careful not to wake him. While getting dressed, she studied his face, shadowed with a bit of scruff, but relaxed. There was no way she could wake him up and tell him what they had wouldn't work. That after everything he'd given her, it was over.

Maybe she was wrong. Maybe everything would be fine.

I need to think about this. I need to make sure I'm doing the right thing.

She couldn't do that here. Not with him so close, making the decision seem so easy. When she looked at him, all she could think about was how much she loved him. On how empty her life would be without him in it.

"Zach?" She leaned over, shaking her head and pushing him down when he grunted and tried to sit up. "I have to go. But I'll call you later, okay?"

"Becky . . ." He groaned and hooked a finger to the collar still around her throat, not pulling, but keeping her in place. "It's early. Are you sure you have to leave now?"

"Yes." She bit her bottom lip as he nodded. "I need to take this off."

He rubbed his face with one hand, his brow creased in thought. "I left the key in the gym. Bring it to me and I'll—"

"I'll do it." She pursed her lips at his frown. "We've discussed *this*, Sir. I had an amazing night, but it's morning. Time for me to get back to my life."

"And that means I can't take your collar off for you?"

"Next time." She knew he hadn't even glanced at the clock yet. And probably hadn't gotten much sleep on the cruise, because he didn't question her further. Just laid back, letting out a low laugh as she tucked him in.

"No worries, Becky. If you feel off today, give me a call. I pushed you a little . . ." He took her hand, kissing her palm without opening his eyes. "But I need you to know you did plenty for me. I know it bothers you when you think you haven't."

"I'll call you if there's anything." She promised, even though she wouldn't. There was no reason to call until she figured things out.

Until she decided whether or not "next time" was worth the risk.

Chapter Twenty

A hard-core beat sounded in the darkness. Zach sat up quickly, reaching for his phone on the night table, hoping the guitar rift of Metallica's "Whiskey in the Jar" didn't wake Becky up. He glanced over to Becky's side of the bed as he answered and frowned. She wasn't there. His brow furrowed as he vaguely recalled talking to her—he looked at the clock. It was only 8:15 a.m. Must have been early.

"Zach?"

By the sounds of it, Tim had repeated his name a few times. Zach scratched his jaw, leaving his room naked to fetch a bottle of water from the fridge even as he spoke. "Yeah, I'm here. What's up?"

"We have a charity street hockey game today with some college kids. I mentioned it to your agent, but she never got back to me."

Zach's laugh sounded hollow to his own ears as he tried to keep things light. For some reason, he felt a little off. He cleared his throat and took a swig of water. "She's juggling details for my contract and a wedding, so I'm not surprised. Why didn't you mention it on the cruise?"

"Honestly? I forgot what day it was scheduled. Madeline just reminded me." Tenderness softened the coach's tone. Nice that things were going so well between him and his woman, but it would be nice if he could pull his shit together.

That last thought aggravated Zach even more than the last-minute invite. He rolled his shoulders, trying to ease the tension coiled around his spine. *Pull it together, Pearce.* He inhaled slowly, nodding. "Sure, I'll be there. What time?"

"Around ten?" Tim sighed. "Sorry about the short notice. I've been a bit distracted lately."

"How come?"

"Madeline and I have been trying for a baby again. She's taking fertility drugs, I'm watching the calendar, and—" Tim snorted. "You don't need to hear this."

"It's all good, Coach." Actually, it was great. Tim would make an amazing father, and the couple had been trying for years. But Zach couldn't seem to work up any enthusiasm about it. *You need a fucking cup of coffee.* "Let me get ready and I'll be right over. Where are we doing this?"

After getting directions, Zach hung up and went to fix himself some coffee. He'd downed a full cup, black, before his conversation with Becky came back clearly. She'd had to leave—hadn't mentioned why. And he hadn't questioned her because they had an agreement. She decided how he fit into her life. Which was fair. She had her daughter and her career. He had the game.

What they had came in the rare moments between.

That worked for him, but still . . . something about her leaving nagged at him. He'd known their scene could trigger things for her. If not right away, then possibly when she woke up. She'd promised to call, he remembered that clearly, and she was experienced enough as a sub to keep an eye out for a drop, but that wasn't the same as *him* keeping an eye out for one. Why should she feel alone, uncertain, sad? He was right here.

Call her.

No. She'd gone because she had things to do. She spent enough time with Bower and Richter for one of them to notice if something was off. Of course, they wouldn't know to look out for it.

He didn't like the idea of going behind her back. He turned his phone in his hand for almost an hour to make sure he was doing the right thing before dialing. Becky's independence could be an issue if she dropped and didn't catch it in time. Better safe than sorry.

Richter answered on the first ring. "Pearce."

"Yeah. How are things?" He went to the small desk in his living room, ruffling through the drawers for a cigar. Lighting it, he dropped into the high-backed wood chair and took a long drag. "How have Silver and the baby settled?"

"Amia is doing well. Silver . . . Silver will be fine." Richter cleared his throat. "The girl thinks she has to handle everything on her own. Much like Becky. I assume she's the reason you're calling?"

"She is. We had a scene last night that might take longer to recover from than she expected." He paused, feeling pride digging in its heels. Ignoring it. "Since she couldn't stay, I hoped you could look out for her."

Richter didn't speak for what seemed like a very long time. Then he sighed. "I had a feeling she didn't tell you. Rebecca asked for some time off—with all she's put in setting things up for the Ice Girls' show, Keane gave it to her. She called him earlier this morning, before her parents left so she could go with them to Gaspe."

"Gaspe." Zach blinked, sure he'd heard wrong. "She . . . did she say how long she'd be gone?"

"Two weeks. Maybe three. Keane doesn't need her until right before training camp."

Two weeks. Zach ran his tongue over his teeth, nodding slowly. "All right. Thanks, Boss."

"Pearce—?"

Zach ended the call. His hand shook as he brought his cigar to his mouth. It was fine. Just fine. She needed time with her daughter. With her family.

She hadn't told him.

Why though? Had she just wanted to get away from him? Nothing in her tone or actions this morning even hinted that, but why else would she go from having a busy day to taking off for weeks? In any normal relationship, a couple would discuss long absences beforehand.

That apparently wasn't the kind of relationship they had. He pushed his chair back carefully, resisting the urge to throw it, and went to the kitchen for more coffee. The bitter liquid burnt his tongue as he gulped it down, but he hardly felt it.

What exactly is it that we have?

Something other than what he'd thought they did. Which didn't change how far he'd pushed her. He wouldn't have pushed her that far if he'd known . . . he snuffed out his cigar and went through his kitchen drawers, looking for—there. Clove cigarettes. The pack was still closed; he didn't indulge in cigarettes often, but he wanted one now. He put the filter of the black cigarette between his lips, staring at the flame of his lighter as he lit the tip. Stupid to smoke this much this close to training camp—he couldn't bring himself to care. He felt weighed down. His brain felt foggy. He had to snap out of it.

In his room, he changed into black jogging pants and a white Cobra T-shirt. He stuffed his phone and his cigarettes into a black knapsack with his wallet and a bottle of water. Grabbed his motorcycle helmet from his living room table. A glance in the hall mirror told him he needed to shave. He looked like shit.

And I give a fuck, why?

He was pissed. But not at Becky. At himself. There must have been clues, must have been something he'd done that had made her want to leave. And he hadn't fucking caught it. What he'd done to her—his neck cracked as he rolled his head from side to side. Any Dom worth his leathers would have known she wasn't ready. Would have realized it was too soon to fucking go there. A flogger and anal play. *Damn it!*

On the way to the school yard where the teams would play, Zach spotted the red flashing lights and cursed under his breath. On top of being an irresponsible Dom, he was being an irresponsible driver. At least 10 miles over the speed limit.

"License and registration," the cop said, sounding bored.

"No fucking kidding." Zach pulled his wallet out of his backpack. He handed his documents to the cop. "Just give me the ticket."

The officer took off his sunglasses. "We gonna have a problem here, Mr . . ." He looked at Zach's license and shook his head. "Why am I not surprised? I guess being a star athlete means that you don't have to follow laws like everyone else, right? All the fucking money in the world—a ticket don't mean shit."

A car pulled up behind Zach's bike. The officer's hand went to his hip, close to his gun.

"Hey, Pearce!" Chicklet stepped out of the car. She frowned at the officer, then glanced over to the passenger side of the car. "Laura, I think one of our boys got himself in trouble rushing to the *charity* game."

Laura came out from the other side. "Is there a problem here, Butler?"

Aw, fuck. Just haul me in. The last thing he needed was to be "saved" by a sub. She would hate him if she knew what he'd done.

"No, ma'am." The officer's lips thinned. "Unless you're going to tell me not to give him a ticket because you're in bed with the team."

"I'll pretend I didn't hear that," Laura said tightly. "If he was going too fast, give him a ticket. If he did anything else, bring him in. I just hope you're not taking this personally because your little sister is fucking one of the players. Which one is it this week? Brookmann?"

"You fucking bitch . . ." Butler hissed through his teeth, then went to his car, returning with a ticket which he slammed into Zach's chest. "Try not to kill anyone, asshole."

Once the cop was gone, Chicklet and Laura approached Zach, both looking concerned. Zach spotted Vanek, getting out of the backseat, and couldn't take it anymore.

"Don't ask." He took off before they could, wishing the route was a little longer when he parked and saw them pulling into the lot behind him. He was in the fucking mood for a fight and he wasn't sure why. His whole body was shaking. He wanted to break something.

He should have stayed home. Alone in a dark room with his thoughts of how much he'd fucked up. *I should have called her.*

Things only got worse when the game started. The teams were divided school yard-style and the dozen Cobras that had come were split evenly amongst the college kids. Late teens, early twenties, all the boys were overexcited about playing with the Cobras. Being downright obnoxious. And the younger Cobras weren't behaving much better. Carter checked Zach, holding him against the brick wall as Vanek swiped the puck and dashed for the net. Zach growled when Carter wouldn't back off. The crowd cheered as the puck hit the back of the net.

"You're gonna have to do better than that if we're gonna make the playoffs. That was pathetic, dude!" Carter smirked and moved to join him team.

Zach latched on to the front of Carter's shirt and slammed him into the wall. "Dude? I suggest you watch it, you smart-ass fucking twinkie. If you were my sub—"

"Jesus, Pearce." Chicklet slapped her hand into Ramos' chest a second before he could lunge for Zach, then pried Zach's hand from Carter's shirt. "Ramos, cool it. Carter, you open your mouth again and I'm gonna flog you myself. Pearce, take a walk."

Ramos took a step back, but his eyes were hard as they met Zach's. "We will speak again, *hombre*."

"I don't think that will be necessary, Ramos." Tim stepped between them. He drew Ramos aside, speaking low.

Ramos' expression softened suddenly. He caught Carter by the back of the neck and led him away. The rest of the team had banded together to distract the curious college boys, giving Zach some space. Which he badly needed.

I don't need space. I need Becky. I have to find out if she's all right.

"I've got it, Chicklet." Tim patted Chicklet's shoulder, nodding as she gave him a look Zach couldn't read. He felt completely out of control. And when Tim turned to him, it seemed like the man knew it. "Go ahead, Pearce. Take a swing. Curse me out. I can't promise I won't bench you for half the season if you're going to be an idiot about this, but if you're itching for a fight, I'm right here."

"I should go." This had never happened to him. He was a loose cannon, and he had no right to force anyone to deal with him like this. He needed to be alone.

But Tim wouldn't have it. "Dean told me Becky left." Tim's brow rose as Zach's jaw ticked. "You two had a scene last night, right?"

"That's none of your business, Coach." Zach clenched his fists at his sides. And kept them there. *What the fuck is wrong with you, Pearce?* He loosened his fists, then went to his knapsack, which he'd dropped on a nearby bench. He pulled out a cigarette, groaning when he realized Tim had followed him. The other players had continued the game without them. Fans filled the lot, cheering from the sidelines with players' wives and kids.

He grunted as Tim took the lighter from his shaky hands to light his cigarette. "Thanks."

"Did you eat today?"

Zach frowned. Just the thought of food made him feel a little sick. "I had some coffee."

Tim laughed. "We'd have words if you gave me that answer before a game. What would you say to a sub if they were behaving this way after a scene?"

"Coach, you can go fuck yourself. I'm fine." Hell, since when did he talk to the coach like that? Tim was the best thing the team had ever had. Zach knew that. But he couldn't stop lashing out. "Damn it. I didn't mean that."

"I know." Tim shook his head and pulled out his phone. He pointed at the bench. "Sit down. And listen to me. There are benefits to being a switch. We aren't expected to be perfect—"

"Believe me, I know I'm not perfect." Zach's eyes narrowed. "What are you getting at? I shouldn't be here."

"This is the best place for you. With your teammates." Tim gave him a hard look when he opened his mouth to protest. "You would do the same for any one of them, Pearce. I wish I'd figured things out in time to do it for Callahan. Maybe he'd still be here." He shook his head. "Just shut up and let me help you."

Zach rolled his shoulders, not sure it mattered one way or another. He wanted to go home, where no one would have to put up with him being a complete asshole. He puffed at his cigarette, feeling the burn deep in his lungs, knowing he'd regret it when the trainers got to him.

Tim gave him a sideways glance as whomever he was calling answered. "The physical conditioner said you couldn't get out in time to make the game, but we need you." He paused. "More importantly, *Zach* needs you."

The call didn't last long. Whomever Tim had spoken to was coming.

And it didn't take a genius to figure out who he was.

* * * *

Scott rolled his eyes as Stephan followed him down the hall, bitching as usual. His voice was thin with exertion as he struggled to keep up with Scott's long strides.

"You're not ready. You waited too long to get in good enough shape for training camp. It's going to be brutal."

"I've been through this before. Fuck, Stephan, by the way you talk I've been sitting on my ass all summer eating fucking nachos." Scott patted his firm stomach. "I'm at the gym every day. I'm being a good boy and cutting back on the red meat. What else do you want from me?"

"Tell me what's so important that you had to blow off your conditioning. People are watching everything you do. That trainer will report back to Keane. He'll think you're not serious about—"

Stopping short, Scott glared back at the little man, fed up of working his ass off and getting no fucking credit. Yeah, he'd earned people not thinking he took *anything* seriously, but when would his actions start to count for something? "I'm in the best shape I've ever been in. Me and Sahara have smiled pretty for all the cameras. When I'm not posing for photos or getting kicked in the nuts by angry chicks with asshole boyfriends, I'm doing promo and charity gigs. I don't have a life. But I do have friends. People that matter to me. If taking some time to be there for them means I'm not serious, then you and Keane can go rim each other in the middle of the Delgado Forum. There's a lot I'll give up for this team, but there's got to be a limit."

"Fine!" Stephan slapped his hand onto the glass door of the gym before Scott could touch it, shoving it open. "Tell me and I can make it work for you. That's my *job*!"

No fucking way would he tell Stephan what was going on. Coach said Zach needed him. That was personal. Beyond his keeper's payroll. But he had to give the man something. "You told me I needed to find a chick for the public to see me with, right?"

Stephan's brow furrowed. "Right."

"This isn't about a chick."

"Damn it. I can't make this look good for you, Scott. The league barely managed to tolerate Pearce coming out." Stephan's expression was fit for a man who'd been told the world was about to go through a full-fledged zombie apocalypse. He took the car keys from Scott's hand, waving him toward the passenger side as though he'd accepted that serving as a chauffeur was the best he could do at this point. "But he's in a position to make some positive changes. You're not."

"And you're repeating this to me why exactly?" Scott smirked as he dropped the passenger seat back far enough so he was almost lying down. He knew it irked Stephan when he looked sloppy and lazy, but hell, he had to have *some* fun! Besides, showing up to see

Zach acting all worried wouldn't do him much good. He'd use the drive and irritating Stephan as a way to tone things down a notch. "I promise, I won't propose to him until after Keane offers me a contract."

The man didn't take the bait. Instead, Stephan cast him a sideways look as he pulled out. "You're going to see Zach?"

"And if I am?"

Stephan shrugged. "You suddenly don't look overly concerned. The shift in behavior is a little surprising. I assume it's not serious?"

"It's serious enough." Scott brought one hand to the back of his neck, massaging the knots out of his muscles. Acting all relaxed wasn't gonna be easy. "But I need to keep my cool."

"I see." Stephan's lips curved up on one side as though he was considering something. "Perhaps some good news will help you both. I received a call while you were on the cruise from the YWCA, the organization that runs the Rose Campaign to end violence against women. They really appreciated your interview discussing what happened to your foster sister. They wanted to know if you'd like to get involved."

Scott sat up, blinking. They wanted *him*? "Are you sure I'd be good for that? I mean, I'll donate money and stuff, but I want to *help* the cause, not—"

"You'll be perfect. Speaking of which, letting the Cobras know that you had a difficult childhood would probably serve you well." Stephan sounded excited now, like he'd finally come up with a way to fix all of Scott's problems. "People will be sympathetic. They'll understand that you were just acting out because—"

Scott cut Stephan off with a sharp motion of his hand. Making up shit wasn't a solution. "Stop right there, Steph. My childhood was fucking fine. You think I was drafted out of the fucking womb? Yeah, I was in foster care, but I've had support my whole life."

"All right. It was just a suggestion." Stephan sighed. "Your behavior sometimes indicates some kind of abuse, but—"

"Abuse?" He sucked his teeth, more than a little pissed that the man would throw a word like that out when he didn't know shit about Scott's past. And even if he did . . . *No. Just no.* "You're joking, right?" Scott rolled his eyes at Stephan's solemn look. "I was spoiled rotten. My foster mother gave me anything I wanted." *Everything.* Scott tugged at the collar of his T-shirt—stupid thing was too tight around his neck. "My behavior is all me. I'm trying to fix it, but don't make excuses for my shit."

Eyes on the road, Stephan gave a curt nod. "Very well. I'm not a therapist in any case."

"No kiddin'?" Scott straightened his seat, opening his door and jumping out before Stephan had finished parking. "You can use my car or bring it back to my place to grab your own. Whatever you want. I'll catch a ride with Zach."

"Okay. But, Scott?" Stephan waited for Scott to look at him before he continued. "Please use discretion, whatever you do. You have made progress and . . . How can I say this in a way you'll understand?" His eyes hardened. "Don't fuck it up."

"Gotcha." Scott saluted, then spun on his runners, needing to get away from Stephan before the man decided they needed to have another heart-to-heart. He approached the lot behind the school at slow saunter. A rather large crowd surrounded the play. Reporters from local stations had cameras set up, locked on the game. The Cobras were putting on a pretty good show.

Sneakers slapped on pavement, but other than that the sounds weren't much different than what you'd hear on the ice. Shouts from the men. The scrape of sticks, then the snap when they hit the orange ball being used as a puck. The way the guys played was like there were points on the line.

Carter hogged the puck, effortlessly looping around the college boys to take a shot on Ingerslov. Then he spotted Scott and tripped over his own big feet.

Guess he remembers. Scott chuckled, nodding at Tim as the coach waved him over. Two cute little Ice Girls cut him off, giggling and shoving cans for donations at him. He pulled out his wallet and stuffed a few twenties into the can. Then he made his way to the end of the lot, close to the back of the school, where grass and flower beds softened the harsh appearance of the school yard. Zach sat on a long, wooden bench, puffing at a black cigarette, filling the air around him with a pungent, spicy scent. Black butts littered the grass around his feet.

The man had sacrificed his lungs to whatever was eating at him. Scott clenched his jaw, his throat tight as he looked at Zach, head bowed, shoulders hunched. Zach was the strongest man he knew. Seeing him like this made Scott feel... powerless. What the hell could he say or do to make things better?

If anything, he'd probably make things worse.

Tim latched on to Scott's arm and drew him back far enough that Zach couldn't possibly hear them. "Ever heard of 'top drop'?"

Scott arched a brow. "Yeah. At the club there was a big debate going on. Chicklet and Callahan were butting heads about it. She was saying Doms should prepare for it before a scene. Callahan seemed to think it was bullshit. A few of the other guys agreed with him. I didn't have anything to add, so I stayed out of it."

"So you have no opinion on the matter?"

"Not sure. I mean, I've never seen a sub drop, so I guess I could be an ass and say that's not real either." Scott knew he was being a bit of a jerk, but seeing all the Doms and subs on the team all in the loop, and knowing he didn't fit in there either, got him feeling a bit defensive. "My opinion doesn't mean much."

Tim's lips thinned. "My question was pretty straightforward. Why don't you just give me an answer?"

Damn. All right then. "Doms are still human, right? I mean, Chicklet said sometimes she feels like she's doing stuff most people think is messed up. She beats her subs. Makes one watch while she fucks the other. It's not that hard to believe that a Dom would need a sub to say it's all good after, right? I mean, a Dom is all about the subs during the scene. Looks out for them after. But..." *Fuck.* His muscles tensed as he glanced back at Zach. It was not okay with him for Zach to feel like he'd done something wrong. *Where the fuck is Becky?* "Who takes care of the Dom?"

"My thoughts exactly." Tim let out a rough exhale. "Zach's in a bad place. I called my brother to find out what was going on. Becky left. Zach asked Dean to keep an eye on her because they had an intense scene, and she'd taken off early this morning. This conversation happened at about eight a.m., so we're talking *really* early. Dean had to tell Zach Becky had gone to Gaspe with her parents. The thing is, Zach was worried about her. Worried that she'd drop. I think he's like the rest of the Doms that go to the club. They're all concerned about their subs dropping but are too macho to admit to what they feel after a scene. Dean's no better. I'm sure he'd spot it if Bower dropped, but there's a lot of snuggling and talking after their scenes with Silver, so I'm pretty sure it hasn't been an issue."

"Are you telling me Becky just left Zach, like right after he ... fuck, what did he do to her?" Scott felt a little sick. He'd seen enough scenes at the club to wonder if Zach didn't deserve to feel like shit. If he'd used a whip on her, made her bleed—screw helping him get past the drop. Unless beating the crap out of him would help? "She's in Gaspe? Maybe I should go see her. And maybe you called the wrong person. If he fucking beat her—"

"Damn it, Scott. Maybe you're right. Maybe I *did* call the wrong person." Tim took a step back. "Do you know Zach at all? He's not a sadist. And what if he was? Would that change how you feel about him?"

Scott inhaled sharply. He knew Zach. He wasn't sure how he'd feel about the man if Zach enjoyed drawing blood like Callahan. But that probably had more to do with how Scott felt about Becky. She wasn't into that extreme. Or ... he didn't think she was.

Being into two people was complicated. How was he supposed to handle this? People at the club talked about trust a lot. Did he trust Zach?

On the ice? Absolutely. With Becky ... he couldn't just *give* that trust. But this was *Zach*. The man who'd pushed Scott away from Becky because Scott couldn't be faithful. Couldn't give her what she needed. Would Zach *ever* risk hurting Becky?

No fucking way. "You're my coach. If anyone else asked me this shit, I'd tell them where to go. But ... fuck! You've got my career in your hands, and I trust *you*. If I'm gonna be honest, I love Zach—" Scott swallowed. Had he really just said that? Did he mean it?

Yes. Great big fucking yes.

"Tell me what to do. I don't really get this whole 'top drop' thing, but I don't get sub drop either. And I'd be there for Becky if she was going through it. Damn, Zach doesn't smoke this much. I get that as a coach you probably don't think any of us should smoke at all, but Zach's all about moderation. I'm not seeing that right now."

"I wish I *could* tell you what to do, Demyan. And you're right. In moderation, Pearce smoking cigars—and even cigarettes—isn't any worse than the other men going to a fast food joint once a month. In my experience as a sub, a drop can make me feel off for a few hours. On a rare occasion, days. I don't know the effects of a top drop long-term—if there are any. But right now, I'm concerned. That's why I called."

"Got it." Scott knew he had been right about one thing back in the car. Going to Zach all serious wouldn't do any good. He needed to handle this with his devil-may-care attitude. He swung at the coach with a feigned left jab, right hook when he noticed Zach watching. "Thanks, Coach."

"No problem." Tim threw a light punch that connected with Scott's gut, laughing at Scott's exaggerated grunt. "I heard that you're going to be the new spokesman for the Rose Campaign. I'm impressed."

"Yeah?" Scott grinned, his chest swelling as Tim gave him a look filled with something he couldn't recall ever being aimed his way. Pride. Coming from the coach, it meant a lot. "I mean, it will be good for my image. But that's not why I'm doing it."

"I know." Tim nudged Scott's shoulder with his fist. "Now go get him, kid."

Zach watched Scott as he approached, his expression more curious than defeated. He nodded in Tim's direction as the coach headed back toward the play. "What was that all about?"

Scott dropped on the bench beside him, still grinning. "I got an offer to be the team's spokesman for this anti-violence against women's group."

"Nice." Zach brought a fresh cigarette to his lips, shook his head, then dropped it to the dirt to crush it under his heel. "I'm happy for you. It'll be good for people to see what a good guy you are."

"Yeah, well, I'm honored to get the offer, you know?" Scott ran his tongue over his teeth. "You don't look happy though. What's going on?"

"I'm sure Tim had some theories."

"Yeah. Something about Becky leaving and you needing to snuggle." Scott shrugged. "I'm good with that."

Letting out a dry laugh, Zach dropped his head back. "Right. You? Snuggling?"

"Sure. But I want to get in on this game first." Scott's lips formed into a crooked smile as he stood. "I'm thinking we should play for something. The winner gets whatever he wants from the loser when we go back to your place."

"Figures you'd make this about sex."

"Who said anything about sex?" Scott asked lightly. "I win and we have a zombie marathon. And you've got to watch them all. Even the cheesy classics."

Zach stared up at him, nodding slowly. He pushed off the bench, pulling Scott to him in a way that would look like a rough hug between friends to anyone watching. But the length of his firm body pressed against Scott's, the way his gruff tone made Scott's balls tighten, had nothing to do with friendship. "I win, you come to my place and you suck my cock. Then you spend the night."

Easy enough. "Done."

"I mean it, Scott." Zach released him, his eyes hard. "No fucking disappearing in the morning."

"Wouldn't think of it, man." Scott slapped Zach's shoulder as they walked side by side back to where the other guys were resting up between periods. "And hey, I'm sure she had a good reason to take off. Don't think the worst until you talk to her."

"I'm not, it's just . . ." Zach shook his head, his brows drawn together as though he couldn't quite figure out what to think. "It's all good. I just need to know she's okay."

"She's fine. You didn't do any . . . permanent damage, did you?" Scott hated to ask, but he needed to know what he was working with. "Accidents happen, and I get that. But if she left when she should have been in the hospital or something—"

"Damn it, Scott! You really think I'd do that to her?" Zach raked his fingers over the hair cut close to his scalp. "A scene can bring a sub to place that leaves them vulnerable. I'm not sure I spent enough time easing her out of that place."

"What about a Dom? Do they go to that place?"

"No. The Dom's in control." Zach frowned at him. "Why do you ask?"

Scott shrugged. "Just wondered. You know I'm trying to learn stuff at the club. I might never be a Dom, but if I played with someone, and felt shitty after, would you tell me I shouldn't?"

"Of course not." Zach put his hand on Scott's arm, stopping him before they were within hearing of the other men. "What are you getting at?"

An ice cream vendor ringing a bell and rolling his cart around the lot to tempt the kids passed. Scott waved to him, then jogged over to buy a couple of Häagen Dazs chocolate-covered bars. He brought them back to Zach, then handed him one.

"You get to be taken care of too." Scott unwrapped his bar, lifting it toward Zach in mock cheers. "And I'm gonna do it, whether you like it or not."

Zach took a big bite of his bar, crunching on the chocolate shell and licking his lips before inclining his head to Scott. He already looked a lot better than when Scott had shown up. He actually managed a smile by the time he finished his ice cream.

"Chocolate?"

"Yeah." Scott smirked. "Thought pulling you into my lap wrapped up in a blanket might not be appropriate."

The roar of Zach's laugh had most of the men staring at them. The team was used to Zach being pretty reserved around them. But those who'd known what was going on looked relieved. Tim gave Scott a thumbs up. Even Chicklet smiled.

Scott left Zach to get ready to play, feeling damn good about himself. Zach was gonna be okay. And one way or another, they'd be together tonight.

Most importantly, Scott had finally done right by the man.

* * * *

Becky's hair was a tangled mess under the motorcycle helmet, but she didn't much care as Zach unbuckled it and tossed it down on the gravel by the bike's wheels. She gasped as he bunched her hair in his fist, holding her still while he ravished her mouth, thrusting his tongue deep into her mouth as he ripped open her leather vest. Her nipples hardened as the sun bathed them in heat.

Zach leaned back against the bike handles, slowly unzipping his leather pants. His dick jutted out, hard and proud as she rose up to take him into her body, shamelessly exposed with her black pleated skirt barely covering her thighs. He stretched her slick folds roughly as his hips jutted up and she arched her back, crying out. Letting him fuck her on his bike by the highway was so perfectly wicked. It made her feel young, wild, and free. She had nothing to worry about other than pleasing this man who could have her anytime. Anywhere.

"Look at those pretty tits." Scott chuckled when she gaped at him, then leaned down to bring one breast up to his mouth. "You want both of us, don't you?"

"Yes!" Becky kissed Scott as Zach rammed up into her body, completely lost in the sensations of the men's hands and mouths and bodies. "Please!"

"Then you know what you have to do, pet." Zach growled, wrapping one arm around her waist to ram her down hard. "Just forget everything else."

"No! No, I can't!" Becky woke, shoving the sheets away, slapping her hand over her mouth when she spotted Casey, sleeping peacefully beside her. Tears clung to her lashes as she pressed her face into her pillow. At least she hadn't woken her daughter.

This wasn't like her, this last minute decision to take the early morning flight to Gaspe with her parents, getting Casey up at 7:00 a.m. to make the trip. She'd packed in such a rush that she was sure she'd forgotten something. And what must Mr. Keane think of her calling so suddenly to tell him she wouldn't be coming in for two weeks? She was lucky that he hadn't fired her!

But she'd had no choice. Her relationship with Zach had become too much to handle without putting space between them to figure things out. She needed to spend time with her daughter. With her parents, who were the perfect example of how a good, strong relationship *should* function. God knows she hadn't managed that in her own marriage.

Her nap had only served to make her feel more tired. Drained. She slipped from the guest bedroom, padding downstairs to the kitchen, smiling groggily at her mother who met her with a cup of freshly brewed coffee.

"Oh, honey." Her mother shook her head, brushing Becky's hair back to look into her eyes. "Maybe you should lie down for a bit longer. You're so pale..."

Becky forced a smile to her lips. "Sleep won't help, *maman*. I just need time out in the sun with Casey. I'll bring her to the park later."

"I see." Her mother gave her a shrewd look. "There are parks in Dartmouth."

"I know *that*." Becky took a few sips of coffee and sighed. "I wanted to spend time with you."

"Don't you lie to me, *mademoiselle*. I spent weeks out there with you and your brother—"

"Are you upset that I came?"

"Of course not! You're always welcome." Pulling her into a hug, careful not to spill either of their coffees, her mother whispered, "but I know you. Before Patrick, you would face your troubles head-on. But ever since... it's as though you must analyze everything and then lock away your emotions before making any decisions. As though the part of you that feels is something to be hidden. Maybe even ashamed of."

Her mother was so wrong. She wasn't ashamed of her emotions. And there was nothing wrong with considering her options before doing anything rash.

And leaving Zach like that? That wasn't rash?

Just knowing she wouldn't see him tomorrow, or the day after, or... a weak sound escaped her before she could stop it. This was wrong. Needing a man was so very wrong.

But she missed him already. And he'd be so hurt, so confused when he found out that she'd left. Guilt made it impossible to sleep well. Or even take in enough air when she breathed. Maybe, if she called him, spoke to him...

You'll want to go home. You should go home!

Her mother's grip tightened around her. "Talk to me, *ma bichette*."

Bichette. Little doe. Becky let out a watery laugh. Her mother and Zach using the same endearment for her should feel weird, but it was just so right. As though Zach had known exactly who she was from the start. A little doe, trapped in a tunnel, not sure if the light at the end was the sun or a car coming to crush her. And because she couldn't tell, she ran.

"I don't know what to say." She sniffed. She might not be sure of much, but she was absolutely certain of one thing. "I've felt off since Casey went to visit Patrick. There are so many distractions back home. I need it to be just the two of us for a little while."

"All right. But, Rebecca?" Her mother's tone was that special mixture of firmness and tenderness. The tone she'd used when Becky was little and slipped out of sight for a few moments, long enough to scare her mother to death. An "I love you, but don't you ever do that again". "Don't hide. Not from me. What you went through with Patrick . . ." Her mother's face crumpled. "I don't understand how you put up with it. How you let him tear you down the way you did. I raised you to know your worth."

"*Maman*, he cheated on me. And he had no respect for me. But something good came out of that hell of a marriage. I can't regret what we had. It gave me Casey."

"He taught you to feel alone. And you're not."

I am. But that's my choice. The only one who should never feel alone was Casey. She was a child and she needed her mother. But Becky told her own mother what she needed to hear. "I know I'm not. I have you."

Unconditionally. And she would give her own daughter no less.

Chapter Twenty One

"Put a movie on, Scott."

Scott froze midway between the door and the sofa where Zach had stretched out. Scott's hands were curled under the bottom of his T-shirt. He'd been all ready to strip and get on his knees—Zach's team had won after all. Apparently, Zach wasn't ready for his prize.

"Sure. Umm . . ." Scott went to the hutch where Zach kept all his movies, then glanced over his shoulder. "Got anything in mind?"

"I thought you wanted to watch some zombie movies?"

Rubbing the back of his neck, Scott studied Zach. "But I lost."

"That you did." Zach's lips twitched with amusement. "Pick a movie."

All the movies Scott wanted to watch were on Netflix, so he closed the hutch and went to grab the remote for the PS3. After pausing George A. Romero's original *Night of the Living Dead* he took a step toward the kitchen. "Want anything?"

"Yeah. Get some popcorn and a couple of beers." Zach snorted when Scott stared at him. "Don't give me that look. I know what time it is. You ever heard that country song? Pretty sure Mason's played it a dozen times in the locker room."

Uh-huh. Must be five o'clock in fucking Ireland or something. Works for me. But Zach was a social drinker. Again with the moderation. Scott glanced over at the black Roman numeral clock on the wall above the front door. "Not even two here, man. You're not still being all destructive because you're kink damaged, are you? Maybe you need more chocolate?"

Zach covered his face with his hands, groaning and laughing. "I'm not kink damaged. Just having a beer with a friend, pal."

"Right." Scott inhaled slowly as he made his way into the kitchen, getting the popcorn ready and snatching the beers out of the fridge. All the muscles in his back felt like molten steel, hardened in an unnatural mold. *A friend. Guess it's something.* He dumped the popped kernels into a red plastic bowl, then brought everything back to the living room, more than ready to suck his *"friend's"* dick and get the fuck out of there. He wasn't even sure why the label bugged him. Maybe because he wanted there to be more between them.

And there never would be.

"Take off your shirt," Zach said, bringing a small handful of popcorn to his lips. "And come here."

Scott practically tore off his shirt, then threw it in Zach's face. "I don't give a shit what everyone thinks. You're a fucking asshole. At least I'm clear when I'm not serious about someone. You've got me jumping through fucking hoops to be your *friend*? Enough with the head games. I know you sadistic fuckers are into them, but they don't do anything for me."

Zach dropped the shirt on the floor by the sofa, looking so damn calm Scott wanted to crack the man right in the jaw. His deadpan tone didn't help. "Are you quite done?"

"Soon as you blow your load down my fucking throat, *buddy*."

"And *I'm* damaged? Damn it, Scott. I saw you were concerned. I appreciate it, but I'm feeling better." Zach turned on to his side, bracing himself up on his elbow. "I'm taking you up on the snuggling."

"You—you're what?"

"You heard me." Zach sighed, pushing to a sitting position. "We both know we're more than friends. I don't know how *much* more yet, but I'd like to find out. I'm not in a rush to get off. I want you here, lying next to me." He pulled off his own shirt and laid it over the back of the sofa. "I just want to feel you. Skin on skin. Nothing else."

"Nothing else . . ." That confused Scott more than the "friends" thing. Yeah, he'd gambled for a movie marathon, but that was because he figured Zach would like him not being all about sex. Didn't mean he got it though. And he'd understood even less after Zach had thrown in the blow job token. "So we're doing . . . what? Platonic shit?"

"No. You owe me." Zach grinned, slouching back on the sofa in a way that drew Scott's attention right down to the well-defined lump between Zach's parted thighs. "But there's no rush. Part of the deal is that you're not going anywhere."

"I'm staying." The words came out like a breath that had been held too long. The pressure building up in Scott's chest evaporated. Finally made sense. Zach needed to know he'd stick around—more so after Becky's disappearing act. Scott gave Zach a crooked smile, shoving at Zach's chest until he was lying down again. "Good thing you've got a big sofa. We ain't small guys. Need our space"

"Not too much space though." Zach dropped his arm over Scott's side as Scott pushed back against him, his fingers running lightly over the trimmed, golden blond hair on Scott's chest. He kissed Scott's shoulder. "Press play. Pretty sure I haven't seen this one."

Scott grabbed the remote and unpaused the movie. He pillowed his head on his arm, eyes drifting shut as he focused on how good it felt to have Zach touching him. Different, because he didn't *do* nice and tender. Or simple affection. But it relaxed him. Made him forget about the rush to get the job done. This wasn't about getting his rocks off. Hell, he didn't think being with Zach in any way could ever be something quick and cheap. There was so much more to it. Emotions and all that crap.

It was fucking scary when he let himself think about it.

They stayed like that during the first movie, leaning up just a bit to take sips of beer. Which was different too, because Scott usually just guzzled beer down—the whole point of drinking was getting numb, right? But it wasn't like that now. He got to enjoy the crisp flavor of the German lager. Zach drank beer the same way he smoked cigars—or cigarettes. To appreciate the flavor. He appreciated the few vices he allowed himself, and rarely overindulged. Scott couldn't help but wonder if he was like those vices. Something to savor on occasion.

Is that a bad thing?

He couldn't say. Drinking or smoking too much could be a bad thing. Ranking on the same level as Zach's clove cigarettes meant they wouldn't be spending tons of time like this. Zach would be the one to pull back, wary of the damage Scott could cause.

I could be good for him.

Scott groaned as Zach's hand wrapped around the front of his neck and his lips slid along the corded muscles of Scott's throat. Zach's other hand was low on his stomach, slipping into his shorts, his boxers.

I will be good for him.

"Fuck, I love having you here like this." Zach let out a low growl as he stroked Scott's dick. "You've dropped the front. You're all mine."

"Fuck!" Scott jutted his ass back against Zach, not sure what was getting to him more. The pleasure of Zach's firm grim on his cock, or the fact that it *was* Zach. Kissing his neck and saying shit that smashed all the walls Scot usually put up when he got with someone. Sex was physical. Just a thing he did when he had the urge. But with Zach, it meant more. And he *needed* to show Zach just how much more it meant. "*Please.* I messed up, man. I'm sorry; I'm so fucking sorry that I—"

"It's over, Scott." Zach's teeth scraped the curve of Scott's shoulder. "I forgive you."

"*I* don't forgive me." Scott rolled over, off the sofa and on to his knees. "I *owe* you."

"You don't. Just stay with me and we'll call it even." Zach lurched to his feet, pressing the heels of his palms to his forehead. "I know that sounds pathetic, but—"

"It doesn't. I get it. That's how I felt when I came to move Becky's stuff. She set me straight, but all I wanted . . . all I wanted was for you both to *let* me stay." Scott held up his hands when Zach gave him a pained look. "I earned it, Zach. She loves you, and she didn't want me to hurt you again. I know I did. And I hate myself for that." He latched on to the back of Zach's legs, then pressed his forehead against Zach's thigh. "Never again. I've never had anything I cared about losing, but I don't want to lose you. Either of you. And I'm trying to prove it."

"You're doing a damn good job, Scott." Zach petted Scott's hair, his tone gruff with passion. "If it was just me, I'd risk it. But with Becky . . ."

"I know. She's got a lot more to lose. And if she's not sure of you—fuck, what chance have I got?" Scott gritted his teeth. "I need . . . I need to know I'm getting somewhere. Don't give up on me, Zach."

"Not happening." Zach framed Scott's jaw with his hand. "I've got you, Scott. I'm not letting you go."

"Good." Scott gave Zach a feral grin. "So is you fucking my mouth going to ruin all this?"

"You are too much. I won't use you. You've got some shit to tell me before I'm comfortable with this."

"What shit? Like how much I want your cock slamming into the back of my throat? Like how it makes my mouth water just to feel how hot and hard your dick is through these jogging pants?" Scott rolled the jogging pants over Zach's hips, exposing his flushed, throbbing cock. "How about how good it feels that you're letting *me* do this to you? Because I know you're fucking picky. You don't do this with someone you don't care about. And you care about me, don't you?"

"More than I can say, Scott." Zach thrust his hips forward as Scott wrapped a hand around his dick. "But I know you. I could be anyone. And I can't deal with that."

"Not anyone, Zach. Not anymore." Scott wanted to suck Zach's dick, make him come hard, but he had to be sure Zach really understood that he wasn't just saying what Zach needed to hear. That he meant it. He stood, still holding Zach's dick, and faced the man. He held Zach's gaze as Zach opened his eyes, staring at him. "When you jerked me off, you asked me to look at you. To remember who was touching me. I see you, Zach. I could have a dozen different men any day of the week. But I've shot every fucking offer down because none of them are you."

"Do you mean that, Scott?" Zach grunted as Scott dropped back onto his knees, his hands clasped at the back of Scott's head. "You'll give all that shit up?"

"For you?" Scott dipped his head down, taking Zach's dick in deep. He made a low, hungry sound in the back of his throat before he lifted his head. "You're fucking right, I will."

At first, Zach just stood there, letting Scott bob his head and slide his lips up and down his dick at a steady pace. But as Scott reached the limits of Zach's control, Zach pushed harder on the back of his head, holding Scott still to fuck his mouth, leaving Scott with no choice but to take him in. Rough, just what Scott liked best, but it was the penetrating look Zach gave him that brought his own arousal up a few dozen notches. As though Zach was being rough not just because it felt good, but because he knew what it was doing to Scott.

Scott used his tongue and the suction of his mouth to stimulate Zach as the man rammed deep into his throat. He held tight to the back of Zach's thighs, breathing through his nose as Zach held him close, coming hard.

The pulse under his tongue, the salty spurt he swallowed, gave him a sense of power. He finally had something to give, even if it was nothing but pleasure. Zach had said a lot of things *Scott* needed to hear, but the man was probably still feeling pretty low. He loved Becky, and Scott might be nothing but the next best thing.

Still, it was something. Scott licked the last of Zach's cum off the tip off his dick and stayed on his knees as Zach dropped heavily on to the sofa. They were even as far as the bet went.

But Scott owed Zach so much more.

* * * *

Rain splattered on the window in Zach's bedroom window, the slight part in the curtains showing the grey morning sky. Zach rolled over to the cold side of the bed and let out a bitter laugh. Things had been good between him and Scott the night before—hell, the man hadn't even pushed for sex. But Scott's promise to stay was like most of his good intentions. Not worth much in the long run.

You giving up on him already, Pearce?

Zach rubbed his scruffy cheek, sighed, and shook his head. He wouldn't give up on the man, but it was hard not to be disappointed.

Maybe his "keeper" called him again. Maybe he was being considerate, not waking me up.

Yeah, and maybe they really would get their hands on the Cup this year.

There was no point in dwelling on what he couldn't change. He was feeling a lot better than he had after waking up to find Becky gone. Between the two of them, he should probably get used to spending his mornings alone.

And being left in the dark.

At around 2:00 a.m., he'd gotten a short message from Becky. Not much to go on, but something at least: *I'm sorry for leaving like that. This is for my daughter. Please understand.*

He understood—not why she'd gone about it that way, but they would discuss that when she called. He checked his phone. If she called. The text he'd sent seconds later had a read time stamp on it. No reply yet.

After fetching a change of clothes, he left his room, ready to shower and start his day. He had to call his agent, let her know that he'd gone off the deep end because there could be repercussions. And then he should get in touch with his personal trainer. Time to up his training to get ready for camp. He never really slacked off, but he liked spending the last few weeks before hitting the ice getting in top shape. Which meant no more smoking. Or drinking. His diet could use some fine-tuning—

The warm scent of cinnamon drifted down the hall, and he glanced toward the kitchen when Scott cursed. Seeing Scott, standing there with a tray of food, had Zach rubbing his eyes to make sure he was actually awake.

"Couldn't stay in bed just a few more minutes?" Scott walked past Zach, back into the bedroom. "Get in here."

Zach laughed, following Scott and climbing onto the bed, legs stretched out so Scott could set the tray on his lap. "What's all this?"

"Food, dumbass." Scott grinned. "You got French toast last time we roomed together on the road. I make 'em pretty decent."

Actually, the French toast was delicious. Zach chewed on the first mouthful, making an appreciative sound in the back of his throat. The hotel had made it a little soggy and bland. Scott's had a nice texture and a fresh zesty taste that Zach couldn't quite pin down, along with just the right amount of spices. He swallowed and cut another piece with his fork. "This is really good. I didn't know you could cook."

Scott shrugged. "Can't do much, just a few of my favorites. Had to learn to feed myself if I didn't want to eat out all the time. After being on the road, it's nice to come home and have a few meals in my own kitchen."

Zach could relate to that. His own cooking skills were little more than functional, but he'd had Sue who enjoyed making elaborate meals when they were together, and his two boyfriends after had been domestic types. He had a feeling Scott had never had anyone who'd taken pleasure in serving him. Whatever people thought of him, he'd learned how to take care of himself.

But had anyone ever taken care of him?

Bringing another bite to his mouth, Zach eyed Scott.

"What?" Scott shuffled his feet. "Is everything okay? I put cream in your coffee. No sugar. I know you drink it black sometimes, but usually when you're in a rush, and you ain't so—"

"Everything's perfect, Scott. I'm just . . ." Zach shook his head. "I'm still processing. I thought you'd left, but instead you were doing this. It's unexpected."

"In a good way?"

"Definitely," Zach said, smiling. He finished the French toast, then sipped at the coffee. "Did you eat?"

"Yeah. I've got that women's self-defense thing today, so I made sure I ate and showered early. Gives me some time to chill with you before I have to take off."

"How much time do you have?" Zach let his gaze travel slowly over Scott, from his bare chest to a pair of loose-fitting jeans that Zach recognized as his.

Scott's throat worked. He followed Zach's gaze to the jeans. "Hope you don't mind that I—"

"I don't." Zach relaxed back against the headboard as Scott took the tray off his lap. "Are you going to answer the question?"

"Ah . . . guess I've got some." Scott's eyes shifted away from Zach. "Want to finish that movie?"

Zach cocked his head. Now this was interesting. If Scott was a sub, Zach might think he wasn't ready for the level of intimacy that came with making love, but didn't know how to come right out and say so. Maybe that wasn't so far from the truth since sex usually meant so little to Scott. Zach nodded. "I'd like that. The movie was just starting to get good."

"Okay." Scott turned, then cursed softly before putting the tray on the night table. He moved toward Zach, speaking through his teeth, "You fucking scare me. I know it will be more than . . . it will be more. I want it, but it kinda freaks me out."

Jerking Scott down onto the bed, Zach quickly rolled over him, grazing his teeth down Scott's smooth jaw. He gave Scott a bruising kiss while undoing the jeans. Smiled against Scott's lips at his groan. "You know what scared me? I thought you would run again. I thought you had. But you stayed." He slid his hands between Scott's thighs, gently massaging his heavy sac. "You had the balls to stay."

"*Shit.* I want you." Scott's hips jutted up as Zach palmed his fully erect dick. "I told you I'd stay. Wasn't for this."

Zach sucked at the side of Scott's neck, running his hand up and down Scott's cock, his own balls swelling and pulsing with lust, his blood pounding along his hard length. "This" wasn't why he'd wanted Scott to be here when he woke up, but it was impossible to let Scott go now that he had the man in his bed. "Do you have any idea how difficult it was to hold you at arm's length all this time? Sometimes I wished I could be like you. Fuck without caring."

"I don't want you to be like that. If you were, I wouldn't love you so damn much." Scott wrestled Zach onto his back, teeth bared, tone gruff, not giving Zach a second to react to the impact of his words. "It was worth the wait, but I can't hold back anymore. Take me or I'm gonna take you."

Sweat broke out on Zach's flesh as he shoved Scott off him, pushing him face down on the mattress. He bit the back of Scott's shoulder hard enough to leave a mark, then let out a harsh laugh. "Not this time."

Fetching the lube and condoms from the night table drawer, Zach took a few deep inhales to calm himself enough to make this good for them both. Last time they'd had sex, they'd both been drinking. He wasn't sure if Scott had ever been with anyone, man or woman, completely sober. Fast and hard would be no different than what he'd experienced so many times before.

He covered himself and climbed over Scott, sliding his lips along Scott's spine. He rose up to squirt some lube into one hand, then pressed one finger between Scott's ass cheeks, sliding it into him slowly. Scott shivered, letting out a muffled sound as he pressed his face into the pillows.

"So fucking hot." Zach worked another finger in alongside the first, pumping his fingers at a steady pace as he pressed his forehead against the center of Scott's back. The grip of Scott's inner muscles around his fingers heightened the urge to slam his dick in to the man's perfectly willing body, but something deep inside him held on to making this better than their first time. Zach withdrew his fingers, spread lube over his length, then slid it into the crease of Scott's ass, one arm wrapped around Scott's waist.

"Jesus, Zach!" Scott panted, thrusting his hips backward. "I need you inside me."

"I know. But one thing first." He lowered so he covered Scott's body completely, one hand on his own dick, the other pressed to the side of Scott's face to turn his head for a long, slow kiss. He made sure Scott was looking at him, then whispered against his lips, "I love you too."

* * * *

All the air went out of Scott's lungs at the same time as his heart skipped about a dozen beats. Zach loved him? His jaw hurt from grinning while pressing his mouth hard to Zach's, trying to kiss the man back. A sharp laugh of relief came out with the little oxygen he had left. He felt light-headed and fucking wonderful. And he never felt *anything* when he got fucked. Nothing real or lasting.

But how could he feel any less with Zach?

The smooth head of Zach's cock stretching him brought a twinge of pain. A bit more pressure and Zach's slowly breached the snug ring of muscle. Scott inhaled, holding it in as the sensation took over.

"Relax, Scott." Zach kissed his temple, rocking his hips to penetrate Scott with shallow thrusts. "I don't want to hurt you."

"I don't care if you hurt me." Scott braced his forehead against the pillow and bucking his hips back to take Zach in all the way. The cotton pillowcase dried the sweat on his brow, but the rest of his skin was slick with it. He wasn't sure what he was saying anymore. He just kept mumbling the same words over and over. "It's you. *You.*"

"Yes." Zach latched on to Scott's hips, holding them tight as he eased out, then in, gradually going deeper. Harder. "You're making this very difficult. I want to be gentle. But I've been waiting for you—" Zach slammed in, lifting Scott up to meet his thrust "—so fucking—" he pistoned in and out, his slick flesh slapping against Scott's ass "—long."

"I don't need gentle. Fuck!" Scott threw his head back as Zach rose up and angled his dick in a way that stimulated the most sensitive spot inside him. Every slick drag in and out forced him open a little more. When Zach rammed in to the hilt, the feeling of fullness caused Scott's balls to tighten and the pleasure building in his spine to billow outward like steam contained in a tightly sealed steel pot, ready to burn everything it touched when it was set free. As Scott clenched around Zach, Zach slowed his pace, hitting that same spot again and again. Scott groaned, fisting his hands into the sheets. "There. Right there."

All that hot, hard flesh pounded into him. He almost lost himself to the pleasure, but then Zach's hands were on his shoulders, pulling him up on his knees, lips pressed between his shoulder blades, slipping as he moved, the scruff on his jaw scraping Scott's flesh. "Don't let go yet. I want this to last."

"Ah!" Scott bit the inside of his cheek, struggling for control as Zach lowered his hand, taking hold of Scott's dick. The loose grip brought him up to the edge. He was going to come. He leaned his head back onto Zach's shoulder, trying to think of anything that would calm him down enough to make it last like Zach wanted. An image flashed behind his closed eyelids, and he had to lock his muscles not to throw himself away from Zach and right off the bed. He was in another time. Another place. Small and vulnerable. The sting of rum scalded his throat. He opened his eyes wide so he could stare at the wall. So he could forget *her* face. "Not now. Damn it, not now!"

Zach went still. "Scott—?"

"Fuck me, Zach! Please!" Scott's eyes burned as he kept them focused on the wall without blinking. Pure white marred only by his shadow. And Zach's. *Zach's!* "Don't stop! I don't want you to stop!"

Suddenly, Scott was empty. His lips parted in protest, but the words caught in his throat as Zach flipped him onto his back, then slid into him.

"I think it's better if you come for *me*." Zach slapped one hand on the bed by Scott's head, thrusting hard. "*Now*."

Scott's back arched as he came, shuddering and snarling. The pressure release like an avalanche in the mountains sent cascading over a cliff with a scream. His mind went blank, but he still felt the urge to get away. To run. There was a reason he rarely fucked or let anyone fuck him sober. Sometimes getting off felt amazing, but so fucking wrong.

He used the sheet to clean the cum off his stomach as Zach pulled out. Then he shoved back, throwing his legs over the side of the bed. "Sorry. I really messed that up."

"Don't you dare move." Zach grabbed Scott's arm and jerked him onto the bed and into his arms. "If anyone messed this up, it's me. I know there's something you're not telling me. I should have made you before letting this happen."

"I'm not a fucking chick, Zach. I don't need to 'share' before getting with someone." Scott stopped fighting and leaned against Zach's chest. "This is just different. But in a good way."

"Is it?" Zach stroked Scott's back, resting his brow on top of Scott's head. "You weren't in a good place at the end. Admit that at least."

"For a second I . . ." *Fuck, I can't lie to him.* Scott sighed. "No. I wasn't in a good place. I'm not sure why."

"We'll figure it out." Zach framed Scott's jaw with his hand, tilting his head back to kiss him. "But . . ." He laughed. "How are you feeling otherwise? I didn't hurt you?"

"Not any more than I wanted you to." Scott shifted, the ache in his ass, the tenderness running up from his balls to the tip of his dick, drawing out a low groan. Just thinking about Zach fucking him was enough to make his cock twitch like it hadn't had enough. But overall, he felt pleasantly drained. And something more. He liked having Zach's arms around him. Liked knowing sex wasn't the beginning and the end of what they had. "It's weird, but for the first time, I'm not looking to get out of bed as fast as I can. If I had nothing else to do . . ."

"I like hearing that." Zach chuckled and kissed his cheek as he eased Scott up to his feet. "But you do have to go. What we have doesn't change what you have to do to stay with the team."

For some reason, it bothered Scott that Zach thought staying with the team was the only reason he was doing this. He gathered his clothes, then paused by the door. "Some of those women I do the self-defense thing with . . . they've been beaten. Or worse—like Akira. Others are scared because they know someone who has been. I can't tell the guys I enjoy putting on that stupid padded outfit and letting the girls beat on me, but . . ." He raked his fingers through his hair, shrugging. "I do. Even when it hurts, them hitting me hard enough to feel it is good. It's not a masochist thing. It's the look on their faces when they realize they have the power to defend themselves." He shook his head, knowing he wasn't making any sense. "There's nothing like it."

"Scott, you might be surprised to know that the guys and I heard about all the different stuff you're supposed to do to look good. We all do the charity thing, but you were the first one to volunteer for this. It's pretty obvious that it means something to you." Zach curved his hand around the back of Scott's neck and shook him, smiling. "You're a better person than you know. But we see it. It counts."

"Yeah, well . . ." Scott wasn't sure how he felt about things getting all mushy between them. His insides were like the French toast from the hotel. Soggy and warm like bread that hadn't gotten solid enough to hold together when the sweet mixture was soaked up. He needed Zach to know he was strong and stable. Not that he'd shown him much of that. "I won't flake out, but it's just an hour long. Maybe we can do something after." His lips twisted in consideration. "Unless . . ."

"Unless what?"

"You wanna come with?" Scott almost wished he hadn't asked when Zach took a deep breath and stepped away from him. "You don't have to. Just thought I'd put it out there."

"It's not that." Zach rubbed the bridge of his nose, shaking his head. "I know why you make appearances with Sahara. Being seen with me could make things difficult for you."

"Hey, you let me worry about that." Scott grinned. It was kinda cool seeing Zach not so sure of himself. His grin faded as he considered *why* Zach would be reluctant to hang out with him. Zach and Becky weren't exactly open about *their* relationship. He hadn't missed that Becky had turned away from Zach's kiss while seeing him off for the cruise. Or that Zach had let her. "You're a private kinda guy. I get that. But we can do stuff and have it mean something to us without anyone knowing. If I hadn't screwed things up with the team so bad, I wouldn't care what anyone thinks about us being together. It ain't gonna be easy for me to keep my hands off you—"

"I understand." Zach turned his back on Scott to tear the sheets off his bed. "But I don't think you do. What we have *has* to be between us. I won't let it affect how hard you've worked to prove yourself."

Scott rolled his eyes. *Stubborn fucker.* "What aren't you getting about 'let me worry about that'? Who's going to question two players doing charity work together? It's simple, man. I want you around. We've got more than sex, right?"

"Of course." Zach faced him, folding his arms over his chest. "But there have to be limits."

"Does there?" Scott smirked. "No one will wonder why management would stick me with a responsible guy like you. You're a good influence."

"True. But I'm also gay."

"Shit, no one really believes that. Not with the way you look at Becky." Scott clenched his jaw when Zach winced. Damn it, he needed to talk to the woman. She wanted to tell him not to screw with Zach? Well, that fucking well went for her too. "You don't wanna come, just say so. This shit is already complicated, I get that. But you're making it more than it needs to be. People will talk. They talk about Carter and Ramos, but they don't know anything for sure. What it really comes down to is who we are on the ice. And that we're not complete assholes out in the world. You've never had a bad rep. I'm working on mine."

"You're right."

Scott smirked. He doubted he'd hear Zach say that often, but he'd take it. "Damn right, I am. Come with me. I wanna share this with you."

"Okay." Zach's lips curved into a hesitant smile. He grabbed Scott's arms, pulling him in for a hug. He exhaled like he'd finally let all his reservations go. "I'd like that."

This felt like giving back. Like maybe Zach needed Scott as much as Scott needed him. The whole "love" thing didn't mean much when one person carried all the weight of the relationship.

Hefting a good part of the heavy load on to his own shoulders was serious commitment, but one Scott was willing to make.

He was in this for the long run.

Chapter Twenty Two

The turnout for the self-defense class was impressive. Fifty some-odd woman crowded the large room on the second floor of the downtown Dartmouth gym, some shying away from the cameras that seemed to follow the Cobras everywhere they went, others preening. Mirrors lined the walls, the reflection making it seem even fuller, and a dozen red mats covered the center of the room.

Zach stood close to the wall, nodding at the women who recognized him while avoiding any attempt to draw him into conversation. He wasn't here to distract them. Thankfully, his reputation prevented anyone from taking offense. Most of the women seemed content to stare at him from afar. How little they knew about him was a big part of his appeal. Not something he'd done intentionally, but it made him uncomfortable to have stranger's adulation. The only woman he wanted to adore him was his sub. And she wasn't here.

He didn't want to disturb Becky's time with her family, but he needed to hear from her. He settled on sending a text.

Me: I've heard Gaspe is beautiful this time of year. I hope you're enjoying the scenery and the time with your daughter. Tell her I say "hi" and I miss you both. Which I really do. We should talk. Soon.

He didn't hesitate before pressing send, but wondered after if he'd said too much. He didn't want Becky to feel pressured. If she was any other sub, he would push for answers, but she wasn't. She was a mother, and he'd never been with anyone with her kind of responsibilities. He had to take that into consideration.

My mother had a life, a job, after she had me. Why can't Becky?

But he refused to let those thoughts fester. His mother also had the father of her child there to support her. Something Becky lacked.

I could—

Could what? Take his place? It would be a very long time before Becky would allow that. If ever.

He pictured little Casey, holding his hand and peering up at him with those sweet, trusting eyes. He'd never considered himself father material, but Casey made him want to take on that role. Made him want to stand by her mother's side and watch her grow into the same kind of strong, independent, loving woman Becky was.

Give it time.

Maybe, eventually, Becky would trust him enough to let him take a permanent place in her daughter's life. It took a lot of trust for a woman like her to scene with any man. It would take even more for the mother in her to let him in. And he would be ready when she did.

He looked forward to it.

Which brought to mind the other person who was slowly letting him in. Zach grinned as Scott took his place on the mats, wearing a bulky, padded red suit to protect him from serious damage. The cage mask over his face was similar to the mask worn by players with facial injuries. Zach was a little surprised that Scott hadn't considered himself too macho to pull on the much gear, but then again his agent might have warned him against anything that risked his ability to show up for training camp.

Either way, the awkward apparel didn't seem to change the women's opinions of Scott. And Zach couldn't blame them. There was something magnetic about Scott that couldn't be hidden by any amount of layers. Zach could feel it pulling at him even now.

Shoving his hands in the pocket of his jeans, he leaned against the wall near the door. Out of the way and far enough to resist grabbing Scott—all the people watching be damned.

The women broke from their little groups and formed a square around the instruction area. The instructor was an older man—at least sixty, but in damn good shape. Wrinkles lined his face and the light shone off his bald head. His neck was thick and his arms and legs were more muscular than the biggest Cobra. Zach couldn't see how the vulnerable women taking the course weren't intimidated. Another woman training them would probably be easier.

The instructor looked over the women, a slanted smile on his lips. Something in his warm brown eyes erased Zach's doubts. His tone was as soothing as any Dom's would be when comforting a skittish sub, with the slight, firm edge that would remind them of who was in control. "Did you all do your homework?"

All the women shouted, "Yes, Carl!"

"Good girls." The man folded his arms over his barrel chest, pacing around the mats, studying the women. He pointed to one in the rows closest to the windows. "Akira, you were too shy to get in front of the class last time. Let's try again, shall we?"

Akira stepped up, head held high, a very forced smile on her lips. She glanced over at Scott as he spoke quietly to her, then nodded. Her gaze flicked toward the door and her eyes lit up.

Zach followed her gaze and grinned as Mason came to stand beside him. "Captain."

Mason's lips twisted slightly. He shook his head. "Still not used to that."

"I can imagine. I wouldn't want to trade places with you."

One brow arched, Mason jutted his chin at Scott, who'd taken his position behind a much more confident looking Akira. "You took on something pretty big. If you can handle him, I think the team would be easy enough." Mason paused. "I could use an alternate the men respect."

"Yeah . . ." Zach watched Akira kicking Scott in the nuts for a while. There was no hurry to give Mason an answer. He didn't want the job, but neither had Mason. Which probably made them better suited than any of the men vying for the positions. He sighed as he looked away from Scott giving Akira a bear hug from behind. "Who's getting the other A?"

"Ramos."

"Ah." Good choice. But surprising. "You choose all Doms for a reason? I like Ramos, but the men might resent someone so new to the team being picked over the guys who've been with us longer."

"Tough. The men need what you two can give them." Mason focused on the attack simulation. Akira dropped Scott to his knees with an elbow jab right to the exposed area beneath the padding covering Scott's ribs. Scott carried on for a while, making Akira laugh. Mason smiled as she helped Scott to his feet and hugged him. "Never thought I'd say this, but I hope Keane keeps Demyan. He's pretty decent. I like how he is with Akira."

"So do I." Zach straightened as another woman came forward. "Damn it, what is Chicklet doing here?"

Mason shrugged. "I think the Dartmouth police force is involved in the program." He gestured toward a small group of women in grey sweats to the right. "Laura's here."

Laura wasn't an issue. Zach had seen the sub with her Mistress at the club. She was always composed, graceful in her submission with a kind of quiet strength he admired. Chicklet was an amazing Domme, but when it came to her pets she was as protective as a lioness over her cubs. Wayne, one of the club's bouncers, had tried to take liberties with Laura weeks ago—apparently under the mistaken impression that being involved in a scene with her once gave him the right to play with her whenever he felt like it. Laura hadn't panicked when the man had cornered her. Simply said "red" loud and clear.

Wayne seemed to think she needed some convincing, so he'd kissed her. His lips had barely touched Laura's when Chicklet sauntered over in her thigh high ass-kicker boots and grabbed hold of Wayne's balls right through his leathers.

"You want to act like a horny sub with no discipline, I'll treat you like one." She'd kept squeezing until Wayne dropped to his knees, then snarled right in his face. *"You ever touch what's mine again without my permission and I'll nail these to the floor. Got it?"*

The big man had been kicked out of the club by Richter shortly after, but Zach doubted anyone would ever forget how Wayne had nodded with tears in his eyes, completely emasculated. Chicklet could be the most easygoing person Zach knew, but once you got on her bad side . . .

Scott was definitely on her bad side. Zach still wasn't sure what he'd done to get kicked out of Vanek's place, but one look at Chicklet and it was clear things weren't settled between them.

A smart man would have backed down. Any sub, man or woman, would have knelt and begged forgiveness. Scott showed no signs of being either as he removed his face mask. Then the rest of his pads.

Chicklet might have her reasons for being pissed at Scott, but Zach couldn't just stand back and watch her beat the shit out of the man. Especially since it was obvious Scott had no intentions of defending himself.

Mason slapped his hand into Zach's chest before he could intervene. "Leave it. They both need this."

"We need him on the ice in a few weeks." Zach wouldn't bother bringing up how it would affect him to see Scott hurt. No matter how much he deserved it. The only thing Mason would care about was what Scott meant to the team. "Taking off his gear is just plain stupid."

"I won't argue with you there." Mason grinned, something in his eyes reminding Zach of who this man really was. The team captain, maybe, but he'd been the team enforcer much longer. His idea of justice was a little skewed. "But I respect him for not tucking tail. So will she."

Like I give a shit. Zach cracked his neck, eyes narrowing as he met Mason's level gaze. He was more than willing to take the man on to protect Scott. And he could probably get Chicklet to back off. Unfortunately, that would only serve to make his feelings for Scott very public. Which would be worse than anything Chicklet could dish out.

Can you seriously just stand here and watch this?

The expression on Scott's face when he faced Chicklet made the choice very easy. Scott let his arms hang limp by his sides, whispering, "I'm sorry."

Damn it, Mason was right. Scott needed this. He done something that he still felt guilty about, and he wouldn't be able to move past it until he'd made things right with the woman.

Chicklet nodded and slapped Scott's shoulder, her sharp laugh making Scott jump and Zach tense. "I believe you. Now let's show these ladies how even a big tough chick can be taken by surprise. And how she can get out of it without getting nailed with an assault charge."

Scott let out a nervous laugh. "You're going to hurt me, aren't you?"

The woman's grin was wicked. She leaned close to Scott, but her tone carried.

"Just a little."

****

Scott caught Zach eyeing him with concern and tried to give the man a reassuring smile, but the way Zach's eyes narrowed, he knew he'd failed. It wasn't like he was scared of Chicklet, exactly. She just reminded him of Xena: Warrior Princess. With spiky hair. And a few more muscles.

Chicklet moved away from him, addressing the women as she paced in a slow circle around the mats. "Some of you might be wondering why I'm here. Well, let me clear that up. I was the victim of an assault in my early twenties. A man attacked me in the alley behind my father's bar." She paused and squared her shoulders. "I spent a few months in jail for 'defending' myself."

Agitated mutters filled the room. The women around them exchanged confused looks. Scott had to stop himself from checking where the exits were. *Jail? Fuck, this woman is going to serve me up to Zach in little pieces when we're done.*

Chicklet held up a hand to quiet them. "Don't get me wrong. It was worth it to take that bastard down, but I know I went too far. I've been training in martial arts since I was very young. There are laws against using excessive force. There's no point in bitching about them. You shouldn't hesitate in doing whatever you have to when threatened, *but*—" Her lips thinned "—the most important thing to know is *if* there is a threat. Wanting to use your skills to teach the fucker a lesson can either land you in prison or worse, put you in even more danger." She nodded to Scott. "Attack me."

No man in his right mind would attack Chicklet, but she was making a point, and it was important that the women around them understood it. Yeah, she could kick his ass. But the ability wouldn't necessarily give her the advantage. *In some alternate universe.* He tipped his head back as Chicklet turned away from him and whispered a prayer to the higher power that was probably laughing his ass off right now. Then he lunged.

Shouting "Help!" as Scott wrapped his arms around her waist, Chicklet dropped her weight and smoothly swept his feet out from under him. Scott grunted as his back hit the mat. Chicklet leaned over him, her hand on his throat, and punched the mat by his head.

The women cheered.

"No." Chicklet shook her head. "Not 'yay!' Akira, come back

here. You do it. Demyan, get padded back up. And don't hold back."

Jesus. Scott pushed up to his feet and shook his head. Akira wasn't ready for this. "Choose someone else."

Akira bit her bottom lip. Looked past him and took a deep breath. "It's okay. I'll be okay, Scott."

Scott shook his head again, then sighed as the women just stared at him. "Fine, but I don't need the gear. Let's just get this over with."

Chicklet grabbed his arm. "You won't be doing her any favors if you're too gentle."

"I don't think I'm doing her any favors anyway."

"You are." She grabbed the chest pads, shoved them at him, then groaned when he ignored her. "Stupid boy. Don't bitch if you get hurt."

With a sick feeling in his stomach, Scott got into position behind Akira. She'd been to a few of these classes. Hopefully, she'd learned enough to put him on his ass quickly.

Akira's waist felt small in his arms. So fragile. He locked on to her just tight enough to make her predicament feel real. He could feel her pulse racing against his cheek as he pulled her close. She whimpered.

From the corner of his eye, he saw Zach block Mason. Akira dropped her weight. Squirmed.

Jabbed her heel into his foot. He cursed under his breath, then found himself on his back. When she swung at him, he latched on to her wrist and jerked her down onto the mat. Rolled over her.

"Perfect." Chicklet patted his shoulder as he stood, waving him aside before he could offer Akira a hand up. She smiled at the smaller girl. "So, my little Amazon. What went wrong?"

"I should have gone for his eyes or something." Akira chewed at her bottom lip. "But I didn't really want to hurt him."

"Not sure why not, but you're wrong anyway." Chicklet chuckled at Akira's blank look. "Scott, grab me again."

Do I have to? Scott ground his teeth, repeating the same attack. The fall stunned him, and he groaned as he slid back, bracing himself for Chicklet to hit him or something.

The women were quiet. He sat up and spotted Chicklet at the other side of the room. "Do you understand? Akira is not a big girl, but she got him down. Which was perfect. But instead of using the opportunity to get away, she attacked him, both giving him another chance to grab her, and opening herself up to charges if she managed to injure him. Notice she wasn't shouting either. Escape wasn't the priority. She was angry and wanted to make him pay. That's a mistake on so many levels."

Escape wasn't the priority. Scott rubbed his hand over his face, backing to the other side of the room to take a few swigs from his water bottle. He stayed far away from Zach and Mason, avoiding their gazes, feeling both watching him. He had these weird moments during the courses sometimes, but he didn't need anyone making something of it. A few minutes to breathe and he pulled on the padding, feeling fine. Perfectly fine.

They went over similar scenarios for a while, then moved on to something else that hadn't been covered before. Carl took over for this lesson.

"Everything you're being taught is meant to help you defend yourself. But in a real-life situation, you might end up being taken down no matter how much you've trained." Carl waited for Chicklet to lie on the floor and positioned himself between her legs, arms barred by her sides. "Chicklet is a big, strong woman. I'm bigger. And once I have her like this." He nodded to Chicklet and she started struggling. "She's trapped. Most of your assailants will be bigger and stronger than you are. They expect you to fight. But they have one goal in mind." He used his weight to hold Chicklet down, his muscles tense, but using little more effort than that to restrain her. He grabbed her wrists when she swung at him. "Getting tired, Chicklet?"

"Yes." Chicklet let out a broken sound and her whole body went limp. She dropped her head back on the mat. "I give up."

Akira stood close to Scott's side, breathing hard, her face pale. He blinked as she moved closer to him, then glanced over at Mason. Mason's lips were drawn in a tight thin line, but he inclined his head, letting Scott know it was okay. Scott put his hand on her delicate shoulder, somehow finding some strength to give her.

Carl stared at Chicklet for a moment. "You what?"

Chicklet didn't move, simply whispered, "I give up. Please don't hurt me. I'll do anything you want, just don't hurt me."

The tiny woman at Scott's side covered her mouth with her hand.

"Good." Carl lowered his hands to Chicklet's hips. "Very good."

What happened next took even Scott by surprise. Chicklet moved fast, dragging her body out from under Carl and sending two quick jabs—that didn't connect—at his face. She was on her feet and across the room before anyone reacted. Suddenly the women were chattering excitedly and clapping. All except for Akira. She was pressed tight against Scott's side, shuddering.

Carl got up, explaining to the women how feigning surrender could be their greatest weapon. But Scott wasn't paying attention to him anymore. He kept Akira close to his side, easing her away from the other women, over to Mason.

"Akira." Mason took Akira's face in his hands. "Eyes on me."

"I fought." Akira sobbed, pressing her face against Mason's chest. "I didn't stop fighting until I couldn't anymore. If I'd—"

"Enough for today. We'll discuss this privately." Mason held Akira close, meeting Scott's eyes briefly before taking her out of the room. "Thank you."

Scott shook his head, rubbing his eyes with his forefinger and thumb. "'Thank you'? Seriously?"

"She hit a trigger, but you helped her in the long run." Zach squeezed Scott's shoulder, then handed him a towel. "You're helping them all. You *know* that."

A little hard to believe since Akira had left, looking more broken than he'd seen her in a while. Scott stripped off the pads, wiped his face with the towel, then turned to tell Carl he had to go. He still had about fifteen minutes left, but he was done. His insides felt raw. And for some reason, those words, "I'm bigger," haunted him. He needed a fucking drink.

"Scott?"

His name, coming from Chicklet, froze him in his tracks. She called all the men by their last names. Even Callahan, who'd known her for years. This could either be very good. Or very bad.

She studied his face in silence for a few beats, then held out her hand. "We're good. Got me? What you're doing here matters more that how stupid you were." She smiled as he took her hand and pulled him in for a rough hug. "Keep it up."

Once she walked away, all Scott could do was stare after her. A stamp of approval from Chicklet was big. He glanced over at Zach, grinning. And found something worth even more.

Zach pulled him into the hall, checked to make sure no one was around, and kissed him hard. Then he whispered, "I'm glad you shared this with me. I'm so fucking proud of you."

Nothing in the world topped that.

Chapter Twenty Three

Zach: It's been almost two weeks since your last text. Call me, please. At least let me know you're all right.

Zach: Thank you for getting that message to me through your brother. It's good to know you're doing well. But I don't understand why you haven't called…

Zach: We really need to talk.

Zach: It's hard not to assume the worst. Why are you ignoring my messages? This will be my last one until you come back. I know there's something you're not telling me. Don't hold back for my sake. You know there's nothing I value more than the truth.

Becky looked over Zach's texts one last time before tucking her phone in her purse and leaving her car in the Delgado Forum underground parking lot. This was her first day back at work after three weeks in Gaspe. From late August to mid-September a lot seemed to have changed. She'd noticed the construction outside the forum to add the new giant outdoor screens was done. The weather was a little chillier. Her daughter had started kindergarten that morning in her new school—late, but the transfer had taken longer than expected since her lawyer was on vacation and she hadn't had all the papers the school had wanted.

Her daughter hadn't gone to day care since there were always friends or family around to watch Casey while she was at work, so this first day of school was hard. For Becky, not her little girl. Casey was a little social butterfly in the making. Before Becky had managed to force herself away from the door to the classroom, Casey had struck up conversation with two little boys and a girl about the Cobra jersey she'd insisted on wearing that morning. The number 20 and the Bower name were partially hidden by Casey's curly ponytail, but Casey wasted no time letting the other children know that the Cobra's goalie was *her* uncle Landon.

Casey seemed happy. Which made it a little easier for Becky to leave her. But only a little. She would be working late today with the team's five-hour practice, including medical examinations and photographs. Since Landon was on injury reserve, he wouldn't be attending camp. So he'd offered to pick Casey up after school.

Everything was scheduled perfectly. She didn't even have to worry about making supper because Dean had invited her and Casey over. But her life still felt like one great big mess. She'd barely made it here in time to grab a coffee before she met with Mr. Keane and the Cobra's staff. They'd all fit in an extra meeting just to update her because she hadn't been at the meeting earlier that week. The season was about to start and she wasn't even close to ready.

Most of all, she wasn't ready to see Zach again. Because all she could say to him was "I'm sorry." And that didn't cut it. She wouldn't have been able to forgive him if he'd done this to her. Disappeared without calling or making it clear that "I love you" hadn't been meaningless words spoken in the heat of the moment. Damn it, she *did* love him. She'd tried to stop, but her heart rejected her best efforts. And found a way to counter every objection her brain came up with.

He loves someone else.

Could she honestly say Scott meant nothing to her?

Casey needs stability.

She'd never met a more stable man than Zach.

It's too soon.

She'd been alone for years. Zach hadn't asked her to marry him. And he'd done everything in his power to fit into her life. Given her all the space she'd asked for.

What if he's not ready to deal with a woman who has a kid?

But she'd seen how Zach was with Casey at the park. She hadn't been sure about asking him to come along, but Casey loved the attention he gave her. And when Casey was bratty, Zach turned to Becky before saying a word to her. He respected Becky as a mother. As a woman. What more did she want?

He's a hockey player. The game will always come first.

The game. Scott. She could think of a dozen things that would take a bigger role in Zach's life than her and Casey. But even then, she knew she was reaching. Digging deep to convince herself this wouldn't work out. She wanted it to work, so very badly, that it scared her. Zach could probably quiet all her fears with a few words, but that scared her even more. Because she could handle being disappointed if Zach couldn't follow through. But Casey couldn't. She already looked at Zach like he was some kind of hero just because he was a Cobra. Every moment he spent with her was like living out some kind of fairy tale. She'd never come right out and said it, but her little girl fantasies, whispered as she lay her head on her pillow at night, told Becky everything she needed to know.

"*I'm gonna marry a hockey player, Mommy.*" Casey blushed and hugged her little stuffed polar bear tight. "*And I want one to be my new daddy. I can have a new daddy, right? My old daddy doesn't like me very much. He said so.*"

"*He wouldn't—he loves you, Casey.*" Becky's heart had stuttered at the conviction in her baby's voice. She brushed her fingers lightly over Casey's hair. "*What makes you say that, poupée?*"

"*He said I was expensive. And messy. I tried not to be messy, Mommy.*" Casey's bottom lip quivered. "*I really did.*"

I could kill you for hurting my baby, you bastard.

All right, maybe homicide was a little extreme, but it was a good thing he wasn't close enough to tempt her though as she gathered Casey in her arms. And choked out the words she had to say in a nice calm tone because it was what her daughter needed to hear.

"*Grown-ups say silly things sometimes, Casey. I get upset when you smear peanut butter on the cupboards, and the fridge, and the floor.*" She tickled Casey until her little girl was wiggling, and giggling, and happy again. "*You know I still love you, right?*"

Becky hauled her purse strap over her shoulder and grabbed a box of files from her trunk. Damn it, she was tired of trying to defend that man. Casey was a smart little girl. And Patrick wasn't very good at hiding how he really felt. He'd lost interest in being a father years ago. He insisted on seeing Casey because he considered it his right. Not because he really wanted to. And a child like Casey would see through his half-assed efforts.

Damn you, Patrick.

Pushing the parking lot door open with her hip, Becky moved into the wide hall beyond, almost getting knocked over by the four men running down the long stretch, dragging stacked plate weights on thick ropes behind them. She fumbled with her folders, smiling gratefully at Tim when he came to her side to take the box from her.

"Thank you." She shook her head as she watched the men slap

the wall at the end of the hall, then turn to run in the other direction. "I didn't realize camp had started already. It's scheduled for 9 a.m."

"It hasn't started yet. A few of the boys wanted to warm up together. The press isn't allowed in here. We make them park outside so the men have a place to kick the ball around, or do stuff like this." He grinned as Luke Carter pulled ahead of the other men, shouting back taunting remarks that had them all pushing harder. Ian White was only a few steps behind him, but Shawn Pischlar and Bobby Williams, one of the team's eldest players, struggled to keep up. "It's good for them, giving more than we ask, getting themselves all worked up before they even hit the ice."

Becky nodded slowly. "True. But this would be good for the fans to see. The reality show Silver signed the team up for is supposed to be all access."

"Becky, I know it's your job to be the go-between with the team and the media, but we've spoken a few times at my brother's place, and I'd like to think I know what kind of person you are." He paused, studying her face like a man who wasn't sure his words would be considered "off the record." At her nod, he smiled. "I'm their coach. I get to decide how much of this they can take. And I'm telling you they need this one space where they don't have to worry about the cameras looming."

As the door opened behind them, Tim shifted over, clearing the way for the team's temporary leading goaltender, Dave Hunt. The young man didn't even acknowledge the other players. Or her and Tim. He simply dropped his bags at the end of the hall and took out a tube of tennis balls. Before long he was bouncing four against the wall, catching and letting them loose in the same focused rhythm she'd seen Landon use with the same exercise.

"Hunt is bad with the press." Tim watched Dave with a solemn expression on his face. "He's a good kid. Very talented. But he doesn't mesh with the team, and the media attention throws him off. I'd like you to keep interviews with him to the bare minimum. He may handle it better as he matures, but for now I'm more concerned with him concentrating on the game and not on explaining how he can replace a goaltender who's already being compared to some of the greats." He gave her an apologetic look. "I know Landon is your brother. And he's earned his reputation. But we don't have him right now. We have Hunt. So I'm going to do what I have to for him."

"I understand." Becky mentally crossed off several of the interview requests she'd received for the young man. She moved toward the door at the other side of the hall. "The media obviously has questions about him, but I can redirect them if that would help."

"It would. And I appreciate this. I understand the press needs as much access to the players as possible, but you've kept them away from your brother. Which I fully support." The heavy metal door shut behind Tim, cutting off the sound of the men ribbing one another as they raced with the weights. "I just hope you can do the same for any other player who can't take the added pressure."

"Just let me know who, and I'll handle it." Becky took the folders from Tim as they reached the elevator. "Speaking of which, are Zach and Scott here yet? Zach is evasive, but the media loves him. And Scott is always good with a mic in his face."

"Not so much anymore." Tim followed her into the elevator, surprising her, his expression remote. "Zach has closed down completely—"

"Closed down?" Her throat tightened and she had to open her mouth just to breathe properly. *What the hell did you do to him, Becky?* "How bad is it?"

"Nothing bad, sweetie. He's just not giving the press anything to work with. I think he's worried about people seeing him with Scott so often."

Oh. Becky nodded, speaking again before Tim could add anything to that. She didn't want to hear it from him. "And Scott?"

"Scott is restricted to the usual player clichés during interviews. Don't expect him to say much more than 'We're giving one hundred and ten percent.' He'll be more open when discussing his charity efforts, but he's under the microscope. We need to focus on the positives with him. Keane has been talking to his agent a lot lately. Not really my business, but I'll do everything I can to give his agent something to work with. Scott's IC has done a lot to make Scott look good for the team. I wasn't sure about the guy at first, but there's no arguing the impact he's had. I went from dreading dealing with Scott to looking forward to seeing what he can do for the team."

"I can see that." A sweet warmth spread through Becky's chest as she thought about how different Scott was from the man she'd interviewed last year. He could still give any reporter a good story, but there wasn't much drama to expose. No bunnies coming forward with photos that would get a few hundred dollars thrown their way. He'd cleaned up his act. Not that it should matter much to her. "So I take it they're not here?"

"No. Zach's giving Scott a lift and they're both stuck in traffic." Tim frowned when Becky gave him a stiff smile. "Becky, I know you and Zach have something. I can't picture him keeping his relationship with Scott from you. I try not to get involved in my players' personal lives unless it affects the game. Zach is one of our best players. I haven't seen anything yet that justifies me butting in, but . . . it hit him hard when you left. You have to talk to him."

"I know." Becky took a deep breath. She'd avoided this long enough. She knew she should have called Zach. Or at least answered his texts. Today was the day she stopped finding excuses to hide from him and laid it all out so they both could deal with whatever the future held. Or didn't. "I'll wait until after practice. I know it won't be just you watching him. I don't want what happens with our relationship changing how he's judged as a player."

"He's not the only player who has a life, Becky." Tim came with her to her office, glancing over at his brother's. The door was closed, but the light under the door made it clear Dean was present. "Life doesn't always make things easy, but the game isn't much different from any other form of entertainment. The show must go on. We all accept that when we sign on."

"To a certain extent, yes. But some players want a family and some don't."

"Some don't." Tim inclined his head. Then fixed her with a hard stare. "But Zach does. And I'm not saying this as just his coach. Becky, you've become part of my family through Landon and my brother. I've tucked your daughter in almost as often as they have. And you never questioned her getting too close to me or Dean or my mother. You know we're not going anywhere." He put his hand on her shoulder. "Zach isn't going anywhere either."

"You don't know that, Tim. I know Dean will never leave Silver.

The way he is with Amia . . ." Her eyes teared. That little girl would never lack for love. "She might as well be his. And you and your mother have accepted that little baby as though she is blood. It's awesome, but it's a lot to ask of any man."

"Not too much to ask of a man who truly loves a woman."

"Maybe. But I'm not ready to ask for that kind of commitment." Becky focused on laying her files out on her desk. They made sense. Everything on those papers was printed out in black and white, leaving no room for doubt. "I will talk to him. But that's all I can tell you. The rest is private, and I hope you can respect that."

"I can. But, Becky . . ." Tim put his hand over hers as she flipped through the files, preventing her from losing herself in the job and all the things that were so very simple. "He loves you. You'd have to be blind not to see it."

"And the game? You're going to tell me he doesn't love it more?" Not just the game either. Scott. How much love did one man really have to give? "You consider my daughter family, Tim? Consider what it will do to her if Zach can't be the man she needs him to be. Forget me. Think of my precious little girl and tell me I should go for it."

Tim pressed his hand to her cheek and met her eyes. "Casey is part of my family. I love her as much as if she was my own. As much as I love Amia. You want an answer? It won't be the one you want to hear. If I had to trust a man to be there for that little girl, to be the man her father can't be?" He let his hand fall to his side, his tone gruff with emotion. "I couldn't give that trust to just anyone. Dean? Absolutely. I've seen how he is with Landon's kid. She will always have him, no matter what happens. You aren't alone Becky. Dean considers you one of ours as much as I do. Casey also has your parents. And mine. But she needs to know her mother isn't afraid to love. There's a big difference between several 'Uncles' and a man she can call 'Daddy.' You can tell by the way she talks about Patrick that 'Daddy' is nothing but a label. I doubt that will change."

"I know it won't."

"Then go for it, Becky," Tim said. He glanced toward the door at a soft knock. "Hey, bro."

"Hey." Dean gave his brother a searching look. "Do you have a minute?"

"Sure." Tim squeezed Becky's shoulder, smiling and nodding at her whispered, "Thank you."

Alone in her office, Becky tried to focus on her work, but her mind kept slipping to how badly she'd screwed up. She'd done all the things to Zach that she'd warned Scott not to do. It would serve her right if he didn't forgive her.

But she wouldn't assume anything. She knew him well enough to figure out that he'd come looking for her once he was done on the ice. But after what she'd pulled, the idea of him needing to search for her didn't sit right. She'd go to him. Tell him everything. And let him take the lead for once.

He wouldn't know that she was done hiding, though. She didn't want to disturb his performance in front of the trainers, but there must be a way to get the message to him before he felt like he had to chase her down.

She pulled a pad out of her top drawer. Took a deep breath. And wrote a message that hopefully wouldn't come across as just another way to avoid him. Because she was done with that.

Dear Zach,

I was so, so very wrong to leave the way I did. There's a lot we need to talk about. I'm ready, but I don't know if we should have this conversation here. I'll wait for your text. Tell me where and when you'd like to meet.

I haven't shown it, but I still love you very much.

Yours Always,
Becky

She read the letter over several times under her breath, her hands shaking as she resisted the urge to crumple it and just send Zach a short text. A text seemed so cold and impersonal. He deserved better.

After folding the letter, she put it in an envelope. Sealed it and went straight down to the men's empty changing room. She could hear some of the men lingering in the lounge and the locker room, so she quickly slid the envelope into Zach's locker and slipped out.

If she wanted to finish early enough to speak to Zach, she had to hustle. Keeping busy made it a bit easier not to wonder what he would think about the note. About how mad he must be. About whether or not he'd be willing to give her a chance.

But she didn't let those thoughts distract her from her work. If there was one thing she hadn't doubted when it came to her relationship with Zach, it was that he respected her devotion to her job and her family. He wouldn't want her giving them less because she wanted to give him more.

If he still wants more.

And if he didn't?

She powered on her computer, typing in her password, done with letting her thoughts sway back and forth. If he didn't want her anymore, it was exactly what she deserved. She'd be alone again.

Her life would go on. The only thing that would change is she'd miss what she'd almost had and she'd always wonder... wonder what could have been if she'd been just a little stronger.

* * * *

Scott's skates glided across the ice, moving him faster and faster as he completed yet another lap across the rink. Coach blew the whistle and had the players stand off to the side near the benches so they could take turns practicing their shots. When it was his turn, he raced toward Ingerslov, feinted five-hole shot, then fired high glove-side.

"Nice!" Tim shouted. "Again!"

Heading in the other direction, Scott fixed his sights on Hunt. The young goalie came out too far and Scott skidded around him, zipping the puck toward the net.

Hunt dove sideways. The puck hit his outstretched glove. And trickled over the line after clinking against the goalpost.

"Fuck!" Hunt pushed to his feet, slamming the back of his elbow into the goalpost. It didn't seem to matter that he'd shut the door on an impressive ninety percent of the shots. Every time one got by him, he snapped.

"Cool it, Hunt." Tim blew his whistle and gestured for the

assistant coaches to take over, skating over with the goalie coach to speak to the rookie goalie.

Scott took his time joining his teammates for face-off practice. Yeah, he was being nosy, but he had to know how Tim was going to handle the temperamental net minder.

"You're not going to shut out every game, kid. How you recover after letting one by is what will determine the outcome of the game—Demyan, get over here since you're not interested in working on the face-off."

Scott ducked his head and skated closer to the two coaches and Hunt. "Sorry, Coach."

"Don't be. You're one of our best shots. Work with Nate and Hunt for a bit," Tim said, inclining his head to the goalie coach, Nate Olive, before joining the rest of the team.

For about an hour, Scott worked with Nate and Hunt, changing directions, taking shots from the point, rushing the net, giving Hunt the opportunity to make saves from different angles. When Tim called for the break, Scott took off his helmet and grinned at Hunt. The kid had to feel better now. He'd blocked most of Scott's shots.

Hunt's lips curved slightly at the edges, as though he wanted to smile but couldn't quite remember how. His black hair was soaked when he took off his helmet and his cheeks—covered spottily with his attempt to grow a beard—was red with exertion. But his eyes were shining with the energy of a young athlete who knew he was at the top of his game.

"Glad you're on *our* team, Demyan." Hunt dropped his helmet on top of the net, then squirted some water into his mouth and over his head. "You've got good hands."

That was the first nice thing Hunt had ever said to anyone on the team. Him saying it to Scott after their scuffle was pretty impressive. "Thanks!" Scott slugged Hunt's shoulder. "You didn't make it easy, rookie."

"So he's good, Demmy? We'll see about that!" With a boyish laugh, Vanek burst on to the ice, zipping around the rink as the men who hadn't left yet called out greetings and questions. Tim stood by the open door to the home bench, arms folded over his chest, failing miserably at his attempt to look displeased about Vanek's cockiness.

The smile he barely contained and the gleam in his eyes seemed like he was trying not to cheer.

Good news?

"Get your helmet back on, Hunt! Want to see if I'm rusty." Vanek circled the rink, kicking a few pucks on to the red line. "I'll even be nice and let you know where each shot's gonna go."

Scott rolled his eyes, sliding out of the way as Hunt and Vanek prepared to face off. "What are you doing here, Vanek? Thought you were holed up with the doctor?"

"I was. But he said I'd better get out here if I want to be ready for the first game." Vanek's blue eyes practically glowed as the men shouted cheers and surrounded him. Someone must have gone to the locker room to tell the other guys because within seconds, the whole team was flooding the ice, hugging Vanek and passing him around like he was some kind of trophy.

Mason grabbed the kid from Carter, trapping him in a bear hug and bumping helmets. "It'll be damn good to have you back, kid. Guess the doc said you need to see how you can take a hit?"

"Yeah . . ." Vanek groaned as Scott gave him a facewash. "Damn it, Demmy! Get off!" He laughed when Scott looped an arm around his neck. "I was worried that no one would want to hit me, but you'll have no problem, right?"

"None at all." Scott glanced back to where Hunt had stayed between the pipes, helmet on, mask down, steadily skating grooves on to the blue ice. He looked ready. Scott shoved Vanek away from the crowd of players, gesturing toward the young goalie. "Let's see what you've got."

Vanek nodded, then glided up to the line of pucks. He rushed at Hunt, his skates moving in a blur. "Top shelf."

Hunt braced himself, dropping at the last second and closing his pads as though sure Vanek would go for a low shot despite what he'd called. The puck hit the mesh inside the top of net. As Vanek had said. Top shelf.

"Did I confuse you?" Vanek asked, spraying up snow as he stopped at the edge of the goal crease. "You do know what top shelf is, right?"

"Fuck you." Hunt dropped his stick and his gloves, skating to the bench without taking off his helmet. The men watched him leave without a word, conversation resuming uncomfortably, the excitement from before slightly dimmed.

The worst thing was, Vanek didn't seem to get that he'd done anything wrong. His gaze trailed Hunt for a split second before he went to chat up White and Pischlar. Scott wasn't all that surprised though. Vanek had every reason to be excited.

But his presence pushed Hunt even further from the inner circle of the team. Maybe that was why he was cool with Scott. More often than not, Scott was outside of the circle too.

"Demyan?" Mason called from just beyond the small group of players that had encompassed Vanek yet again. Mason caught Scott's eye and jerked his chin in the direction Hunt had disappeared.

Right. Us outcastes have to stick together. But it didn't bother Scott as much as it would have once. Spending all the time he had with Zach over the past few weeks got him used to the guys being relaxed with Zach, but not overly chatty. Zach kept a professional relationship with the other players unless he considered them friends. And he picked those carefully. Being among the few Zach let close meant a hell of a lot more to Scott than being Mr. Popular.

Most of the guys would say "Hey" to Scott and go on with their day. At least they weren't giving him dirty looks anymore.

He ditched all his equipment by his stall, then found Hunt in the training room doing his fitness test. On a bike with tubes and wires all hooked up, the team doctor, a physical therapist, and a research director taking notes of his endurance and heart rate and all the fun stuff. After a torturously long span of going at full speed, the doctor turned off the machines, removed all the monitoring stuff, and let Hunt cool down at a slower pace for a few minutes.

When Hunt got off the bike, he immediately tore off his shirt and used it to dry the sweat from his face. Scott stood in the doorway, thumbs hooked to the pockets of his shorts, really looking the rookie goalie over for the first time. For a twenty-year-old, he was pretty big. An inch or so shorter than Scott, but at least ten pounds heavier. He doubted the kid had even five percent fat. A few of the guys in the locker room were going to have to bust their ass to get back in game form, but Hunt seemed like the type who had two modes. Playing the game and getting ready to play the game.

Hunt inclined his head in thanks when the doctor handed him a bottle of water. "How'd I do?"

"Excellent. Thirteen minutes and you're the first one who's come in here that I don't have any advice for." The doctor grinned and patted Hunt's shoulder. "Whatever you're doing, continue."

That perked the kid up. Hunt nodded and smiled at the doctor in a way that made it even more obvious how young he was. He soaked in the praise like a dried-out sponge dropped in a bucket of water. "Thanks, Doc." His smile faded, his brow furrowing slightly. "But I've been trying to put on a few more pounds. Nothing I do seems to—"

"Son, at your age, you're lucky to have this much bulk. Work on maintaining, not building. As you get older, you may gain more weight, but it will be harder to stay in shape. It'll be a few years before we have to worry about that though," the doctor said. "Go take a break, then get back on the ice. I've got to deal with the slackers." He turned to Scott, his expression showing that he'd know Scott was there all along. "Speaking of which . . . Mr. Demyan, since you're here, let's see what we've got to work with."

"I think you're gonna be surprised, Doc." Scott smiled, pretty confident that all his time at the gym would pay off. He stopped by Hunt's side before the boy could walk out. "Hey, you wanna wait for me? Thought we could chill for a bit."

Hunt shrugged. "Guess so. We're off until one, right?"

"Right." That settled, Scott climbed on the bike. The thing to measure his oxygen intake was stuffed in his mouth and a padded clamp pinched his nose closed. Once the other monitors were set up, the research director told him to get started, reminding him to keep the pace at 80 RPM. Scott pumped his legs hard, muscles burning as he fought to keep the reps up. His eyes squinted as moisture dripped into them from his forehead.

"Keep going. Don't ease up now, Demyan," Doc said.

His thighs were nothing but bone and wet flesh encasing pulsing flames. He grunted as he forced himself not to slow down just to lessen the heat. Then the resistance on the bike was increased.

"Bring it up to 80. Push it!" The director instructed.

Fire and pain and nothing but a blind need to reach the goal. Scott stared at the monitor in front of him. *76, 78, 73, 75 . . . 80! Go, go, go!*

The agony in his muscles dissolved and a rush of pure energy took over. Scott felt like he could keep going forever. Then like he *had* been doing this forever. That burst of energy burned out and he huffed into the tube as his lungs seared in his chest.

83, 79, 73, 65 . . . Fuck!

"All right, slow it down." Doc removed the tube and the clamp. "Not bad, Mr. Demyan. Nine minutes. Do you smoke?"

Scott panted as he leaned his forearms on the bike's handlebars. It took him a while to get enough air to speak. "Not usually. I might have once or twice this summer."

"Hmm." Doc went over the report with the other two experts quietly, then brought Scott a bottle of water. "You're in decent shape, but I'd like you to work on your cardio. Morning runs, time on the bike, whatever you can do for at least an hour, pushing yourself harder at intervals of about ten minutes. The trainer may have more suggestions for you, but in any case, you're going to have a hard time lasting for a thirty second shift. We don't want you getting tired out there."

"No, sir." Scott did his best to climb off the bike without falling and making himself look even *more* pathetic. His legs were shaking, but he made it to the door and out of sight of the doctor before he needed something solid to hold him up.

"Damn, did you sleep all summer?" Hunt finished off his water and tossed the empty bottle into the big metal trash can against the wall. "My dad would kill me if I did that bad on the test."

"Yeah, well fuck you, Hunt." Scott grinned so Hunt would know he was joking. "I ain't got anyone on my ass, so I've got nothing to worry about. I passed."

"Barely." Hunt led the way toward the locker room, lowing his voice as he paused in front of the closed door. "Your boyfriend won't be mad? I mean, he made the twelve-minute mark and he smokes *cigars*."

Scott winced, both because Zach might be disappointed, and because Hunt shouldn't know enough to bring up "his boyfriend".

"Hey, Zach and me aren't what you—"

"Fuck, I'm not gonna tell no one. Honestly, I don't think the people that know give a shit, and most aren't paying enough attention to have figured it out. You're fine." Inside the locker room, Hunt put on a clean T-shirt. The room was empty, which seemed to put him at ease. He wasn't usually this talkative. "I run if you want to tag along. I mean . . ." He ducked his head. "I could help you."

"Sure." Scott changed his own soaked shirt for a fresh one, then grabbed his wallet. "Where you staying?"

"Just a few blocks away—with Olsson."

Olsson? Damn, the man doesn't even speak English! Scott studied Hunt as they made their way up the stairs to the main floor. "There's no one else for you to stay with?"

"White, but he's a jerk." Hunt shrugged. "Me and Olsson get along pretty good. Stay out of each other's way."

"Got it." Scott stepped out on to the sidewalk, inhaling deeply, positive his lungs were writing him thank you cards as they spoke. The air was nice and crisp, a little on the cool side. Perfect. "So . . . about you flipping out on the ice—"

"Don't fucking lecture me, man. It was stupid. Won't happen again." Hunt's strides widened, forcing Scott to ignore the ache in his thighs and quicken his pace to keep up. "You're the last person who should be telling me how to act."

"True." Scott reached Hunt's side just as he hit the lights. Thank God, they were red. "But I'm working on it. You're starting out, kid. They don't have to like you, but with how hard you're working, they should respect you."

"I don't fit into their little clubs." Hunt scowled. "And I don't want to."

"Fine, but you really want to let them see you all messed up? You're physically tough. You want to make it in the league?" Scott liked that Hunt's scowl faded, that his expression turned thoughtful as he nodded. The kid was smart. And finally ready to listen. Scott tapped the center of his forehead with a finger. "You gotta be just as tough up here. You don't wanna make friends on the team, then don't. But we've got to trust that you're not gonna freak if a bad bounce gets past you. We. Need. You."

"You've got Ingerslov."

"Seriously?" Scott rolled his eyes. "Ingerslov is a great guy, but we know—hell, *he* knows—he's not a starting goaltender. You are."

Hunt nodded slowly. Then he frowned. "Hey, why are you being so nice to me? I messed with your girl and—"

"She's not my girl. She is a friend, but I know you tried to make things right. You paid for what you pulled, so me and you are good."

"Okay . . ." Hunt said, hesitating before he continued. "Still. You've got enough shit to deal with."

"Buddy, I'm not all that complicated. The game is one of the few things in my life that makes sense. I want this team to make it, even if half the guys act like arrogant pricks and the other half wants to be just like them. With a few exceptions." *Zach.* Scott took a deep breath as his face heated. Even a brief thought of Zach was enough to trip him up. He wondered if Zach would be okay with him spending the night again. He'd said they'd have to cool it a bit when the season started—Scott should be spending time with his "girlfriend"—but the season hadn't started yet, so . . . "Anyway, Lord Stanley is end game. We ain't gonna get our hands on him without someone solid between the pipes. That's you."

"But Bower—"

"Won't be back until what, January? If that?" Scott shook his head. "This is all on you, kid. You up to it?"

Hunt squared his shoulders. Inhaled. Then inclined his head. "Damn right, I am."

"Good." Scott stopped in front of the Tim Horton's, shoving the door open. "We better hurry."

"Timmy's?" Hunt scrunched up his face. "Dude, I don't do coffee and donuts."

"*Dude!*" Scott repeated in a mocking tone. This kid was too much. "They serve fucking salads. Suck it up."

They ordered, found a table, then ate in companionable silence. Hunt checked his phone a few times when it buzzed, clicking ignore. He polished off two salads with chicken strips and no dressing.

Crazy rookie.

Scott finished his panini, then downed the last of his iced cappuccino. He gestured to Hunt with the empty cup. "It was cool, hanging out with you. Wanna go for a beer sometime after camp?"

Hunt considered for a moment, looking embarrassed when he answered. "Demyan, you're—you're a great guy." He paused. "But I'm straight."

After he'd managed to stop laughing, Scott slapped Hunt's shoulder. "I won't hold it against you, sport. Straight guys drink, don't they?"

"Yeah... but..." Hunt groaned as his phone buzzed again. "It's my dad. He's gonna flip if I keep ignoring his calls." He stood. "Catch you back at the forum?"

"Sure thing." Scott waved Hunt off, then looked down at his chocolate-glazed donut. Hell, he loved snacking on sweet stuff, but he'd gained seven pounds in the off-season despite all the workouts. He wasn't going to start stocking his fridge with greens, but cutting back on junk food might help.

A hand with long, graceful fingers, manicured nails painted a subtle pink, appeared in front of him, stealing his donut. His head shot up and the sight of Becky smiling at him was like a punch in the gut with a fistful of lust.

"I was privy to your test results. I figured it would be charitable of me to remove temptations." She took a big bite of the donut and made an appreciative sound in the back of her throat. "Oh, this is good."

"You're horrible." He chuckled as she took the seat across from him, licking chocolate glaze from her lips. The gesture was damn sexy, but his blood cooled as he thought of Zach. Of how shitty Becky had treated him. Sitting around joking with her just felt wrong. He moved to stand. "I'll let you finish that."

"Scott, please don't go." Becky set the rest of the donut on a napkin by a tray holding four cups of coffee. She worried her bottom lip between her teeth. "I... uh... saw you with Dave Hunt on my way here. I wasn't trying to eavesdrop, but I heard everything you said to him. He needed that."

"Yeah, well..." Scott didn't want to care what she thought. She'd hurt Zach, and the worst thing was that at the sight of her, he'd almost forgotten all about how bad it had been. She looked so fucking beautiful in her white suit, her rich mahogany hair pulled away from her face in a fancy bun. He usually liked his women fast and loose, but this was Becky. She'd managed to do more than get under his skin. Try cracking his ribs open to reach straight into his heart. But Zach was there too. So Scott kept his tone carefully neutral. "I do what I've gotta do."

Becky sat back, her gaze fixed steady on his face. "You're mad at me."

"Why would I be mad at you?"

"Because I'd be mad at you if you treated Zach the way I have."

"How's that?"

"Damn it, Scott!" Becky's eyes glistened as she pushed away from the table and stood. "Never mind. You don't want to talk to me, fine. But just say so. I can't handle you being all cold. I wanted to tell you I'm sorry. It was wrong of me to say what I did—"

Whoa. What? "To me? What did you say to me that you need to be sorry about?"

"You're not a snack. That's what I wanted you to be. Because I'm afraid of the competition. You're so much easier for him to love."

"When is love ever easy? Should it be?" Scott had to clamp his lips shut to keep any more shocked words from coming out. Becky considered him competition? Was she crazy? "If anyone should feel threatened, it's me. All you have to do is tell Zach how sorry you really are. That you'll be his good little sub. That you were scared and that I'm a problem for the two of you." His throat tightened. He took her hands in his. "He'll choose you. No fucking doubt about it."

"Don't do that, Scott. Don't try to make how he feels about you into something that can be thrown away." She hunched her shoulders and stared at the table. "It's real."

He sat back and let out a bitter laugh. He knew how this would end. If she wanted Zach back, she'd have him. "He has to decide between us."

"Does he?"

"Not from my end." Scott placed his hands on the table, palms down. He wouldn't fight her on this. He knew how she felt about Zach. How Zach felt about her. He wouldn't complicate things by sticking himself in the middle. "I get it. Zach is everything you need, so long as he can let me go. I can make him." He couldn't look at her as he spoke. It killed him just to say the words. "I will, because it's what's best. For both of you."

Becky stood and picked up the coffee tray. "I have to go, but you need to think about what you're saying. I pushed you toward Zach because I knew there was something between you two. He gave in *only* because he knows there's something between you and I. I made a mess of everything, but that changes nothing."

Scott frowned. "How do you figure?"

"Scott, you're not a snack. It was despicable for me to put that label on you. You've worked so hard to make yourself into a better player. A better *person*. And I undermined that." She turned her hand to hold his. "I'm disgusted with myself for what I said to you. But I'm asking . . . I'm *begging* for another chance. I have no idea how this is going to work. But . . ."

"You want it to?"

Her grip tightened on the edges of the cardboard tray. She gave a sharp nod. "Yes."

"Good enough for me." The pressure on his chest diminished. He didn't have to let Zach go. And he had a shot with a woman he couldn't forget, no matter how hard he tried. It was like a goal in overtime of game seven of the first round in the playoffs. Enough to stop his heart and get him thinking about the impossible. The unbelievable. But even after that goal, there were still a ton of challenges to face. To overcome. And he, Becky, and Zach would be dealing with no less. "You need to tell him all this. It won't be easy."

"I know." Becky pulled herself up straight, looking like she could take on the hardest check from the biggest man in the league and not even spill the coffees she held. "I left him a note. I hope you're there when he reads it. He'll need someone who gets what's going on. Someone who can support him whether or not he decides to put up with me being a head case."

"You're not a head case, Becky. You're a mom and you married an asshole."

Scott suddenly understood why this sweet woman struggled so much with a relationship that should be so perfect. And the understanding came like a wrecking ball crashing right into the center of his chest. If Becky felt like she had to make a choice, Casey would always come first. Which was good. That precious little girl had all the love she needed. And it didn't cost her a thing. Shouldn't. Because Casey was a good kid. Not like he'd been.

But this wasn't about him.

"Casey's birthday is in October, right?" His tongue ran over his teeth. "I got her something."

Becky stared at him. "You did? Why?"

No way could he explain how he'd spent the past few weeks making Casey's gift. That he'd gotten the idea when he'd helped move the furniture into the freshly painted room. But he spoke before his brain kicked in. "Because she's special. She's yours. She's a Bower and Landon . . . Landon fucking rocks. I know he doesn't like me, but he's the man. Don't you dare tell him I said that!"

She laughed. "I won't. But it means a lot to me that you think so much of my family. Scott . . . you're more than I expected. More than I could have hoped."

"All right, so . . ." Scot held the door open for her as they left Tim Horton's. "Whatever Zach decides . . . can I drop her gift off the night before her birthday? It's kinda big and I wanted it to be a surprise first thing, you know?"

"That's fine." Becky held the coffee tray with one hand and touched his forearm. "But . . . no expectations. You won't be coming over for—"

"Christ, Becky. I'm not using your daughter's birthday as an excuse to fuck you."

"I know that!" Becky held his wrist, forcing him to stay by her side. "It's only . . . until he decides otherwise, Zach is my Dom. His rules. If . . . or *when* anything happens between us, I need to be sure he's okay with it."

"No one wants to know if *I'm* okay with it?" Scott cut his laugh short when Becky stared at the sidewalk. She wasn't playing around. He might not completely understand the dynamics in the whole lifestyle thing, but he accepted it. "Zach's call. Got it."

He walked with Becky to the elevator in the forum, leaving her to go up to the offices while he went down to the rink. He managed to focus on the instructions from the trainers and the coaches until training was done and all the men were back in the locker room. Zach lingered on the ice as the coaches went over plans for the season, open to suggestions from Zach and Mason, both who'd spent a lot of time with the players in the off-season.

But the game and everything else became meaningless when he saw Zach take the envelope out of his locker. Zach spent a long time reading it over before setting it on the bench by the towel he'd used to dry his hair. He dressed in the black jeans and the plain black T-shirt he'd worn to training. His breath, his tone, was slow and measured as he faced Scott.

"Would you mind hanging around for a bit? I need to . . ." Zach raked his short fingernails over the close-shaved brown hair on his scalp. "I need to see her. And I need you around when we're done."

You won't be done. Ever. Scott had to believe that. Because Zach would always be missing something if he let Becky go. And Scott wasn't about to let that happen. "I ain't going anywhere."

"So you know what I have to do?"

"Yeah, I do." Scott framed Zach's jaw with his hand, pressing their lips together, fucking grateful that everyone else was gone so he didn't have to hold back. "But I don't think you know. Not yet. Hear her out."

"I will. But I want you to understand something." Zach curved his hand around the back of Scott's neck, holding his gaze until Scott could feel the intensity of it deep down in his core. "You are not an option."

"Zach—"

"You're not an option. When I told you I love you, I meant it. Nothing she says or does will change that." Zach closed his eyes and sighed. "I have no idea what that means for the three of us. If you asked me to leave her . . . I couldn't. The same goes for her asking me to leave you. I'm torn. It's not fair to either of you, but it is what it is."

"Zach. Shut up." Scott kissed Zach again, harder. Longer. Until he knew the man didn't have enough air in his lungs to talk any more stupid shit. He'd get exactly what he wanted. If Scott could get past him and Becky trying to make sense of things in a conventional way.

Sometimes life didn't fit into a neat little box. He could deal with that better than either of them. "You two chat. But don't decide anything. Because that's where I come in. I've got this."

"Really?" Zach arched a brow, his gaze intent. "How so?"

Hell, don't ask. I'm winging it. Scott shrugged, feigning that he had it all figured out, hoping that he wasn't too far off. "Trust me."

"I do, Scott," Zach said. "I shouldn't, but I have to trust someone."

This is not good. Scott watched Zach text Becky, his jaw hard as he shook his head at whatever reply she sent. Zach called her, pacing away from Scott as he spoke.

"You don't need to leave work early to speak to me. I'll come to your office." He paused, his brow creasing slightly. "Is there any reason either of us would be shouting? Whatever the outcome, this will be a civil conversation." He nodded. "Yes. I'll be there in a few minutes."

Zach dropped his phone into his sports bag. He picked the bag up by the strap and handed it to Scott. Then he made a rough sound in his throat, pulling Scott close, his lips sliding over Scott's in a soft kiss.

"Swear you'll talk to me before taking off again." Zach drew in a sharp inhale. "Hell, wake me up in the mornings you're at my place, no matter how early it is. I can't keep doing this—can't keep wondering what I've done wrong."

"I swear it." Scott grabbed Zach's shoulder before he could back away. He stared at the man until Zach met his eyes. "Hear me?"

"I hear you."

"Good." Scott let him go. Then he grinned. "Now go schedule our first threesome. I'll wait for you in the lounge."

Zach's eyes widened as he choked back a laugh. "You're too much. Who says there'll be a threesome?"

"What else is there gonna be?" Scott shrugged, but his lips turned up a little at the edges as he thought about holding Becky. Kissing her. Waking up to her all grumpy pre-coffee, wearing nothing but one of his T-shirts. Zach probably thought he was eager to get in her pants—okay, he *was*—but there was more to it. All that other stuff he hadn't cared about before Becky and Zach. He cleared his throat. "She won't do anything with me unless you approve. Easy enough if you're there."

"Granted, but your relationship with her won't revolve around me." Zach arched a brow when Scott opened his mouth, shaking his head, confused. "Did you think I was going to have you around as a spare, Scott? You're not going to be an addition to my toy bag, you're going to be the other man in her life. Which means romance and your own spot in the doghouse when you piss her off."

"Oh joy. I get a share of all the fun stuff?" Scott gave Zach a dry smile. "I can't wait."

Snorting, Zach headed out of the dressing room. "You're going to love every second and we both know it."

Damn right, I will. Scott pictured Becky stealing his donut. Her sweet smile and throaty laughter. Yeah, he'd love the good and the bad. Love just knowing she'd belong to him too.

Chapter Twenty Four

The office was nice and bright, the walls a crisp white with an ultra-modern glass and metal desk cutting the room in half, a white bookshelf built into the wall on one side, huge windows on the other. A potted Lady Palm sat in one corner and several ferns perched on the window sill.

Nothing about the room even hinted at the sport. No, that wasn't true. There was one picture on the bookshelf of Landon as a teen on the ice in his Bulldogs uniform among about a dozen school photos of Casey. But the office could easily belong to a lawyer. An accountant.

I thought she loved the game. What else was I wrong about?

Zach waited patiently by the closed door as Becky held up her finger, finishing up the phone call she'd been on when he came in, her eyes on her desktop screen. The air conditioning chilled his damp skin as he observed her, but he ignored the cold. Actually, he felt a little numb. She'd only glanced up at him once, and she couldn't seem to meet his eyes as she mouthed, "One second."

How had this happened? How had things gone so wrong between them? The sinking sensation that had sucked him under after their last scene pulled at him, but he wrenched himself free. No matter how often he mentally went over that scene, he couldn't find anything he'd done that would have made her want to get away from him. Until she told him what had driven her, he wouldn't speculate.

Becky hung up the phone, glanced at him again, then stared at her desk. "Can you please sit down?"

He was so tempted to say "No." He'd rather stand. But his need to make her comfortable, to make it easier for her to open up to him, prevailed. He pulled out one of the leather and metal chairs angled in front of the desk and sat.

Then he leaned forward, forearms braced on his knees. "What's going on, Becky?"

"I . . . I ran. I was confused and I should have talked to you." She turned her head to the side, still not looking at him, and whispered, "I'm sorry."

"Why though? What did I do?" He sat up a bit, hands on his knees, forcing himself not to stand and start pacing. *Let her explain, Pearce.* "You asked to speak with me. I'm listening."

She winced. "I'm not sure how to tell you this. It's . . . I guess it started when I saw Casey with my brother. God, the way she looks at him with Amia, it just breaks my heart. Part of me knows that the only father she'll ever really have is whatever man I'm with. And I have to be so careful about who I choose." Her brow furrowed. "You're amazing with her, but I can't help but feel it's too soon to expect you to take on that role in her life."

He had a hard time not dwelling on the "it started when"—which implied *before* their last scene, but he managed. He knew how important Casey was to her. That was never an issue. He took a deep breath and nodded slowly. "Did you feel like I was pressuring you? I've tried to be careful when I'm around her. To be no different than any other player she might spend time with. If I've overstepped—"

"You haven't. Zach, you've been perfect." Becky finally met his eyes and shook her head. "That's the problem."

Zach blinked. "What?"

She put her hands over her face, groaning with frustration. "It's not you. It's me . . . ugh. That came out wrong. I love you, and it was so easy to see our future together. But then I had to consider how that would work out for Casey. I got over the game being an issue. It's your job. It's part of you. Casey watched almost every Cobra game last season, and I think she'd understand you not being around because you're playing. But . . ."

He had a feeling he knew where this was going. His gut twisted and he felt a little sick. If he was right . . . he ground his teeth. "Go on."

"Scott. I saw how you were with him after the cruise. But to be honest, I think the two of you becoming serious bothered me before that. I even . . . I talked to him and I made sure he knew I was okay with you sleeping together. Because I hoped that would be it. That you could have sex with him once in a while and—"

"*What?*" Zach practically knocked over his chair as he stood. He didn't shout, but he was tempted. "What did you say to him? And why did you tell me you were fine with it—?" He groaned. How stupid could he have been? She'd mentioned that things didn't have to be serious between him and Scott. Because she'd figured Scott could be an outlet. For what? His "gay" urges? Did she really think he could just use Scott that way? "Becky... I love Scott. Do you understand that? I thought I made it clear that I don't just *fuck* people. That I wouldn't be involved with him—or *you*—unless there was more than sex."

"You did. But you were with him and I didn't want you to feel you had to hold back for me."

"I was holding back for *me*. Yes, part of it was for us because I've seen you together. I didn't want him to hurt you, but I never thought..." Zach ran a hand over his face, repeating slowly, "What did you say to him?"

"I told him I was okay with it... no, actually, I encouraged him to go after you. I already apologized to him for what I said." She spoke in a rush. "It wasn't right. He means more to you. To me. And I—"

"What *exactly* did you say to him?"

Becky's throat worked as she swallowed. She hugged herself, the tendrils of hair that came loose from her bun hiding her face. "I said something about it not always needing to be a full-course meal. That you needed a snack."

"You called him a snack? You..." *Breathe, Pearce.* He kept his tone cautiously level. "Is that how you see him? Is that really what you think I need?"

"No. But I was afraid you couldn't love us both. And if you did, he'd do something to—" She shook her head and sat up straight. "There's no excuse for what I did. And you have every right to be angry. But—"

"I'm not angry. I'm very, very disappointed. I thought you could be honest with me and you weren't." His lips thinned. "But there's more. This all happened before our scene. You seemed fine when I came back from the cruise. Only, you weren't, were you?"

She blinked fast. Shook her head. "No."

He pressed his fist against his mouth, inhaling through his nose. "You put on a good act. When did you decide you were going to leave?"

Her words were so quiet, he had to stop breathing to hear her. "When you told Scott there was more."

"And that changed how you felt about me? About whether or not I could be the man for you—be the man your daughter needs? Do you really think I'm so limited that caring for Scott would make me love either of you less?"

"I don't think that—not anymore. But I did. I can accept coming second—or even third—in your priorities." She stood, clasping her hands in front of her skirt, moving like she wanted to come to him, but wasn't sure she should. "I can't accept that for Casey."

Why not say so then? He didn't understand. Apparently, her feelings had changed, but the fact remained that she'd sooner leave and cut him out of her life completely than have a simple conversation. And maybe they could work on that. Do things differently from this point on. Except . . .

"You'd decided to leave before I tied you up. Before I . . ." He ran his tongue over his teeth and glared at the ceiling. A good act? How about the performance of a lifetime? He considered himself an observant, attentive Dom. He might as well have blindfolded himself before taking the flogger to her. "Do you realize you have triggers because you've played with 'Doms' who didn't care if you were scared, or hurt, or not in the mood to be *fucked*? I have done *everything* in my power to avoid being one of *them*."

"You're not, Zach!" She approached him then, reaching out, but he couldn't let her touch him. Couldn't let her think anything she said would make this okay. A tear spilled down her cheek, and it took all his strength not to pull her into his arms as she hugged herself. "You didn't do anything I didn't want you to."

"You *lied* to me, Becky. Again and again. Not only with your words, but with your body." He saw her again. Bound. Exposed. *Helpless.* He'd pushed her limits, thinking she trusted him. But she didn't. And he had no reason to trust her. "I'm scared for you, Becky. You seem to think a sub's responsibility in a scene ends the second a Dom chooses her to play with. But you can't simply let things happen to you. The way you play is downright dangerous."

"But I trust you, Zach! I wouldn't have done anything with you if I didn't!"

He gave her a hard look. "First of all, don't shout at me. You aren't right because you speak louder. Second, you don't trust me or you would have been honest about your feelings."

"So that's it? You're done with me?" She let out a broken sob. "I love you. I made a mistake. Tell me how to make this right." When he didn't answer, she dropped to her knees in front of him. "Please, Sir. I—"

"Get up." He held out his hand, pressing his eyes shut as she placed her wrist in it like a sub giving over control. He couldn't handle her doing that right now. He pulled her to her feet. "You only kneel to me when my collar is around your neck. And I can't say when I will put it there again."

"Sir—"

"Zach. I can't be your master, Becky." Damn it, he couldn't stand to see her crying. And he didn't want to let her go. He should. If he was smart, he would. *Screw that.* "Shh. Tell me what you want. You've told me what you've done, and why, but not what you want from me now."

"I ruined everything." Her whole body shook as she wrapped her arms around his waist and pressed her forehead against the center of his chest. "I want another chance. I want you to forgive me. But I have no right to ask that of you. No one would blame you for walking away from me."

"I can't do that. I still love you." He kissed her hair. As a Dom, he knew letting this go was wrong. But as a man, all he saw was the women he loved, coming back to him. "I gave Scott another chance. Do you really expect me to give you any less?"

"Scott . . . you have to know I don't want you to give him up. And before you argue that I shouldn't make it okay to make you happy, I want to make this very clear. I tried to pretend that I accepted him for you, but there's something between me and him." She tipped her head back, fine lines forming around her eyes. "I don't know what it is, but I'm done trying to figure out how it fits with my role as a mother. Because I'm more than a mother. Casey doesn't need to know everything I do. She won't be calling you both Daddy."

"She doesn't have to call either of us 'Daddy' for us to be there for her."

"Right. So . . . if it's not over—"

"It's not over." Zach managed a thin smile. He wasn't sure what they had anymore, but he wasn't ready to give up on it completely. "You were saying?"

"Can we try this? The three of us?" She sniffed and swiped away her tears with an impatient gesture. "I think we can make it work."

"So do I." Zach cupped her cheek in his palm, studying her face as he spoke. Which might be pointless. She was very good at hiding how she really felt. "I'll tell you the same thing I told Scott. Your relationship with him doesn't revolve around me. I believed that you were comfortable with me moving forward with him, and I have. Feel free to do the same, at your own pace. I won't tell you what to do with him, but I'll always be here if you need to talk to me. And I hope you will." He paused. If she was going to have a relationship with Scott, she had to know it wouldn't be easy. "He's shared a bit about his past. The interview where he spoke about his foster sister. He told me about his brother's gambling addiction once when he was drunk. But there's more he isn't ready to share yet. He says he wasn't abused, but . . . I'm not sure I believe him. Something happened to him. He might not even remember it, which would explain a lot."

"He needs you. I don't think anyone's ever cared enough to see that there's a reason for the way he acts." She frowned. "Actually, I never considered it, and that makes me feel like even more of a bitch. I did stories on him, exposing all his antics because the viewers loved it. I . . . I only ever refused to dig deeper when it came to you. I respected what you did for Luke."

"I can handle bad press. I have a brand-new, solid contract that should keep me with the team for years. Scott's future with the team is still uncertain. If we're going to be with him, we need to help him get through this. He's so close, but . . ." Zach shook his head. "One wrong move could ruin his chances."

"We'll make sure he behaves." Becky smiled as though relieved that they'd found some common ground. There was hope in her eyes. "So . . . are we okay? Maybe after I finish we can—"

Not yet. It's too soon. This time he was the one who couldn't meet her eyes. "I have a meeting with my agent in an hour. Then I'm going to the food shelter with Ramos. Tonight's no good."

"Oh." Becky moved away from him. "I have a busy week too. We can always meet at the club this weekend and—"

"No." Zach sighed. He wouldn't react to her dishonesty with more of the same. He had to be up-front with her. "Becky, I'll need some time before I can play with you again. To make sure we have the trust we need to explore the lifestyle."

"Will we ever?" Becky tucked her hair behind her ears, the pallor of her skin even more apparent with the black smudges of mascara under her eyes. She looked worn out. "Do you think I can regain your trust?"

He nodded, taking her hand and bringing it up to his lips. He kissed her knuckles, praying it would be enough to let her know the situation wasn't hopeless. Because he couldn't give her more right now. "If you really understand why pretending everything all right when it's not is a problem? Yes. But I need to see you being honest, Becky. Be open with me about your feelings. And give me some time. It's not just my trust in you that's been shaken."

"It isn't?" Her eyes widened. She frowned. "Did Scott—"

"Not Scott." He took a deep breath and released her hand. "Myself. However well you hid your fears from me . . . I can't help but think I would have noticed if I'd been paying more attention. If I hadn't been so confident in my 'skills' as a Dom." As he spoke, it became clear to him that he wasn't entirely blameless. Maybe she'd been right all along. Maybe he'd been lying to himself about how much he'd wanted Scott from the beginning. And if he couldn't be sure of his own feelings, how could she? "If we ever play again I need to—"

"*If?*" Becky shook her head. "Zach, this is something we both need. Are you going to scene with someone else?"

Zach let out a bitter laugh. At this point, the last thing on his mind was playing the Dom again. "Not without supervision. But if you want to go to the club, I won't object. Just . . ." He rolled his shoulders as the muscles within drew taut. He hated the idea of her sceneing with another Dom, but he wouldn't force her to go without the release she needed just because he couldn't give it to her. "Just be careful."

"I don't want anyone else, Zach." Her cell phone buzzed on her desk. She checked it, then pressed ignore, keeping her gaze on it as she spoke. "I want you."

He had no idea what to say to that. This would take some time to process. So he stepped up to her and kissed her cheek. "You should get back to work. I'll give you a call when I'm free. Maybe we can go to a movie or something this weekend."

"Zach . . . ?"

"Yes?" He paused, hand on the door, and glanced back at her.

The pleading in her eyes cracked the cement shell encasing his heart, leaving his once solid defenses nothing but dust. If he stayed any longer, he might let her talk him into just about anything, if only to see her smile again.

Tough it out. You can't be the Dom she needs. Not yet.

"Becky, you have to work and I have to see my agent. I can't—"

"I love you." She wrapped her arms around her ribs, looking down. "That's all I wanted to say."

He swallowed and managed to smile. His pulse pounded hard in his skull. "I love you too."

But when is love ever enough?

* * * *

For about half an hour, Scott had totally immersed himself in playing *Red Dead Redemption* on the Xbox 360 hooked up to the flatscreen TV in the lounge. But the second the door behind him opened, he let the poor bastard he'd been trying to save hang. He dropped the controller on the cushion behind him, twisting around to watch Zach picked up his bag and turn to leave.

"Uh . . . do you need to talk or something?" Scott stood and walked around the sofa, not sure what to make of Zach's distant expression. He didn't looked as bad as he had that day he'd dropped, but it was damn close. "Or we can go out for supper." Scott slapped his stomach, trying to keep things light. "I could use some advice on how to lose all this flab."

Zach's brow rose, his steady gaze clearly saying "Are you serious?" Then he shook his head. "Not tonight, Scott. I'm sorry I had you wait, but I really need some time to myself." He pressed his lips together, clenching and unclenching his fist at his side. "If anything, you should go make sure Becky's all right."

Aw, fuck. "You didn't dump her, did you? I told you to—"

"I didn't dump her. I asked for some time." Zach's eyes narrowed. "Why didn't you tell me she called you on the cruise? That's why you were drinking that night, isn't it? Because of what she said?"

Scott rubbed the back of his neck, thinking fast. Had he somehow screwed things up for them? *Wait, when did I sign up for full disclosure?* He stared back at Zach, his brow furrowed. "So let me get this straight. Me and Becky can be together, so long as we provide transcripts to every conversation?"

"That's not what I'm saying."

"Then what *are* you saying? Yeah, we talked. She made sure I knew she was okay with everything." Scott shrugged. "Nothing wrong with that far as I can tell."

Zach tipped his head back and groaned. "Damn it, Scott! She told you it was okay for me to *fuck* you! She implied that it would be nothing more, and it bothered you—you didn't think that was something I should know?"

"It *is* okay for you to fuck me. She didn't tell you to stop, did she?" Scott was a little confused. After his discussion with Becky earlier, he doubted she'd do that, but who knew anymore? "I thought me and her were good."

"She called you a fucking snack. You're more than that."

"You've made that perfectly clear, and I'm happy with where things are going with us." Scott rolled his eyes as Zach made a frustrated sound and disappeared into the hall. He followed after a few seconds, making sure there was no one around before he shouted, "I'm missing something here! I'm supposed to be okay with you leaving her over something this stupid?"

Dropping his bag by the garage door, Zach strode back up to Scott and latched on to his shoulder, giving him a hard shake. "If you had said something like that to her, if you made her feel like that,

I'd fucking knock you on your ass. All I did was ask her for some time."

"And what would you do if I hurt her and left you to pick up the pieces?" Scott shoved Zach's hand off his shoulder. "All because of something she said? To *me*?" He let out a sharp laugh. "I'm a big boy. And I've had people call me worse. Get over it."

"It's not that simple. She wanted to leave me before the scene we did. She wasn't honest with me and—" Zach scraped his nails over his scalp. "I don't expect you to understand. Do what you want."

"Always do, buddy." Scott retreated a few steps, not liking the idea of letting Zach leave all pissed off. Zach had told him that his relationship with Becky was between the two of them. He guessed that worked both ways. If Zach and Becky had issues, maybe he needed to let them work it out. And make sure they both knew his door was always open. He spoke before Zach could pass through the garage door. "Hey, Zach?"

Holding the door open with his shoulder, Zach stopped, but didn't look back. "Yeah?"

"You don't want me taking off on you, don't do it to me." Scott's lips quirked. "I expect at least a call tonight."

Zach looked taken aback. But then he laughed. "I'll call. I promise."

That felt like a win. Scott ambled down the hall, feeling more than a little pleased with himself. Quite the change, Zach and Becky needing him to be the reasonable one. Not time to celebrate just yet though. He hesitated by the stairs, then changed direction, heading for the elevator. He should conserve his energy. He had a feeling it would be a long night.

And not in a good way.

* * * *

A single tear plopped on Becky's keyboard. Then another. She rolled her chair away from her desk, blinking fast and swallowing against the urge to break down and sob. If she started, she wasn't sure she'd ever stop.

Zach might say he'd give her another chance, but she wasn't sure he could. Things had been so wonderful between them. She'd never forget their time together. And at this point, all she might have was those memories. Because she doubted Zach would ever look at her, ever hold her, the same way again.

What did I do? The sob tore out of her chest and she couldn't hold it in anymore. *What the hell did I do?*

Her office door opened and she quickly shot out of her chair, facing the window and drying her tears with her fingertips. Damn it, the last thing she needed was for Mr. Keane to see her like this. Bad enough that she'd taken off for three weeks. She couldn't help but wonder if he'd let her absence slide because of Landon. Keeping her around *might* motivate her brother to return to the team, but if she didn't pull herself together, Mr. Keane could decide she was more trouble than she was worth.

"Becky?"

Oh God. Scott saying her name, his tone rough with concern, smashed through the dam on her emotions like high tide in a storm. Her knees folded and she braced to hit the floor. But he was there before she could fall. His arms came around her and he made a soft, hushing sound, kissing her cheeks a few times before tipping her chin up.

She expected him to claim her lips, but instead he stroked her bottom lip with his thumb and shook his head.

"My tough little woman. I hate seeing you like this. Makes me want to hunt Zach down and drop the fucking gloves."

A watery laugh escaped her. "You're not wearing any gloves."

"You know what I mean." Scott scowled. "He went too far."

"No, he didn't. I did. He's earned my trust and respect, and I gave him neither. You can't expect him to be okay with that." She put a finger over Scott's lips before he could argue with her, but it was sweet to see he wanted to. "I'll just have to take your example and prove that I can do better."

"Oh boy." Scott drew her toward her desk, dropping onto her chair and pulling her into his lap. He nuzzled his face into the mess of her hair. "If you're following *my* example for anything, we're all in trouble."

She rested her head on his shoulder, knowing cuddling with him in her office was inappropriate, but not really giving a damn. She hooked her fingers into the collar of his white T-shirt. "And why's that?"

"You know why. I'm a bad, bad man." He ran his hand up and down her arm. "You gonna be okay, sweetie? You know this isn't over, right?"

"What Zach and I had before is over." She pressed her eyes shut, grateful that the cotton of his shirt soaked in her tears. And that his arms around her made her feel less broken. She let out a weary sigh. "It will never be the same."

"It will be even better. You've got me now too." Scott laughed and gave her a little squeeze. "Come on, Becky. He's pissed, but he'll get over it. And you're not dealing with this alone. If you really need someone to spank you in the meantime, I'm sure I can manage." He took a deep breath, shifting uncomfortably as he hardened against her hip. "Time to change the subject. You done here?"

"Yes." There was no point trying to work anymore, and she wanted to get back to her daughter. Find out how her day went. She might be a horrible girlfriend, and a lousy sub, but at least she could be a decent mother. She checked her watch. Landon had texted her about two hours earlier to let her know he had Casey and she was fine. Made sure to remind her that Dean was expecting her for supper. A few minutes more with Scott wouldn't hurt though. "Don't move please. I'm enjoying this."

"Yeah?" Scott continued running his hand along her arm. Then he snorted. "Carter is such a dumbass."

Random much? She peeked up at him. "Why?"

"He's always going on about flowers and candy. His go-to whenever he gets on Jami's bad side." Scott pressed her head back down to his shoulder. "Sometimes a woman just needs to be held."

Who is this man? She sighed as her phone buzzed. Dean wouldn't be happy if she let her food get cold. He was constantly reminding her not to work too much. To eat properly. She had a feeling Landon had hinted that she sometimes made meals for her daughter and worked at the dinner table while finishing up paperwork. Sometimes her own supper ended up being the next day's lunch.

Easing off Scott's lap, she stood and checked her phone. A message from Dean. And from Zach.

Zach: I shouldn't have left the way I did. But I meant the last thing I said.

She felt Scott come up behind her and leaned back against him as she typed in her reply.

Me: So did I.

Zach: Are you okay?

Me: Yes... She hit send. Then figured if she was going to prove herself, she should let him know she wasn't alone. *Scott's here.*

Zach: Good. Give him a kiss for me. I'll call you both tonight.

Her face heated. Such a casual response. If it was going to be the three of them, Zach's request shouldn't be a big deal, but kissing Scott could lead to a whole lot more. And she couldn't do *that* here.

"What is it?" Scott took a step back, watching her face in a way that made it clear he hadn't read the message. "He's not still being a dick, is he?"

"No, I was just thinking..." She tongued her bottom lip, thinking of a way to distract him from coming down on Zach without sharing the details of their texts. She gathered her suit jacket, her briefcase, and their conversation about Luke came back to her. Glancing over her shoulder, she smirked. "For future reference, blue hydrangeas are my favorite."

Scott blinked, "Blue what?" He swiped a pen off her desk and held it to his palm. "Spell it? This is gonna be important."

She shook her head and laughed. "If you don't remember, I'll know you aren't that sorry."

"Aw, come on!" He grinned, joining her in the hall and waiting as she locked her office door. "Does it count if the flowers are blue?"

"Depends how bad you've messed up." She headed for the elevator, then held her breath most of the way down. Zach wanted her to kiss Scott. Which she couldn't do without throwing herself at him. Which would give him the wrong impression. Besides, Scott would eventually make a move. Actually, she almost wanted him to. Until he did, she wouldn't know how to handle it. Their first kiss had made an impact, but hadn't been anything life-changing. This one would be.

But she ended up standing by her car, pressing her lips together to keep from asking what he was waiting for. Even without knowing what Zach's message said, Scott had to have seen at least one opening. All those times he'd hit on her, and now he needed an invitation?

His lips twitched with amusement when she faced him, hands on her hips. He spoke as her lips parted. "Mind giving me a lift? Zach kinda left me stranded."

She frowned at him. "No, I don't mind, but—"

"Want me to drive?"

"*No!*" She made an exasperated sound when he went around the car to wait by the passenger side. "Ugh, you've got to be kidding me."

He gave her an innocent look. Then slapped his forehead. "Oh, damn. You're right. Sorry." Coming back to her side, he took her keys from her hand, unlocked the door, then held it open for her. "Chivalry ain't dead, babe. It's just slow."

He was too cute, with his helmet hair and his mischievous smile. And he was most definitely messing with her. For a split second, she considered the two years she had on him, and the decades of maturity, and wondered if maybe he wouldn't be better off with a younger woman.

Someone like Sahara.

A little, nasty green thing that reminded her a lot of Gollum hissing about the one ring reared its ugly head. She got in behind the wheel and tried to sound blasé as Scott sat in the passenger seat. "So how's your girlfriend? Don't you think you should run this by her before you commit to anything?"

Scott smirked. "Nope. Her, Jami, and Akira just found a new place together. I've reclaimed my bachelor abode. It's awesome. I can be a total slob again."

She really didn't like the idea of his living in a messy house. She tightened her grip on the steering wheel and glanced over at him at a red light. "I don't have time today, but maybe tomorrow—" Not tomorrow, the Cobra's staff had another meeting. "—or the day after, I can come over and help you—"

"Oh, hell no! When you come to my place, it's gonna look nice.

And I'm cooking you dinner." He rubbed his chin with his thumb and forefinger. "I hope you like lasagna. It's one of the few foods I can brag about making pretty good."

"I *love* pasta. It's a date." She focused on the road as he gave her directions to his condo. When she pulled up in front of it, she watched him get out, nodding and muttering "goodbye" as he collected his bag from the backseat. She was looking forward to their date, but who knew when that would happen? Preparing for the season would monopolize most of their time. She wasn't sure why it mattered that he still hadn't kissed her. Was she really that insecure that she needed big displays of affection? Hadn't he done enough? Hell, the way he'd held her—and even before that, the way he'd listened to her problems . . . he was doing everything right.

But there was that one final line they hadn't crossed. Not in any way that counted. And she had to go there with him Had to do it just to convince herself this was real. She could get out and tell him Zach had asked her to, but that wouldn't be the same—

She jumped when he rapped his knuckled on her window.

"Open the door," he said.

Hand on the door latch, she unbuckled her seatbelt as she opened the door, staring at him as he slid close to her, his hand on her cheek, leaning down with a soft smile on his lips. She swallowed and put her hand over his, trapped in the intensity of his level gaze. Scott didn't look at her like this. Like she was everything. Like she was the *only* one that mattered to him. When he undressed her with his eyes, it was down to the skin, not down to her soul.

He'd changed.

"Our first kiss. This is it, Becky. The one before doesn't count." He brushed his lips over hers, the brief touch like a lick of flame. "This is ours. It's not proving anything. It's not a way to get you naked or to show you can have any man you want. It's me showing you exactly what you mean to me. For the first time. But not the last."

A bit of pressure, the slight press of his tongue, and she was his. He pulled her to her feet, held her against him, slanting his mouth and dipping in a little deeper, teasing her tongue with his, smiling against her lips as he tasted her. His teeth tugged at her bottom lip.

He explored her mouth as though he could find everything he was looking for in kissing her. Holding her. And that little stopwatch inside her, the one that measured every event, every passing second for its worth, shattered. All that had passed between them from the moment they'd met had come to this. It was like a puzzle piece made of steel, welded into place, fitting just right. Too hot to touch, but already secure. Strengthening as it cooled.

The kiss, however, didn't cool. He had her standing on the street, her door open wide, stealing her breath and restraint, not letting up even when she whimpered, needing more. She fisted her hand in his shirt, refusing to let him go as the intensity of the kiss lessened. It wasn't enough.

It would never be enough.

He pressed his eyes shut as his lips left hers, breathing hard. "I don't want to be good. Responsible. Tell me I don't have to be. Tell me we can both tell the rest of the world to go to hell and just be together."

Her brain somehow found its way back into her skull. Fully functional. She could practically see Landon lifting Casey up onto her booster seat and pushing her chair close to the table as Dean fixed her plate, giving her a small helping of the vegetables she hated. She could hear Casey asking about training camp, about how each player had performed like she was a miniature authority on the game. Dean and Landon would nod as she quoted all the sports blogs she looked up every morning, trying to humor her as she took every words as gospel.

And then she would ask "Where's Mommy?" Becky refused to leave Landon and Dean to make excuses for her. She touched Scott's cheek. "You are good. And you know 'the rest of the world' includes my daughter. I can't—"

"I wouldn't ask you to." He bit the tip of his tongue and shook his head. "Sorry. Me being selfish. Go be a mommy. Her birthday is in two Fridays, right?"

"Yes." Becky managed to compose herself and settle down behind the wheel. "So you'll be there Thursday night?"

"I'll be there." He held on to her door, bowing his head and letting out a rough laugh. "Cold shower time. Damn, I want to kidnap you—with a blindfold so you won't notice the mess. I'll behave when I come to your place. I can't wait to see what you think of the gift."

"What is it?"

"You'll see." He winked. "Gotta make sure it's perfect before I bring it over. But I think you'll like it." He scratched his scruffy jaw. "I hope she does."

"She will. One thing I can say about my daughter is she appreciates everything she gets. She's not one of those kids who unwraps a gift and tosses it aside to get to the next one." Some of her friends had kids like that. She'd been amazed when Casey was three and she spent so much time admiring a pair of socks with cow print that Becky had to take them away and give her another gift to open. Her grandmother had tears in her eyes as Casey stared, open-mouthed, at the little gold cross she'd been given. Casey was the one who'd privately told Becky later that night to put it away until she was a "big girl."

"I'll break it, Mommy. I don't want to break it," Casey said.

A gift from one of her heroes would be even more precious. She was happy Scott would be there to see Casey's reaction. Unless . . .

"You're not coming early because you can't be there for her birthday, are you?"

"No way. I wouldn't miss it." His eyes gleamed as he gave her a secretive look. "Not a single man on our team will miss her birthday. But don't tell her. It's a surprise."

Becky pursed her lips. What did the men have planned? And why was this the first she'd heard of it? "It's not my surprise, so why don't you—?"

Scott shook his head and placed his finger over her lips to quiet her. "I was asked not to. So I won't. But trust me, she'll love it."

"Scott—"

"Hey, you wanna keep pushing, deal with Richter." He cocked his head. "Actually, that's not a bad idea. If Zach won't play with you—"

"Dean is involved with my to-be sister-in-law. Playing with him would be weird." She wrinkled her nose as she considered exactly *how* weird. The man shared a bed with her brother. She shuddered.

"Don't even joke about that."

"All right, got it." He rested his forehead against hers. "Thursday, latest. We'll do the text, email, phone call thing until then unless we get some free time."

"Sounds good." Actually, it sounded horrible. But their schedules didn't leave room for more. She planted a smile on her lips. "Get some rest. And if you want a snack, stick to fruit."

Scott snorted, trailing his fingers down her throat before backing away with obvious effort. "So many ways I could misinterpret that. But I'll be good." He stood on the sidewalk, hands in his pockets as she settled behind the wheel. As she pulled out, she glanced at her rearview mirror, and spotted him mouthing something like, "I'll miss you."

When she got to Dean's house, she took her phone out of her purse and texted Scott before going inside.

Me: I'll miss you too.

Scott: You caught that, huh? <g> Have a great night, babe.

Me: I will. And thank you for being there. It really helped.

Scott: I'll always be there. <3

Me: Awww

Dinner was wonderful, as always. Dean cooked better than any man—or woman—she knew. She felt much better about having shown up late when Casey drew her into the conversation about a prospect she'd heard Landon mention without missing a beat. Becky didn't know much about the young man, but she shared the little she'd read about in the papers. She glanced over at the door a few times as she polished off her spaghetti, not sure whether or not she should ask why Silver wasn't with them. Amia was fast asleep in her swing close to where Landon sat at the head of the table. He fussed with her light, pale pink baby blanket a few times, but other than that, ate and spoke with the adults in a relaxed way that told Becky he had gotten comfortable with parenting. He didn't smother his daughter, but she would know he'd never be far.

Him and Dean. She knows their voices, responds to them. But what about Silver? Amia didn't share the same bond with her mother as she did with her fathers. But now wasn't the time to bring that up. Not in front of Casey.

But soon.

Finally, talk turned to Casey's birthday. She gave both Landon and Dean level looks, her tone very serious. "I want a hockey theme for my party, but—and you have to promise not to laugh—everything has to be purple." She pursed her lips and turned to Becky. "Can we do that, Mommy?"

Becky hesitated, glancing over at the men, not sure what to say. She was fairly certain a local party store would carry Dartmouth Cobra-themed party decorations, but in purple? "I'll see what I can do, *poupée*, but—"

"Consider it done, sweetheart," Dean said, winking at Casey. "I can make a few calls. Your mother and I will discuss the details."

God, I love this man! Becky smiled at Dean and he inclined his head. He was like the older brother she'd always wanted, perfect for Landon, amazing with Amia, with Casey, and always there for her family. He took everything in stride and handled every situation, with the team, and in his personal life, with dignity and compassion. As she helped Casey tie her shoes by the door, she studied him. He was in the dining room, arguing quietly with Landon about the dishes. She ducked her head to hide a smile as he told Landon he didn't want him putting too much pressure on his leg.

"But you bitch about me not spending enough time with the physical therapist?" Landon snorted. "You cook. I clean. It's not up for discussion."

"Really? I beg to differ," Dean said, taking a pile of plates off the table.

Landon held his hands out for the plates. "Beg all you want. I don't reward obstinacy."

Dean's lips thinned. "Big word, goalie. You sure you know what it means?"

"Yes, you arrogant, stubborn . . ." Landon paused and glanced over at Becky when she cleared her throat. "Damn it, Dean. I can load the dishwasher. And tidy up. Take care of our daughter while I do it. The doctor said she shouldn't sleep in the swing for too long. And she needs a bath."

"We're leaving!" Becky called out, grinning when Casey giggled. "Bye!"

"I'm sorry, Becky." Dean carefully lifted Amia from her swing without waking her, carrying her over and smiling as Casey rose up on her tiptoes to kiss the top of the baby's head. "You know how your brother is."

"I heard that!" Landon rolled his eyes, his lips curving slightly as he glanced up from wiping down the table.

"You were meant to." Dean kissed Becky's cheek, then Casey's. "Be good for Mommy. I love you, sweetie."

"I love you too, Uncle Dean." Casey gave him one of her I-mean-business looks. "And you really need to consider going after Richards. It would be a big mistake for you to let another team grab him."

"I'll take that into consideration." Dean looked at Becky. "All this talk of prospects and birthdays—I haven't had a chance to ask how you've been doing. I hope your time away did you some good?"

"Yes and no. But I've figured some things out," Becky said, kissing Amia's forehead. "And you? Are you doing well?"

"Yes. Silver's on some new medication that is helping her quite a bit . . . it makes her tired though. She would have come down to see you otherwise."

"That's okay. I'll see her next time." Becky bit her bottom lip. "Is she seeing someone about . . ."

Dean shook his head. "Not yet. But we're working on it."

"All right, well, let me know if I can help." Becky took Casey's hand, said her last goodbyes to Dean and her brother, then headed out to her car. She was worried about Silver, but wouldn't dwell on it. She was in good hands. And she knew Dean wouldn't hesitate to call if they needed her.

Once they got home, she and Casey did the bedtime routine that hadn't changed since Casey was an infant. Bath time, PJ's, then some mother-daughter chat while Becky brushed Casey's hair—Casey did most of the talking. Becky read Casey's current favorite book, *Curious George at the Aquarium*, for the umpteenth time. Tucked her in. Sang "*Ah! Vous dirai-je maman*," as requested. And managed not to cry as she finished the lullaby.

"Daddy wants me to reason, like a grown-up person." Why that song of all the ones Becky sang to her? Damn it, her little girl wanted a daddy so badly.

And she didn't have one. Not really. Patrick hadn't called since before he'd sent Casey home, and that was just to let her know what time his mother would by flying down with Casey. He ignored Becky's emails telling him how Casey was doing in school. The most recent ones asking if he could make it for her birthday. But Casey didn't ask about him anymore—she did speak to her Nanny every weekend though. Which seemed to be enough. For now, at least Casey had two loving uncles to partially fill that role.

Over the next two weeks, Becky spoke with Zach and Scott every night. One morning, she opened the door to her office to find a bouquet of blue hydrangeas. She laughed when she read the card, signed by both men.

> *I remembered the color! Zach finally took mercy on me and told me the name of the flowers.*
>
> *Xoxo,*
>
> *Scott*
>
> *Every night I think of you, long after I hang up after speaking to you. Things will be okay.*
>
> *Love,*
>
> *Zach*

Things would be okay. She had to believe it. Her job and Casey kept her busy enough not to worry too much about not spending time with the men, but... there was something missing in her life. Moments when she felt like she was standing in a big, empty room alone. Waiting.

She wasn't even sure what she was waiting for. Maybe just some assurance that the emptiness wouldn't last for long. That she still had something to give to the two men in her life.

That they still needed her as much as she needed them.

Chapter Twenty Five

The fresh bite of wood stain scented the air as Scott carefully wrapped Casey's gift in the paper provided by the GM. Richter had stopped by the day before to make sure he'd be at Casey's party, and Scott had nervously spilled both his intention to bring the gift early and told Richter what the gift was. The man spent a lot of time with Casey, so he'd know if she'd like it.

"She'll love it, Demyan. It's . . . you made this yourself?"

"Yeah. I'm pretty good at stuff like this." Scott shrugged, uncomfortable sharing that little tidbit with the GM, but kinda hoping the man wasn't about to tell him it was a good thing he could play the game. "I made all my own furniture, but I don't usually make stuff for other people. It's just a hobby."

"Well . . . if you're not too busy—this can't take you away from training—"

"It doesn't," Scott said quickly.

"Good. Then maybe you could make something like this for Amia? I'd pay you of co—"

Scott shook his head, barely resisting hugging Richter, speaking in a rush. "I'd love to. And you don't need to pay me. I didn't get Silver or the baby anything, and it would be awesome to give them something they'll like. I mean . . . if you like it?"

"Scott." Dean gave him a hard look. "Know your worth. You're very talented. You have another twelve years at best in your hockey career. It's good that you have something you enjoy doing to focus on after."

"Thank you, Mr. Richter," Scott said, a little embarrassed by the compliment, not really comfortable talking about life after hockey. "I'll see you Saturday."

Richter hesitated by the door. "Scott, I know you and Sahara are not together. The way she looks at Keane . . ." He sighed. "That aside, I've seen how you are with Pearce. And the way you watch Becky when she's rushing around, herding the press. I have to tell you—"

"What, Richter? I'm not seeing how what the three of us do is any of your business."

"It isn't. But Landon won't trust you not to hurt his sister." Richter's jaw hardened. "I'm not sure I trust you, but I can deal with my misgivings. Landon has enough stress. I'd simply ask you not to add to it."

"So no PDA?" Scott's tone was sharp, but he was done having everyone dictate his life. What more did he have to do? He scoffed as he held his front door open for Richter. "I don't think Becky's into making out in the parking lot like teens. But she's not going to let her little brother tell her who to be with. She's made that pretty clear."

Nodding slowly, Richter took his cane from where it rested against the wall by the door. The sky was cloudy. His knee seemed to be bugging him. "Forget that I mentioned it."

Now Scott felt like an asshole. Richter was just looking out for Bower. They had their own issues. He sighed. "We don't need to flaunt anything. I've got it."

"Yo, Demmy, you gonna make me load this into your car by myself?"

Carter nudged Scott's shoulder with a fist, bringing him back to the present. Scott glared at him. "Don't call me that. I put up with it when you were drunk, but—"

"Ugh, can we not talk about that?" Carter hunched down at one end of the heavy gift. "You don't bitch when Vanek calls you Demmy."

"Yeah, well no one bitches when Vanek does anything." Scott picked up his end. "I'm glad he's back, you know?"

"I know. But he's starting to be a pain in the ass." Carter backed carefully through the open front door, easing into the hall outside Scott's condo. "I'm glad Tim told us to hit him as hard as we can to make sure he's ready. Vanek chirps at me one more time about the *one* time I let Chicklet Domme me and I'm gonna do more than nail him into the boards."

"I hear you." Scott took a deep breath as they placed the gift on the floor of the elevator, pushing the button for the basement level. "I swear, the kid's using his mouth to make up for lost time."

"I'm gonna enjoy watching his Domme put ball stretchers on him at the club this weekend." Carter winced. "So long as it doesn't give Seb any ideas."

"Fuck off. I should tell him you said that." Scott smirked. Carter was a fucking pain slut. It had freaked him out the first few times he'd seen Ramos use clamps or a riding crop on him, but Carter clearly enjoyed everything the big man did to him. "You so into being shared, maybe Ramos should ask Chicklet—"

"No. I don't think Jami would be cool with another woman . . . fuck, Demyan, about when I was drunk—"

Oh, hell no. "Forget it."

"I can't."

"Did you tell, Ramos?"

"Yeah. I woulda anyway, but Pearce made sure I didn't put it off." Carter lowered the gift, waiting for Scott to unlock the backseat of his car before lifting it again. For some reason, his face was really red. And not from the weight. "I told Seb . . . fuck, it would be weird if me and you did anything. After Bower, you're one of my best friends. We'd have some hot, wild fucking sex—"

"Ramos never put speech restrictions on you?" Scott felt himself getting hard. His agent, Zach's, and Stephan needed to be locked up somewhere for at least an hour so he and Zach could do more than crash at the end of the night. Two weeks without any was killing him. And Carter had a nice ass. Friends or not, he couldn't take much more of this. "He should."

"And here I am, baring my soul to you." Carter shook his head and ducked into the passenger seat. He didn't speak again until Scott started driving. "Seb and Pearce talked a few times."

"So?"

"If Pearce . . . if I did a scene with him, would it bother you?"

Scott took a deep breath. The answer should be easy, but it wasn't. Zach was his and Becky's. But being a Dom was part of him. Ramos getting him to even consider doing a scene was a good thing. Would it bother him if Zach fucked Carter?

Hell yes.

But the other stuff? He wasn't sure. Watching Carter suck Zach's cock would be fucking hot. Seeing Ramos and Zach tie Carter up and torture him a little, not letting him come, touching him and using floggers and stuff on him . . .

I need a bath. Full of ice. Or kill me now. He cleared his throat. "Naw, I guess it would be okay."

The last thing Scott wanted to be thinking about when he got to Becky's place was sex, but his chat with Carter made it hard to think of anything else. And when he tried, all he could think about was whether Zach playing with Ramos and Carter would bother Becky. He carried the gift up to Becky's porch, set it down, then rang the doorbell.

When she opened the door, it was like . . . he couldn't find the words. Damn, he wanted her. But it wasn't mindless lust like what his talk with Carter made him feel. He wanted to step inside, slam the door in Carter's face, and pull her into his arms. Kiss her in a way that might express all the things he couldn't say. Long and slow, like he'd never let her go.

I don't have to let her go. If I don't fuck this up, I'll have her tomorrow, and the day after, and the day after that . . .

Or would he? It still made him a little nervous because, if she could take off on Zach, what reason would she have to see this through with Scott involved?

"Hey!" Her tone was bright, but something in her eyes made him feel like she could see his every thought branded right on his forehead. She pressed her lips together, then seemed to come to some kind of conclusion as she waved him and Carter inside, laughing when they whispered their greetings. "You don't have to worry about waking up Casey. She's not here—Dean's mother picked her up earlier since she can't come tomorrow. She's bringing Casey to Dean's so I can decorate tonight." Her eyes were wide as she looked over the present. "That's quite the gift. Wow. Dean pulled off the purple Cobra paper! We've both been so busy with work, I wasn't sure he could!"

"Yeah, not much that man can't do," Scott said as he and Carter carried the gift into the living room.

"Would you boys like a drink? Coffee? Soda?"

Carter asked for a soda, then made himself comfortable on an armchair as Scott hovered by the large, wrapped package. He started wondering if the stain he'd used was too dark. Or if the thing was too big.

What if Becky hates it? Or Casey does?

Becky put her hands on her hips, shaking her head. "Something's bothering you, Scott. What is it?"

Scott shrugged, shuffling his feet and staring at the floor. "Just . . . could you take a look at the gift? I want to make sure it's okay."

"But it's wrapped so nicely."

"Yeah, but . . ." Scott ran his tongue across his teeth and glanced over at Carter. Who just sat back in the chair and smirked. Helpful bastard that he was. Scott knelt by the gift. "The paper won't rip much if we're careful."

He'd wanted the gift to be a surprise for Becky and Casey, but why disappoint them both? If Becky didn't like it, he might have time to get Casey something else.

Becky bit her bottom lip, her eyes seeming a little sad. But she simply nodded.

They'd need more tape to wrap it up again, but he managed not to ruin the paper. He smoothed the wrapping out over the floor, taking a deep breath before glancing up at Becky. Then he cursed and shot to his feet.

She was crying.

"I'm sorry. I didn't mean to . . ." He swallowed, holding out his arms, relieved when she stepped up to him and leaned against his chest. "It's okay. I'll get rid of it. I just thought—"

"Get rid of it?" Becky let out a shocked laugh. "Please tell me you're joking!" She eased away from him, dropping to her knees in front of the maple toy box, tracing one of the unicorns he'd carved into the lid with a fingertip. "She's going to love this. How did you . . . you did this, Scott? For my baby?"

"Yeah." *Is that really so hard to believe?* "I told you; I think she's awesome."

Shaking her head, Becky continued to examine the toy box, running her hands over the wood he'd sanded so carefully, checking the special hinge he'd gotten so the lid wouldn't slam shut. Then she went back to staring at the carved unicorns.

"I don't know what to say." She shot to her feet and threw herself at him, practically knocking him off his feet as she hugged him. "Thank you. Thank you so much."

He rubbed her back and kissed her hair. "So it's good?"

"It's better than—" Becky laughed and playfully slapped his chest. "It's amazing! What happened to that ego, Mr. Demyan? You have no problem showing it for the press."

"I don't care what *they* think of me," Scott said.

"Ah . . ." Becky gave Carter a pointed look. "Thank you for helping Scott bring that in, Luke. Are you finished your drink?"

Carter frowned and glanced at his empty glass. "Yeah, but—"

"It's been nice seeing you. Give Jami a kiss for me." Becky took the glass from Carter.

"Becky, Landon won't—"

"Lucas Isaiah Carter, don't you *dare* go there."

"Hey!" Carter scowled. "Only my mom gets to call me that."

"And she probably does it when you're being a pain in the butt. Landon has no say in this. And you can tell him I said so."

"Really?" Carter stood and folded his arms over his chest. "You really think that would be a good idea with all that's going on?"

Becky took a long, deep inhale, shaking her head. "Maybe not. Don't tell Landon. I will when the time is right. But *that* doesn't change what I'm going to do with my life."

"Fine." Carter rolled his eyes and headed for the door. "It's Demyan's funeral."

After Carter left, Scott distracted himself meticulously rewrapping Casey's gift. Becky didn't say anything for a long time, simply went through the two bags of decorations, looking up at him once in a while as though she wanted to speak. The silence was getting weird. Almost like they were strangers.

He didn't like it.

So he went over to the table and picked up one of the rolled up streamers. "Purple? I thought Casey's favorite color was pink?"

"It's her *second* favorite color now," Becky said with a light laugh. "She's been going back and forth for years."

"Ah . . . so her room . . ." His brow furrowed. "If you want, I don't mind helping paint it again. Unless that's something you and Zach—"

"She *loves* her room. But I'm not finished painting the basement if you want to help."

"Sure." He rubbed the back of his neck and held up the streamers. "Want me to start hanging these?"

"Soon." Becky stood, holding on to a banner she'd just taken out of the package. She brushed by him, leaving sparks on his skin with the brief contact. "Can you help me with this first?"

"Okay." Scott went to get a chair from the kitchen, inhaling and exhaling slow, even breaths, trying to stick to the task at hand. He returned to the living room, stood on the chair and taking thumbtacks from Becky to pin the banner on one wall. They continued for a bit, Becky asking him about training camp, telling him about her job. Then how well Casey was fitting in at school. He found himself more interested in the conversation when Becky complained about how a teacher had already called her to recommend she encourage Casey to find another interest besides hockey.

"If Casey were a boy, I doubt anyone would have a word to say about it. I'd rather her be interested in hockey than Pokémon or Skylanders or . . ." Becky gave him a sharp look when he chuckled. "What's so funny?"

"Nothing. I just wouldn't want to be that teacher." He grinned as he stepped off the chair, done with the last of the streamers. "Is Casey good with everything else? Reading? Math?"

"Yes. And she speaks two languages fluently. I think the teacher just needed something to complain about because Casey's ahead of her level in everything. It's not that she's not making friends—just most of them are boys."

"She doesn't seem like a tomboy."

"She's not . . . really. She loves dressing up, but only one or two other little girls are interested in hockey. Casey takes offense to anyone not knowing who 'Landon Bower' is." A soft smile on her lips, Becky glanced over to a large photo of her brother and Casey on the mantle. Bower was in uniform and Casey was about three, sitting on his knee and beaming for the camera. "He's her hero. And all the most important men in her life have been part of the game. Her father hates it, but . . . sometimes I wonder if that doesn't make her love it more. They aren't close."

"He's an idiot." Scott paused, then cleared his throat. Maybe he shouldn't have said that. It was one thing for Becky to say things about her kid's father. It was different for him to do it. "I mean—"

"It's all right." She put her hand on his arm. His heart stuttered as she peered up at him, something vulnerable in her eyes. "As long as you don't say that in front of her... it's just... sometimes I wonder why he can't be a better father to her. She deserves so much more."

"So do you." That didn't make any sense. He swallowed as she shifted closer to him. Fuck, her soft warmth felt damn good against his hard chest. *Cool it, Demyan.* "I mean, you deserved better from the man you married."

"I knew what you meant." She met his eyes. Pressed her hand to his cheek. Her hot gaze was a lick of flames straight from the center of his chest to the tip of his dick. "Scott... I won't have what I have with Zach with you. But I can't take control and—"

So not a problem. He slammed his lips to hers, groaning against her lips, lifting her up against the wall. She tore at his shirt even as he lifted hers over her head. Both ended up tangled together on the floor. He hissed in a breath as he kissed her throat, and her nails dug into his shoulders. He had her pants undone. Bent to pull them off. Straightened, claiming her lips as she worked on his belt.

His dick pulsed pure heat as her fingers wrapped around it. Raw lust clawed at him as he brought her up again. Her hand left him and her arms wrapped around his neck. He held her hips with one arm as he grinded against her.

"Condom." She gasped, shoving at him with one hand, holding him against her with her arm looped around the back of his neck. "My purse."

When did he *ever* forget a condom? Hell, thankfully she had some, because he hadn't even put one in his wallet. He put her down and tripped over their clothes, halfway across the room before he realized he had no idea where her purse was. And to top it off, there was *no way* he was going through a woman's purse.

Becky found her purse before he had to worry about invading her privacy. She dropped to her knees in front of him, then rolled on the condom. When her lips slid over him, he buried his hands in her hair. Not moving. Hardly breathing. This was Becky. *His* Becky.

All the times he'd come on to her, all the times he'd pushed for some cheap, torrid affair between them—*fuck*, he's was glad she'd shot him down each and every time. Because it wouldn't have been like this. The way she gazed up at him as she took him in deep brought more than unbelievable pleasure. It pierced his heart, injecting his love for her straight into his blood until he could feel it flowing through his veins, thick and pure. That love had been there from the first time he'd laid eyes on her, but he'd been too messed up to see it for what it was. And he'd almost ruined it.

Being with a woman almost always came with the risk of him seeing . . . someone else. No matter what they did, flashes of the past would sear the inside of his skull, burning straight into his brain if he didn't numb it with about a dozen shots first. But he was sober now. Sober and all he saw, all he felt, was Becky.

The second he closed his eyes, the second he gave into the pleasure—he couldn't see her. All he could feel was lips around his cock. The sensation was too clear. He forced his eyes open, gulping against the strained sound coming from his throat. Becky. He pulled her to her feet, staring at her as he lifted her up against the wall. He held her gaze as he slid into her body.

She gasped, her legs wrapped around his waist, pressing her eyes shut as she took him in deeper.

"Look at me, Becky." He kissed her, thrusting in, whispering against her parted lips as her eyes met his, "Becky. Becky."

Her fingers dug into the back of his neck. She bit his bottom lip hard, panting, never looking away from him. "That's right. Becky. I've got you, Scott. Ah! God! I've got you!" She whimpered as he hammered into her, dragging her nails across his shoulders. "Ah!"

She undulated around him, screaming, gasping into his mouth. He tried to hold back a little longer, but she clenched down hard and pleasure erupted, numbing his brain, so fierce and abrupt his mind never had a chance to go anywhere else. He leaned into her, fighting to hold her up as a merciless, fiery fist gripped the base of his spine, blazing up and around his cock, spreading along his muscles until the effort to stand had him shaking.

Their bodies were both slick with sweat as he gently pulled out and set her on her feet. He removed the condom and went to the kitchen to toss it in the trash. When he got back to the living room, she was gathering all their clothes. He watched her for a beat before laughing and sweeping her up into his arms. He managed to grab her purse before he headed up the stairs.

And he was halfway up before she made a shocked sound of protest.

"Hush, babe." He strode up the last few steps, then kissed her until she didn't seem like she much wanted to talk anymore. "We're not done yet. Not even close."

* * * *

The sweetest, softest kisses eased her awake, making her smile sleepily and let out a contented sigh as the scent of coffee greeted her. She laughed as weight pinned her legs and scruffy cheeks rubbed between her breasts.

"Scott." She tipped her head back as he drew a nipple into his mouth. "Mmm . . ." *Feels so good . . . why do I have to stop him again?* She slit her eyes open and glanced at the clock on the nightstand. 10:15 a.m. She nudged Scott's shoulder, quickly sitting up. "I slept in. Damn it! I've got to get everything ready!"

Scott made a face, looked like he might protest for a minute, then nodded, handing her one of the cups of coffee he'd left by the clock. "Drink your coffee first. What time is everyone supposed to be here?"

"My brother and a few other people are coming early for last-minute things. Ten thirty? Eleven?" She groaned as the doorbell sounded. "Now?"

"Ah . . ." Scott went still at the sound of the door opening downstairs. "Who has your key?"

"Landon, but don't worry, I'll—"

"Becky! Where do you want the cake?" Landon called out.

"Shit." Scott dragged his jeans up over the boxers he'd slept in. He gave her a quick kiss, ignoring her surprised stuttering, and headed toward the window. "Stall him. I'll disappear."

"Scott, you don't need to—" Becky ground her teeth and hurried to grab her robe as she heard Landon on the stairs. She opened the door a crack. "I'm coming!"

"Are you still in bed?" Landon sounded shocked. No wonder. She *never* slept in like this. "You feeling okay?"

The window opened and closed behind her. She braced her

forehead against the doorframe, wondering if Scott was more likely to break his neck if she went and shouted for him to get his ass back in here. Was he really that scared of her brother?

"I'll be right out." She smirked, knowing from experience exactly how to get her brother to back off. "I just started my period last night and—"

Landon grumbled something and his footsteps sounded down the stairs twice as fast as he'd come up. She hurried to the window, opening it quietly and sticking her head out to try and see Scott. She spotted his hands on the ledge. They disappeared.

No scream of pain. He was all right.

But by the large crab apple tree in her backyard, stood Zach. His expression shifted from relief to anger. He met her eyes briefly before moving forward, probably closer to Scott.

And there was no mistaking that look. He thought she'd used Scott, treated him like the snack she'd called him, then kicked him out. Damn it, she needed to let him know . . .

Only, she couldn't. Not until after the party. She wished he knew her well enough, that he'd trust her enough—and yet, she'd already proven he didn't. He couldn't.

She had no one to blame but herself. She just hoped he'd give her a chance to explain.

* * * *

Zach rolled his shoulders and inhaled slowly, forcing a smile as Scott righted himself from his dangerously high drop. Fine, it was no different than a teen jumping off the monkey bars in the park, but no less stupid. And said teen wasn't inching close to thirty, with a professional hockey team that needed him healthy and whole.

Damn it, I need him healthy and whole.

This wasn't the time or place to come down on Scott about being careless, or Becky for being . . . what exactly? Heartless? She wasn't that. And yet, a big part of their issues were about her making Scott feel like he was a negligible part of the relationship. Or not part of it at all. He didn't expect her to announce what went on in her bedroom to the world, but would it have been so hard to say Scott had shown up early to help?

Scott stared at Zach, barefoot and shirtless, a blush staining his cheeks. He cleared his throat as he pulled on the pale blue T-shirt he'd had tucked into the back of his jeans. "Ah . . . hey, Zach."

"Hey." Zach shook his head, laughing as he reached out and pulled Scott against his side, one arm draped over his shoulders. "You dumbass. Tim would kill you if he saw that."

"Yeah, well Landon would freak if he knew I spent the night." Scott glanced toward the front of the house as another car pulled up, then drew Zach closer to the house, out of sight. "You're not pissed, are you? I'm not sure how this is supposed to work. You said it was okay and—I don't have to ask every time, do I? That would be—"

"No. You don't have to ask." He fisted his hand in Scott's shirt, brushing his lips over Scott's, not quite kissing him. "So long as you always come back to me."

They didn't have much time. He shouldn't be doing this here. But Zach couldn't help himself. He slid his hand up to Scott's throat, feeling the rapid pulse under his palm. Teased the crease of Scott's lips with his tongue until Scott groaned and let him in. And then did the best he could to show Scott exactly how much he meant to him.

"You coming, Pearce?" Tim shouted from the front of the house.

Zach eased away from Scott, his hand on Scott's shoulder, not ready to let him go just yet. He replied loud and clear, "I'll be right there!" Then locked his eyes with Scott's passion-glazed blue ones. "I hope you enjoyed your night. And I'll tell you the same thing I told her. I won't get in between you, but—"

"We've all got to be open and honest. Got it." Scott gave himself a little shake. "You two are gonna drive me nuts. All this talkin' can't be healthy." He winked to show he was joking, then adjusted himself in his jeans and strode out to meet Tim and the next car pulling in. "Carter! Long time no see!"

The group converged on Becky's living room, talking loudly, all excited for the birthday girl to get there. Zach was a little surprised to see both Landon and Dean there without Amia. Neither seemed to leave the baby's side for long. Dean spent most of his time on the phone—likely organizing last minute details for Casey's *other* party.

Laura left Tyler and Chicklet with Landon, arguing about the cameras and video recorders, and joined Becky in the kitchen to help set up lunch. Scott followed her and, after a moment, Zach did as well.

"Thank you so much!" Becky smiled at Laura as she took over peeling cucumbers. She gave Scott a shy look, handing him a plate of pigs in a blanket. Then her smile faded as she turned to Zach. "Umm . . . we should probably talk."

He agreed, but it could wait. Casey didn't need to see her mother stressed-out because of him on her birthday. So he shook his head, giving her an easy smile. "Later, little doe. What can I do to help?"

Becky looked uncertain but quickly pulled it together and nodded at the fridge. "I made sandwiches. Five different kinds. Can you put them on those trays?" She gestured to a stack of trays on the counter. "And bring them to the dining room table?"

"Sure." Zach stepped up to her side, kissing her cheek and whispering in her ear. "I meant what I said on the card. Things are going to be okay."

That brightened her up considerably. She flushed, then scurried off as someone rang the doorbell. Soon the house was even noisier, with little boys running around, demanding autographs and chatting with the players. He had to stop his task several times to sign hats and jerseys. But, by the time Casey arrived with Jami, Silver, and Amia, everything was in order.

Casey screamed as she stepped into the living room, bouncing up and down and pressing her hands to her cheeks. She spun around in a circle to take in all the streamers, the signs, and the party accessories with Cobra logos on every available surface. She ran up to her mother, hugging Becky's legs and screaming "Thank you!" over and over.

The excitement startled Amia and she burst out in shrill cries. Silver patted her back awkwardly, looking ready to cry herself. The second Landon took Amia, Silver excused herself and hid in the kitchen.

Becky's hand went to her throat. She glanced at Casey who had been distracted by Carter furtively handing her one of her gifts. Then she slipped away from the crowd as though to follow Silver. Dean caught Zach's eye from across the dining room. Shook his head before going after Silver himself.

Zach reached Becky by the doorway, his hand on her arm, speaking low. "Silver will feel even worse if she thinks she's taken you away from Casey. Enjoy the party." He kept his arm around her as she nodded, knowing how hard this would be for her. Nothing was more important than her family. Yes, her daughter came first, but she'd be torn, seeing how distracted Casey was and how broken Silver looked. But she listened to him. She stayed. And seemed to find strength in having him at her side.

Which somehow made it easier for Zach to breathe, to relax and enjoy the party himself. He ate a few sandwiches, grinning when Becky laughed at the face he made when he stuffed a banana and peanut butter one in his mouth. She rescued him with a glass of root beer as he scraped his tongue with his teeth and wiped his mouth with a napkin.

"Not a fan of bananas?" She asked.

He shook his head. "Peanut butter. I can't stand the texture. It's an insult to the banana to put them together." He gulped down the root beer, then took an egg salad sandwich. "These, however, I could eat every day."

She bit her bottom lip. Her blush made her adorable as she whispered, "I'd make it for you, Sir."

He took another and winked at her. "I may take you up on that."

When it came time for presents, he took Becky aside, speaking quietly as he pulled an envelope out of the back pocket of his jeans. "I meant to ask you earlier—I figured I should before I give it to her. With how passionate she is about hockey, I thought she might like to join a minor novice team. I got a gift certificate to cover the equipment and paid the registration . . . it can all be refunded if you don't like the idea, though, so don't worry about—"

"Oh, Zach, it's too much!" Becky took a deep breath, staring at the envelope as though he'd just signed over a million dollar check. She covered her mouth with a hand. "I know how expensive it is—I looked into it last year when she asked to join."

In other words, you shouldn't have. Seriously. Idiot. He kept his smile in place. "I can get her something—"

"I could strangle you and Scott. No, you don't have to get her something else." Becky folded her arms over her breasts, giving him a stern look. "Yes, my pride is grumbling because I couldn't afford to do this for her, but I won't let it deny her the opportunity."

"All right." Zach frowned at the envelope. Would a six-year-old really understand a gift like this? Maybe he should have gotten some equipment to go along with the papers, but he'd thought she'd want to pick it out with her mother. He handed the envelope to Becky. "This doesn't fit with everything else she's gotten, so—"

"Oh yes, it does." Becky snickered as Casey unwrapped an Under Armour shirt and leggings. The little girl looked confused for a bit, but when Chicklet explained what it was for, she got excited and decided she needed to try it on right away. Becky stopped her daughter from stripping right there. "*Poupée*, not here. Unwrap the rest of your gifts, and then I'll help you try them on upstairs."

"Sorry, *Maman*." Casey giggled, then tore into her next gift. Hockey books from Carter and Ramos. She gave Ramos pretty eyes, scooting up next to him on the sofa as she asked him to read *Z is for Zamboni* to her. At Becky's shrug, Ramos cleared his throat, and the other children all sat on the floor around him.

The way Jami was staring at Ramos—Zach glanced over to where Richter stepped in with Silver tucked to his side, then exchanged a look with Becky as Richter shook his head and loosened his tie as though it was suddenly strangling him.

Scott sidled up to Zach's other side, nudging him with an elbow. "I think boss man's going to be a grandpa soon."

"I think you're right," Becky said, jutting her chin toward Carter, who was standing at the other side of the room, cooing to Amia who he'd temporarily gotten Landon to hand over. "One way or another."

"You're going to be the next Karen Koch. Yes, you are. You are." Carter didn't seem to notice there was anyone else in the room. And only Vanek seemed likely to tease him about the baby talk.

Vanek's lips barely parted when Chicklet leaned close to him, a smile on her lips, but her eyes hard enough to crack cement. A few quiet words from her and it didn't look like Vanek would open his mouth again during the party.

When Ramos finished reading, Casey grabbed her next gift. New skates from Landon and Richter. Becky moved forward to stop her from stuffing her feet in them. Had her open the next few gifts, leaving Zach's and the largest one for last.

"This is from Scott," Becky said as Casey knelt in front of the huge present.

Casey swallowed, opening the gift slowly, peeling off each piece of tape as though to prolong the reveal. The chatter around the room quieted as Casey let out a loud gasp. Her eyes were bright as she ran her hand over the wood. Stared at the unicorns on the top. Opened it and peered inside.

"Oh, Mr. Demyan! All my babies have a home now!" She jumped up and launched herself at Scott. "You are the bestest!"

Surprisingly, Scott didn't look uncomfortable with Casey hugging him. He crouched down, hugged her back, and flicked one of her ribbon-tied pigtails. "I'm glad you like it, pipsqueak. But it's either Scott or just Demyan if you want to call me what all the other guys do."

"Demyan, then," Casey said after careful consideration. "That's what I yell when you miss an easy shot."

The men and Chicklet burst out laughing. Becky let out a surprised "Casey!" in her mom voice. Scott snorted, then picked Casey up to sit on his shoulders. He grinned up at her. "I'll keep that in mind next time I'm on the ice. I wouldn't want you to be disappointed in me."

"Besides Uncle Landon, you're the best player in the league." Casey giggled at the chorus of "Hey!" from the other men. "You're all a close third."

"All right, last present. This is from Zach." Becky handed the envelope up to Casey. "Then we'll have some party games."

Casey clutched the envelope, then glanced over at the small pile of equipment by the sofa. Her lips parted, but she quickly pressed them shut and went to work on opening the envelope. She blinked at the papers after pulling them out, sounding out the words slowly since she often had trouble reading out loud. "Minor no . . . vice. Hockey . . . hockey team?" She seemed confused at first. Then her mouth formed a wide O. "Really? Really, truly I can, Mommy?"

"Yes, Casey," Becky said, beaming up at Zach in a way that made him feel like the king of the freakin' world. Like he'd just offered her daughter the moon and the stars. His chest swelled, and he laughed as Casey shook her head like she still couldn't believe it.

"*Arrête ton char, maman! Vraiment?*"

Landon choked back a laugh from across the room. "Casey, that's rude. Your mother wouldn't bluff about something like this."

Wiggling until Scott put her down, Casey came over to Zach. She was much more hesitant with him than she'd been with Scott, but something about her tone squeezed his heart. "Thank you, Zach. I love all my presents, but . . . this is something I've wanted for so long."

"You're very welcome, sweetie." Zach bent down as she held her arms open, biting his bottom lip as she looped her arms around his neck and gave him butterfly kisses. She was so delicate. So precious. It felt like she wanted something from him, and at that moment, there was nothing he wouldn't give. He eased her back and kissed her forehead. "There's another surprise though. One that even Mommy doesn't know about. Ask Uncle Dean."

"What?" Becky gave Richter an accusing look when he cleared his throat. "What surprise, Dean? I'd appreciate it if you'd run anything involving my daughter by me first and—"

"I understand that, Rebecca. But I knew you'd try to organize everything yourself if I let you in on my plans. And I wanted it to be enjoyable for you as well." Richter held Becky's gaze. "Can you trust me?"

Becky opened her mouth, glanced over at her brother, then closed it and nodded. "Of course."

Zach hadn't missed the hard look Landon had given her. As though to tell her Richter had more than earned her trust. Which brought back the very reason things had changed between Zach and Becky.

It didn't matter what a person did to earn her trust. She couldn't give it.

And he wasn't sure they could continue together if that didn't change.

****

The look on Becky's face when the entire team greeted Casey in the locker room was priceless. And Casey's little scream was like off-key music to Scott's ears. Not in a bad way either. He couldn't stop grinning as she raced with the other kids around the room, pointing out players and quoting stats. She hugged Mason and had to be stopped by Becky when he pulled out a small gift for her as she spun around.

"Oh, Mr. Mason, I mean . . . Captain?" Casey glanced over at Richter, then continued when he nodded. She held up the silver chain with the hockey stick pendant. "It's so cool! Can you put it on me?"

"Sure thing, doll face." Mason took a knee, then clasped the necklace behind her neck. "Did you bring your skates?"

"Yeah, but—" She gaped at him. "I get to skate? *Here*?"

"Yep, but you better hurry. We only have the ice for an hour." Mason straightened, turning to Becky as she moved closer, thanking him in a soft, overwhelmed whisper. "You're welcome, sweetie, but we try to do something like this every year for the players and their families. Richter just changed the date so it would be on Casey's special day."

That was exactly the right thing to say. Becky seemed to relax as Zach went to help Casey put on her brand new skates. Scott was a little surprised when she slipped up to his side, gazing over at Zach and her daughter with longing in her eyes.

Rubbing his hand up and down the base of her spine, he spoke quietly. "He's good with her, isn't he?"

"Yes, but . . ." Becky took a deep breath and shook her head. "It doesn't matter. Not now. She's happy. All that matters to her is what she has—not what she doesn't."

"That's right. So maybe stop worrying so much, huh?"

Scott knew very well that wasn't going to happen, but maybe she'd take a break from it for a little while at least. He stood by her as she watched over her daughter. Soaked in the smell of the ice coming from the door to the rink being opened and closed as players brought their children to the rink.

"Tracy! You came!" Zach straightened and held out his arms.

A tiny woman with long, dark brown hair ran up to Zach and hugged him. Beside her was a boy of about ten, who looked a lot like Zach. The woman looked like him too. His sister?

"I wasn't sure I could get time off, but Mathew really wanted to see you, so I used some of my vacation time." Tracy smiled as Zach ruffled the boy's hair. She nodded to Casey. "I guess this is the birthday girl?" Her smile shifted slightly as Becky joined them. "And you're Becky."

"Yes. It's nice to meet you." Becky held out her hand, and after a brief pause, Tracy took it.

While his mother talked to Becky, Mathew wondered around the room, stopping close to Scott's side. Scott looked to Zach for help when the kid cleared his throat, but Zach just smiled and helped Casey to her feet, leaving Becky with his sister and Scott with his nephew.

"Uh, Mr. Demyan?" Mathew shuffled his feet, pulling his hockey skates off his shoulder by the laces. "This is gonna sound lame, but I kinda need help."

"It's not lame, sport." Scott laughed nervously, but he couldn't make himself take the skates. Something with the consistency of a Brillo pad had lodged in his throat. Mathew was ten. Ten. Looking at the boy made him think of himself at ten. *Fuck, was I ever that young?* He felt a little sick and he couldn't say why. "I... uh... never helped anyone put on skates. Maybe—"

A firm hand settled on his shoulder. Tim took the skates from Mathew. "I think I can help you out. Take a seat."

Mathew gave Tim a grateful smile and dropped onto the bench in front of Carter's stall. When Carter came over to chat the kid up, the boy's eyes widened and he lost his ability to speak.

Finished with Mathew's skates, Tim took the opportunity to draw Scott aside. "You need a minute. I don't know what's going on, but you're fucking pale. Do you want me to call the doc?"

"No. I'm fine." But Scott didn't feel fine. His body was moving, but his mind was somewhere else. He got to the bathroom all right, but then his stomach had a fucking fit and he ended up on his knees, puking out his guts. A cold sweat covered him. He pressed his eyes shut, hands gripping the toilet seat as the last of his strength spewed out with dry heaves.

"I'm fine." He choked back a sob, then laughed at himself. *What the fuck? Get a fucking grip, Demyan.*

He was drowning. He struggled against a flood of images, shoving the heels of his hands against his eyelids to drive them out. His face was slick with tears. He could taste them on his lips. Dropped hard onto the tiled floor and leaned against the wall of the stall.

"Never. I was never that young." His bottom lip quivered, but he kept shaking his head. "Never."

Chapter Twenty Six

The rink echoed with the joyous sound of the children's light laughter mingling with the deeper laughter of the men. Landon had come out with Amia to show her off, then shocked Becky by laying his daughter in her arms so he could put on his skates and join in the fun. He moved very slowly and Dean hovered close to him as though unsure if his leg had healed well enough, but Landon simply grinned at him, taking one of Casey's hands while Zach took the other. Casey had never worn hockey skates before and she was a little unsteady, but gained some confidence with the support of the two men.

Today was absolutely perfect. Exactly what my baby deserves.

Becky put her finger in Amia's little hand, holding her niece close to her chest as she perched on the hard wood player's bench. She glanced over as Silver sat beside her. The young woman had dark circles under her bloodshot, green eyes. There was tenderness in her eyes as she gazed down at her daughter, but when the thick, pink flannel blanket slipped off Amia's little kicking legs, she moved as though to fix it, then dropped her hand.

"It gets a bit chilly down here; I don't want her to—"

Nodding slowly, Becky fixed the blanket, tilting her head slightly as she studied Silver's pale face. "Silver, sweetie, talk to me."

"I don't know what you want me to say." Silver inched away, hugging herself. "I don't know what anyone wants from me. I'm trying."

"I know you are." Becky cradled Amia in one arm and took Silver's hand. "I just need you to know you're not alone."

Silver inhaled deeply, then inclined her head, a tight smile on her dry lips. "Thank you. I don't deserve that with how nasty I've been to you. I really do appreciate everything you've done for me."

"You're family." Becky smiled as Silver leaned over, resting her head on Becky's shoulder. She kissed the top of Silver's head, then kept perfectly still as Silver freed her hand to touch Amia's cheek. Amia's made a little cooing sound.

"She's so comfortable with you," Silver said.

"She knows she has a lot of people who love her." Becky lifted her head and searched out Casey on the ice. She frowned as Casey stood by Scott, taking shots at the net with her new stick. She couldn't hear what Casey was saying, but she looked angry. Her face was red and she threw her stick down after missing the net. "Oh, boy. Can you take her, *chérie*? I need to see to my little angel."

"Ah . . . yeah. I guess." Silver held her breath as Becky placed Amia in her arms. When Amia didn't wake, she seemed to relax a bit. "Go ahead. I'll be fine."

By the time Becky reached the door to the player's bench, Zach was there, carrying Casey. Casey was crying, whispering sorry over and over.

"My head hurts, Mommy. And my throat hurts." Casey covered her mouth and let out a dry cough. "I didn't mean to be a brat."

"Oh, *poupée* . . ." Becky brushed Casey's cheek with her fingertips. She was a little warm. "It's okay. Let's get you changed. Zach, would you mind . . . ?"

"I've got her." Zach's tone held some surprise, as though he'd expected her to take Casey from him. He gave Becky a hesitant smile, then carried Casey into the locker room. He knelt to take off Casey's skates. "Do you want me to drive you to the hospital?"

Becky grinned. She had a feeling Zach would be just as bad as Landon if he took a permanent role in Casey's life. Landon wanted to bring Amia to the hospital every time she got a little cranky. Thankfully, Dean had enough experience raising Jami to talk him down.

"No, but you can drive us home if you want. I'll have Landon drop my car off later."

"You sure?" Zach put his hand over Casey's forehead as she let out another weak cough. "She has a fever."

"Children get them sometimes. It's probably just a cold—maybe the flu." Becky crouched down in front of Casey. "Want me to make you some of my special chicken soup? It made you feel all better last time."

Casey pouted. "I'm not hungry." She wrinkled her nose and looked at Zach. "Maybe later, but only if Zach stays to have some too."

"I'm sure he wouldn't mind." Becky glanced at Zach, pleased when he nodded. He still seemed worried, but he'd feel better once Casey was tucked in her bed, resting peacefully. It warmed her heart to see how he reacted to her baby not feeling well. She had to be careful about letting him get too involved too quickly, but she wouldn't worry about that now. Right now he needed to know Casey would be all right. And Casey would be happy to know he wanted to stick around.

That was all that mattered.

* * * *

That was . . . pretty easy. Zach combed his fingers through his hair—which badly needed to be shaved again. He felt awkward standing in Becky's kitchen as she fixed them up some coffee. He had to admit, he'd panicked a bit when he'd realized Casey had a fever. Sure, Mathew had gotten sick before, but he was such a tough little kid. Casey was delicate. So tiny.

Becky had handled everything perfectly. She gave Casey a purple strip of medicine, tucked her into bed, then had him sit with the little girl while she fixed her a green tea with honey. He'd read her *The Hockey Sweater*—the other book from Ramos—and smoothed her sweat-soaked curls from her forehead. While Becky had set up the humidifier, Casey had asked Zach for a lullaby. He didn't know any, so he sang her "Mama Said" by Metallica.

Any second, he'd expected Becky to tell him it wasn't appropriate. But she'd simply taken a seat at the other side of the bed, holding Casey's hand, and looking at him in a way that made him sing all the way to the end of the song. Even though Casey had fallen asleep. Even though there was really no reason for him to stay.

And yet . . . every reason.

"Zach, please sit down." Becky put a heavy, black stoneware mug in front of him, then pulled a chair up close. "I have to tell you . . ."

Zach lowered into the chair, keeping his eyes on Becky's as he took a sip of coffee. The uncertainty in her level gaze shifted his thoughts from how badly he'd handled her daughter being sick, back to the issues he had with the precious little girl's mother. "Go ahead."

"You don't have to do any of this. Read to her, sing her lullabies. But when you do, I can't help but think . . ." She dropped her gaze to the table. "It scares me how much I want this to continue. I'm still waiting for the other shoe to drop. The first Dom I played with after my divorce wanted complete honesty too. I was very upfront with my expectations—which were that I had none. He knew I was a mother and that I wasn't looking for a daddy for my daughter. That I wasn't looking for a long-term relationship. I wanted to explore the other side of myself, but I was determined to keep my needs separate. I still am. I just don't know how that works. I never thought I'd have to figure that out. But now . . ."

Zach rubbed his jaw, nodding slowly. "Is BDSM all we have, Becky?"

Things were going well. They were finally talking, and he felt good about where this was going. But her next words were like a solid kick straight to his guts.

"I don't know . . . maybe."

He refused to lose his temper. He refused to take it as an insult. She didn't know . . . well, he'd wanted honesty, hadn't he?

"Let me know when you do." He set down his mug and pushed away from the table. She stood, shaking her head and looking like she wanted to say more, but he couldn't listen. He couldn't sit here and have her tell him he was nothing more than her Dom. Because he couldn't be that to her. He held up one hand and shook his head. "Becky, your daughter is sick. We can have this discussion some other time. Maybe when I get back from the preseason road trip."

"Zach, you'll be gone for over a week!" She grabbed his arm. "Please don't leave like this. Let me explain."

"Not now." He glanced down at her arm, his lips in a thin line. She let him go. "In a week, maybe you can clear things up for me, because at this point, I have no idea what else I can do. Training has me worn out and this—" he gestured from her to himself "—has me exhausted."

"Are you serious?" Becky followed him to the door and stared at him as he put his shoes on. "You asked me to talk to you, and when you don't like my answer, you run?"

He straightened, shaking his head and laughing bitterly. "I'm not running. I don't know how you expected me to react. You told me you loved me. Apparently you only 'loved' what I could do for you as a Dom."

"I didn't say that."

"You said you don't know. I don't think it's unreasonable for me to need a clear answer," he said in the most controlled voice he could manage. "If I told you I only loved you when you were on your knees, you'd call me an asshole."

Her eyes narrowed. "So now I'm an asshole?"

"Don't put words in my mouth."

"You know what, fuck you." She held the door open and gave his shoulder a little shove. "Get out."

"Gladly." He strode out, almost walking right by his car, grinding his teeth as he got in. What a fucking mess. This wasn't at all how he'd wanted their conversation to go. He'd completely lost control of what needed to be said.

Which fit. He'd never had any control when it came to Becky. Only the illusion.

* * * *

In his suit, all ready for the road trip, Scott sat on the edge of Casey's bed, leaning across the tray set up over her lap and opening his mouth wide for a spoonful of chicken noodle soup. Casey giggled as he made an appreciative sound in the back of his throat. He grinned at her, licking his lips. The soup was freakin' good. Nothing like the canned kind. The flavor of the spices warmed him from the inside out. And so did Casey laughing even though she didn't feel well.

Becky sighed as she stepped into the room. "Scott, you're going to end up catching her cold. If you want some soup, I'll get you some."

"Ha! A nasty little cold don't bother a big tough hockey player." Scott let Casey feed him another bite of her lunch. Of course, Becky was right, but Casey had been so excited about him trying her mommy's soup he hadn't even considered that he might get sick.

And hell, even if he did, no big deal. Maybe Stephan would get off his ass about being early for *every* practice to make up for the ones he missed last season if he got a cold and still played. He really shouldn't tempt fate though. He gave Becky his most charming look. "I'd love a bowl though, sweet thang."

Casey giggled again as Becky huffed. "Really, Scott? 'Sweet thang'?"

"Honey pie? Dearie?" He chuckled, holding up his hands before Becky gave in to her obvious urge to smack him. "I've never tasted anything so delicious." *Liar.* But he wasn't going to bring *that* up in front of her kid. "May I please have a bowl, Becky?"

"Yes, you may." Becky started for the door, then paused, giving him a look that had his heart doing funny little flips. "Thank you for coming over. Casey wanted to see . . . wanted to see you."

Now Becky was lying. Casey had probably wanted to see Zach, but the man was in a mood. He hadn't even answered his phone last night, and this morning he'd just curtly told Scott he'd see him on the plane. Scott had a bad feeling there was something going on between Zach and Becky that hadn't been worked out. And seeing as they were leaving in an hour, probably wouldn't be.

While Becky was getting his soup, Casey offered him a few more bites of hers. She was having so much fun feeding him, he decided to throw caution out the window. A cold wasn't gonna kill him.

His phone buzzed. Stephan, letting him know he'd meet Scott at the airport with some new suits. *More suits? Ugh. How many do I need?* Scott turned his phone off and shoved it in his pocket. He didn't have much time left. When Becky returned with his soup, he ate as fast as he could, kissed Casey's forehead, told her to get better quick, then walked with Becky to the door.

"Hey, you wanna talk about it?" He frowned when Becky refused to look at him and pressed his fingertips under her chin until she did. "It's none of my business, but I can't go unless I know you're okay."

"You have to go, Scott. It's not an option." Becky dropped her stern tone and shook her head. "This is my mess. I don't how to fix it, but I'll figure it out. I'm still angry, and I know I have no right to be. So—"

"Don't give me that." Scott folded his arms over his chest. "Screw it, I'm gonna be nosy. What happened between you two? Everything seemed cool yesterday."

"Yes, until we actually spoke to one another, alone. I feel like he's never going to forgive me—he took something I said the wrong way. Wouldn't let me clarify. He said he'd give me another chance, but then he doesn't want to hear a word I have to say and—" Becky groaned. "It's not all him. I'm just not sure where we go from here."

"Forward." Scott closed the distance between them, kissing her before she could counter his very logical answer. Her lips softened under his and her hands flattened against his chest. He whispered, his lips brushing hers as he wrapped his arms around her. "See how easy it is? We're facing each other. One of us takes the first step—"

"Life doesn't work that way, Scott. It's complicated."

"It doesn't have to be. You two love each other." He lifted one hand to tuck her hair behind her ear. "Take it from there. I think you've both got some ideas on how it's *supposed* to work. Forget all that shit and focus on how it's *gonna* work for you."

"If we could limit it to the lifestyle, that would be simple. We'd have our time when all I'd have to do was submit. That's not what he wants."

"Is that all *you* want? Really, Becky?" He put a finger to her lips and made a hushing sound. "Don't answer yet. Don't tell me what I want to hear, or what you think is the right choice." He took her hand and placed it over her heart, holding it there under his. "Answer from here."

Becky's bottom lip trembled. "From here? From here is where the brilliant idea of marrying Patrick came from. I thought I loved him too. Hell, I *did* love him. Which made me miserable and left my daughter without a father. I can't do that again."

"You know, I kinda get how the whole trust in BDSM thing works." Scott cocked his head. "Would you ever have let Patrick tie you up?"

She gave him a horrified look. "No!"

"Those other Doms—you ever play with them alone? Bring them home or go to their place?"

"Of course not."

"Then why did you do that with Zach? What made him different?"

"I knew him as a man. I felt... I felt like I could trust him." Becky sighed and leaned her forehead on his chest. "I do trust him, but—"

"Becky, I think you need to learn to trust *you* a little more. You're older and wiser than you were when you were with Patrick, right? It was, like, a learning thing." He hugged her tight, one last time, before moving toward the door. "Use this week to think about that. About what you want to say to Zach." He glanced up the stairs as Casey coughed and cried out for her mother. "When you're not working or doing the mommy thing I mean."

Becky laughed, quickly wiping away the sheen of tears under her eyes. "When did you get to be so smart?"

"'Bout five minutes ago." He cuffed her chin lightly. "Now it is my sorry task to go have this chat with Zach. Not about what you said; that's all on you." He sucked his teeth and stepped out on to the porch. "There's no reason you shouldn't have been able to tell him all this. It's all good that he wants you to talk to him. But that man's got to learn to listen."

Chapter Twenty Seven

The sun bore down, blinding as it reflected off the bus windows straight into Zach's eyes. He squinted, inconspicuously peeling the front of his white dress shirt from where it had plastered itself to his skin. He had to get out of this suit.

Taking his luggage from one of the assistant coaches, he mumbled his thanks before trudging toward the hotel. The atmosphere of a five-game losing streak hung heavy on the team. He'd only played three of the games, but sitting back to watch their young prospects being hammered by the equally young opposition was another kind of hell. These games didn't count for anything, but if it was even a hint at what the season would look like, their chances of getting anywhere near the playoffs were grim.

Nothing's set in stone. The men will adjust.

Only, he wasn't so sure they would. The rookies weren't the problem. There was no leadership on the ice. Mason was out with a bad stomach flu—the doctor and Coach refused to let him play no matter how much he argued. Which left Ramos and Zach to pick up the slack. And there was plenty of that.

Every game started the same. Tim had a way of pumping up the men so they hit the ice with a winning attitude. The last loss didn't matter. Play *this* game, one shift at a time.

A bad penalty, a soft goal, and everything fell apart. They weren't a team anymore. They were nineteen men suited up, and the way they played, they might as well have been skating in nineteen different rinks. Zach managed not to make things worse by letting his personal drama affect his play, but the result was he and Scott were just as distant as every other man out there.

Three or four players managed to bounce back, managed to leave the arenas after a loss talking about how different the next game would be. Carter and Scott often hung around for a bit to speak to the coaches about what had gone wrong. White seemed to be taking down names for each insult he'd let pass after Tim's threat to bench him if he racked up any more penalty minutes. The other team's goalies loved how he made the posts sing for them, but it didn't stop him from hitting the rink early every morning to practice his deadly hard shot. And Vanek . . .

Vanek needed Chicklet here to put his collar back around his neck. Zach paused in the hotel lobby, glancing over at the entrance as Vanek ran in behind the team's newest acquisition, eighteen-year-old Braxton Richards. He slammed into the boy hard enough to knock his phone—which he'd been texting on—out of his hand.

"See, Braxie, *that's* how you take a check." Vanek laughed as Richards bent down to pick up his phone, slapping the kid's bare shoulder. The loud *Crack!* made the receptionist gasp. "Try *taking* them instead of avoiding them and maybe you won't lose the puck every time the big guys come at you."

A blush stained Richards' smooth cheek. He hunched his shoulders and hurried to the elevator.

"Aww, come on!" Vanek shouted after him, ignoring the dirty looks he was getting from the other players. "Just trying to help you out, kid!"

"That is *enough*, *hombrecito*." Ramos stepped up to Vanek's side, his tone hard and cold. "It is not on you to teach him."

"Hey, at least I'm scoring. It's not my fault our goalie can't—"

"*Enough!*" Zach moved closer to Vanek, trapping the arrogant little shit between him and Ramos. He managed to lower his voice even though he wanted to deck the kid as Hunt strode by them, his face tense and white. "I suggest you cool it."

"Or what?" Vanek glared at him, challenge in his eyes. "What are you going to do about it, Pearce? We need that kid. With Callahan and Perron gone, we're short on forwards. If he can't make it as a pro, we better find now."

The players that remained in the lounge didn't even bother pretending not to listen in. And surprisingly, despite how obnoxious Vanek had been since his return, most looked like they agreed with him.

Zach's lips thinned. He gestured at the elevators. "We'll discuss this privately."

"No, we won't." Vanek adjusted the strap of his duffle bag on his shoulder. His chin jutted up. "You're not a Dom here, Pearce.

You're just an alternate."

Aw, fuck. Zach sucked in air through his teeth. All around him, men were nodding. Vanek had turned this into him being unwilling to submit. Every player who wasn't in the lifestyle probably understood why he'd have an issue with that.

Except, Zach hadn't been trying to get him to submit. He wanted the kid to stop being a prick.

"Guys, I happen to like this hotel. We've been coming here for five years." Tim ambled around the players clogging up most of the lounge, the assistant coaches close behind him. "You're making the other guests uncomfortable. We can have this conversation during the team meeting tomorrow." Tim shook his head when Zach opened his mouth, then turned to Vanek. "I think your mom's waiting for you to call, tiger." He grinned when the guys snickered. "No teasing him about it, boys. You don't want to see how he plays when he *doesn't* call."

Vanek ducked his head to hide his beet-red face before darting off to take the stairs. Carter came to stand behind Ramos as the men cleared out, scowling after Vanek.

"I used to like him."

Tim laughed and reached out to squeeze Carter's shoulder. "Hey, give him a break, kid. He's been working his ass off for a year to get back in the game. He'll calm down once he realizes he still has a place here." He lowered his voice. "He's also been pretty much 24/7 for a while. I think part of the posturing is him proving to himself that he can manage without Chicklet. Let me work on that with him."

"I've never had that problem." Carter stuffed his hands in his pockets, his jaw tense.

"Yeah, well, you're a switch, sport." Tim grinned at the younger man. "That gives us a special perspective." He shifted his focus to Zach and Ramos. "As Doms, you both trigger something in him he's fighting. It won't help."

"I understand." Ramos inclined his head to Tim and Zach, then spoke quietly to Carter, saying something that made the kid's lips twitch and his eyes sparkle with mischief.

Carter strolled up to the elevator, taking out his phone, his tone light as whoever was on the other end answered. "Hope you're free tonight, boo."

He and Ramos disappeared into the elevator. Zach looked around the lounge as all the coaches but Tim headed up to their rooms.

"Scott's stuck outside with some adoring fans." Tim motioned for Zach to walk with him to the elevator. "Leave him. He's handling it well. His interviews have been textbook lately, and it's not only puck bunnies and tabloids hounding him now. I meant to ask . . . is everything all right with you? You seem off lately. It's not your sister, is it?"

"Tracy's doing good. So is Mathew. They both loved coming down for Casey's party." Zach gave Tim a stiff smile. "Everything else is private."

"Got it." Tim pressed the button to call the elevator. After the doors opened, he hustled his luggage and briefcase inside. "But I've spoken to my brother, and Becky looks just as miserable as you do." He didn't speak again until the elevator stopped on their floor and they both stepped into the hall. "I have a feeling you're both having the same issue Vanek is, in your own ways."

"Yeah? How do you figure?" Zach really didn't want to have this discussion with his coach, but he was curious.

"The structure of a scene can make things seem very clean-cut. You have the Top and the bottom. Or the Dom and the sub. In any case, what comes after can be messy. Becky knows she can't be a sub all the time. Managing her life and her job and her submissive urges is a juggling act, and I have a feeling I know which ball she'll let drop first." He gave Zach a shrewd look. "You've got two balls, Pearce—you know what I mean. I'm not talking about the ones hanging under your junk. I think you can handle three or four, but you keep tossing up the same two, keeping the rhythm going, all nice and neat." Tim dropped his bags in front of his door, then took out his phone and his wallet. He started juggling them. "Player. Dom. Player. Dom."

This is ridiculous. Zach laughed, shaking his head. "Coach—"

"Player. Dom—" The perfect circles became uneven as Tim fought to keep the rhythm going. "You're not overconfident about either, which means you're always trying to improve. Which is great." Tim caught both the phone and the wallet. "But you're more. You know to push a sub's limits. Learn to push your own."

Zach chuckled. "If you were a sub . . . but you're my coach. So I'll take the odd lecture with a thank you and a have a good night."

"Sometimes I *am* a sub. Sometimes a coach. Sometimes a husband." Tim shrugged. "I can see you're not getting the point. But you will." His lips slanted. "Just like you'll eventually hit the net. You got pretty close at the last game in Jersey."

"Ha-ha." Zach's brow furrowed. He hadn't missed the point. But he disagreed. If they were talking about his relationship with Becky, Tim was wrong. He'd been more than a Dom to her. She refused to see that. *Fuck, I miss her.* He swallowed, speaking up as Tim opened the door to his room. "She's miserable?"

"She hides it about as well as you do." Tim shrugged, hand on the door. "So you tell me."

"Right." Zach stared at Tim's closed door for a long time, then bowed his head and pressed his eyes shut. Maybe he should call her. They'd exchanged a few texts over the past week, mostly consisting of him vaguely telling her about his day and her doing the same. There was a distance between them that couldn't seem to be crossed, and the coldness of short-typed sentences wasn't helping.

He went to his room, dropped his bags on his bed, and called her cell.

"Zach?"

"Hey. I . . ." He took a deep breath and rested his hip against the large black dresser. "I needed to hear your voice."

"Really?" Becky sounded so unsure it made him feel like a complete dick. How could he have let this go on for so long? She continued before he could answer her. "The last time I asked if I could call you, you said you were busy."

"We had a team meeting."

"All night?"

"Late enough. I didn't want to disturb your sleep when I saw the time," His brow furrowed at the length of silence. "Can we just talk for a bit? I want to know how you're doing. Is Casey feeling better?"

"Zach, I can't talk now. The phones been ringing off the hook at the office, and I have a lot of paperwork to do. Casey's all better. How do I say this..." She let out a bitter laugh. "I'm busy too. Maybe we can schedule a meeting when you get back."

"Becky—"

"You know, when I took off for three weeks, I knew you wouldn't be happy, but I didn't realize how much it hurts to be treated like that." Her tone was the sharp edge of a razor blade. "Thank you for showing me *exactly* how much it does."

The dial tone came as a shock, even though it shouldn't have. Part of the reason he loved Becky so much was her strength. Her independence. And how much it took for her to depend on anyone, even a little. He pulled off his suit jacket and shirt, tossing both onto the bed before making his way into the bathroom to take a shower. Shave.

Something.

I want her to be able to depend on me.

She might have considered it if things hadn't gone so far off track. He wanted to do things for her, to be there when she needed someone, provide for her so she didn't have to work so much.

But she loved her job. And she could provide for herself and her daughter all on her own. All he could give her was that taste of giving up control at the club. Without that... maybe she was right. Maybe they had nothing else.

The door to the hotel room opened. Closed. He didn't need to look to know who it was. The new collective bargaining agreement between the players and the league granted each player their own room on the road. Keane had to give them the option, but Tim took it on himself to encourage the men to pair up as much as possible. Not so much to save the team money, but to instill the closeness rooming together on the road provided. For some, it wasn't an issue. Ramos and Carter.

Zach and Scott.

"You ready to talk?" Scott leaned against the doorframe, arms folded over his chest, his black shirt and tie giving him a bad boy appeal, but his expression completely no-nonsense. He watched Zach through the reflection of the mirror above the sink, then sighed as Zach braced his hands on the edge of the sink and nodded. "What about listen?"

The porcelain warmed under Zach's hands, but goose bumps rose on his flesh from the cooled air around him. "I guess you've spoken to her? That's good that . . . that she has you." He pressed his lips together, shaking his head. "All this time I was worried about you hurting her."

"So you finally done sulking? Ready to face that storming out of her place and not letting her explain herself was a dumbass move?"

Brow furrowed, Zach looked at Scott over his shoulder. "Yeah. Rub it in why don't you."

"Naw, I'm done." Scott's lips twitched at the edges. "It's a relief actually. I've been practicing a whole bunch of speeches—none of them were all that good." He pushed away from the doorframe and stepped up behind Zach. Wrapped his arms around Zach's waist. "We all get second chances. Even you."

Letting out a rough laugh, Zach met Scott's eyes in the mirror. "I don't think flowers are going to cut it."

"Nope."

"I could go home." The idea warmed him a little. So did Scott's solid hold. "Stand on her doorstep and refuse to leave until she speaks to me. Short of that—"

"Tim will kill you if you leave. And you'll make her believe you think you have to give the game up for her." Scott grazed Zach's throat with his teeth. His breath was hot on Zach's skin, but the frisson of pleasure made him shudder. Scott spoke low, close to his ear. "That's not what she wants."

"I know." Zach had to struggle not to pant as Scott kissed his throat, hands moving down to undo the top button of Zach's pants. Drag the zipper down over his rapidly swelling cock. He practically strangled on his words as Scott traced a finger above the waistband of his boxer briefs. "I'm not sure I know what she wants."

Scott chuckled, nipping Zach's earlobe hard enough to add an edge of pain to the sensations already on the verge of driving him mad. "She wants the same thing I do. You. Just you."

Zach shook his head. Scott didn't understand. "She needs more. She needs a Dom who can teach her how to trust, who can see when she's holding back, who can—"

"It's still you. Her Dom is the man she loves, not someone separate." Scott slid his hand into Zach's boxer briefs, then fisted it around Zach's dick. "Now shut up. I'm fucking tired of you pushing me away because you can't deal with your shit." He bit the curve between Zach's neck and his shoulder, breathing hard. "Not going to let you do that anymore."

Gritting his teeth, Zach moved to turn, to face Scott. He let out a rough sound when Scott pressed his hand down between his shoulder blades, forcing him to stay as he was, with his hands gripping the sink.

"Don't move. *Sir*." Scott gave him a feral smile in the mirror, then pulled something out of the pocket of his black slacks. He held it up between his thumb and forefinger. A small black package. He opened it and inside was a condom and a sample of lube. "It's my turn."

Arms shaking slightly, Zach struggled to stay in place, to not shove back and twist around to grab Scott. Make the arrogant fucker get on his knees. Zach didn't bottom often. Not that he didn't enjoy it, but he found it difficult to guide a sub from such a submissive position. The effort it took to give directions when he just wanted to be fucked ruined it almost every time.

But Scott wasn't a sub. He didn't ask permission before pushing Zach's pants down over his ass. He held Zach's gaze as he lubed up his fingers. As he pressed them against Zach's tight hole. As he thrust them in deep.

Groaning, Zach jammed his hips backward, needing more. *Now.* The rough, burning feeling of Scott stretching him was exquisite. His whole body was humming. His cock twitched, the head swollen and hot. He pressed his eyes shut, turning all his focus to hauling himself back from the climax that already tempted him.

If Scott wanted revenge for all the times Zach had made him wait, he was close to getting it. Zach cursed as Scott's fingers left him, pressing his eyes shut as Scott reached around him to wash his hands. The throbbing in his dick was almost painful. He heard the distinct sound of a condom wrapper being ripped. Then the pressure as Scott slowly pushed inside him.

So fucking full. Rough friction as Scott eased in all the way, showing he'd used just enough lube to slick Zach up, but not enough for him to feel nothing but the wet glide. The Dom in Zach took note, knowing most gave what they liked to receive. If the notes had been physical ones, they would have been barely legible scribbles. Zach's hand slipped on the sink as he tried to reach for Scott's hip. To get him moving.

"No, Sir." Scott put his hands over Zach's, rocking his hips at a languorous pace. "I want to take my time." He flatted his chest against Zach's back. His silk tie stuck to the sweat beading up on Zach's flesh. "You're not in charge."

Snapping his teeth together and his eyes open, Zach glared at Scott in the mirror. "Then stop calling me 'Sir.'"

"I thought you liked it." Scott thrust in a bit harder. Then he dragged out, panting with his lips on the side of Zach's neck. "Fuck, you feel good."

Scott smiled at him, still cocky as ever, but there was something different in his eyes. Something that stole the urge from Zach to rush things. He was looking at Zach as though he'd found everything he would ever need right here. Right now.

Pressure built up gradually at the base of Zach's spine, in his balls, as Scott slid and out, his rhythm faltering before long. His grip on Zach's hands tightened. He groaned as he pistoned faster and faster, still staring at Zach in the mirror. Pleasure rushed through Zach's core, barely contained, like a can of soda shaken up with the top cracked but not opened completely. He could feel it sizzling, ready to burst.

Scott slammed in and brought one hand to Zach's dick, stroking even as he came. Zach tensed, letting out a sharp cry as the climax erupted, stealing the strength from his arms and legs. His cum spurted into the sink, and he clenched down on Scott as the nerves inside him ignited. He held on to the sink with everything he had left so he wouldn't crack his head on the porcelain on his way to the floor. Which didn't seem all that solid at the moment.

"Fuck, ah . . ." Scott rested his head on the back of Zach's neck, gasping for air. "Don't . . . don't move for a bit."

"Not sure I can." Zach laughed breathlessly, feeling like he'd just finished a double shift—or maybe a triple—on the ice, going full speed without stopping. And some asshole had iced the puck, trapping him there. "Damn it, I'm glad you're not a sub."

"Yeah?" Scott took a deep breath, wincing as he eased out. He braced one hand on the sink beside Zach's. "Why's that?"

"Because I needed that. Needed to not be in control." Zach straightened, kicking off his pants and boxers so he could take a shower. A quick one because he needed to crash. Hopefully in the bed. If he made it that far. He gave Scott a rueful smile, sure he'd shocked him. "Strange thing for a Dom to say, huh?"

Scott shrugged. "Not sure why. You sign up somewhere agreeing to be a Dom and nothing else?"

Strange question. "Of course not."

"Then, the way I see it, we had some hot fucking sex. Me and you. No one surrendering, not one of us giving while the other takes. I get kink. I get that some people need it all the time to get off and that's cool." He moved in close and gave Zach a lazy kiss. "Not so sure you're one of them. And neither is Becky." He smirked against Zach's lips. "Which works out pretty damn good for me."

"Clearly." Zach snorted, shaking his head. "I'm going to take a shower. *Alone.*" He added when Scott's lips curved. "Get some sleep."

After his shower, Zach climbed into bed, pleased to see Scott was still awake. Waiting for him. Zach pulled Scott close, aligning their bodies. He loved the feeling of Scott next to him, all that solid muscle relaxed, the tough guy gone, leaving one who actually like to snuggle.

This guy was easy to talk to. Zach didn't have to hold anything back. "You're getting to know me pretty well, Scott. How about you tell me what I'm gonna say next."

Scott laid his head on Zach's chest and let out a contented sigh. "'You're a very wise man, Scott. I don't know why I would ever argue with you—you're pretty much always right.'" He paused. "'And I love you.'"

Smiling, Zach buried his face in Scott's mussed up hair, breathing in his clean, masculine scent. Then he whispered, "Close enough."

Chapter Twenty Eight

Chugging down coffee between periods wasn't Scott's thing, but he couldn't seem to shake that sleepy feeling. He drank two cups, careful to tip the mug at the side of his mouth that wasn't taped. Florida was playing pretty rough, like they wanted to leave an impact. His whole body felt like one huge aching, throbbing bruise.

He grinned at White as Doc cleaned up his bloody knuckles. That last dirty check might have stunned Scott, might have left him looking like a rag doll tossed on the ice, but the other guy looked much worse after White was done with him.

White gave him a salute, then held still as Doc taped a cut under his eye.

Tim paced back and forth across the locker room, his suit rumpled, his eyes snapping with rage. "We're holding our own. It's tied up at one, but they're walking all over you out there. How about we try throwing some checks instead of just scooping ourselves off the ice after they nail us into the boards?"

Carter hunched over, holding a bag of ice to one of his two black eyes. He chewed hard on his mouthpiece and scowled. "Sorry, Coach. You said discipline, right?"

Stroking his jaw, Tim observed the men for a moment. He stopped in the center of the room, then hooked his thumbs to the pockets of his grey slacks, giving an offhand shrug. "Be hard on the forecheck. Don't let up. They may have some brutes, but you guys are faster. Wear them out, and if you can figure out how to make them hurt without spending time in the box—" he directed a pointed look straight at White "—do so." He squared his shoulders, eyes narrowing slightly. "Vanek."

Vanek froze with his water bottle halfway to his mouth. "Yeah, Coach?"

"You don't get more points for the goal being pretty. Shoot or fucking pass." Tim waited for his nod, then turned to Richards, giving the kid's shoulder a squeeze. "That goal was perfect. On and off your stick, nice and clean. Keep it up."

Richards ducked his head, his cheeks flushed. "Thanks, Coach."

"All right, boys, get back out there!" Tim's face broke into a wide smile as he regarded them all like he knew they wouldn't disappoint him. "You're playing a tight game—better than you've played so far. Bring it home!"

The men shouted and cheered, hustling back out to the ice. Scott bumped shoulders with Zach in the hall, pumped up and ready to win their last preseason game. Zach grinned at him, lightly tapping his helmet before they sidled onto the bench. Second shift, Scott took the face-off to Hunt's left. The young goalie had made some awesome saves. Tim had met with him before the game, and whatever he'd said had restored the kid's confidence. Hell, Scott was pretty sure he'd seen the kid crack a smile once or twice.

Head up, Scott waited for the signal from the ref. He felt rather than saw the puck touch his stick, then swept it back to Palladino, his right winger. A smooth pass to Pischlar and the three of them were racing across the rink with the Panthers on their heels, one defenseman all that stood between them and the goalie. Pischlar slid the puck over to Scott. Anticipated him picking up speed and crossed the zone a step ahead of the puck.

Offside. Face-off in the neutral zone. Scott won again and cut straight through the offense, skidding the puck through the defenseman's legs. Pischlar cupped the pass. Lifted the puck high. It soared over the goalie's shoulder.

Goal! Scott and Palladino slammed into Pischlar. They skated by the Cobra's bench to knock fists with all the players. The next line hit the ice, practically trampling the Panthers after Manning won the faceoff. The Panther's goalie made a miraculous save, passing on the puck rather than freezing it. Scott sat forward on the bench as the Panthers' top line cut straight across the ice. Zach swiped the puck, legs pumping as he sped across the neutral zone. A Panthers' defenseman skidded into his path, sending him flying with a low hip-check. Scott tensed as Zach dropped to the ice, holding his breath when the man stayed there. His heart stuttered, but then Zach pushed to his feet, quickly catching up with the play. In their zone.

Too late. Richards had traded places with Carter. Fumbled the puck when Hunt stopped a soft shot and let off a rebound. A crowd hit the net, stabbing at the puck, the Cobras trying to clear it, the Panthers trying to poke it past Hunt.

Richards fell into Hunt. The puck glided over the goal line.

The Panthers whooped. Hunt shoved Richards, growling something. Richards shook his head, pointing at the celebrating Panthers.

"Time-out!" Tim called. He gestured at the ref, then put one foot on the bench beside Mason as the men gathered around and in front of the bench. His eyes were on Hunt. "Take a deep fucking breath, Hunt. You're a fucking professional. Act like one."

"Kinda hard to do my job with that stupid shit sitting in my fucking lap!" Hunt jabbed his stick at Richards. "You're seriously going to blame me?"

"He's not throwing a fit. Ingerslov's out with the same flu Mason had, but I'm more than willing to give Sampson a shot." Tim nodded toward the backup goalie, brought up from the minors just for this game. "Calm down or I'm pulling you."

"You can't fucking pull me with five minutes left to the game!"

Tim gave the kid a level look. "Watch me."

With the time-out over, the third line resumed the play. But the atmosphere seemed to have changed. Scott tried to focus on the game, but it was hard with the trainer and the assistant coach talking to Zach about who knew what. He lifted his head, watching as the trainer helped Zach stand, then walked with him away from the bench and out of sight. Only a hand on Scott's shoulder kept him from following.

"Go see him after the game, Demyan." Mason kept his gaze on the ice, but his lips slanted slightly, as though he understood. He patted Scott's back when Tim called for a line change. "Tell him all about the win."

Win. Right. Scott hopped over the boards, taking a deep inhale of the fresh, ice-nipped air. He tapped his stick on the ice and Carter sent him a swift, precise pass. They both lunged forward, Vanek only a pace behind. Scott sent the puck back to Stills, who snapped it to Vanek. Vanek did some fancy stick work, twisting around a Panthers' defenseman. Then shocked Scott by passing the puck over. He jumped when Scott riffled a shot stick side on the Panthers' goalie.

The goalie knocked it down. Carter dove to catch the rebound with the tip of his stick.

The puck crept over the line. The goalie dropped to stop it.

A little too late.

More hugging and cheering. Carter even knocked his helmet with Vanek's, all forgiven.

Vanek laughed, skating with Carter to the bench. "Facedown, ass up. You're a needy fuck, Carter."

"Damn straight." Carter snorted, giving Vanek a quick face wash with his smelly glove. "Don't be jealous, kid. You'll see Chicklet soon, and I know what kind of toys she's got."

"Fuck you, you fucking perv!"

Scott rolled his eyes as they all got to the bench and he heard Carter whisper something like "Ask my Master, pretty boy."

"You guys better stop it." Scott's lips twisted as the two young men stared at him. Yeah, he was being the mature one. "Makes the other guys uncomfortable when we talk about that stuff. Keep it off the bench at least, 'kay?"

"I couldn't agree more." Mason inclined his head to Scott, giving Carter and Vanek a look that would likely shut them both up for the rest of the night.

At the other end of the bench, Ramos shook his head, shoulders shaking like he was laughing. The mood seemed to have improved a bit. Winning elated the men and there was a lot more friendly chatter in the locker room after than there had been in a long time. The guys were still split into their own little groups, but no one was fighting. A definite improvement.

Good enough for Scott. His face hurt from grinning, and he couldn't wait to tell Zach everything. But he couldn't find him anywhere. His grin faded as he went to the coaches' office, waiting outside as Tim packed up his things, nodding at whatever the assistant was saying.

"It was better, but the team's still disconnected. I want to have a few morning skates. Another team meeting." Tim sighed. "Work out whatever issues they've got."

"I'll tell you what the issue is." The assistant slapped his briefcase on the desk and leaned over it. "Perron was the goddamn heart of this team. Losing Callahan was bad enough, but both?"

Tim lowered his voice. Scott held his breath to hear him. "There's no guarantee that we've lost Perron. I won't get their hopes up, but he dislocated his shoulder at a rodeo in Calgary. He hasn't signed yet and there are rumors that he fired his agent. I have a feeling he wasn't so sure about leaving. My brother and Keane have been talking to him directly."

"And?" The assistant sounded excited. "Do you think—?"

"What I think is we've got to get this team to pull together, whether or not he comes back." Tim cleared his throat. "Mr. Demyan, I expect you to keep this to yourself."

Stepping into the office, Scott nodded, a rueful smile on his lips. "I won't say a word. Be good to have him though."

"It would." Tim gathered his things, glancing at Scott as he made his way out. "Zach's already gone. The doctor was on the first flight out, and the travel coordinator was able to get Zach on the same flight. It's nothing serious—left thigh contusion. We have a few days before the first regular season game, so we wanted to make sure it was taken care of right away. He'll have an MRI tonight. Start therapy in a day or so if possible."

Scott frowned. "Yeah, all right. But can't I head back tonight too?"

"Honestly? I'd rather you didn't. It won't look good and—" Tom groaned, shaking his head. "I hate saying shit like that, I hope you know. If he was in bad shape, I'd tell you to fuck appearances. But it's not worth it."

Shit. Scott swallowed, but didn't bother arguing. Zach would be telling him the same thing if he were here.

Hours later, Zach called and confirmed that it really wasn't a big deal. So minor the doctor was already telling him he might be back in the lineup for their first regular season game. Zach made Scott promise to follow Stephan's instructions, hit the gym, maybe go see Becky?

Scott was ready to promise Zach just about anything. So long as he'd be able to see him. And hell, since it wasn't so bad, maybe they could see Becky together. Scott smiled a little, thinking about how she'd fuss over Zach. This injury could be enough to break the ice.

"I want to see her—and you. I'll call you both tomorrow, but it's just... fuck." Zach's soft curse dimmed the bit of optimism Scott had managed to work up. "With therapy and everything my agent has planned for me... I don't know how much I'll be around, Scott. You know it's not because I don't want to see you, right? Because I do."

"I know you do, pal." Scott sat on his packed suitcase, holding in a sigh. He did know. And he wouldn't let Zach feel bad because life fucking sucked sometimes. "We've only got two games that week. We'll have plenty of time after."

"We will. But call me every night anyway—doesn't matter what time." Zach let out a bitter laugh. "Damn it, it sounds like we're gonna be in two different countries."

"Could happen. Hell, Zach, I'm not new at this. I know how it is. We'll be fine." Scott knew that wasn't what Zach wanted to hear. He forced a smile Zach would hear in his tone. "I'll be fine."

That night, the bed seemed big, cold, and empty. Scott got up to turn off the AC, then lay on top of the sheets in only his boxers, skin sticky with sweat. He got up and turned the AC back on. Flicked on the TV. Couldn't find anything to watch. Turned it off.

His phone buzzed. He smirked, sure Zach couldn't sleep either. He answered without checking the number.

"Hey, babe, miss me already?"

"Babe?" Jimmy snorted. "Some chick you're serious about, or were you expecting a booty call?"

Scott sat up, throwing his legs over the edge of the bed. Ice slithered over his damp skin. His stomach turned into a clenched stone fist. "What do you want, Jimmy?"

"Some way to talk to your brother. What do you think I want?" Jimmy snapped out each word, his bitterness seeping through his tone. "You don't have to be a dick about it. Not all of us are so lucky and—"

"Fuck you, okay? I'll send you some fucking money!" Scott stood, jabbing his thumb down to end the call. His guts flipped, twisted, and his head spun. He tossed his phone, hearing it shatter as he cut across the room and opened the minibar. He grabbed a few small bottles. Chose one.

Rum. He dropped it, laughing as his eyes teared. How pathetic. How fucked up. Ever since Becky and Zach had come into his life, it was like he couldn't deal with anything properly. Couldn't shut things off when he needed to. Since when did he freak out like this when Jimmy called? He had the money. Jimmy didn't. Pretty fucking simple.

Only it wasn't simple. His brother hated him.

And he had every reason to.

* * * *

So many girls in the Ice Girl uniform, standing in the hall, waiting to go out on to the ice. Many wouldn't return. The fans would vote and some of the young women would go home with nothing but fond memories.

Akira couldn't be one of those. She'd worked too hard. They all had, but the other girls didn't have their whole futures riding on this. Most were hopeful, but realistic. They chatted about school. Boyfriends. About what they would do if they didn't make it because that would be okay. The theme was "I'm not gonna cry."

Can't say the same. Can't . . . She was going to be sick. Ten minutes to stand in the hall, waiting to put on a three-minute show that would make or break her. Her bottom lip quivered. She slipped by the other girls, feeling for the door, sure her makeup would be ruined by her tears.

The forum was sold out, which didn't happen often. The event coordinator had stressed that their performances had drawn people from across the Maritimes, from Quebec, even from New York—and the Rangers fans weren't coming all this way just to watch their team. Other teams had Ice Girls, but they played a small part. The Cobras Ice Girls were becoming celebrities in their own right. They could be a big part of their team's success. All the media attention would help the team nail down a few more years.

Yet another thing for Akira to worry about. She sprinted for the bathroom, not sure if she should head to the toilet to puke or to the sink to make sure she was presentable. Her stomach settled a little as she looked at herself in the mirror. Not too bad. Just a few smudges.

She knew her routine. She'd worked hard with her team to perfect it. They would put on an amazing show.

What if they don't? What if I *don't?* She pressed her eyes shut. And saw Dominik. Telling her she could do this. As he had again and again. She hadn't seen him for almost a week, but the impact of his words hadn't faded.

"Believe in yourself. At least half as much as I do." He'd kissed her, his big, dark hand so comforting and warm as it cupped her cheek. *"And yes, that's an order."*

"Akira?"

Akira spun around and threw herself into her best friend's arms, knowing Jami would understand. Needing a moment to be weak, needing to know she could and that it wouldn't last.

Jami framed Akira's face in her hands, drying her tears. "Hey. You didn't think I wouldn't show, did you? Just got off an early shift. I hate using Silver and my dad to get time off, but I wasn't going to miss this. Someone else can cook the fucking hot dogs."

"Jami . . ." Akira swallowed back a sob. It didn't need to come out. She felt the strength return to her muscles, solidify in her bones. "I'm so happy you came. I just wish you could be out there with me."

Grinning, Jami took her purse off her shoulder, quickly taking out some lip stain and blush. "Hey, I'll try out again next season. How about we make sure you're one of the people who gets a say in whether I make it or not?"

"That works for me." Akira held still as Jami fixed her makeup. She mentally went over her routine. The tension eased from her brow as Jami swept a soft brush over her cheeks. "I can do this."

"That's right. But I thought you might need your own cheering squad." Jami grinned as the door opened. "He wasn't *too* busy."

Dominik. Larger than life in his uniform and even taller with his skates on, guards covering the blades. The harsh bathroom light cast a glow on his dark, black-scruffed cheeks. His lips curved into a warm smile.

Akira sobbed and ran to him, forgetting about her makeup and everything else. His arms around her, his solid chest, felt so wonderful. She knew, right then and there, that he would always be there to catch her. It didn't matter that they didn't have some big, long-lasting romance. Besides her father, he was the only man she'd ever been able to count on. He made the earth seem stable under her feet.

"I'm here, little one." He held her close for a moment, then stepped back, his hands on her shoulders. "They're waiting for you. They need you to lead them."

Akira blew out air to cool her face as Jami came to her side, clucking her tongue and repairing the damage done by her renewed tears. Staring up into Dominik's dark eyes, Akira felt her heart take on a steady rhythm. She smiled up at him. "Like the Cobras need you."

"Exactly. All the men will be on the bench, watching the show. And I think you know who the favorite for the Ice Girls' captain is." He tapped her nose and winked. "No question about you making it. The crowd decides how far. Don't leave them with any doubts."

"I won't." She stiffened her spine, walking ahead of Jami and Dominik into the hall, ready to lead her girls and get as many of them as possible on to the team. Every single one deserved it.

That was all that mattered until she saw who was waiting for her. Ten minutes was a long time to wait. The coaches would give any girl who needed it a few minutes. Amy had obviously taken advantage of that. And had found someone to give her a little moral support.

Ford set Amy away from him when he spotted Akira. He shook his head and opened his mouth.

She didn't want to hear it. She gave him a cold smile, ignoring Amy. "It's sweet of you to come down to support us, sir. The girls *love* how involved the owners are."

"Akira." Ford stepped toward her.

Dominik cut him off. "Akira, he's management as a courtesy. Not an owner. Don't give him too much credit."

"I'm not." Akira turned to Dominik, blocking out the *other* man as much as she could. Even though she was all too aware of Ford. So close. For some reason not going away like he should. She smoothed her hand over Dominik's jersey, tracing the big C with her fingertip. "I'm going to work on getting me one of these."

"You'd better." Dominik kissed her forehead, then stood by the door, preventing Ford from following when it looked like he might. He called out before she let the door close, "After the game, I will see you."

She placed her hand on the door, trying to keep her eyes on Dominik. Trying not to see Ford. She refused to give him any more of her time. "After the game, Sir, I'm all yours."

The pain in Ford's eyes didn't bother her. Not in the least. She kept the image of him with Amy in the back of her mind in case the little voice within decided to be stupid. To forget. Of all the things he could have done to make this easy, being anywhere *near* Amy was at the top of the list.

Amy caught up with her before she could join the rest of the Ice Girls. "You put on a decent act, but I'm not blind. You want him."

Akira stopped. Faced Amy, her tone level and cold. "You must be pretty desperate to try to use him against me. But I'm not surprised. There's no way someone like you could care more about a friend than about a hot guy with a big dick."

"I've heard he has a *huge* dick. From the girls who had fun with him on the cruise." Amy covered her mouth, giggling. "Not that you were missing out. Props to you, you sleazy little chink. Fucking the Cobras' captain does give you a bit of a head start. But I don't think the fans care who you're sleeping with."

"For once, you're right, Amy." Akira joined her girls, smiling sweetly at the bitch who trailed her, the racial slur doing nothing more than stiffening her spine with resolve. "The fans will be looking at what we do out there. So good luck."

"I don't need it. But hey, if it's any condolence, my dad owns a few Chinese restaurants. I'm sure I could get you in as a waitress. I hear the tips are good."

"Amy, will you shut up?" Sahara stepped away from her group, shaking as though it took everything she had not to slap the other woman. "I wish the fans could hear this. No way would they vote for an ignorant little cunt like you. When you say shit like that, I just want to—"

Grabbing Sahara's arm, Akira drew the tall blond aside, Amy's laughter nothing but white noise, like the excited clamor of the crowd beyond the steel doors. "Hey, don't do that. Don't react. That's what she wants."

"I know, but—" Sahara pursed her bright red lips. "You're right. I'm the veteran. I should be saying this to you."

"Hey, you've had my back through everything." Akira hugged Sahara, so happy they weren't really competing against one another, even though it would look like they were. "I've got yours. Always." Her cheeks heated. She lowered her voice. "I probably won't be home tonight. Neither will Jami. If you are, can you take care of Peanut?"

"Jami already asked." Sahara laughed. "Will do. That bird is everything a single lady could ever want." As Keane's voice boomed from the speakers, announcing the competition and thanking all the fans for attending, her lips thinned. She laughed again, the sound overly bright. "I'm thinking some ice cream and *The Notebook*. In case you decide to come home early." She batted her eyelashes. "And if you do, I will *so* bug you about it all night!"

"Won't happen." Akira wrinkled her nose at Sahara's knowing smirk, then went back to her girls, squeezing a few hands and whispering words of encouragement to the ones who looked like they needed it. Amy's group went first.

Each group consisted of seven girls. Only the top ten voted for by the fans—either online or by text, would make up the core team. A second vote would pick the captain. Silver Delgado's original plan had been to start with a small squad, but Mr. Keane had taken over, scouting for experienced girls like Sahara to add. Sahara, and whomever was chosen as captain of the team, would get the final say on any new recruits.

Amy was good. Very good. As much as Akira hated to admit it, she still had a chance of getting that coveted C.

The doors leading out to the rink were left open, giving all the Ice Girl finalists a clear view of what they were up against. The Jumbotron over the rink provided a close-up of Amy's gleaming, toothy smile before the lights went out. A golden spotlight came on. Forming an arrowhead on the dance mat spread over the ice, with Amy at the center, the seven girls began a slow, provocative sway to Britney Spears' "Criminal."

Not a bad show, the audience seemed to like it, but Akira felt bad for the girls on Amy's team. Their moves were uniform, and they were nothing but backup dancers to their leader's elaborate, erotic performance. Maybe it was just bitterness on her part, but Akira was a little surprised Amy hadn't asked for a pole to go along with her routine.

Doesn't matter. It's time to get out there and show them what you've got. Akira glanced back at her girls, gave them a bracing smile, then took off running onto the ice as Amy's group cleared the way. The grips of her shoes were specially made to prevent slipping, but she was still a little nervous about falling on her butt as her legs shook.

Her girls formed a circle. The spotlight pulsed, giving the rink a club feel. "S.O.S." by Jordin Sparks kicked up, and she threw herself into the music, thrusting her hips, tossing her hair around, lifting her arms up high. All the girls spun to face the crowd, jumping up and down as the chorus began.

The words to the song gave them so much to work with as a group, but one part of the song did more. Akira had worked with the choreographer to give every single girl a chance to move to the center of the circle and show off her unique skills. The movement never stopped, but the girl in the center drew the spotlight. The attention of the crowd. One girl grinded low. Another did a breakdance move. A ballet specialist did a pirouette that ended in the splits.

At the climax of the song, the girls widened their circle. The finishing move had been decided on by a unanimous vote. Akira backed up a few steps, praying she didn't let them down. Without much space, she couldn't run far. But she had enough space for her layout.

Two long strides and she flew into handspring, then a backspring, giving herself enough height for a nice twist and a smooth landing. Her pulse echoed in her ears along with the roar of the crowd. Her team took their poses around her. Adrenaline had her trembling like a wet puppy sitting out in the cold. But in seconds she was surrounded, the girls hugging her and chattering enthusiastically as they herded her off the ice.

A coach gave her a thumbs up, handing her a big grey Cobra

sweater as she returned to the hall. Her girls huddled around her, quiet now as Sahara's team lined up on the dance mat. No music. No lights. Sahara started clapping and stomping a familiar beat. The other girls followed her, and soon the crowd had joined in.

You bitch! Akira thought without menace, laughing as the girls in the hall started clamping and stomping as well. "We Will Rock You" by Queen. Sahara screamed the opening line, most of the crowd singing with her. The music blasted and Sahara's girls threw themselves into the dance, perfectly coordinated, stopping at the chorus to clap and stomp, then gesturing for the crowd to sing louder.

Not a fancy routine, but everyone in the stands stood at the end, revved up, involved, and ready for the game. Which was the point.

Sahara and her team took a bow, then bounced around, waving for the crowd to keep cheering as Amy and Akira's teams returned to the dance mat. The announcer reminded everyone to "Vote! And vote often!"

As Akira headed for the Ice Girls' changing room, she heard the anthem starting up on the rink. If she hurried, she might be able to see the puck drop from the owner's box. Mr. Richter had invited her, Sahara, and Jami, and she was looking forward to watching Dominik play. Sahara waited for her as she pulled on a pair of jeans. They ran all the way to the elevator together, smothering giggles with their hands before opening the door to the owner's box.

The blood left Akira's face as one of the men near the large window overlooking the rink glanced back. Ford frowned as she took a step backward, then turned to face the glass. Akira hugged herself and bit her bottom lip as Sahara guided her to the other side of the room.

Jami came to meet them, an apologetic smile on her lips. She pressed close to Akira's side, speaking low. "Akira, you don't have to talk to him. I promise, he won't bother you."

Damn it, Akira refused to let Ford make her feel uncomfortable here. She would be around often, and they'd have to learn to deal with seeing one another occasionally. *And he has to deal with the fact that I will* never *let him close to me again.*

She jutted her chin up, shaking her head. "Don't worry about it,

Jami. I should talk to him anyway. There are a few things we have to clear up."

Sahara opened her mouth, exchanged a look with Jami, then patted Akira's shoulder. "We're here if you need us."

As the American anthem trailed off, Akira approached Ford, a lot less anxious than she'd thought she'd be. Mr. Richter was there with his assistant, his gaze like a steady, supportive hand on her back. She wasn't alone.

Ford was. And she almost felt sorry for him.

But just a little.

"You've decided to stop giving me the silent treatment?" Ford folded his arms over his chest, not looking at her.

"I spoke to you earlier."

He snorted. "Right. You *appreciate* my presence."

"Amy certainly did." She bit out the words, then shook her head, inhaling slowly. That made her sound jealous and she wasn't that. *At all.* She licked her bottom lip. "Look, we will never be friends, but we can be civil."

"Civil?" Ford unfolded his arms, glancing over at her as he tucked his thumbs into the pockets of his navy blue pants. "You sure you can manage?"

She pursed her lips. "As long as you're not being an asshole? Sure."

"Akira . . ." He lifted one hand toward her, then dropped it to his side. His brow furrowed as she stared at him. He finally met her eyes. "Tell me what I have to do. I want to—"

"I'm with someone, Ford."

"Dominik?" Surprisingly, he didn't laugh. Concern filled his eyes. "Shorty, he just broke up with my sister."

"I know that." She crossed her arms over her chest, not wanting to care what he thought. Wishing she didn't feel like she needed to explain. But she did. Her gaze shifted to the ice. "He's a good man. A good Master. He's giving me what I need, and that's all you need—no, *more* than you need to know."

Ford's throat worked as he swallowed. His head tilted slightly. "Is that what you need, Akira? You're into all that . . . stuff?"

"Yes, but that's not the point."

"I think it is. I think it would be different if I was a Dom." Ford shook his head, his tone softening. "I would do that for you. I could be what you need."

She rolled her eyes, cocking her head as she turned completely to face him. "Could you?"

"Absolutely."

"That's funny, because one thing that's most appealing about a Dom is his control." She lifted her head, the cold from below finding the bare flesh under her sweater and making her shiver. She had the strangest urge to move forward, but she forced herself back instead, rubbing her own arms through the thick cotton. "I need a man who's in control of himself, his life. You're not. I'm not sure you ever will be."

He shrugged, something in his eyes seeming resolved. Like he'd accepted defeat. For now. "I think I'll surprise you."

"I doubt it." *Not that it matters.* "I'm going to watch the game. Just remember what I said."

"Which part?"

"We will be civil." Her words sounded stiff. Lifeless. Damn it, she needed to put some space between them. "Have I made myself clear?"

The edges of his lips slanted up. "Yeah, shorty." He inclined his head. "You made yourself very, very clear. Enjoy the game."

Damn him. She retreated back to the other side of the room to sit with Jami and Sahara. To munch on some popcorn, sip soda, and do her best to forget Ford was even there. He'd purposely misinterpreted her words. He thought he still had a chance.

A guy like him was just arrogant enough to think he could bide his time and wear her down. He could try all he wanted, but it was useless. She'd keep him at arm's length. Or farther.

Much, much farther.

Chapter Twenty Nine

Scott swore he was slowly sinking into a coma. His brain pounded against the inside of his skull. Swallowing saliva stung the raw insides of his throat. Something heavy was weighing on his chest.

But he'd be damned if he'd let Coach know. The flu was going around. He hadn't puked yet. He could make it to the end of this game. He grinned as he recalled the meeting with Keane and his agent earlier that day. His brand spankin' new two-year contract. His agent had wanted to push for more, but gave in when Scott threatened to fire him. The man was a bit of a jerk—he wasn't stupid.

As for the game, Scott had to do something to get past the sluggish feeling. Coffee made him desperate to piss for about ten of the twenty-minute periods, so he switched to Red Bull. White always had a few, which he was always happy to share. Scott cracked open his can, touching it to White's in cheers, then gulped down the medicinal-tasting, fizzy liquid. It took a few minutes, but he was pretty sure the dizzy rush as he stood was the figurative wings all the ads promised.

"Whoa, you good, Demyan?" White held Scott's elbow as he swayed. He leaned close, lowering his voice. "You been drinking? Coach'll flip if he catches you—"

Scott shook his head. "Naw, I think I caught Mason's bug. Just keep quiet, 'kay?"

"'Kay." White stuffed his mouthguard in as Tim came to give his little speech about how they were doing decently but couldn't let up. Had to keep pushing.

I can do that. Scott trailed after the other men, swiping away the sweat beading up over his lips with his glove, clearing his throat to stave off the urge to cough. His padding was a goddamn furnace. It was a relief to get waved on to the ice for the face-off.

The ref threw him out of the face-off. He wasn't sure why. He found his spot, almost losing his stick as the opposition's right winger pressed against him. He gave chase, his skates sinking into the ice melting under his feet. The blue blur under him moved up as something hit him hard. The wall smashed into him. Or a body.

For a second, things cleared up. A linesman was shouting at him. Zach asked him if he was okay. Only, it wasn't Zach. Zach was in the press box. Or somewhere . . . fuck, when had it gotten so cold?

He squinted as Ramos hauled him to his feet. Yelling. Scott snorted, not sure what he was saying. Maybe something sexy. In Spanish.

"No speakin' the . . . the . . ." He shivered. Black flashed across his vision. He was sliding and someone was pulling at him. Touching his face. He snarled, slapping away the hand. "Don't. Lemme alone."

"He's burning up."

"Damn it, Demyan." Tim's face was suddenly right in front of his. So close Scott could smell the mint on his breath. "Come on, get up. Go with the doctor. He'll check you out."

"Naw, don't need the Doc." Scott inhaled, shoving at his helmet. Too freakin' heavy. "Put me in, Couch."

"Come on, buddy." Ingerslov's ugly mug replaced Tim's. He hefted Scott up, half carrying him to the hall, a trainer on Scott's other side. They both vanished and everything went dark.

Someone was pulling at his clothes. A palm pushed something into his mouth. He thrashed blindly, panic seizing his guts like a hawk's talons ripping into a rodent's soft belly. He shouted, snarling as he was pushed flat on his back.

"Scott, listen to me, son." Doc's wrinkled face appeared over him. His tone was soothing. Nice. He put a cool cloth on Scott's head. "You're running a dangerously high fever. I'm sending you to the hospital. I've given you something that might help, but I'm not messing around with this."

"Don't go." Darkness threatened the edges of Scott's vision. His heart was busting through his ribs. His shirt was gone. His skates, all his equipment. When he blinked he could see *her*. They couldn't leave him alone. "Doc . . . Doc, where's Zach?"

"I'll have him meet you at the hospital." Doc nodded to a strange man and Scott was being moved. "Try to relax."

"No. No you don't understand." Scott tried to sit up. He was forced down. He twisted his body. There were faces, voices everywhere. People holding him. Hands on his bare skin— "Get the fuck off me!"

"Scott?" The sweetest voice in the world. A beautiful face, clearing through the black smog. Her soft grey eyes met his and she made a gentle sound, stroking his cheek, her lips parting slightly as she moved her hand up to his forehead. "Oh, Scott. You're so hot."

"Mmm, you too, babe." He groaned as the room swirled around her. He felt a little woozy, like he'd just downed a full bottle of tequila all by himself. Not smart before a game. "Becky, was I drinking?"

"I don't think so, sweetie." She bit her bottom lip, moving with him. Or maybe the room was moving. He wasn't sure, but she was there. Right beside him. She had a fresh cloth, nice and cold, and was wiping his face with it. "How long have you felt sick?"

"Not really sick. Little tired." The air took on a strange, sweet scent. He gulped, staring at Becky as he recognized it. Rum. God, he hated rum. His eyes watered and his whole body shook hard. His mouth went dry and he tried to tell Becky—no, ask her. He had to ask her to stay with him. And that was the only word he managed to get out. "Stay?"

"I'm not going anywhere," she said in her wonderful, firm tone. Her bottom lip trembled as he shivered. She took his hand and held it tight. "Just talk to me, okay? They're putting you in the ambulance now. I'll be right with you the whole time."

"Ma'am, unless you're family or—"

Becky lifted her head, her eyes hard. "I'm the closest thing he has right now. Please don't argue with me about this. Take care of him."

Scott smiled, even though he was pretty sure someone had just injected ice into his veins. He'd never been so cold. But Becky was here. Staying. She was all he needed.

But . . . He inhaled and exhaled through his open mouth, not sure why he couldn't breathe right. "Z-zach. You'll call Zach?"

She squeezed his hand hard, nodding quickly. "I think the doctor called him, but if he didn't, I will."

"Good. And, Becky . . ." It was dark again. The smell returned, but he could still feel Becky. She wouldn't leave him. But he had to tell her something . . . something important. The people had talked about family. They wouldn't fucking get it, but Becky . . . he could trust Becky to do this for him. "No family. Don't let . . . any *family* take me. They aren't real."

"Shh, don't worry, honey. I won't let anyone near you." She kissed his forehead. "Just me and Zach."

Eyes drifting shut, Scott smiled. *Her and Zach. I'll be okay.* He'd be safe.

* * * *

"Your husband is resting, ma'am. His fever was at 104.8 degrees, but we managed to bring it down considerably." The doctor paused. "Are you aware of any health conditions he may have that his team doctor wouldn't be aware of?"

Becky opened her mouth to tell the doctor Scott was *not* her husband, but then decided against it. So far the hospital staff was telling her anything she wanted to know. She would be his wife if it would get them to talk to her. "Not that I know of. Several of the men had a stomach flu, though. Could this be . . . ?"

"I don't believe so. We're doing some blood tests . . . his doctor did mention the possibility of Scott having caught something that may have compromised his immune system." The doctor made a face and fidgeted with his clipboard. "I would advise you to get some blood tests as well, ma'am."

Her cheeks heated. She shook her head. "I've had blood tests within the last three months and . . . we used protection."

"Becky?" Zach came down the hall, running. He pulled her into his arms, kissing her forehead and breathing hard. "Where is he? Do they know what it is?"

"Not yet." For a split second, Becky considered slipping out of his arms. Putting some space between them—and not just because of the look the doctor was giving her. He'd stayed away from her for so long, been so cold and distant . . . it shouldn't feel this right to be held by him. But it did. She clenched her jaw as all the strength she'd managed to hold on to for Scott splintered. She blinked fast, resting her head against Zach's chest, the rapid beat of his heart making her feel so much better. He wasn't calm either. He was scared. "They brought his fever down. They're doing tests."

Zach nodded, then turned to the doctor without letting her go. "Can we go see him?"

"He's resting." The doctor gave Zach a hard look. "I suppose his wife may decide if *you* can see him."

"His . . ." Zach shook his head, then glanced down at Becky. His lip quirked when she shrugged. "May I go see him, Mrs. Demyan?"

Damn, that sounds weird. Her throat was still tight, but she couldn't help but smile as Zach waited for her answer, like he needed *her* permission. The lines around his eyes and lips were deep. He was trying so hard not to show how worried he was. There was no way she could say no. "Yes. He'll be happy to see you."

They went into Scott's room together, Zach a step behind Becky. She felt him hesitate near the door and reached back to take his hand.

Scott was spread out on the bed, his hospital gown twisted around his waist as though he'd fought to get it off. A fine sheen of sweat covered his broad chest and darkened his blond hair. His tanned skin had lost most of its color. He looked very young with his eyes closed, sleeping peacefully. The heart monitor showed his pulse had steadied. An IV was taped to the back of his hand.

"Fuck, how could I have . . . I should have noticed something was wrong." Zach rubbed his lips with his hand, approaching the bed, speaking softly as though he was afraid to wake Scott. "He must have been feeling crappy before it got this bad. If I hadn't been so busy doing my own thing—"

"He's been trying to prove himself, Zach." Becky stroked Zach's palm with her thumb and hugged his arm. "No one knew. Not even Tim, and he's been keeping an eye on the guys ever since Dominik and Ingerslov got sick."

"But I'm—"

"His lover?" Becky tipped her head back to meet Zach's eyes. If either of them had Scott close enough over the past few days, maybe they *would* have noticed he wasn't feeling well. She shook her head, placing her hand on Scott's chest to feel the steady rise and fall as he slept. "So am I. And I wish I'd seen more of him, maybe dug a little deeper when he sounded tired—but I'm not about to beat myself up, thinking about everything I should have done. I have my job, my daughter, and Scott understands that."

Zach's brow creased. He brushed her cheek with his fingertips. "So do I. And I'm sorry if it didn't seem like it, Becky."

"That wasn't the issue, Zach." She didn't want to talk about this now, but they might as well get it out of the way. "What I did—the way I left—was wrong. I get that. But you were wrong too. You can't expect me to open up to you if you walk away when I say something you don't want to hear."

He shook his head. "That's not what I was doing. I love you. I needed to know we had more than my being your Dom."

"And we couldn't have discussed it? Decided together what we *do* have?"

"We can. But at that moment, I wasn't sure if I could be calm. I was angry, hurt, and a Dom doesn't—"

"Ugh, I want to... to slap you. Not something a *sub* should want to do, but fuck, I'm tempted!" Becky jerked away from Zach and hugged herself. "Is that what's going to happen whenever we have a disagreement? If you can't handle it as a 'good Dom,' you won't deal with it at all?"

"No, that's not..." Zach pressed his eyes shut, nodding slowly. "You're right. I just don't ever want to be like your husband. I won't get into a screaming match with you. Not now. Not ever."

"You don't need to scream at me to be angry with me." Becky scowled. He might say she was right, but it wasn't much better than the dismissive "Yes, dear" Patrick used to give her whenever he didn't want to discuss things anymore. "I'm not always right. I *know* that. But I need to know you care enough to tell me. That you care enough to let me know you're angry or hurt. Let me know that I've made a mistake, but you still love me."

"I do still love you. I never stopped."

"But you didn't forgive me. Not really. So you saying you love me doesn't mean much."

A rustling of sheets from the bed brought both their eyes to Scott, who was trying to sit up. Zach rushed to his side, speaking quietly, trying to get him to lie back down.

Scott groaned and dropped back onto his pillow. "I'm dying here, and all you guys can do is fight?"

"You're not dying, Scott." Zach paled, looking at Becky for reassurance. She quickly shook her head and went to Scott's other side. Zach cupped Scott's cheek and gave him a shaky smile. "I'm sorry it took me so long to get here. The press blocked my car in the parking lot, asking me about my leg, about the game."

"You're here now, so it's all good." Scott's eyes drifted shut. "But you two have to make up. It's my last request."

"Stop it, Scott." Becky stroked Scott's arm. "You have some kind of virus." *Let it be something small. Something that he'll recover from.* She wouldn't think the worst until the doctors gave her a reason to. "Zach and I will work out our issues. You focus on getting some rest so we can get you out of here."

Chuckling, Scott let his head flop over, facing her without opening his eyes. "So we can have our hot threesome? It's on my schedule."

Becky rolled her eyes. Then laughed. He must be feeling a bit better to be talking like that. "We'll see."

"Not a no. I'll take it." Scott huffed in a breath. "Did we win?"

"In overtime. Hunt saved us in the shoot-out," Zach said.

"Good. He's a good kid." Scott's words were getting slurred, like he was fighting to stay awake. "What about Akira? And . . ." He let out a soft laugh. "My girlfriend? Did you know I have a girlfriend *and* a wife, Zach? I'm the fucking man."

The fucking dead man if you don't shut up. Becky checked his forehead for a fever, deciding to forgive him since he still felt a bit warm.

"Your *wife* might disagree if you keep talking like that." Zach gave her a hesitant smile. "Akira made captain. The compilation shown of Amy's last few weeks as one of the nominees for captain wasn't . . . flattering. She didn't even make the team. Sahara was already on, but she made a close second for captain even though she wasn't nominated. A lot of fans put her name up."

"I like that." Scott settled into the bed. "She'll be happy here."

"Yes, she will."

"Do you think she'll be too busy to take care of me when I go home? Can you ask her if she can stay with—"

Okay, that's enough. Becky made a rough sound in her throat, putting her hands on her hips as Scott's eyes shot open. "*She* won't be taking care of you. I will. And you will do everything I say, Scott Demyan. You will sleep, and drink plenty of fluids, and we will follow the doctor's orders to the letter. Understand?"

Scott's lips parted. He nodded. Then shook his head. "Becky, you've got Casey to take care of. And work. You can't—"

"When I'm not with you, Zach will be. We aren't discussing this." She paused, tonguing her bottom lip, not sure she should assume Zach would agree to that. "If that's all right with you?"

"It is. But Scott's right. I'm here if you need to go home to your daughter." Zach pulled a chair up to the side of the bed. "We can take turns."

"Jami has Casey. My mother came down to help out when Casey got sick, but she had to leave today. Jami's great with her, and Casey loves visiting Sebastian's house so she can play with Luke's puppy." Becky stepped away from the bed to fetch her own chair. She'd called Casey earlier and her little girl had made it perfectly clear that she'd be fine as long as she could come visit Scott tomorrow. "It's Saturday tomorrow, so I don't have to work. I'm not sure the doctor will like us both being here all night, but . . ."

"Well, since you're Scott's wife, he'll probably ask me to leave." Zach's jaw hardened. "Which I have no intention of doing."

Was he angry about the whole "wife" thing? Becky watched Zach pull the sheets from under Scott and spread them over him as Scott fell asleep. Zach fussed with Scott's pillow, then watched the heart monitor, then stood to pace. He went out to talk to the doctor. Came back and settled into his chair for a few minutes before getting up to pace again. He seemed to favor one leg, not quite limping, but tensing a little when the weight hit his left side.

"I wish someone would tell us something. What's taking them so long?" Zach rubbed the back of his neck, stopping near the window to stare out into the darkness. "They'd know if it was just a virus, wouldn't they?"

"They'll tell us when they know, Zach." She left her chair, hesitating before finally deciding just to go to him. She hated seeing him so upset, but at the same time, it made him easier to approach. She didn't need him being a Dom now, all controlled, shutting down his own feelings to take care of her. It was nice to know he needed her strength once in a while. "I haven't gotten a chance to ask how your leg is. Does it still hurt?"

"Just a bit."

"Why don't you sit down . . . actually, I could open up that chair for you." She gestured to the large grey armchair in the corner. "It turns into a bed."

He shook his head, but then went still. Smiled at her. "Are you trying to take care of me?"

"I am. It helps calm me down . . . Sir." She bit her bottom lip, bracing for him to tell her he wasn't her Dom and didn't want to be. They still hadn't figured out if they had a relationship. Never mind one like that. "I'm sorry, I know I shouldn't—"

His features softened. His hand curved around the side of her neck. "It's all right, little doe. We've both made some mistakes, but we can work on fixing them. I like knowing you still want to call me 'Sir.' That I haven't screwed up so badly that I'll never have you looking at me the way you are right now."

"Damn it, I hated not speaking to you. It was hard. I missed you and I kept wanting you to show up and tell me I had to talk to you." She fisted her hand in his shirt. "I waited for you to call, and when you didn't, I told myself it was over."

"I did call, Becky."

"It was too late. I was too angry." She pressed her eyes shut. "And hurt."

"I'm sorry I hurt you." He bent down, brushing his lips over hers as he spoke. "I promise, I'll never hurt you again."

"Don't promise that, Zach. You'll hurt me. And I'll hurt you." She tugged at his shirt, kissing him hard enough to bruise her own lips against his teeth. "We can promise never to go to bed angry. I've always liked that one. Patrick and I never made that promise—not that any of our promises ever meant anything to him anyway. Our fights usually ended up with me sleeping on the sofa if I couldn't let it go."

"One of these days, I think you and I should sit down and have a little chat about this fucktard you called a husband." Zach kissed her again, smiling against her lips. "I want you to feel comfortable talking to me."

"I'm getting there. And I think I understand a little more why it bothered you that I wasn't more open about things." She moved away reluctantly, then opened up the chair for him. She rubbed her arms as he sat on the makeshift bed. "Scott... he was out of it for a while, but something he said really got to me. He doesn't want his 'family' to 'take him.' I'm not sure what he meant. He said they weren't real. There's something he's not telling you or me, and I wish he felt like he could."

"Maybe he needs time too. I do know that his relationship with his brother is strained. Not so much anything Scott said, but the way he talks about him. He worries about his foster sister, but that's the only family he speaks of." Zach massaged the bridge of his nose. "Between the two of us, I'm sure we can find a way to make him feel comfortable sharing that part of his life. He's never been in a serious relationship. Never had people he *could* talk to. This is new to him."

"I think this is new to all of us, Zach. But I really believe..." She wasn't sure saying it out loud was a good idea. It could jinx everything. But looking into Zach's eyes stole the urge to hold anything back. "I believe we will be good together. All three of us. It's not just trying it out anymore. It feels right."

"It really does." Zach laughed, pulling her with him as she tried to get him to lie down. He kissed the top of her head as she curled up in the small space next to him. "Different, but right."

For most of the night, she lay there with Zach, half asleep and too comfortable to move. At one point a nurse came in and Becky carefully slipped away from Zach, whispering to him when he reached for her without opening his eyes. She'd hoped he would go back to sleep, but his eyes were on her and Scott as she spoke to the nurse. The nurse checked Scott's vitals, then assured Becky that he was doing well. She clucked her tongue, letting Becky know that only one person should be in here.

Then she leaned close to Becky, letting out a soft laugh as she spoke too quietly for either of the men to hear her. "I won't make him leave, but I will say you're one lucky woman. Let me know if you ever get tired of either of them."

Becky gave the nurse a shocked look, then gave up the pretense and just shook her head, grinning. "I won't. Ever. These two are mine."

Mine. Long after the nurse left, and Becky was snuggled up to Zach, her eyes on the steady rise and fall of Scott's chest, that same word echoed like a sweet melody playing over and over again in the back of her head. One she would never get tired of. *These two are mine.*

Chapter Thirty

Zach met with the rest of the men in the lounge the next morning, sure he looked like crap but not really caring. He'd slept decently, all thanks to Becky. She'd gotten up a few times, ever the mother, such a light sleeper that the nurse just had to touch the doorknob to get her awake and alert. He'd tried to stay awake for a bit so she could get some rest, but it wasn't until the doctor had arrived for morning rounds and delivered the diagnosis that Scott stopped needing to be checked on every hour.

Carter barked out a laugh after Zach shared everything he knew. "Chicken pox? Are you serious? I had that when I was two!"

"Shut up, Carter." Vanek pulled away from Chicklet, his eyes narrowed. "My mom got it a few years ago. She never had it as a child either. It was pretty scary." He looked at Zach. "Is he gonna be okay?"

Nodding, Zach put his hand on the kid's shoulder after a glance at Chicklet to make sure it was okay. The boy may be cocky as hell, but he cared about his teammates. "He'll be fine. The doctors gave him a vaccine, so he should recover pretty quick. They're keeping him for another day—mostly to make sure his fever didn't do any damage. He's miserable because the spots have started cropping up all over, but other than that, he's not doing too bad."

"He's welcome to come back to Tyler's place once he gets out," Chicklet said, stepping up behind Vanek, kissing his cheek and smiling at the boy. "It's probably better if he's not alone."

Zach inclined his head to show he appreciated the offer, even though Scott didn't need it. "He won't be alone. Becky wants him to stay with her. She and I will take care of him. He'll be happy to see you all, but . . ." He looked from Chicklet, to White, to Mason, who stood near the door. Then glanced over at Tim as he returned with coffee for them all. "I hate to ask this, but could you come back later? Becky is finally sleeping and—"

"Becky noticed you were gone." Becky came up behind him, wrapping her arms around his waist. "He's awake and he wants more details about the game than I can give him. The nurse said no more than two people at a time, so you'll have to take turns." She paused as Hunt slipped into the lounge. "He heard about how well you did in the shoot-out. He wants to congratulate you."

"Yeah, well . . ." Hunt stuffed his hands into the pockets of his jeans, hunching his shoulders. "Let his friends go in first."

Carter snorted and went over to shove Hunt toward the hall leading to Scott's room. "You're one of them, stupid. Come on."

"*Nino.*" Ramos gave Carter a level look. "Behave yourself."

"Absolutely, Sir. On my best behavior." Carter grinned, then leaned close to Hunt. "Demyan is a big pussy when he's sick. We'll have some fun with him."

"You will not, Luke!" Becky groaned and trailed after the two young men. "I swear, they need to hire this team a babysitter. Luke, you better not—"

Her last words were overpowered by the laughter of the players who remained in the waiting room. Tim waved Zach over and they walked down the hall, Tim asking a few questions about Scott's condition. His reaction was closer to Vanek's than Carter's.

"It's good that Demyan's straightened up, but I'm glad he finally got that contract. He's been pushing himself too hard." Tim gestured to the door leading outside and Zach nodded. Some fresh air would nice after long hours spent breathing in the hospital air that always had the faint odor of sickness under all the disinfectant. Tim found a bench away from the small group of smokers and sat with his hands braced on his knees. "I've been trying to keep an eye on him ever since Casey's party, but with so much going on—"

"Casey's party?" Zach frowned, trying to remember anything that had happened at the party that might concern Tim. He came up blank. "That was over two weeks ago—probably when he caught the virus. Casey got it from a kid at school, but she'd already had the vaccine, so it was fairly mild. Becky hadn't thought to mention it until the doctor brought it up. But . . ." He shook his head. "Scott wouldn't have been feeling sick then."

"No, but something was bothering him. I was hoping he'd spoken to you about it." Tim shrugged. "He knows he has you and Becky now. Maybe he'll open up eventually."

"Yeah . . . eventually." Zach folded his arms over his chest, hating that he couldn't just go in there and demand Scott tell him everything. After his conversation with Becky, he knew he had to be patient. Funny how it was so easy for him to show patience with a sub in a scene but so difficult when it came to the people he loved. When something hurt them, he wanted the power to make it better. But sometimes it was out of his control. And he had to accept that.

To some extent.

"Hey, you're the Cobras' coach, aren't you?" A tall, lanky man in his mid-twenties with long, greasy, dirty blond hair stopped in front of Tim. He thrust his hand out as Tim stood and nodded. "I'm Jimmy. Scott's brother."

Tim smiled as he shook the man's hand. "It's very nice to meet you. Your brother is an excellent addition to our roster. We're very happy to have him."

"Yeah?" Jimmy snorted, scratching his scruffy jaw. His lips twisted with amusement. "That's not what I heard. Did he finally get a contract?"

All the open friendliness in Tim's features faded. He was still smiling, but there was something guarded about it. "Yes. But I'm sure he'll want to share the good news with you himself."

"I'm sure he will. Wanna tell me what room he's in?"

Like hell. Zach stepped forward before Tim could answer. "No."

"No?" Jimmy stared at him, the nostrils of his sharp nose flaring. "Who the fuck are you to tell me no?"

Maybe it was none of Zach's business, but Scott had asked Becky to keep his family away. And Zach had no doubt that included Jimmy. Something about the man made his skin crawl. He met the man's stare with a level gaze. "Your brother and I are close. His girlfriend informed me that he wasn't interested in seeing 'family' right now. I'll let him know you stopped by."

"Like fuck you will." Jimmy tried to step around him, but Tim cut him off.

"Give me the number where you're staying, and I will personally see to it that Scott gets it," Tim said, obviously trying to keep the peace. "He can decide whether or not to call you."

"Where I'm staying? I'm staying in my goddamn car." Jimmy jutted his thumb over his shoulder at the parking lot. "Which is where I'mma be until I see my brother. You tell him I'm here. He knows better than to brush me off."

"Really?" Zach fisted his hands by his sides, grateful for Tim's presence. Something about the coach being there made it a bit easier to keep his cool. "And why's that?"

"Because he fucking owes me." Jimmy's tone was cold. He stepped up to Zach, baring his teeth. "Ask him about it. How he became such a good player. He might have some talent, but it was all the training, the teams that cost a shitload for him to play on, the expensive equipment, that got him where he is."

Zach's brow shot up. Was the man taking credit for Scott's success? "He's been playing since he was quite young. You're younger than he is. How can he owe you for anything?"

"Our foster parents . . ." Jimmy's lips curled into an ugly sneer. "They weren't rich, but 'Mommy' made sure Scott always had the best of everything. Not me. I had nothing and Scott knows it wasn't fair. You remind him of that when you tell him I'm waiting. You remind him of how I had shit clothes and never enough to eat because even at that age he was such a pretty boy."

Cold washed through Zach's veins. Bile rose in his throat. It couldn't be what he thought. Not even this bastard would figure his own brother owed him if . . . His jaw ticked as he moved into Jimmy's personal space. Like Scott, Jimmy had a few inches on him, but Zach was much heavier than this scumbag. He relished in the hint of fear widening the man's eyes.

"What exactly are you saying? Scott was the favorite?"

"Of course he was. Her little fucking whore. He was born that way." Jimmy let out a nervous laugh, his gaze shifting. "He's always known how to work people. I can tell he's gotten to you."

No. Just no. Zach inhaled roughly. "How long was Scott with this woman?"

"Until he was thirteen. And she got bored of him, so we were both shipped off. She never wanted me—"

"You disgusting son of a bitch." Zach's tenuous control snapped like the stem of a cheap wine glass in a massive fist. His vision flooded with flaming red. He lunged for the man, snarling as Tim hauled him back. "Your brother! Your own brother and you use something like that against him? You're sick! I'll fucking—"

The pathetic piece of shit ran as Tim dragged Zach back, waving off the hospital security as they came to see what was going on. Tim was stronger than he looked. Or maybe part of Zach held back because he didn't want to hurt him. But he wanted to hurt someone. Scott's brother. Or that woman . . . fuck, he'd never wanted to wrap his hands around a woman's neck before.

"Goddamn it!" Zach slammed his fist back into the wall. His chin quivered. He clenched his jaw. "How could she have—why didn't he say something? This is . . ."

"I know." Tim took hold of Zach's shoulders and shook him hard until Zach met his steady gaze. "I know, but beating the shit out of his brother won't help him."

"Then what will, Tim? I can't force him to talk to me about this. It didn't help when I expected Becky to tell me why she was scared to be with me and this is worse." Fuck, he was going to be sick. How could anyone do that to a child? Any child? He rubbed his lips with his fist. "This is worse. So much worse."

"Scott needs someone who knows what happened and doesn't blame him. You can't force him to talk to you, but you can tell him what his brother said. And how you feel about it." Tim swallowed hard, looking at little sick himself. "Then just listen. I think, deep down, Scott knows what she did was wrong. But he's spent his whole life being told it wasn't. By his brother. By *her*. This explains a lot. He's been living down to what the people he should have been able to trust expected him to be." He pressed his eyes shut. "Jesus, help me. I've been so fucking hard on him. Always on his case about how out of control he is. He needed—"

"You couldn't have known, Tim. None of us could have." Zach inhaled slowly. Losing it wouldn't fix anything. Not that anything could really be fixed. There was plenty of false blame to hand around, but doing that would be pointless. Tim was right. Zach watched Jimmy's car speed away, positive that the man wouldn't go far. He'd be back, and Scott needed to be prepared to deal with him. And not alone. "I'll let Scott know you were here. That way he has both of us. And Becky, if he's comfortable telling her—which I hope he is."

"You have my number. You let him know he can call me whenever he needs to." Tim's lips were white, but he straightened, jerking at his suit jacket, his resolve firm in his eyes. "You let him know he's not that little boy anymore, with no one—" His voice caught. He cleared his throat. "He has you and Becky. Me. The team. We'll help him work through this."

"I'll let him know." Zach frowned as Tim turned toward the parking lot. "You're not coming in?"

"Naw, I'll swing by later. I need to see my niece. Maybe it sounds weird, but after that I have the strangest urge to hold Amia and promise I'll never let anyone hurt her."

"Doesn't sound weird at all." Zach inclined his head at Tim, then pulled his phone out of his pocket. He tried to keep his tone as normal as possible, but Tracy knew something was wrong. He couldn't tell her, but she seemed to understand when he asked, "Can I talk to Mathew for a minute? I just need to tell him I love him. And that I'm always here . . . don't ask."

"I won't. It's always good for a kid to hear that anyway." Her tone was full of understanding. She was good like that. "Mathew, your uncle wants to talk to you. What?" She paused. "Yes, the one that totally rocks. You can tell him all about how awesome he played. I'm sure he'd like to know that you were watching. And he's got something to tell you too."

* * * *

Scott laughed as Carter and Hunt lingered by the door, blocking Mason and Ramos from coming in, Carter once again asking to see his spots. Little pain in the ass. Scott secured the sheet over his waist and pulled down his hospital gown to reveal his chest. He poked at one particularly itchy mark, already starting to scab over, using the opportunity to scratch at it while Becky wasn't looking.

"Nasty, aren't they?" He dropped his hand to his side as Becky glanced up from her magazine. He was only allowed two visitors at a time, but apparently, Becky didn't count. The nurse seemed to think it would be good for his "wife" to keep an eye on him. He gave her his most charming smile. "They itch like hell, but I'm being a good boy and not touching them."

"Liar!" Carter snickered as Ramos dragged him out into the hall. "If you need someone to tie him up, Becky, I'll so do it."

"Freak." Scott gave Carter the finger, then sat forward to listen to Ramos and Mason's recount of the game. He'd already heard it, but he couldn't get enough. Damn, he wished he could have been there! He grinned as Ramos described a fight Mason had gotten into after one of the Rangers' brutes had slashed Carter. Ramos gave Mason a nod of thanks as he finished with how Mason had taken the man down. Carter had shown off the stiches on his jaw. Less self-conscious about his scars than he once was. Ramos had done that.

Carter was doing really well with the big Spaniard. Scott had to admit, he used to be a little jealous of what Carter had with Ramos and Jami, but now it was just awesome to see Carter being the same, easygoing, smart-talking, little shit he'd always been. More confident. More comfortable in his own skin.

'Cause I'm getting there too. Yeah, he'd started off needing to prove himself to stay on the team, but Zach and Becky had motivated him a lot. And he finally believed he was good enough for them. Part of him knew they'd be fine without him, but they wanted him. Best of all, he'd helped them too. Waking up to see them cuddled up on that small chair-bed had made him feel big enough to conquer the fucking world. But he didn't have to go that far. All that mattered was making sure the two people he loved more than anything were together. And with him. And happy.

Zach slipped into the room, standing near the door, looking a little grey—like someone had just told him he was being traded to the Bruins or something. Scott's smile slipped as Zach asked Ramos and Mason if he could speak to Scott. Alone.

Fuck, if he's been traded, I'm . . . I'm going with him. Even if I have to give up the game. The thought made his muscles tense as though his whole body objected. Never stepping onto the ice again? Never scoring another goal? Could he do it?

It wouldn't be easy, but he could. He *would*.

What about Becky?

Leaving her would . . . no. He wouldn't leave her. He'd talk her into coming too. The three of them could figure things out. There must be good schools for Casey in Boston?

Who said anything about Boston?

Okay, he was thinking worst-case scenario here. He had to rein it in and wait for Zach to tell him what they were dealing with. People in relationships made decisions like this together, right? Zach could say no. Fight the trade or . . . damn, what if it was something else? Something worse?

"Scott, I need to tell you something." Zach's features stiffened, as though he was trying not to show how upset he was. He wasn't covering very well. Becky stood, moving toward Zach, reaching out to him. Zach hugged her, then whispered something. He looked at Scott. "It's up to you whether or not you want Becky to stay."

"Of course I want her to stay!" Scott didn't feel good lying in bed while Zach was being all serious and weird. He moved to stand, then shifted to the other side of the bed when his IV tugged at his hand. His stomach rolled. He couldn't wait to get the damn thing out. "It's the three of us, right? There's nothing you can say that I'd want to keep from her. Just spit it out, you're scaring me."

Zach rubbed Becky's arms, then nodded and came to sit on the edge of the bed. He took a deep breath. "I saw your brother. Spoke to him."

The earth did a nosedive under Scott's feet. He reached for the bed and latched on to the rail. Jimmy was here. What did he want? Scott had sent him twenty-thousand dollars. Maybe he should just send him a clean million and tell him to take a hike. But it wouldn't be enough. It would never be enough.

"Where is he?"

"I asked him to leave."

Oh, fuck. Scott knew Jimmy. Jimmy wouldn't have just walked away. He had to be desperate to come all the way down here. He owed people. And those people would agree that his rich brother should be able to cover him. They'd sent someone.

Scott pulled at the IV stuck into his hand, making a frustrated sound when Becky grabbed his wrist. "Babe, you have to let me go. I'll go see my brother. He just needs a bit of help, then he'll go away."

"Why would you want your brother to go away?" Becky looked

from him to Zach, not letting Scott go. "Someone please talk to me."

"Jimmy wants money. He always wants money from you, Scott." Zach blinked fast, his eyes shiny, his lips pressed together so hard they turned white. "He thinks you owe him. He told me why."

"No." The whole world froze. His heart stopped beating. He twisted away from Becky and backed into the bed. Something warm oozed between his fingers. He shook his head. Kept shaking it. Jimmy wouldn't have done that. He wouldn't have told anyone. No one needed to know. "You're lying. Jimmy told you he wanted money. I can see that. But that's it. I'll give him the money. I don't need it."

"Scott . . ." Zach came closer, but Scott couldn't let him. Not if he knew. He wouldn't get it.

If he knew, he wouldn't want Scott anymore. He'd see him for what he was. Someone who would take any opportunity given to him. Someone who was only good for one thing.

But Zach should know. He should know everything. Scott's bottom lip quivered. He bit it hard. He wouldn't be weak now. He'd be strong enough to admit that Zach deserved better than him. That Becky did. They both deserved better.

"Get away from me." Scott held his hand up to keep Zach away. Zach stayed where he was. "How much did he tell you? Did he tell you how I sold myself to play the game? For nice clothes and good meals? Did he tell you how I wanted it so much that I would do anything? Because it's true. It's fucking true and I don't—" His words caught. He forced them out. "—I don't regret it. It didn't matter. I loved the game. I *love* the game. I'm here now, and that's all that counts."

"That's not true, Scott." Zach shifted as though he was having a hard time not closing the distance between them. "You were a child. You were ten years old, and she was supposed to take care of you."

"I knew what I wanted. Don't look at me like that!" Scott voice cracked as Becky's hand hovered over her throat and her lips parted. She held out her hand, tears streaming down her face, face pale with shock. He shook his head. "Don't pity me. It wasn't bad. She loved me and she *did* take care of me. But not Jimmy. I tried to help him, but it wasn't enough. It will never be enough because she had something with me she didn't have with him. She gave him more when I—" Becky's tears were killing him. A fucking blunt dagger stabbing straight into his heart. "Don't. Becky, please don't. You're seeing it all wrong. I wanted it. I was . . . mature for my age. You're not seeing it right."

"Scott, you were a baby." Becky made a soft, hushing sound. "Please listen to me. I know you're upset. You have every right to be. But you have to see—"

"See what?" Scott ground his teeth as the nurse rushed into the room. Fuck, they might as well broadcast this to the whole world. The press would love this. Poor him. He'd had sex young. *So fucking what?* "Please give us a minute."

"Sir, you really should . . ." The nurse took a deep breath and shook her head. "The doctor will be signing you out shortly. I'll let you finish this."

Finish this. Damn right, they would. He waited for the door to close, then sat on the edge of the bed, head in his hands. "Becky, you don't know what I was like back then." He let out a sharp laugh. "I bet you can guess though! I was sneaking peeks at the pornos with the older kids. Wondering what it would be like. To have a woman want you, to have them touch you . . . You two apparently want the truth, so here it is. I liked it when she touched me. It felt good. I didn't . . . I couldn't go all the way for a bit, but she waited. She took her time with me. Gave me what every young man fantasizes about." Becky's expression made him want to hold her. To explain things to her gently. To tell her that men were different. Fuck, she had a little girl and she was probably thinking . . . but it wasn't the same. Not at all. "Becky, you can't . . . I know it's hard, but picture me. Just a bit smaller. It's really not a big deal. Boys want to be men. She helped me become a man."

"Do you really believe that? You didn't ever want . . ." Becky gulped in air like she was drowning. Shook her head. "Want her to just love you without asking for anything in return?"

"She took in two kids when our parents couldn't take care of us. She didn't have things easy. Her husband was mean. He couldn't do it for her. I did." Scott pressed his eyes shut. He didn't want to see how things had been. He didn't want to go back there.

But he did, because maybe it could help him make things clear. He remembered the first time she'd come to his bed. Crying, telling him that her husband said she was ugly because she was fat. She wasn't fat. She was soft and warm, so different from his mother who had been skinny. Hard. Cold. His mother held him to shut him up. She'd covered his mouth and hissed at him to be quiet because his father was talking to important people. His foster mother had let him cry. Let him ask about his mother and his father. And she'd told him the truth.

His parents were losers. But he didn't have to be like them. He was good looking. Strong. Talented. And she knew he would be someone. She just needed him to be there for her like she'd be there for him. To make her feel loved. Worth something. Yeah, sometimes it felt weird. Like when she'd made him call her "Mommy." When he just wanted to sleep and she wouldn't stop. When . . .

Damn it, he couldn't let what Becky and Zach thought change what had really happened. He'd been a bit skinny at the beginning but never a little boy. She'd given him treats. And the rum. He took a deep breath, staring down at his socked feet. Little boys didn't drink rum.

"You must think I'm disgusting. To find out I was like this, even then." His lips formed a hard smile. "It just sucks, you know? All that work 'improving' myself, but I can't change what I've already done."

"What she did, Scott." Zach grabbed a towel from the small pile on the table by the window. He latched on to Scott's wrist, then gently cleaned the dried blood from his hand. He held tight when Scott tried to pull away. "And that doesn't change how I feel about you. Not in the least."

Becky sat on the edge of the bed, reaching out as though to touch Scott's hair. Pausing as though she wasn't sure he'd want her to. "This has changed nothing for me either, Scott."

He shook his head, taking her hand and pressing it to the side of his face. "Then why are you afraid to touch me?"

"I'm not." Fresh tears spilled from Becky's eyes. She moved her hand down a bit and stroked her thumb over his bottom lip. "I'm afraid with all this being brought up, you might not want me to."

Oh God. How could she even think—he let out a sharp sound, speaking without thinking. "I'm not some kind of victim, Becky. I want you to touch me. You're not like any other woman I've ever been with. And you're *nothing* like her. It never feels wrong when I'm with you."

Neither Becky or Zach said a word. Becky just kept her hand on his face. Looking at him with . . . not with pity. More like she was waiting for something. Zach's expression held more of the same.

He rolled his eyes, sneering as he felt the warmth of tears spilling down his own cheek, moistening Becky's fingertips. "Is that what you want to hear? That it felt wrong?" He bit into his cheek hard, hoping the pain from that and the dull throb in his head would toughen him up a bit. He didn't need anyone feeling sorry for him. "It did. Sometimes it made me sick. But I never said no. I never fought." He turned away from Zach's level gaze. "I could have stopped her if I'd wanted to. I never tried."

"Never, Scott?" Zach asked, quietly.

"Not loud enough. Not hard enough." Scott recalled the weak efforts he'd made. They didn't count for anything. "Look at me, Zach. You really believe she overpowered me? Forced herself on me?"

Zach pulled out his phone. Tapped the screen and revealed a picture he must have found before coming to the room. Scott went perfectly still as he stared at a picture of himself. He couldn't have been more than ten or eleven, a scrawny little thing. Posing for a picture with his brand new hockey stick, holding it all wrong, but something about his expression . . . it was like he thought someone would take it away. And he had. He'd believed all the good things would be taken away.

"I believe that she was a horrible woman. That what she did to you was despicable. She had no right to . . ." Zach took a deep breath. "And somewhere, deep inside, I think you know that too."

The doctor knocked at the door. Just in time, because Scott really didn't know what to say. He tried to listen to the doctor's instructions, took his prescriptions, then signed all the necessary paperwork. Had Becky and Zach wait in the hall while he got dressed. Didn't argue when an orderly came with a wheelchair to roll him out. He felt utterly drained. This whole stupid conversation had taken what little energy the stupid virus had left. He was glad that Zach didn't demand that he talk more when they got to Becky's car. Or when they got to her house.

But it wasn't over. There was still Jimmy to deal with. And eventually this would all come up again. Whether it was Becky or Zach just wanting to make sure he was okay. Or a nightmare that woke him up screaming. Screaming those words he'd whispered as a child.

No! Don't, please don't!

Because somewhere deep, deep down inside, he'd known then as he knew now.

It was wrong.

Chapter Thirty One

"*Stop.*" Becky rolled over and took a deep breath as she stared at the baby monitor she'd set up on her nightstand. Neither Scott nor Zach knew she'd hooked one up in the den and in the basement. Zach had been too busy making sure Scott was comfortable on the sofa bed, then distracting Casey while Becky made sure Scott took his meds and covered all his spots with calamine lotion. The image of Zach sitting across from Casey on the floor, sipping iced tea from a teacup he looked afraid to break, had made drifting off to sleep a little easier.

Poor Casey. Her baby felt so bad about Scott being sick. She blamed herself for feeding him soup and giving him her germs. Then insisted Becky make him more since he liked it so much.

Through the baby monitor, Becky could hear Zach speaking softly. Trying to calm Scott without waking him. Letting Scott know he was there. That Scott was safe.

"Stop! I said stop! I said it!" Scott let out a choked sob and raw pain clenched deep in Becky's chest. She hurried across the room to grab her housecoat, slipping by Casey's room with a glance in to make sure her daughter was still asleep.

Part of her had wondered if she was doing the right thing. She needed Scott here. Where she could take care of him. Where she could make sure that he'd really be okay. But was she doing the right thing as a mother? Without giving any details, she'd called her own mother to see what she thought. He mother had been with the same man most of her life, but she'd faced her own obstacles. Issues with her family, with Daddy's, letting her brother, and once her cousin stay with them during hard times. Becky couldn't recall any of those long visits affecting her own schedule.

But she wasn't her mother. And Zach and Scott weren't family... not in any way those looking in would care about. They would judge. They would call her a bad mother.

What if Patrick finds out?

Becky hurried down the first flight of stairs. Then cut across the kitchen to head down to the basement. She focused on her mother's words.

"*Do they love my granddaughter? Are they good with her?*"

"Of course. I wouldn't bother with them otherwise." Becky hesitated. "But it's too soon to—"

"*Too soon? For what exactly? To show your daughter what you're willing to do for the people who matter to you?*"

Letting out a sigh into the phone, Becky shook her head. "No. For my daughter to know how much they matter. I haven't been seeing Zach for that long. And Scott... how do I explain this to her?"

Her mother chuckled. "*Cherie, you don't. They aren't strangers to her. For now, they are Landon's friends. And yours. To Casey, you're taking care of a sick friend. That's it. When they move in for good, we'll have this chat again.*" She paused. "*And then I will tell you a child can never have enough love. Which is exactly what I told your brother.*"

"Landon was worried? But Amia will grow up with the three of them."

"*Yes. With two men who are very close. Who are both 'Daddy.' Landon refuses to let Dean be any less. To let Akia call him uncle or something else for appearances. But he is worried that he's making things more difficult for her.*"

"What did you tell him?"

"*What I'm telling you. Every child has their own story. Their own hardships. Being the most important little person in many people's lives will never be one of them.*"

And that had settled it for Becky. She'd gotten all worked up about Zach not being able to love her, and Scott, and Casey. As though love was a pot of stew, very filling, but with only so many helpings to dish out. Even with how worried he was about Scott, when Zach sat across from Casey to play tea party, he gave her his all. And he always would. Becky didn't doubt that. Not anymore.

By the time she got to the den, Scott was awake, letting out an amused snort as Zach uncapped a bottle of water and handed it to him.

He took a few gulps, then shook his head. "Aftercare for a bad dream?"

"Do you want to talk about it?" Zach moved to cross his arms over his chest, stopped, then hooked his thumbs to the waistband of his boxers. The gesture made Becky's mouth dry. The way his hands framed the carved slope of his pelvis, darkened with soft, springy hair...

She made herself look away, annoyed with herself. Scott needed her full attention.

But Scott simply let out a low laugh, his eyes hooded as his gaze trailed over Zach's hard body. "He's something else, isn't he? If I had the energy, I'd grab him and—"

"Well, you don't." Zach's tone was rough, but his lips curved in a way that made it obvious he didn't mind having them both stare at him. He shook his head and nudged Scott's shoulder to get him to lie down. "And you didn't answer me."

Scott blinked innocently. "I didn't? Sorry, was busy stripping you with my eyes."

That made Becky smile. Nothing held Scott down for long. But she knew Zach wouldn't let him flirt his way out of the discussion.

"Do you—" Zach leaned over Scott, the hint of mirth from before gone from his features "—want to talk about it?"

"Damn it, back to that?" Scott dropped onto the pillow, hands behind his head, glaring at the ceiling. "No. I don't want to talk about it." His nostrils flared. "Ever again. How's that for an answer?"

"Scott, holding this in has been hurting you. It's the reason for—"

"Don't even fucking go there." Scott winced as if his own sharp words were hurting his head. He let out a pitiful cough. Scratched at his belly. "This is horrible. Itchy, sore, sick, and all you do is nag at me." He turned his head and gave Becky a weak smile. "Do you think I can have more of that soup? And maybe you can sit with me for a bit. His snoring is disturbing my much-needed sleep."

"My poor baby," Becky said, teasing him a little as she gently nudged his hand away from his stomach. "Don't do that."

"Sorry, sweetie. Can't help it."

Zach grumbled, pacing away and lacing his fingers behind his neck. The man didn't seem to like not knowing how to fix things. He was worried about Scott and tended to revert to treating him like a sub. Not the best approach. Not for their hardheaded, damaged but still so strong, Scott.

She knew a better way.

Bending over the bed, she patted Scott's cheek. "I'll get you some soup. And something to help with the itching. But you have to answer one question first."

"Another one?" Scott frowned—actually, it was closer to a pout. He was cute when he was sick. "I'm really tired, sweetheart. How about you just climb up here and snuggle with me. That will make everything better."

Behind her, Zach mumbled something like "Milking it for all it's worth."

Not bothering to hide her grin, she petted Scott's hair. "One simple question, and I'll get your soup, then snuggle for a bit. But I can't stay down here. I don't want Casey going to my room and wondering where I am."

"No, no, of course not. I wouldn't ask . . ." Scott's brow furrowed. He tongued his bottom lip. "What's the question?"

"Those girls you work with at the self-defense class have been through a lot. They have all been strong enough to get past what happened to them. They joined the class, not only to learn to protect themselves, but to take back some of the power stolen from them." She held up her hand when Scott opened his mouth to interrupt. "Yes, you're big and strong and no one can ever take advantage of you again. Just like they have different skills that will help them."

Scott nodded slowly. "Right, but . . ."

"There's damage that was done to them that wasn't just physical. Would you suggest any of them keep it bottled up inside. Never mention it again?"

Rather than scoff and tell her it wasn't the same—which she'd prepared for—Scott pressed his eyes shut. Inhaled deeply. And let it out with a sigh. "You're right. I wouldn't tell them that. We have therapist we recommend, so maybe I should . . . maybe I will." He opened his eyes. Looked from her to Zach. "I get what you're both trying to do, but you've got to leave it at that, okay? If I decide to go, then I go. You don't make a big deal about it."

"Agreed," Zach said without hesitating.

Becky pulled one of Scott's hands out from under his head. Kissed his palm. "I'm fine with that."

"Good." Scott held her hand, his lips curving in a warm smile. "And keep looking at me, just like that. Not like I'm some broken thing. I'm not broken. Just a little messed up."

"Not any more than the rest of us, Scott. You might be a little out of control sometimes." Zach moved in close to Becky, his lips brushing her cheek, his hand lightly resting on her hip. "But that's just a small part of the man we love so much."

"Love, huh?" Scott glanced up at Becky, a flicker of hope in his eyes. "Do you love me, Becky? Not because you feel sorry for me, but because . . . just because?"

"Just because." And she did. She felt it, not the first sparks, because those had been lit inside her a long time ago. Like kindling letting off nothing but smoke, the small twigs red and charred, showing no signs of a flame. A breath of air, cupped hands to shelter them, and they caught, feeding off any fuel, spreading, glowing hot and fierce. Still, saying the actual words didn't feel right now. Not yet. So she did the next best thing. She kissed him and whispered, "I don't feel sorry for you. I'm happy you're here. And that you're mine."

"I love being yours." Scott tugged at her hand, rolling over until she laid down next to him. "Forget the soup. I'll have it for breakfast. Just stay with me for a little while."

"All right." Becky nestled her head against the side of his neck, her eyes drifting shut as she felt the mattress dip where Zach sat beside her. Being between them both was lovely. So comfortable and warm. She could stay here, like this, and sleep peacefully for the few hours left until dawn.

No, I can't. She opened her eyes, determined to watch Scott's face until he was out for the night. Then go back to her own bed. Wonderful as this was, she couldn't have her baby waking up thinking she was alone.

Zach spoke low, close to her ear. "Relax for a bit. I'll keep an ear out for her. She usually gets up around six, right?"

"Yes, but . . ."

"I'll get you up before then."

"You need your sleep too, Zach." She tilted her head to the side and frowned at him. "I don't want you to—"

"It may sound odd, but I want to stay up. Watch over both of you. It will make me feel better." He met her eyes, something in them making it clear he really needed her to understand. "Can you trust me?"

"Yes." She muffled a laugh at his shocked expression. It wasn't funny, but she was tired and it was true. She trusted him to do exactly as he said. He would wake her up. He would listen for Casey. And she had no doubt he'd check on her baby a few times just to make sure she was sound asleep. He was good like that. "I love you so much. You look good in my house." She was talking nonsense. But exhaustion loosened her tongue and she didn't want to stop. "All this nice stuff, all the rooms, all pretty. But it was missing something."

Zach smiled and bent down to kiss her forehead. "I thought so too."

* * * *

Two weeks went by and things had settled into a pleasant routine. Zach stood by the pantry, resisting the urge to grin as he pulled out the box of Cheerios. He showed it to Casey.

"How about this?"

"No!" She giggled, shaking her head. "Guess again!"

"This one?" He held up the Corn Flakes, knowing full well she'd want the Mueslix. They played the same game every morning. Becky sat across the table, nursing her coffee, a serene smile on her lips. Casey could be grumpy for a while after waking, refusing even her favorite cereal when her mother simply took it out and poured her a bowl. For some reason, Zach doing it this way put the little girl in a good mood pretty quickly. He replaced the box, brow furrowed in concentration, then whipped out the Mueslix. "It *has* to be this one!"

"Yep!" Casey bounced in her seat as Zach came over to fill her little plastic Dora the Explorer bowl. After he added milk, she took a huge spoonful, shoving it in her mouth and speaking around it. "You're so smart, Zach!"

"Don't tell him that, Casey!" Scott came into the kitchen, shut the basement door behind him, then stepped up to plant a kiss on

Casey's messy curls. "Hockey players are born with oversized egos."

Zach motioned for Casey to finish what was in her mouth before she spoke. She nodded and he caught Becky giving him one of those smiles he'd come to love. One that said she appreciated how he got along with her daughter. It had lost some of the wistfulness of before, the hint that she wished the man who should be sharing these little moments with Casey cared enough to want to.

His loss.

Mouth cleared, Casey tipped her head back to give Scott a serious look. "Oh, I know. That's what Uncle Landon always says about you."

Becky hid her mouth with her hand, eyes sparkling with laughter. Zach chuckled.

Scott shook his head. "Yeah, well Uncle Landon is . . ." He stopped, glancing over at Becky before she had to interrupt, and quickly changed whatever he'd been about to say. "He's smart too."

"He's the smartest. You know he told me spiders aren't really bugs? So when Mommy says she hates bugs, spiders shouldn't count. But she doesn't agree, do you, Mommy?" Without waiting for an answer, Casey continued, telling them in-depth exactly what the difference between bugs and spiders was. Zach drank his coffee, and a refill, nodding as she tried to quote exactly what her uncle had told her, helping her with some of the big words when she couldn't pronounce them. Scott sat on Casey's other side at the round table, shuddering every time she said "spider" and making her giggle.

The little girl soaked up all the attention but hesitated every once in a while and glanced at both men as though wondering if they were bored. Seeing they weren't, she chattered on, her longest pauses when she at another bite of cereal at Zach's pointed looks.

After fixing Scott some coffee, eggs, and toast, Becky took a seat, completely at ease as she joined in the conversation. It was Friday, so she'd be heading off to work soon. Casey had a Ped Day and her grandmother would be coming to pick her up to spend the long weekend in Gaspe in about an hour. She'd already been told this would be the last day he and Scott would be staying here. They were back on the roster for the game tonight and would be on the road starting Monday. Rather than crying, or sulking, Casey enjoyed the time she had left.

Tough little kid. She seemed to take whatever life threw at her and make the best of it. Hopefully, this situation wasn't yet another she'd have to just take in stride. If he had his way, she'd be able to count on his presence. Not all the time, because some road games could keep him away for weeks, but she'd hear from him every day. And she'd know he'd always come back to enjoy moments just like this.

He wanted to be a constant in her life. And he truly believed Becky wanted that too.

Tonight, he'd know for sure.

A faint buzzing had the three adults checking their phones. Scott pulled his out, stood, and backed away from the table. He took a deep breath, flashed a smile at Casey when she gave him a curious look, then slipped out of the kitchen.

Zach glanced over at Becky and she nodded, distracting Casey by bringing up the zoo her grandmother would bring her to. They'd both seen the way Scott had paled. Zach could only think of one person who would get that reaction from him, a fact that made Zach's blood boil.

He found Scott in the living room, staring at his phone which was set on the center of the coffee table. After all the talk of spiders, and Scott's obvious distaste for them, one would have thought his cell had just grown eight spindly legs. He actually jumped when it buzzed again, like it would crawl right off the table. This time, a text flashed on the screen. Zach couldn't read it from where he stood, but Scott's jaw hardened as he silently read the words.

"He's at my house." Scott hunched his shoulders, rubbing his hands on his cargo shorts. "So's most of my stuff. He knows I'm playing tonight. He knows I'll show up eventually."

"What do you need, Scott?" Zach approached Scott slowly, knowing that he wouldn't want to be held right now. One of the things that seemed to bother the man the most was feeling weak. Helpless. As much as Zach wanted to pull Scott into his arms to comfort him, he had to let Scott deal with this in his own way. Let him make the first move and call all the shots. "Your equipment is at the forum. You can borrow one of my suits."

The edge of Scott's lips quirked up slightly. "Stephan would kill me. The pants will be loose and too short."

"Gotta start bulking you up a bit, boy," Zach said with a smile.

"Boy?" Scott moved toward Zach, sliding his hand from Zach's waist to the small of his back. He glanced at the hall, cocking his head as though listening for little footsteps, then pressed his lips to Zach's, whispering, "You call me boy and I get to call you babe."

"Babe?" Zach snorted, hooking his fingers into Scott's collar to pull him in for a hard kiss. He teased Scott's bottom lip with his teeth. "I like it better when you call me 'Sir.'"

"I'm sure you do." Scott drew away from the kiss as his phone buzzed yet again. He swallowed, then lowered his forehead to Zach's shoulder. "Fuck, I don't want to see him."

"Then don't." Zach wrapped his arms around Scott, gathering him close, barely holding in a sigh of relief when Scott let him. Damn it, Scott's cheek felt cold against the side of Zach's neck. Zach hated that Jimmy still had the power to do this to him. And Scott wasn't ready to take that power away. He'd recovered from the virus, had gained back some of the weight he'd lost over the first week when his appetite was next to nil. But the scars of his past were like fresh wounds with the scabs ripped off. And those would take some time to heal.

Seeing Jimmy today would be like tearing open stitches just set to parted flesh. Scott would be all too ready to take the blame for his brother's failings.

Zach refused to let that happen. He shifted back a bit to study Scott's face as he spoke. "I'll go—" He hushed Scott before he could interrupt. "I swear to you, I won't lay a hand on him. I'll tell him you don't want to see him. That he's got to deal with his own shit." He grabbed Scott's chin when Scott shook his head. "He does, Scott. You've done more than enough for him."

Creases formed on Scott's forehead as he met Zach's eyes. "He's my brother."

"By blood only. You have twenty Cobras that deserve the title more." Maybe not so many, not yet, but they'd get there. "It's time to end this."

"How pathetic is it that I want to say yes?" Scott rolled his eyes toward the ceiling, blinking, gulping as though he needed to swallow air just to get enough. "This is my problem."

"It's not yours alone. Are you going to tell me you won't step in if Patrick hurts Casey again?"

"Becky won't let us."

"Becky had me answer the phone when he called the other day." Zach ground his teeth as he recalled the conversation. The bastard hadn't wanted to talk to his daughter—Becky had told Zach just to pass the phone to Casey if he did, she just couldn't speak to the asshole calmly after he'd failed to call Casey on her birthday or return Becky's calls while Casey was sick. Patrick had simply given Zach a message for Becky. The child support payments would be late. He was sorry, but something had come up.

Fucking piece of shit. Zach was pretty damn proud of himself for being civil with the man. He could manage so long as nothing Patrick ever did stole the smile from Casey's sweet face or brought tears to her eyes. If that happened... he couldn't make any promises.

"Becky's such a tough chick." Scott was breathing a little easier now, the subject of Becky and Casey seeming to relax him. "I'm surprised she—"

"Why? She wasn't in a good place to deal with him. You're not in a good place to deal with Jimmy." Zach held tight to Scott's shoulders, never shifting his gaze even when Scott did. "Say yes."

"Yes." Scott let out a rough sound, half between a laugh and a groan. "Get my stuff. Tell Jimmy I'm fucking done." His shoulders shifted as though a massive weight had just been lifted from them. He tipped his head back. "I'm done."

"Good." *No. Fucking perfect.* Zach hugged Scott, then went to tell Becky he'd see her tonight.

She worried her bottom lip with her teeth, glancing over at Scott as he returned to his seat with a bowl. Casey offered him her cereal, and Scott nodded, letting her pour him a huge helping. Becky pulled Zach aside as the two bent their heads together to talk smack about the Sabres, who the team would be playing tonight.

"It was Jimmy, wasn't it?"

"Yes. But don't worry, I'm handling it."

"What about Scott? Is he okay?" She lowered her voice, even though they were both already speaking too quietly for either Scott or Casey to hear. "Should I stay with him? If I call Mr. Keane and explain—"

"No. This stays between us. The only other person who knows is Tim, and I trust him not to say anything." Zach smiled as Scott used his spoon to snap a piece of cereal off the table into Casey's bowl. "Scott's got a full schedule today between seeing Stephan about the Rose charity and the fan meet and greet before the game. He'll be fine. You go to work. Keep things as normal as possible."

"All right." The doorbell rang and Becky hurried down the hall to open it and let her mother in. Zach kissed Casey's cheek, patted Scott's shoulder, then went to say hello and goodbye to Erin before pulling on his shoes and heading out. He made one stop, then went straight to Scott's place.

Jimmy sat outside in his beat-up, once red Toyota POS. He watched Zach climb off his bike, rolling his window down about half way as Zach strode toward him.

"Hey, I don't want no trouble, man." Jimmy scooted back in his seat, eyeing the door as though to make sure it was locked. "I just wanted to make sure Scott's okay."

"Sure you do." Zach's lips curled away from his teeth as he stared down at the despicable excuse for a man. Much as he wanted to beat the fucker to a bloody pulp, Jimmy wasn't worth risking even one game to busted knuckles or a night in a jail cell. "We both know why you're here. You want money."

"He owes me—"

"He. Owes. You. *Nothing*." Zach practically spit out each word. He could feel the bile rising in his throat as he braced his hand at the top of the rust-eaten door. Being near this man was about as pleasant as trudging through manure. Actually, he'd prefer to be knee-deep in shit. He stuffed his hand into his pocket, pulling out the cashier's check he'd had made up at the bank. He reached through the open window and flicked it into Jimmy's face. "Take this. Consider it your final, get-the-fuck-out-of-his-life, payment. And don't you dare come back begging for more, because you won't get another cent. If this isn't enough to pay off the people you owe, they can fucking bury you. Scott is done. Got it?"

Jimmy's eyes were wide as he held the check in front of him and gaped at the amount. He nodded quickly. "Got it. This is . . . thank you. It's plenty." He gave Zach a yellow-toothed grin. "Fuck, he's still got it. He really nailed you, didn't he?"

All the muscles in Zach's body tightened like thick steel cords fused around his bones, the way they did before he dropped the gloves on the ice to defend a teammate. He straightened, not sure he wanted to test his control by being any closer to the man than necessary. "Don't thank me. This is for him."

"Whatever." Jimmy folded the check carefully and slipped it into his pocket. "You tell my brother that he's not gonna have the game forever. Or his good looks. One day he's gonna be a nobody, and he'll have nothing because he's never had any business sense. You tell him, if he's real nice, I may consider helping him out. Because I'm gonna make it big. Maybe I'll end up buying the stupid team he loves so much, and then I'll give him a cushy job because that's the kind of brother I am."

If that ever happens, Scott will have the strength to tell you where to go himself. Zach gave Jimmy a cold look, not willing to waste another breath on the loser.

Jimmy shrugged. "I'd wish you luck for the game tonight, but I'm a gambling man and all odds are against you. Just try not to embarrass yourselves."

For a moment the man sat there, as though waiting for some kind of reaction. When Zach didn't give him one, he shrugged again and pulled out. Zach stood at the side of the street, watching the red car until it turned. Then stayed a little longer, not sure why the tension within hadn't eased with Jimmy gone. Scott had told Zach how much money he usually gave his brother. What Zach had given Jimmy should tide him over for a very long time.

Or it could be tossed on a table that very night and lost. Zach shoved his hands in his pockets and crossed the street, making his way up to Scott's condo to collect Scott's things. He knew very well he might have just exposed himself as someone else Jimmy could leech off of, but he had time to figure out how to deal with it. Jimmy was his problem now.

It was worth whatever the cost to protect Scott. Money meant nothing compared to seeing the man he loved smile again. To see the shadows fade from his eyes. To see him finally free.

Chapter Thirty Two

Scrambling for the puck, Scott threw his body into the Sabres' center, leaning all his weight into the other man as he scooped the puck out from beneath his own skates for a pass to Pischlar. Ramos charged up from behind them, brushing off a hard check to receive a pass from Pischlar and drive into the offensive zone. He snapped the puck to White, well prepared when it came back to him as two hulking defensemen crowded the tenacious left winger.

Cobras were on a power play after Vanek received a vicious slash from Nelson, the Sabres' captain. For a bit, it had seemed like the Cobras might lose a man to roughing when the teams had crowded in the corner, not a single man willing to put up with Vanek becoming a target after his long absence. But Vanek had wrestled his way into the center of the tussling group to let Mason and Ramos know he was fine. He had a bloody lip, but he shrugged off the trainer, determined to let the team know they had to get back at the Sabres where it counted.

On the scoreboard.

That, Scott could handle. He drove hard to the net, angling his stick blade as Ramos took a hard shot. The crack of the puck on the base of his stick reverberated through his arms. The lights flashed. The sirens sounded. And Scott couldn't believe it. He missed his opportunity to do some showy kind of celebration as the ref signaled that the goal was good. His teammates were all around him, shouting at him and pushing him toward the bench for congrats from the rest of the guys.

This was the first game in a while that they had enough of a lead for the Cobras to feel good about. Hunt wasn't letting anything by him. The score was 5-0, end of the second period. The fans were going crazy, and he could practically hear the front rows jabbering about the Cup already.

Awesome, but part of him was waiting for this period to end. Because between the second period and the third, he knew what was coming. Something that would have a bigger impact on his life than raising that silver trophy over his head. Not much could top that, but this would. He felt himself shaking as the puck was dropped, and he touched it with his stick without any real effort because there was less than a second left. As most of the men headed off, he held still, watching the scoreboard. The cameras fixed on Zach as he stepped onto the ice.

A murmur from the crowd had the men heading off, those that didn't already know, pausing and looking around curiously. Those that were in on this hadn't moved. Ramos, Carter, Vanek. Pischlar and White. Tim, leaning over the boards, a broad grin on his face. Mason by his side, his smile a little sad.

Zach took a knee as the song "Have You Ever Really Loved a Woman" by Bryan Adams played loud on the speakers. Well-timed, the big screen switched to Becky, in the press box.

God, she looked beautiful, her dark brown hair pulled away from her face with a few loose strands left to frame it. Her grey eyes were wide. She'd taken off her harsh grey suit jacket, and her pearl colored shirt brought out the beautiful shade of pink coloring her cheeks. She brought her hand to her mouth.

A microphone was pinned to Zach's collar. Zach held out the ring he and Scott had chosen together, taking a moment to look down at the words engraved in the rose gold, across from the four embedded diamonds. Then he looked at Scott, smiling.

That smile served to engrave those same words in Scott's heart. *The four of us. Always.* He bit the inside of his cheek to keep from showing more emotion than he cared to let the cameras catch. The words came as close to everything Scott wanted to say as anything could. Zach was in a position to have Becky and Casey for his own. But he wouldn't leave Scott out. And, for the first time ever, Scott truly felt like he belonged.

He let out a laugh as the screen showed Casey and Erin Bower—who hadn't left for Gaspe as "planned." Then Landon, standing with them in the space just past the benches. He was holding his baby and his smile was just as big as anyone's. He was happy for his sister. He'd seen the ring before the game and knew exactly what those words meant. And he'd hugged Scott just as hard as he'd hugged Zach, calling him his brother. He didn't doubt that

Becky would say yes.

But Zach, Zach had his doubts. And he'd shared them with Scott.

"What am I doing?" Zach had paced the locker room for fifteen minutes, not half as long as he'd paced after picking up the ring they'd gone to customize the week before, but long enough to get Scott's heart pounding. What if Zach chickened out? Scott couldn't see himself being a good husband, but Zach had made it clear that's what he was agreeing to when the words were set in gold. Not legally, but in every way that counted. If Zach was uncertain, where did that leave Scott? Scott was the last man any woman should want to spend forever with. And Zach hadn't made it any easier when he'd kept talking. "I've done this before. The woman said yes. But neither of us followed through."

"She wasn't Becky." Scott cut Zach off, stopping his pacing because he couldn't stand it anymore. "And you didn't have me."

"True." Zach scraped his nails over his freshly shaved head. He held up the ring. "Do you really think she'll like it?"

"I know she will." Scott smirked, well aware that it would get Zach's balls in a knot. His nice, heavy, tasty balls. Scott was looking forward to having them in his mouth before the night was over. Much easier to deal with than all this uncertainty. He snatched the ring to admire it. "Hell, I chose it. You've been with too many men since that 'one' you thought was the end all. If you're still hung up on her, I'm gonna take this ring back to the jeweler's and switch the words to 'The three of us.' This ring is so Becky. Not too showy. More meaning than flash. I'm so taking all the credit."

"Scott, those words, do you really get it?" Zach had faced him, shiny beads of sweat on his temples. "Always. Forever. Long-term."

"Yeah, I graduated, Zach, I know what those words mean."

"Do you? I mean really. Seriously. Because when I stand in front of the judge, I'll be speaking for us both. This includes you." Zach gave him a long, passionate kiss, and every man in the locker room saw it. There was no mistaking the implications. "Forever."

"Zach, I'm here." Scott pressed his hands to the sides of Zach's face, wondering if the man wasn't a little damaged himself. He repeated those same words, not sure he could say it any better. "I'm here."

The sound of Zach clearing his throat quieted the crowd in the stands. Overhead, the screen was split in half to show Zach and Becky, side by side. Becky had tears in her eyes. Scott ran his finger under the collar of his jersey, sure it had gotten a bit snugger.

"Rebecca Bower, I love you more than I ever thought myself capable. We didn't make it easy for one another, but all that trial and error showed me one very important thing. Nothing feels right without knowing I'll be coming home to you."

Zach paused, his cheeks reddening slightly as the crowd let out a unified "Awww." He stole a look at Scott, and Scott gave him an encouraging smile. Zach squared his shoulders. "I rehearsed a much longer speech, but Scott told me getting straight to the point would be best." The edges of Zach's lips quirked into a half-smile as the screen showed Casey again, bouncing up and down, waving. "I see you, baby girl. You think I should ask your mommy to marry me?"

Casey let out a scream that could be heard across the forum without a mic. She tugged away from her grandmother and ran on to the ice. Scott sped across the ice, swooping her up into his arms even as he skidded to a stop with a showy spray of snow. He held Casey against his hip, motioning for her to wave at their audience.

He skated up to stand beside Zach, and the huge image of them overhead was almost perfect. Zach, Scott, and Casey. All that was missing was Becky. The screen switched to her, frozen in place in the press box, tears flowing freely now, her smile making her whole face glow.

"So how about it, Becky?" Zach held up the ring a little higher, the gold flashing in the bright forum lights. "Would you do me the honor of becoming my wife?"

Becky's lips were moving, but it was impossible to tell what she was saying. She held up a finger, then disappeared. She reappeared at the player's bench and Carter gave her his arm to help her make her way across the ice to them.

"Yes." Becky bit her lip as Zach slid the ring on her finger. She ran her finger over the four diamonds, more tears spilling as she looked at Scott. She whispered yes again before Zach lifted her up in his arms and kissed her.

Casey looped her arms around Scott's neck, speaking quietly in his ear. "We're gonna be a family. Isn't that awesome?"

Scott grinned and kissed Casey's cheek, hugging her tight. "It is."

He had a feeling the little girl was including him, which was pretty damn awesome in itself. How she knew was anyone's guess, but that didn't matter now. Carter had retreated back to the benches, so it was just the four of them on the ice. Becky and Zach turned, still holding on to each other, and drew Scott and Casey into a firm embrace.

Becky didn't kiss him in front of the cameras. They wouldn't announce what they had to the world and he understood that. But she did something even better. Once they were in the hall leading away from the ice, she motioned for Casey to go with Zach.

She pulled off his gloves, dropped them, then laced their fingers together. A few players lingered by the rink door, others down the hall, all cutting off the press, giving them some privacy. His heart pounded as he gazed into her warm grey eyes, and he finally got what Zach had been saying.

Forever. Forever to make this woman happy. To be the man she needed because he couldn't expect her soon to-be husband to pick up his slack. Together they could—they would—give her more than either could alone.

"I love you, Scott." Becky drew his hands up, kissing their clasped hands. Her eyes repeated the words with so much intensity his breath caught. She smiled, rising up on her tiptoes to reach his lips. "I was waiting for the right time to say it."

"It's always the right time, Becky." He kissed her, freeing one hand so he could delve his fingers into her hair, holding her still so he could kiss her harder. Deeper. He smiled against her lips. "I expect to hear it often."

Becky laughed, smacking the center of his chest. "You jerk. You're supposed to say it too."

"Am I?" He chuckled, hauling her back when she moved to storm away. He kissed her cheeks, the tip of her nose, the length of her throat, breathing hard because he really didn't think just saying it would be enough. His voice was rough when he spoke again, trying to put all his feelings into those three simple words. "I love you."

She was crying again, those happy tears that messed up her makeup even more, making her look as undone as when he made love to her. He dried her tears with the sleeve of his jersey, keeping her close to his side as they headed to the locker room. Maybe those words *were* enough.

Because he meant every single one.

Chapter Thirty Three

This night had been planned for a week—or so the men had told her as they'd left the forum after the game—but Becky had no idea what to expect when she stepped into the club. In the day-to-day flow they'd eased into, things had become so... normal. She'd made love to Zach, quietly in her bed. Had a quickie with Scott in the shower after washing the calamine lotion from his body. Wonderful, all of it, but there was nothing kinky. Nothing besides their relationship going beyond the status quo of one man, one woman, to make what they had any different. Not even a threesome to add a bit of spice.

Then again, she hadn't expected the proposal either. Her men were sneaky, and she'd come to love their little surprises. Whether it be flowers, stolen kisses between the three of them behind closed doors after a press conference, or a sudden trip to a BDSM club.

But... at the same time, she wasn't sure what they were doing here. Zach hadn't given any indication that he wanted to be her Dom again. She'd tried to regain his trust by being open about her insecurities. By sharing everything from her bitterness about Patrick losing interest in his daughter, to how she felt when he spent the night in the basement with Scott, instead of sleeping by her side. He'd been quiet for a while after she'd admitted she wished both he and Scott could sleep with her but was afraid of the questions from Casey if she came in and saw them together. Then he'd told her to do whatever she felt was best, with a subtle reminder that Casey was perceptive and would ask about the three of them either way. Becky had to be prepared for that.

And maybe she was.

Sometimes she worried that he'd get tired of her going on about *everything*, but all she saw in his eyes was compassion. And, more importantly, his reservations about their future had slowly dissolved until none remained. Clearly, since he'd placed his ring on her finger, committing himself to her for the rest of his life.

The rest of our life.

She couldn't help but be a little concerned that Zach would want to play here, the first time it was the three of them together. It made her feel horrible to think she'd damaged his confidence so much that he'd feel the need to be supervised to do a scene with her. She'd never hide from him again. She'd done her best to prove that.

"You better get rid of that worrywart face before Zach decides to start the night off with a spanking," Scott whispered in her ear as he took her long, white wool coat. He shrugged off his own jacket, then handed both over at the new coat check that had been built near the door, narrowing the once open entrance. An influx of new people vying for membership had Tim—who was temporarily running things for Dean—making a few changes to protect the privacy of the players who made up a good third of the regular attendees. Becky took a deep breath as she peered into the darkened club, seeing little more than the bar from where she stood.

You don't belong here. Becky stiffened her spine, even as Zach's past words made her steps falter. "The way you play is downright dangerous." He'd been right. But she'd changed. Learned from her mistakes. A tiny, sharp voice in her head thought otherwise. *Have you? Really?*

With a mental sock stuffed in to shut that voice up, she gave Scott a sly look. "If he's going to spank me, it won't be because I seem worried about something."

"Oh really?" Scott grinned, drawing her away from the entrance to the bar where he sat and stood her between his parted thighs. He unbuttoned her silk blouse, then stroked the bare expanse of her stomach with his fingertips, making her shiver at the frisson of pleasure. "What are your intensions, my naughty girl?"

"You'll see, Sir." Becky dropped her gaze when she caught Chicklet glancing over at her from behind the bar. She couldn't help but feel like every Dom in the place was watching her, like that little voice had spit out the sock she'd stuffed in its mouth to laugh and whisper that they needed to. Because she couldn't be trusted.

I'll show them. I'll make my Master proud.

If he ever wanted to be that to her again.

"Hey, lovebirds. Wanted to say congrats." Luke came over, a lot of swagger in his walk even though he was wearing nothing put a pair of low-riding, snug silk boxer briefs, his feet bare, a decidedly submissive outfit. He winked at Chicklet when she met his gaze with a hard one of her own, as though assessing his behavior. Chicklet shook her head, grinned, then came over to serve the drinks Scott ordered. Three shots of tequila. Luke stared at Scott, then tapped his finger by his shot glass. "Uh, I really shouldn't . . ."

"You get to play with my man, I get to corrupt you." Scott gave Luke an easy smile as he lifted Becky's wrist to lick it. He sprinkled salt on her wet skin, then held her wrist out for Luke, his lips brushing Becky's neck as he spoke. "Taste her. She's delicious."

Luke shuddered, his gaze still on Scott as he licked the salt. His tongue was hot on Becky's flesh, and for some reason, having Scott hold her while Luke had his mouth on her had hot liquid pooling in her core.

"Open." Scott picked up Luke's shot glass and tipped it to Luke's lips, a positively wicked glint in his eyes. He put a possessive hand on Becky's shoulder when Luke's gaze shifted to the exposed swell of her breasts above her cream-colored bra, then fed Luke a lemon slice. "One shot for courage. You better go. They're waiting for you."

"You sure you're not a Dom?" Luke asked, sounding a little breathless as he dropped the lemon slice on a napkin. "'Cause . . . damn."

"Naw, I'm pure vanilla, boy." Scott chuckled at Luke's doubtful look. "Can't you tell?"

If that's true, I think vanilla just hit the top of my favorite flavors. Becky squirmed as Scott idly traced the waist of her suit pants, fiddling with the top button.

"Right. Vanilla." Luke snorted. "With sprinkles, chocolate sauce." His eyes glistened with amusement. "Maybe a few nuts."

"Ha!" Scott watched Luke as he drew Becky's loose hair over one shoulder. He undid the front clasp of her bra, brushing aside her hands when she moved to stop him. "I don't envy your nuts tonight, pal."

"*Niño.*" Sebastian called. Luke turned, a flush spreading across his skin as Sebastian gave him a hooded look. Sebastian pointed to the spot beside where Jami knelt at his feet. "Come."

"Fuck, I think I'm gonna." Luke mumbled before quickly

crossing the room to kneel in front of his Master.

Scott pressed his hand to Becky's cheek, bringing her gaze back to him. "We have a few minutes before we have to go. Pretty slaves get their drinks last, right?" He cocked his head as he lifted her bare breasts in his hand. "I think I'll take my time with mine."

"Go . . . ?" She whimpered as his thighs gripped her hips tight and he flicked his tongue over one nipple. Then the other. A sprinkle of salt and his mouth was on her again, the sensation of the salt adding a slight scrape to the smooth press of his lips. He sucked her nipple into his mouth, holding her still as her knees buckled. The zip of pleasure traveled down like a sharp electric pulse straight to her clit. Moisture dampened the plain white panties she'd worn under her pants.

He gave her other nipple the same attention, then dipped his finger into his shot glass. Sucked it dry. Eyed her as he tipped a quarter of the liquid over her breasts. "I don't drink and drive, but I can't leave you all wet."

He squeezed the lemon over her breasts, lapping up the cool droplets as they drizzled down. Then he kissed her, his mouth sweet and sour all at once, making her taste buds sizzle almost as much as her skin.

"Lick." He offered her his palm. His skin tasted fresh and clean from the shower he'd taken after the game. She eyed him as she took her time running her tongue over his rough flesh. The control he'd displayed so far faltered a bit. His hand wasn't quite steady as he shook the salt shaker over his hand. She sucked rather than licked off the salt.

Her shot of tequila burned all the way down. Every single inch of her was aroused. She pulled at the lemon slice he brought to her mouth, using her lips and the gentle press of her teeth to show him what she'd do once she had her mouth on him.

"Damn, woman." Scott stood, his arms still around her to keep her close enough to feel his erection through his pants. "Keep it up and I won't wait for Zach."

"We have to, Scott. Tonight, I need—"

"I know. So do I."

Zach returned from where he'd been speaking to Sebastian, his eyes on her as he took hold of Scott's wrist and sucked his fingers. Then he pressed her against the bar and lowered his head to clean the droplets of lemon and tequila Scott had left on her breasts and stomach. He rose to kiss her.

"Get the keys to Ford's bike, Scott. I'm ready to go." The edges of Zach's lips quirked up as Becky stared at him, confused. "You didn't really think we'd share this special night at the club, did you, little doe?"

"Actually, I did." Becky dropped her gaze to Zach's shoes, not sure she could take the disappointment in his eyes once he heard how badly she'd misjudged him. "I hate that I made you feel lacking as a Dom. But I know I did. And—"

"No, Becky. I let myself feel that way. We've both learned a lot about one another since then. I'm not perfect. I can't read minds." He tapped a fingertip under her chin, then waited for her to meet his eyes. "You've made it clear that I don't have to. I want this for us. Want what brought us together. And so much more."

"I was scared that I'd ruined it. I couldn't stand to see you here, feeling like you needed to be watched over with me." She gave him a hesitant smile. "So we aren't staying? Why is Scott getting Ford's bike?"

Zach leaned against the bar, a crooked smile on his lips. "Because I left mine here and he needs a way to get where we're going. Do you remember the dream you told me about? You on my bike, both of us touching you? The dream aroused you until I told you to forget everything else. As though you had to choose between your life and what we share?"

"I remember." She hadn't liked telling him about that dream. How could anything positive come of it? But she didn't keep things from him anymore. She whispered her thanks as he did up her bra, then her blouse. Being dressed made it easier to talk openly. "I know you'd never ask me to do that—"

"Yes, but it's a shame to waste such an erotic setup. We've both been working to replace some of Scott's negative memories with good ones. Scott and I plan to do the same for you." He rested an elbow on the bar as Scott returned with Ford. "Are you ready?"

"I'm not sure *I* am." Ford fisted his keys in his hand. "You sure this man can drive, Zach? My bike's my baby. Scott's my friend and all . . ." His eyes narrowed at Scott's frown. "Hey, I saw footage of you ripping up the side of a rented Camaro against a brick wall street racing. Sorry if I need a second opinion from someone sane."

Becky smiled, snuggling close to Zach's side, liking Ford a little more for his assessment of her Master. Maybe he was smarter than he looked.

"You have it, Ford. He'll get your baby back to you without a scratch on it," Zach said, slapping Ford's shoulder. "That aside, how are things going here? You feeling it?"

"Ah . . . let me get back to you on that. Experiencing everything from the side of a sub is a little weird. It feels wrong." Ford took a deep breath as Chicklet called out for him to take a tray to a waiting table. "The Cobras and their crew are enjoying this way too much. Becoming a Delgado came with a price. Mason sends his order back one more time and I'll—"

"I wouldn't suggest you doing anything besides saying 'Yes, Sir.' He's one of the most respected Doms here." Zach gave Ford a pointed look. "And he knows *exactly* why you're doing this."

"Yeah, well he can go fuck himself." Ford grumbled, picking up the tray Chicklet slid across the bar. "With all due respect. Which I won't repeat."

"Good idea." Zach casually slung his arm over Becky's shoulder, grinning when she shivered at the proprietary gesture. "Most of us have been through this, boy. If you're meant to be a Dom, this will make you a better one."

"As an aspiring Dom, can I tell you to suck my dick?" Ford balanced the tray on his hand with experienced ease, a dark scowl on his face.

Zach gave him a biting smile. "Not unless you plan to follow through. Don't forget, you want to be acknowledged as a Dom here in the future, you have to go through me as well. So play nice."

"Got it. And no." Ford shifted away from Zach. "I'm cool with you swinging both ways, but I'm not going there."

"So noted." Zach drew Becky away from the bar, watching Ford until he handed his keys to Scott. "You'll have your bike back tomorrow morning. With my thanks. And Becky's and Scott's as well."

"Hell, you've got my thanks now." Scott grabbed Ford's shoulder, then pulled him in for a rough hug. "You'll be fine. And give me a call later. I get what it's like—trying to prove yourself."

Becky wanted to wrap her arms around Scott. Remind him he'd succeeded. But Zach was already leading her out. He retrieved their jackets, then held her hand as they crossed the small parking lot beside the bar. By his bike, Zach took her helmet off the handlebar and placed it on her head. The face shield was dark enough that she couldn't see much at night with it down, so she was surprised when it was lifted to reveal Scott, instead of Zach.

Not that she minded, at all, but she couldn't help but glance over to make sure Zach hadn't left without her. The idea of playing out her fantasy had her feeling a little uncertain. Sex in the club was the closest she'd ever gotten to exposing herself in public.

Scott leaned close, speaking against her lips. "If you don't want to do this, you should tell him now."

Straddling his bike, Zach met her gaze with a reassuring smile. He would accept whatever choice she made.

I want this. I want to take his lead and not worry about where he'll take me. Because no matter where it is, I'll be safe. She took a deep, bracing breath and smiled at Scott. "I'm good. Was that all you wanted to say? Because I wanted to tell you—"

"You did tell me, Becky." Scott gave her a soft kiss. "The way you looked at me when I mentioned proving myself made it clear that I have."

"Yes." She pressed against him, catching his bottom lip with her teeth. He still tasted like salt and lemon. Delicious.

Scott groaned, deepening the kiss, chuckling when Zach revved his bike's engine. "We better go before he decides to play right here. My fault. I've been teasing him with erotic details about the scene we planned whenever I get him alone. His dick's probably rock hard in his leathers."

Becky grinned mischievously, stroking Scott's erection through his pants. "He's not the only one."

"Oh, you're mean!" Scott laughed, tapping down her face shield. He gave her a playful shove toward Zach before going to mount a big black and gleaming chrome Harley parked a few feet away.

Zach reached back to help her up onto the bike behind him. He looked at her over his shoulder. "Everything okay?"

"Everything's perfect!" She shouted to be heard over the purring engine, hugging his waist. "I just had to get back at him for teasing you!"

Chuckling, Zach brought his hand down to squeeze hers. "That's my girl!"

The ride in itself was thrilling, with the dark aroma of Zach's leather jacket mingling with the damp ocean air, the wind whipping at her as they sped through the night. Streetlights danced in a yellow blur for the first few miles, but then there was nothing but the headlights from the bikes to illuminate the street. No sound but the animalistic roar of the engines. The vibrations beneath her had her blood racing to her core where it pulse with a steady, needy rhythm.

She tightened her grip on Zach's waist, wondering if his bike would get her off before he could. The arousal winding up within made it likely. Memories of the dream, no longer as frightening as they'd once been, had her whimpering. She knew the feeling of both men's hands, their mouths, on her body. But not both together.

Zach pulled to a stop just as she pressed her eyes shut, ready to let go. He killed the engine, then lifted her right up without warning, holding her flush against his body as he lowered her to her feet. Her heels made her unsteady on the rocky surface. She squinted as Zach brought up her face shield, the headlight of Scott's borrowed bike practically blinding her.

"You were driving me insane back there, clenching your thighs, moving in that way you do just before you're about to come." He studied her face, his pale green eyes glowing with passion. The wind rustled through the leaves of the trees around them, but the space where they stood had an aura of stillness as though Zach controlled the very atmosphere around him. "Did you?"

She shook her head, licking her lips as her core gave a mournful throb. "No, Sir. But I was close."

Sliding his hand up between her breasts, he held her gaze as his hand curved around the base of her throat. He added a bit of pressure, enough to make her gasp at the rush of fear. Of desire.

"Let's cool you off a bit then."

As he stepped back, Scott moved forward, his lips slanting slightly as he unbuttoned her blouse. Then unclasped her bra for the second time that night. He tossed both to Zach, then took a knee to remove her pants, drawing her panties down with them. He left the helmet on, which made watching what he was doing a little challenging. But she could feel him. Becky's legs shook as he remained on his knee, his face so close that his breath caressed her freshly shaved pussy. He couldn't resist touching her, tasting her—could he?

But he did. He stood and took her things from Zach and went to stuff them into one of his bike's saddlebags. Zach removed his leather jacket and dropped it at his feet.

He pointed at the jacket. "On your knees, little doe."

Movements unsteady, Becky went to him, finding some practiced grace as she eased down to her knees. The leather kept the rocks from cutting into her knees, but the hard, jagged edges still dented her flesh. Not bad enough to complain about—*yet*—but she would tell Zach if he intended to keep her like this long. She also wouldn't be *too* upset if he took off the helmet. It wasn't heavy, but the way it restricted her vision annoyed her. She couldn't see where Scott had gone.

She turned her head to look for him.

Zach clucked his tongue, then patted the top of the helmet. "Eyes on me, pet. He'll join us in a moment." He gave her a slow, positively wicked smile. "Not that you'll see much of him. Or me."

One headlight went off. Then the other. The silence, increased by the padding of the helmet, gave her the sensation of being deaf. Her pulse quickened as she stared up at Zach.

"You seem nervous, pet. Perhaps uncomfortable?" Zach arched a brow. "What color do we use?"

"Yellow." She didn't even hesitate before saying the word. She trusted him, but she needed an idea of what they were going to do to her. "My knees are a little sore on the rocks. And . . . where are we? What if someone—"

"We're on a stretch of property owned by Mr. Keane. He was generous enough to let us use the place for the weekend." Zach placed a hand on her shoulder. "And you won't be on your knees much longer. Can you handle another minute or so?"

Privacy and a limit to how long she'd be on her knees. She inclined her head. "Yes, Sir. That's fine."

"Good." He held out his hand beyond her vision. "Thank you, Scott."

"You're welcome, Zach," Scott said, a hint of humor in his tone. "Now hurry up."

Zach shook his head, letting out a soft laugh. He winked at Becky. "He's so impatient. Maybe we shouldn't let him play."

Batting her eyelashes, Becky gave Zach her sweetest look. "I'd like him to play, Sir. But only if it pleases you."

Scott snorted. "Suck-up."

"If it pleased me to have him leave, would you object?" Zach asked, his tone indecipherable. "Would you still do anything I ask?"

Becky frowned. That wasn't even funny. But Zach wasn't laughing—or even smiling anymore. Did he seriously expect her to let him get rid of Scott when they'd all been anticipating their first time together? Did he think putting his ring on her finger made her love Scott any less?

If he does, he's got another thing coming. "No, I don't think I would, Sir."

"Wouldn't object, or wouldn't do anything I ask?"

"Zach, that's enough." She scowled, shifting to stand. "I don't know what you're trying to do, but—"

"Relax, firecracker." Scott's hands were on her shoulders from behind her, keeping her in place. "I think our big, tough Mr. Dom here just needs some assurances. We're all in this together. Agreed?"

"Yes! I love you both!" Becky met Zach's eyes, relieved that there was no doubt in his. "Sir, I would have told you if I was unsure of him. Or you. I'm not. Not anymore."

Zach let out a rough exhale, as though he'd been holding his breath. "Good, because you may kneel for me, but you both stand by my side. I wouldn't feel right putting this around your neck if it made him any less to you."

The collar. Becky's vision blurred with tears as Zach brought the collar to her throat. Clasped it even as Scott lifted her hair out of the way. The leather felt soft and warmed readily to her flesh, but it was the implication that made her heart swell. She'd managed to regain Zach's trust. They wouldn't play a timid kinky game with him. He was truly taking his place as her Master.

"All right, up with you." Scott helped her to her feet, then smacked her butt. The shield went down over her face. "This is all lovely, but if we keep you out here too long, you're gonna start getting cold."

The temperature was mild for fall, but Scott was right. Even though her skin flushed with pleasure, with arousal, the slight breeze wasn't exactly warm. There were so many ways she could say what the ring, the collar, and both men meant to her, but she needed to do more. She needed to show them.

Without another word, one of the men lifted her up by the hips. She was carried a few steps. Placed sidesaddle on the motorcycle seat. Chain clinked behind her. Cuffs were placed on her wrists and ankles. Then she was leaned back until she was draped over the seat, her arms spread wide, her feet resting on the pipes which were still warm, but not hot. Testing the restraints, she realized she was securely bound to the bike.

"Fuck, that's hot." Scott made a low sound of admiration in his throat as fingertips trailed along her inner thigh. "I'd love a picture. Would you mind, Becky?"

Becky relaxed her neck as much as possible, the helmet weighing enough to put some strain in her muscles if she tried to lift her head. She envisioned Scott standing by Zach, both their eyes on her, seeing how open and ready and wet she was for them. She needed them near her, touching her.

But first, she'd give Scott his answer. Maybe surprise him a little. "As long as they're just for you and my Master, I don't mind at all."

"Damn straight," Scott said. Footsteps moved around the bike, softer than the heavy clunk of Zach's boots. A faint click came, telling Becky Scott was taking pictures. "I'll use these to torture him while we're on the road. I guarantee he'll beg me to suck his cock after just one look at them."

Her entire lower half had become pure liquid heat. She hissed in a breath at the image Scott painted in her mind. "He'll beg you to suck his cock because you've got an amazing mouth."

"Oh yeah?" The footsteps stopped in front of her. Between her parted thighs. And she felt Scott's breath on her stomach as he spoke. "Not sure I've used it on you often enough for you to say for sure, sweetheart. How 'bout I fix that?"

His smooth cheek slid along her thigh. Her pussy moistened a little more as she pressed her eyes shut, waiting for the touch of his tongue. His lips, then his teeth, teased the shallow along her hip. His hands curved around her inner thighs.

Another set of hands stroked just above them. Zach's. She let out a little pleading noise as he used his fingers to part her pussy lips. To hold her wide open as Scott's tongue finally came to her, licking along one side of her folds, then the other. He homed in on her clit, and her hips quivered as she struggled against the restrains to rise to him. To demand a bit more pressure . . . *there*. Right there!

"Scott!" She snapped her lips shut as something slapped the top of her thigh. Zach's hands had left her. Scott was holding her open himself now, but the sting of the slap couldn't have been from Zach's hand. It was too long, too thin.

It wasn't until the sting faded to a length of pure, painful heat that she was able to really react to the sensation. *That hurt!*

"Be still, pet. And speak only when spoken to." The heat of Zach's body covered one thigh and her hip, as though he was leaning over Scott to look down at her. "Do you like the cane? I enjoy the marks it leaves on your pretty, pale skin, but I have other toys to play with if you prefer."

Becky wasn't sure how to answer that. The cane was a bit much without warm-up, but she did like how the bite of pain drew her back from the brink of climax. She wanted this to last. "I'm not sure I like the cane, Sir. But I do like that it helps me not be so easy."

"Easy?" Scott nibbled lightly on her outer labia, then sucked the flesh into his mouth. He breathed out a laugh when she clenched at the sensation of his feasting on her. "Hmmm, not sure I'd call you easy. Tasty. Responsive. Not easy."

Scott speaking with his lips on her pussy sent jolt after jolt of pleasure deep inside her. He lapped up her folds like they were covered in honey, delving into her with his tongue as though he wanted more.

"Ah!" Becky's lips formed a wide O as he thrust in faster and deeper with his tongue. Another snap of pain hauled her away from the edge. She whimpered at the next strike, which hit her other thigh.

Snap! Snap!

The pain was almost unbearable. Then . . . not. Heat spread from each lash, melding with the fire Scott stroked with his tongue.

Snap!

Her body quivered. Her resistance became a twig, bending and bending until it finally splintered, breaking in two. Her screams echoed in the helmet as her pussy milked Scott's tongue, which he kept inside her until her inner muscles undulated weakly around him.

Then he moved, and she couldn't feel either man near her. She swallowed, listening for them. She heard two sets of footsteps by her head. The shield was flipped open and she whimpered as she watched Zach kneel in front of Scott. Scott stood like a soldier at attention, a little to her left with his back to her as Zach unzipped Scott's pants, freeing his cock.

Zach met her eyes as he fisted his hand around Scott's dick. "You didn't get to see us make up, pet, but now you can watch me get him ready for you."

Oh. My. God. Becky flushed as she watched her Master take their lover's dick into his mouth. Her men were beautiful together and the connection they shared wound around her, making her feel part of what they shared even though neither touched her. Her mouth watered as Zach slid his lips slowly over Scott's length, taking him in, inch by inch.

Groaning, Scott brought his hand to the back of Zach's head. He froze when Zach drew back. "Zach, please—"

"No. We discussed this." Zach smiled pleasantly at Scott even as he flicked his tongue over the tip of Scott's dick. "You take what I give you. Nothing more."

And you're not a sadist, Sir? Becky bit back a grin, barely managing not to laugh at Scott's frustrated expression.

"You can't Dom me, man." Scott cupped Zach's cheek, his tone tender despite his words. "I'm not into that."

"I'm aware. But you are—" Zach swirled his tongue around the head of Scott's dick, taking it between his lips, then grazing up to the tip with his teeth. "—'into' this."

Tipping his head back, Scott's jaw hardened. His knees locked and Becky could see the effort it took for him to keep from thrusting into Zach's mouth. "You pushy fucking—oh fuck!"

Becky almost came again just watching Zach taking Scott in all the way. She muttered a curse along with Scott when Zach released Scott and rose to his feet. Zach took something out of his pocket, his lips slanted in an evil grin.

"I think you need this." He opened the plastic wrapper. Becky thought it was a condom at first, but then she saw the black ring, which looked like it was made of some kind of leather. The ring was about the size of a circle made with her thumb and forefinger. The Velcro holding its shape made a ripping sound as Zach opened it. Zach fitted the ring around the base of Scott's dick, under his heavy balls. "She needs you to last."

Scott inhaled through his teeth. "Damn it, that feels weird."

"Not too tight?"

"No. No, I'm okay." Scott shook his head, then latched on to the back of Zach's neck, planting a firm kiss on his lips. "You are one twisted man." He grinned. "I love it."

Letting out the breath she'd been holding near the end of their exchange, Becky's gaze followed Scott until he disappeared around the other side of the bike. As she felt him between her thighs, Zach came to her, reaching into the helmet to touch her cheek.

"We'll both take you now, little doe. One day I hope we can both be inside you, feeling each other, and you, but I don't think you're ready for that yet."

Not long ago, she would have said "No." But she wasn't so sure anymore. She wanted to try it with them, at least once. He was right though. She wasn't ready yet. Teeth denting her bottom lip, she smiled at him. "This, what we're doing, is perfect. I want you, Sir. Any way I can have you."

"Good girl." Zach leaned down, kissing her, which was different in and of itself since her head was upside down. He nipped her chin, then straightened to unzip his leathers. "Open for me, pet."

She opened her mouth wide, relaxing her throat as he pushed in all the way. In this position, taking him in that deep was easier. So long as she swallowed against the gagging sensation. He eased out, then back in, leaving her mouth completely as the head of Scott's dick pressed between her folds. Zach entered her mouth again with short thrusts, stroking her cheek with his thumb as Scott slowly filled her. Ever since he'd gotten well, she'd been having sex with Scott without a condom. All the blood tests had come back clean, and there was nothing better than feeling him without a barrier between them.

This time was different. With every long stroke he seemed thicker, hotter. The head of his cock stretched her, blazing hot, every single time he drove into her. She tightened up around him, gasping around Zach. The combined sensation of the men using her was indescribable. She tried to focus on tensing around Scott, on using her lips and her tongue on Zach, on heightening their pleasure any way she could, but finally just gave in and let them take her. She dropped into the erotic flow, into the rhythm, coming closer and closer to the peak with every thrust into her body, her mouth.

Her hands fisted as Scott lost his rhythm, slamming into her harder, his fingers finding her swollen clit. She went rigid as Zach's pace faltered. Salty warmth coated the back of her throat as he made a rough sound and drove in. Scott cursed, trapping her clit between his fingers. He thrust into her almost violently, but she could tell he was holding back, waiting for her. The knowledge pitched her into a shuddering climax and she felt him come as she spasmed around him.

Another sharp jab of Scott's dick had her convulsing all over again, and she screamed as Zach left her mouth. The chains restraining her rattled as she thrashed, the sky and the trees and the earth shattering around her. Scott was deep, so deep inside her, and the only thing that held her together as the sensation tore at her was Zach's hand on her face. His soft whispered words that she couldn't quite make out.

All she knew was that as she came back to level ground, he was with her, keeping her from falling too fast. After Scott unclipped all her cuffs, Zach picked her up, cradling her in his arms as he carried her to where his jacket was spread over the dirt road. He sat with her and Scott plunked down beside them, looking as boneless as she felt.

Scott unbuckled her helmet, set it aside, then kissed her forehead. "Just think, we've got a whole weekend of this."

Zach smiled, leaning over to kiss Scott. "Hmm, very true. Tim's going to want a word with me when he sees how worn out you are when we show up to practice Monday morning."

"I think Scott and I will have you pretty worn out too, Sir." Becky rested her head on Zach's shoulder, reaching out to run her thumb along Scott's bottom lip. "He's younger than us both—I think he's got the endurance to outdo us."

"Damn right I do." Scott caught her thumb between his lips, watching Zach as he sucked at it. "I'm thinking Tim will be on my ass about wearing *you* out, Zach. And Keane might have something to say about it too. Becky will be a little sore by the time I'm done with her."

"You said Mr. Keane owned the property? Including a house, with a bed?" Becky asked, feeling a little sleepy. She was going to be sore—pleasantly so. But hopefully she'd get some rest first. "I wish I'd known we'd be staying somewhere. I have nothing to change into."

"I brought you a few things, love," Zach said, helping her to her feet as he stood. "Not that you'll need much. I plan to keep you exactly like this over the next few days."

Becky yelped as he swooped her up in his arms, then laughed. "Naked, aching in all the right places, with my feet always up in the air?"

"Works for me!" Scott took Zach's saddlebags off the bike and slung them over his shoulder. "Don't expect to get much sleep this weekend, honey."

Zach's muscles hardened around her as he carried her along the trail leading to a large, rather modern-looking cabin. His tone was gruff as he slowed his pace so Scott could catch up. "She'll need time to recover, Scott."

Frowning, Scott shifted the saddlebags. "I know. I was just—"

A sly smile slid across Zach's lips. "Eventually. After we try out the bed he bragged about. Solid iron with thick posts. I brought extra chains with plenty of ideas of how I'll use them."

"Zach!" Becky couldn't stop smiling. This weekend was going to be amazing. She couldn't believe she was lucky enough to spend this time with them both. But she playfully smacked Zach shoulder. "When I mentioned a bed, it was for actually sleeping. I need recovery time now!"

Arching a brow at her, Zach snorted. "Not if you have enough strength to smack me, naughty girl."

Scott bared his teeth in a broad smile, winking at her. "I'd call him 'Sir,' sweetie. Or Master." He cocked his head. "Your Royal Highness might be a good idea." He patted the saddlebags. "You haven't seen what he packed."

She swallowed, quivering with nervous energy, equally thrilled and afraid. Fully aroused. She couldn't wait to see. But she wasn't stupid. She gave Zach her most humble, most submissively sweet look. "I'm very sorry, My Lord."

With a wicked glint in his eyes, Zach brought his lips to hers and whispered, "Oh, you will be."

Chapter Thirty Four

The cold snapped at Scott as soon as he stepped out of his car on to the sidewalk. It was late November, but it felt more like January. A light coat of sparkly white snow already covered the sidewalk. His dark grey, wool jacket might be "stylish" as far as Stephan was concerned, but Scott was ready to start wearing a parka. He'd always hated the cold.

He stared at the big office building, then double-checked the address on the card Chicklet had given him at the last self-defense class. She'd gotten it from Laura, who apparently knew this person. They both thought someone who understood the lifestyle would be best, no matter how little involved in it he really was.

This meeting had been scheduled for days. And he'd been having nightmares ever since. Thankfully, he'd handed over his condo to Hunt for a pretty damn low rent, seeing as he liked the kid, and had been staying at Becky's for about two weeks. At first, he hadn't been all that sure about living with the newlyweds. Yeah, they were all together, but Becky and Zach were *official*. He'd been a little grumpy for a bit that they'd decided on a small wedding with the justice of the peace. He thought Becky deserved something big and elaborate. Zach agreed, but Becky said she didn't have time for it. Stated that they could have something big for their tenth wedding anniversary.

Fine, but they should at least have had a decent honeymoon. His arguments didn't get him very far with them. And he was secretly happy that they didn't. The at-home honeymoon involving the three of them while Casey stayed with Landon, Dean, and Silver was pretty amazing. Lots of sex, kink, and plenty of naked lounging around feeding Becky her favorite treats. Absolutely perfect.

As had been every day and night since. His bedroom might be in the basement, but he could pretty much count on either Zach or Becky—sometimes both—spending at least a few hours with him down there every night. Actually, since the first nightmare, Zach had been by his side from the second he closed his eyes until he woke. Becky had tried to talk him into moving into their bedroom.

He was still thinking about it.

Both had offered to come with him today. And he'd almost said sure. Almost, but hadn't. Because he needed to do this alone. Needed to know he was strong enough to get past all this crap without anyone holding his hand.

He pushed open the big glass doors, heading straight for the elevator, ignoring the security guard's, "Can I help you?"

I don't need help. Not even this, but I'll fucking do it, okay?

He jabbed his thumb on the elevator button, then shoved his hands into his pockets. The ride up seemed to take forever. Like that whole day had, from the quiet breakfast after he'd gotten up too late to eat with Casey before school, to the moment he'd finally dragged his ass out to his car. The traffic had been bad. He'd been sure he'd be late for his appointment.

No such luck. He was right on time.

When he stepped off the elevator, a familiar face had him stopping in his tracks. He blinked just to be sure. "Silver?"

Face red, holding tight to a piece of tissue that she was using to dry her tears, Silver started, then stared at him. "Scott?"

"Yeah." He shifted, looking around, wondering if there were any other kinds of doctors here he could claim to be seeing. Maybe he could be getting his prostate checked. Yeah, that would be less embarrassing. "Uh . . . you okay?"

"I think so." She sniffled, then shook her head, letting out a sob. "No. Physically, I'm better, but mentally?" A sharp laugh escaped her. "I'm a mess. But I'm seeing someone. Pretty pathetic, right?"

"Why?" Not that he didn't agree. He felt like that too. Talking to a shrink was the last thing he'd ever thought he'd be doing. But if Silver needed to talk to someone, she shouldn't feel bad about it. "I've met your dad. After a few minutes with him, I swear, I needed therapy. Or antidepressants."

Silver gaped at him. Then burst out laughing. "Damn. You're so much more than I thought you were when I saw you in that magazine."

"I can say the same, sweetie. You've been good for this team." He held out his arm, giving her a firm hug, shushing her when she started crying again. "Did it help? Talking about whatever it is?"

"A little." She shrugged, easing away from him. "It won't get better overnight, but it will get better. I'm actually looking forward to seeing my baby. For the first time. I don't feel like I need to stay away."

"That's good." He nudged her chin with a fist. "Go see your baby. Tell Landon I said hi, but . . ." He frowned. "Not where you saw me."

"Got it." She sniffed. "Whatever it is, Scott, just know that it does get better. You have to believe that."

He nodded, then went to tell the receptionist he was here. She directed him to the office with the right name on the door. Inside, a small, elderly woman who reminded him of Betty White gestured to the leather lounge chair. When he hesitated, she pointed at the big, high-backed leather armchair.

"Perhaps you'd be more comfortable there?"

"Uh, yeah."

She waited for him to get comfortable, leaning forward in a chair that matched his, setting her notepad and pen aside. She shocked him by giving him a short lecture on how he needed to make his passes sharper. They chatted for a bit about hockey before she finally got down to business.

"Scott, we spoke a little on the phone, but I think it's important for you to tell me, clearly, what happened to you. Know that I won't judge you. I just need to see where you are with this so I can help you."

Scott nodded slowly, staring at his wet dress shoes. Gulping against the sick feeling rising in his throat. He couldn't look at her. But he could say it. "I was . . . I was sexually—fuck!" He stood, shaking his head. Why was it so hard?

"Some terms used to diagnose things come with certain stigmas. Don't use them if they make you uncomfortable. Use your own words."

Hands fisted by his sides, Scott faced the therapist. He licked his bottom lip. "The woman who should have been a mother to me . . . she did things to me. And it fucked me up." He rolled his eyes, blinking against the burning sensation. He wasn't going to start blubbering. She couldn't do that to him anymore. He took a deep breath. "I was a little boy. And she was a sick bitch."

The therapist's kindly old face wrinkled as she gave him a broad smile. "Good. Very good. I won't ask you how that makes you feel. It's obvious. But I will ask you how it's affecting your life. And give you some tools you can use to move forward from here."

"That sounds good." He sat back in the chair, liking the woman already. "That's what I'm all about. Moving forward."

* * * *

Shirt off, Amia tucked close to his chest, Landon lifted his head, still a little drowsy from his nap, smiling as Dean laid on the other side of their baby girl. Dean casually rested his head on the arm Landon had stretched over the pillows, then lightly ran a finger over Amia's soft cheek as she stirred. Their daughter seemed to sense the moment Dean was near, which was pretty awesome.

"Want me to bring her down for lunch? You were up early for PT. You're probably still tired," Dean said quietly.

"In a bit. Stay here for now." Landon rubbed his face with his free hand, putting it over Dean's when Amia's eyes popped open. She smiled, kicking her feet and smacking both their hands with hers, looking from him to Dean before letting out a happy sound. "You've been working a lot lately. She misses you."

"She'll be with me all day." Dean arched a brow. "Are you certain she's the one who misses me?"

"We both do, you fu—freakin' workaholic." Landon let out a dramatic sigh. "I'm home, cleaning and cooking and—"

"Calling my daughter to bring you lunch is not considered cooking, you big oaf." Dean snorted. "And neither is opening a jar of baby food."

"Still. It would be nice to feel appreciated once in a while."

"You know I appreciate you, Landon." Dean's brow furrowed. He circled Landon's wrist with his hand. "I know this isn't easy. But you're making the right choice—you'd miss the game if you never played again. You're still very young."

"Not that young, but you're right." Landon worried his bottom lip with his teeth. He was glad Dean was still holding his wrist.

Something about having the man near calmed him. If not for Dean, he wouldn't be able to sleep through the night. Especially when Silver started sleeping on the sofa. With how much she'd pulled away from them all—him, Dean, and worst of all, Amia—it was hard not to feel completely alone. Yeah, his dad had seen them in bed together once and freaked out. So fucking what. He didn't care what anyone thought.

Dean was the one who'd helped him through everything. It was Dean who'd stood by his side when he visited his son's grave. Who'd taught him how to change diapers and test the temperature of the milk since Amia had been bottle-fed since birth.

The first few times they'd touched, or sat too close, had been a little weird. Because straight men didn't do that. But that was his father talking. Dean was a strong shoulder to lean on. A comforting arm around him, a warm body at night to keep those haunting thoughts at bay. Ever since the doctor had told Landon that Silver was suffering from postpartum depression, he'd been doing research on it and some of the stories scared him. That she refused to get help only made things worse. He had to have an armory's worth of shields up around his heart just to deal with being in the same room with her since it had gotten to the point where she barely looked at him anymore.

Better than the way she looks at our daughter. Which he didn't know how to deal with at all.

"Do you think she's serious about going to stay with her sister in Calgary?" Dean asked, putting his finger in Amia's hand, still smiling, even though the lines around his eyes had deepened. "Oriana would be a sound voice of reason. She may be able to talk Silver into taking care of herself, but—"

"I know. I don't want her to leave either." But it was getting harder to say that with any conviction. Silver didn't want him, or Dean. And the way she treated Amia sometimes . . . fuck, he knew it wasn't her fault. But she acted like her own baby had come from someone else. Like she didn't know her. And it was hard not to pull away from Silver a little himself because of it. He was always honest with Dean, so he said exactly what he was thinking. "Maybe it's for the best. We've done all we can."

"Yes. You have." Silver's voice came from the doorway. He lifted his head to watch her approach the bed, her eyes so full of longing that his heart, which had hardened somewhat lately, cracked a little. Fuck, it hurt. She held up her hands before either he or Dean could speak. "Before you say anything else, I need to tell you something."

"Go ahead, dragonfly." Dean's hand shifted from Landon's wrist to his hand, as though he sensed that Landon needed something to hold on to.

"I—" Silver glanced at their hands, then hugged herself, turning her head to stare out the window. "I'm not going to Calgary. Me and Oriana had a long chat and . . . she got me to talk to your mom. I think I needed some tough love." A smile crossed her lips so quickly Landon was sure he'd imagined it. "I saw the doctor. The heart meds are working. As long as I'm careful, I should be fine." She shook her head when Dean sat up. "Yeah, it's great, but more importantly, I was finally able to admit that it's not just my heart that was damaged. I don't know me anymore. Actually, I think I hate myself a little. So I went to a few appointments to work things out. I'm on some medication to help control my hormones—or something like that. And I went to see a therapist today. I'll be seeing her twice a week, and she's going to make it so I can find a way to be Amia's mother. I'm s-sorry—" Her face crumpled. She took a step away from the bed. "I'm so, so sorry I fucked things up so bad."

"Silver—" Dean's lips thinned when Landon didn't say anything. He withdrew his hand and stood. "You know we both understand that it wasn't you. You didn't 'F' up anything."

It's better if I don't say anything, man. Landon swallowed, trying not to stiffen up since Amia was still sleeping next to him. He couldn't honestly say Silver hadn't fucked things up. Or that he hadn't by not doing enough.

"I did. But at least Amia had both of you. I know she'd be fine without me, but—" Silver moved closer to Dean, wrapping her arms around his waist. Se rested her head on Dean's chest, then slowly turned to face Landon. "I'm her mother. And she's going to have me too. I'm going to get better—*stronger*—for her."

"Damn it, Silver." Landon felt his eyes tear as hope burst

through his chest, shattering the last of his shields. He cradled Amia in one arm, sliding off the bed, hating the tightness in his gut that made him have to fight to get any closer. But then Dean put an arm over his shoulder, drawing him in. And he found himself kissing Silver. Finally seeing the woman he loved. He handed Amia over to Dean so he could hold Silver. So he could dry her tears and tell her all the things he hadn't for so long. "I love you so much. I missed my fiancée. Our daughter missed her mother. She wouldn't be fine without you. Her fathers did their best though."

"I know you did. It makes me feel a bit better to know she was being taken care of while I was going off the deep end." Silver pressed her wet cheek against his bare chest, one arm still around Dean's waist. "And that you were being taken care of too, even though I'm starting to think you guys won't need me for *anything* if this keeps up."

"Silly girl." Dean laughed and kissed Silver's cheek. "I'll take your soft body over this brute's any day."

Silver giggled, giving Dean an innocent look. "You sure about that? Maybe the problem is you haven't gotten him on his knees yet and—"

Landon made a sharp sound in his throat, gently covering Amia's ears, which made his baby girl wiggle and laugh. "Not in front of our daughter please."

"Later." Silver nibbled at her bottom lip, moving away from Landon to look at Amia. "Can I hold her?"

"She'd love that, *mon amour*. I think she missed her mother." Landon smiled as he spoke, but he had to meet Dean's eyes for a moment to be sure. Dean was the reasonable one. The only one who really knew what he was doing. Landon despised even the brief thought that Silver needed more time before she could take her rightful place as Amia's mother. At least Silver didn't see his doubts.

Dean did. But he squeezed Landon's shoulder as though he understood. Then he placed Amia in Silver's arms. "My mother is visiting. Amia likes going for a walk in her stroller every day around this time. Why don't you bring her down and help Mother get her ready?"

"You're not coming?" Silver held Amia to her shoulder, glancing over at Landon as she headed toward the door.

Before Landon could answer, Dean spoke. "No. He needs to rest his leg. He'll take a nice, long, hot bath."

"And you'll help him?"

"Brat." Dean smiled at Landon before following Silver into the hall. "No. I'll be coming along. I just have a few calls to make first. I took the day off to spend time with our daughter."

"All right, well, I'm looking forward to spending some time with you too. There are a few players that I've been looking into—"

"Silver, that's my job."

"Hey, I got us Scott. And he turned out to be a good choice."

Their voices drifted off as they started down the stairs, but Landon could still hear them. He left the bedroom to watch them descend.

"I agree, but you will not be signing any players in the future," Dean said. "There are procedures to follow and—"

"Fuck that. I say—"

"Young lady, unless you want your daughter to go to preschool speaking that way, I suggest you stop using words like that around her," Dean's mother said. Then her tone softened. "You look happier, sweetheart. And the way you're holding her . . ."

"Thank you for being here so much . . . Mom." Silver leaned into Dean's mother, smiling as the older woman kissed her forehead. "And for talking to me. I followed your advice."

"Good girl." Dean's mother grinned. "Most find life gets much easier when they do exactly as I say."

For the first time since Amia's birth, Landon felt himself believing those very words. Verity had said them to him a few times. "Life gets easier." Not only when people did as she said, but in general. It hadn't been easy, but he'd learned to take one day at a time, enjoying all those peaceful moments with Dean and Amia. Sharing their daughter's firsts with someone who he could trust would always stand by his side.

Now there would be someone else. The woman who'd given them that precious child. He couldn't lie to himself—or Dean, when they talked about it, probably later that night—and say he felt sure of her yet. Whether or not it was her fault, she hadn't wanted him,

Dean, or . . . or Amia, for a long time. But that would come. They had the rest of their lives to find that place where their family would feel whole.

And one good thing had come of all this. It was no longer Dean and Landon standing on opposite sides, nothing in common but the game and the woman and child they both loved. They had their own connection.

And Landon would need that strong connection to lean on while he rebuilt all he and Silver had lost. They had a solid foundation to start from in the man they both loved.

Epilogue

Mid-December

The air whitened with every breath Becky took, but the coffee in her hands and Zach's arms around her kept her warm. She'd had a long day at the office, had almost begged out of the promised trip to the skating rink with Casey, too tired to slip on skates and try to keep up with her energetic little girl.

"Becky, you are mentally exhausted. Physically . . ." He guided her to the front door of their house, helping her dress warmly as though she was just as young as Casey. *"You need some exercise. And fresh air."*

She grudgingly agreed, but dug in her heels before they walked out the door. *"My skates—"*

"Scott has his. Chicklet is going to be there with Jami, Vanek, and Carter. They promised to show Casey how to do a slap shot." He grinned, rubbing her arms. *"We simply have to stand off to the side and cheer her on."*

Becky did just that as Casey swung back and shot at the net, cheering even though Casey had hit the post. Hunt had shown up along with the others, standing in net, pretending to be ready to block the shots. Becky knew he would let them by him, but so far the closest her baby had gotten was the post. And Hunt slid the puck back to her as Scott and Chicklet tried to show Casey how to hold the stick properly and aim.

Casey was on a team, but she'd faked being sick a few times, admitting to Zach, rather than Becky, that she wasn't as good as the other kids. And a few of the little boys were mean to her because she was a Bower and her uncle didn't even play anymore. So maybe she wasn't tough enough to hack it either.

Whatever Zach had said to Casey had her ready to pull on her skates and pick up a stick again. After a few days of practicing, she was getting better at carrying the puck. Could dodge a soft check without losing it. Chicklet was pretty good at pep talks, and she'd told Casey in a loud whisper that she'd been the smallest on her team for the first few years. Until she hit a growth spurt. Then she'd been the biggest and fastest.

With wide eyes, Casey had stared up at Chicklet. Then she'd tightened her grip on her stick and shown how fast she could go without losing the puck.

Backing to the approximate place the blue line would be on a real skating rink, Casey's small mouth twisted with concentration. She scooped up the puck and skated hard, racing toward Hunt, swinging her stick—then swooping to the left, lifting the puck just like Scott had shown her.

Hunt dove dramatically, right under the puck. It hit the back of the net.

All the men and Chicklet cheered. Becky clapped, shouting "That's my girl!" Casey stood there with her mouth opened wide. Then she dropped her stick and slid across the ice on her knees, mirroring a move Vanek had done just last week after he'd scored against Philly.

"Did you see, Daddy?" Casey jumped up, almost falling over before skating up to them. She tugged on Zach's jacket sleeve when his lips parted and he just stared at her, his grip tightening on Becky as she went completely still. "Daddy, Daddy, did you see? I *scored* against a pro goalie. One of the best in the league. Besides my Uncle Landon of course."

Zach was still speechless. Coming over to grab one of the coffees, Hunt grinned at Casey, his face red. Chicklet came over to pick Casey up, speaking in a mock whisper, "I think your daddy is stunned. How about you show him again?"

Everyone took their places. This time, Vanek and Jami positioned themselves in front of Hunt, playing defense. Scott passed the puck to Casey, accepted the return, took a shot—Hunt blocked. Vanek slammed into Scott, knocking him on his ass. Chicklet nudged Casey as she went for the rebound. Fell back as Casey pushed by her. Casey poked the puck past Hunt.

Others on the rink who had stopped to watch clapped and Casey grinned, bowing. Vanek helped Scott to his feet, ribbing him affectionately. "Good thing she's on your team, Demmy, she got more points than you have in the past five games."

Casey frowned. "Hey, only I get to call him Demmy. He said so."

"But—" Tyler shut his mouth at Chicklet's hard look.

Becky covered her mouth with her mittened hand as Casey inclined her head at Chicklet in thanks. Casey was very possessive of the men in her life. She often called them 'Her Demmy' and 'Her Zach' when they went out and she introduced them to people. Drooling puck bunnies got dirty looks, and both men would politely excuse themselves without even offering autographs to any woman who was too forward in front of her daughter. Or her for that matter. Becky wouldn't admit it, but she'd done a few searches online and the "bunnies" weren't happy with how she and her daughter had claimed two of the most sought-after men on the team.

Despite how unconventional their life together was, it fit them all perfectly. But Casey calling Zach "Daddy" was a first. Becky didn't mind, but she needed to know Zach was comfortable with it. And she had to figure out quickly how to dissuade Casey if he wasn't.

"Daddy, did you see this time?" Casey skated over, peering up at Zach, something in her eyes causing Becky's heart to stutter. Casey wanted Zach to take that role in her life. He did in every way that counted, but apparently Casey needed more. Needed to call him something other than his name to show who he was to her.

What do I say if he's not comfortable with it? A lot of men wouldn't be. Casey had a father. He just wasn't part of her life.

Zach cleared his throat. He smiled and bent down to Casey's level. His eyes were shiny, either from the cold, or with emotion. His tone proved the latter. "I saw, baby. And I'm so proud of you. Come here."

Casey giggled and threw herself in his arms, holding him tight as he stood. Then she peeked up at Becky. "Is it okay, Mommy? My father won't be mad, will he? I didn't think he'd care. He's *not* my daddy. Zach is."

Damn, what's the right answer?

Jami stood close, shifting from side to side, mouthing "Sorry."

"Why?" Becky's eyes narrowed, and she held up one hand, forcing a smile for her baby. "One moment, *mon petite*." She turned to the younger woman, pulling her aside. Casey making this decision on her own was one thing, but she didn't want anyone else influencing it. "Did you tell her to call him—"

"No! Of course not!" Jami shook her head quickly. "She heard me talking on the phone with the *woman* who gave birth to me. I didn't realize she'd followed me. I called her 'mother' and then sat with Silver for a bit. I swear, I thought Casey was still watching TV." She bit her bottom lip. "I told Silver that she's not much older than me, but she's more of a mom than mine has ever been because she's the one who's there for me. I only call her 'Mommy' to bug her, but maybe that got Casey thinking . . . fuck, I'm sorry."

"Don't be." Becky hugged Jami, then returned to her daughter, who was still in Zach's arms. She kissed Casey's cheek, then looked from her to Zach. "As long as it's okay with him, you may call Zach 'Daddy.'"

"Is it okay?" Casey leaned back to look into Zach's eyes. "Can I?"

"Yes. God, yes." Zach grinned, then kissed Casey's forehead. "You're giving me something very special in calling me that."

"Special enough for you to get a goal tomorrow? Just for me?"

"Just for you." Zach looked over at Scott as he joined them. "Think you can help me with that—what is it she calls you? 'Demmy'?"

"Yes," Casey said, her tone very serious. "Because it's close to 'Daddy.' But it's just for him. I love you both and I'm very lucky. Grandma said so."

"She's right." Becky shifted so she stood between Scott and Zach, resting her head on Scott's shoulder as he put his arm around her. She wanted to laugh and cry all at once. How was it even possible that this strange relationship had ended up being exactly what both she and her daughter needed? "We're both very very lucky."

Everything she felt was reflected in Scott's eyes. And in Zach's. Neither man could have predicted that they'd all be together in the end. So many things could have gone wrong. Things still could; who knew what the future held?

But . . . maybe she did. The beginning and the end was right here, all of them together, smiling and laughing, where they'd been yesterday. Where they'd be tomorrow. This was their life and it was right.

Complete.

THE END

Visit the Dartmouth Cobras
www.TheDartmouthCobras.com

Game Misconduct

THE DARTMOUTH COBRAS #1

The game has always cast a shadow over Oriana Delgado's life. She should hate the game. But she doesn't. The passion and the energy of the sport are part of her. But so is the urge to drop the role of the Dartmouth Cobra owner's 'good daughter' and find a less . . .conventional one.

Playmaker Max Perron never expected a woman to accept him and his twisted desires. Oriana came close, but he wasn't surprised when she walked away. A girl like her needs normal. Which he can't give her. He's too much of a team player, and not just on the ice.

But then Oriana's father goes too far in trying to control her and she decides to use exposure as blackmail. Just the implication of her spending the night with the Cobras' finest should get her father to back off.

Turns out a team player is exactly what she needs.

"Ms Sommerland takes us on an extremely incredible journey as we watch Oriana's master her own sexuality. She comes to realize that there is more out there that she craves and desires, than she has ever realized." Rhayne —Guilty Pleasures

"With a delicious storyline and kinky characters outside of the norm, Game Misconduct pushes you outside of your comfort zone and rewards your submission with phenomenally erotic sex. If you're a fan of hardcore BDSM, then this book is going to top your list of must reads!" Silla Beaumont — Just Erotic Romance

Defensive Zone

THE DARTMOUTH COBRAS

Silver Delgado has gained control of the Dartmouth Cobras—and lost control of her life.

Hockey might be the family business, but it's never interested Silver. Until her father's health decline thrusts responsibility for the team he owns straight into her hands. Now she has to find a way to get the team more fans and establish herself as the new owner. Which means standing up to Dean Richter, the general manager and the advisor her father has forced on her. The fact that their "business relationship" started with her over his lap at his BDSM club shouldn't be too much of a problem. Their hot one-night stand meant nothing! But how can she earn his respect when he sees her as submissive? Can they separate work and the lifestyle she's curious to explore?

Balancing her new life away from Hollywood, living among people who see her as the selfish Delgado princess, has her feeling lost and alone until Landon Bower, the Cobras new goalie slips into her life and becomes her best—and only—friend. The time they spend together makes everything else bearable, but before long his eyes meet hers with more than friendship, reflecting what she feels. Which could ruin everything.

Two Dominant men who see past her pretty mask and the shallow image she portrayed to the flashing cameras. A gentle attack from both sides that she can't hope to block unless she learns how to play.

But she's getting the hang of the game.

Breakaway

THE DARTMOUTH COBRAS

Against some attacks, the only hope is to come out and meet the play.

Last year, Jami Richter had no plans, no goals, no future. But that's all changed. First step, make up for putting her father through hell by supporting the hockey team he manages and becoming an Ice Girl. But a photo shoot puts her right in the arms of Sebastian Ramos, a Dartmouth Cobra defenseman with a reputation for getting any woman—or, as the rumors imply, man—he desires. And the powerful dominant wants her...and Luke. Getting involved in Seb's lifestyle gives her a new understanding of the game and the bonds between players. But can she handle being caught between two men who want her, while struggling with their attraction to one another?

Luke Carter's life is about as messed up as his scarred face. His mother is sick. His girlfriend dumps him. When he goes to his favorite BDSM club to blow off some steam, his Dom status is turned upside down when a therapeutic beating puts him in a good place. He flatly denies being submissive—or, even worse, being attracted to another man. He wants Jami but can't have her without getting involved with Sebastian. Can he overcome his own prejudices long enough to admit he wants them both?

Caught between Luke and Jami, Sebastian Ramos does everything in his power to fulfill their needs. His two new submissives willingly share their bodies, but not their secrets. When his own past comes back to haunt him, the fragile foundation of their relationship is ripped apart. As he works to salvage the damage done by doubt and insecurity, he discovers that Jami is hiding something dangerous. But it may already be too late.

About the Author

Tell you about me? Hmm, well, there's not much to say. I love hockey and cars and my kids...not in that order of course! Lol! When I'm not writing—which isn't often—I'm usually watching a game or a car show while networking. Going out with my kids is my only downtime. I get to clear my head and forget everything.

As for when and why I first started writing, I guess I thought I'd get extra cookies if I was quiet for a while—that's how young I was. I used to bring my grandmother barely legible pages filled with tales of evil unicorns. She told me then that I would be a famous author.

I hope one day to prove her right.

For more of my work, please visit: www.Im-No-Angel.com

PRAISE FOR BIANCA SOMMERLAND'S BOOKS

"I just have to start by saying that this book is not for the faint of heart or the easily offended. Secondly, I have to say to the author, Bianca Sommerland, I give you a standing ovation. Deadly Captive was dark, sinister, erotic, intense, sexy and dangerous. Wow!"

–Karyl
Dark Diva Review of Deadly Captive

"My heart broke a little for Shawna. The entire set up made sense and from a personal note, I've been in the same situation. That's when I completely connected to the story and I was moved to tears."

–BookAddict
The Romance Reviews review of The Trip

Made in the USA
San Bernardino, CA
03 November 2017